Praise for *The Divine Husband*:

"A rich and sensuous new novel. Taking as its starting point a mysterious poem by one of Latin America's greatest men of letters and of action, Goldman creates a fascinating adventure story. At its center is not the historic José Martí—the author of the poem—but the enchanting, eccentric, intellectually ambitious and fiercely independent muse Goldman has invented for him, María de las Nieves. Her entrapment in a pretentious backwater society, her tentative, often disastrous romances, her dialogues with a supporting cast of improbable characters who are nevertheless completely believable, are all told sympathetically, delicately, carefully. The result is an engrossing and entertaining book, meticulously imagined, beautifully told." —Alma Guillermoprieto

"[A] beautiful third novel . . . rich . . . deft . . . seamless . . . Goldman is completely bicultural, steeped in two literatures. . . . The voices he gives to each of his characters are in perfect pitch. . . . One could go on ad infinitum, reading the novel as if listening to a grand Baroque concerto." —*Globe & Mail* (Toronto)

"A soulful story about love—from the religious to the romantic . . . Goldman will cast . . . [a] formidable shadow, judging by [its] breadth, scope, and lyrical orchestration. . . . Nearly every page has a moment of lyricism so neatly put it makes you pause and read the passage again. . . . [A] brave and bighearted book." —John Freeman, *The Orlando Sentinel*

"Richly imagined in a double sense . . . [*The Divine Husband*] combines intimacy and reach . . . and a subtle defense of the magic of the imagination. . . . [It] invites us to think about what we are doing when we decide which countries or stories or lives are large or small, significant or insignificant. . . . All the known history in this book is scrupulously respected and represented—indeed, the invented portions would not be so delicate and interesting if it were not. . . . Goldman also knows that the imagination offers its own varieties of experience, and he respects the reach of his characters' dreams." —Michael Wood, *The New York Review of Books*

"A classic Latin American novel, written in English . . . Goldman is a maximalist, and his challenging novel of love, migration, class, and corruption shows off a gratifying literary dexterity." —*Los Angeles Times*

"His best. *The Divine Husband* embraces great themes, without which, as Melville once wrote, you cannot have a great novel—in this case, the relation of the individual to history, love and death, language and reality, among other motifs. . . . Everything he does with [the] historical character [José Martí] feels exactly right. . . . Goldman's book demonstrates that the dream of the Great American Novel is still alive."               —Alan Cheuse, *Chicago Tribune*

"From shards of literary and historical evidence, Goldman's novel re-creates an interlude in the life of José Martí, the great Cuban patriot and poet. . . . Goldman's Martí is indeed wildly popular with his female students, one of whom . . . is able, through prayer and intense meditation, to transport herself from one place to another—an ability that provides an apt metaphor for Goldman's sense of both a country at a cultural crossroads and an exotic lost world."
                                                                 —*The New Yorker*

"José Martí—patriot, poet, and lover—is at the center of Goldman's complex, sprawling novel, and the secret stories that carry the gossipy fictional truth are woven around his weighty presence. . . . Goldman possesses the extraordinary ability of telling a story as if its many facets could all be shown at the same time. It is as if the focus of his lens could simultaneously render background and foreground, side wings and center stage. . . . To write such scenes in all their baroque complexity seems impossible. Goldman performs the feat flawlessly."
                                  —Alberto Manguel, *The Independent* (London)

"A level of writing, very rare, that takes your breath away . . . *The Divine Husband* is an alchemist's brew of history, fiction and legend. . . . The soul of the sweeping plot, however, is José Martí, the driven, charismatic poet and revolutionary who is the fire behind Cuba's insurgence against Spanish rule. . . . Who or what constitutes a divine husband? Within these pages, some find the answer in faith, others in a poet-hero, still others in home and country, or in the embrace of long-sought kinship. Their journeys make for a uniquely ambitious and enlightening read."                                       —*Houston Chronicle*

"With breathtaking originality, [*The Divine Husband*] paints an elliptical portrait of the Cuban poet and revolutionary José Martí and investigates the mystery of his famous love poem 'La niña de Guatemala.' . . . Extraordinary."
                                                                —*Brick* (Toronto)

"Not only does Goldman use an intricate net of storytelling to dredge from the sea floor of history forgotten ways of living (some now ironic in hindsight) that once shaped our hemisphere, but he also brings to the surface a glimmering specimen, a flashing hint for the present literary scene to follow in his very book: to now write the Great American Novel, an author will have to take into account the Big Picture. . . . If that sounds epic, even romantic, then all the better. For it fits the tone—baroque, musical, passionate, even playful—of *The Divine Husband*."
—Oscar Villalon, *San Francisco Chronicle*

"*The Divine Husband* is not only a love story, but a testament to the richness and diversity of the Americas . . . told with my, droll humor."
—*St. Louis Post-Dispatch*

"Wildly inventive . . . engaging and soaringly lyrical."     —*The Seattle Times*

"[A] kaleidoscopic historical saga . . . [that] vividly brings the Americas together."                                         —*Details*

"*The Divine Husband* is a novel to get lost in, a sweeping work of history and imagination that is set in the late nineteenth century in Central America. . . . A tale of intrigue and love that is juxtaposed against the loss of innocence and tyrannies that tear apart a small country."     —*Pittsburgh Tribune-Review*

"*The Divine Husband* presents the peculiar crossroads where love and imagination meet politics and history. . . . *The Divine Husband* is . . . a great miscegenating carnival of ambition and desire. This is why rubber is at the heart of the book— the rubber of plantations, of balloons, of condoms; rubber that stretches, changes form, accommodates, facilitates pleasure, and accepts. . . . [Its] stories . . . pour out of a sly, tender imagination. Tales within tales, they are lushly written, vibrant with lovely descriptions of seascape and landscape."
—*The New York Times Book Review*

"A meditation on the slippery nature of life to art and on the simultaneously artificial and essential nature of storytelling itself . . . Goldman echoes Flaubert, García Márquez, and even DeLillo . . . but he remains his own literary master, and in this book succeeds in making the novel new. . . . A voice of audacity and gravitas that serves as inspiration to writers and readers alike."
—Claire Messud, *Bookforum*

"A novel that, like Central America, connects North and South America and suggests new ways of understanding their long, complicated embrace."

—*Austin American-Statesman*

"Ambitious, rich in period detail, animated by dramatic events and colorful characters. It ably links past and present, underscores the ambiguous connections between fact and legend, imagines the destinies of Central America and the Colossus of the North as inextricably entwined. . . . There is very little that Goldman's sprightly writing cannot bring to life. He makes us feel a nun's zealotry, a politician's ambition, a girl's jealousy." —Dan Cryer, *Newsday*

"A historical epic . . . Goldman's novel sparks with life—with passions, fears, loves, ambitions, jokes, songs, poetry, art. . . . There is plenty of conflict and suspense, failed romances and genuine heroics, but the novel's deepest pleasures come from savoring the subtle characterizations and surprising cultural insights that highlight each episode. . . . His novel speeds through the narrative water with the high-powered assurance of a luxury liner. . . . Goldman has discovered a style that fits his manifold talents and, in this ambitious saga that spans a century of the Western Hemisphere, a story that piques his imagination. . . . When readers reach the end many will choose to flip back to page one and [begin] again." —*Nashville Scene*

"A romantic epic." —*Latina*

"Ebullient, mischievous, and sensual . . . A multifaceted, brilliantly satirical tale populated by compelling and diverse characters, and laced with piquant riffs on everything from miscegenation to hot air balloons. Ultimately, Goldman not only dramatizes the fate of one lush but unlucky Central American country, but also conjures the very spirit of humankind in all its perfidy and splendor."

—*Booklist* (starred review)

"[An] extraordinary beautiful new novel." —Esther Allen, *Bomb*

# The
# DIVINE HUSBAND

# The
# DIVINE
# HUSBAND

A NOVEL

*Francisco Goldman*

GROVE PRESS
NEW YORK

Most of the quotations from and commentary on the writings of Sor María de
Agreda in chapter one are taken from the book *The Visions of Sor María de Agreda:
Writing, Knowledge and Power* by Clark Colahan, published by University of
Arizona Press in 1994. Further quotations are taken from T. D. Kendrick's
translations of Sor María, from his book *Mary of Agreda*, published by
Routledge & Kegan Paul in 1967; the short quotation on page 49 is from
Antonio Rubial García's *La santidad controvertida*.

Frontispiece photo by Yoshua Okon

*Published simultaneously in Canada*
*Printed in the United States of America*

FIRST GROVE PRESS EDITION

Library of Congress Cataloging-in-Publication Data
Goldman, Francisco.
The divine husband : a novel / Francisco Goldman.
p. cm.
ISBN 0-8021-4221-4 (pbk.)
1. Martí, José, 1853–1895—Fiction.   2. Cubans—New York (State)—New York—Fiction.
3. Teacher-student relationships—Fiction.   4. Revolutionaries—Fiction.   5. New York
(N.Y.)—Fiction.   6. Single mothers—Fiction.   7. Guatemala—Fiction.   8. Authors—Fiction.
9. Ex-nuns—Fiction.   I. Title.

PS3557.O368D585 2004
813'.54—dc22        2003063647

Grove Press
an imprint of Grove/Atlantic, Inc.
841 Broadway
New York, NY 10003
05 06 07 08 09   10 9 8 7 6 5 4 3 2 1

*For* Yolanda Molina, my mother (my *Niña de G.*)
& *four accomplices:* Amy, Beatriz, Bex, Esther
& Aura *por el arranque nuevo*

*El sol despierta:*
*Un alma de mujer llama a mi puerta.*
The sun awakens:
The soul of a woman is calling at my door.
—José Martí

# The
# DIVINE HUSBAND

# Chapter 1

When María de las Nieves Moran crossed from convent school to cloister to become a novice nun, it was to prevent Paquita Aparicio, her beloved childhood companion, from marrying the man both girls called "El Anticristo." Of course that is not the version known to history. María de las Nieves became one of "the English Nun's" last two novice nuns, and took as her religious name Sor San Jorge—Slayer of Dragons, Defender of Virgins. She did understand that she was living in a time that called for acts of selfless valor, and that by her own self-sacrifice she was eternally sealing Paquita's sacred vow not to engage in conjugal relations until she—María de las Nieves/Sor San Jorge—had first.

The upholding or breaking of that vow between two thirteen-year-old convent schoolgirls would not only influence the history of that small Central American Republic but also alter the personal lives of some of our American hemisphere's most illustrious men of politics, literature, and industry. What if we read history the way we do love poems, or even the life stories of sainted Sacred Virgins? What if love, earthly or divine, is to history as air is to a rubber balloon? I'm holding a balloon inflated more than a century ago, the nearly weightless globe still supple and warm with the human breath inside. What if I unknot it and let the ghostly air escape, or better yet, take it into my own lungs . . . ? (Maybe this balloon, at least for now, should be regarded as metaphorical.) This project, which you did not live to see completed, Mathilde, had its origin in an old newspaper photograph that, more than thirty years ago, first brought me to your door in Wagnum, Massachusetts. That photograph in the *Wagnum Chronicle* was a reprint of one that had appeared earlier in *Le Figaro* in Paris, and it depicted a Wagnum man bearing a remarkable resemblance to one of Latin America's greatest poet-heroes not just of the nineteenth century but *of all time,* and forever and ever. As a result of that visit, I've spent the ensuing years unearthing and writing this story of María de las Nieves Moran and the people who were closest to her.

One afternoon when they were both still students in the Convent of Nuestra Señora de Belén, Francisca Aparicio—Paquita, familiarly—summoned María de las Nieves to a secret rendezvous in one of the school pavilion's superfluous stone patios. She wanted to share with María de las Nieves the latest note she'd received from her terrifying suitor, smuggled into the convent by his secret ally and friend, the eminent Canon Priest Ángel Arroyo: "*. . . It won't be long now, Paquita, before we close the convents. Then you won't have anywhere to hide from me. See how love conquers all, mi dulce monjita?*" Paquita laughed, though the unfolded note trembled in her hands. The patio smelled of rainy season mold and the urine of little girls who never made it, in the deep hours of the night, from the dormitories to the privies in the rear garden. "His sweet little nun!" she exclaimed. "But this man is so impudent and pernicious, little sister! Look what he calls me! Look at the diabolical messages he sends!" She spoke as if she'd just discovered a new, haughtily adult way of speaking, as if she should have been covering half her face behind a deftly wielded fan as she spoke.

Alarmed, María de las Nieves snatched the note from Paquita and hotly announced, "This I am bringing to the Headmistress General *ahorititita!*" (Double dimunitives, "little-little right now," usually signifying, in that local vernacular, *more* of something, in that case a more immediate immediately.) Paquita's hands reflexively lashed out to grab the letter back, and tore it in half. As if in mirror images, each lunged at the other's half of the letter. Standing stiffly inside their petticoats and identical ankle-length brown serge jumpers and high-collared white blouses, the interned students' uniform, they ended up entwined like Spanish gypsy dancers, slowly circling, each with one arm cocked behind her head to hold half a letter as far back as possible from her rival's reach and the other groping forward, fully extended, fingers wriggling—one girl, Paquita, with skin as white as a sliced almond and black eyes glossy with tears, already ample breast rising and falling, her abundant hair a swooshing avalanche of ebony ringlets down to her waist, her elegant, ladylike nose up in the air like her own avenging angel; and the other, María de las Nieves, damp-cinnamon-colored and skinny as a puppet made of hinged sticks, with no chest at all, and the thin, straight, rust-streaked hair of Indio-Yankee miscegenation, her small flat nose flared out with fury, and strikingly opaque eyes under slashing scimitar brows, swampy mud-hued eyes which, like those of an intelligent drunkard's, seemed always to be intensely staring outward, inward, and nowhere at the same time. Four hands now entwined into one writhing fist, they hovered face to face, until María de las Nieves let go, pushed Paquita away, and flung her balled scrap of the letter to the floor. Paquita staggered backward, righted herself, flopped down on top of it, and, looking up, was run through by María de las Nieves's look of cold pity and disdain.

"I don't need the letter, little-little leadhead. I'll just tell the Madre Headmistress about it." María de las Nieves spun to go, and almost crashed forward onto the floor as Paquita's arms closed around her knees. And so Paquita found herself kneeling before this daughter of an Aparicio family employee (an Indian, albeit a landowning one) begging, pleading: "But it's just a lot of wind! He always says things like that! Close down the convents? He couldn't even if he wanted to. Hermanita mía, you know as well as I that as long as the President's wife is our Madre Prioress's patrona . . ." and so on.

María de las Nieves's expression softened, turned thoughtful, until finally she said, "Bueno. But you have to promise me just one thing."

"Claro, claro, anything."

"You will remain a virgin until I no longer am one myself."

"Sí, sí, claro, I promise." And she grabbed and kissed María de las Nieves's hand.

That had felt like a return to the tortuous method of some of their childhood games, when Paquita had learned to fear María de las Nieves's occasional bouts of perversity, until she'd discovered that she could always reduce "Las Nievecitas" ("The Little-Snows") to a fit of remorseful giggles with a well-timed smile of bemused and tolerant love. But this time all Paquita's smile seemed to accomplish was to further incite her fanaticism: María de las Nieves grabbed Paquita's wrist, jerked her to her feet, and pulled her, almost running, back into the school and to the oratory dedicated to La Virgen del Socorro, she of breast and erect nipple bared to succor her Divine Infant with her Divine Milk. She pushed Paquita down onto her knees and kneeled closely alongside her to seal the vow in prayer. Paquita obeyed, but stole a sidelong glance at her childhood friend, certain

that she would be met by a playful look of conspiratorial mirth. Instead
María de las Nieves answered with a theatrical stare of righteous anger and
sorrow, and Paquita bit the inside of her cheek to keep from laughing. But
in the next instant she was filled with fear: María de las Nieves roughly
grabbed her by the wrist again, lifting the back of Paquita's hand to her
own tear-soaked cheek to hold it there as if it were a handkerchief before
thrusting it back against Paquita's lips with the command "Lick my tears!"
No, said Paquita, she would not lick her tears. María de las Nieves whispered, "Francisca Aparicio, harlot of the pigsties, lick my tears or I will
scream!" And Paquita audibly gasped.

Only when Paquita finally licked the other's salty tears from the back of
her own trembling hand did María de las Nieves release her grip on her
wrist, telling her: "It's a Holy Vow to La Santísima Virgen María and can
never be betrayed without damning us both. So now he can never make
you his wife. I swear that I won't free you from this until he's dead, which
I hope will be soon—" And having expressed such a perhaps sinful desire,
María de las Nieves quickly crossed herself, whispered an act of contrition,
lifted her slender arms around Paquita's rigid shoulders, covered her
cheeks with soft kisses, and murmured, "Ay my poor hermanita, now we
even share each other's sins."

That was how the historic vow—heretofore unknown to history—was
made. If the vow was broken, history and the lives of illustrious men would
unfold one way; upheld, history and men would turn out, at the least, a
little-little differently.

TWO YEARS BEFORE, Juan Aparicio had dispatched his daughter to the
convent school in the faraway capital of the Republic to put her beyond the
reach of her despicable suitor, a man nearly thirty years her senior, the new
revolutionary Liberal government's governor and military commander of
the department of Los Altos. María de las Nieves was also enrolled in the
school by the Aparicios so that their daughter would not be too homesick,
and to be the family's trustworthy informer. Also to advance both girls'
educations and refine their feminine domestic skills and Christian
virtues—it was well known that there was no better school for girls in all

Central America than that of the Convent of Nuestra Señora de Belén. Juan Aparicio often told his daughter and María de las Nieves that no woman was beautiful unless the light of intelligence and learning showed in her eyes.

Los Altos was the country's most Liberal department, at least if the mostly opposite loyalties of the Indian majority were discounted, and the Aparicios, who lived in Quezaltenango, the provincial capital, were among its leading Liberal *criolla* families. They were dutiful Roman Catholics who even sent their sons to study with the Jesuits, there being no better educational option in Quezaltenango, but they worshipped the ideals of Progress even more. Nobody had been happier than they when the Liberal rebels, invincible with their new breech-loading rifles and Mexican sanctuaries over the border, triumphantly entered their forward-looking little city; Juan Aparicio was among the first to sign his name to the decree expelling those same Jesuits, those "Perpetual Assassins of Thought," and closing their school. But at least one trait set the Aparicios apart: despite their untainted Iberian heritage, they seemed immune to the native-born elite's faux-aristocratic disdain for hard work. When coffee was still the crop of the future, Juan Aparicio had established the family's first coffee plantation in the tropical wilds of the Costa Cuca piedmont with "his own bare hands," alongside a drafted army of Mam Indian laborers. Now coffee was the crop of the present, and Juan Aparicio's two-story Italianate mansion was one of the grandest in Quezaltenango, if not all Central America. When the Conservatives were finally driven from power in the capital of the Republic, the Aparicios were immediately comfortable with the Liberals' first President, the affably hedonistic General "Chafandín" García Granados, who declared that although the dark ages of more than three decades of nearly theocratic Conservative dictatorship had turned him into a revolutionary, he was adamantly not a Utopist. Naturally, the new Liberal governor and military commander of Los Altos, the Revolution's indispensable radical rabble-rouser, had become a frequent visitor to the Aparicios' mansion. During several of those visits the eleven-year-old Paquita had obediently entertained the legendary mestizo warrior, who was nearly forty, at the piano, her playing rudimentary but energetic. The Aparicios had been prepared to let themselves feel honored by a friendship with the man who, despite his scandalous and even criminal youth, had already made his mark on the history of the Americas on the side of en-lightenment and progress. But the man of the people had thrown dirt on the family's generosity by setting his rapt heart and marital ambitions on their daughter, still in most pure and innocent girlhood. Paquita's father had resisted with tempered but resolute disdain. It was well known that El Anticristo had threatened Juan Aparicio's life for his refusal, and begun to make trouble for the family in countless irritating but ominous ways in the city in which the Aparicios had lived for four generations. Soon after dis-patching Paquita and María de las Nieves to the convent school, Juan Aparicio went to live in New York City, in order, the two girls were later told, to establish a firm that would import his own coffee to the United States, and export Yankee products to Central America.

In the nearly three years since, Paquita had laid eyes on her reprehen-sible suitor only once, during her second year in the school, when the revo-lutionary government had convened public examinations of Nuestra Señora de Belén's interned students in order to judge whether the girls' minds and spirits were being deformed by the nuns' medieval regimens, and to decide whether the school should be allowed to stay open or immediately closed. So there he was that day, El Anticristo, who'd come all the way from Los Altos, seated along with President General García Granados and his wife, Doña Cristina, a former student of the school and now the convent's most eminent patron. Madre Melchora the Prioress and Sor Gertrudis, also known to history as "La Monjita Inglesa"—the foreign nun was still the school's Headmistress General, though the following year she would be elected Novice Mistress—faces veiled, were the only two nuns present in the school salon that day. Paquita spotted him at the end of the long row of government delegates rising almost in unison from their chairs as she entered. He was still dressing as he had whenever he came to their house in Quezaltenango: in a short jacket—Paquita's mother said he wore it only because a military officer's frock coat made his legs look comically short—and straw jipijapa hat, though for once he wasn't car-rying his notorious bullwhip. The hat, brim pulled low over his eyes, may have hid the donkey bristle of his haircut, but his pair of horizontal mus-taches, square graying beard, and side whiskers could not obscure the sun-baked swarthiness of his mestizo skin or the strict thinness of his lips, though all contributed to his overall air of trying to hide himself behind an elaborate disguise, of which his martial stiffness and fearsome reputation were aspects. Paquita recited a sonnet by Quevedo—*"Mírale el cielo eternizár lo humano"*—and calmly solved all the arithmetic problems posed to her, was quizzed in geography and Spanish but not Latin grammar, spoke a few simple phrases in English, and performed a fairly brief, modestly enunciated oration on Christian virtues as they should be embodied in the home by a loving Christian mother and wife. One of her examination books was passed among the dignitaries so that they could examine her penmanship, as were samples of her needlework. There were no questions on theology or Church history. She was aware of his eyes fixed on her the whole time, his head tilted back as he stared through the shadow under the brim. Halfway through the exam she reflected, surprised, that she hadn't even blushed, as she always had in his proximity back in Los Altos, before she'd even understood what was happening. In detached wonder, she told herself, There is the man who by going to my father and declaring his intention to marry me made himself ridiculous and caused unending calamity for my family—and for María de las Nieves too, because if not for him, neither of us would be here, we would still be living at home, we would still just be day students at the Belemitas' school. At last nearing the end of her speech on the God-fearing wife and mother, she saw him extract a small diary and pencil from inside his jacket and drop his eyes as he jotted something down, releasing her from his stare, and only then did her face blaze with confusion and shame. When she was finished he was the first to erupt into applause, and all the others, rising to their feet, followed, which could have given the impression that both her performance and his approval had saved the school, which was not in the least true, because everyone knew that the school was in no realistic danger of being closed as long as the President and Primera Dama's own daughters were enrolled as day students. Later María de las Nieves told Paquita that when it was her own turn to be examined, El Anticristo dozed through the whole thing, head jerking up and down, finally snoring so explosively that she forgot the words to her own oration on a Christian woman's domestic duties and stopped and looked pleadingly at Sor Gertudis and Madre Melchora, while the President's wife whispered to her husband, who looked sleepy himself, and who finally lifted his long, languid, frock coat–clad frame from his chair, walked over to El Anticristo, and, taking his hat by the crown, picked it off his head and set it back down, waking him. El Anticristo had not liked that at all, darting a look like a snarling dog's at his master's retreating back; he collected himself and smiled at María de las Nieves, his even row of little teeth flashing between his whiskers like a piece of yellowed bone.

During the students' Wednesday afternoon walks to one or the other of the hilltop churches at either end of the city, El Calvario or El Cerro del Carmen, Paquita was always expecting her appalling suitor to appear at any street corner, standing among the clusters of schoolboys, clerks, and soldiers who regularly lined their route, whistling and even calling out some of the girls' names while the servants and lay matrons shepherding them scolded, *Eyes down and forward, niñas;* she imagined him looming over the crowd on horseback to stare at her from under his hat. But he never turned up anywhere, not once. Yet hardly a day passed when she didn't receive at least a tersely affectionate or merely informative sentence printed in his own distinct hand, or even a message discreetly confided to her by a stranger, as just a few weeks ago, when the new barber who came to the school, pruning the knotted ends of her hair, had whispered a sentimental message of affection and salutation from "El Héroe of the Battle of Malacate." His most trusted emissary was still the rooster-faced Padre Ángel Arroyo, whose breath always smelled of stale liquor and the heavy sweetness of the anise seeds he chewed to hide it. As a priest, he was allowed to visit her without chaperone in the interned students' visiting parlor. Padre Ángel claimed to be a longtime intimate of Paquita's family, a ruse to which there was not a crumb of truth. During only Paquita's third week as a student there the priest had passed her a note through the visiting parlor's wrought iron bars, which she read later in the dense shade of the amate tree in a corner of the garden. The then-thirty-eight-year-old military hero of the Liberal Revolution, leader of its most radically anti-clerical faction, had written to his eleven-year-old paramour to inform her of the expulsion of the Jesuits from the Republic. So she'd known even before Madre Melchora, though the Company of Jesus had provided the convent with its preaching clergy and confessors, including the stuttering little Irish priest who came solely to confess Sor Gertrudis—La Monjita Inglesa—in English.

That night of the historic vow, Paquita penned by far the longest letter she'd ever written to her exasperating suitor—El Anticristo, as she often teasingly addressed him, even in a serious missive like this one, know, that he liked it, knowing that she did not like him for liking it reawakening that itch to feel furious with him, to scold and rebuke, so strangely, deeply pleasing—pouring out her confusion over the whole incident with María de las Nieves. *Perhaps it will be better if for a little-little while you stop sharing your little-little secrets with me,* she wrote. A few days later Padre Ángel delivered his reply, rolled up into a thin tube, tied with a pale blue ribbon, and pushed through the visiting parlor's bars. In that letter El Anticristo assumed the comforting tone of a doting father, telling her not to worry, white dove of my heart, though it was precisely because of vows like that, so redolent of the Dark Ages and against nature, that he was going to send all those crazy humbug-stuffed harridans to the same place, far from our shores, that they'd sent the Jesuits, who'd been followed into exile soon after by all the other useless monks and friars of the male religious Orders, and also the Archbishop: *Soon their vows and professions will mean nothing here anymore. Tell your misbegotten so-called sister, in my name, that if in the little time you have left there she causes you any more difficulty, I will make her pay. I think she knows what my bullwhip is made of.*

Paquita was unable to resist sharing this letter with María de las Nieves as well. They met in a corner of the orchard, which was also off-limits to the students, though all knew the way in through a door in the storage rooms behind the school kitchen. Paquita watched tensely as María de las Nieves, holding the letter, read it over more than once. Smiling calmly, handing the letter back, María de las Nieves said, "Bien. You've become a heretic?"

"Claro qué no. Qué no, qué no, but I felt a duty to warn you."

"When he says in his own name, which name is he referring to?" María de las Nieves then asked, because she knew that before the war El Anticristo's name had been José Rufino and now he had changed it to Justo Rufino. Rufino the Just!

Paquita folded the note and tucked it inside her sleeve. When she looked up again, María de las Nieves was already walking away through the orange trees. Not even two weeks later María de las Nieves stupefied everybody by leaving school to become one of Sor Gertrudis's two remaining novice nuns. The gray-eyed, pale, and freckled Novice Mistress was by then already renowned throughout that city and even beyond as La

though her heritage was not English but Irish and she
⟩m Yonkers, New York. In her judgment, María de las
⟩ nearly three years as a boarding student, had revealed
⟩idence of a vocation for a life of chastity, poverty, obedience,
⟩rayer, and so the convent's twenty-three nuns voted unanimously to
accept her, with dispensations for her young age and lack of dowry. That
Sor Gertrudis had only two novices to train was a reflection of the decline
all the female religious communities were experiencing during those years
of insecurity and danger. The Liberal government might forbid any further
taking of vows and professions any day. The death of the individual personality, so zealously and prayerfully sought by those interred in convents,
being a kind of suicide, went the radical Liberals' reasoning, wasn't it immoral not to put a stop to it? For woman was formed to be man's companion, not to bury the treasure of her beauty and grace in the sad solitude of
a convent.

Slightly more than half a century later, in 1927, in Madrid, Spain, Padre
Santiago Bruno would publish his *La Monjitia Inglesa,* his hagiographic life
of Sor Gertrudis de la Sangre Divina. The Spanish Jesuit's book provides
the only known historical account of events inside that convent during the
cataclysmic last year of the convents, including a description of María de
las Nieves's veiling ceremony in the convent chapel:

*Then how can religion be coming to an end in our Republic if He still summons this
virgin to dedicate herself to a life of penitence for all our sins and to be His bride? Give
thanks for Sor San Jorge's taking of her vows, for her humble obedience placates
God's ire, and through her prayers and devotion our sweet little country's anarchy
shall be tamed* ... So went Bishop Julian Ibes's sermon, delivered while
María de las Nieves lay prostrate on the stone floor before the altar, legs
straight and arms out from her sides (she was a shadow of the Crucifix,
waiting to be filled in by His suffering). *Ponder for a moment the immense difference between the place this Sacred Virgin today leaves behind, and the one to which
she comes to live, where austerity shall be her constant companion, fasts her only ban-
quets, mortifications and disciplines her only luxuries and gifts. What shall be her re-
wards? The tranquillity of a good conscience, and the eternal gratitude of pious
patriots* ... This sermon of the soon-after-exiled Bishop Ibes, in the form
of a clandestinely printed pamphlet, was swiftly circulated among those
loyal to religion and the Conservative party. According to Padre Bruno, for

many months afterward, in rich and poor Christian households, obedient little girls knelt before private oratories, altars, and domestic saints to say a prayer for the famous sermon's little novice nun, who had taken the name Sor San Jorge.

So maybe María de las Nieves's initial conception of her calling and vocation really wasn't so contradictory, in spirit if not in scale, to Padre Bruno's historical version after all. On that day of her veiling ceremony, as she lay, face burning with embarrassment, against the cold stone floor while Bishop Ibes pronounced his sermon, hadn't she wanted to leap to her feet and stare defiantly toward where Paquita and the other boarding students were sitting behind their own screened tribune and shout, Let's see if you dare to marry El Anticristo now?!

Bishop Ibes had then come down from the pulpit and, taking María de las Nieves by the arm, led her toward the rear of the chapel and the door to the lower-choir. Carrying her newly consecrated white veil in both hands, she walked with her eyes straight ahead, posture erect, shoulders back, a dreamy smile fixed upon her face—*I am promised in marriage to Our Lord!* (Oh, maybe that was the last time any of this had felt right!) Behind the lower-choir's opaque grille her new Sisters were intoning the *Regnum Mundi* in the very hushed manner of those trying to disguise the imperfection of their voices. She stooped through the lower-choir's door with an abrupt little stumble and the veil unfurled from her hands; inside the nuns closed around her, jostling to be the next to embrace her, covering her face with their foul-smelling kisses, a few with upper lips, even cheeks and chins, nearly as bristly as a man's. (*It was horrifying,* she would recall so many years later, describing that moment as she never could have then. *I was a feed trough in a barn full of starved animals.*) Prodded down onto her knees, she watched her hair, sliced from her head with a large shears, falling in thin splashes to the floor. Sor Gertrudis ordered her to keep her eyes closed while two of the most elderly nuns vigorously stripped the layers of her student uniform from her body for the last time, and then her new religious garments were being roughly pulled over her head, that first touch of scratchy wool against startled skin prompting a feverlike shiver that ran down her torso and made her nipples ache. She felt so transformed by the somber weight of her habit and the thick linen headdress tightly hooding her head, blocking her ears, swaddling her neck and chin, that she put her hands out for balance, even as the white veil was ceremonially lowered over her eyes and Sor Gertrudis intoned, "You no longer need to see, Sor San Jorge, because you will see everything in heaven." At that moment she'd wanted nothing more than a mirror. But mirrors were prohibited in the cloister; she was never to look at herself in a mirror again for as long as she lived. From that day forward she was to have no other mirror than her Sisters in Religion and the starry examples of holy and sainted nuns through history. The first book her Novice Mistress, Sor Gertrudis, assigned to her as spiritual reading was filled with accounts of the horrifying fates of young novices who, against the will of God, decided to return to the world. Those stories often came vividly to mind, causing her to squeeze her eyes shut and clench her fists while twitchy shudders ran all through her.

Because María de las Nieves was a probationary novice nun, wasn't she still free to renounce her vows? Poor and innocent belief! She owed absolute obedience to the Novice Mistress and to her Confessor, now the sole guardians of her conscience and will.

WHEN BOTH WERE still students in the convent school, María de las Nieves and Paquita were taught to manage the hypothetical expenses of a Christian household, paying with the nearly edible hardtack coins baked by the nuns for that purpose. The two girls had then elaborated those lessons into their own game of "*shop*"—they especially liked that English word, *shop*—always played around one or the other's bed in the dormitory. "Let's make a *shopping in the shop*." The bed was the shop and the merchandise was the assortment of personal belongings arrayed over it, though mostly these were extremely ordinary, in keeping with the school's strict regulations on personal possessions. Because in the dormitory all but the most necessary conversation was prohibited, it was a quiet and subtle game, requiring caution and tact. If caught, they would be forced to kneel on hard corn kernels in the school patio with their arms out straight and a rock in each hand for hours—or worse! But any Madre Monitor nun or student observing María de las Nieves and Paquita only saw the two inseparable girls standing as if in transfixed meditation or stupefied boredom or idly pacing around a bed upon which lay, for example, a pencil box, a tortoiseshell comb, and a catechism book. The "shopkeeper's" role was to decide what more desirable item each of these ordinary ones would be changed into, and that was really the heart of the game: a catechism book might be changed into a crystal bottle of Parisian perfume with India-rubber tube and bulb attached, and so on. The strolling shopper, circling the bed, having stopped to eye "the window," would almost always decide to enter—declining to enter ended the game immediately, though that had hardly ever happened. Whenever it had, it had always been María de las Nieves who'd declined, which is not as surprising as it might seem, for in this way she could compensate a bit for Paquita's much greater knowledge of luxury items; but it was also because she was prone to such seemingly bewildering rebuffs, as if really she disliked being treated with gentleness and affection and could endure it for only so long before she had to put a stop to it, sometimes grossly. Once inside the shop, if the shopper could not remember what an ordinary item had been turned into, she wasn't allowed to ask, not even for a hint. With a gesture, a raised eyebrow, she could ask the price, and with held-up fingers or even a whisper, a price would be given; they never haggled like people did in the markets; each girl paid from her own savings of real coins.

Paquita had shown María de las Nieves how to hold the perfume bottle in one hand and the pink little bulb in the other, squeezing it to make a misty cloud of perfume fly from the bottle's atomizer onto her neck like a kiss. She'd paid six centavos for that, and thereby acquired Paquita's worn, lambskin-bound volume of Padre Ripalda's *Catechism*.

When María de las Nieves became a novice nun, that slender volume was the only personal item from her secular life that she was allowed to bring with her into the cloister. It was kept inside the plain pine box at the end of her narrow bed of planks and straw-filled mattress, along with her breviary, book of meditations, the *Contempus Mundi*, her *cilicio*, and rosary beads.

Now she had been a novice nun for five months. It was the first Thursday after Pentecost, only weeks into what would be one of the rainiest winters in memory. In the cell she shared with the Novice Mistress and Sor Gloria de los Ángeles, her sole sister novice, María de las Nieves had just awoken—*before five, but well after four*, as according to the Rule of the Order. Silently, in the predawn park, she recited the prayer points assigned by the

Novice Mistress the night before and stepped to the end of the bed to begin dressing herself *with profound Modesty, while giving thanks to the Lord, who guarded you through the night.* Her religious garments lay folded atop the box. Crouched beneath her habit of night-dampened wool, she wriggled-hopped out of her sleeping chemise, reached for the sackcloth tunic folded atop the box, and wrestled it on. Only then could she straighten up and push her head out through the habit's collar, her arms down the sleeves. She pulled on her hood, pinned on her white veil, and knotted her black cord belt. She glanced across the darkened cell and saw Sor Gloria still struggling inside her habit like a headless, limbless beast, and that profane image provoked a silent puff of laughter that hung inside her like one small cloud in an otherwise leaden sky; a little cloud, she ruefully reflected, full of sin instead of rain. She lifted the lid off the box and reached inside for her manual of Meditation Points, but picked up Paquita's old catechism book instead and brought it to her nose.

Was it still a perfume bottle from Paris, or had it turned back into Padre Ripalda's *Catechism?*

Only You know the truth, my Lord, she dutifully prayed. Oh, *please* let it be a catechism book.

María de las Nieves's harsh and submissive new life in the cloister, during those first months, had passed like a deep dream in which she watched herself growing ever weaker and more infirm, slowly fading away like a mild patch of afternoon light on the forest floor. But just look at what a droopy and dejected little thing I've become in here, she admitted to herself one day, with an inward shiver of lonely truthfulness and self-pity. I, who in childhood was so brazen and sharp-tongued that even adults were wary of me! But did that mean her personality was dying? Shouldn't she rejoice that her future Bridegroom had decided so quickly to favor her? Still, whatever it was she was losing had yet to be replaced by even an inkling of the promised radiance of His divine love.

Every day she prayed: *Please, my Lord, please let me feel something of what I am supposed to feel.*

In the five months since María de las Nieves had become Sor San Jorge she hadn't seen Paquita Aparicio once, not even a glimpse, nor had she received any message from her, nor had she even heard her name spoken. She hadn't received any visitors from home either: not from her own

mother or Paquita's mother or Paquita's older brother, Juan, who'd all occasionally come from Quezaltenango when she was a student; nor had she
received any letters. As a novice nun she was forbidden all locutory parlor
visits and all correspondence, even from her mother, for a year.

Every day she prayed also for some bit of news of Paquita. But it was
obvious that she had no gift for prayer, or even any ability.

THE STORY OF how María de las Nieves had first come to live with
Paquita and her family when both girls were six was a peculiar but fascinating one, and Juan Aparicio never tired of telling it. Over the years many
people, in many parts of the world, would hear it from his own lips, and those
listeners often remembered it, so that it spread the way a good traveler's tale
does, routinely provoking head nodding and heartfelt commonplaces about
fate and the way things can go in the American tropics, and sometimes even
stirring imaginations in more private ways. How there had been a legend, or
rumors, brought down by Indians to Quezaltenango, that far away in the
mountains two women and a little girl were living on their own deep in the
forest. The little girl had golden hair, one of the women had leathery black
skin, and they spoke among themselves, the Indians claimed, in an unin-
telligible demon language. After a few years of hearing those stories, Juan
Aparicio had finally hired a Mam Indian to lead him to the mysterious females. For more than a full day, and all through the night, they'd hiked
across a terrain of forested ridges, mountain slopes, and valleys. When they
finally arrived at the rustic little forest compound, they found a little girl
standing alone in the dirt yard. A spotted fawn, tamely standing by her,
bright brown fur nearly the same color as her skin, scampered away at the
sound of the men's approach, and the girl turned and stared at Juan
Aparicio so directly yet calmly that it was he who was startled. The scent
of a still-smoldering cooking fire hung in the air, though there was no sign
of the legend's other two women. The little girl wore a begrimed smock of
coarse cloth, her hair was braided into numerous limp sprouts tied with
rag ribbons, and she was puffing on a crude cigar of wild jungle tobacco.
From one hand she dangled a strangely buoyant, elongated, yet gelatinous
object, a sort of ghostly idol fashioned, it appeared, from some smudgily

translucent material that it irked Juan Aparicio to be unable to identify. But the girl's stare was every bit as disconcerting. Her eyes had the dark radiance and mossy hue of deep forest light, steadily and fearlessly watching as Juan Aparicio slowly approached, speaking to her in a tone he might have used to soothe a panicked animal. She called out a burst of gibberish and held the idol out as if to warn him away with it—because of its size and the way she now balanced it upon both palms, oddly tremulous and almost floating, the thing, he realized, was nearly weightless. It appeared to have a little face painted on in red blood or perhaps cochineal paste, and long ears. Juan Aparicio had then needed a long moment to recompose himself. Meanwhile the little girl's expression, wide-eyed and grinning, had become one of excited hope and emotion.

"Muddah and Lucy gon git wadah, Dada," she screeched, as emphatically as before. "Yuh brin me panqueques made av sno like yu promis me, Da? Jaja! Look da rabid Pakal Chon make me!"

The demon language was English. The little girl's hair was not golden but a rust hue that would darken as she grew older. The idol turned out to be a plaything, a sort of anthropomorphic doll, made by one of her Indian neighbors from the inflated intestines of a peccary, ingeniously twisted and tied together into the crude form of a rabbit. Juan Aparicio was the first white man María de las Nieves had seen since the death of her father, Timothy Moran, almost three years before. Though she knew that her father was dead and where he was buried, in her confusion and excitement—probably abetted somewhat by the slightly psychotropic effects of wild tobacco upon such an immature brain—she also thought that her father had somehow returned from his long journey to New York City, where he was originally from. In New York City, her *Da* had liked to tell her, the little girls ate pancakes made of snow. When he'd named her Mary of the Snows, hadn't he been thinking of those special pancakes and the fortunate girls who ate them? In her fantasy she had always known that when her Da returned, he would bring her pancakes made of snow. So María de las Nieves herself would recall many years later in *My Forest Memories*, her brief unpublished memoir, handwritten in the simple style of a children's story and composed for at least one very young reader. (There it was one morning, inside a plain manila folder, laid upon the desk at which I'd been invited to work.)

So that was how Juan Aparicio found María de las Nieves, and the black servant from British Honduras, Lucy Turner, and a young Indian woman, Sarita Coyoy, mother of the girl and "widow" of the Yankee immigrant Timothy Moran, who'd brought them to that remote place, intending to start a coffee farm. Timothy Moran had barely even begun to clear the land when he'd perished, stranding his female dependents there. He'd died, Sarita Coyoy soon after told Juan Aparicio, from a mule kick to the stomach. At least he'd had the time to build his family their wooden huts first, roofed with durable oilcloth. All three females almost constantly smoked those hand-rolled cigars, their teeth stained dark with the juice. They grew their own corn, squash, and chilies, but were undeniably dependent on the frugal, bartering generosity of their Indian neighbors. They dressed in the rustically woven fabrics and clothing of the Indians of the mountain forests, but also in tattered remnants of the garments of civilization. Timothy Moran had left behind, among other personal artifacts, a burlap sack filled with bottles of Irish whiskey; the sack of bottles, buried in the dirt, was dug up by Lucy Turner on the day of the rescue. He'd also had a leather-bound two-hundred-page notebook in which, mystifyingly—though it is not the only mystery in this story that I was never able to solve—he'd scrawled only the names of four kinds of orchids in misspelled Latin, leaving the remaining pages utterly blank. In his trunk there was also a small collection of by then nearly rotted magazines, mainly *Harper's Weekly* and *Punch*, from which Lucy Turner had taught the little girl to read in English.

Sarita Coyoy said she was from the Yucatán, and that she'd met Timothy Moran when he was managing a henequen plantation there. They were all Christians, Sarita insisted, though they possessed no Bible or even prayer book. Her daughter had been baptized a Catholic, Sarita Coyoy said, just after her birth and just before they'd fled the Yucatán because of the murderous Indian uprising against foreigners and whites there, crossing the border into this country and settling first in Amatitlán. Many years would pass before Juan Aparicio would finally begin to distinguish what was true and what was false in the accounts that Sarita Coyoy and Lucy Turner gave of their pasts. Born on August 5th, feast day of Mary of the Snows, the remarkable little girl could speak and read in English and Spanish and also spoke an Indian language, Mam.

Juan Aparicio brought the trio back with him to Quezaltenango, where he was raising his own family, including a daughter, Paquita, the same age as the rescued girl. Lucy Turner was soon the Aparicio household's head inside servant, although Sarita Coyoy's position as an inside servant with few chores was even more privileged: she was given two rooms of her own next to the stables, where she lived with her daughter, who was otherwise treated by the Aparicios as nearly a family member.

Paquita and María de las Nieves together attended the day school of the Bethlehemite nuns in Quezaltenango and, during the weeks and months they spent at the Aparicio coffee farm, roamed and played as freely as if both had grown up together in the wilderness. Paquita freely shared her clothing—even her childhood dresses came from Paris—with María de las Nieves, and all her other belongings. María de las Nieves's isolated up-bringing had made her a precocious reader, despite the limited reading material at hand there. Books were new to her, but she was immediately as comfortable with them as if in the mountain forests books in at least two languages had grown on trees. She never needed to be asked twice to read out loud, and often she didn't even need to be asked. Juan Aparicio began searching out suitable books for María de las Nieves in the hopes that she would impart to his daughter some of her bookish enthusiasm and habits, along with her familiarity with English, the language of Progress and the Future. María de las Nieves and Paquita did indeed spend many hours reading together. Subsequently Juan Aparicio sometimes even found his daughter secluded in some corner of the house with a book of her own, and then he knew that he was being rewarded for having taken the stranded fe-males into his home. On rainy afternoons, whether in the city or on the farm, María de las Nieves and Paquita liked to climb into one or the other's bed and lie closely together under one of those coarse and hairy Momostenango Indian blankets woven from mountain sheep's wool, fas-tidiously but relentlessly pinching and plucking at the blanket, holding woolly tufts to their eyes, scrutinizing and discarding until finally one girl or the other found a single bristle of wool long enough to insert inside her nostril while twirling it between thumb and forefinger, tickling the mem-brane until her eyes began to water and all the nerves in her face began deliciously to contract and dissolve into one blissfully prolonged itch that finally became unbearable and she explosively sneezed. That pleasurable vice, their shared secret, once reawakened, often became insatiable. María de las Nieves and Paquita passed many rainy-season afternoons together under scratchy Indian blankets, sneezing until their heads ached and their limbs felt achingly hollow. How many blankets did they leave looking entirely moth-eaten, picked clean of fuzzy wool, until all that was left was the denuded weave underneath?

IT'S A CATECHISM book, María de las Nieves silently, decisively told herself. It's what He made it and intended it to be, *not* a perfume bottle. She laid the book back into the box and took out her volume of Meditation Points—*Spiritual Exercises of San Ignacio, Adapted to the State and Profession of the Virgin Brides of Christ*—and carried it over to the weak glow spilling from the niche holding the small Sanctuary Lamp. Both the Novice Mistress and Sor Gloria de los Ángeles also stepped into that dim light, books open in their hands, though none spoke any word. *Once dressed, read your Meditation Points, and meditate on them for a while. Pray until Prime.* Birdsong and rooster clamor poured in through the still-darkened rectangular window high in the wall, along with the wet smells of night just beginning to lift off the earth. She tugged lightly at her hood, adjusting it under her chin and, rolling the tip of her tongue in and out through the gap in her upper teeth, found her place in the manual. The Meditation Points the Novice Mistress had assigned were on *The Rule of Chastity, and its two poles: Love only your Husband. Do not love with particular friendship any living creature . . . Point One: Consecrate to God your body and senses, renouncing all bodily delight . . . Point Two: The supreme eminence of Virginal Purity. Virgins are Angels on Earth, just as Angels are Virgins in Heaven . . . Third Point: Ponder this Point. Virginity, perfectly guarded, is a prolonged martyrdom. Firstly, because of the temptations with which the Devil battles it. Secondly, because of the war waged inside ourselves, by our own body, soul, imagination, et cetera. Who will defend you from such enemies? The arms of the enemy are the same features and charms which God gave you for His delight. If you surrender, you are making war on God with the same beauty, health, graces, and charms which He gave you. And if He taketh them away, with a grotesque and contagious sickness, as He has done to so many, what will happen to you then? Ponder it well . . .* A certain poor Indian *anciana* with her nose rawly devoured by mountain

leprosy is what María de las Nieves now recalled, and futilely pondered . . .
When the Novice Mistress shut her book, that was the signal for the two
novices to follow her out of the cell and through the cloister to the upper-
choir for Prime, Terce, and Mass.

PAQUITA, THAT NIGHT, as she did almost every night, had crept from
the school dormitory to crawl into bed with the servant Modesta Sabal.
Ever since she was a little child, Paquita had been crawling into bed to
sleep with Indian servants. How could any girl, as a few of the other students actually did, prefer sneaking into the cloister at night to sleep in a
hard, narrow bed alongside a bony or flabby old nun reeking of candle wax,
incense, rancid breath, and dirty hair, or even one of the younger Sisters?

The approaching dawn had yet to penetrate the darkness when Paquita
was woken in the shuttered, pitch-dark room by the door opening and air
swooping in, striking her steamy skin like chilly ocean spray as she lay with
her chin nestled between the sleeping Indian woman's hard shoulder and
soft, tangy neck. Modesta's nostrils were clogged by a perpetual rainy-
season cold, and the saliva flowing from her wide-open mouth had so
soaked Paquita's cheek that when she lifted her head to stare blindly toward the door, that side of her face tingled in the air.

"Niñas, today bring back three," said the voice speaking into the darkness. "Three Inditos, eh?" After a moment the voice repeated, "Three
Inditos," and added, "Do you hear me, you lazy donkeys?"

Paquita went rigid with confusion and terror. The small, brittle-sounding
voice belonged to Madre Melchora. She knew she was about to be discovered in the servant's bed, and horribly punished. But it seemed incredible
for the Prioress to have left the cloister at such an hour, through the only
door leading into the school ground, just to walk all the way to the servants'
room to deliver that message.

Ordinarily Paquita and the interned students saw Madre Melchora only
during religious retreats or during her visits to the school on the first Friday afternoon of every month, when she liked to make the girls run around
the garden until they were out of breath, hitting at their legs and rears with
a stick as they went past. Afterward she would sit under the garden's peach

tree, improvising villancicos and other religious rhymes out loud, and challenging the girls grouped around her to improvise their own. During those Friday visits, Madre Melchora's small, lusterless brown eyes, which had the pretty shape of garlic cloves, would often brighten, and a faint blush would seep into her age- and austerity-scourged cheeks, and a thin smile of penetrating sweetness would animate her coarsened, though delicately shaped lips, and Paquita would remember that Madre Melchora really was the same exquisitely featured, adolescent aristocrat depicted in the portrait hanging in the school's visiting parlor, wearing a crown of fresh flowers on the day of her profession more than half a century before, when the Republic itself was still in its infancy. Back then, the professing of a new young nun, especially when she was from the wealthiest and best of families, with so much more to give up for God than an ordinary girl, had been an occasion for citywide rejoicing, with fireworks and elegant balls.

Paquita stared into the dark, not even daring to blink, listening to the pounding of her heart and to the sucking stewpot of Modesta's breathing as if it were also her own. But maybe this is a dream, she told herself. I'm dreaming with my eyes open. Even if it is a dream . . . Dreams lie, she'd learned in theology class, but some tell the truth. San Agustín's mother, Santa Mónica, had the gift of being able to tell when a dream should be ignored and when it was a message from God. If this was the Prioress appearing to her in a mystical dream, then Paquita knew why. Yes, it wasn't hard to imagine what might be worrying her. Of course I'll help and protect you, Madre Melchora, she silently promised, tightly clutching two fistfuls of her chemise. I'll do everything I can . . . She squeezed her eyes tightly shut, feeling how they ached almost as if punched from the pressure of building tears: I'm going to marry El Anticristo. I said yes a week ago. Not even my mother knows.

"Sí, Madre Reverenda. Three," said Josefa Socorro, the other servant, speaking from the nearby bed. So it really was the Prioress at the door.

"The most repugnant you can find, hija mía," said Madre Melchora.

"Of course, mi Madrecita."

The Prioress said softly, "Blessed be the Sacred Heart of our Most Holy Mother in Heaven."

And the servant responded, "Blessed be the Sacred Heart of our Señor."

Paquita heard the rustle of the Prioress's habit as she turned in the doorway, the door quietly closing, and the soft click of the latch, gently lifted and released. She exhaled, but her relief was fleeting. The secret of her engagement to El Anticristo, which by day was often like a dangerous fairy tale silently and thrillingly telling itself in her very blood, felt now like the mouth of a bottomless cave inside her.

Only a week ago Paquita had hesitantly murmured yes in the confessional to her future husband's latest emissary, Padre Josefat Trevi, who guaranteed her a lavish wedding in the Los Altos Cathedral, despite Rufino the Just's strained relationship with the Church. The young, pink, utterly hairless, native-born diocesan priest came to the school twice a week only to confess the boarding students. "Because by then, Francisca," Padre Josefat had whispered, "your future husband will undoubtedly have ascended to the Presidency." It might be a matter of days, weeks, a few months at most. Everyone knew that the radicals of the Patriotic Junta had grown impatient with the slow pace of reforms, with the first Liberal President's appetite for compromise, his cozy friendships among the old Conservative elite. Back in February, El Anticristo had briefly assumed the role of Interim President while Chafandín García Granados was away at the head of the troops repressing a new Conservative-Jesuit rebellion in the eastern part of the country: only then—by the Interim President's irrevocable decree—had the remaining male monastic Orders and the Archbishop been expelled.

"He'll need you, Francisca, and we'll need you too, so that he doesn't go too far, so that you can intercede on our behalf when he does," Padre Josefat had continued. "You will be the Queen of Central America, Francisca!" The lowly diocesan priest looked like a pink India-rubber ball with round pinkish eyes painted on. Padre Josefat even lacked eyebrows. Were these priests who were allied with El Anticristo apostates? Or apostles of a more just Kingdom of God here on earth? Who was there for her to ask or confide in? Not a soul!

So her three years in Nuestra Señora de Belén seemed to have accomplished the school's stated mission after all: filled her with terror and love of God, and prepared her to be a modest, devoted, and virtuous Christian mother and wife—to El Anticristo. Yet she'd sworn to the Holy Virgin not to enter carnal relations until María de las Nieves, now promised in holy matrimony and chaste eternity to the Divine Redeemer, had done so first.

The future was sometimes like a mirror in which her imagination exulted, delighted, or even wept, but now it was curtained in black. She silently prayed: You made me this beautiful for a reason. Madre Melchora was once as beautiful as I, and You made her beautiful for Yourself. So I was made for someone else. Perhaps I will never comprehend why.

Paquita would never forget Madre Melchora's portentous, predawn visit. Indeed, seventy years later, in the last letter she would ever write to María de las Nieves, her nearly lifelong friend and sometime nemesis, she would confide: *Something inside my heart froze forever that night, mi hermanita.* Guilt and terror like a splinter of glacial ice lodged in her heart, which her own long life of loves and sorrows would never thaw.

"But who could the third Indian be for?" Josefa muttered in the dark. "Surely it's not just an ordinary penance."

Modesta Sabal loudly snorted mucus in her sleep. She had slept through the extraordinary visit.

"Wake her, patoja!" Josefa lit the lamp by her bed, casting a light that filled the low-ceilinged little room like a dirty-gold, quivering liquid.

Paquita sat up and shoved the pretty young servant. Modesta woke gasping and sputtering, and Paquita leaned over and gave her a good-morning kiss on the cheek. Modesta's shining dark eyes always seemed to smile on the world no matter how she was awoken! Josefa and Paquita told Modesta what had just happened, and then both servants speculated out loud on what it could mean, and who the third Indio might be for.

"What do you mean, *for?*" asked Paquita. "What does she do with them?"

"Our Madre's purpose is most sacred, Señorita Francisca," said Josefa. "But it is not for you to know."

The Prioress's unprecedented visit seemed even more ominous to the two convent servants than it had to Paquita. Every Thursday, near dawn—always after shooing Paquita back to her dormitory before the students were woken for morning Mass—Josefa and Modesta went into the city streets to look for destitute Indian men. Before, for as long as each had been a servant there, they had always had to return to the convent with just one Indian, but in February Sor Gertrudis had been elected Mistress of Novices, and had soon after convinced the Prioress to let her join in her weekly rite: from then on two Indians had been required. Now the Prioress had come all the way to their room in the dark to tell them to bring back three. Though they were just servants—*las mandaderas,* the only ones allowed to come and go from the cloister on errands—they knew that such abrupt changes in routine were only supposed to happen outside, and that inside the cloister, it was the serene timelessness and order of heaven that was to be emulated. So it seemed like one more sign that religion really was in danger of coming to an end in their world. But it was also one more sign of the growing influence of the foreign Novice Mistress over the Prioress. Madre Melchora del Espíritu Santo had been reelected Prioress every three years for nearly three decades without ever before having shown such favoritism, her love for her professed Sisters and Daughters in religion—as Padre Bruno acknowledged in his *vida* of Sor Gertrudis—*as evenly dispersed, nourishing, impersonal, and unfathomable as the Divine Light and Dewdrops of Dawn.*

"Grosera!" scolded Modesta, slapping Paquita on the shoulder, for she had just induced a magnificent sneeze, quaking the bed. The servants thoroughly disapproved of this business of making yourself sneeze with blanket hairs. Paquita wiped her watery eyes and nose with her sleeve, sat up, and blurted:

"The third Indio is for María de las Nieves." As soon as the words were out of her mouth, she knew they must be true. "Sor San Jorge, I should say." She'd wanted this last to sound lightly derisive, but her trembling voice betrayed her. Nothing filled Paquita with more unease than the thought that María de las Nieves was truly holy and favored by God.

"Santa Cecilia y Santa Rosa de Lima!" exclaimed Josefa. "I think not!" And she added a feminine growl of disdain that gladdened Paquita's heart. Josefa had the classic features of a jowly Mayan Queen, eyes like enormous dark seeds, sagging earlobes, fat lower lip lugubriously curled, regal anteater nose. She rarely smiled but when she did, as now, the effect was incredible, for Josefa was missing exactly every other tooth in both her top and bottom rows, and her every single intact tooth was situated beneath or atop a gap. It seemed impossible that such an arrangement of teeth could be accidental, but it was.

"You think not?" asked Paquita. "Why do you think not, mi querida Josefa?"

"Because that muchachita is a little devil. Everyone knows that."

"Apparently Sor Gertrudis does not know that."

"Pues síííí, niña. But Sor Gertrudis is very wise. She is destined to be Prioress."

"But Josefa, you just said—" She should try to hide how cross this conversation was now making her. "Josefa, then why do you think Sor Gertrudis has such a high opinion of Sor San Jorge? Last Friday, when she came to school with Madre Melchora, she told us that since entering the noviatiate María de las Nieves has become like a little girl returned to a state of innocence. For such are her simplicity, humility, and obedience. That's what Sor Gertrudis said. What do you think of that?"

As all three contemplated those words, the long silence was broken by the startled clatter of another convent's bells—the Clarissas, now ringing their own dawn Angelus a few long blocks away.

"Then it must be so," Modesta said softly

Modesta began to work with her fingers at the sleep-knotted ends of Paquita's hair, which fell in loose, lustrous tangles to her tiny waist. Paquita pulled a handful of her tresses down over her eyes, pressing them beneath her spread hand while her tears soaked into them, seeping and falling in tart droplets onto her extended tongue, flavored—salty, sweet, bitter, and sour!—by the rose-petal, orange-blossom, and almond-oil mixture she worked into her hair every night before bed, and by the vinegar she rubbed into her face. She lifted her hand away just long enough to say:

"Because La Monjita Inglesa likes talking to her in English, that's how they became friends. That hardly makes María de las Nieves ready for sainthood, eh?"

When Paquita joined her schoolmates for morning Mass in the chapel, conducted by the convent chaplain Padre Lactancio Rascón, the black lace mantilla she wore over her head was her most recent gift from El Anticristo. Woven in Paris by the inheritors of the secret methods of the Chantilly lace makers beheaded during the French Revolution for having served the aristocracy, the shawl consisted of an intricate pattern of railroad tracks and locomotives pulling trains in and out of tunnels. So far the nuns hadn't noticed it, and Paquita, though she knew that Pope Pío IX had issued bulls condemning Progress, Modernity, and Liberalism, had dared not ask whether or not the mantilla counted as a blasphemy.

"THE ROME OF Central America" and "Pope Pío IX's Favorite City," these had been the Conservatives' civic-minded nicknames for their pious capital. Everybody knew that in the intimacy of his personal oratory in Rome, the Pope prayed every day before a crucifix carved in the former colonial capital, Santiago de los Caballeros, from the native wood of an orange tree by the native-born master sculptor Juan Gamusa. Irreverent foreign travelers inevitably remarked that the Conservative Citadel resembled *a colossal convent;* they marveled that a visit to a New World city, set down amid so much verdant abundance, could leave the soul feeling so penetrated by gloom. Yet it was one of the youngest capital cities in the Americas. Not even a hundred years had passed since the former capital, among the oldest, had been devastated by earthquake for the third time in less than a century and its surviving population, by royal decree, ordered to move to the nearly uninhabited Valley of the Cows to found and build a new city—along with the uprooting of several entire Indian villages to provide labor, to carry the rocks and rubble the forty-five kilometers from the old to serve as the foundation of the new. But the work of building a new city from scratch, interrupted by Independence and the constant convulsions of civil wars throughout the Isthmus, had proceeded with dreary slowness anyway, despite the seemingly inexhaustible supply of Indian labor. Another half century passed before the most essential buildings, public and ecclesiastical, were more or less completed, including the Cathedral, which had to wait twenty more years before it was finally provided with bell towers, a chaste neoclassical facade, and a mechanical clock face that still had no hands. But how radiant and blessed the city could look, when approached from the mountains and across the plains on a clear day, the domes and belfries of its thirty-eight churches, monasteries, and convents shining pink and gold in the sun!

Unlike Nuestra Señora de Belén's nuns—even the nuns who taught in the school were otherwise strictly cloistered—Josefa and Modesta went out regularly into the streets and markets of the city the Liberals had now begun to call "the Paris of Central America" and "La Pequeña Paris"; out into what the ecclesiastics referred to merely as "*el siglo*"—literally, the century, but also the world. And the century did seem to have been turned inside out, and upside down. Every day Josefa and Modesta saw or heard about some new outrage. Clowns costumed as priests entertained in the new state schools, sprinkling Florida Water instead of Holy Water from their hyssops, and dispensing pale marzipan cookies shaped like the Host in order to infuse children with disrespect for the mysteries of the Eucharist. Confessionals had been removed from emptied monasteries to the gardens of fashionable Liberals, where they served as flowering-vine-draped booths for coquetries and dalliances. The new military academy was situated in the emptied Recollect monastery; the new telegraph office in the former church of the Franciscan friars; the Bureau of Liquor and Tobacco in the Dominicans' vast old cloister. A new law was passed prohibiting clergy from naming their illegitimate children heirs to any church property or wealth whatsoever.

Josefa and Modesta wanted to believe that what they often heard was true: that because most Liberals had wives, mothers, grandmothers, and sisters who'd been nurtured and educated in girlhood by nuns, they would never dare to close the convents. Nuestra Señora's nuns, of course, had always had their own sources for keeping up with events in "the century": students, parents, visitors to the locutory parlor, patrons, including the president's wife, Doña Cristina. They were resisting the daily sacrileges and threats, they always reassured their supporters, by the most effective means they knew: through prayer. La Monjita Inglesa's Spanish was flawed, and spoken almost entirely without articles. "*Prayers stronger than men,*" Sor Gertrudis, voice ringing out, had reminded the schoolgirls during her previous Friday visit alongside the Prioress. That very conviction was the source of her fame.

When El Anticristo's marauding predecessor Serapio Cruz and his Liberal-rebel horde had seemed poised to conquer the city four years before, just weeks after their murderous sacking and burning to the ground of the departmental capital of Huehuetenango, Sor Gertrudis had placed a tiny tin rifle in the crib of the Divine Infant in the little oratory outside the sacristy, and prayed to Him to defend the city better than men could. For three days and two nights, the freckled foreign nun had fasted and prayed before the crèche, until word arrived that Serapio Cruz's head, fried in oil, wrapped in moss and oak leaves, and carried in a sack slung over a captive

Liberal student's back, was being marched across the plains toward the city gates by victorious Conservative troops. The somber city had responded to that news with its greatest outpouring of public rejoicing since that set off years before by Pope Pío IX's declaration of the Immaculate Conception as church dogma.

The Archbishop was the first to call Sor Gertrudis "La Monjita Inglesa," at High Mass in the Cathedral the following Sunday, proclaiming her feat as equal in holiness to that of the nun whose prayer vigil had been credited by Cardinal Richelieu with the French victory over the British at the Bay of Biscay. Soon La Monjita Inglesa was known throughout the country and, credited with a miracle, was even prayed to—daily people pushed rosaries, medals, scapulars, mantillas, and other articles through the convent's revolving turngate with notes and names attached asking "the English Nun" to bless and return them.

But the defeat of Serapio Cruz was Sor Gertrudis's last battlefield victory. It was the Liberals' country now. Upon their triumph two years later, the exhumed head of he who in life was Serapio Cruz was granted the Church's most solemn posthumous honor: burial in the Cathedral crypt, alongside the Conservative dictator who had ruled the country for thirty years and whose Indian followers had begun calling him "the Son of God" when the former swineherd was still in adolescence and leading them into war with a personal mandate from the Queen of Heaven to drive out all foreigners and heretics.

BRING BACK THE most repugnant Inditos you can find, Madre Melchora had mandated. But Josefa and Modesta understood this to mean they only had to be as wretched in appearance as those brought before the Prioress and the Novice Mistress the week before, the week before that, and so on, and also sober, if only relatively so. Sober enough to promise suitably respectful, even fearful, comportment in the presence of the Prioress, the Novice Mistress, and whomever the third Indian was for—that is, no eruptions of violent, obscene, satanically heathen, or otherwise outrageous behavior. All of that had been known to occur anyway, because when bringing Indios, or indeed any men, including priests, into close proximity with nuns, you could never be too vigilant, no matter how docile or polite they initially, externally seemed.

The two mandaderas left through the convent door adjacent to the turngate, the nun who was Portress closing it behind; Josefa with a basket of hard-boiled eggs and bread rolls balanced atop her head, Modesta with a clay jar of warm, sweetened *atole*, ladle and stringed drinking gourds dangling. The dawn was so fog-thickened that it might as well have been night, for all they could see ahead and around them. Josefa and Modesta turned the corner to walk along the convent's long, windowless southern wall instead. A tallow street lamp still burned up ahead like a single ripe orange floating in the pearly-gray mists. The city's streets had originally been laid, in accordance with Spanish colonial policy, at slightly downward-sloping grades running east and west from the central Calle Real, so that rain and sewage would drain from the most elite neighborhoods down through progressively poorer ones. But many of the old clay drainage pipes and midstreet gutters were so clotted and collapsed by rot that during the rainy season some of the most important intersections, worn concave by traffic, turned into impassable pestilential swamps.

One of the portable bridges spanned the avenue they were walking toward, and Josefa and Modesta could hear the rumble of cart wheels, the clatter of hooves, the softly resounding thumps of so many sandaled and bare feet crossing the sodden wooden planks; also the domesticated and wild animal sounds of what could have been a fog-shrouded Noah's Ark passing up ahead, mixed with the cries of human babies. Passing down the avenue and over the bridge was a human stream of Indians on their way to the market behind the Cathedral, Indians from the villages outside the city gates, and from far beyond, bringing the city its food and labor.

Otherwise, the only signs that the city had begun to stir were the smell of pine-fat-kindling and cooking-fire smoke in the damp, night-flower-sweetened air; stripes of lantern light in cracked shutters. As the sun rose, the fog would lift too, and the city, as it had for two rainy weeks now, would feel lost under low gray skies that erased the usual horizon of mountains and volcanoes, creating the illusion that they were alone at the bleak top of the world, instead of in a lush valley plateau.

In front of the recently opened El Moro y el Oro tavern men lay prostrate; as they hurried past, Josefa and Modesta could see—*chis!*—faces completely blackened with ants. One drunkard had rolled across the muddy swath of street into the sewage ditch running down its middle. *The stench of shit is as the sweetest aroma from heaven to one immersed in loving devotion to God.* Sí pues, Madrecita, but not to those who would have to rouse El Hombre Caca to his feet in order to bring him to you. Taverns, cantinas, billiards halls and gaming rooms, and other by-the-glass liquor establishments opened weekly now, to say nothing of brothels, which before had been confined to a few easily avoidable alleyways and the proximity of barracks.

Josefa and Modesta turned left onto the unevenly paved avenue and, walking along the convent's eastern wall, merged with the market-bound traffic. Most Indians carried their wares on their backs, kept in place by straps across their foreheads. Women also balanced bundles, baskets, and jars atop their heads, and their daughters followed obediently behind, looking less like children than like diminutive women, dressed the same as their mothers, in long woven skirts and embroidered *huipiles,* and wearing necklaces and earrings made from red beads and punctured, now defunct coins bearing the image of the late Conservative dictator. The servants set basket and jar down on the sidewalk of the Plazuela Habana and stood scrutinizing the passing multitude for appropriate candidates.

Paquita had guessed right: the morning's third Indian was to be for María de las Nieves. Sor Gertrudis knew that her newest novice's first months in the novitiate had left her demoralized and full of doubts. She'd counseled María de las Nieves that her feelings of inadequacy were not only to be expected, they were even laudatory, so long as they presaged a true death of the personality and self. Rather than to a complete lack of vocation, the Novice Mistress ascribed her young charge's spiritual troubles to her immaturity and ordinary native indolence, stubbornness, and pride. A girl had to grow up before she could learn to die. After much prayer, meditation, and discussion with both the Prioress and the nuns' Confessor, Padre Lactancio, she'd decided to guide María de las Nieves onto a path of rigorous penitential self-mortification—so years before, as a young Carmelite novice in Havana, Cuba, Sor Gertrudis herself had been guided—one that would elicit authentic reactions and emotions one way or another, impossible to fake, if also difficult to manage. That morning's session in the lower-choir with Madre Melchora's Thursday Indians was to initiate María de las Nieves's harsh new regimen.

It didn't take long for the servants to collect their three Indian volunteers: corpulent Antonio Kaal, a goiter the size of a partridge under his chin, who'd come to the city in search of a son who'd joined the army two years back and hadn't been heard from since, and Domingo Toc, wearing his hangover like a reeking suit made of broken eggshells. The third Indian was Juan Diego Paclom, and his name was destined to leave at least a trace of his existence in recorded history. Only five years later he would die in the mountains of Momostenango, a rebel chief fighting against the Liberals in the doomed Indian uprising known as the War of the Caves. By then Juan Diego Paclom would be a full-fledged *chuchkajawib*, or "mother-father" shaman-priest, one of those with the especially dangerous ability, albeit useful in wartime, to summon the ancestors from within sacred mountains during séances in pitch-black caves in order to send death to their enemies. But that morning, when Modesta and Josefa plucked him off the street, he was still a young aspirant, fulfilling the pilgrimage to which a dream had called him, so that he could begin his apprenticeship: searching for the woman who would be his Spirit Wife and to whom he was to bring the gift of a lamb. A Spirit Wife was more important than a real wife because without one he could not commence his training, neither in the hard world at hand nor in the spirit one. Indeed, all the providential and calamitous signs that Juan Diego Paclom was destined to be a *chuchkajawib* were present. Lightning spoke in his blood (flashing, forking-twitching). Mundo, the mother-father Earth, kept trying to clutch him to her-his breast, and thus he was always stumbling and falling; earlier on his long journey to the capital, he'd broken his foot.

When the servant Modesta saw the young Indian limping along, hair falling to his shoulders around his slender, solemn face, and leading a scrawny lamb at the end of a knot-repaired length of rope, one of his feet filthy bare and the other wrapped in mud-caked rags, she immediately called him over: "Want some eggs and bread? A drink of atole?" Mixing Cakchiquel, her own first language, with Spanish, she explained, as she did to the other candidates, that Madre Melchora, a very holy woman, had invited him to her home. La Madre had a supply of paid Indulgences issued by the Santísimo Padre Pope Pío IX, and she would give him enough to shorten his stay in Purgatory by thirty days. Did he understand? Did he know what Purgatory was? Josefa exclaimed: "Thirty fewer days of waiting and torture!"

Until they were admitted by the Portress, Sor Inés de la Cruz, into the convent's dimly lit reception vestibule, Juan Diego Paclom had never even seen a nun before. The Portress's faceless black executioner's hood terrified him, but her cheerful voice singsonged from inside: "Cálmate, Don Señor. Our visitors always come out alive." Quill pen held in three poised fingers, the Portress recorded the three visitors' names in her book with delicate flourishes, demonstrating an artistry that was the result of countless hours of practicing penmanship in the dark. (The names can be confirmed in the Archiepiscopal archives, in one of the bound volumes in which Nuestra Señora de Belén's Portresses inscribed the names of every visitor, including every one of Madre Melchora del Espíritu Santo's Thursday Indians from 1847 to 1874.) The Portess told Juan Paclom that he had to leave his lamb at the door because animals were not permitted inside; she sternly warned the three Indians that as long as they were in the cloister, they had to keep their eyes fixed on the ground, or God would be angry and would cancel their Indulgences.

The three volunteers were led by the two servants through the gloomlight of the cloister, down corridors like tunnels, to the lower-choir. Inside, on the floor, were three earthenware bowls as if for animals to drink from. Furtively raising his eyes, Juan Diego Paclom saw an ornately carved and gilded altar built around a lavishly dressed Our Lady, its niches filled with objects made of precious metals and gems, and many smallish bearded santos who he knew must be the true owners of this house of holy women: within such images the most powerful spirits often resided. The pretty, dimpled servant caught his eye, made herself look cross, touched her eye with a finger, and jabbed it down at the floor. When he heard movement in the lacquered wooden shell of the room's spiral staircase he raised his eyes again and saw the first monjita coming into view around its curve, slowly and unsteadily, as if descending on stairs of floating logs. Her black veil was pulled back around her white hood: she had a parched, ancient face and feverish, small brown eyes. She was followed by another descending nun, and he glimpsed her large foot in stocking and sandal kicked out from under her hem as she stepped off the bottom step—*Indio! Bajo ojos!* blasted her strangely accented voice, and he dropped his eyes again and raised them just in time to see the hem of a third monjita's habit alight onto the floor, so oversized it hid its wearer's feet completely. And then the Indian with the goiter was summoned forward by the pretty servant to stand beside one of the bowls, and the broken-toothed servant helped lower the ancient Madre onto all fours on the floor. None of what happened next bore any resemblance to the dream Juan Diego Paclom had faithfully followed to this room—the Indian fearfully blurting, "No!" the pretty servant scolding, "Ishto! Por Dios! Shhhh!" and then the ancient Madre kissing and washing that Indian's feet, and the strange words she pronounced—but he knew that often it was a dream's elusive essence one had to decipher and heed, rather than its deceptive details. The big-foot monja who'd shouted at him, her massive face so pallid and speckled it looked painted on, eyebrows like daubed licks of flame, followed, and she performed the distressing ritual with the second Indian in the same manner as the first, only more energetically. Even before he was called, Juan Diego Paclom swung his low gaze toward the crooked folds of the brown habit stepping toward the third bowl. And she also lowered herself onto all fours, and now it was a white veil, not a black one, blocking his view of his own feet: his bare shredded foot caked with layers of dirt, toenails cracked open, and the other rag-wrapped, stinking with infection, steadily throbbing with pain. How skinny she was, inside her hanging folds of brown wool! Her oversized sleeves puddled on the floor, hiding her wrists, but her hands emerged, propped on their heels, the young, bitten, brown fingers tensed as if ready to scratch. The white-draped head slowly sank toward his feet, but then stopped. He felt her veil brush against his bare foot like a trickle of chilly water. Was that her breath on his skin? He felt sick with shame and suspense. Were those her lips, that soft little pat? He heard a faraway groan in her throat. "I am lower than the lowest," went the girlish smatter of a voice, "slave of the slaves." They were the same words the other two monjitas had spoken, though by the end she was nearly inaudible. The second nun again spoke commandingly: "Sor San Jorge . . ." but everything else was in an incomprehensibly barked gibberish language.

For a long moment the niña nun held herself perfectly still over his feet. Then her body shifted decisively backward, though she did not lift up her head enough for him to be able to see her face; with shaking hands, she began to unwrap the mud- and blood-stiffened rags around his injured foot, at first tentatively, then with firm tugs. He lifted his foot off the floor to help her. Cool air enveloped the swollen foot's pain-inflamed skin and chilly lightning ran up his spine and shuddered warmly down into his groin as slowly his penis began to grow. The second nun spoke again—"*Besar heridas como besar heridas de* Jayzoocristo, *Hermana!*" (Kiss wounds as if kiss wounds of . . .) And then the niña nun did the unforgettable thing. She raised her face just enough so that he saw the thin arcs of her brows beneath the white band, and a pair of tear-glazed, molasses eyes met his own with a direct and desperate girlish honesty that swept through him like an unfathomable caress, binding her to him in befuddled complicity. ("I can still feel this thing that she left inside me, this mute little stone that knows everything," Juan Diego Paclom would assert, five years later, to his fellow doomed rebels in the War of the Caves. "I knew she was the one I had come looking for, my Spirit Wife . . .") The niña monjita held his gaze a paralyzing moment longer. Then she lowered her head, her lips, to his broken stinking foot, and did what that other nun had just commanded her to do.

HANDS CLASPED BENEATH her chin and tongue out like a thirsty cat's, María de las Nieves was following several paces behind the Novice Mistress as they returned to their cell. She felt just as she had as a little child whenever her mother had tried to make her vomit up the sickness in her stomach by tickling the back of her throat with the rancid tip of a rooster feather dipped in castor oil. Ahead in the dim light of the corridor, a crimson-glowing lamp in a niche marked the draped entrance to the Chapel of Death. Whenever she passed this way she always succumbed to a brief, inwardly spiraling wonder, as if the corridor were dissolving beneath her feet from stone paving into one made of time running on and on: *In seventy, sixty, fifty years, or much sooner, I too will be carried into the Chapel of Death . . .* And where would Paquita Aparicio be? Would she ever know what María de las Nieves had been made to do that morning at that obscene Indio's wretched feet?

Eyes fixed on the trailing hem of the Novice Mistress's habit, she dropped her hands and feverishly scratched through layers of coarse wool and sackcloth at an outbreak of ferocious itching in her rash-smeared skin while silently reciting an act of contrition over the pleasure found in scratching. She was startled by the nearby bleating of a lamb—because animals have exposed genitals, openly fornicate, and often overtly invite touching (petting, stroking), their Constitution forbade domesticated animals inside their cloister, though there were small entrances cut into the full-sized doors of the food storage rooms so that cats could come and go hunting rodents; it wasn't even uncommon for a nun to wake deep in the night to the purring weight of a cat or even kittens nesting atop her head; the truth was that cats were everywhere . . . The Novice Mistress seemed not to have even noticed the bleating; her bearing and pace were unaltered. They had entered the corridor running alongside the square garden of the professed nuns' cloister, its four sides lined by semicircular arches. Though doing so was prohibited by the rule governing the manner in which a nun should return to her cell from the choir, María de las Nieves turned her head to the side far enough to see past the edge of her veil. Just beyond the flower bed of glossy red anthuriums planted in the shape of the Sacred Heart stood a small grove of banana trees, the dark emerald shadows within beckoning like the secret entrance to a subterranean world—

"Sor San Jorge!"

*Caramba!* She pulled in her tongue and snapped her eyes forward and found Sor Gertrudis looming in her path like an enormous draped statue. A few more steps, they would have collided. She raced through a horrified act of contrition for having profaned their holy house with that silent *caramba* of any lost girl of the world or any muleteer—no better to use a seemingly innocent exclamation like *camarón!* because God would know you really meant caramba and not prawn—and, gaping up at her teacher's broad, freckled face, said,

"Yes, Mudder. Oh, I am sorry, Mudder."

But the Novice Mistress's placid gaze, as usual, hid her feelings as completely as headdress and veil hid her fiery red hair. Itching all over, wan with defeat, María de las Nieves waited; and felt a weak pang of clinging love, an almost irresistible—and, of course, forbidden—urge to embrace her Nana Madre Gertrudis, to bury her face in her woolly habit and dissolve in a flustered, exhausted little girl's tears.

"You were, Sor San Jorge, so deep in contemplation of this morning's exercise that you forgot yourself?" The Novice Mistress's voice was flat and distant.

María de las Nieves thought for so long, so fruitlessly, about how to answer this that Sor Gertrudis finally broke the silence anew: "Your thoughts, Sister."

"Gee, Mudder, I dunno whadda say." She lowered her hands, busily whirled them in front of her chest, and said, "It was ... Gee!" She shrugged helplessly.

"That's all, Sister. *Gee?*" The Novice Mistress's *gee* fell like a heavy drop of cold soup. María de las Nieves's father's native New York Bowery, primary source of her emphatically heaved *gee* and also *Mudder* (though Lucy Turner, the servant from British Honduras, had always pronounced it "mother") was a world apart from the genteel Protestant Yonkers of Sor Gertrudis's upbringing.

"Yeh, Mudder." Something else she might say dawned on her and she almost floated up onto the tips of her toes as she hurried to get the words out: "I'm not wordy of such a gift, Mudder Gertrudis! Oh, so unwordy!" Oh, perfect!

"Well, that is at least a thought, Sister," the Novice Mistress finally replied. "Unlike simply *gee*. Which is not actually a word, but an ignorant yelp. Most likely derived from a blasphemy. It's better when you do your thinking out loud in Spanish, mi vida."

The other nuns always used such everyday endearments, but the Novice Mistress never did. María de las Nieves, stunned to the core, had to stop herself from grinning.

"By visible things do we come to the knowledge of the invisible, Sor San Jorge," the Novice Mistress continued, assuming her pedagogical tone, her eyes as blank as those of stone angels. "Our Husband can only reach us via our senses, and via that which we know how to perceive and comprehend. And so we need our senses and our minds to die, so that they exist only for Him."

They resumed their march. María de las Nieves (Sor San Jorge) and the other novice, Sor Gloria de los Ángeles (Immaculada Concepción Loreta Lucena) shared the Novice Mistress's cell—only the Prioress's was larger—in a far corner of the professed nuns' cloister. The smaller, separate, prettier novices' cloister, reached via a short passage off the patio behind the refectory kitchen, stood empty now but was maintained as if the nuns perpetually expected it to fill with white-veiled young virgins tomorrow. Every morning the vacant cloister's kerosene lamps and candles were lit and every evening before the Great Silence extinguished by one or the other of the two novices; daily, the two girls swept, mopped, and polished there, and picked flowers from the garden for its little chapel and another bunch to be blessed by the Prioress and delivered to the President's wife, Doña Cristina, at her home; every morning but Sundays and solemn feast days they followed the Novice Mistress inside for their three-hour novice class, and returned in the afternoon for their spiritual reading.

To Sor Gertrudis, her only two novices, both being formed in religion by herself, were the first true daughters of the austere "Reform" of the convent's Constitution that she had been patiently planning and working toward for years. Even more so than a Vicaress, who led the nuns in prayer in the choir, a Novice Mistress, especially if she was able to shape an entire generation or two of new nuns, was usually regarded as next in succession to become Prioress. But now that Sor Gertrudis could finally foresee the day when she would be able to implement her Reform, the convent, all the convents, were faced with the threat of closure. It was as if her own and the Liberal radicals' opposite ambitions had been inching in tandem for years toward a day of reckoning that loomed so closely now they were living in its inscrutable but all-darkening shadow.

Converted in Yonkers, New York, to the One True Religion at the age of nine, Sor Gertrudis (back when her name was Anne Louise Rowley) was sixteen when she realized that what she most desired in her convert's zeal was a contemplative choir-nun's absolute forsaking of the world. The Vicar of the New York Archdiocese, a Cuban priest and seminary professor exiled from Cuba for his antislavery views, had offered to help the articulate and tenacious young convert with ecclesiastical-red hair. His cousin was Prioress of the Carmelite Convent in Havana, and that Order had a tradition of welcoming converts: their great founder, Santa Teresa de Ávila, was herself from a Hebrew *converso* family. The Havana Barefoot Carmelites were renowned for the rigor and holiness with which they pursued the ascetic Teresan ideal in the middle of that most sinful, sensual, and pagan of cities, still under the rule of the Most Catholic King of Spain. Despite the torrid and humid Caribbean climate, they wore coarse, heavy wool habits. By the age of twenty-five Sor Gertrudis de la Sangre Divina—she'd taken

that name for the German saint and mystic celebrated for her devotion to
the pulsating, flaming, bleeding heart of Jesus—had been carried by fevers
to the brink of death three times. The passion with which she scourged
herself in order to love God better so shattered her formerly robust constitution that her Confessor and Prioress forbade her anymore mortifications,
even non-bloodletting ones. By then a persistent inner whisper was already
beseeching the Yankee nun to seek transfer to a sister convent where she
could give her Lord more pleasure. Why did that voice keep repeating, like
mosquitoes covering her soul with inflamed little bites, the obscure names
of the tiny republics of Central America?

Permission for Sor Gertrudis's reassignment was granted. Disembarking
at Livingston on the Atlantic coast, she made her way, face and hands hidden from view beneath layers of capes, blankets, veil, and gloves, in the
company of a small group of travelers, by riverboat and mule train, through
jungles, quicksand trails, and burning plains, before finally ascending to the
chilly high plateau of the Conservative Citadel. The Carmelite convent
there had a reputation as the strictest in the world; Sor Gertrudis never
found any reason to doubt that this was true. She spent the next eight
years there plunged into an impenetrable spiritual lassitude—the most
severe spiritual crisis she would endure in all of her long life in religion—
that was rooted in her guilty and terrifying conviction that that convent
couldn't be made any more perfect or austere without turning every last
one of its nuns to stone. One day the Carmelite Prioress mentioned that
the Prioress of Nuestra Señora de Belén was expanding her community's
mission to the educating of girls wealthy and poor, her teaching nuns assuming their new duties without any slackening of their vows or cloistered
reclusion. Upon hearing the name of that convent for the first time, Sor
Gertrudis understood her destiny. For fate often reveals itself among
monastics as it does among secular lovers: a name speaks to us, and we feel
compelled to hide that name away in our heart, where we find that a nest
of love has already been prepared and is waiting, and we forget that just a
moment ago everything had seemed so dull and hopeless.

Sor Gertrudis had little trouble arranging her transfer to a new Order
and convent. Once more, and in the firm belief that it was for the last time,
bundled and wrapped, the future Monjita Inglesa broke cloister to set foot
in *el siglo* for the walk to Nuestra Señora de Belén. Though the walk was

brief, during it, according to Padre Bruno, Sor Gertrudis was lastingly pierced by a sense of the world's desolation.

The former Carmelite found much to busy herself with in her new convent, and was soon vigorously restored to the certainties of her faith. Madre Melchora appointed her Mistress General of Boarding Students, her first task being to teach the girls to prefer sleeping in the new dormitories of the just-expanded school rather than in the nuns' cells. One incandescent night, while praying, Sor Gertrudis conceived a Reform of the convent's Constitution, which she wrote down in Latin. During the Archbishop's inspection visit, she offered him her new book of laws and customs. The prelate concurred that it was indeed divinely inspired, but, without a doubt, too strict and austere for her Sisters. He counseled prayer and patience and told her that she would recognize her moment when it came. Sor Gertrudis had been waiting for eleven years.

FOR THE PAST week, María de las Nieves had been reading the *vida* of Sor María de Agreda during her afternoon periods of directed study in the novice cloister library. Nothing she had ever read before had so impressed or stimulated her, or awoken such concentrated yearning. In deep prayer trances, Sor María de Agreda had traveled from her convent in Spain to the other side of the world, to remotest New Mexico, where she went among the heathen tribes, converting souls, teaching catechism, inspiring the Indians to go in search of Spanish priests to come and baptize them, walking hundreds of miles, for days and weeks, often across the territory of the Apache, unredeemed and murderous spawn of Satan. Sor María was often wounded on these missionary journeys, and more than once she received holy martyrdom from our Lord. Yet because she was in both places at once, in New Mexico without leaving her convent in Spain, she never broke her vow of perpetual cloister.

When Sor María de Agreda's mystical travels began, María de las Nieves told herself, she was just an adolescent novice, like I am now. That was almost three centuries ago. But I doubt I'll be elected Abbess, or Prioress, by the age of twenty-four, like she was. More than two months had passed since María de las Nieves had for the first time taken part in Madre

Melchora's Thursday Indian ritual—she'd obediently done so every other Thursday since, alternating with her sister novice, Sor Gloria de los Ángeles.

Of course Sor María de Agreda had told her Confessor about her missionary exploits, and soon, all over Spain, people had heard of them. Padre Benavides, the director of the Franciscan Missions, was dispatched by his Spanish superiors to find and investigate the tribes the miraculous nun was said to have visited. The Indians told him about the beautiful girl in blue robes who came down out of the sky and went among them preaching. Padre Benavides said that he'd even found rosaries that the Spanish nun had distributed among the Indians. When the Franciscan friar returned from America he went directly to Agreda to interview the young nun. She has a beautiful face, Padre Benavides wrote in one of his reports to his superiors, very white, although rosy, with large black eyes. Her habit is just the same as our habit. It is made of coarse gray sackcloth, worn next to the skin, without any other tunic, skirt, or underskirt. Sor María de Agreda was able to describe in detail for her visitor many of the places they had both been to in New Mexico. My dear Fathers, wrote Padre Benavides, I do not know how to express to your paternities the impulses and great force of my spirit when this blessed Madre told me that she had been present with me at the baptism of the Pizos and recognized me as the friar she had seen there.

Padre Benavides's reports on his encounters with Sor María de Agreda and her visits to the Indians in New Mexico, printed in many languages, were widely read, eventually drawing the attention of Pope and King. A century later in the Bethlehemite monastery in Santiago de los Caballeros, Fray Antonio Labarde wrote and published his *Vida de Sor María de Agreda*, containing lengthy excerpts and descriptions of those reports, as well as of the nun's own writings; this was the volume in which María de las Nieves was now immersed. Of the several provocative parallels between her own life and that of the mystically bilocating Spanish nun, the one concerning her habit seemed far from the most remarkable, but María de las Nieves also wore prickly sackcloth against her skin, a sackcloth tunic beneath the rough wool of her habit. That this was a constant mortification was evidenced by the rashes and sores, some infected, that now covered her torso. The past months' regimen had not only worsened some of these infections but had drained her body of strength while slowly poisoning her blood; she was exhausted and anemic from the agonizing lack of sleep, the aching hunger of regular fasts. She shivered constantly with chills, even on the rare days when the afternoon sun came out, when she could sit in the garden or orchard for a while, steaming inside the bearskin of her habit.

The old, desiccated vellum-bound volume and its moisture-stained, partially eroded pages lay open on the library table between María de las Nieves's propped elbows while she hunched over it, hidden inside her veil, one hand cradled against her nose, the other propped visorlike over her eyes. She had pulled a perfect, nearly straight, inch-long fiber of wool loose from her habit and, pinching it between rolling thumb and finger, had worked its delicate point deep inside her nostril, and was expertly tempting a sneeze, though without distracting herself from her reading.

Three barred windows high in the wall overlooking the cloister garden let in the gray afternoon light. Now Sor Gertrudis sat at one end of the table, her freckled brow furrowed in concentration, an index finger tracing the lines of Latin text in a theological treatise. Sor Gloria de los Ángeles, assigned Padre Nierenberg's *The Temporal and the Eternal,* sat nearly opposite, gaping down at her open book, her lids, as if finally relinquishing their long struggle to stay afloat, slowly and peacefully sinking over the reddish jelly of her sleepless eyes beneath the golden shimmer of her brows, while her hands absently caressed the purring cat on her lap.

From childhood, wrote Padre Benavides, Sor María de Agreda felt great grief for those who are damned, and particularly for the heathen, who, because of the lack of light and preachers, do not know God, our Lord—. María de las Nieves sneezed, deliciously, into her hand, and so loudly that the cat in Sor Gloria de los Ángeles's lap woke and sprang to the floor.

"Jesucristo," said Sor Gertrudis, flatly, without looking up from her book.

"Jesucristo," repeated Sor Gloria a moment later, whose drowsy voice was softer than a dove.

María de las Nieves remained hunched and rigid, soaked palm clasped over her nose and lips, blinking back tears, waiting to see if the lingering sensation would resolve itself suddenly into another sneeze, as often happened. She dropped her hand and hoarsely intoned, "Blessed be His Name, forever and ever." The cat, slate gray, yellow-eyed, having streaked partway across the floor before stopping in its tracks, was glaring over its shoulder, back arched. Such explosive sneezes almost always seemed to set off an aching echo in the very marrow of her bones, and María de las Nieves let her arms hang loosely at her sides until it passed. She wiped her hand on her sleeve, turned a page of Fray Labarde's book, and began furtively groping and plucking at her habit, along the underside of her thigh, hunting another perfect piece of wool, pausing to scratch her rashes through the fabric. But another sneeze rocked her as she turned her face into her shoulder just in time and she heard the cat hiss and the rapid thumping of its sprint toward the door, which was closed.

"God is sending you a catarrh, Sor San Jorge," added Sor Gertrudis, after the usual obligatory exchange.

"Yes, Mudder, indeed maybe He is."

The Novice Mistress said, "You know that our Lord does not like us to be delicate, Sister, but please make sure that you don't sneeze onto the book. It is one of the few books in this library that was rescued from the rubble of our first convent in the old capital. Our predecessors must have loved it very much."

SIX WEEKS EARLIER, in June, El Anticristo had finally ascended to the Presidency of the Liberal Republic, triumphing over the incumbent in a constitutional free election from which Conservative candidates were excluded. The transfer of power was peaceful. Soon after, the former President's wife, Nuestra Señora de Belén's most devoted alumna and patron, met with Sor Gertrudis and the Prioress in the latter's office, decorated with large, dark oil portraits of her predecessors and other religious figures and scenes. Doña Cristina had come to deliver the startling message from the new ruler that he hadn't forgotten the excellent performance of the students at the public examinations that he'd attended in the convent school so many months before. Would Madre Melchora and the famous Monjita Inglesa be willing to advise his government in the establishing of the new state schools for girls?

"Then the convents are saved?" asked Madre Melchora, withholding her answer. Doña Cristina said that she suspected that the new President's anti-clericalism had already been sated. Now he would have a new hunger to feed: ultimate power. He would want to be loved as much as he was already feared. Of course he must know that even most of the men who'd voted for him were at least secretly against expelling nuns . . . When the former First Lady finished her analysis, Sor Gertrudis gruffly complimented her on her political astuteness and frankness. Doña Cristina, savoring a long sip from her gourd-cup of hot chocolate, had a mischievous twinkle in her eye as she regarded the Monjita Inglesa's humorless visage. Then she set the gourd back in its silver, monkey-shaped holder, and remarked, "Everything my husband has achieved in politics he owes to what I learned as a schoolgirl in this convent, especially from my Nana Melchora. He did not always govern as I would have wished, but he would never have persecuted our female religious Orders. But if our new President truly despises nuns as much as some claim, not even Cardinal Richelieu and Santa Catalina de Siena together would be able to dissuade him from whatever he has planned."

During the afternoon hour in the community parlor, when speech was allowed to flow freely as long as it related to spiritual and strictly communal matters, such events as the rise and fall of political chieftains in *el siglo* were rarely mentioned. The two novices were kept even more isolated from the world. But during one of their novice classes Sor Gertrudis, without meeting either of her two students' eyes, told them that during their conversation the former Primera Dama had confided that she thought the new President would leave the convents alone because from now on he would want to turn his attention toward enriching himself, and to finding a wife. At the word *wife* María de las Nieves forgot to breathe. Her heart lurched and plummeted through her airless self. Had the Novice Mistress said wife because she knew something about Paquita? She waited tensely for her teacher to say more. The misery flooding her now was guilty and unconfessed confusion, and a longing to hold her lost Paquita in her arms. Her own imperfect sacrifice was supposed to keep Paquita's vow of virginity unbroken; if that wasn't true, then there was no reason to marry God. That was the pact she'd made.

And now all this time had passed and she still hadn't received any message or even sign of life from Paquita. This was how you began to die, from this hurt of being forgotten and unloved and knowing it was because of what you'd done.

So, as if nothing else could ever again matter as much, she sat reading about Sor María de Agreda, a consoling voice, like a balm on all her blistering unhappiness and shame, and then something more. María de las Nieves now lived for these afternoon library sessions. In her meditations, interior prayers, and as she lay awake at night, she lost herself in methodically narrated adventures and inner dialogues inspired by the mystical travels of the Spanish nun. These imagined flights were becoming so vivid that in her high excitement she sometimes wondered if they might not be the anteroom to the actual experience, as the antechoir was to the upper-choir; the antechoir, where hot chocolate–making equipment was kept so that nuns could refuel themselves before and after exhausting sessions in the upper-choir, where those who had the true gift of prayer flew as close to the radiance of their Husband's love as possible without having to leave their bodies behind forever. Whenever she could now, María de las Nieves tried to lose herself in meticulously guided day and night dreams of mystical bilocation. She went home to Los Altos to see her mother and Lucy and to eat limón and guanabana ice. She traveled to New York City to visit Paquita's father, and to see where her own father and Sor Gertrudis had been born. She even made the entire Convento de Nuestra Señora de Belén, with its school and walled-in orchard, lift off the earth like an enormous aeronaut's balloon and navigated it through the stars. Were they going to heaven? Perhaps someday, if they were martyred. But they were looking for Purgatory, to bring cool water to all the thirsty souls waiting there, enduring its flames. Was it right that these hours in the library should pass so pleasurably, reading, dreaming, tickling her nose? María de las Nieves knew that if her contentment was noticed, the Novice Mistress might decide to banish her from the library.

That was why she now faked a loud yawn. Silently and a bit contritely, praying for mercy, she weakly bobbed her head up and down and let her mouth droop open in imitation of Sor Gloria de los Ángeles's sleepy stupor. As if following a secret logic, the cat now leapt up into her lap. If she allowed herself to sneeze, the cat, jolted by the earthquake, would dig its claws deep into her thighs before springing away. Yet, depending upon Sor Gertrudis's mood, it could also be looked upon as a too free assertion of her own will were she to noticeably nudge the cat off her lap.

Sor María de Agreda was befriended by King Felipe IV of Spain. The Spanish monarch was so enchanted by the young Abbess's stories, by her mystical and trained intelligence and learning, and by her beauty, that he frequently came to the convent to sit hour after hour at the locutory grille, conversing with her. Sor María de Agreda's habit often emitted the scent of fresh dawn roses. According to Fray Labarde, the scent of the actual roses in the royal gardens were enough to fill that sin-wracked Christian warrior of a King with such emotion that he would need to sit down as if exhausted by life, staring at the ground, nodding to himself and making gestures of supplication with his long, pale hands. They exchanged more than six hundred letters over the subsequent years, slowly growing old together, for time moves as slowly inside palaces as it does inside convents. The King always wrote on the right-hand side of a sheet of paper and Sor María always replied on the left—two separate handwritten columns lying as if shoulder to shoulder on every sheet that traveled between them.

Everyone deceives the King, Sor María de Agreda wrote in one of her typically frank letters. Lord, this monarchy is coming to an end, and everyone who does not try to set this right will soon be in hell. She was the King's most trusted adviser. The King knew he alone was to blame for all of Spain's calamities. He was a libertine, a lecher, a perpetual adulterer. In every bad thing that happened, from military defeats at the hands of English infidels to common crimes in the streets of Madrid, he saw displayed God's wrath against himself. The King wrote to Sor María: It is a great comfort to me in the middle of all these worries to know that there is someone who is trying to lessen them by so safe and certain a method as prayer; only, I fear, Sor María, that I am the one who wastes all the pains you take, because in the measure that your efforts increase, my sinfulness increases, so that I am unworthy of the good you seek for me. The nun answered, My Lord, no man can truly be a King who is not ruler of himself, controlling and having complete mastery over his desires and passions. It is by crushing them and refusing to be ruled by them that a King's heart is put in the hand of the Lord. The hand of God is strong and presses hard, which is why God said, *Whom I love, I correct.*

Though Sor María de Agreda was declared Venerable by Pope Clemente X, her beatification process was stopped, for too many bishops thought her heretical and crazy, Sor Gertudis had explained in novice class one

morning, launching into a tirade against Spain. For in Spain, she said, they
were now embarrassed by nuns like Sor María de Agreda. "Why? Because,
dear girls, I want you to know that the spiritual daring and genius of a nun
like that only provokes the insecurity, self-consciousness, and spiritual
smallness of that now terribly reduced race of people. Those Spaniards
have been hiding behind their silly, haughty mimicking of reason for generations now, ohhh they are such mannered little sardines, ashamed of
their lost glories, their imperial *crimes*—for bringing the Word of God" (and
she roughly cleared her throat) "to pagans and cannibals—a past which
now seems *tooooo* intimately bound up, let us say, with the visions, levita-
tions, divine flights—nowadays called hysteria, lunacy, heterodoxy, subver-
sion of ecclesiastical authority!—of our most glorious Sisters. Well, at least
here in the cloisters of the Americas, we resist such *contra*-mystical, effete ra-
tionalist revisionism. Ohhhh those little Spaniard *monsignors,* they do test our
obedience and humility, don't they? They want us to be small. I'd rather
take on our own Liberal *sans-culottes* any day. They just want to guillotine us."

When the Novice Mistress had finished her disconcerting outburst she
fell silent, her eyes hard as snail shells imbedded in the solid putty of her
blanching face. María de las Nieves, as always whenever the Novice Mistress spoke in English, quietly and somewhat perfunctorily translated the
lesson for her sister novice. Sor Gloria de los Ángeles sat silently, an aching look of concentration on her face and her lips silently moving, as if by
mental exertion she was reconstruing the foreign nun's unusually histrionic, galloping cadences and trying to fit them to María de las Nieves's
abridged and neutral version, stretching and pulling at the latter like taffy;
then she turned to the Novice Mistress and tremulously asked:

"Do they really want to guillotine us, Nana? Do they really want to cut
off our heads like they did to the Carmelitas and Ursulinas in France?"

"That is impertinent question," the foreign nun answered in her awkward Spanish, still staring straight ahead as if at nothing at all. "You pray
every day that we deserve happiness of martyrdoms give to our French
Sisters!"

María de las Nieves, of course, under the Novice Mistress's tutelage,
had already learned much about the renowned nuns and mystics, their
hard-earned visions and ecstasies. (Santa Teresa de Ávila as a levitating
young nun, grabbing onto the iron bars of the chorus as she rose up to the

ceiling, crying out to her sister nuns to hold her down.) But it was Sor María de Agreda who really illuminated those most difficult days of her novitiate, and helped to guide her. María de las Nieves knew now that such flights and visions were won only through the most heroic discipline, suffering, and selflessness, and by the twinned powers of reason and faith. In her daily novice classes and spiritual reading, in her slow learning yet surprising aptitude for abstract study, training her intellect on the mysteries and divine attributes of the Holy Trinity and the complex demands of interior prayer, she was beginning to understand what was actually required to become one of the great nuns. She knew that learning had to be counterbalanced by brutal obedience, and also by daily contemplation of the will as the only means to the spiritual perfection that opens the door to the seraphic world of visions where nuns can finally become *living metaphors of sacred fire and wedded bliss.* Perhaps the Novice Mistress really was finally succeeding in shaping María de las Nieves into a true *Jesuitona.* She was no adviser to a King, but secretly thought herself suited to such a role. Oh yes she did. Well, at least she was doing all she could to set things right! For if Paquita Aparicio and El Anticristo . . . *ahhh* (here it comes) . . . pues, not *her* fault . . . *ahh*—

A jarring sneeze. María de las Nieves had to bite her lip to keep from crying out, such was the searing pain caused by the clawfuls of flesh the cat had torn away with.

"God blesses you, Sor San Jorge. We have to be grateful for everything our Lord sends us. A bad cold can be a trial, but it can also be the first sign of something more severe."

"Oh yes, Mudder!"

As a young novice, Sor María de Agreda had also been made miserable by her own sense of sinful inadequacy and self-doubt. One day, in novice class, while discussing Sor María's youthful trials, Sor Gertrudis had gravely said: *She made of her soft young flesh a slaughterhouse.* Through ascetic penitence and self-mortification the Spanish novice had finally found the means of escaping her worldly self. Her prayer trances had begun almost immediately, conveying her to the farthest corners of New Mexico and even beyond without removing her from her convent. And her own blood, seeping into her habit, had imbrued the sackcloth with the smell of roses at dawn. But María de las Nieves's rashes and wounds gave off a smell more like the emanations from a pile of sun-rotted, blackened mangoes. So far, at least, she'd been spared the Agreda novice's phantasmal and demonic carnal torments. Though Sor Gloria de los Ángeles, apparently, had not. Just the other night Sor Gloria had woken them in their cell, screaming that she felt invisible hands on her body, the scrape of invisible beard, and hot breath on her face. María de las Nieves, shivering from sadness and fright along with her usual fever chills in her hard and narrow bed, lay awake listening to the Novice Mistress trying to calm the sobbing novice. Poor Sor Gloria! How she wished she or Sor Gertrudis were at least allowed to lay a comforting hand on Sor Gloria's writhing back or shoulder. After only a few more minutes, the Novice Mistress had scolded, "Now that is enough, Sor Gloria, you cease this right now, foolish girl, Sor Gloria you will now *stop*," and without another word she'd turned and gone back to her bed, while poor Sor Gloria's sobbing had grown even deeper and more choked.

Now the fly-drone-laced silence of the library was dashed by the first splatter of afternoon rain, which, within seconds, became a pounding downpour, so suffusing the room with the smell of wet earth and vegetation that María de las Nieves imagined winged cherubs flinging handfuls of torn-up garden and mud in through the windows. Meanwhile she went on bringing herself to the verge of a sneeze, and then letting it subside, dexterously twirling her pinched length of wool as she read.

My heart never delighted in earthly things, for they did not fill the emptiness in my spirit, wrote Sor María de Agreda, looking back on her own early days as a novice. For this reason the world died for me in my youngest years, before I really came to know it. —María de las Nieves wondered, And how well did I ever get to know it? An image of her Confessor Padre Lactancio's face on the other side of the confessional grille suddenly bloomed, his tensely staring eyes, the damp, taut skin over pursed lips like a thin scrap of undercooked meat on a grease-sheened plate. The next thing she thought of was that shop with a sign over its door reading, *Umbrellas Repaired. Don José Pryzpyz, trained in London.* She'd been in her last months as a student when she'd spotted it on one of their weekly outdoor excursions, when the boarding students of Nuestra Señora de Belén were led through the muddy city streets in a long double row of shawl-draped schoolgirls holding hands, past the clamoring men and boys

who lined their route. At the bottom of the hand-painted sign, smaller
script announced that Don José Pryzpyz also repaired caucho-weatherproofed and India-rubber cloaks and capes. The shop was as small as any
tailor's, with only a single, barred vertical rectangle of a window in its strikingly narrow facade, the shutters pulled open. That afternoon there was a
group of men and boys clustered in front of that window, and though all
their heads had turned as one to direct the usual ardent stares and mating
calls at the schoolgirls going past, what first caught María de las Nieves'
alert eye was the way those men and boys had been postured around the
window just a moment before, obviously absorbed by whatever there was
inside that window to look at. By the downward tilt of the taller men's
heads, and the way some of the tallest even had to remove their hats so
that these wouldn't topple over their faces as they looked down, she could
tell that it was not something well inside the shop that they were looking
at, but something right there, at the bottom of that window, though she
was unable even to glimpse whatever it was through that wall of frock coats
and trouser legs. Then the little shop was past.

María de las Nieves had barely turned her head while squeezing Paquita
Aparicio's hand to ask, "Did you see?" The students were supposed to
maintain silence until they reached the grassy slopes of the Cerro del
Carmen.

"Quién?" asked Paquita without moving her lips, for if they were caught
speaking in line, they could be punished.

"Not who. That. That new *shop* we just passed! Bueno. *Zaz!* It's past."

The next week they went to the muddy meadows behind El Calvario for
their recreation, and so didn't take the avenue leading past the mysterious
shop. The week after that, in order to evade the increasingly ribald male
uproar along their route (another clear consequence of Liberal atheism),
their lay matrons and senior student monitors led them back to the Cerro
del Carmen along a different avenue, and the following week they took
that route again, and the next they returned to El Calvario. A week later
María de las Nieves left school to become a novice.

So, in truth, her heart had delighted in *earthly things*. She still wondered
about that shop where a man with an unusual name, trained in London,
repaired umbrellas and caucho-weatherproofed capes, and displayed in his
window something sufficiently remarkable to have drawn such a crowd. Of

course it was sinful to occupy your mind with such things as umbrellas and mysterious windows when you were in choir, chanting the five psalms of Lauds. *When you recite psalms and hymns, you must hold in your heart what you say with your mouth—*

"Jesucristo."

"Jesucristo."

María de las Nieves looked up from her book, hand still pressed over her nose and mouth, and knew—the intuition filled her like ink poured into water—that this time Sor Gertrudis's quietly alarmed gray eyes had settled on her even before she'd sneezed. Face flushing, she looked down at her *Vida de Sor María de Agreda.* She tried to read the same few lines again and again but now they made no sense, as if this new atmosphere of danger required an entirely new method of reading. Her chest silently rose and fell as if she were out of breath from running. Only when she finally risked a glance at the Novice Mistress and saw her returned to her own book did she feel calmer. Soon the printed words began to absorb her attention almost as before, though she resisted the urge to pull another piece of wool from her habit.

The light of God, wrote Sor María de Agreda, coming out to meet me as I entered life through the door of rational thought, showed me the beauty and importance of truth. God raises up those who humble themselves. He keeps His secrets hidden from the proud, but He reveals them to the little people. —When the Most Holy Virgin decided to reveal the true story of her life as Mother of God and Co-Redeemer, wrote Fray Labarde, she chose Sor María de Agreda to be her scribe. The Queen of Heaven, via the Holy Spirit, told Sor María everything that the Bible leaves out: how she was also immaculately conceived in the womb of her mother Santa Ana; how it was her own idea that her Son by God should take human form and be sent to earth to redeem mortal humanity, even though she foresaw her own maternal sorrow; her ascent into heaven alongside her resurrected Son, and her return to earth to lead the Apostles—Sor María de Agreda wrote it all down, enough to fill eight weighty volumes. When she was finished, she destroyed every page, and then rewrote it from memory and left only one copy in the possession of her loyal friend the King, who considered it the most important book written since the New Testament; it was titled *The Mystical City of God, the miracle of Her omnipotence and infinite grace.*

*Divine holy life of the Virgin Mother of God, our lady and queen María Santísima, redeemer of Eve's sin and mediatrix of grace.* Sor María successfully defended her great "autobiography of the Virgin" before separate tribunals convened by the Holy Inquisition and the skeptical Doctors of the Sorbonne; both subsequently condemned it, but only after her death. Among nuns the world over *The Mystical City* became one of the most beloved of books. Fray Labarde's *vida* contained only tantalizing descriptions, a few excerpts and paraphrases. Soon María de las Nieves would be finished with the learned friar's life of the Agreda nun. She wondered if there was any way of convincing Sor Gertrudis to assign her *The Mystical City* as her next spiritual reading. She would certainly have to conceal the intensity of her yearning, for the Novice Mistress also taught that reading, incorrectly practiced, was among the forbidden pleasures of the body.

Two afternoons later, Friday, in the library—on Monday she would be assigned a new book to read—while anxiously poring over parts of Fray Labarde's book that she'd already read at least once before, she came upon a sentence that stupefied her: *He gave me as much snow as my wool would bear.* It was disconcerting that she'd somehow missed this sentence before. She understood its obvious meaning—God had given Sor María de Agreda as much suffering as she could endure—yet she found herself rereading it as if she didn't, as if these words concealed a personal yet mysterious significance it dared her to decipher. She felt frightened to have come across such words, which seemed to menacingly hint at her old secular name—a name she'd previously loved, because of the magical resonance of *snow* and its association with her Da's faraway northern city—in mocking juxtaposition to *wool*, a word that now projected a menacing shadow into every corner of her existence. This seemed an unjust end after all the loving attention she'd lavished on this book, and she felt irked and even slighted. María de las Nieves now sneezed, and squeezed her eyes shut, as if flinching against an inevitable blow. But the Novice Mistress subjected her to nothing more than the usual subdued call and response. She felt a thorough self-disgust with her own spirit and soul and mind and name and body, this sneeze-addicted, unwashed, itching, burning, sweating mass with its recent distraction of newly swollen little breasts and a perpetual dark fizzing inside, down there between her legs, and even deeper inside. *He gave me as much snow as my wool would bear.* It was as if her own depraved physical being, this skin and blood flashing hot and cold, hair, teeth, bones, moisture, filth, had *all* been crushed, boiled, and reduced down into an inky substance just to print those few words that kept their secret hidden . . . *Ay Madre, ay Jesucristo, I'll do anything, pound me into powder, just make me a saint!*

The light in the room had yellowed and thickened into a suffocating and translucent gelatin. Sor Gertrudis sat at her end of the worm- and termite-eaten table, immobile behind the peaceful rhythm of her index finger tracing lines of Latin text. María de las Nieves's heart felt frozen with terror. She sat paralyzed in her chair until the sensation subsided, leaving her feeling tremulous and drained.

That evening it was Sor Gloria de los Ángeles's turn to leave the library early to ring the bell for Compline, and when María de las Nieves heard its muffled tolling, that was the signal to close her book, rise from her chair, and return the book to the shelves. Still feeling weak from that fit of fright, she said her prayer to God, giving thanks for the divine gift of reading and asking for help in learning to love knowledge without vanity. She knew that it might be a very long time before she would hold Fray Labarde's *Vida de Sor María de Agreda* in her hands again and so she clasped it tightly. Goodbye beautiful, beloved book, good-bye, I love you. She set it back on its shelf, her eyes filling with tears.

Sor Gertrudis, having taken a few deliberate steps toward her, said, "Sor San Jorge. One moment please. Just right there, hold still for one moment. Thank you, Sister."

Her stare was fixed on María de las Nieves's habit, roaming over it. Bending forward, hands on knees, the Novice Mistress lowered herself for an even closer inspection, searching as if she'd lost something very tiny in the habit's picked-at, threadbare fabric, smeared and encrusted all over with dried mucus, especially the sleeves. María de las Nieves stood with her arms limp at her sides. Not having seen herself in a mirror for so many months, she didn't know that her sneeze obsession had begun to disfigure her face. Her nostrils were perpetually flared, the membranes inflamed and visibly swollen inside the rims, and her lips were always slightly parted and pulled back into a frozen, cheerless near grin. She looked as if she was perpetually on the verge of a sneeze.

The Novice Mistress straightened up and asked, "Moths have been feasting on your habit, Sor San Jorge?"

"Perhaps dat is so, Mudder Gertrudis," she answered in a barely audible tone. "But I have not been seeing too many mods."

"You have been making yourself sneeze with wool pulled from your habit."

"Dat is so, Mudder."

"Is it because you consider it a mortification, Sister?"

"Yes, Mudder."

"It is not because it gives you pleasure."

"I . . . Oh, no, Mudder."

"And do you expect to be given a new habit, when this one has been reduced to shreds?"

WITHIN WEEKS OF El Anticristo's assumption of the Presidency, a new decree was passed forbidding priests from wearing clerical garb into the streets unless leading religious or funeral processions. The old Concordant signed with the Holy See by the Conservative regime, which had obligated the state to uphold Catholicism as the One True Religion, was severed; freedom of religion was declared as yet another inducement to immigrants. The first Protestant marriage in the country was celebrated at the American Legation, uniting a Yankee railroad engineer and a recently converted cigar roller from Barrio El Sagrario. There was already one Hebrew with an umbrella-repair shop in the city and now, on the old Calle Real, another opened a floral shop, selling flowers that everyone had previously gathered freely from the meadows beyond the city gates; so why was this business such a success? Then El Anticristo dealt the Church a devastating blow, decreeing the nationalization of all Church-owned property without exception. The expropriated wealth would be administered by the government for the purpose of "*developing agriculture.*"

In the past, Sor Gertrudis would have been able to bring her questions about whether or not María de las Nieves's sneezing might be a mortification or a sin, and if a sin, what degree of sin, to a Jesuit Confessor or some other learned friar, and would have soon received a decisive answer, complete with theological citations. But Padre Lactancio Rascón, Nuestra Señora de Belén's chaplain since the expulsion of the Jesuits, like virtually every other native-born, diocesan priest, had not been educated in Salamanca, Paris, Rome, or the Angelópolis of Puebla; his erudition provided for little more than quotations from the Bible and methodical renditions of the Latin Mass. Sor Gertrudis had inherited a Jesuit's distrust of such priests. Hadn't Napoleon, scattering his agents throughout Spanish America in a plot to arouse the colonies against the mother country, instructed them to gain the aid of the American-born lower clergy, perceiving their natural sympathies?

Padre Lactancio had no answer to her questions about María de las Nieves's sneezing, but assured Sor Gertrudis that he would deliver them to the Ecclesiastical Council and the Curia for their consideration. He advised patience, however. The bishops were lately much preoccupied.

"I put in your hands," the foreign nun obediently responded. "I know do this I put in hands of God too." (*Yo poner en vuestros manos. Yo saber hacer esto yo poner en manos de Dios también.*)

"It might be a long wait, Madre." The priest was unable to repress a malicious smile. "They might have to send all the way to Rome for an answer."

"Our Lord wait long time on Cross too," she sternly replied. "Impatience a great sin." Padre Lactancio's face darkened, and he dropped his gaze. It broke his heart to be so frequently reminded, day after day, of his own inferior intelligence and even piety, and of the disappointment he knew he must represent to these learned nuns who had no choice but to rely on and obey his spiritual guidance. Thank God they no longer wished to be confessed once a day, as apparently some had back when their Confessor was a Jesuit.

During novice class one afternoon María de las Nieves finally dared to ask if Sor María de Agreda's "autobiography" of La Virgen María could be her next spiritual reading. The Novice Mistress replied that it had been one of her own favorite books when she was young and promised to meditate on her request. But even before the end of that same class, Sor Gertrudis switched to English to announce, "It is certainly not up to me to decide whether the Most Holy Virgin did actually dictate *The Mystical City* to Sor María or not. But it being true of this book that its author does openly identify herself with the heroism and even person of our Most Holy Blessed Virgin, I wonder if it makes suitable reading for a mere novice who *does* seem to identify just as strongly and openly with its mortal author. Hmn? What do you think about that, Sor San Jorge?"

Of course it moved María de las Nieves to be spoken to so thoughtfully just when she was feeling so despised and low. So those words touched her almost like maternal caresses she'd never expected to feel again, though she also understood their meaning: that she was not going to be allowed to read the book. Submitting to the Novice Mistress's authority in this as in all other matters, she answered, "I don't know, Mudder."

"Well, I think it is not suitable reading for you just now. If God wills it, perhaps there will come a time." And then, dropping her voice into an unusual whisper, the Novice Mistress confided: "You know, Sor San Jorge, we women of the Church have always been told that we are too essentially weak and flawed to be counted on to find or recognize the truth on our own. Maybe that is indeed true, mi preciosa, for how is it that I was not able to decide on my own about your sneezes? I did not have to leave this matter solely to Padre Lactancio. I could have told him what I thought about it, and I am sure he would have agreed. But I hesitated. I proceeded as I was taught to proceed, by Jesuits and Carmelites. Well, too late! It is now too late."

María de las Nieves was astonished to see an apologetic little smile quivering at a corner of Sor Gertrudis's lips and a darting shyness in her eyes as she turned her mottled face away. *Mi preciosa!* It was only the second time the Novice Mistress had addressed María de las Nieves with such personal affection. Only the second time in nearly a year. But now, instead of secretly filling her with bliss, it made her sad, and then despondent, and she sat staring blankly at her own hands clasped in her lap.

IT WAS DURING that time that a basket of fresh, seemingly exquisite beef was delivered anonymously to the convent of the Recollect Sisters. Their Madre Superior had the good sense to feed a piece of the meat to one of their dogs; suffering horribly, the dog promptly died—no doubt poisoned by Freemasons. (But there were also those who, recalling how the Jesuits had justified murdering monarchs to keep their kingdoms free of Protestantism, observed that the most likely consequence of a convent of fatally poisoned nuns would be widespread violent uprising against the Liberals.)

The menacing developments in the world outside, along with the saturating dampness of the rainy season, had accelerated Madre Melchora's decline into a disconcerting frailty. Her walk had become perplexingly unsteady, she was many times thinner than before, and her trembling hands, in their parched wrapping of bruised skin and veins, resembled withered, pulled-up roots. No matter how much water she drank, she remained thirsty; she hardly ate, but her breath was always foul. Sometimes the venerable Prioress seemed to find the simplest choices or problems bewildering or even terrifying. At such moments, she always cried out for her hijita Sor Gertrudis.

Ominous signs were everywhere: After their nine days of heartrending laments in the home of the deceased, the black-clad women who worked as professional mourners still went door to door throughout the city, asking for eggs to bring to the convents. In exchange for each *florin* of three dozen eggs, the nuns would pray a novena for the recently departed immortal soul. Funeral bells tolled no more frequently than usual, but eggs were arriving at Nuestra Señora de Belén's front gates in greater quantities than ever before. María de las Nieves was frightened by those overflowing baskets, almost too heavy to lift, a few eggs inevitably spilling and breaking as the baskets were lurchingly carried inside. What was known out there that now made people want to donate so many eggs to nuns? The two novices spent many hours sitting on the floor of the kitchen, out of the way of the Sisters and servants working at the wood-burning stoves, weighing eggs in buckets of salted water. Eggs that sank directly to the bottom were the freshest and were set aside for Padre Lactancio and his sacristan or sent to the Archiepiscopal Palace, where the exiled Archbishop's relatives were still residing; those that floated to the top had been laid at least five days before and were given out in the free morning school for poor girls; eggs that hovered in between were kept for the convent and boarding school.

María de las Nieves was sitting on the kitchen floor weighing eggs with Sor Gloria when she overheard the nuns and servants talking about three fourteen-year-old students who'd been caught in a storage room in the school stripped naked to the waist and expelled. They'd been meeting there weekly to bare, measure, and compare the size and shape of their blossoming breasts by candlelight. Paquita, with an ample chest well before other girls her age, had not been among them. Her own——. But a nun was not ever even supposed to think about her own just emerging little turtle-head breasts and sprouting hair, which the Novice Mistress said was a sign of women's fallen state like *mala madre,* the horrifying leaking filth inside her. Still, in the kitchen Sor Gloria de los Ángeles gravely whispered to her, "Sorita San Jorge, you are finally getting some chichitas too." And then Sor Gloria slumped backward onto the floor with her hand over her own mouth, writhing with silent laughter, which she fought to stifle, until she ended up lying on her back, staring emptily at the ceiling and panting for air.

... *POINT SEVEN: CONTINUOUS meditation on the inviolate guarding of the senses, those of eyes, ears, tongue, and nose, through these windows the Death of Chastity enters* ... Standing before the Sanctuary Lamp with her book of spiritual exercises open in her hands, María de las Nieves remembered the remote consistory of Church wise men now supposedly weighing her fate. She sighed bleakly, and told herself, They are going to fry me in oil like chicharrón. Should she escape? Did she dare? But where would she go? Before, if a nun or novice ran away, the government would send soldiers and police to capture and return her, but could any Prioress ask such a thing now?

Her attention was caught by a black shadow sinking vertically through the dark light in the window. A few moments later she saw it again and realized it was a pigeon, floating straight down in front of the window, wings out and unmoving, like a dark, descending Cross. When it flew up again, she glimpsed and heard its flapping wings. Moments later it descended in front of the window a third time, holding the same posture. She could smell its tart droppings on the sill and saw a wispy column of steam rising between the bars. She had broken out in a cold sweat. Small pebbles of pulsating light danced inside her head and before her eyes.

THE CONVENT SCHOOL'S main entrance faced the corner of a street that, because of the steeper grade of its incline, often turned into a torrential river during the rainy season. The October rains were so heavy and continuous that one night the street overflowed as never before, so flooding the school that the interned students woke in beds standing in a foot of steadily rising muddy water and debris. Bringing their mattresses and hastily packed trunks, the students and servants came to stay in the vacant novice cloister. María de las Nieves couldn't bear knowing that Paquita was so close by. But for as long as the emergency lasted, no member of the community who was not a Teaching Sister or Monitor nun was allowed into the novice cloister. Night and day nuns in shifts marched an image of the Miraculous Virgin through the corridors, chanting litanies against the steady crash of rain and howling winds, imploring her to spare their cloister from the flooding.

*Oh, Sor María de Agreda,* prayed María de las Nieves, *prayer carried you to the other side of the world, but my prayers can't even get me into the novice cloister to see Paquita.* If only they could speak face to face, embrace, and forgive each other. She felt sure that their mutual vow of virginity, which her nun's martyrdom would make lifelong for both, must be weighing terribly on her old companion. Then she would release her from it, but only as long as Paquita didn't marry El Anticristo. She resolved to sneak into the novice cloister to find Paquita. The Sister Monitors should not be impossible to trick or evade. According to their Constitution, the nighttime Monitors had to be their community's most elderly nuns. They were older, much older, than the century, doddering and even senile.

María de las Nieves spent the day outside in the wintry downpour, with the nuns assigned the task of seeing what could be salvaged from the quicksand of the devastated gardens and orchards. Down on all fours, drenched and chilled to the bone, she groped in mud up to her thighs and elbows for submerged clusters of carrots and heads of cauliflower. That night, exhausted and overwrought, babbling about so many drowned kittens, she sobbed herself to sleep; later the Novice Mistress and Sor Gloria were unable to wake her for Matins. When Sor Gloria carried her in her arms to the infirmary the next morning, María de las Nieves was unconscious and burning with fever.

She woke sometime later to the weight and feel of a large, warm hand on her bared belly, and the smell of tobacco, and a deep, self-assured male voice talking about the long-ago first convent of Indian nuns in Oaxaca, New Spain. Opening her eyes, María de las Nieves found a man in a black frock coat, with salt-and-pepper beard and mustache and still-youthful ruddy cheeks, sitting by her bed. Standing alongside were Sor Gertrudis, stonily scowling down at the man's hand on her belly beneath her rolled-up chemise, and the Infirmarian Sor Micaela. "They wanted to prove they could endure all that the white gachupina and criolla nuns could," the man continued; he punctuated his remarks with softly resonant drum taps of his fingers against her hollow belly. "But their Indian-princess skin was too delicate for sackcloth and they fell as gravely ill from skin and blood infections as this poor novice of yours has, Madrecita. Like her, they also never complained. Medical knowledge was still in the dark ages, and they were not even bled until it was too late. An entire convent, every last soul, sacrificed to God in this way. But the Lord must have illuminated their Archbishop, because he had their *Reglemens* altered so that their successors would wear less abrasive fabrics. I suggest the same for this little novice of yours, Madre. She is clearly allergic to wool."

"Yes, Dr. Yela, I ask Madre Melchora," the Novice Mistress answered in a leaden tone. "But our Rule is strict obedience to divine command of God."

"She is also emaciated and anemic. When she has recovered her strength, she needs to eat more, and should be excused from fasting for at least one year. In the meantime I will send over some bottles of Vino Pepsona de Chapotauet. This is beef, Madre, first-class beef, which has been scientifically treated in a solution made from the gastric juices of animals and mixed with a little wine, so that it can be easily drunk. Very fortifying. It comes from France, of course, but Don Simón Goldemberg has it in his pharmacy on the Street of the Capuchins."

María de las Nieves was in the second week of her convalescence, wearing a new long-sleeved, ankle-length linen tunic beneath her wool habit and back to making herself sneeze almost as frequently as before, when a much awaited shipment of Breton lace, silk brocade, and several bolts of satin and velvet arrived at the convent spoiled with mildew, mold, and a low-tide stench. It was the third week of November, a season of clear skies and brisk, ebullient breezes. By that time of year the nuns were usually producing a steady flow of Christmas decorations and ornaments along with semestral prize ribbons for the school and their normal work of sewing vestments for the sacristy. Before, they had always ordered their finest fabrics from Europe, but this year they had heeded the prudent advice of Don Valentín Lechuga, the convent's secular majordomo, to be more frugal: in San Francisco, California, "Breton lace," sewn by Chinese women, could be had for half of what it cost in France. Shipping costs were much lower too, down the Pacific coast by steamer, rather than from Le Havre to Aspinwall, across Panama by rail, and up the coast by steamship again; or by sail from Europe around Cape Horn. That afternoon in the community parlor the distraught nuns wept in desolation over the spoiled fabrics. They would have to celebrate the Birth of the Savior in a sparsely and dingily decorated convent, the figures in their Nativity crèche dressed in last year's robes. Madre Melchora, trying to rise from her chair in order to speak, became entangled in her string of rosaries, which snapped, sending beads rolling across the floor, chased and batted by a black cat that pounced out of nowhere, and it all seemed yet more ominous proof of God's irritation with his servile Brides, for no one could remember any nun, never mind one so revered as their Prioress, ever having had such an accident.

The next day Don Valentín delivered a letter, imprinted with the official seal of the Legation of the United States America and penned in a vice-consul's hand, which the Prioress was to cosign so that it could be mailed to San Francisco in the expectation of the convent eventually receiving reimbursement. ". . . European goods never arrive damaged with water," Sor Gertrudis read aloud from the letter. "To compete in this market, United States merchants and shippers must improve in the art of packing. Textiles and cotton goods generally should always be subject to steam pressure and wrapped in coarse blankets or India rubber–treated coverlets, for which there is no duty—" A shriek cut her short. One of the nuns, turning to examine the slovenly Yankee burlap packing, had discovered that the ruined "Breton lace" was now white as purest snow, every green blemish and patch of mold vanished. The silk brocade was also pristinely restored, though the bolts of fabric were still ruined. The nuns jubilantly gathered around the table upon which the lace and brocade were laid, taking turns touching the restored articles. Some jumped up and down in their excitement, others dropped to their knees in prayer, for there was hardly a nun in that room, no matter how young or old, who had not been waiting all her religious life for just such a manifestation of their Señor's divine love.

"Oh my Sisters!" crowed Sor Gertrudis. "If the seculars only knew of the joy hidden in convents, they would storm the walls to live here too!"

María de las Nieves, holding a piece of the restored lace over her nose to investigate what a miracle smelled like, inhaled the familiar mustiness that over time, their cloister gave to all fabrics, including those she was wearing. The Novice Mistress snatched the lace away with such a re-proachful look that María de las Nieves was about to cry out that she hadn't been trying to make herself sneeze. The look's message stopped her cold: Sor Gertrudis no longer loved her at all.

ON THE FEAST day of the Immaculate Conception, Madre Melchora was moved from the infirmary, moaning from the malignant tumors devouring her insides, to her cell to await the death that Dr. Yela said was imminent. Sor Trinidad the Night Monitoress was on her inspection rounds two nights later when she came upon Madre Melchora sprinkling the doors to the nuns' cells with Holy Water. The next day Sor Trinidad would tell her anxious Sisters about the corona of light that had illuminated their Holy Madre throughout the encounter, and how she seemed to have recovered her long-lost sprightliness, though she was still as thin and wasted by ill-ness as before. According to Sor Trinidad, the Reverenda Madre told her: "I've been waiting to talk to you, hijita. You know that very soon I will be with my Husband. We both want Sor Gertrudis de la Sangre Divina to succeed me as Prioress."

Although the morning found Madre Melchora back in her bed, too weak even to lift her hand, Sor Trinidad's story seemed all the more credible because up until then she'd been the leader of the nuns' faction conspir-ing to ensure that the anti-Reform Vicaress, Sor Filomena del Niño Jesús, would succeed Madre Melchora as the next Prioress.

Madre Melchora's prolonged death agonies were surely a sign that she had lived a blessed and holy life: her Señor was lovingly rewarding her with suffering before summoning her to His side. The Death Candle was lit, and no other light was allowed to penetrate her cell.

"Sí Madre mía, querida, voy, voy," Madre Melchora whispered, her eyes barely flickering open. "Muchas gracias, niñitas, por sus preciosas flores . . ." They were her first intelligible words in days. A mandadera was immediately dispatched to fetch Padre Lactancio, for this might be her last chance to receive the final Sacraments while still coherent. When the priest had left the cell only hours before, he'd been disconsolate, blaming himself for already having waited too long.

"To who you speak, Madre?" asked Sor Gertrudis, her lips close to the Prioress's hooded ear. "Who the little girls bring you flowers?" María de las Nieves leaned in closer between the nuns sitting in vigil on the floor around the bed.

"La Virgen Santísima has come to see me, hijita," answered the Prioress, though her lips did not seem to be moving. "And here are all the little girls I prepared for first communion who died from the cholera later that terrible year. Oh look, how beautiful! I'm coming, niñas!"

That year in Nuestra Señora de Belén the feasts and octaves of Advent and Christmas overlapped with mourning rites. An impending death and its aftermath provided Padre Lactancio with the opportunity of repeated visits inside the cloister, during which he always managed to corner and pester María de las Nieves with remarks about her sneezing and the Vatican tribunal weighing her fate, and the gratitude she already owed him for having interceded against the Novice Mistress in the matter of whether she could wear a linen tunic, all the while touching her shoulder and arm like a cat pawing a candle flame. Five days after speaking her last words, the lime-dusted corpse of she who in life had been Madre Sor Melchora del Espíritu Santo, crowned with the same now withered and preserved flowers she'd worn on the day of her profession sixty-six years before, was borne from the Chapel of Death to the lower-choir.

Sor Gertrudis was elected Prioress one day after the feast of the Circumcision of the Infant Jesus, and ceremoniously presented with the convent seal and keys by Canon Molina, the acting Ecclesiastical Governor. Her reign was formally initiated that same day with a reading out of the new Constitution and Book of Customs. No detail of convent life proved too insignificant for Madre Gertrudis's Reform. All personal hot chocolate–making equipment and braziers were to be immediately removed from the nuns' cells. Because the Lord said that she who loves her father and mother more than she loves Me is not deserving of My love, even family members would no longer be permitted to visit the locutory parlor; indeed, the locutory was now closed to all but clergy on prescheduled missions of spiritual guidance. Even Doña Cristina was no longer allowed into the cloister. Never again would any male who was not a priest defile the lower-choir, nor would any pagan Indio; from now on the nuns would even do the masonry themselves when burying one of their community in the crypt. No nun or novice would ever again be exempted from wearing a sackcloth tunic, for the Lord bestows skin allergies on His Brides as an opportunity to share His suffering—

Within days one of the younger nuns, Sor Cayetana del Niño Salvadór del Mundo, dismissed herself during recreation to visit the privy and went directly to the front doors, opened them, and stepped out into the street. The doors were always closed during the midday hours, and it had never occurred to anyone that they should be locked so that they couldn't be opened from the inside. It was the first time in memory that a nun had escaped a convent in that city by the obvious means of leaving by the front door. The new Prioress summoned locksmiths.

On the ninth of February, the Liberal government issued a decree ordering all the female religious communities to be consolidated into a single convent in eighteen days. It was more shocking than an outright order of expulsion because it was so unexpected, and in some ways even more dreadful, for how were nine convents of nuns, all following different Rules and Customs, to coexist inside a single convent? That same day the further professing of nuns was also outlawed—finally, according to the Liberal press, putting an end to the coercion of young women into unproductive slavery, suicide in life, and perversion of the laws of nature, medieval practices having no place in a democratic republic of free citizens.

Every afternoon now Madre Sor Gertrudis tried to prepare the terrified community for the moment when soldiers would come to expel them. The history of the Church's female religious Orders was a luminous galaxy of Blessed Virgins who, rather than commit suicide or submit to the depredations of convent-sacking infidels and barbarians—Vikings, Goths, Franks,

Saracens, Magyars, Moors, Tartars, the armies of Voltaire and Benito
Juárez—had resisted to the last: entire communities of nuns cutting off
their noses or lips or secreting rotted chicken meat inside their orifices or
finding some other way to make themselves repugnant to their attackers,
provoking the glorious martyrdoms that dispatched them, *intactum*, to their
Señor's Bridal Chamber.

"Although God can do all things," Madre Gertrudis quoted from the
sacred writings of San Jerónimo, "He cannot raise a virgin after she has
fallen."

María de las Nieves blurted, "Madre, do you know if—" and stopped
herself. "Yes, Sister?" asked the new Prioress. "Nothing, Madre," she answered, lowering her gaze, brusquely apologizing. But Sor Gertrudis's
narrow-eyed stare bored into her. That evening in the refectory María de
las Nieves was given beans dressed in lamp oil for dinner; she ate them
without even a grimace, thanking her Lord for having let her off so lightly
and asking for forgiveness, though she was unable to stop herself from again
silently posing her question: Why would You be able to raise the dead and
restore sight to the blind and trade hearts with nuns and not be able to
repair a virgin? Oh Señor, did You ever try?

The acting Ecclesiastical Governor, Canon Molina, instructed all the
Prioresses to inventory their convents' valuables, and arrange for their storage in the homes of trustworthy seculars. But each Prioress was allowed to
send a formal letter of protest on her community's behalf to the Liberal
government, with a copy to the Curia. From Nuestra Señora de Belén came
a female monastic's Apostles' Creed declaring the nuns' willingness to die
as martyrs. Padre Bruno included that letter in his *La Monjita Inglesa*, and
listed the twenty-two nuns who signed it: the novice Sor Gloria de los
Ángeles's signature is among them, but Sor San Jorge's is not. On the next
page the Spanish priest reported that Madre Sor Gertrudis had received
instructions to release her *sole remaining novice* in as secret a manner as possible. Limp with terror and grief, in secular dress and hooded cloak, Sor
Gloria was escorted at midnight by the Portress, Sor Inés, and the
Cellaress, Sor Guadalupe, to the door leading from the cloister into the
school—at the school's front gate a coach was waiting to bear her home to
her heartbreakingly indifferent family.

But where was the novice Sor San Jorge?

"—*AND ALL THOSE* pícaras novicias *and young nuns, hearing themselves called* señoritas *and other gallantries by the soldiers escorting them out of their convents, forgot their grief and smiled like the coquettish* doncellas *that a true and just God, who delights in nature, wishes them to be* ... Are you listening to me, Mamita of my heart? What a marvel!" Paquita Aparicio was reading out loud to her mother from the newspaper *El Tren de la Tarde* (though it would be decades before Los Altos had its own train). "Mi queridísima, Madre, can there be any doubt that one of those flirty novices was our Las Nievecitas?"

During her first three years as a boarding student, Paquita had always had to stay behind in the convent school during holidays, along with María de las Nieves. Now that El Anticristo was President of the Republic and living in the capital, Paquita had been allowed to come home, and then hadn't even returned for the new school term. She'd told her mother, and written to her father in New York, that she and Justo Rufino intended to wed in July, as soon as she turned fifteen.

"I suppose Las Nievecitas will want to come back and live with us again."

"I think it would be best for her to stay with the monjitas, mijita mia, wherever they go next," said Doña Francisca Mérida de Aparicio to her daughter in her flat, muffled voice, which always sounded as if it came from the bottom of a well.

But Paquita insisted on sending a coach for the mandaderas Modesta and Josefa so that they could be her servants when she was married, and if María de las Nieves wanted to come home with them, all the better—

*El Tren de la Tarde* sneered that it was obvious that Church authorities had ordered the Prioresses to dispose of their notorious instruments of torture, though what had obviously been a dungeon was found in one convent, and in another, iron bolts in the walls, the remnants of broken chains, and shackles. But the only reference to Nuestra Señora de Belén was a mocking description of a mural in its refectory portraying San Agustín weeping over the death of his mother, Santa Mónica—*a total falsehood*, asserted *El Tren de la Tarde*'s correspondent, a former Jesuit seminarian, because in his *Confessions* San Agustín admitted that he had not wept.

In the next day's newspaper Paquita read that the government had now decreed the Santa Catalina convent open to the public during the workday hours. When the acting Ecclesiastical Governor announced that any secular person trespassing into Santa Catalina would be excommunicated, Rufino the Just reacted to the threat as if to an act of war, declaring the immediate extinction of all female monastic Orders. The nuns were given just three hours to vacate Santa Catalina and go home to their families. Any nun who refused could be arrested and shot. Those events were days past by the time Paquita read about them, but the realization that it was too late now to send a coach paled in comparison to the most recent development reported, however derisively, in that same edition: the Ecclesiastical Council, declaring *our lost brother José Rufino* to be an apostate and anathema to all Christian humanity, a Pharisee of modern times, accursed and placed outside the mercy of God, had ordered his immediate excommunication. *And let the fate of the excommunicated follow all those who willingly lend him their support—*

*Salve, María!* gasped Paquita. Tears fell onto the backs of her hands, which her future husband had yet even to touch with his own fingers. Am I excommunicated too? What about our Cathedral wedding? And how will we baptize our children? She returned to the newspaper and read through a blur that the priests had also prohibited him from taking the name of one of the saints of the Roman martyrology, Justo . . . *—accursed and placed outside the mercy of God!* Well, go and find crueler words than those, if you can!

FOUR DAYS BEFORE the Sisters of Nuestra Señora de Belén were to abandon their convent, María de las Nieves, as she did every Friday afternoon, had gone to confession in the lower-choir. The small mahogany door of the confessional window was decorated with an exquisite painting, in oils and gold leaf, of the Lamb of God nestled inside a corona of flames; when she pulled it open she found Padre Lactancio already waiting on the other side. The priest's eyes were tremulous pools of lonely pessimism. She sneezed so suddenly she didn't even have a chance to lift her hands.

"Jesucristo," said the priest in a quietly stunned tone, nearly gaping at her.

"Blessed be His name, forever and ever."

"Impious and disgraceful niña," he said, in his suffocated voice of torturous, unconfessed love. "Why, of all possible moments, do you choose to sneeze now?"

"It wasn't on purpose, Padre," she answered. "It must be because today is a cold, gray day, and I also feel cold and gray inside. Soon we'll be leaving our cloister."

"That is not among the causes of sneezing mentioned by Aristotle." Padre Lactancio pronounced the philosopher's name with an acid trace of personal resentment. The judgment, he told María de las Nieves, had finally arrived.

"All the way from Rome?" she asked, as brightly as she could.

He didn't know. The judgment was unsigned, but it had been slipped under the door of his sacristy in an envelope sealed with the emblem of the Curia. "What I think, Sor San Jorge," he said, "is that some very learned theologian or canon, knowing that this is a critical and historic moment for our Church in this country, one certain to be studied by scholars for all time, did not wish to have his name attached to a disquisition on sneezing. But I confess, I had hoped for a more compassionate interpretation. I trust the writer felt guided by God."

María de las Nieves felt the stirring of pitch-dark panic, but managed to ask calmly: "Does our Madre Priora know?"

"Pobrecita, she is running in circles, trying to see to a thousand matters at once. We are to discuss later today what is to be done."

Padre Lactancio had brought the letter, which he unfolded and began to read out loud from in his earnest, stumbling manner. Padre Famianus Strada, the author of a seventeenth-century treatise on the sneeze, was cited as the fundamental source for much that was to follow, beginning with the myth of Prometheus, who, while making a clay statue that he wished to endow with life, stole a beam of sunlight from Apollo and absent-mindedly put it up his nose, causing himself and then the statue to sneeze violently. As soon as María de las Nieves heard the words "Aristotle wrote, It is very pleasant to sneeze, and the pleasure is felt in all parts of the body," she had no doubt about her fate. The judgment's author next cited a seemingly binding precedent. A little more than a century before, in the former viceregal capital, when the sneeze-provoking inhaling of snuff was endemic in the convents, the Archbishop had declared the use of snuff by nuns to constitute a mortal sin of the flesh. The possession of snuffboxes and the practice of accepting pinches of snuff from visitors to the locutory was prohibited inside all the cloisters from that day forward.

" . . . The novice Sor San Jorge's habitual sneezing is of the gravest category of mortal and monastic sin because it is a debauched bodily self-pleasuring and, in the satisfying of lechery by a less obviously proscribed means, a ridiculing of her most solemn vow of virginal purity."

María de las Nieves, eyes cast down, felt indignation growing inside her. Her brow flashed hot. When she finally spoke, she managed to sound calm: "Why now, Padre Lactancio, if the convent is to close in four days, and all novices are to be freed from their vows? You're not really going to show it to Madre Gertrudis, are you, Padre Lactancio? It isn't even signed. Somebody is playing a trick on us. Don't you think so?"

But the priest was again reading from the judgment in a low, rapid voice: "The angelic doctor San Tomás de Aquino wrote that the reason can be consumed by the vehemence of such pleasure until there is no room for intelligent activity. Because the novice Sor San Jorge has only been vehement in the pursuit of her vice, she should be confined and observed. We pray that it is the loss of reason, more than wickedness, which explains her. There it ends, Sor San Jorge." With a momentous nod, he concluded, "So perhaps it is the loss of reason, and not wickedness, which explains you. You know I cannot defy the orders of my Superiors."

When the new Prioress read the verdict, she ordered María de las Nieves confined to a punishment cell in the novices' cloister. But Padre Lactancio assumed that the imprisoned novice had simply been freed, that she, like Sor Gloria, had been discreetly slipped out of the convent before the move to Santa Catalina. He was sorry that there'd been no chance to say good-bye. María de las Nieves, he knew also, must now consider him an odious fool, and he blessed her for that. But priests share with God the great vocation of bringing happiness to others: at least twice a day, Padre Lactancio went to Santa Catalina to visit Madre Gertrudis and her nuns. But it was not until the second day that he finally dared to ask her about Sor San Jorge's whereabouts.

"She left behind in punishment cell, Padre," was the foreign nun's cold-hearted reply. "The authorities find and send home. But Padre, no call her Sor San Jorge. Sor San Jorge is no more her name."

ONE MORNING MARÍA de las Nieves woke to bells ringing Prime, which, being imprisoned, she would not attend; the next to the reedy squawking of a soldier's cornet. She'd been stripped of her habit, veil, and headdress. It was impossible to pull a sneeze-worthy piece of thread from her sackcloth tunic. She could hear the clamor of soldiers in the professed nuns' cloister and knew it was just a matter of time before they finally found her, for the convent was not a labyrinth; they would only have to explore a little more. That morning the little door at the bottom of the locked door to her cell did not slide open for her daily ration of hard bread and water. But the previous dawn someone had delivered three oranges as well, and then tried to push something else through the opening, but it was too large. Then she'd heard the shriek of the bolt being slid open, the door opening and closing, footsteps receding. When she woke again, the morning light pouring through the high barred window, she saw the big box left just inside the door. But it was not a box. It was a fat single-volume edition of Sor María de Agreda's *The Mystical City*, the "autobiography" of the Most Holy Virgin. All that day and the next she read without stopping. No more food or drink was pushed into her cell, but she felt indefatigable. She slid the open tome across the floor, chasing the fading light until she was down to just one small diluted patch penetrating through the crossed iron bars. It truly was a book of marvels: the divine unborn Infant in the Holy Virgin's suddenly transparent womb, waving to the future Apostles being carried in the mortal but also transparent wombs of their mothers; and the Holy Virgin's adventures in heaven.

But the Bible and liturgy and the *vidas* of saints and nuns that she'd been reading and listening to for a year were also full of marvels, if not so realistically told. Sor María's book went thoroughly into matters lightly passed over in the Bible and everywhere else, so much so that it was as if the screen of divine instruction had been ripped away, and she was now reading about biblical events as they had actually occurred. This idea disturbed her so much that as soon as it became too dark and she had to set the book aside, she sat on the floor sucking and chewing orange peels, scratching at her rashes, and thinking about what she'd read late into the night. Such was her absorption that she didn't feel afraid. She could smell wood smoke and meat roasting in the air, and something foul, as if fabrics, or even hair, were being burned. She heard glass smashing. Some of the soldiers became drunk the way Indians do, querulously shouting and arguing with their own sorrow, fear, and shame. Then she almost forgot to breathe, because it was as if those same violent, unhappy voices were sending her an archangelic revelation about one of the chapters she'd read earlier that day, the one in which the Holy Virgin is early in her pregnancy and her husband, José, notices. *For being most perfect in the proportions of her body, the slightest change was the more apparent.* Sor María de Agreda related, page after page, what the Bible leaves out: José's prolonged anguish over his much younger wife's infidelity. As his suspicions grew, the carpenter became more melancholy, and sometimes spoke to his adored wife in a severe and unkind manner, something he'd never done before. But the Holy Virgin maintained her usual sweetness, and went on making his meals and attending to all his wants. After passing two more months in unendurable uncertainty, José came to a decision. He prepared a bundle of clothing and took a small amount of the money he'd earned from his carpentry, leaving the rest. He told God he was going away, not because his wife had committed a sin but because, seeing her condition, he was ignorant of the cause, and could bear it no longer.

So she lied to her husband to keep him from abandoning her to face the scandal alone, thought María de las Nieves. He pretended to believe her, because it gave him an excuse to stay, though he was devastated, because he knew now that she'd also lied when she'd told him that she loved him. Maybe she even secretly despised him, and loved someone else. María de las Nieves sat in the pitch-darkness of her punishment cell as if at the bottom of a bottle of ink, and prayed: Queen of Heaven, send me a sign, because I know that Satan prepares you for himself by giving you satanic thoughts. It was just before dawn when the bolt in the door was slid open, and she told herself to accept the horrors that were about to befall her as just punishment. But it was only Padre Lactancio. The priest led her out of the novices' cloister, while she carried the enormous book against her chest in both arms. In the kitchen a soldier was crouched in front of the stove working a bellows and did not even glance up as they passed. Padre Lactancio took hold of her elbow and ordered her to close her eyes when they entered the garden—but she disobeyed, and saw soldiers and even women asleep in the open corridors, some using the satin robes of saints' statues as blankets. She saw the rag-shrouded, leathery, long-haired skeleton of a nun, pulled from the crypt and propped up against the base of the fountain, an empty aguardiente bottle between her splayed thigh bones.

# Chapter 2

$\mathscr{F}$ive days after the glorious battlefield death of El Anticristo, and only one after his burial in the General Cemetery, Francisca Aparicio and her seven children fled the country. Despite the young widow's pious entreaties, the remains of he who in life had been the unappeasable persecutor of Jesuits were flatly denied what even Serapio Cruz's severed head had been granted: entombment in the Cathedral crypt. Paquita would travel by Pacific Mail steamship from Puerto San José to San Francisco, California, and then by train to New York City, now the much preferred route even in winter, when the long transcontinental journey was often impeded by snow. She would never risk, certainly not with her children in tow, the quick trip through revolution-riled Panama and the miasmal fever port of Colón, where the cemeteries were filled with the hasty graves of abruptly rerouted travelers of all nations. Who could forget the time her late husband's Vice-Minister of Works had disembarked at Colón with three Yankee teachers and a butcher, expert in the latest slaughterhouse methods, whom he'd recruited during a trip to New York? They were delayed when heavy rains interrupted the running of the trans-Panama trains, and by the second morning all but one of the New Yorkers was too ill to leave the hotel. One teacher subsequently recovered, but the healthy one succumbed, was the first to die, and the third teacher, widow of the first, perished next. After ten days in Colón, the German-born butcher declared himself convalesced and the reduced party finally traveled across the Isthmus to Panama City, where they boarded a Pacific Mail steamship sailing up the coast, and two nights later, in the suffocating quarantine berth to which he'd been confined by the ship's surgeon with a diagnosis of scarlet fever, the butcher also died, and was buried at sea off the coast of Nicaragua, wrapped in the Stars and Stripes of his adopted country. The following evening another Yankee passenger, a four-year-old girl, the favorite of all the first-class passengers and officers, a little songstress with a prodigy's ear and memory for popular melodies and opera alike, suddenly fell ill; she breathed her last before dawn, and the solemn funeral rites were repeated, this time with a ship captain's hat laid upon the child's tiny breast and to the accompaniment of a sailor's accordion playing a romantic ballad she'd performed on deck on her last night of good health—and thereafter, the young Vice-Minister of Works later recounted to Paquita, that voyage was pervaded by a most pensive and poetical gloom . . . All in all, a tragic end to the good work of the Vice-Minister of Works, and a blow, pues sí, to the Supreme Government's efforts to lure immigrants. Never before had their country's name been so vehemently shouted and defamed by the army of newsboys in the streets of New York, bawling perverse scenarios of foul play into the infernal air as if trying to incite the homeward- and saloon-rushing male masses into rioting for war—insinuating blame even for the death of the little girl, though she'd been traveling with mother and siblings to join her father, a mining engineer, in Sonsonate, El Salvador. (But who cabled the information to the newspapers? Justo Rufino suspected the diplomatic agents of certain European powers, trying to inflame Yankee fears of the coveted Isthmus's native treacheries.)

As if in New York people never perished from fevers or unintentionally contaminated foods! As if there were not miserable swamps of contagion even in the heart of that great metropolis, which Paquita had come to love as much as she did her own native Quezaltenango. *So that you can see it with your own eyes, Monsieur and Madame President,* she and Justo Rufino had been taken one summer night on a carriage ride through the swarming neighborhoods where poor immigrants lived, the stifling heat so noxious, so like an Indian market inside a lidded chamber pot that they'd had to take turns holding her perfumed handkerchief over their noses just to breathe!

Nearly a decade later Paquita was still encountering New Yorkers who, as soon as her nationality or status as Primera Dama was introduced, ungraciously recalled that notorious episode of the dead married teachers, the little girl, and a butcher. She always replied, with appropriate sincerity (are you watching, mi Rufinito? This is how you conquer those who think themselves superior to you) and never apologetically, lightly grasping each of her interlocutor's forearms and looking directly into their eyes: Yes, that was very sad, and such a terrible loss, which my husband and I remember every year with candles and prayers. But you know, corazón, many of us no longer take the risk of traveling the Panama route, and we encourage visitors to avoid it as well. Though I am sure you will be happy to learn that the one teacher who did survive that tragedy, Miss James, decided to continue her journey, and now she is the headmistress of the Instituto Nacional de Señoritas, located in our former Convent of Nuestra Señora de Belén, where I myself was once interned as a student under the rule of nuns. Miss James has lifted up our little secular school in her own hands in order to hold it closer to the sun, except that sun is inside of her, and its radiance is the Yankee can-do spirit, and the progressive educational philosophies that formed her.

Another New York butcher, Mr. Henry Koch, was also eventually lured to La Pequeña Paris, and so prospered that now there was not another butcher in the city who did not have to buy meat from him, or rent his butcher's stall in the market from him. Even her husband's Chief of Police, Colonel Pratt, was from New York, and one of her governesses, Jane Pratt, hired to tutor the children and herself in English, was his niece.

Earlier in their marriage, during an official visit to the United States, Justo Rufino had purchased a five-story mansion in New York in his wife's name, situated on a newly fashionable stretch of Fifth Avenue, facing Central Park. Ever since, Paquita had spent as much time there as her husband and her duties as "La Presidenta," the beautiful, refined, and fertile spouse, mother, and symbol of the young Liberal Republic, had allowed. Paquita's father was still living and doing business in New York as well.

The entourage accompanying Paquita out of the country that day included María de las Nieves and her seven-year-old daughter, Mathilde (who shared her mother's surnames). No one associated with the slain dictator in despotism, plunder, or even family connection was safe from wildest vengeance now. But the former novice nun had long dreamed of going to live in New York. In her luggage that day she carried her copy of a document that scholars and others have long believed to be lost forever, or at best to have been misplaced, buried, and forgotten—in the diplomatic archives in Madrid or in the archives of the old Pinkerton's National Detective Agency, or in some other archive or private collection in Spain, the United States, Cuba, somewhere.

At the train station, before boarding her private presidential railroad carriage for the last time, Paquita turned to address the crowd and military guard that had come to see her off. Vigorously shaking out the long black trains of her mourning dress like a haughty Andalusian dancer, she shouted in her grief- and fear-flayed voice:

"Do you see? Not even this country's dust or dirt will I take with me!"

Not the dust or the dirt, María de las Nieves would in later years relate, but all the country's *pisto*—pues, eso sí! Incredibly, Paquita believed, or seemed to, that it was money her husband had honestly earned, in the mighty spirit of the times, like a Central American Carnegie or Gould, even as he'd increased and spread through personal example and bold governing the country's prosperity generally, waking it from centuries of Spanish-Indian torpor, wealth that was now most rightfully hers, considering all that she'd contributed to his reign, and all that she'd endured.

At the last moment Dr. Joaquín Yela rushed onto the train to press a sealed porcelain jar into the young widow's black-gloved hands, gravely announcing that it contained her late husband's heart preserved in alcohol. Standing next to Doña Paca was a brown-skinned woman in a dress of black percale fitting loosely over her thin frame, a dark-eyed, solemn little girl leaning back into her skirts; despite the woman's murky stare, slashing black brows, rust-hued hair worn in a lax chignon, the bearded physician did not recognize in her the fourteen-year-old novice nun whose allergy to wool he'd diagnosed more than a decade before on a visit to her convent infirmary.

When the train began to move Paquita gave the porcelain jar to the broken-toothed servant Josefa Socorro to hold and sat with her youngest children enfolded tightly against her, as if all were trying to squeeze within the frame of a photographer's portrait. Miss Pratt, the governess, sat with a ceramic bowl in her lap, peeling green oranges with a knife and handing pieces to the children. María de las Nieves absently stroked her daughter's head through her hair and stared in sullen fixation at the jar cradled in the Josefa Socorro's fleshy arms. Could there be a heart more unlike Sor Gertrudis's beloved, flaming, pulsating Sacred Heart of Jesucristo than the one floating inside that jar? As they descended toward the coast, the train filled with the heavy, fragrant lowland heat and the drifting smoke of burning sugarcane. María de las Nieves fell into a nodding, sporadic sleep, and kept finding herself back in the choir, before a radiantly gem-festooned golden altar, praying to a heart boiling in a thin, scarlet, poisonous broth inside a clear glass bowl, slowly strangling on its fumes.

The scattered and remote lights of Puerto San José and the torches on its pier were still visible through the bilious green-yellow twilight when Paquita carried the porcelain jar to the rail and dropped it overboard into the frothing waves churned by the steamer's bladed wheel. María de las Nieves shouted to be heard over the rancorous clanging of the machinery:

"You should have opened it and fed his heart to the sharks."

Paquita, hands on the rail, went on staring at the dimming coastline of the country she would never see again, her hair in the wind like a distant shadow of the long black cloud pluming into the darkening sky from the smokestack. Then she turned with a tolerant smile, her cheeks moist with spray and flecked with cinders, and took hold of María de las Nieves's arms, only to see her friend avert her eyes from her own earnest, tear-clouded gaze.

"Ferocious fool," said Paquita, leaning closer. "He had everything but God's love, which this last and greatest ambition of his was not likely to have won."

Ándale, chuladita, thought María de las Nieves. Keep up this pretty show, Paquita, I know you can't believe your good fortune. She felt nauseous with inexpressible ill will.

El Anticristo had died in the very first engagement of his campaign to reunite all of Central America into a single federal republic by force under his rule. Anticipating the failure of the French efforts to build the canal across Panama, and knowing that the Yankees or even the British would end up putting one through Nicaragua regardless, Justo Rufino could not allow that country to subsequently become Central America's wealthiest and most dominant, his own reduced to a beggar's role on the margins. Possessing the military might to prevent that, wasn't it his right, his obligation and destiny to do so? His Central American Republic, with the long-dreamed-of canal connecting the oceans running through it, would be a nation of consequence in the world long after he was gone. Except he'd failed even to lead his troops across the border into bellicose and treasonous little El Salvador, shot off his horse by sniper fire, his panicked, disconsolate army routed—well, that was the official version, and María de las

Nieves and Paquita still knew no other. The Kentucky-bred stallion, Relámpago, which had borne him into his last battle that day, was also traveling with them to New York; there was the horse, white mane streaming in the hot wind, a humiliated Pegasus, wearing blinders, penned and tethered beneath a tattered canopy on the foredeck among crates of poultry.

Soon Paquita would be a regular sight in Central Park, out riding, side-saddle, atop her late husband's thoroughbred war horse. Enveloped in such an aura of exotic romance and wealth, it was no wonder that the beautiful young widow would rise so swiftly to the peak of Manhattan society. Despite his self-styled image as a Garibaldi-like man of the people, her husband's fortune had grown so immense during his twelve years of absolute power that at the time of his death there was six million dollars in his New York accounts alone, willed solely to his widow, along with his many properties and businesses at home and abroad. In New York, titans of North American industry and politics and their wives would come to Paquita's lavish but tasteful entertainments as equals, crediting their lovely hostess with having introduced into their society a discerning Latin warmth and hospitality.

But even during the last years of Rufino the Just's reign, Paquita's Fifth Avenue mansion had already become a fashionable gathering place for wealthy and distinguished foreigners, from Latin America but also Europe and especially from Spain, despite her husband's avowed sympathy with the cause of Cuban independence. At the time, Spain was trying to crush a new outbreak of seditious conspiring and insurrection in her most precious colony, and had hired the famous Pinkerton's National Detective Agency to spy on rebel conspirators among Cuban immigrants and exiles living in the United States, in the populous cities of the eastern seaboard especially. One evening in the winter of 1881, Paquita's friend the Spanish Consul General, Don Hipólito de Iriarte, heir to the Condado de Perrogruño, had spontaneously entertained a gathering of guests in her salon by reading out loud from the Pinkerton reports of a Yankee spy who'd managed to rent a room in the same small New York boardinghouse where an impoverished young Cuban rebel leader was living with his unlikely, elegant young wife and infant child. Eventually Paquita realized that the compromised Cuban in question was none other than José Martí, the same loquacious "Dr. Torrente" who, in 1877, had arrived in her country in order to teach in one of the progressive new schools established by her husband's government; among the many broken hearts he left behind a year later was that of María de las Nieves. She did not possess beauty, wealth, or surnames but had other qualities sufficient to have drawn the interest of a few surprisingly suitable suitors, and seemed to be returning the feelings of at least one of these until the impassioned, stirringly talkative, and learned young Cuban poet-seducer had entered her life. María de las Nieves's reputation and marriage prospects had ended up in the mud, of course, as soon as her pregnancy was noticed. Malicious tongues even linked the controversial Cuban to her baby, though she was born many months after he'd already left the country under a dark cloud (his also pregnant Cuban bride in tow), an allegation that, whenever Paquita confronted her with it, she vehemently denied. María de las Nieves could have protested that for the slander to even have a possibility of being true her daughter needed to have been conceived during Martí's final days in their country, so small was the window allowed by the settled measure of time between impregnation and birth; yet the existence of those few days could not be denied. One of Martí's most famous and perhaps most regrettable verses, composed more than a decade later, would recall a good-bye kiss and a beloved face like burning bronze. If we could know and classify what sorts of kisses have marked the conception of all children ever born since the beginning of universal human time, the offspring of good-bye kisses have probably been far more numerous than those of hello kisses.

As the Pinkerton operative's confidential report, at least those brief portions that the Spanish Consul read aloud to her friends, did not cast Dr. Torrente—the extraordinarily verbose Martí's nickname in her country, Paquita had explained to Don Hipólito, who'd responded with a knowing smile—in a dignified or enviable light, Paquita requested a copy, and told him why. Her dearest childhood companion, María de las Nieves, had paid a severe price for her mystifying folly and carelessness and had since grown hard inside her youthful womanhood; it had been years, she was sure, since Las Nievecitas had last heard words of even light flirtation, to say nothing of expressions of sincere romance from any man. Perhaps reading this report would help, a little-little, to soften that stone inside her. The Spanish diplomat said that in that case she could have it, for it was no longer needed and, at any rate, there was another copy at the legation in Washington. Surely his enchanting hostess and friend did not do him the dishonor of thinking that he would have read state secrets out loud for the amusement of her guests?

Upon Paquita's return home later that year, she gave the document to María de las Nieves. (There it was, upon the worm-eaten table at which I sat and worked, among all the other books and bundles of papers heaped there for my perusal, including María de las Nieves's extremely rare copy of Fray Labarde's *Vida de Sor María de Agreda;* and a London first edition of Casanova's *Under the Leads,* given to her on her birthday in 1899, a black velvet ribbon marking the pages where the immortal libertine narrates his own entranced reading of Sor María de Agreda's "autobiography" of the Virgin while imprisoned in a prison cell in the Doge's Palace in Venice; and, of course, María de las Nieves's own copy of the nun's massive tome, the same one she'd carried away from Nuestra Señora de Belén that morning in 1874; and a well-worn edition of Padre Bruno's *La Monjita Inglesa;* Sainte-Beuve's *Celebrated Women* inscribed "with fraternal affection" by "Pepe Martí"; and a copy of his *Versos Sencillos,* published in New York in 1891, also affectionately, if unrevealingly, inscribed . . .)

That night on board the *Golden Rose,* after the children had been put into their berths, María de las Nieves and Paquita stayed up talking in the sitting room of the stateroom suite taken by the late dictator's immediate family, the ship's most luxurious, next to the gentlemen's smoking saloon, from which came the sounds of manly drinking and gambling. María de las Nieves and Mathilde were staying in one of the small first-class cabins toward the front of the deckhouse. The two women were sipping brandy diluted with water, eating soda crackers and tinned sardines, and fanning themselves against the heat as they reminisced about their days, together and apart, in the convent. María de las Nieves was smoking paper-rolled cigarettes; the widowed Primera Dama, heeding the New York model of female comportment, had renounced that vice—nevertheless, with a pickpocket's feathery touch, she kept plucking cigarettes from María de las Nieves's fingers, bringing them to her own lips, returning them; back and forth, like dizzy fireflies, from one pair of lips to the other, went María de las Nieves's cigarritos and she didn't even seem to notice.

"By far the eeriest thing I witnessed in all my time in the cloister was Madre Melchora on her deathbed, speaking her last words without moving her lips," declared María de las Nieves.

Paquita kept refilling the other's snifter too. María de las Nieves was unaccustomed to such a steady flow of liquor, and her eyes were glassy and gay. The constant weight of melancholy and self-torment of the past years seemed to have miraculously lifted. Of course she was excited to be traveling out of the country for the first time, toward a new life, and the possibility of a happier one. She even dared to think that she was not a traveler but a true emigrant, one who might never return, or at least not for a very long time. So words were spilling from María de las Nieves, as she sat with her legs crossed, her hands clasped over a knee and that knee moving relentlessly up and down, causing her upper torso to do the same. That Japanese circus that came to the National Theater only a few weeks ago? With the sixteen acrobats forming into one kaleidoscopic tower of torsos and limbs that tipped over and ran around the stage like a giant centipede; and those two kimono-clad monkeys who conducted an extremely high-pitched and coquettish conversation via the "voice-throwing" artistry of that pig-tailed Japanese girl—

"—Do you think it's possible that Sor Gertrudis knew how to do that? It's the only explanation I can think of. That la Madrecita really passed away only moments before, and what we heard was Sor Gertrudis throwing her voice."

Paquita solemnly answered, "You know very well, mis Nievecitas, that the Holy Spirit is the greatest ventriloquist of all."

"And is the Holy Spirit the explanation for Sor Trinidad's role as secret agent provocateur?" said María de las Nieves, voice rising. "*You*, Madame Francisca, know that we've both learned a thing or two about conspiracy in our lives, but our Monjita Inglesa was the unsurpassable master."

"Unsurpassable master!" Paquita, with an incredulous expression, pushed herself partly out of her plush chair. "That does make me laugh. Now *you* expose the commonness of your own perceptions, María de las Nieves. A conspiracy among nuns must be as mundane as cheating at dice. How much of a master was your Sor Gertrudis, if it took her twelve years to plot a Reform that didn't even last two months?"

"Hmm . . . Sí . . . Sí pues." María de las Nieves slapped her fan closed against her lap. "Camarón! Of course, you are right." She nodded glumly and said, "But I can't see her so clearly as you do, fíjase. When Sor Gertrudis began to hate me because she thought that I thought she'd switched the lace, you see, *that*, my dear Paquita, hurt at least as much as any other love I've ever lost. Including God's. So it is difficult for me to see her as you do, with your infinitely greater detachment and clarity. As you see her, Doña Paca, with your even greater knowledge of conspiracy and machination, the poison fruit of so many years of access to the reports and lies of spies and traitors. Yes, Paquita, the poison fruit!"

Shiny-eyed with happy malice, María de las Nieves inhaled her cigarette and took a fast drink of brandy and, swallowing wrong, began to cough, lifting a hand to her mouth.

Paquita smiled thinly, like a blind woman lost in her thoughts, waiting for the coughing fit to pass. "Las Nievecitas. You know when we get to New York you can't speak to me like that anymore, not even in jest. People there won't understand our comedy. What about Dr. Torrente? Didn't it hurt even more to lose his love?"

"Pepe didn't love me. So I didn't lose it." Like many Josés, Martí liked to be called Pepe—derived from the double *P*s of the biblical Pater Putativus.

"What really happened between you and Martí? Please tell me, María de las Nieves."

"There's not so much to tell. Hardly anything."

"Is he Mathilde's father?"

"Oh Paquita . . . please."

"Some day, María de las Nieves, you will have to reveal to your daughter who her father is."

"One can always invent a story. A story can certainly be a better father than a real one, Paquita."

"In such a case, both are far from ideal, mis Nievecitas."

"I don't know that I agree. It depends." If I were *your* children, she thought, I'd much rather have a story.

"If you tell me, I promise to tell you what I know about Martí and María García Granados. Half the servants in Chafandín's household were paid spies. That doesn't surprise you, does it?"

Chafandín—General Miguel García Granados, the Liberal Revolution's first President—and Doña Cristina's daughter María was the same age as María de las Nieves and Paquita. About a year after Martí had first arrived in their city, and soon after he'd briefly returned to Mexico to marry and then come back, accompanied by his Cuban wife, to resume his teaching appointments, María García Granados had died—it was said of pneumonia or of consumption, either way a sad fate but one that could befall anyone at any time. Even before her death, the common gossip had been that the general's daughter had lost her heart to the Cuban, and that he to some degree had returned her affections, and perhaps her passionate love. Now that the whole sad episode was almost forgotten, leave it to Paquita to bring it up. It was cruel of her to want to talk about María García Granados—whom María de las Nieves had been friendly with, jealous of, whom she'd felt so sad for when she'd died after taking to her bed, coughing and coughing herself to death, as could happen to anyone—; María de las Nieves felt uncomfortable and confused thinking about María García Granados now. What right did Paquita have to be offering her these years-old secrets? The reports of informers and detectives who were just as likely to be peddling lies and secondhand gossip.

"But we're not so good at keeping our vows, are we? Vows we make to our Santísima Virgen de Socorro, no less!"

Paquita grinned speechlessly at her suddenly cold-eyed tormentor, flushing.

"What use are spies who repeat gossip and make up stories, Paquita?" Had she been obsessed with the dazzling young Cuban too? Or, apart from money, was this all that was left of power, and so she had to love it like self-love? "Tell me, why should a spy be any more credible than any other gossip?"

"Justo Rufino used to say you had to know how to listen to a spy. If you weren't sure whether he was telling the truth or not, there was always the *stick*."

"You're going to have to learn to listen in a whole new manner now, in a world without your husband's torturers to rely on. And without God too."

"I still have God. I'm not like you, who—"

"I meant the God that makes *other* people afraid to lie, squash head." Now she felt calmly restored to her familiar ill will.

"You met Martí at a party at Chafandín's house."

"Yes, that is true. And one reason I gladly went was that now that Don Miguel and your husband were enemies, I knew you wouldn't be there."

She liked poetry more than she liked stories. Ideally, she did—but how many times could one listen to the exiled Cuban José Joaquín Palma, the Bayamés Bard, recite yet another Ode to the Liberal Republic or sing about his valiant Cuba in chains? Yet of all the poets at "the Literary Society of 'the Future'" evenings of recitations—since the revolution it seemed as if every young dandy and intellectual in the city was a poet *of the future*—he was then the most esteemed. She'd read and listened to far better poetry in the convent. Even Madre Melchora's improvised villancicos had more charm and interest. There was La Presidenta, as always in the chair of honor, the Muse who makes the Doves of Parnassus lay their eggs. Back then, it had still made her stomach ache to be in the same room with Paquita, even with nearly a hundred other people to hide behind, so she'd left, but not before hearing José Joaquín Palma's florid announcement regarding the imminent arrival in their country of an exceptionally gifted young poet and heroic compatriot who would bring honor to the name of the Literary Society of "the Future."

"I saw you that night," Paquita said. "I still hated you too. But even hating you, I wouldn't let Rufino throw you in jail or hang you up in a net. He wanted to, because he thought you knew where Sor Gertrudis and her nuns were hiding."

El Anticristo sometimes arrested women connected to the old Conservative families or to the Church, women he suspected of knowing about conspiracies, or of spreading gossip about the President or his wife, or whose aristocratic presumptions and bearing seemed to cry out for violent humiliation. Sometimes he ordered that the women be suspended inside string nets from the rafters in the stables of the Casa Presidencial, the same nets as those the Indios carried on their stooped backs, filled with huge loads of avocados and such. For days the prisoners were left hanging, sometimes naked or nearly so, until the cords, ever tightening around the weight they held, cut bloodily into the women's skin. Salt was sometimes applied to those cords, milk cows allowed to lick at the netted load of women. Paquita had protected her from such a fate, she knew. And that had eventually helped her to forgive, or at least put aside—justly humbling, given her own compromised existence, her presence on this California-bound steamship being proof enough of that. What would Pepe Martí, with his novice mistress–like harping on purity of conscience, purity of everything, say if he could see her now?

One day, seemingly out of the blue, Paquita had even sent her a handwritten message offering her a position as governess and tutor of her children, inviting her and Mathilde to accompany them during their months-long residences in New York—María de las Nieves had bluntly refused; yet once or twice every year, La Primera Dama had repeated the offer (and only days ago, María de las Nieves had finally accepted, at least the invitation to New York). That was the same woman who'd stood alongside her husband on the balcony of the Casa Presidencial, presiding as the Muse of Massacre over the executions in the Central Plaza of all those whom her husband had accused, not in each case wrongly, of having plotted the murder of the Presidential Family.

"Did you know where Madre Gertrudis and her Sisters were hiding?"

"Not exactly. I could have found out, I think."

"Would you have told?"

"If he'd hung me up in a net, or thrown me to Rosario Ariza?" Ariza was the warden of the women's prison established in the former Carmelite nuns' convent, a notorious harpy and sadist. "Yes, I would have told! Did you think I would suffer to save Sor Gertrudis? Is it true that he wanted to put her in front of a firing squad?"

"I thought you would, yes. I thought you were still a complete fanatic, that you were just pretending to have changed. That you were just waiting for a chance! But Rufinito never said that. Perhaps in jest, he did. Execute La Monjita Inglesa, imagine! Even if she deserved it, even if she was complicit in one of the conspiracies to murder us, to murder not just the President but, do not forget mis Nievecitas, his wife and children too—oh, corazón, that would have caused many more problems than it *ever* could have solved."

"A crime, but a greater blunder. Didn't someone in history say that?" She lightly sucked her lip, widened her eyes, and lied, "Madame Roland."

"Back when you met Martí, you had suitors. You might have married one of them. I marvel sometimes at your serenity, María de las Nieves. Doesn't it ever bother you to think how differently your life could have turned out?"

"The only ones I was aware of were old or homely or dull or widowed or foolish or lonely or some combination of those," she answered. (Serenity! Anything but!) "And a few disreputable foreigners, the type who would even stop you in the street and try to talk to you, usually drunk. But never the handsome men, never the immediately impressive, dazzlingly vital ones. Of all those candidates, let's say lonely had the best chance to force open a slight angle of vision, through which I might judge, without anyone else knowing, the quality of light that appeared."

"O Dios, Dios mío! Grant me patience! Sor San Jorge and her eternal Jesuit sophistries!" Paquita laughed, then said, "That blond Englishman wasn't so terrible. You could have done worse than him."

"Oh? Do you even remember his name?" After a moment, she hinted, *"Wehhh . . ."*

Paquita again shook her head no.

"Wellesley." Spoken as almost three syllables (a bit contemptuously, like a foot sliding into a shoe as you're pushing up to leave). "Wellesley Bludyar. And, yes, he was lonely. He had the bluest eyes, but he was not handsome. Children even used to make fun of him in the streets, poor Wellesley, shouting at his back, El Chino Gringo!"

The parcel of land on the high Pacific slopes of the Sierra Madre, at the far eastern frontier of the Costa Cuca, which María de las Nieves had inherited from her father, Timothy Moran, she had sold only one year after leaving the convent, when she was still living in Quezaltenango with her disgraced mother and the Indian sheep farmer in his squalid family compound in Barrio Siete Orejas. She received much less for the land than it was worth, and gave half of the sum to her mother, who had left the Aparicio household to live with the sheep farmer. (But he was not a poor Indio, and grazed his sheep at several pastures within the city limits.) Though she could hardly foresee ever having the capital to begin planting coffee or anything else there, she did know it would have been wiser to have kept the land—if she'd had any way of preventing it from being stolen from her. The deed had been signed under the old Conservative regime. When she got there, it was being farmed by Mam Indians, who claimed it was theirs. From the beginning of time, they said, it had been part of their ancestral lands. But what if the Mam were lying? Her father had signed a deed. Going to the pregnant young bride of the President of the Supreme Government was out of the question. She refused to even approach the Aparicios, after the way they had forgotten about her and treated her mother. Who did she have to turn to? She, just another refugee of the historic de-cloistering of the nuns, enduring the humiliation of living with her mother in the Indio sheep farmer's compound, sleeping on a mattress of piled corn husks in a corner of their dirt-floored hut, fighting for space with chickens and mangy dogs in the smoky hut; back to nun's hours, roused out of bed well before dawn to grind corn; waging futile war against fleas and lice abounding everywhere, steaming herself in the sweat bath so excessively that her fingers and toes felt perpetually like mealy potatoes, her skin tart tasting from the vapors of medicinal herbs, her hair as slimy as if washed with algae. From an itinerant vendor in the market she bought a moldy volume titled *American Popular Lessons,* with which she was able to practice and improve her English, and that book became the sun at the center of her life, just as Fray Labarde's had for a while been at the center of her previous one. Finally she wrote to Padre Lactancio, and her old Confessor telegraphed her the name of a Los Altos priest, who, when she went to see him, had already begun to negotiate on her behalf with the head of a Bavarian household of laborers; the proper paperwork was prepared. Selling the land hadn't been wise but it had saved her, kept her out of danger. It was her father in heaven, his land, and being able to sell it, that gave her the life of a romantic heroine in a novel rather than of an ordinary *mengala* in the city, with no other escape but marriage to anyone who would take her, or perhaps a servant's job, or some other even more sordid circumstance; hers was a mystical escape as wondrous as any she'd read about in Sor María de Agreda. Her share of the money allowed her to buy a small house on a narrow callejón near the Plazuelita de las Beatas; the modest amount left over was placed with Padre Lactancio for safekeeping. She had a boarder, Amada Gómez, widow of Zeno, a seamstress with a job at a dressmaker's, who rolled cigarettes at home to earn a little more and cried herself to sleep every night, and one Indian servant from her girlhood home in the mountains, María Chon, the niece of Pakal Chon, the maker of rabbits from inflated peccary intestines. Another new phenomenon of the era: women living on their own in the city, who in order not to seem backward had to wear at least an inexpensive Parisian-style hat like an inverted flowerpot with artificial flowers, instead of a lace mantilla. María de las Nieves had recently purchased such a hat, a few secondhand, refitted French-style dresses, and other required accoutrements. She often walked unescorted in the streets, as usually only foreign women did, or any India or lower-class mengala. At sixteen, though lacking a formal school degree, she'd been hired by the British Legation as a translator. She spoke and read English, Latin, a little French, and Mam, possessed a convent schoolgirl's and ex-novice's manners and clerical and domestic skills, and was also giving lessons in Spanish to Mrs. Gastreel, whose husband, Mr. Sidney Gastreel, was British Minister Resident to the five Central American Republics (also, covertly, to the rebel Mayan Republic over the border in Quintana Roo, and to the dormant Kingdom of Mosquitia, on the Nicaraguan Atlantic coast.) María de las Nieves nearly lost her employment at the legation when the inevitable gossip finally reached Minister Gastreel, via Mrs. Gastreel, about her childhood relationship to the wife of the President of the Supreme Government. Minister Gastreel did acknowledge that Doña Francisca was just a child, imprisoned by marriage to an ogre old enough to be her grandfather, but obviously a charming girl, and even a civilizing force on her spouse, though only slightly, but how can we be certain, María de las Nieves, and absolutely certain we must be, that you are not a spy?

On first impression Minister Gastreel looked like a farmer or woodcutter in a fairy story, with coarse steely hair, strong, knobby features, weather-roughened face, and small, alert eyes; his manner was sharp and condescending, but sometimes very kind. Also present at her impromptu interrogation that day in the Minister Resident's library was the legation's young First Secretary, Mr. Wellesley Bludyar, who looked so much like a colorless, nearly albino, tall but plumpish blue-eyed Chinaman that, in an odd echo of her former nun-mentor's popularly misattributed nationality, he really was known around the city as El Chino Gringo (or, in certain rarefied circles of La Petite Paris Centro-américaine, as Le Chinois Anglais). She told the two British diplomatists that she hadn't spoken to Paquita, *not a word*, since they were schoolgirls together in the convent. Her indignant eyes filled with tears. They had seen for themselves how happy she'd been over the outcome of the Consul Magee incident, when Minister Gastreel had so easily imposed his degrading terms against El Anticristo's insolent pretensions. Colonel González, commander of the garrison at Puerto San

José, a boorish Spaniard, the President's friend and ally, was relaxing on the beach with his soldiers one evening when he was approached by an Englishman with a series of minor requests and complaints that he seemed to want resolved immediately, all the while holding out papers, which the irritable port commander was too drunk to read. His smoldering Iberian resentment of Englishmen instantly aggravated by this one's supercilious manner, Colonel González had him jailed and flogged. The Englishman was Mr. John Magee, and the papers in his hand identified him as Her Majesty's recently appointed consul at Puerto San José. The British Legation had then respectfully informed the President of the Supreme Government that, in order to avert the immediate dispatching of British warships, several demands would have to be satisfied. So the Union Jack was raised over the port and honored with a twenty-one-gun salute by troops of the Republic after their own flag had been lowered onto the mud; the obnoxious Colonel González was sent to prison, lashed and pummeled so severely he must have received his death as a blessing from a forgiving God; and the Supreme Government was forced to pay fifty thousand pounds in reparations, divided between the government treasury of Her Majesty the Queen and Consul Magee, converting the former British merchant sailor, overnight, into a man of means, one said to be already looking into purchasing a coffee farm.

"I rejoiced in all of that!" María de las Nieves concluded. "I am second to no one in this country in my detestation of this despot! I didn't even go to him to save my father's land. Don't you think I could have?"

Wellesley Bludyar then remarked, "We are employing the most unusual translator of any legation in this country, if not in the whole world, Your Excellency. A Yankee-Indian, anti-Liberal, anticlerical who often speaks like a Freemason yet also seems to admire the Jesuits and certain apparently monstrously gifted nuns of centuries past. O Virgin of the Snows!"

She thought, A pícaro, that Señor Bludyar. During their idle hours at the legation, she'd let herself converse too freely and vainly.

"Like so many other young people now, I am not sure what I believe," María de las Nieves passionately responded. "So much has been torn down, and so quickly. But has anything yet replaced it?"

Hands in pockets, Mr. Bludyar stood studying the floor, his dull ivory-yellow hair (straight as a Chinaman's) hiding his eyes. Minister Gastreel wore a stopped-clock expression. She hadn't meant to cast such a mood of gravity, which she felt settling over them like a net in which the afternoon light was slowly dying.

Wellesley Bludyar looked up, and with an air of stifled mirth said, "How very superficial of you, Snows."

And Minister Gastreel said, "But no one has ever accused Mr. Bludyar of being profound. I'm sure you are right, Señorita Moran, and that for the thoughtful young people of this great Republic life here now presents a perplexing conundrum, with only a cynical despotism and the hardly abated spectacles of popery and priestcraft offered as exemplary. What is the faith of this nominally Christian government, Wellesley? It is hard to believe they are not the enemy of all religion. I am continually telling the members of this government that if they would provide the small number of Protestants here with a church, then the people could witness a more decorous and sincere form of worship, from which might originate a *true* reform of this country. You will not lose your employment, Señorita Moran, but it was not proper of you to have concealed this extraordinary personal connection."

One night soon after, Wellesley Bludyar escorted María de las Nieves, outfitted as a pirate in seaman's clothes borrowed from the legation, to a costume party at the home of General García Granados, the former President. Bludyar was astonished at the warm welcome María de las Nieves received from Doña Cristina—but the former Primera Dama and enthusiast of intrigues, whether political, conventual, or romantical, was fascinated by the former novice's personal connection to the current Primera Dama, and knew about her conflictive relations with the vexing and now clandestine Sor Gertrudis as well. In keeping with Chafandín's aristocratic, Liberal, and "bohemian" sensibilities, his parties were always eclectic gatherings: government ministers and members of the old Conservative elite, fashionably libertine poets, ambitious young military officers, the diplomatic corps, eminent clergy, the impresarios and performers of whatever opera or drama company happened to be installed in the National Theater as well as those from visiting circuses and bullfights, political exiles, coffee planters, foreign travelers and adventurers, the occasional low-born young dressmaker dazzling the city with a just-cresting perfect beauty, or any character at all who captured the interest of the general or

of anyone else in his family. Chafandín's house was the only place in the
city where María de las Nieves could have mixed with such people. On
other nights, the social life of the wealthy and powerful went on as usual,
much of it revolving around public adoration of the dictator's beautiful
young wife.

In the elegant *sala*, ablaze with chandeliers and Venetian mirrors full of
golden light, a slight, curly-haired young man with flashing almond eyes
was declaring that Napoleon's officers at the Battle of Waterloo owed their
uniform's brilliant scarlet coloring to *cochinilla* dye (cochineal, in English)
from this country.

"So do our small, weak countries participate in the great historical
events of even the most powerful nations," he said. "As blood circulates
through the heart and brain through the extremities and back" (pronounced in his softly Antillean-accented, liquid, yet precise diction, the
recollection of which, as María de las Nieves sat consuming brandy and
sardines and talking with Paquita in the stateroom of the steamship, still
could make her feel as if a feather were being drawn lightly back and forth
over her skin). "Of course *Le Rouge et le Noir*, the title of Stendhal's celebrated novel, refers to the red of those same French officers' uniforms, as
*le noir* does to the cassocks of the clergy," the eloquent young stranger
continued. "So even the title of one of the most notable novels written
in Europe in our century has also been steeped in our . . . cochinilla . . .
our"—he swept his hand before him, as if everyone listening was a
cochinilla cultivator who now had reason to feel pride in his connection to
an important work of French literature—"in that same native Central
American red in which our resplendent quetzal first dipped and dyed her
feathered breast . . ."

The stranger smiled quietly, as if not completely satisfied with his per-
oration, while his eyes beamed like those of a bemused, intelligent child's,
seeming to confide that he couldn't help himself from talking this way,
though he eagerly awaited a sympathetic response. His listeners, women
in costumes and men who mostly were not, did not immediately provide
it. Who was Stendhal? Why was he mixing up cochinilla and the ancient
legend about the quetzal and the slain Mayan cacique Tecum Uman's
blood? Who wanted to think about cochinilla, evocative now only of lost
fortunes and livelihoods?

"And the philosophers who conceived the French Revolution," he added, more softly, turning his palms up as if he'd spoken these words many times before, "might not have done so had not our coffee, our own divine American nectar, been present to illuminate their thoughts and quicken their ardor. According to Voltaire—"

Was this, wondered María de las Nieves, the very Cuban so lauded by the Bayamés Bard? Most of the women simply stood there, intrigued behind their masks and fans by such loquacity, and by this slender young man with a philosopher's broad pale forehead, a poet's dramatic gaze and swept-back black mane, and the effortless good manners, dashing mustache, and electric energy of a true metropolitan. The men, less sure, looked around, seeking some signal in each other's darted glances to tell them whether to feel derisive or impressed. But some had already heard that the young Cuban had been imprisoned by the Spanish for revolutionary activities in Cuba, and that later in Paris he'd been received by Victor Hugo in his own home, and so they were regarding him accordingly, as if they could already sense that his mere presence among them meant that fate (as one young poet and future diplomatist among those men expressed it years later) had unexpectedly laid a path down amid their obscurity leading into the sunny foothills of greatness; one by one, most of the other men began adjusting their own expressions to match those of the knowing few.

Of course the worldly young foreigner's strange claims were actually plausible, because in the time of the Napoleonic Wars their country had been one of the world's leading cultivators and exporters of cochinilla, the tiny dye-producing beetles cultivated on the broad leaves of the nopal cactus, meticulously harvested and then baked in clay ovens. But the invention of aniline dyes in Germany had finally put an end to the once enormously profitable, if always uncertain trade, to which María de las Nieves owed so much: when they had first come to this country her father had worked as the administrator of a cochinilla plantation in Amatitlán, where he'd saved the money to buy his own plot of land for the new enterprise of growing coffee.

So it had been María de las Nieves who spoke first, unconsciously imitating his maddeningly infectious intonations even then: "I grew up on a cochinilla plantation. And then I was a novice nun in a convent. So I come from two worlds that are now obsolete. Two ways of life that have vanished from our Central American . . . our . . . Well, I mean to say, these are two things we no longer do here. We no longer cultivate cochinilla, and we no longer imprison our women for life in convents."

The stranger paused to politely exchange introductions—José Martí, he said, at your service—before adding with a smile: "From a nun to a pirate—let's hope that doesn't prove to be the characteristic transformation of our epoch, Señorita Moran."

"What should I have transformed into instead?"

"Into a schoolteacher, no? That too is a sacred calling."

"Oh! I've had quite enough of sacred callings, Señor Martí." Flustered, she murmured, "I was being trained to become a teaching nun."

"Our times also require martyrs and ascetics, but of a new kind—"

But at that moment a man standing behind her interrupted in a strong voice: "So she's part bug, part nun—that's a new kind of *something.*"

"—willing to give up everything," Martí continued, while María de las Nieves turned to look at the man of rude voice and words and found a sturdily built, thick-necked young Indio in a frock coat, grinning at her as if he expected her to be overjoyed to recognize him. She was sure she'd never seen him before. Something about his preposterously eager face was like a big rock you instantly want to pick up and hurl into a pond. —Willing to give up everything for what? But when she turned back the young Cuban was being pulled off into another conversation.

María García Granados made a late entrance costumed as Cleopatra, her long, bare arms decorated with bracelets, her low-cut satin tunic exposing her pearly collarbones and the yellow-gray shadow of her cleavage, and her long ebony hair silkily opulent; but María de las Nieves did not notice that night's fateful first meeting between Martí and the former President's daughter. Also that night, Wellesley Bludyar, witnessing how María de las Nieves had lit up before the garrulous Cuban, and the evident strain of her effort to impress him, felt an all too familiar dread and a novel bewilderment as he realized that she was as capable of devastating his starved heart as any English girl had ever been. That night María de las Nieves also had her first encounter with Marco Aurelio Chinchilla, the brash Indio "nun-bug" interrupter. So it was a significant party in more ways than one, as has been certified by *history.*

Later, she read the very book the Cuban had mentioned, as she would try to read any book she could find that he praised, and in it encountered the impressive "Mathilde."

"Ay Paquita, I'm tired and you've made me drunk; I am going to bed."

"But you've told me nothing at all, desgraciada! I already knew that, about how you met him."

María de las Nieves went to bed; and her story—much more than she would ever confide to Paquita—went on sailing up the night-obscured coast without her.

RUMORS THAT JOSÉ MARTÍ left behind at least one illegitimate child during his year in Central America have always centered on the subject of Poem IX of *Versos Sencillos,* one of forty-six untitled, often overtly auto-biographical poems that the future hero of the Cuban Revolution against Spain published as a single slim volume in New York in 1891, during his decade and a half of exile there. That famous poem's tragic *"niña de G—"* is known to have been, or to have been inspired by, María García Granados, the daughter of the first President of the Liberal Republic, and of Doña Cristina, the late Madre Melchora's most devoted former student and patroness. María García Granados passed away at the age of seventeen on May 10, 1878, from pneumonia and/or tuberculosis or, as the poem suggests, from the debilitating, wasting effects of a devastating heartbreak, which, of course, could have provoked the mortal onslaught of either illness or both together; unless, as claimed by rumor and legend, she died in childbirth; or even from all four phenomena combined into a single fatal cataclysm, if she really was heartbroken, and pregnant, the Koch bacilli dormant in her lungs, and, as the poem explicitly, perhaps metaphorically, suggests, threw herself into a river one afternoon and caught a deathly chill (the River of the Cows, winding through the Valley of the Cows); or else, as according to the skimpiest biographical record, she caught that chill by visiting one of the popular hot spring baths outside the capital on a Sunday afternoon when she was already running a slight fever, exposing herself to the fatal evening air on the way home. She and María de las Nieves really had known each other and were even, somewhat, friends. (But who outside the closed circle of the García Granados family, her mother and sisters especially, ever knew what truly occurred between the love-smitten girl and Martí, if even they did? Spying household servants? The Cuban poet José Joaquín Palma, such good friends with both Martí and María García Granados? But the golden-bearded Bayamés Bard was totally in love with the general's ethereal and willowy daughter himself, so perhaps neither would have told him anything.) María de las Nieves knew as well as anyone how much you could get away with hiding even in the small, joyless, informer-infested world of La Pequeña Paris. Yet thirteen years after "la niña's" death, when the incident was finally fading into the past and no longer inspired gossip or speculation and few outside the García Granados family ever spoke of it anymore, Martí would be the one to bring it up again, this time so that it would never be forgotten, in his appalling poem of tortured remorse and confession and morbid longing, sung like a fairy-tale song about a sad little princess who dies of love.

An entire long lifetime later, in 1959, indeed, the very faraway year of our heroine's death, the Cuban-American actor Cesar Romero, famous for his "Latin lover" supporting roles in thirties and forties Hollywood movies—though his greatest period of popular stardom was actually still ahead, playing the Joker on the sixties hit television series *Batman*, followed by his role as the debonair, elderly costar of the seventies prime-time melodrama *Falcon Crest*—appeared as a guest on the *Jack Parr Show*, that week televised directly from Havana, Cuba, in the aftermath of the romantic revolution there, and confided to the American nation that José Martí was his grandfather; though for that to be true, Romero's mother, María Mantilla, born in 1880, near the beginning of the fifteen years during which the "Cuban Apostle" made New York City his home, would have to have been Martí's illegitimate daughter. Hagiography, exalting, puerile, and prudish, is what most of the biographical literature about José Martí consists of. Now the subject of the "Husband of Cuba's" secret offspring was, for a while at least, more or less openly and widely discussed, though before long the official guardians of the hero's idealized image on both sides of the Straits of Florida would again intimidate scholars into the new-old attitudes of restrained and silenced speculation, at least so far as that specific event in Martí's private life was concerned. Some accused Romero of a cynical publicity stunt (as if having learned from television that he was grandson to the Cuban patriot-martyr, Americans would now clamor to see Romero in starring movie roles!). "The only paths to the luminous inner fountains of my grandfather's immortal verse," Cesar Romero insightfully told the pioneering talk-show host that day, "are the winding, hidden ones of his amorous history, which can only be explored with the torch of compassion held high." The actor also quipped, "Of course my grandfather, whose statue is all over the place in Cuba, was himself no statue." (Addressing Romero by his inside-Hollywood nickname of "Butch," Parr asked that he recite some of Martí's verse, but all the actor offered was the well-known fragment, *Yo soy un hombre sincero / De donde crece la palma*, in a native New York accent nearly as strong as Sor Gertrudis's.) It was Martí himself, one of the founding poets of Hispanic American modernism, who in his seminal prologue to Pérez Bonalde's *Poema de Niágara*, regarded as a kind of manifesto of the movement's poetics (which Cesar Romero is not likely to have read, though some publicity agent or literature professor pal, preparing him for his appearance on the *Jack Parr Show*, could certainly have summarized for him) wrote, *in these times, with personal life so full of doubt, consternation, questions, unease and battle-fever, life—intimate, feverish, unanchored, impulsive, clamorous life—has come to be the principal theme and, along with nature, the only legitimate subject of modern poetry.*

Though Martí was only twenty-four when he came to Central America, his life was already following a path that, from the perspective of his heroic martyr's death in battle eighteen years later, would seem as predestined as any saint's. Barely into his adolescence, he began authoring anti-Spanish tracts in the Cuban separatist clandestine press (and attempting translations of *Hamlet* and Byron, his English self-taught at home from a book of *American Popular Lessons*—the same manual that the fifteen-year-old María de las Nieves, living with her mother and the sheep farmer in Quezaltenango, would immerse herself in). Imprisoned by the Spanish authorities and charged with treason at sixteen, he served a sentence of hard labor in the notorious San Lorenzo penal quarry under the infernal Havana sun, with a heavy iron chain running from his waist to a shackle above his ankle, causing festering sores and abrasions. Martí's prison experience ruined his health forever, leaving him with, among other ailments, a recurring inguinal infarction and strangulated testicular hernia, caused by the constant pull and friction of prison chains against

groin and infected wounds, which would require several apparently inef-
fective surgical operations over the course of his life, and which must have
been the cause of considerable intimate discomfort, for years later he wrote
that with those chains his jailors' had left him damaged in his decorum as
a man. (An autopsy performed by Spanish authorities on Martí would plau-
sibly record a missing testicle; in that era removal of the testicle was a
common though futile surgical procedure for a testicular hernia.) From
Cuba the teenaged rebel was deported to Spain, where he studied law and
literature, wrote poetry, enjoyed his first passionately requited loves, and
made speeches that among his fellow students and exiles won him the
nickname "Cuba Weeps." In Paris he called on Victor Hugo, and before the
visit was over the epoch's incomparable literary giant and universal cham-
pion of freedom had presented the young exile with a copy of his book of
poems *Les Filles* to translate into Spanish. Martí's parents and sisters had
moved from Cuba to Mexico City in the hopes of better economic circumstances; joining his family there, he found them living in humiliating poverty and grieving over the death of his beloved younger sister, Ana. In
Mexico Martí wrote journalism as well as poetry, published his translation
of *Les Filles,* enjoyed another precocious literary success with the staging of
his romantic light verse comedy *Amor con amor se paga,* conducted love affairs (consummated and not) with actresses and the city's most notorious
muse fatale, made speeches, and took part in public debates over the most
polemical issues of the day (spiritualism versus materialism, during which
he argued for a position in-between.) He also became engaged to marry a
young woman from an aristocratic and wealthy Cuban family temporarily
residing in Mexico, whose lawyer-businessman father was opposed to the
match. Having become embroiled in Mexican political tensions, needing
to prove that he could earn a living on his own, drawn to and curious about
the Liberal Revolution in the little country to the south, and stirred by ardent ideas and visions of Pan-American liberty and fraternity, Martí decided to go there, promising his beautiful young fiancée that he would
return to marry her and bring her back with him as soon as he was well
established in the *Land of the Quetzal.* In a letter to General Máximo
Gómez, the military leader of the Cuban rebel army that had been waging vicious and doomed war across the island since the "battle cry of
Yara" nine years before, Martí , referring to himself as *el mutilado silente,*

wrote that he was sick with shame that his weak health prevented him from fighting.

Martí landed on the Central American coast at Livingston—named (he wrote in his diary) for the jurist, not the explorer, but an honor to both!—in the spring of 1877, continuing inland via Izabal and Zacapa, following the same route an equally young Sor Gertrudis de la Sangre Divina had traveled thirty years before. Like the famous Monjita Inglesa, Martí also crossed the lush valley plateau atop a mule and, seeing the church and monastery towers and domes rising into view like fantastic minarets against an indigo twilight horizon of darkening volcanoes and mountains, knew that he was being carried toward the gates of a city of fate. Like the Yankee former Novice Mistress and Headmistress General, he was a visionary educational reformer; like her, he would be a teacher there. Martí's voice would also penetrate deeply into María de las Nieves's memory and heart and stay forever. The poem in which Martí dreams of a marble cloister at night and of speaking by the soul's light to the immortal heroes reposed in the divine silence is one that might have stirred Sor Gertrudis's own feeling for martyrdom. One could go on listing similarities between Martí and Sor Gertrudis, though, of course, a list of their differences would be longer.

On that inland trip, Martí had an encounter with a lithe but voluptuous Indian girl who emerged like a *crowned Venus* from the crystalline tropical river in which she was bathing, unself-consciously displaying herself to the thirsty traveler, who drank in her charms, his senses awakening to a new idea of American beauty; writing about the incident a few years later, Martí would confide that he *loved and was beloved* that day, before continuing on his way. What did he mean? That their eyes locked, until she shyly lowered them—and noticing in her physical manifestations of attraction and excitement corresponding to his own, he stepped closer to her? She did not splash back into the river, or run away, but allowed herself to be embraced. Her skin was sweet with the smell of her youth and the river water, which did not completely erase the traces of cooking-fire smoke in her hair, the sharp tang of tobacco on her breath, while he, scratchy shirtsleeves closing around her waist, was overripe with the stench of long, hard travel. Where were his guides or traveling companions and their mules? Did this occur in Izabal, before catching a river steamer, when he took a walk, following a stream into the jungle? She laid a quick bed of broad palm or banana leaves over the mossy, mud-oozing ground, and there they lay, ignoring or spared the fiery bites of ants. Or did he mean love in a transcendental sense, two sets of yearning, curious eyes, black and brownish, Amerindian and Spanish, there in the jungle shadows, chastely loving and desiring each other's youth, loving and discovering perpetually virgin America yet again? But who is to say that an anonymous child was not engendered in that fleeting encounter, one whose ancestors, perhaps Mayan-featured but with the striking forehead of the Cuban Apostle, shaped like a swollen heart, or like the upturned buttocks of a diving neoclassical nymph, are now, at this moment, living somewhere on this earth, in that country or, just as likely, given the migratory nature of these times, in this one, oblivious of their encoded heritage, yet feeling strongly stirred by some vague or wordless recognition in a photograph or illustration in a history book—or perhaps not wordless at all; perhaps they say, "Hey, my forehead is just like that!"—or by a bronze or marble bust mounted on a pedestal in some obscure park or courtyard or gloomy hall anywhere in the Americas or even the world, or by the enormous equestrian statue at an entrance to Central Park in New York, depicting a mild-looking man of wide forehead and flapping three-piece suit in the final moments of his life as the first Spanish bullets hit, tumbling him from his rearing horse. On the secret side of his death, Martí eternally rides a "question statue" too.

It was only years later, when the myth spawned by his death began to spread over the Americas like a hemispheric cloud of pigeons looking for statues to land on, that those who'd known both the general's daughter and the young Cuban exile understood that the poem about the girl who died of love and its author were now linked in immortality. But what if it was all just a fiction, a story, dressed up as a poem of tragic love and confession? A lie told for the sake of art, but with the consequences of a real lie. A poem that tricked you into hearing a confession when maybe it just wanted to be a poem. Or did Martí want something else from that poem? For example, to cruelly confront his wife with it. Why write it if not to wound her? Or, while she sat sobbing with the sheaf of his treacherous, soon-to-be-published verses in her lap, did he kneel at her feet babbling, "But it's a poem, mi querida, it lies in order to finds its way to another truth . . ." In another poem he mentions a woman with black brows and dark aquatic eyes, but not with so much feeling and with a different kind of regret,

which is one of the ways María de las Nieves could tell that he sometimes
wanted his poetry to lie. But that night, when she and Paquita conversed
on the California-bound steamship, that poem did not yet exist, it was not
yet María de las Nieves's invincible rival; that poem's ascension was still
far in the future, when Martí became Martí, and his crucified love—for
that is how he portrayed it—his perhaps fictional love, was *resurrected,* in
order to become, forever and ever, throughout the Spanish-speaking
Americas, a love poem memorized and chanted by schoolgirls. And an
unending source of rumor, scandal, and indignity. Even that scented silk
pillow mentioned in the poem, into which she'd wept her brokenhearted
tears, the one she'd embroidered herself and given him as a going-away
present so that he could travel up to Mexico to marry his wife with his
"niña's" fragrant pink-and-yellow silk pillow tucked under his arm, that
same lachrymal pillow, more than a century later, is displayed in the museum to El Héroe Nacional in Havana, a silly teenaged girl's pillow worshipped like the relic of a saint!

IN THE PARQUE de la Concordia, where there was now a flower garden
in one corner, cultivated roses in another, and jungle plants around a
little lagoon in the shade of a thirty-year-old African palm tree recently
transferred from La Sociedad Económica's experimental farm, all protected from "the nervous excesses of curiosity" by wood and iron
fences—the fencing in of plants being a widely remarked and controversial novelty—four kiosks had also been erected. One of these, the larg-
est, open to the air, was to shelter musicians such as Colonel Dressner's
military band, which performed twice weekly in the afternoons. Another
housed the park's guardians. A third, yet to open, would offer a buffet,
fresh desserts, and drinks, as well as selling toys for children and other
such articles. The fourth kiosk was a "reading room," with two sturdy
writing desks, wooden chairs, and a box for posting letters. Originally
there had been writing implements and stationery, but these had been
stolen and not replaced. Steamship schedules for the ports of San José
and Champerico were posted on the walls, though these were not always
current, along with shipping rates, customs fees and tariffs, coffee prices,

and other announcements. There was a bookshelf, but the only book it held was *Táctica de guerrilla*, used by the cadets at the new military academy in the former Convent de la Recolección, the vast garden where the nuns had cultivated their famous cabbages now converted to parade ground and shooting range. There was also a rack with portable sticks for holding foreign newspapers, the latest to have arrived aboard the steamships that now called at their ports from all over the world. Local newspapers were stacked atop one or the other of the writing desks, and María de las Nieves did like to read these whenever she stopped into the reading room in the mornings on her way to the British Legation, which was just across the street on the southern border of the park. Minister Gastreel and First Secretary Bludyar were not fluent readers of Spanish and were often impatient with the local newspapers and she knew they were grateful, however much they concealed it, for the information she provided without their having to ask.

The reading room was not a disreputable place, but it was generally perceived as a gentlemen's sanctum, though not so strictly as El Jockey Club, which was where such men, if they were members, went if they were really interested in reading newspapers; there, or La Sociedad Económica. No longer a novelty, the reading room kiosk was usually deserted. From their windows across the street, her employers could see directly into the park. A well-bred, respectable dama never walked alone through the streets, as María de las Nieves usually did; nevertheless, she knew it made a proper impression for her to arrive at the legation every morning accompanied by her servant. Most mornings María Chon went with her to the reading room as well, and then dropped her off at the legation door and continued on to the market.

A well-bred, respectable dama was never to return any male greeting in the street either, no matter how polite, for even a lightly tipped hat was a flung-open door to scandal and much worse. She would never sit alone with a foreign umbrella mender in his little shop for hours, as María de las Nieves liked to do. Nor could she eat garlic, onions, limones, chilies, or anything sharp, tart, or spicy enough to stir or heat the body and awaken lust. Having gone to such strident lengths to separate God from his Virgin Brides, the ruling Liberals seemed to want to keep women—but only *their* women—as strictly cloistered as before, and were as suspicious of their wives' and daughters' innate licentiousness and sinfulness as the most zealous novice mistress or confessor priest.

Yet since returning to live on her own in the city, María de las Nieves had yet to do anything that could cause her much social harm, or even anything that she was too ashamed of. She considered herself pure in her heart and in her body—even more so than she had as a nun, now that she was no longer required to regard her own incarnate self as a poisonous swamp and she wasn't so addicted to sneezing anymore either (there was no bristling Indio blanket upon her bed now, so if she wanted to sneeze in the old way, she had to pluck some wool from her boarder's or María Chon's blankets, risking great embarrassment if she were caught). She knew that her own circumstances excluded her from being counted among the well-bred respectable anyway, despite her convent education, and re- gardless of how sincerely her well-bred respectable compatriots professed to believe in the new democratic principals of la *revulución* (the fashionable pronunciation). And so she also understood—in the vague yet burdensome manner by which such unpleasant and rarely voiced knowledge is received and stored—that she was not really required or even expected to be "pure" by society generally, or by those whose eyes fell on her when she walked alone in the streets. There were many dangers she was not immune to, but so far she had been adept and nimble enough at deciphering and moving among them, even when she did not really comprehend what it was she was so instinctually avoiding. Los Gastreel y Bludyar, perhaps blind and deaf to these local nuances, certainly seemed to regard her, at least in com- parison to other local señoritas, as well-bred and respectable enough!

María Chon was darker, shorter, even skinnier than María de las Nieves, three years younger, and her smile revealed what looked like two rows of perfect little milk teeth. Usually she covered her mouth with her shawl whenever she laughed or smiled, and often when she spoke, although she was not in the *least bit* shy. Walking in the street, market basket balanced atop her head, María Chon always had her lips hoisted into a dismissive little pout, while her intense black eyes seemed to look out at the world as if accurately weighing the good and bad in every passerby, with predict- able results. It was good to have María Chon by your side when walking out: her double sniper's stare and angry little mouth unnerved people, made them careful, reluctant to be bold. Which was all a bit ridiculous because María Chon knew so little about anything—no surprise in a niña her age, an Indita Mam no less, whose family had lived near María de las Nieves, her mother, and Lucy Turner in the forest. City life was a swarm of befuddlements to her, and there was little consistency or usefulness in her judgments, although she was rarely reluctant to voice any of them.

While María Chon waited on a park bench, shawl draped over her head and an unlit cigar in her mouth, basket at her feet, María de las Nieves went into the reading room kiosk. That day there was only one foreign newspaper hanging in the rack, and when she lifted its damp-saturated front page to see which it was, the corner tore off in her hand as softly as if it had been floating in a pond. It was a three-week-old *Panama City Star & Herald*—not a newspaper that excited a sense of romance or desire to daydream herself into the life of a faraway city.

There was also a small, elevated brazier for lighting tobacco in the reading room, and María de las Nieves, before sitting down to her local newspapers, took a rolled maize-leaf cigarette from the small leather sack in her purse. The age-blackened mahogany of the writing desks exuded a humid aroma that always made her feel hollow and a bit bleak: she could smell at least a century of monastic tedium and misery emanating from those old desks as surely as if they were the ghosts of unwashed friars. That morning, as she leaned down to the brazier, instead of hopefully blowing tepid ash back into her own face, she fanned a flame from the coals with just her second breath, let out a little shout of triumph, and carried her lit cigarette out to María Chon so that she could light her cigar. Back inside, she sat down with that week's edition of *El Progreso* spread open on the desk before her, slowly savoring her cigarrito and thinking about Wellesley Bludyar, whose bold and obvious yet definitely uncertain wooing of her could no longer be ignored or incredulously disbelieved. He was her first ever legitimate suitor, surely a significant event in any girl's life, one requiring the most serious contemplation and examination of her own feelings—feelings that should include some discernible metamorphosis at the core of her being, or no? (Bludyar, in those days, was also spending much of his time reflecting on that bewildered courtship, sometimes even out loud and within the hearing of others; perhaps even now, on rare days when the rain suddenly tastes tropical instead of like cold black stone and mussel beard, the emerald grass growing over his grave in a Norfolk churchyard still mulls that unlikely yet persistent love; though the grass, however much it drinks, can't weep.)

*"The notorious Spanish decadence began with the addiction to smoking tobacco in the Americas"*—Wellesly Bludyar, just the other day, had cheerfully read that aloud from a book, the memoir of an Englishman's travels in Central America, published in London, as they sat in a corridor facing the central patio on a not atypically idle afternoon at the legation. The notorious Spanish decadence, María de las Nieves had countered, began with the betrayal of Spain's own best religious, mystical, poetic traditions. A large argument to try to make in just one sitting, especially considering Wellesley's manly Anglo-Saxon distaste for such conversation—but then, in the most disconcertingly intoxicated if quiet manner, she'd spoken for many minutes to the moon-faced First Secretary as she never had to anyone in her life about her year as a novice nun. No day passed without her having some reason to recall how much she'd despised her time in the cloister, yet here she was talking to Wellesley Bludyar as if she still loved that way of life better than any other, cherished its memory and lessons above all others—while he gazed at her with such overflowing humor and affection that it was as if she could feel her own heart filling with the sparkling blue sky of his eyes. This is not me, she'd thought, this is like having a talking foot! From which liquid words are gushing as if from a radiant fountain of truth. What is happening?

"I almost think I'd give anything to be locked away in a convent with you, Snows," Wellesley Bludyar had jovially remarked when she was finished. "The two of us rising side by side, up-up into the air, over the mountains and ocean, all the way to . . . where was it? New Mexico. Hahaha. Aha . . ." Then he'd winked at her! Suddenly and perplexingly, the ebullience had drained from her heart. A moment later, reverting to his pompous tone, he'd added, "Your Spanish mystics must also have smoked, then. That is your opinion, is it. Or were they addicted to putting snuff up their noses, and levitating on sneezes!"

When Wellesley Bludyar saw María de las Nieves's expression (as he later confided to a sympathetic Mrs. Gastreel; and many nights later, though quite inebriated, and not so explicitly, to others; and within hearing of yet others, for the city was so infested with secret police, informers, and spies that another foreigner living there at that time, who kept an eventually published diary, famously wrote *here even the drunks are discreet*—

though not always Bludyar) he thought his little joke had impressed her as
cheeky and clever, and he felt unaccustomedly and gratefully thrilled. An
instant later all had subsided into a feverish chill in his intestines. Could
he really be falling in love with the odd little half-breed legation translator, with her crooked, gapped, discolored teeth, and tobacco-fouled breath
and tobacco-stained (nearly vermilion) fingers? He gazed at her, smiling
soporifically, and imagined himself telling his mother: Yes, an American
Indian girl, rather well educated, you know, in a convent . . . No, they do
not wear feathers and war paint . . . Anyway, not properly an Indian, she's
what some call a *mess-teezah* . . . She does walk fairly well into a room,
Mother, yes, and with a little instruction and practice, I'm sure she will
walk into a room splendidly . . . Perhaps he should never leave the diplomatic service, though with such a wife, his next posting would be an even
more obscure one. What would that be like, living with her in London? He
saw himself moping through the cold wet, feeling misunderstood and
mocked by everyone on earth except for María de las Nieves, and eagerly
rushing home to the soft embrace of her skinny naked limbs. He would
know how she smelled, how she tasted, what she dreamed, what she liked,
disliked, feared, her private opinions of this person or that, what she—
everything! He would live only for his Snows, for her kisses and intimate
pleasures, in a secret world of—in and out of the little gap in her teeth he
would slide his tongue—. How long was any man expected to do without
love? Bludyar felt dizzy with soaring hope. He crossed a heavy, trembling
leg over the opposite thigh, grabbed the tip of his raised shoe and pulled
it toward himself like an oar, and frowning down at his knee, thought, The
new Minister Resident of the United States, Colonel Williamson, is married to a lady from Cuba. So it can be done. Start anew in Canada. Not
Australia. Oh why not just bunk off to California—. Did they dare? He gave
her his warmest, sweetest smile, as if she'd just said yes yes yes—

     The surprised gape on María de las Nieves's face was really one of ap-
palled anxiety: Was the clandestine Sor Gertrudis, from her hiding place in
the city wherever that was, sending out stories about her humiliating disgrace? Or was it Padre Lactancio? But the First Secretary's look of feverish devotion convinced her that his remark must have been coincidental.
She laughed, and he responded with a sweet titter of his own, blushing,
nodding, looking very happy, not meeting her eyes, tucking his head down

into his neck and shoulders like a giant dove. Then a giddy sensation settled over her like the vast shade of a ceiba tree on a sleepy, warm afternoon. Pues, qué cosa, what was happening that afternoon in the legation garden, what strange spell was this? That providential moment of intimate well-being might have lasted had Wellesley Bludyar not ruined it by taking up his travel book again.

"The indolent decadence of Central American women," he read out loud, picking up where he'd left off, "perched in their barred window seats, gaping out at the street, with their drooping lips, glazed listless eyes, and unwashed faces, inwardly intoxicated as drunken bees by their wanton daydreams of romance . . ." Bludyar stopped himself, apologized, and said, "I don't see you hanging about in a window seat like that, Snows. Do you have such a window seat?"

"Dirty faces," she said. "Sí pues." Now, why should this annoy her? It wasn't untrue.

"You wash your face, María de las Nieves, I know. Really, a lot of this book is complete nonsense. He has a theory about why Central America has so many earthquakes. Because of the equatorial region's greater proximity to the sun. The sun's rays, refracted by the ocean like a magnifying glass, you see, bore with a more intense heat into the ocean floor than at other latitudes. Thus the molten earth beneath our feet, and the steaming fumaroles of the volcanic landscapes, and such."

"That sounds sensible." All over this country, boiling water was perpetually seeping and spurting up from the *mundus subterraneus.*

"Yes, but Mr. Gastreel says it's all rubbish. There is some other explanation."

Dirty faces, wanton romance, she wondered, was that what the foreigners saw, framing you with their gazes in the street? Wellesley Bludyar too? How do you see what's inside a man? Look at him now, looking at me, desperate for something to say, words of his own, not from a book. Why shouldn't what we think of the foreigners matter just as much? So now respectable women no longer smoke in public, and because of the foreigners' often expressed disdain of our reluctance to splash our faces with water, many women now regularly do that also, even in full belief that a wet face is like a door flung open to sickness in our world of battling hot and chilled winds that don't have to travel very far from sweltering coasts to stony mountaintops to reach us, of blazing sun swiftly covered over by massive black clouds, full of thunder and lightning; drenching tropical rain one second and frozen hail the next, steaming mists at one end of the street and frigid fogs down at the other. They fall sick and know it's because they washed their faces and let in the hot or cold. But she had also been taught to wash her face, on sunny mornings always, by Lucy Turner. She remembered being very small and sitting in forest shade with her madre and Lucy Turner, all three smoking cigars of wild jungle tobacco (even cruder than the one María Chon is smoking now) as darkness fell, and the saraguates howled and the trees seemed to melt and swarm into the most pleasant patterns, entangling their dark branches in the glowing stars and pulling them closer to the earth. As soon as she woke, always in the predawn still-dark, her mother, before sending her out into the forest to gather kindling or fill the water jug, would make her take lung-filling puffs of her cigar, to protect her from catching a sudden fright inside: with her head so dizzily spinning, colored lights pulsing in her brain, she wouldn't even notice any malevolent nighttime spirit still out there. If she caught a fright and it stayed trapped inside, she could fall ill and waste away; that was how children died. In the forest everyone believed such things. I am also the daughter of foreigners. Half-breed mengala, by a superstitious India from the Yucatán, and a gringo who didn't know better than to shove a maldita mule from behind—

There was a pleading look in Bludyar's eyes. Asking what? For friendship? For her to understand that he was unhappy? For her to believe in him? For her love? So, twice in her life, though several years apart, she'd apparently awakened more than just a passing longing in a man—first poor Padre Lactancio, who, pathetically unable to hide his feelings, had thankfully never dared to express them, and now the young British diplomatist. A longing that looked like weakness. A desire to reach out and comfortingly stroke Wellesley's blunt nose. Yet look how he loomed over her, this hulking blue-eyed dove! That afternoon she felt confused and alarmed in a new way. So she rose from her chair and with a soft "perdón" and a lump in her throat walked briskly toward Minister Gastreel's office, as if there were a letter to translate waiting for her there, which there was not. Every day since, the First Secretary had become a little bolder with her in his conversation, while his eyes grew hungrier and sadder. It was as if he wanted her to know he was suffering—that he was suffering nobly! But why was he suffering? Just last Thursday, hadn't she let him escort her home in a carriage from the García Granados costume party? She did sometimes feel an impatient pride in her looming victory over all those who would never have thought it possible for her to awaken the love of a British Legation officer. He had not yet asked to call on her one evening, but she sensed that this extraordinary development was imminent. She'd already discussed it with her dour boarder, Amada Gómez, who reluctantly agreed to act as chaperone.

"You haven't gone and had a spell cast over Señor *Gueyeslee* or me, have you?" she'd confronted María Chon, assuming her most autocratic manner. "Because I don't believe in that! I would die of shame and melancholy and disgust if such a thing were ever to be the cause of my thinking myself in love or loved. Do you understand me, María Chon? If I ever learn you've been paying visits to witches, I'll have you arrested by the police. You know what can happen now to insolent servants when they are arrested by the police, don't you, María Chon?" She knew that María Chon knew; she was the one who'd first brought the terrible gossip back from the market, how Don Rufo Zarco had turned his unruly servant over to the police, and the police had put her in one of Doña Carlota Marcorís's brothels. Thus the new epoch of Revulución, Progreso, y Orden: under the Conservatives the police would capture escaped nuns and return them to their convents, but under the Liberals they hunted down any girl who ran away from a licensed house of tolerance. María Chon, wide-eyed, had hotly retorted, "What would I pay such a witch with, mi doñacita? With money? Maybe I could steal one of your madre's husband's sheep. Qué tal? So that you can go live in England with fatty Chino Gringo."

My little love for Wellesley Bludyar is a tiny blue flame, she decided, wishing it to be larger. But who is supposed to make it larger, him or me? This image of a tiny blue flame was one she'd held inside her for days now, like a meditation point, like interior prayer after all; *ponder this point:* Are you going to flame up, little blue love, or be extinguished? Her fingernails dug tightly into her own palms, and she was biting her lip. *Ea*, what are you so afraid of? She stared down at *El Progreso*, without registering anything she might have read, and turned the page.

So if no European ever actually marries an India, she mused, then where did all the mestizos come from? If we are so ugly, then how can it be that this blond Englishman desires me? As if I'm the only one who is not ugly! María Chon is so pretty, with her zapayul eyes and lips as haughty as any Parisian mademoiselle's that sometimes it makes me happy just to look at her. You will say, Well, it's her character that delights you. Pues sí, she is so funny, so impossible! But it's not just that—. María de las Nieves rose again from the writing desk and went to stand in the door just to spy on María Chon smoking her cigar and sitting on the park bench, and laughed out loud when the girl returned a puzzled scowl. The first mestizos came from the first María Chons, for who could resist them—! In the mountains, even pretty girls are worn and withered-looking by thirty, but here in the city, not always. What good luck that my Maricusa works for me, and not as a servant in a house with husband and sons who doubtless would be unable to resist using her as they do even serving girls who are not one-fifth as adorable—. Disturbed by this thought, she turned back into the reading room kiosk, sat down, and turned a page of *El Progreso*, turned another page, and another—though only one memory of what she read in the newspaper that day would survive.

*El Señor Martí is a collaborator of the youth of our century, which in both American continents is pronounced with these words: Forever Forward.* It was an account of the Saturday night tertulia at the Normal School, where Señor Martí had apparently dazzled and which she, anticipating the presiding presence of the pregnant muse of all poets of the Republic, had avoided, staying home to play cards with her boarder, Amada Gómez, and María Chon, and a friend from Nuestra Señora de Belén, though she'd hardly known her there, Vipulina Godoy, the former Sor Cayetano del Niño Salvadór del Mundo, the young nun who'd escaped the convent simply by leaving through the front door. The article on the tertulia was followed by a small announcement:

*At the Academia de Niñas de Centroamérica, the recently arrived Cuban professor and poet José Martí will be conducting free evening classes in literary composition, that art which so elevates a woman's merit.*

As if she'd just tasted some subtle flavor in the air, she felt a quiver inside her throat—and then she was holding herself very still and all her shadowy excitement fled and she found herself at the bottom of an abyss of sullen dissatisfaction, hating her own delusions and pretensions, the absurd lie of her specialness, and she sat blankly staring at the announcement in the newspaper, her clenched hand propped so rigidly on a corner of the page that it began to resemble the taxidermied hoof of a fawn. She stayed that way until a clump of ash fell to her lap from the dwindled cigarrito between her lips. Now, here was a problem. She carefully raised her thighs by slowly lifting her heels off the floor and lowered her head and blew steadily on the ash, which instead of flying off the yellow muslin all in one piece exploded into a fine gray powder that was going to leave a smudge in the fabric no matter what. With both hands she shook her dress in her lap and, averting her eyes, swept at it with the back of her hand, and stood up to go, and had hardly taken three steps toward the door when she saw a figure rapidly approaching from outside like a storm at sea—a storm that somehow cleaves a sailing ship exactly in half, port side sailing off in one direction, starboard in another—; she knew she had to turn back and tear the announcement from the newspaper and leave at once, and she had to leave at once because it was that same Indio in a frock coat who'd interrupted at the party where she'd met Señor Martí.

Before whirling around she glimpsed him removing his hat and a flash of teeth-and-grin and heard that resonant metallic *cloc-clic* that lately she heard everywhere. In her agitation she tore away more than half the page of the newspaper, too big a piece to neatly fold in such a hurry, and, still holding her cigarrito, she balled it into her palm, and turned—

"Señorita Moran—" She gasped and dropped the cigarrito and took a step backward, for he was standing right inside the reading room, with his hat over his broad chest, pomaded black Indio hair combed straight back over his large square head, showing his fleshy smile, blunt cream-colored teeth, and a steady but worried stare, and as if this was the only explanation required he proffered his hand to show her the little iron noisemaker known as a *cri-cri,* saying: "Good day to you, Miss Moran!" He pronounced it the original Yankee way (More-anne) rather than as everyone else did (Mor-án); even her own tongue resisted the awkward exertion and vanity of pronouncing it as her father must have (his own name).

And he quickly stooped to pluck the moist tail of her cigarrito with the thumb and index finger of the same hand clasping the cri-cri and she veered around him and walked quickly out of the reading room without another word. She was almost out of the park, by the rose garden, lifting her skirts over the muddy ground, the rhythmic rustle of fabrics like the beating wings of geese, when María Chon caught up to her, running in her clattering sandals, clutching a corner of her shawl in her teeth, both hands holding on to the basket atop her head, and before María de las Nieves could scold her for not having leaped to her side as soon as she saw that impertinent Indio approaching the kiosk, María Chon was actually scolding *her:*

"He wanted to give you a cri-cri! He smiled and tipped his hat and showed it to me before he went inside and when he came out after you left with ants in your underwear he showed it to me again and I said, I'll bring it to her, Señor! *That* one is a gentleman!"

"That one is just a grosero jocicón from the mountains, who thinks with a little English—"

"Ah, sí pues, we're not from the mountains, vaya, how dare a jocicón try to give a cri-cri to Doña Sholca!"—fatty-lips give a cri-cri to Doña Missing-her-front-teeth—and there in the middle of the rough-paved street approaching the legation, María de las Nieves whirled and slapped at her little servant's face, though María Chon was so nimble she jerked backward just in time, and grinned maliciously, and María de las Nieves lunged forward and slapped at her again, this time barely scraping her cheek. But at least now María Chon looked frightened, and stammered an apology in Mam, and around them she heard the whistles and shouts of mockery, even the shrill voice of a boy bootblack calling, "Look at Queen Victoria beating her little servant!" And someone else: "Anda Indita chuladita, give it back to her, smack that uppity mengalita!" And a resonant baritone: "It's a massacre! Ayyyy, a massacre!"

María de las Nieves could see Don Lico, the legation concierge, on his stool by the front doors, watching from under the bent brim of his straw hat. Oh, don't let the Gastreels or Wellesley look out any of the windows! María Chon, lower lip pushed out like a little girl about to cry, was staring down at the little metal cri-cri in her hand. María de las Nieves said, "Ven," she didn't want to leave her outside on her own, but María Chon clucked her teeth and turned and strutted off with her basket hoisted back atop her head, through a stream of hilarity and whistles, rapidly thumbing the metal tab of the cri-cri in her hand, her trail of sharp metallic clacking answered by numerous people in the street with cri-cris of their own. Astonishing instruments! Imported from France! One day no one had ever seen a cri-cri before and the next, all over the country, one in every child's and fool's hand or vest pocket like a plague of metal locusts!

Don Lico, still sitting with his chubby legs splayed and his hands on his knees and cackling, did not budge from his stool until María de las Nieves, blinking back tears, was standing before the doors.

"Don Lico," she squeaked desperately.

"Ay chula," he said mirthfully, "we all have to be like soldiers ready to die for the patria every day!"

She walked directly through the vestibule with its polished white marble floor like the mirrored reflection of a milky cloud, through the antechamber and the wrought iron doors, into the central courtyard and around two sides of the shaded corridor hung with small bird cages and baskets of flowers and lined with slim white columns and heavy marble urns holding jungle plants, spilling trumpet vine and hibiscus, and sat in a straight wooden chair with leather-padded armrests outside the closed door of Minister Gastreel's office. She pulled the wadded newspaper page from her purse, unfolded and smoothed it out on her ash-smudged lap. The Academia de Niñas de Centroamérica was where the daughters of the wealthy went; even an evening class there could only be for respectable damitas living at home with their respectable families. Yesterday she'd never even imagined the possibility of such a class, but look—. Now she felt like she no longer even wanted to live because she knew she was going to be prevented from attending this class offering a solution to everything tedious, choking, and small about her existence—including her own confusion and inarticulateness regarding weighty matters requiring some degree of inward eloquence and clarity of expression, her inability to decide if what she felt for Wellesly Bludyar, and he for her, was beautiful or mediocre, for example—right now she didn't even know if she adored or wanted to kill María Chon!

Although we know that, in the end, José Martí, of course, did welcome María de las Nieves into his class at the Academia de Niñas, at that moment she could not have felt more convinced that it was impossible, and life had never seemed so unfair.

Presently Mrs. Gastreel entered the corridor opposite from the interior garden and living quarters, where Wellesley Bludyar, being a bachelor, also resided. The Minister Resident's wife (Wellesley called her "the

Chiefess") was eighteen years younger than her husband, and was just showing the first signs of being pregnant with their first child. She was wearing a red-and-white striped dress, an undecorated wide-brimmed hat against the sun, and was carrying a large garden shears in one hand and a packet of letters in another, and was followed by one of her indoor servants, Chinta, her arms full of fresh-cut flowers. Mrs. Gastreel's hair was nearly as red as Sor Gertrudis's and her eyes were an even brighter shade of blue than Bludyar's.

"Hello, Señorita Moran, a very good morning to you, I'll be with you in just a moment"—often Mrs. Gastreel liked to get her Spanish class out of the way first thing in the morning—"but look, dear, I did just want to give you these. These are all our lovely Christmas cards from this past season; there are fifty or so, many from England. I was going to throw them out and thought, Oh, what a terrible waste, and then I remembered that an excellent use for Christmas cards is to put them in a packet just like this one, you see. Then, whenever you have the opportunity, you can lend them to invalids and old people to look at. It really takes so little to cheer such people up, and I think we do forget that rather too easily. Oh well, not you, María de las Nieves, we all know that you are an angel from heaven."

ABOARD THE *GOLDEN ROSE* that afternoon, in the sitting room of her opulent stateroom suite, Paquita's two oldest daughters, Elena and Luz, put on a show of handkerchief telegraphy, proceeding through the semaphoric display, which they had spent hours practicing, like well-drilled naval cadets. They wore colorful Japanese silk kimonos and glittering gold slippers that Mathilde, sitting quietly, followed with rapt eyes. Elena and Luz, directing meaningful stares toward an invisible object in the middle of the room, announced in unison: "This means I wish to begin a correspondence with you," and each slid a flowing white handkerchief across her lips as if delicately wiping away a crumb. Next each girl touched her forehead with her handkerchief, gave a sideways glance, and said, "This means we're being watched." A handkerchief held against the right cheek meant "Yes"; against the left, "No"; clasped to one shoulder, "Follow me"; rapidly daubed from one cheek to the other, "I love you"; wound tightly around an index finger, "I'm promised to another"; wrung with both hands, "Indifference!"; pressed to the right ear, "You are unfaithful"; pulled with an insolent flourish through the left fist, "I detest you!" Elena and Luz each struck a blindfolded pose and dramatically sighed, "Mamá will answer for me." (María de las Nieves nearly blurted, Very pretty, but do you expect any man worth knowing to have memorized all of that? He'll just think, What fidgety girls—but she stopped herself, and thought of Martí; because Pepe Martí was so curious about everything he probably had memorized the language of handkerchiefs, of fans and flowers too, though nowadays dandies who were virtuosos of such frippery and interested in *nothing* else were everywhere.) María de las Nieves did laugh out loud when each girl, biting into her handkerchief, growled through clenched teeth, "I'm jealous!" Then, draped over the head like a mantilla, "I'll see you in church"; patted against the base of the neck, "This cough has me in a bad mood"; dangled like a banner in front of the chest, "My heart is innocent"; waved over the shoes midcurtsy, "I'm going to marry a foreigner!" Mathilde, watching from her chair in the corner, face as somber as a ripe brown pear, sprang forward in short white dress and bloomer-trousers and snatched the handkerchief from Luz's hands. She dropped to one knee and flung her arms straight up, holding the handkerchief taut like a canopy over her head, and called out, "I'm going to marry a cat!" She spun agilely into a ballerina's pose, her leg and foot arched so high behind her that she was able to leave the handkerchief draped over her toe while spreading her arms, and said, with a flicker of a smile, "Mamita, someone who loves you has just woken up from a dream about you." Then Mathilde stood facing them, holding the handkerchief between her elbows and peering out through the V of her forearms, and gravely announced, "This means if you desire to speak to me, you will have to remove your head."

Luz started toward Mathilde, arm raised to strike her, lips in a sneer—but Paquita's vigorous applause and shouts of "Bravo! Bellisima! Bravo!" made Mathilde skip forward into the safety of her "tía's" embrace, leaving Luz holding up her hand as if a bee had stung it. Meanwhile María de las Nieves sat there, still only gaping at her daughter. Was Paquita a naturally superior mother, or just a more practiced one? Luz and Elena stood sulking like usurped predators until Paquita began lavishing praise over all three performers, this time with María de las Nieves obediently chiming in.

In her stateroom suite Paquita slept in a four-posted bed bolted to the
carpeted floor, and there were gas lamps on the walls that she was free to
burn any hour; her children and the governess Miss Pratt had berths in the
adjoining rooms. The small first-class cabin María de las Nieves shared
with her daughter had a glass-enclosed candle she was not allowed to light
after eleven at night, a rule she ignored. But now it was nearly midnight
and María de las Nieves, having just left Paquita's sitting room after another night of conversation and brandy drinking, was leaning on the ship's
rail. Mathilde, she thought, has the hermetic air of a girl who might forever
remain a mystery even to herself. One day, hopefully, she'll be sought and
found, but the H. M. Stanley role can hardly be performed by the mother,
who tends to regard her daughter as the artifact of all her own worse failings and flaws.

She knew her daughter would be lying awake now, waiting for her.
Mathilde was terrified of the ocean. Boarding the ship at Puerto San José
had scared her out of her wits; shamed her too, because Paquita's children,
experienced travelers, the oldest so poised in their fixed attitudes of historic grief, had taken it so calmly. But Mathilde had never seen the ocean,
had never set eyes on such violence: the long waves rolling in, exploding
like thunderous cannonades, sun-blazed water shooting high into the air;
thick swaths of foam washing in crunching stones; the debris of shattered
fishing boats and the timbers of larger vessels strewn up and down the
black sand beach like wreckage of war; the horrible deathly stench of tidal
rot and fish. Their steamship had been waiting at anchor more than a mile
out, beyond the treacherous surf. A black iron pier extended two hundred
yards into the ocean and the train ran directly onto it; looking down, they
could see enormous sharks swimming just outside the barnacle-encrusted
iron pilings. A shed at the end of the pier sheltered infernally clanking and
grating steam hoisting engines, two of which, via their pulleys and ropes,
delivered cargo to the boats waiting below—including the late President
General's white war stallion, strapped around its girth, eyes covered with
blinders, ears and tail twitching, legs straight down in the air, its defeca-
tions inciting thrashing skirmishes among the sharks. A third engine lowered passengers five at a time inside an iron cage to the launch below,
including an already weeping Mathilde. A muscular Indio wearing only a
loincloth helped women and children out of the cage; they tumbled and

flopped down among the coffee sacks piled into the wave-rocked launch. A slow tugboat towed them out to the steamship, the passengers blinded by ocean spray and oily black smoke, their vessel so violently pounded by the waves, lifted up and dropped over and over, that its shattering into sticks and splinters seemed imminent—. She held on to Mathilde tightly, felt her hard shivering, and pressing her lips to her daughter's ears to soothe her, heard Mathilde reciting her incompletely memorized rosary, and she joined in, reciting the words aloud for the first time in years . . . claro, to give comfort to her daughter . . . Passengers had to be hauled up one at a time inside a roped barrel lowered by sailors from the deck of the *Golden Rose*—one at a time, the women forced to shed all modesty, lifting skirts high while the nearly naked Indio helped them struggle into the dangled barrel and their boat rose and fell away from it, rose and fell away on the waves—. Who should go first, she or Mathilde? Both options incited wailings of panic and doom.

Every night since, Mathilde had climbed down from her bunk to sleep with her mother, despite the bed's narrowness and the heat. But right now María de las Nieves needed a bit of air. She had to admit that she liked this constant humid stickiness, this salty film of faintly rancid ocean covering her skin. Every now and then she took a little lick of her own forearm, the back of her hand; in private, she touched herself here and there, brought the small pungent smells to her nose; long-ago convent smells, really (it was inconvenient to bathe on the ship; one had to rent a little stall behind the barbershop, and pay Mr. Frank, the Negro barber, for soap, extra for hot water). Starlight foamed across the sky like butter in a cast iron skillet, and tonight the almost eerily tranquil ocean was filled with phosphorescent sparkles and flames, bursts and flickers of colored light like silently exploding fireworks as far as the eye could see. Unlike the most spectacular sunsets, she thought, these light effects don't enrapture the soul in a religious way. It was more like the nocturnal magic of a fairy story, one that was a little bit frightening. Of course it made you want to know the scientific explanation too. It was a delight, a complete privilege, to be on a ship at sea. But shouldn't she be able to derive some lasting lesson from so much beauty and surprise?—an insight into the universe corresponding with something good and necessary inside herself; something that could help her, that she could resort to during the trying times undoubtedly waiting ahead, in the cold, mysterious, frightening, thrilling, winter-dark and improbable city they were headed to? Something she would always remember and be able to pass on to Mathilde like a family heirloom of *knowledge*. Why was it so elusive, why did she feel so full of intelligent feeling, yet incapable of expressing the utility of any such feelings in words? Her old friend Martí had known how to transform moments like this into words he could possess and share—always in the manner of a brilliant and ardent young man, at least, dazzling himself as much as others. What would he be like now, nearly eight years later? He had reasons to be bitter, both personally and in his political passions; she knew that much from the Pinkerton detective's report. And if she managed to find him again, how disappointing would Martí judge her? He'd sometimes spoken so excitingly and exaggeratedly of the high expectations he had for her. Who else had ever spoken to her that way? Who else? Now here she was, taking her daughter to New York, to live like an opulent dung beetle off El Anticristo's plunder. Whenever she caught herself smiling like this, so confidingly and with such sad resignation to *no one*, she felt a wave of embarrassment and disgust. She wondered if she would always feel so alone in life as she did now, as she had for years.

In the morning, if the ship had a roll, she was going to feel horribly sick from the brandy, and would just want to sit all day. She wouldn't even want to take a turn with the binoculars watching the dolphins, the spectacularly colored schools of fish in the transparent turquoise water, or the changing geography of the coast. Yesterday they'd sailed through a wide stretch of ocean paved like a road of gleaming black stones with sea turtles.

As soon as she came into their darkened cabin, Mathilde, a sleepless grackle in her covered cage, squawked softly that she couldn't sleep. María de las Nieves pulled aside the double curtain and, regretting her warm brandy-tobacco-sardine breath, leaned in and kissed her daughter's damp cheek and said, "Do you want to come outside and see the stars and the ocean? They are so beautiful!"

"I want to pray my rosary." Paquita had given her rosary beads and now every night she wanted to clutch them and pray.

"Not now, chulita. Come outside with Mami."

Mathilde, in her sleeping smock, was still small enough to be carried, her arms wrapped around her mother's neck. María de las Nieves knew little about constellations, but she found two especially bright stars, among the lowest on horizon, looking as if they'd strayed from the rest. "Look at those two stars," she said. "Do you see them, Mathilde?" She described where to look. "Those are two little pearls my mamá gave me when I was little. She told me to put them away there, so that when my own daughter is old enough, I can take them down and give them to her."

"Abuelita doesn't have pearls. She has Indio beads and Abuelo's locket," replied Mathilde, her hot cheek pressed against hers. "Those are stars, Mamá, nothing more."

"Camarón! Whatever happened to childhood?"

The one piece of jewelry Timothy Moran had given Sarita Coyoy: a copper locket with a shamrock inside it. Lucy Turner had once explained the symbolism of the little trifoliate plant pressed beneath the glass, but if she'd ever actually spoken the word *shamrock*, María de las Nieves had long forgotten. One day at the legation Minister Gastreel had announced: "Today is Saint Patrick's Day, Señorita Moran. Shouldn't you be wearing a shamrock in your hat?" Her incomprehension had invited an explanation, leading to the revelation that her paternal surname apparently revealed her father's Irish origin. But he'd been born in New York, he was a Yankee, and when she'd reminded the Minister of that, he'd jovially replied, "Well, you are noticeably lacking in the Irish sentiment, Señorita Moran."

"Then do you want to take a little stroll with your mother, Doña Mathilde?" That was the night María de las Nieves took her daughter up onto the hurricane deck, when she first saw the sailor who looked so *familiar*. The hurricane deck's long expanse was interrupted only by the ship's two funnels and masts and the gaslight-glowing pilothouse forward, and along the sides, lifeboats fastened over the rails. During the day, exposed to the harsh sun, the deck was an all but empty desert, but by night, a transient population formed, shadowy even in starlit dark, mostly composed of passengers escaping the suffocating heat and crowding of steerage and the below-deck cabins. Many lay down to sleep on the deck, stretched out with their feet toward the rail, and couples, asleep or not quite, lay in tight embraces, barely covered by their sheets and blankets; here and there María de las Nieves's gaze skipped over a bare white leg, a shoulder, some other fleshy portion. Some hung hammocks in the rigging. Negro and Chinese waiters, stewards, and kitchen workers stood along the rails smoking;

boisterous Yankees with their happy-sounding arguments and quarrelsome laughter, spitting tobacco everywhere; over there a group gathered around an accordion player sang bawdy ballads in a strangely stirring cacophony of voices. Of course she, and certainly Mathilde, really didn't belong up here: she'd already turned back toward the stairs when she noticed a young sailor in white uniform and cap lounging against the rail, following her with his eyes, and her heart jumped and she stopped in her tracks and returned his stare with what must have been, she realized later, cringing, the most astonished expression. The other sailors were whites but he was not, he was a Mexican or Central American sailor, his smooth face a long oval, with high cheekbones and deep-set, flammable black eyes that lit up as if someone had just tossed a match in, and he broke into an impish grin—*he* didn't need handkerchief telegraphy to express himself—and, tightly gripping her daughter's hand, she resumed her walk back across the deck to the stairs.

# Chapter 3

When he heard the skinny, cinnamon-colored mestiza at General García Granados's fantasy party costumed as a pirate announce that she'd grown up on a cochineal farm and later become a nun, Mack Chinchilla immediately deduced that this must be the same girl he'd first heard told about some three years before in Mr. Jacobo Baiz's office on Williams Street in Manhattan, down in the dockside district where most of the coffee and tea traders were located. Mack had begun working for Mr. Baiz as an office boy but had risen to junior clerk by that sweltering summer night when Don Señor Juan Aparicio, soon to purchase the firm—he would retain the firm's reputable name and Jacobo Baiz as a full partner, for nobody understood the secrets of the tropical American trade better—had stopped by for a visit, and stayed to talk long after the closing hour. Don Juan Aparicio seemed glad that night to be among countrymen—the two Hebrews, Mr. Jacobo Baiz, who considered himself more or less a compatriot and had recently been appointed consul by the Liberals, and Salomón Nahón, Mack's fellow clerk and inseparable young friend, sent to New York City by his father to learn the tropical trade under Mr. Baiz's tutelage; and of course Mack himself, who had no memory of the country of his birth. Don Juan Aparicio's daughter, though still in girlhood, had recently by marriage become First Lady. The already wealthy and numerous Aparicios were on the verge of a personal business empire through that connection, though anyone could tell Don Juan was melancholy about the match, having a personal distaste for his arrogant, tempestuous, and crass son-in-law, though he did not deny that he was just the man to pull and whip and lead his indolent and superstitious people into the future.

Well, this was a small country, a smaller metropolis, and if the girl in Don Juan Aparicio's story was still alive and residing here, he'd been bound to run across her. But so what anyway, Mack had told himself just after making his not very warmly received quip about a nun-bug, because look at the way she's hanging on that showoff Cuban's every word, the two string-beaniest people at the party. Of all the girls in this country raised on cochineal farms, probably no small number entered convents, especially after the European markets' demand for the tiny dye-producing insects collapsed. Later that night Mack realized that if the silver-tongued Cuban masher wished to seduce anyone—though to succeed, there would come a moment when he would need to stop talking—it was General "Chafandín" García Granados's daughter, "just presented in society last year" and looking like a languid and virginal night nymph of the Nile in her costume of airy veils, gold bracelets shimmering the length of her slender arms. A vision of the unattainable female if ever, thought Mack in the shadows of the garden, in the jasmine-scented paper-lantern-lit dark as he watched her dwelling upon the Cuban, her dark gazelle eyes flashing merriment one moment, dissolving into melancholy pools of sympathy the next. You wouldn't think that the Cuban would dare, a former president's daughter, but maybe the Cuban is very moneyed as well as clever and society gifted—such were Mack Chinchilla's impressions of (the impoverished) José Martí that night—and this house does have the reputation of being an abode of libertinism. Contrary to all that society's inherited traditions of noble Spanish reserve, the shutters and drapery of the many windows in the García Granados mansion were normally left open and tied back behind the iron grilles on nights when there was a party, though most of the guests did their best to stay out of those rooms with windows facing the street, for the citizens who liked to gather outside to stare in at such a late hour usually only wanted to shout satiric commentary and drunken insults. There were many people, many of them hypocrites, who spoke now as if all the dissipation and amorality supposedly afflicting their society emanated through those very windows, as if all one had to do was convince Chafandín to keep his shutters closed, and women of all classes would go back to spending their nights sewing little costumes and dressing up statues of saints.

Mack went back to watching the nun-bug, though he wouldn't have another opportunity to speak with her that night. Ears poking out through her thin hair, peach-pit breasts beneath the red-striped jack-tar pullover, she was not even a little voluptuous, but he liked her, the impression she made, her nervous good humor, her air of hermetic and lean self-reliance, a tension about her, and there really was something fetching in her posture, the way she stood with her shoulders back, the long poised arch of her back, her slender but not overly delicate fingers, the hands of a girl raised in the tropical wilds, hands that had dug in the dirt for edible roots and climbed trees for fruit, a girl rescued from the tropical wilds who knew how to behave in society but retained inside herself a fearless American wildness, hardy as any pioneer lady or squaw, a niña who might even hold up a train if she were desperate enough, disguised as a nun, a legendary desperada of the Frontier West!—such was the personage Mack was feverishly inventing. Even if she wasn't the same girl as in Don Juan Aparicio's story, and of course she must be, the monja-bicho was just the sort of young woman he'd been waiting and searching for—. Nobody could accuse Mack of a grasping vanity. They had characteristics in common, of course, which she might consider mean, but which he would show her were not.

Now Mack slurped his oily soup, lifted his eyes toward the ceiling and silently chanted *nothing nothing nothing* and returned his gaze to the soup and thought, She will have nothing to do with me. Yes sir, of course he felt like a clod! Stooping to pick up her cigarette! He rarely spoke to the other guests at the dining table in his hotel, and if he did meet their eyes he stared boldly, daring them to ask the tedious and infuriating questions he knew polluted their minds. (How is it that you, a thoroughly Indio-looking fellow, speak like, and seem to consider yourself, a Yankee? And for that reason alone every sallow-skinned criollo dandy or wicked preening Spaniard or other degenerate European of the lowest sort, which this part of the world seemed to attract like flies to manure, every puffed-up little mestizo traveling merchant—men who filled their mouths with drinking water at the end of their meal, swished it around, and spat it out onto the floor!— or born Yankee liked to regard him with superiority and skepticism.) After dinner Mack went to his room, as was his strict habit, to compose at least three sentences, never fewer, rarely more, in his diary, on whose first page he had written the title "The Return." That night he wrote, My time will come. He should have titled his diary that, crossed out "The Return" and written "My Time Will Come," so frequently did he begin his daily entry with those very words. Today I suffered a discouraging defeat, he wrote. In my present employment, an opportunity is bound to present itself. This last sentence, nearly as common an entry as the first, he wrote just to sandwich the weighty information in the middle. Because that was what had occurred in the reading room kiosk, this day's only significant event. He stretched out on his narrow bed with his boots off and stared into the circle of candlelight upon the ceiling, an insect-populated moon, rubbing his itching feet together and trying to decide what to do next. He was not so naive as to believe that he had furthered his cause by giving the cri-cri to her little servant. If only he could have impressed her with the information that he was Juan Aparicio's and Jacobo Baiz's agent for the importation of cri-cris from France to Central America—except they had their own agent here, Don Juan's son, Juanito, who in turn employed an agent in the capital, a German immigrant no less, Gerhardt Hockmeyer. He had read in La Sociedad Económica's weekly newspaper that "people of taste" now considered the inexpensive noisemakers a vulgar nuisance that should be outlawed in the schools and at all musical performances. But people were making money off cri-cris all over the world! A rectangular little box of copper-oxidized lead with a slightly convex piece of sheet iron across the top, which, when rapidly pressed and released by the thumb, emits a resonant clatter—the inexpensive, democratic, little iron cricket, the most successful overseas export item in world manufacturing history! Mack was a student of international commerce. In France, he'd read in a newspaper, as crinolines became obsolete, as the women of France and other nations forsook the wearing of underskirts bell-shaped by metal hoops, steel prices had plummeted into a depression, but were again soaring on the success of the cri-cri!

There was no denying that, so far and in all respects, it had been a bitter *return*. His seemingly impulsive ambition to make the young half-Yankee mestiza his woman had helped Mack feel less alone in the world all the same. Though he did not personally know Señorita María de las Nieves, his awareness and judgments of her, his own manner of thinking and feeling about her, nevertheless provided affirmation, to himself and what of it, that he was indeed a man of good and virile ideals and hopes. He knew that loyalty, self-reliance, endurance, resourcefulness, and even dependable intelligence were not traits for which the more ephemerally endowed and passionate Spanish-American female was renowned—one was much likelier to find them expressed in Yankees, Anglo-Saxons, Hebrews, and in a sturdy India like his own mother; but if Mack could ever find such traits in a woman kindred to himself—such as he believed Señorita María de las Nieves to be—then he would fight to make a space in this hard world for the two of them, and would not relax a single day of his life until that goal was attained. Mack had first felt a thoughtful sympathy upon hearing about María de las Nieves years before in Mr. Jacobo Baiz's office, so this could not be classed as anything so sentimental and dreamy as love at first sight. There was no denying—by deployment of the rather feminine but nevertheless useful device of *hindsight*—that at least the idea of an ideal love had first asserted itself then, though all such energies had soon been diverted into the long, wintry, fateful courtship of his darkest New York years. (In hindsight, he should have left Reyna Salom alone. Hindsight was often useless.) An athlete was Mack, a ballplayer, a pugilist, an inexhaustible competitor in this endurance race his birth and life had marked him for. (Born Marco Aurelio Chinchilla, he had taken in boyhood the Yankee moniker Mack, and sometimes employed other surnames, including Cody, Crocket, Caleph, Cohen, Nahón . . .) And so he'd let his imagination inhabit his worthy and sensible romantic purpose, had even ridden on horseback to the lakeside town in which she'd been raised, formerly the center of the cochineal trade (he was adamant about using English words rather than Spanish even for native products such as cochinilla), not so much to spy on her—how could it be that, if she hadn't been there in some fifteen years?—as to establish a place for himself in the imagined setting of her past, and to see for himself where the incidents of Don Juan Aparicio's story had occurred (an old stablekeep in town had directed him to the well where the first Mrs. Moran had drowned, the deep steamy hole in the volcanic earth in which she had boiled herself into nonexistence).

Don Octaviano Mencos Boné, a squat, wrinkled asthmatic, his soft white beard falling like an apron bib into the white silk waistcoat he wore beneath his coat that night at Chafandín's party, was Mack's "Jefe" at the Immigration Society. Mack had been hired there for his indispensable English and clerical skills and had been given the same grand-sounding title as Wellesley Bludyar's at the British Legation, First Secretary, though his job was more similar to María de las Nieves's, if somewhat better paying. He was astonished to learn that Don Octaviano was forty-eight—that did not seem old enough to be such a wheezy and wrinkled Santy Claus!

That night Don Octaviano gave him a ride in his carriage from the party to his hotel. Mack still knew nothing for sure about the girl dressed as a pirate (the nun-bug), other than where she worked; nor did Don Octaviano really know anything more when Mack inquired in the immaculately appointed carriage, which was like sitting in the snug palm of a hand wearing a black glove of the finest kid leather, more luxurious than Mr. Baiz's carriage in New York, to say nothing of his team of splendid white Arabian horses. Don Octaviano so casually remarked that she must be that portly blond British diplomatist's *traida* that Mack had shrugged indifferently in reply, not wanting to let on that he didn't know that word and assuming that he must be implying that her position was lowly and subservient; he didn't realize until weeks later that his boss had used a common colloquialism for a disreputable lover (he'd simply never heard that word, not from his mother or from anyone else he'd spoken Spanish with in New York; not even Salomón Nahón, as far as he could remember, had ever said *traida*). In the carriage Don Octaviano recounted his own *interesting and useful conversation with that recently arrived young Cuban who is causing such an impression*— the Cuban newcomer had effusively praised the quality and flavor of their country's rustic cheeses. In the amazing Cuban's opinion there was no reason that those same rural peasant artisans could not be taught to produce exportable Roquefort and Camembert, in other words, world-class European-style cheeses; they needed only to invite a European cheese-master to immigrate. The government had already granted a sizable portion of the department of Verapaz to the Californian-Frenchman Don Pedro Sanservain so that he could re-create the success of his California vineyards and wineries here, and Don Octaviano agreed with the Cuban that a cheese industry would be most complimentary—Don Octaviano, who'd put away a good amount of Chafandín's champagne, clapped him on the thigh and exorted, "Pues no, vos, young Mack? Someday our Central American wine and cheese will be renowned throughout the world. Tomorrow you will write to the Minister of Haciendas informing him of our search for a master European cheesemaker." Mack waited inside the door of his hotel until Don Octaviano's carriage had been driven away; he tipped the sleep-dazed porter, who, after much pounding, had finally come to let him in, and then he went back out into the warm and windless sewage-stinking night, letting his footsteps carry him down the rutted, roughly paved streets sporadically lit by old tallow lamps to the Café de Paris, which was not a café in any sense of the word but the most fashionable of Doña Carlota Marcorís's dozen licensed first-class *burdeles* (her empire included all the second-class ones too). Among the men there indulging in late-night drinking, gambling games, prolonged coquetries, and negotiations, he would find someone who could tell him about the "traida" dressed as a pirate. But then he sat alone at a small table in the corner of the ornate parlor filled with shaded lamps, chandeliers, and mirrors, nursing his sole whiskey in tight-lidded silence and a sullen miser mood, deflecting even the parrying of painted eyes, which, despite the sordid circumstances, were full of startling dark beauty and soft feminine tenderness—this, Mack had decided, was the most striking difference between a brothel here and one in New York: the persistence of the Spanish-American woman's need for the illusions of romance—for they had small chance of finding love except when they were working, rarely getting to sleep before dawn yet prevented by law from leaving their brothel houses after two in the afternoon, kept inside making and winding bandages for hospitals, and always desperately dreaming of finding among their clientele any man who would buy their freedom from Doña Carlota and take them away, even to another country, as, once or twice in the universal history of whoredom, had supposedly occurred. Mack told himself it was his abhorrence of losing money that prevented him from joining the game of dice at the bar, though by doing so he would have the chance to make a friendly male acquaintance. Some of the men playing were Yankees, he overheard, with the railroad company bringing the railroad from Puerto San José to the capital. He recognized no one but the giraffe-tall gentleman in a string-tie with silky gray-blond mustaches and apricotlike head and features, Mr. Doveton, formerly the Southern Confederacy's diplomatic representative in Mexico, now residing here; he'd come to the Immigration Society one day to petition Don Octaviano for a land grant on behalf of fellow dispersed vanquished refugees who wished to form a farming colony. In New York Mack had been no genius at striking up friendships, but he'd known how to, had been familiar with a range of places, from saloons to Turkish cafés and athletic clubs, where he could find conversation, and hadn't had to sit there alone in a corner like an empty eggcup when he did not wish to, yet now he felt crippled in even this essential manly ability. Resolving to correct the matter, but not tonight, Mack finished his whiskey and left without saying good-bye to anyone, not even to Doña Carlota, just tipping his hat to that one señorita he was acquainted with, who, though there was already plenty of room there for hosting a visitor, was sliding over on the sofa, patting the empty space beside her, smiling her slice-of-pineapple-and-cherry-lips smile, fan fluttering—the dutiful theatrics and vulnerable loneliness of whores suddenly making him feel as melancholy and restless as if he'd just spent the entire night with one, though of course not as sated; he went out into the night, perfume still lingering in his nose, and walked back to the hotel beneath a clear sky so thick with blazing white stars it was like looking up into a snowstorm falling away, down upon some parallel world where people walked upside down in the snow.

It was the mender of umbrellas, parasols, and caucho-waterproofed clothing articles, Don José, a Polish-English-Hebrew immigrant from Manchester who now went by the perverse-sounding surname of Pryzpyz instead of his birth one of Ginsburg—he had thought the solidly Polish Pryzpyz, transplanted to the American tropics, would possess an exotic magician's mystique, a touch of Old World allure, good for business; it was Don José Pryzpyz who assured Mack that María de las Nieves was indeed that same girl rescued from the jungle by the First Lady's father.

From his shop, though only well past his regular business hours, the gangly umbrella mender also sold India-rubber condom sheaths, manufactured by himself in his cluttered back workroom—by hand of course, one at a time, as he'd learned to in Manchester, England, preparing the caucho at his iron stove in the usual way, cooking and smoking raw sap with sulfur and ammonia and then flattening the reeking mass with a baker's rolling pin into the thinnest possible sheets, from which he later cut the member-shaped pieces, using a flat mold. He matched the pieces, slightly smaller cuts of linen laid in between, one atop the other on a heated cast iron tray, fused them together by hammering all the way around the edges with a blunt iron chisel and hammer, and trimmed the rough edges with a cobbler's knife, finally producing an elongated India-rubber sack that held water without leakage, from which the linen could then be removed. They came in three sizes, were all the unappealing color of smoke-smudged fish belly, and were reusable—to be washed out with warm water and soap after each use, and hung upside down in a cool place; turning them inside out risked tearing the seams. Of course the sheaths inspired much more complaint than praise: they slipped off easily during the act if you were not practiced in their use, and deadened sensation even if you were; and they smelled like rotten eggs (the sulfur)—but wasn't that preferable to bringing a filthy disease home to your wife? With the Liberal Revolution had come an extraordinary brothel boom, but also, among progressive and scientific types, an unprecedented enthusiasm for public hygiene. One day, some four years before, Don José had simply displayed one of his wares in his window atop a white cardboard pedestal hand-printed with the motto *Protect yourself and your wife. You may grow old and weak before she does, and upon whose gratitude and mercy shall you depend then?* He had calculated on there being enough pedestrians who would recognize the India-rubber article immediately, and others who, looking at the curious thing and drawing other pedestrians into low conversation, would eventually deduce or find out what it was for. Don José had calculated correctly. Mounting the display in his shop window for one day only, he succeeded in attracting enough of a clientele to not ever, he was sure, need to advertise again. By day he plied his respectable trade and by night sold his condom sheaths to those who knocked at the door of his darkened shop between the hours of ten and midnight only. Mack Chinchilla had developed a loyal fascination and sympathy with Hebrews in New York City, and having heard beforehand that Don José Pryzpyz (né Josip Ginsburg) was of that race, he'd stubbornly lingered inside the darkened shop's door that first night when he came to make a purchase, determined to initiate a friendship.

Mack liked to talk about business and all matters related; to him some stupendous titan's launching of a new empire or monopoly was no more interesting than the story of an immigrant merchant's studious and intuitive discovery of even a modest business opportunity in a place where no such thing had existed before. To Mack there was something mystical and blessed about that process: hidden angel patriarchs stepped out from city shadows, unrecognized by the great majority, but whom the predestined and deserving one, however humble his status, sees blaze up before him into articulate light. Mack communicated this nearly fanatical enthusiasm in no overt way, but it was there in his dogged, bright-eyed questioning, which kindled the seemingly taciturn and solitary, middle-aged Hebrew's own nostalgia and musty pride, and that night, after they stood inside the door for some time, Don José (as he insisted on being called) invited Mack to have a seat, so that they could continue talking and wait for customers together, apologizing for the necessity of their having to converse in a darkened room—the umbrella mender did not wish to "illuminate" his semiclandestine nighttime trade—and offering Mack a glass of hot tea, which he went back into his rear living quarters to brew. Yes, his had been a long, gambling, adventurous journey. Though born in Poland, as a child Don José had immigrated with his family to Manchester, England, and had grown to adulthood there, learning his trades, including an apprenticeship at the famous Macintosh factory. Nearly twenty years ago now he had set out for the American tropics in search of fortune, freedom, and happiness, some of which he'd found, even if in perhaps small relation to what he'd originally dreamed. Still, he regarded himself as far from bitter. But he'd left a baby son behind in Manchester. His wife no longer loved or desired him, yes, she'd deceived him, Mack, and that had had a good deal—but not everything!—to do with his leaving. Now his son was nearly grown, and Don José hoped to return to England one day soon and present him with a gift of all the money he'd saved. Then he would look around a bit and catch up on the latest methods of working with India-rubber, for he'd heard that astonishing industrial advances were being made. But he would not remain in England one hour longer than necessary. He would turn around and come right back. He was not like so many other immigrants here who spent their day staring out at the rain, eating themselves up with memories and sighs and talk of returning home, and then never did; or else they did finally go back, selling everything, Good-bye forever! Good riddance! *Auf Wiedersehen!* and a year or three later, they reappeared, and joylessly began again, looking for a business to start up or agricultural land to buy at a price dearer than what they'd sold their original holdings for, but with no apologies or explanation other than that they had simply gotten used to the way of life here, and it had ruined them for life in Europe, or even in the United States.

"The way of life here," Don José would repeat, releasing an infectious, rumbling dark laugh that seemed to belong to a much stouter man. "Oh yes, my *God,* the way of life here. That is good. How are you enjoying the way of life here, Mack?"

This had not been the first stop of Don José's extended tropical American migration. He had first settled in Port Royal, followed by Cartagena de

Indias, and then Greytown, before discovering this mountain city of long, rainy winters, of umbrella-crushing downpours and spoke-snapping, fabric-ripping monsoon winds, of innately conservative, stingy citizenry, Parisian pretensions, and the unreliable availability and high price of imported umbrellas in the shops—an umbrella mender's paradise. Often he was asked to repair umbrellas, sturdily made in the old European way, with thick wooden handles and whalebone spokes, that had been in the same venerable family for three or four generations. The sign outside Don José's shop advertised his London training because he'd originally presumed that Manchester would lack commercial allure. Though he realized now that any customer for an umbrella mending or waterproofing was almost certainly among those, by now a majority in the capital if not the country, who ate with knife, fork, and spoon, and so were likely to be aware of the reputation of Manchester steel cutlery. Those who scooped up their food with a folded tortilla or ate with their fingers were more likely to protect themselves from the rain beneath a cape of braided palm, or by simply holding a large banana leaf over their heads—but one day the Indios would also use umbrellas and India-rubber capes, coats, and boots, for wasn't that promised by the era of progress on which the Republic was now embarked?

"But it is also the best city I've yet found in which to be a Jew," said Don José, "at least a nonworshipping one, Mack, because since our great Liberal Revolution, everybody is equally welcome here, and everybody despises everybody else equally. Not only is every immigrant from Europe with an unfamiliar-sounding name suspected of secretly being a Jew, but everybody suspects every other family here, no matter how old and supposedly pure their Spanish lineage, of hiding such a secret as well."

Mack had met Hebrews like Don José before, who wished not to call attention to their race, or even tried to hide it—wished to while being unable to. As for himself, Mack, who in some circumstances even introduced himself as Mack Caleph, Cohen, or even Nahón, had taken many lessons from and even tried to copy the iron-willed, assertive, and often droll style of the men he'd most admired in the Turkish-Hebrew colony and cafés of New York City. No Hebrew, Mack had learned from them, could ever afford to display weakness. Disarm prejudice with unflappable composure, aloof good cheer, dangerous wit; never allow them to infect you with their disdain; study the persecutor and ask: Is he so perfect?

Remember, no good or worthy man ever allows bigotry to lodge in his heart. But weren't those the lessons that any father should pass on to his son? Might not Mack, a Roman Catholic, have learned similar lessons among Irishmen? But Mack had no father, and he had no friends among the Irishmen of New York. He'd learned his lessons from the men he and young Salomón Nahón both regarded as exemplary (there were also, of course, many who were far from exemplary) among that community of immigrants from places as far flung as Salonika, Bucharest, and Tangiers, many speaking an old-fashioned kind of Spanish not so different from that spoken by Mack's own mother. Thanks to his years of apprenticing and clerking in Mr. Baiz's firm and his friendship with Salomón Nahón, Mack, a fatherless Yankee-Indio who felt as if he belonged nowhere, had found unlikely comradeship and acceptance among that immigrant colony that belonged most of all to itself. There he'd developed his idea of how he, the Yankee son of an ancient, conquered, and despised American race—yet believed by many expert men of religion and science to be descended from the lost tribes of the biblical Hebrews—should comport himself in the world. Mack vowed that when he got to know the self-effacing umbrella mender better, he would share this knowledge with him. He would reprimand him for not being more self-confident, more assertive and visionary with his talents, for just take a look around, Don José, at the inept and corrupt scoundrels who have the run of this country! There are honest fortunes to be made here. Everyone knows that Central America is destined to become the fruit orchard of the United States, and the great terminal of world commerce!

It turned out that Señorita María de las Nieves was a friend of Don José's and a regular visitor to his shop, always during the afternoon hours. As much as Mack sought to press this matter, the umbrella mender was reluctant to provide much detail or explanation. Mack visited at night, not to buy sheaths—he'd bought one that first night only—but because such was the ritual of their friendship. He didn't need to be subtle to perceive that were he to leave the nighttime aspect out of this still evolving ritual, it would be like a magician neglecting to tuck a certain handkerchief up his sleeve: no more magical illusion, no more friendship.

"I like that you come at night, Mack. It's a good hour to have visitors, especially during the dry season, when work is slow."

"So she visits you, Don José. Frequently?"

"Yes, she does. She is a good girl, of course. Just a bit of a stray cat, I suppose."

"What do you mean, a stray cat?"

"María de las Nieves doesn't have very much in the way of family, you know, Mack—that is all I mean to imply," said Don José almost apologetically.

"But what about her mother? And are not these Aparicios like a family to her? And Doña Francisca, whom she grew up with? Weren't they even sent to the convent together?"

Don José shrugged. "I don't know. Maybe they have grown distant. That would be inevitable, I suppose."

"Why you? Why does she visit you? Oh, Don José, you are an excellent sort, the personification of the decent merchant, an exemplary man, but why you—when by making the smallest effort to exploit her ties to the Aparicios, she could belong to highest society here? She would not be the only woman of low origin so elevated by a connection to the Liberals. You've seen some of the President's military generals and their wives, some of them belonging every bit as much to the native race as I."

"You would have to ask her yourself, Mack, what the reasons are."

"Perhaps there is a reason, Don José, for some in this society to feel they have a right to exclude and censor her."

"She has done nothing deserving of censure."

"Something she may not even be aware of herself, but for which she is unjustly censored . . . by the Aparicios!" What if only Mack and the Aparicios knew the details of the story that Don Juan Aparicio had told in Mr. Jacobo Baiz's office in New York?

"María de las Nieves forms innocent attachments. You would have to ask her yourself why me in particular. But she doesn't just visit me, you know. She visits other merchants too, J. J. Jump the photographer and Olivier Partagas the bookseller, for example. She is my dear and intimate friend—a bit like a daughter, Mack, you might say. There, that is all."

"She visits other merchants too? And they all regard her as a daughter? And she is not loose in her morals?"

"She is not in the least loose in her morals—"

"Forgive my crudeness, Don José. You regard her as a daughter, then that's all, eh?"

"Mack Chinchilla, if you have set your heart on this girl, you have nothing to fear from me. I am hardly a fit rival," he said with a new laugh, which had something unpleasant about it, like a melted caramel hardened and stuck to the inside of a pocket. "Though, of course," the umbrella mender finally added, "I would not want to see her paired with a brothel man."

"Don José, I am not a brothel man. I purchased one of those . . . things . . . as a way to make your acquaintance . . . Okay, it's true that I've been to the Café de Paris, but just to play a little dice with the other fellows there. A young fellow's got to get out a bit, you know."

"Well, she has other suitors, Mack. Are you aware of that? You should take it into consideration, Mack, that she does have a very serious suitor. The leading candidate being none other than one of Her Majesty's diplomatic agents in this country. A gentleman, young and blond. You know the high esteem in which people of fair features are universally held here—" (Mack Chinchilla certainly did know, for it was the prevailing mission of the Immigration Society to import them to the country.)

"You mean the one they call El Chino Gringo? *Him?* You're joking, Don José! He's serious about her? Serious enough to marry her?"

"You would have to ask María de las Nieves about that, Mack."

"Well—hang it, then!"

That was how Mack Chinchilla learned of the serious intent of the *usurper*, a turn of events that nearly drove him to a frenzy of indignation over the sheer injustice of the impediments that could block a man's willed path to contentment. Why should he have to contend with a romantic fairy tale? Why not a frog-prince? Why couldn't the Englishman find a wife among his own kind? At the time it had seemed as drastic a turn as the terrible surprise that had awaited him at the end of his arduous journey, when he'd first arrived from New York and traveled out to the lowland village where his friend Salomón Nahón, his father, and two uncles had their home and business. That sad visit had been a blow from which he'd not yet nearly recovered, whereas the heaviness in his heart since that last demoralizing conversation with Don José Pryzpyz was at least lightened weeks later, when, at the bar in the Café de Paris, he'd encountered Wellesley Bludyar, so inebriated that he was even greeting strangers with Hello, Old Chum and Hello, Old Avocado, and inviting them to a glass of Scotch whiskey, grasping at shoulders and baying to anyone who would listen about his frustrated wooing of María de las Nieves.

Mack suspected that El Chino Gringo's behavior that night was not typical of the British Legation First Secretary. He was unusually familiar with the manner and conversations of diplomatists and not just because Mr. Baiz, due to his expertise in all matters related to commercial shipping in the port of greater New York, had been appointed consul by the new Liberal government. Mack Chinchilla's mother, born Petronila Calvario in the village of Mixco, an Indian pueblo just outside the capital, had been servant and cook to Don Sínforoso Revolorio for twenty of the nearly thirty years he'd served the Conservative regime as Chargé d'Affaires, Consul General, and Minister Extraordinary to the United States of America. There being little business on his country's behalf to occupy him in Washington, Don Sínforoso had lived in New York, in a four-story house on State Street in Brooklyn, in the Heights, overlooking the harbor, and that had been Mack's childhood home.

According to his mother, Mack had also been born in Mixco, and his father, Gaspar Chinchilla, had died fighting as a foot soldier with the troops the conservative dictator, the Defender of Religion, had dispatched to join the triumphant campaign against the North American filibusterer Walker, who'd already conquered Nicaragua and sought to turn the Isthmus into a slavery republic. There were medals, no paper proof, but Mack accepted the legend of his pedigree. He had no memory of any childhood home other than the one on State Street, where he lived with his mother and the long-widowed and childless Don Sínforoso until the august diplomatist's death, at the age of eighty-nine, one year after the ending of the United States' war of secession. Mack was twelve then. His mother next found work as a servant in the home of a Cuban-born ship captain, a recent widower, with two children, nearby on Amity Street, and Mack left school to apprentice himself to Don Sínforoso's younger friend and business associate, Mr. Jacobo Baiz, who owned a firm specializing in imports and exports between New York and the American tropics, and was then beginning to focus particularly on the burgeoning trade in Central American coffee.

Prosperity had given Mr. Baiz's business the air of a happy family party: the constant hum of voices, the manic and joyous activities of money and commerce, the smells of coffee beans and tobacco smoke, the clamor of the nearby port, young office boys racing (as Mack had) down South Street on errands (Go to Mr. Garretson, would you Mack, and ask him if he will not shade his price; We have a sale, Mack, go and learn today's price of gold) beneath a thrilling canopy of bowsprits and the amazing female figureheads reaching nearly all the way across the street, dangling naked sea-smoothed breasts above the multitude, office boys spending their meal hours (as Mack had) at the wharves, watching the cargo being unloaded from the great clipper ships and schooners, listening to the tales and banter of tattooed sailors of every conceivable nationality and race, and the often incomprehensible pitches with which they tried to sell the curios they brought to the New York wharves from the remotest corners of the earth— once Mack had held in his own hands a delicate bone sculpture of a canoe paddled by a grotesque but charming trio of animals, a monkey, a parrot, a lizard, and two strange, seed-eyed human figures in serpent-feather headdresses; according to the sailor, it had been carved by the ancient Indians of Central America and depicted a fire brigade of pagan gods hurrying across the sky to put out a massive flaming meteor headed for their hidden jungle city—alas, the sailor's price was far beyond Mack's means, and he felt the heartbroken covetousness of a child for another's toy when he had to hand the magical canoe over to Mr. Wing, of the great foreign fruit house of Wiley, Wicks & Wing, who bought it on the spot (and only a year later new signs appeared on the sides of that company's wagons, depicting a nearly naked, vixenish, and seed-eyed Indian woman, wearing a flamboyant serpent-feather headdress, standing in a canoe piled with fruits and paddled by monkey, parrot, and lizard, but the exotic image caused such a scandal among the city's virtuous sectors that it soon disappeared from view; and reappeared decades later, metamorphosed into a strikingly similar woman with fruit piled high on her head on the little stamps adorning every one of Mr. Samuel Zemurray's bananas; that mechanical method, invented at one of his Honduran plantations by an ingenious native engineer, of inexpensively branding individual bananas with the image of the fetching "Chiquita" allowed Sam "the Banana Man" to distinguish his bananas from the naked sameness of all other bananas on earth, and changed the foreign fruit trade forever, that nearly anonymous and soon forgotten Honduran's invention as revolutionary in its way as any of Mr. Edison's!)—and office boys arriving back at Mr. Baiz's office (as Mack had) carrying fragrant sacks full of coffee samples from the warehouses, and shouting like messenger gulls an order from broker Such & Such, the price of Santos coffee, the latest cables received at the Exchange announcing the London or Hamburg market up or down, and So and So, that rascal, is trying to sell his inferior Angostura bean as the best Boca Costa peaberry! A handful of peaberry should feel heavy like a handful of shot, and, look here, this is like holding dried rabbit turds! Or whispering to Mr. Baiz, Mr. Garretson says he will not shade his price, sir—. Or Mr. Baiz, just back from the Downtown Club, sharing coffee merchants' gossip and quips heard there while lunching with the visiting Vice-Minister of Works from the Supreme Government—Mack, this young gentleman, the Vice-Minister of Works, is eager to import a cylindrical printing press, take him out to Newark, would you, to this address, I've arranged . . . et cetera. You're in good hands with our Mack, Señor Don Vice-Minister, he is our most dependable boy—

Salomón Nahón arrived during Mack's second year, boarding with Mr. Jacobo Baiz and his family on East Eighteenth Street. "Never forget a face or a name, and do as you're told, and pay good attention to everything young Mack here has to teach you, and you'll do fine"—with those words, Mr. Baiz had introduced Salomón to the business, and to Mack, who led the novice on his first runs as a messenger that morning. By the time they went for their first midday meal on the wharves, the two boys were fast friends, though it would take a week of dining on potatoes and bread with apple butter for Salomón to give in and join Mack and the other office boys at the oyster counters. Salomón spoke a little English, which he'd taught himself at home from a book called *American Popular Lessons* (yes, the same indeed popular manual in which both Martí and María de las Nieves had studied the language) and had practiced with his father and uncles, who'd lived in California. His pronunciation was hopeless, but the warmth and enthusiasm of his voice turned his words into whirring hieroglyphs, which people often seemed happy to make an effort to decipher, leaning in, closing their eyes, gesturing for him to repeat himself, nodding, smiling, as if it were all some engaging guessing game. Mack was willing to speak Spanish, but Salomón usually insisted on giving his English a try—and how quickly he learned! Salomón was two years younger than Mack, and though an inch or two taller, he was still short by American standards, and slight, in fact every bit as slight as that wispy and loquacious Cuban, though of a completely different physical type, his agile limbs as sinewy hard as jungle vines, because he'd grown up entirely in *el campo,* in the wild country of grasslands and tropical forests of the southern plateau, just between the Pacific lowlands and the coffee foothills of the Sierra. Salomón's cashew-brown skin seemed suffused with tropical sunlight even in the malignant depths of the New York winter. Despite his vehement detestation of the cold, he looked as if he radiated heat. His hair was a messy mass of black curls, and he had a swarthy, narrow face that already, at fifteen, had grown the beard of a baby goat, and slightly protruding dark eyes that seemed always in hyperbolic motion, and a mouth usually set in a jaunty, expectant half smile, and a Hebrew's nose, though not such a pronounced one—not so different from an Indio's nose, from Mack's in fact. More than once, when both boys were wearing winter hats pulled down low, collars raised to their ears, scarves covering their chins and mouths, they were asked if they were brothers. It came as no surprise that Salomón was precocious with the opposite sex—he, the Hebrew country boy, charming and adroit with the girls, and Mack, the metropolitan Catholic boy, a stammering boob!

An extraordinary story lay behind the life of Salomón Nahón, and that story itself was full of stories, and it seemed that no day ever passed without Salomón adding some new one—but that central story, from which all the others branched, was the one about how and why the unmarried Nahón brothers, Moisés, León, and Fortunato, had decided together, ten years after all three had settled in the village of Cuyopilín, that Salomón Nahón needed to exist. "Yes pues, they call me come to life, Mack, like the Indios make a ceremonia so come the rain!"

The Nahóns were from Fez, Morocco: the first to leave the family home in that holy fortress city's Hebrew ghetto had been Moisés, the oldest of the brothers, who signed aboard a French guano schooner in Marseilles, jumped ship in Lima, and gradually made his way to San Francisco, California, where he worked in a paisano's general store. León and Fortunato, after their father died and they had settled their mother with relatives in Tangiers, joined Moisés there. After much study of where the next best American opportunities might be found for entrepreneurs of such boundless energies but limited means as their own, the brothers made their care-

fully prepared move to Central America. They chose Cuyopilín because it
was just inland from the unlivable Pacific port of Champerico, near a river
and hot and cold springs, perfectly situated at the foot of the higher elevations of the southern coffee piedmont, and connected to roads, mule train,
and old Indian paths leading to the port, up into Los Altos, and to the
growing nearby agricultural towns of the coastal plain, and even to the
capital. The brothers Nahón built a general store in Cuyopilín, acquired
two small peddler's carts and mules to pull them, and were soon supplying an assortment of wares shipped from California to sugar plantation
owners, cattle ranchers, and the coffee pioneers beginning to settle nearby
in the Costa Cuca and Costa Grande and throughout the piedmont. It
would not have been easy to lead the life of an observant Jew in Cuyopilín,
and the Nahóns did not try. Of course it is not the devout and studious Jew
of stereotype who typically strikes out for the American tropics, a trail
blazed by such notables as the South American railroad builder Henry
Meiggs, Peter Goldfarb "the Macaw King," and Salomón Casés, the Moroc-
can Hebrew and ex–British Army warrant officer who led a ragtag "Foreign
Legion" of fellow Amazon rubber traders in a successful armed uprising
against the illegal taxation and corruption of the Peruvian authorities in
Iquitos (also, decades later, Sam "the Banana Man" Zemurray, of the eventually infamous United Fruit Company)—to say nothing of countless ped-
dlers and umbrella menders, their descendants, the descendants of their
descendants; the even more numerous descendants of those first unions
between Inquisition-fleeing converso conquistadors and Indian women;
and the offspring of Santa Teresa de Ávila's nine converso brothers, who
also settled in New Spain, where they collectively fathered at least ninety-
seven known children, to whom one contemporary Carmelite scholar has
recently been able to trace five hundred and forty-six legitimate offspring,
who in turn produced some two or three thousand more, all born before
the end of the seventeenth century, thereby widely dispersing the family
genes of that greatest of Carmelite mystic saints into the unfathomable
mongrel river of the Americas. That levitating Hebrew-blooded hottie,
most favored and adored of all God's Holy Virgin Brides (as anyone only
familiar with the famous Bernini statue in Rome of Santa Teresa in divine
ecstasy, her beautiful face rendered in voluptuous orgasm, might easily
deduce), author of the most rigorous and influential convent Constitution

and Rule ever written ("God is in the pots and pans") and of a disquisition on the Song of Songs so sensual a theological adviser ordered her to burn it, and of her own now classic *vida* (composed in an unaffected and collo-quial Golden Age style and which the young José Martí studied at univer-sity in Madrid, and later recommended to his students in composition at La Academia de Niñas de Centroamérica, though of course María de las Nieves had already read it and was aching for inspiration and example from any other source), Santa Teresa de Ávila is by now ubiquitous in our hemi-spheric DNA—much more so, thanks to her nine brothers, than Washing-ton, or Franklin, or Jefferson, or anyone like that, at least as far as has been documented. (By the way, María de las Nieves's old favorite, the bilocating Sor María de Agreda, sometimes called the "Santa Teresa of the Baroque," was also the daughter of conversos.)

Every morning the brothers Nahón said their prayers, poured water over their hands, thanked God for having made them men and not women. They lit candles at dinner on the Sabbath, but had no time or inclination to rest. In ways overt and more subtle, they sought to be charitable. Some-times somebody remembered that it was a holy date, and, perhaps, an appropriate song. Or one of the brothers read aloud a Bible story from the Spanish-language Haggadah that León had found at a secondhand bookseller's during a business trip to San Francisco. On the Great Day of Atonement, they sometimes fasted. They refrained from eating *chancho*, or pig. It was difficult to be much more observant than that. The only women around were Cuyopilín's Indian women, of the Pipil tribe, who went bare-breasted in the lowland heat, and a small number of mestizas living nearby. The Nahóns built a rustic and relatively cool house, a giant Indio hut was what it really was, with green bamboo instead of cane walls and a high-peaked palm-thatched roof and hard-packed dirt floors. They planted a shady grove of mango trees in front, and coffee trees, of poor quality at that low elevation, all around the house, and an orange orchard, and raised bees for honey, and they bought milk cows, and eventually horses and donkeys to breed mules—León had developed into a masterful breeder and trainer of mules—which they sold, along with their oranges, at the farmers' market in Retalhuleu. Though the Nahóns were making and saving money, they knew it was nothing compared to what some of the criollos and European immigrants, Germans and British especially, were starting to earn from coffee. But coffee was truly profitable only when farmed on a large scale, and establishing such a finca was enormously expensive and time-consuming: land, equipment, a drying patio and soaking vats and a good supply of water, plus you had to buy thousands of saplings just to get started, and the young trees were fragile, and you had to know just what you were doing, it required study and experiment, or at the very least the hiring of a trustworthy administrator with expertise, and such men were in *great demand*, and you had to build a hacienda house as grand as those of neighboring fincas or else lose the respect of your workers. And then you had to wait at least three years to see if your coffee trees were going to produce any profits. Only Indios, to harvest the berries and so forth, were easily had and affordable. And you needed assistance—the government tried to help the wealthy criollos and the immigrants it considered most desirable, and the Germans, with their Los Altos German Association, especially helped each other. Nevertheless, the Nahóns dreamed of seeing their family name installed among the emerging coffee aristocracy. It might not be possible in their lifetimes, but if they worked hard and saved their money, wouldn't it be for their heirs? But what heirs?

"Ahh? *Puuuú-chica!* What heirs, amigo Mack? The dozen or so little half Indios, the little Hebrew-mestizos, that Moisés, León, and Fortunato has fathered with all the naked-chichi Indias? All my little half brothercitos y half sistercitas? Choose one to be Salomón Nahón from so many? And circumcise where, how? With machete? Jaja. Pues, you see this problems, Mack."

Even if all three of the brothers were to marry and each produced a legitimate heir, there would not be nearly enough money to buy three coffee fincas. Nor could three Nahón heirs each become a wealthy and powerful coffee patrón by sharing the single finca that the brothers' life savings should be able to provide. But what if there was only one prodigal young Nahón, who would inherit all three brothers' life savings? What if that sole Nahón heir was raised to found a coffee empire in redemption of all three, with a chance to preserve and perpetuate the Nahón name and line among the coffee aristocracy for all generations! A good plan, no? But who would be the mother to the heir? What about Herr Weisselberger? There were Hebrews among the German coffee pioneers, including Herr Weisselberger, who had a marriageable daughter, not even a little bit good-looking—. Imagine the brothers' visionary excitement, as they sat out at night on their crude verandah by the light of pine-fat torches to keep mosquitoes away, amid the insect and frog uproar of the tropical nights— chanting *Weisselberger!* Who else will marry Charlotte Weisselberger? At least her name is beautiful, Charlotte, mother of Salomón-future. But who will be the husband (groan) of Charlotte?

"So goes legend of my familia, Mack. Weisselberger girl look like danta, a long curve nose and fat fanny up—danta is name for animal live in the swamps and lagunas, Mack, Spanish also call tapir. Do you know their meat, especially when smoke, is good eat, and very good ropes make from . . . their . . . piel, Mack, what is piel? *Hi-des.* Good ropes from the hi-des, and clean, burn-slow oil from the grasa. And my uncles and father-future for sometimes think lot about this idea of domesticar this animal, the danta. Why not? They study it, yes. They study the turkey, a wild of the tropic but the Indios domesticar. They domesticar the turkey, Mack. And you take a a jabalí—a boar, yes, a boar baby wild from forest, and you bring up with chanchos, the pig-es, Mack, it do just like the pig. Everything just like same! But just like pig, danta is not beast kosher—but los three Nahones only remember after they partakes of the meat manymany time. The no clove-foots. This is example, Mack, of profound strategy of American tropics on the Hebreo— what? On the Hebreo mind and spirit, which have be shape for epocas on one side of globe, and take all way round to this sun tropical primitivo side, Mack, where invent thing like domesticar the danta, which I think is one perfect idea. Why not? And why not also taste the native girl, sweet and juicy like papaya, Mack, poor lonely desgraciados fellow-es, with their muchachas India, the brothers Nahón. Oh, poor fellow-es! Maybe one God make one piece of globe, and other god-es make the other piece. Sometimes I think, yes pues, only explanation. Hebreo God angry, but cannot come to tropics and punish. One more thing about danta. Miembro, miembro?—member. Manly member more longer than any other animal, more longer than horse or bull! Fold up against stomago like *Z*, a flatted *Z*, and urinar straight back! So if you stand in back the danta, oh, yes, you get it, the urinar in your face. And when hard and straight for fuck! Uff! Not believe, ja. Claro, the Indios know, yes pues. Many legend about great giant fucking of danta!"

Such was Salomón's storytelling manner, that one chattered out on a long omnibus ride down Broadway while he hugged himself against the cold, not even any overhearing Puritan voicing offense because they couldn't be sure of what they heard anyway, and as Salomón liked to say, Who is going to bite my tongue?

A formal offer of marriage was made to Herr Weisselberger: he and Charlotte could select any one of the three Nahón brothers to be her husband, and thereby become the beneficiary of the life savings and ongoing earnings of all three. The offer was indignantly rejected—when it was time for the danta-girl to marry, the Weisselbergers, if need be, would travel back to Germany to find Charlotte a suitable husband.

"But so why no choose one clever boy to be Salomón Nahón from these manymany little half-Indio sons, Mack? Is that the way of America? Is justice. Ahhh, and so many trouble save. So manymany tears never comes. But then, I no exist. So I no can gruntle. Imagine never see this sweet life? Never all the love beautiful muchachitas. The Pipil girls have firme little chichis, oh Mack, deliciosas. Never come to this maravilla New York for live with Don Jacobo. Never know my friend Mack Chinchilla!"

It was finally decided that Fortunato would travel back to Tangier and find the mother of the heir. The two older brothers would never marry, but would continue to seek satisfaction and comfort with the local women in their accustomed manner, one not entirely free of emotional entanglement. A year later Fortunato returned with the beautiful and beloved Estercita, his wife, who soon after gave birth to Salomón. Oh, what rejoicing! All the way to Mexico City traveled the new little family so that infant Salomón could have his foreskin snipped by a mohel. "Ay Dios mío, no hay bien que por mal no venga!" Just a year later Estercita died after giving birth to his seven-month sister Gracia, whose own life lasted little longer than a falling star in the night sky. Fortunato, who'd never loved any woman but Estercita and had never even dreamed of the happiness he'd discovered inside their not quite two years of conjugal intimacy, was devastated by his double loss. From then on, Fortunato would seem like a man always near tears, and never partook of the local women again, dedicating himself instead to a noble plan: first he attempted to identify every natural child he thought he or his brothers might have fathered so that he could send them all away to boarding school in the capital at the Nahóns' expense; but then, fearing that it was inevitable that at least one of those children would be overlooked—thereby condemned by discretion, forgetfulness, or simple fate to a life of dark ignorance—he decided to build a school where all the children in the village could be educated, including his sole legitimate son, Salomón, and imported a teacher, Rubén Abensur, from the Alliance Israelite in Tangier. The two uncles doted on Salomón, pampering his every want. But Fortunato was determined that his son should be brought up like a young prince who is never allowed to ignore or forget the weight and responsibility of his predestined kingdom. He wanted him to study hard in their little school, especially mathematics, but also to learn the secrets of nature and, especially, of coffee, and so he took Salomón with him on all his peddling trips into the piedmont. Not even the most prejudiced and arrogant Prussian coffee patrón could intimidate Fortunato into losing his composure, or successfully repel his polite and disarming attempts to engage that patrón in conversation, if it meant providing his son with a chance to learn something new about coffee farming. Of course Fortunato understood that it was good for his son to grow up close to the Indios too, because their knowledge of nature was a treasure that most of the European and even criollo patrones disdained to consider. The Indios should be his son's indispensable allies, as long as he treated them as employees who were also equals—only natural and just, considering that many of Salomón's schoolmates were his half siblings, no? Salomón also inherited the sexual exuberance of his uncles, fathering his first child, a son, named Máximo, when he was twelve, a misdemeanor for which his father mercilessly whipped him—no joke, solemn truth!—with a tapir whip, just as elastic, twice as long, as one made from a bull's member.

When he was fourteen, Salomón Nahón was sent to New York to learn about the coffee trade in the firm of Jacobo Baiz. Three years later, when he was finally ready to return, Salomón said to Mack: "We go into coffee together. You come and be partner-administrator, Mack, and when you ready to start finca of your own, I help you as if you are my *only* brother."

Four years in a row Mack Chinchilla had received a letter from Salomón Nahón repeating the offer, every year with the same instructions on how to get to Cuyopilín, and even what to pack for his journey, and warning him to not even *think* about traveling through the countryside without a weapon, such as a good Colt .45 revolver. By then Mack had risen to the position of head junior clerk in Mr. Baiz's firm, of which Don Juan Aparicio was the majority owner. The sedentary life of a well-situated clerk, if he

was careful to save, could provide a secure life. Before long, Mack would be
ready to look into buying his own home in Brooklyn or far uptown, no small
achievement for the immigrant son of an Indian servant. Though Reyna
Salom's fig-colored eyes had lost none of their placid regard when Mack
asked her, in Spanish, if she did not believe him, so unimpressed did she
seem by his proud assertion of imminent home ownership. Reyna answered
that it was not up her to believe him, that Mack should tell her father, and
if it was true and important for her to know, her father would tell her. She
was the daughter of Mojluf Salom, who worked for a Java coffee and fire-
cracker importer on Water Street and had befriended Salomón and Mack
and sometimes accompanied them to the Café Constantinopolis in the
afternoons; the Saloms were Seffardim from Sarajevo, and Reyna and her
mother, Ricca, spoke exclusively in the antiquated Spanish they called the
*vero castellano*, a language Mojluf spoke hardly at all. Reyna was diminutive,
fine-boned, and soft-looking, with a sallow-brown complexion, curly brown
hair falling to her waist, and a mole like a glistening scarab beneath a
corner of her innocent lips. Her demeanor was reliably pleasant if a bit
listless—she smiled with sleepy-lidded eyes, curled up, dressed like a
Saracenic doll, in the sofa cushions of their dark, cramped little parlor.
Salomón had become besotted with Reyna the very first time he and Mack
had been invited to the Salom's home, and afterward, with Mojluf's permission and Ricca's unobtrusive vigilance, the two friends had regularly
visited Reyna in the evenings. After Salomón went away, Mack kept on
coming by himself, astonished and encouraged that there was no change in
Reyna's agreeable but vague manner. Since no one ever discouraged him—
neither Reyna nor Mojluf nor Ricca—he persisted in his sedate but stubborn courtship routine for nearly four years, calling on her once or twice a
week, investing too much of his earnings in little, sometimes gaudy gifts.
After all, she sometimes allowed him to hold her warm and damp little
hand in his, and later it would seem that her quiet perfume lingered in the
creases of his palm as if she'd been sleeping there. He was sure that he'd
found his wife, that this snail's-pace courtship was how it was done in a
respectable Hebrew family, not so different, his mother allowed, as in her
own country. Reyna still occasionally teased him with the same coquettish
folk sayings and verses—*Morena me llama / el hijo del rey / si otra ves me llama
/ yo con él me iré*—which, familiar as they were by now, always excited his

hopes and a thrilling lust he believed could only be quelled by marriage. In an attempt to solicit some providential signal from her, his conversation had finally become boastful, and that had made him feel ashamed. One afternoon, a cold leaden winter Sunday, Mack made an impassioned speech, promising to adore Reyna forever and even convert to her religion if she would marry him. Reyna Salom answered with calm conviction that great loves and grand passions were for stories in books. She would marry whomever her father told her to marry. Mack would never forget his long trudging afternoon walk to the Fulton ferry port, a light snow falling as the slate darkness fell, then standing outside on the ferry deck despite the cold, burning wind and snow, and climbing up the hill and walking all the way to Amity Street, and entering the ship captain's house as always through the service entrance, where, finding his mother in the kitchen, he'd finally burst into tears. He kneeled with his head in his mother's lap for a long while that night, but was unable to answer her when she asked him what was wrong; he couldn't, Madrecita, because he had no words for what was wrong. He never called on Reyna Salom again, and Mojluf never asked him why. A few months later he would hear that the Saloms had abandoned New York to try their luck in Buenos Aires.

One afternoon soon after that incident Mack stood up from his desk and felt himself swaying dizzily and he put his arms out and heard a faint voice, his own, dreamily yet firmly say, "Petroleum jelly." He came to on the floor with clerks, salesmen, office boys, and Mr. Jacobo Baiz peering down at him. Mr. Baiz told him to go home and to take the next day off—he said Mack had a nervous condition, that his constitution was not naturally suited to the strain of so much mental work, that he needed exercise and fresh air. But Mack was athletic and was not suffering from any such lack. He understood what he needed as soon as he hit the sidewalk. There was no grand future for him in a business where the owner, Juan Aparicio, looked after his own family and their connections first of all. He didn't want to be a clerk. He wanted out of this end of the business of business. Greatness happened out there in the world, and everything Mack wanted was out there; just around the corner on lower Wall Street, in a building of mostly tea and rice merchants, was the immensely profitable Chesebrough Manufacturing Company, which made and sold only one product, petroleum jelly, or Vaseline, its founder an ordinary Brooklyn chemist, but one with the initiative and push to have traveled on a hunch to the Pennsylvania oil fields, where he noticed the filmy petroleum residue collecting on the pump rods of the oil wells, a dense slime that many of the workers, scooping it directly off the rods with their hands, rubbed onto their own bruises and cuts. That same day the chemist had somehow managed to transport, by coach, train, and ferry, half a dozen heavy buckets of the crude petroleum jelly back with him to Brooklyn, and within an hour of arriving home, using his wife's flower vases as beakers—so went the awed lower Manhattan legend—was experimenting on the salubrious qualities of the substance in his own kitchen.

Both Mr. Baiz and his mother gave their blessing to Mack's plan to join his friend Salomón Nahón in coffee farming. This was an era that rewarded bold enterprise and risk. As the economic, military, and maritime power of the United States grew, Mr. Baiz predicted, so would that of Central America right along with it. The fare via the transcontinental railroad and Pacific Mail steamship was far too expensive for Mack, even though that route led virtually to the Nahóns' door. But he could sail directly from New York via New Orleans to Belize, and from there to Livingston, for barely a fifth of the cost. So Mack Chinchilla had reentered the country of his birth at the same tiny port where Sor Gertrudis had disembarked decades before, and where young José Martí would land only months later. Mack did not travel their route to the capital, however, diverging from it to head all the way across the country, through jungles and over mountains, to the Boca Costa southern piedmont, and further down to Cuyopilín.

The young man who landed at Livingston, who never before had even ridden a horse or struck another man in anger, to say nothing of using a pistol, was certainly not the same weary, even somewhat traumatized one who finally arrived in Cuyopilín three weeks later. Mack would never really be able to separate the memory of that journey from the bitter association of its ending, nor from some of its more disagreeable episodes along the way. Adventurous as his trek "across the continent" by riverboat and horseback was, Mack's own experience of it more closely resembled a mole's progress through an underworld of his own secret fears, disquiet, and loathing.

Mack could easily have written a travel memoir about that trip, though in later years he rarely spoke about it. So what should be told now? That nothing he'd ever heard from any of his compatriots prepared him for the beauty of the landscapes—everywhere flowers and birds of astonishing plumage, and jungle rivers full of alligators, and green paradisical valleys and dramatic volcanoes with the glowing sludge of lava and flames rising from their remote craters, and everywhere the Indios' humble cornfields climbing mountainsides into the clouds as if they were growing food for angels rather than humans. But nothing had prepared Mack for the country's abundant horrors either, which, whether natural or human, seemed to issue from the same malignant, inexplicable source . . . Steadily ascending a long trail of slippery clay through the forested cordillera in ink-black night and mountain fog, the trail abruptly ending at a steep precipice with nothing to alert the rider to the fatal plunge waiting just ahead: only his mare's ability to see in the dark and stubborn resolve not to take another step forward had saved Mack's life, though he'd sat atop her spurring and slapping like a drunk mounted upon a statue, until his *mozo*, his Indian porter, caught up, and gave a shout of warning (only green-eyed horses can see in the dark, the man who'd sold him the mare in Izabal had boasted, which Mack had dismissed as just a colorfully tropical version of the universally fraudulent character of horse sellers) . . . A forest village of pretty homes of white-washed adobe, with neatly thatched roofs, entirely abandoned to vampire bats at dusk, dead animals lying in the tall grass, and a terrible stench, and so many bats whirling in and out of the windows and doors of the tidy little huts that Mack didn't dare enter any even for a quick look, and though he and his mozo quickly escaped that village, an enormous bat alighted on the mare's rump and clung there while Mack, turned all the way around in his saddle like a trick rider in a Wild West show, scream frozen in his throat, swatted and jabbed at the hideous creature with his pistol until finally he dislodged it, the bat flying up on a brief geyser of blood . . . In another deserted but springlike and festive stretch of rural landscape, traveling through green meadows filled with noisy flocks of parakeets feasting on wild peach trees, Mack and his mozo came upon a dead Indian lying faceup in the road, his clothing on fire: smothering the flames with a blanket, tearing away smoking rags with their bare hands, Mack and the mozo quickly put out the fire. The nearly naked corpse was black with soot and burns but otherwise seemed free of wounds. His broad face, with serenely closed eyes and swollen lips slightly parted, looked peaceful, as if the flames hadn't hurt at all. He did not look much older than Mack. Who had set this Indio on fire and why? If they buried him and went on their way, his family might never learn his fate. But it seemed just as terrible to leave him to the vultures and wild animals. Mack and the mozo kept their vigil until nearly nightfall, when finally they agreed that there was nothing else for them to do but continue on their way.

A few days later, at the entrance to a busy little hilltop town where he planned to find food and lodging for the night, Mack had a distressing encounter with a group of drunken Indian soldiers. At first sight their mismatched, disheveled uniforms and the morose expressions with which they observed his approach did not seem ominous or even irregular in comparison to the dress and comportment of other soldiers he'd so far encountered. They were clustered outside a little guardhouse by a rustic wooden bridge spanning a roaring river. On the approach to the bridge, the road was muddy clay; on the other side, ascending into the town, it was paved with stones that resembled the shells of giant black beetles. Mack dismounted from his mare, removed his hat, and presented himself and his papers in the usual way, but the soldiers refused him permission to pass. They didn't demand bribes or ask that he pay exorbitant duties, as soldiers had been doing throughout his journey. When Mack called attention to his passport with its seal identifying him as a citizen of the United States of America, their mystifyingly belligerent attitudes were not in the least pacified. He gave his name as Mack Cody and challengingly held the passport out to them, having learned on his journey that it was extremely rare to find a soldier who would be able to read it. "I am a citizen of the United States of America," he announced in a strong voice—then, heeding a fearful intuition that they might steal or destroy it, he quickly put the passport away beneath his India-rubber poncho, and repeated, "My name is Mack Cody." One of the soldiers, as if diffidently attempting to pronounce what he'd just heard, responded, "Coatimundi?" That was the native name of a sort of jungle rodent with which, Mack allowed, the name Cody might be confused, and so he said, "No, pardon, it's *Cody*"—and now the soldier answered, in a querulous tone, "Sí pues, Señor Coatimundi," and another soldier chimed in accusingly, "Vos sos Indio Coatimundi, verdad?" The soldiers seemed to savor that nonsensical phrase, repeating *You are an Indio Coatimundi*, laughing like lunatics, asking again if he was an Indio

Coatmundi and threateningly shouting, "Sí o no? Contesta Señor!"—until
at last they all fell quiet, and Mack hoped that they were now going to
cease their appalling japing and let him continue into the town, and he was
searching for the correct words to renew the discussion when another soldier sullenly announced, "Vos sos mozo, verdád?" This soldier seemed to
be their leader, if only because he was taller and sturdier, his fixed gaze
and voice heavy with solemn authority, and the other soldiers echoed that
taunt, "Vos sos mozo," but without laughter now, and with something ag-
grieved in their stares, and they began to poke at him with the long barrels
of their outdated, rusted rifles, while Mack held up his hands and exasper-
atedly bellowed, "I am not a mozo, I am Mack Cody, a commercial traveler
from the United States of America." But the soldiers kept on saying, "Vos
sos mozo" and "Coatimundi" and poking him with their rifles and roughly
shoving him in the chest with their hands as he stumbled backward. It was
as if they were simply trying to make him turn around and go away, and
Mack did realize that such a retreat was his most sensible option. But his
legs felt weak from fear, and he was nearly nauseous with indignation,
which somehow made it impossible for him to do anything but continue his
preposterous show of stern civility, insisting that there must be a misun-
derstanding, that the soldiers must allow him to pass, or else take him to
their comandante and justify their behavior. But they kept on drunkenly
repeating their taunts, and poking, jabbing, shoving. Mack, growing wea-
rier, calmer, and noticing the first fireflies of dusk in the brush alongside
the road and realizing that this might continue without any change deep
into the night unless he gave up, finally decided to do just that, mount his
mare and retreat while maybe there was time to find another village with
food and lodging, however primitive, and he even signaled his disengage-
ment by holding up his hands and taking a firm step backward. Just then
the mozo appeared, carrying Mack's heavy trunk on his back, supported by
a thick leather strap running across his forehead; the mozo was also leading the mule packed with the rest of Mack's supplies, which, on account
of the mule's rebelliousness, it had taken them nearly all morning to load.
The soldiers rushed at Mack's mozo and knocked him to the ground. With
clumsy-looking but determined brutality, they kicked and punched the
mozo about his head and face, and pummeled him with their rifles. Before
Mack could decide how to react—whether to take advantage of this mo-

ment when they were concentrating their fury on the mozo to run away and seek help, or to risk shouting for help right now—two soldiers turned and grabbed the mule by its halter and pitched it over the riverbank with such force that for a split second the mule hovered weightlessly in the air, ears straight up like a hare's, then crashed down into the rushing water. Mack stepped forward and struck the soldier who seemed to be the leader, his fist landing solidly on his ear, and the stunned soldier dropped to his knees, and then remained there like a penitent, head bowed and blood trickling from his ear. But the others were still torturing the mozo, whose wailing screams of pain were mixed with the strangled screeching and thrashing of the crippled mule in the rushing river. Mack had an intuition and pulled the Colt .45 out from under his poncho and, in imitation of a murderous desperado of the Wild West in a dime novel, sharply called out for the soldiers' attention, sneered, and aimed his cocked pistol deliberately at each in turn—his intuition was that their old rifles were not loaded, or were useless as firing weapons. He commanded them to flee—Vete! Zape!—but they remained standing over the felled mozo, mostly gazing back at Mack over their shoulders. He whirled and fired two shots down into his crippled and drowning mule, and when he turned back to face his tormentors they were all running away, down the road and away from the village.

Mack felt no pride in this sordid victory. He ached with pity for his quiet Indio mozo—this one's name was Pedro—who was so badly beaten his eyes were swollen shut. Like every other traveler, Mack was required to pay the authorities of each town he passed through for an Indio mozo to carry his baggage as far as the next town with mozos for hire. So far, all of his mozos had been good fellows, and his first mozo, hired at Izabal, had even taught him how to ride the horse he'd purchased there, a worn but reliable see-in-the-dark mare, though set in her ways, stubbornly stopping for a mouthful of grass whenever she wanted no matter how hard Mack pulled on the reins. He was hardly happy to have lost the mule and, with it, some of his luggage. The incident had been in every way degrading, and he was deeply unsettled by it, and felt filled with a heavy despair he lacked words for. Were these the famous lessons of travel? With a handkerchief, he tried to clean the blood from the mozo's face. His medicine kit had been lost in the river with the mule, but it so happened that in a pocket, as a good luck charm commemorating his decisive epiphany in New York, he carried a tin of the famous petroleum jelly, and he rubbed some on the mozo's battered eyes and face. The trunk was too heavy for Mack to carry in his own arms up the steep road into the village, and there was no way for him to load it onto the back of his mare, but his mozo, still prostrate in the road, was obviously too injured to resume. Mack knew that the decent and compassionate thing for him to do now would be to carry his own trunk up into the town, even if he had to do so in the beast-of-burden manner of a mozo. The possibility of assuming the mozo's load after the soldiers had just taunted Mack as a mozo filled him, of course, with some revulsion— but also with a defiant and willful compulsion, an odd sensation of irresistible anticipation there was only one way to satisfy.

He sat down in the road and experimented with the strap, a long leather oval, until he'd readjusted it across the bottom of the trunk, and then positioned the small of his back against the trunk as he'd so often seen mozos do. He took off his hat, lifted the sweat-blackened loop over his forehead, and slowly pushed himself to his feet, feeling the weight pulling his head backward as if to snap his neck; he grabbed the strap on both sides, pulled up on the bottom of the trunk, and lurch-leaned forward just enough to balance it. "Pedro, get up," he said. Mack nudged the mozo with his boot and almost fell over from the shift in weight. The mozo stood silently swaying and staring at Mack through the narrow slits of his swollen eyes, to which the petroleum jelly gave a lurid aspect. "You take the horse," said Mack. "Pedro, please, get on the horse." And Mack began his staggering climb up into the town, the strap across his forehead and the heavy trunk on his back, while Pedro slowly moved ahead atop the mare. When he neared the entrance to the town there were people, and Mack felt a burst of humiliation. He set the trunk down by a whitewashed, mossy wall and rested against it with his eyes closed. Of course he realized what a curious and even suspicious spectacle he and the mounted, blood-caked, jelly-greased mozo must be, and he wished there was no need to explain to the townspeople who they were, or what had happened, or that he needed lodging and a fresh mozo to carry his trunk. He wished he could just remain standing against the wall with his eyes closed and fall asleep listening to the peaceful sounds of the town and the forest and the evening cacophony of the birds and the river rushing around his murdered mule far below, and go on deeply breathing the night air, so deliciously and invitingly smoky from so many humble cooking fires.

Later that night Mack couldn't rid himself of a feeling of sorrow over the entire incident at the bridge—*a mute sorrow*, a fancy poetic phrase he'd heard somewhere—a sorrow that could not explain itself. Mack missed the comforts of home, he understood that: his mother's affection, the stove, a hot bowl of stew on a winter night; perhaps it was only his loneliness and nostalgia that allowed these probably routine incidents of travel to amplify into such a dark mood of crisis—incidents, after all, that he might one day be able to laugh at, or recall with virile pride. That night, Mack sat down to the usual grim dinner of the corn griddle cakes called *tortillas,* a food that he'd heard his mother recall countless times, but that she never made in New York (tortillas were much more palatable, Mack had discovered, if one toasted them directly over the fire until they were a crisp brown, charred around the edges), and black beans cooked in a rancid lard, and eggs, and the drink the natives called coffee, or *un cafecito,* made from coffee beans burned in a pot until reduced to a tarry black tincture and kept in bottles corked with corncob, from which drops were spilled into boiled water to brew a bitter, insipid concoction. Afterward Mack went directly to his bed, that is, lay atop what passed for a bed—a hard wooden bench, chickens roosting underneath—in the *posada* where he'd found lodging, in a filthy room that he also shared with his wounded mozo, a pack of restless, flea-infested dogs, and several members of the landlords' family, including a great-grandmother with the dreadful hair of a dissolute hag, who in the middle of the night got out of her hammock and sat on a small stool, her withered breasts exposed, taking turns smoking a cigar with a naked little girl of no more than six. Lying awake, Mack confronted again the riddle of his mute sorrow. It was as if the Indio soldiers at the bridge had not been human. It was as if they were made of mud and straw. As if it had been a supernatural encounter. How else to explain their subhuman brutality? And he wished that they had not been human, he wished that they had been some other thing that one could kill without needing to confess it to a priest afterward, or even to feel remorse.

Of course they had thought he was an Indio too, they had called him *Indio Coatimundi* and *mozo.* Soon Mack wasn't even noticing landscapes, flora and fauna, or making his usual inquiries about business opportunities.

He saw only Indios watching him wherever he went, or saw himself watching Indios, or saw non-Indios scrutinizing the Indio in him, and heard something deep inside himself wailing like a cruelly abandoned child. As a game of mental self-torture, he imagined himself dressed in Indio clothing, and slipping easily into their village lives. Yes, he would pretend he really was mute, until he learned their language and ways. He would teach himself to be civilized and uncivilized inside his single mind at the same time. Would he then be a success, a leader, among the Indios?—having the advantage of his New York education and skills, knowing what he knew about bookkeeping and clerking, and being able to converse about the interesting engineering details concerning the spectacular new bridge being built to join Manhattan and Brooklyn? Mack even tried to imagine himself as one of the drunken Indio soldiers outside the town who'd felt such brutal rage at the sight of the Indio-featured traveler, with his Yankee Doodle manners and accent, giving his name as Mack Cody: yes, he could imagine feeling provoked, but he still considered their behavior unforgivable.

When he saw Indio children picking and eating lice from each other's hair he felt the return of his mute sadness, like a trumpet repeatedly blasting one long, sorrowful, silent note inside his chest. But nothing in his life as a fairly dutiful Catholic in Brooklyn had prepared Mack for the spectacle inside the dirt-floored churches, the crudely carved and painted statues and dolls which the Indios worshipped with a grotesque pagan devotion that seemed to have nothing to do with the mortal death and eternal life of our Savior. The tin shrines and crude altars decorated with evergreen branches and rank-smelling fruits and flowers; the black-magic smoke pouring from censors swung by wizardlike old men; the old men chanting prayers and filling their mouths with aguardiente and spitting into the sputtering fires at their feet; the votive and devotional candles covering the dirt floors like lined-up armies of self-immolating toy soldiers; the starving skeleton-dogs wandering in and eating the candles; and the Indias on their knees wailing their drunken-sounding prayers: all of it filled him with a tight-lipped shame and a heart like rain in a dark swamp.

But didn't the praying, kneeling women look beautiful too, in their long loose blouses woven with colorful symbols and patterns, the long red ribbons in which they wound their long black hair into a disc atop their heads, or into a long braid down their backs? Aren't they beautiful too? Come on now, Mack, you know they are! Did the beautiful Indian girls see in him, whenever he rode into a new pueblo, a handsome and mysterious Indio stranger who might capture the heart of the prettiest girl and take her away, or settle down there and marry her? Did they see any such thing when Mack rode into town in his India-rubber poncho, on his green-eyed mare, with his mozo following somewhere behind?

In church he interrupted an India, a young and pretty maiden, and frankly asked what it was she perceived in the unrecognizable crude wooden doll she was worshipping with such devotion; she smiled delicately at Mack, but she could not speak Spanish. Another India standing nearby could, a little, and she told him that the statue was San Antonio and that it had a soul—maybe she said it was the soul of winds, or that the wind was a soul disguised as the wind, or maybe Mack heard all wrong, but there was enchantment in that moment, her softly enunciated attempt to explain, the kind and honest gleam in her eyes, and though he barely understood, it made him feel better. The tight fist inside him relaxed a little. As he rode off into the twilight, he felt the stirrings of fascination, a cautious revival of his traveler's interest in all he saw around him. From now on, Mack vowed, he would watch and listen to the Indios carefully. He would try to keep following this wispy trail of fascination. But it was only fascination. Wasn't it just like wishing he knew the names of all the fantastic birds, flowers, and trees?

And the Indian girls bathing naked in the rivers and pools, with their lithe, graceful figures, and their breasts, and their lack of shame before a stranger gaping from the bank atop his mare, their shy but unguarded smiles; how could he not feel a racial pride in their firm and supple beauty? Here was a beauty that deserved to be displayed among the forty beauties of forty nations at any international exposition! He could not imagine that his own mother had ever bathed this way, but perhaps she had, perhaps his own father had once stood on a riverbank, looking down upon the bathing jungle nymph who would soon become Mack's mother. And that girl, that half-Indian half-Yankee wild girl in Don Juan Aparicio's story? Did she look like this without her clothes? Wouldn't that be a fine thing, an India who was also a Yankee, who looked like one of those bathing girls, with firm buttery-brown breasts and even darker nipples silently sharing with him— as he watched from atop his mare—their shy wish to fly through the air to his lips! Thinking how when he reached Cuyopilín he would tell Salomón about what he'd just imagined, Mack laughed out loud, his first moment of robust joy the entire journey.

Nearly everywhere he went Mack also found Yankees and Europeans, the majority of these foreigners as far from being rich coffee planters as he was. This town had a drunken blacksmith from Maine, who nevertheless made a fine job of reshoeing Mack's exhausted mare; that town had a post-master from Kentucky, with whom Mack mailed terse letters to Mr. Jacobo Baiz and his mother; this one a telegraph operator from Scotland, who tapped out Mack's telegram to the telegraph office in the port of Champerico, hoping it might be delivered from there to Salomón Nahón in Cuyopilín. Mack found himself meditating on a long-ago and unhappy incident that, before this journey, he'd had little reason to recall. As a small boy he'd been taken by his mother to a Bowery dime museum to see a captured Mayan Indian Chief and his two little children from the recently discovered hidden Central American city of Ixmaya, deep in the jungle, where the Maya still lived as they had in the days before Columbus. The little boys and the Chief all wore long white smocks, and the boys' hair was cut short so that they looked like altar boys, but the Chief's hair fell to his shoulders, and he wore an erect crown of green parrot feathers, and was holding a spear, and all three stood upon a small elevated stage with a painted backdrop of stone pyramids and palm trees, above which flew colorful birds with long, undulant tail feathers. The youngest of the little boys was about Mack's age, and he remembered recognizing the resemblance of his color and features to his own, and feeling a tense relief that both boys looked so healthy and cheerful. The Mayan Chief began to deliver an impressive lecture about life in Ixmaya and the brave young American explorers who'd discovered the secret capital, yet his words excited loud hooting and mocking hilarity from the audience, utterly bewildering Mack, who did not then understand that the cause of the uproar was that the Chief spoke in the baritone voice and accent of a practiced Yankee thespian. The Chief's speech was a terrible debacle, yet the captive little boys went on smiling merrily, while Mack turned into a tiny, tightly lidded cauldron of fury. And looking down from the stage while answering the audience with ribald-sounding taunts of his own, the Mayan Chief's eyes alighted on Mack's mother, and he smiled at her, and then smiled right at Mack, and then the Chief, his expression salacious and amused, said—and there was no mistaking his words, or whom they were directed at—"Why don't you and your son, Madame Señora, come up here onstage so that we might all make one happy family together?" And Mack, plunged into the most complete incomprehension by the bizarre remark, gaped up at the stage, but then his mother, her head down, was pulling him away by the arm, aggressively using her shoulder to open a path through the roaring crowd. And in all the years since, he and his mother had very rarely mentioned that incident, and then only in order to jokingly recall it as one of those preposterous humbugs so popular in New York.

Three weeks into his journey, Mack came over a final mountain ridge late one afternoon and looked down upon the most splendid landscape he'd yet seen, a vast vista he felt as if he was actually hovering over like a hawk: the densely planted, dark green slopes and folds of the coffee piedmont at his feet, and spread out far beneath that, the forests, grasslands, and sugar plantations of the lowland plain, a vastness of infinite shades of green interrupted, here and there, by oasislike villages—one of which must be Cuyopilín—and the white cupolas of churches, and shafts of golden light shining down on the plain through breaks in the clouds, and rivers and streams running to the Pacific, and beyond it all the hammered-silver shimmer of the wide ocean merging into the high haze of the curving horizon.

When he reached Cuyopilín it was night. A whitewashed wooden arch stood over the entrance to a long dirt road lined with the slim trunks of almond trees. The wafting smell of smoke, and firelight through the slats of huts, and tireless village children, running, shrieking, flashing through the darkness and trees as if through the viewing slots of a zoetrope, and the shadowy figures of adults never running, and of a young couple deep in the trees like sentries at the entrance to their own shadowy forest, and the glinting eyes of dogs, and muffled voices drifting out through the hot nighttime air, which always feels so buoyant compared to the daytime heat, mixing with the heavy green smells and the placid barking of the dogs and pulsating insect and frog noise—Mack loved riding into such a village at night, like just another shadow moving through the dark, though now he felt as if there must be a warm red lamp glowing in his excited chest. He asked a boy just inside the gate for the home of Salomón Nahón. But the boy gazed up at him with a ghastly smile, and Mack said, "Don't worry, I'm a friend," and the boy pointed down the long dirt road, and turned and ran back into the dark, and Mack hadn't ridden very far ahead before he heard that familiar ripple of village voices spreading the news of a stranger's arrival behind him, except he noticed something different this time, as if trapped inside those voices there was now a frantic beating of many tiny wings; and he felt uneasy.

And then he was standing by his mare in front of the darkened house with the three Nahón brothers, one of them holding a lantern, all in white trousers and collarless shirts, as if they were just home from a day in the office, one with a long beard and the other with his beard clipped short, both standing stiffly and looking not at Mack but past him into the night, as if each had a hand on a tiller during a dangerous passage at sea. Fortunato was holding the cork helmet in his hands, flipping it upside down to show Mack how Salomón's blood had coated the inside of the crown and spread to the underside of the brim, while in a voice rough with grief he explained that Salomón hadn't come home one night, and that they had found him in the morning just over there, beyond the orange trees, his cleanly severed head resting inside this helmet, which had been placed next to the torso. —A machete probably, maybe a very sharp knife or even an ax. Well, you know how it sometimes goes here, Señor Mack. If it isn't fever it's bandits, or some jealous son of a whore. Perhaps we will never know. Perhaps, one day, we will know.

Salomón Nahón had been murdered some nine months before, not long after Mack had received his last letter. Yes, Mack's telegram from Cobán had arrived. Yes, Salomón had spoken about him. The brothers' manner with Mack was tepid. Stay for the night, they offered; you can't go riding off at this hour. Mack told himself: They hate this country now. Around them stood the people of the village, including the schoolteacher Rubén Abensur and his wife, the India Felipa, all observing with owl-like eyes the anguished and awkward scene. How many of them were Salomón's half siblings? Which was his little son, Máximo? Later, whenever Mack tried to remember back through the cloud of sadness and fear still enveloping those moments, his memory saw curly-haired young Indios like melancholy cherubs carved into a mahogany lintel of forest and night.

In the morning, the middle brother, León, walked with Mack out to where Salomón was buried, near the graves of his mother, Estercita, and sister, Gracia. Like the other two, Salomón's was a small grave of white-washed cement, a few stones laid on top. Mack would add his own stone, linger at the grave awhile, and then be on his way. The Nahóns had not invited him to stay any longer. But León gave him a sack of oranges and offered to be of help in any way he could for the remainder of Mack's stay in the country. Did Mack know his plans yet? Mack answered that he was headed to the capital, and would do a good deal of thinking there, and beyond that had not yet decided anything. But a mad idea had occurred to Mack in the middle of the night, and now, at Salomón's grave, it spilled from him:

"Don León, I never had any brother in my life but Salomón. I would be willing to do everything in my power, anything you might ask of me, including take the name Nahón as my own, Don León, to fulfill the expectations you and your brothers had for Salomón. After all, I already understand the coffee trade. I was a rising clerk under Señor Jacobo Baiz, and I know he would attest to my abilities and character. And I've just ridden alone across this country, and am beginning to learn what it takes to master living here."

For a long time León was silent. Mack couldn't tell if he was thinking his offer over, or of something else entirely, something that caused a slight smile to flicker at the corner of his lips. Finally León gave him a soft clap on the shoulder and asked, "Señor Mack, were you being a good brother to Salomón by pursuing that muchacha, that Reyna Salom, after he left New York? I know Salomón felt betrayed. He received a letter from Reyna."

Never before had it been made so clear to Mack that his perception of reality could be so opposite from that of others. At first he was too stunned to feel anything but a trite, face-scalding embarrassment. Why was he so often nagged by the sense that his understanding of emotional events was always superficial, as if others knew how to go on turning page after page in that mysterious book, while he remained forever stuck at the one with a promising but probably misleading title? He stood looking from León to the grave and out past the treetops at the blue morning sky. When he spoke, he was surprised at how his voice trembled: "I didn't realize, after

Salomón left, that Reyna still interested him. No one ever said anything to me. Honestly, Don León."

After a moment, León chuckled dryly. "Pues, he forgot about it too after a while, I think. But, at any rate, as I suspect you already know, it's not as if Salomón didn't have a great many young relatives to choose from, here in Cuyopilín, if it was our intention to select a . . . someone to inherit Salomón's role. But as soon as the winter rains begin, my brother Fortunato is going back to Tangier to find himself a new wife." León shrugged. "Yes, Señor Mack, that's right, my brother is determined to begin all over again."

But when they were walking from the orchard to the stable where Mack's horse was waiting, León returned to the subject again: "Fortunato wants to start a new family. But who knows how much longer we can survive in our business? The Nahóns cannot just become mule breeders! It is getting more and more difficult to sell our wares to the European coffee planters, Señor Mack. It is the European way of doing business, you see. The Europeans have figured out how to link the coffee trade to their own shipping and commercial enterprises. Señor Mack, the German and British shipping lines and trading houses have their own resident wholesale merchants here now, and to the German and British farmers, they offer long-term credit at low interest. Yes, they make loans to the coffee farmers in advance of their harvests, very generous loans—and so what happens? The farmers are obligated to buy only German and British goods from those same merchants in return. As you know, that's not the American way of doing things, or our way. How can we compete, Señor Mack, when loyalties built up over years suddenly don't matter anymore? Perhaps it is just that the Americans are still far behind the European maritime and commercial powers in these matters, and will catch up. The Americans build splendid ships, but they haven't learned to coordinate their trade in the European way, Señor Mack. Merchants don't even want to ship merchandise with the Americans because they say even their packing is shoddy, and that goods will arrive ruined. Do you know, Señor Mack, that there are merchants here who still import goods made in the United States via Liverpool and Hamburg ? Yes, all the way over there, on British and German ships, with British and German packing, and then back across to Central America, even if it means going through the Straits of Magellan or around Cape Horn."

MACK'S LAST TANGIBLE remnant of his connection to Salomón Nahón and the initial promise and dream of "The Return" was María de las Nieves, the half-Indio, half-Yankee girl in the story he and Salomón had heard Don Juan Aparicio recount one night in Jacobo Baiz's office, when he'd spoken with such amused and paternal affection about the intelligent little wild girl he'd rescued from the jungle. In *retrospect*, with the aid of *hindsight*, this was clear to Mack, though he also sometimes heard another voice inside warning that in the end he would be forced to admit that, really, this connection, this infatuation, his solid and unfounded devotion, was all just a desperate fabrication, the strained figment of a lost soul, one doomed to a lonely life. Maybe someone else, such as his rival Wellesley Bludyar, would someday reveal yet another version of this story, and Mack would once again be forced to realize that what he thought, or at least hoped, he perceived was actually the reverse of truth.

After they had listened to Don Juan Aparicio's story that night, Mr. Baiz had invited him and Salomón to a nearby saloon for a glass of beer; he wanted to talk to them about Don Juan's astonishing offer to purchase his firm. And there Salomón had turned to Mack and said, "Wouldn't that be an excellent sort of woman, for either you or me, Mack, a half India who is also half Yankee? But only if she was really at home in both worlds, as you and I are, because you would not want her to be half India in blood, Mack, and not in civilization. But of course I have to marry a woman of my own religion. So she is yours, if you can get her to leave that convent in which Don Juan says she has hidden herself. Jajaja. And I'll keep after Reyna." And the two boys had laughed and clinked their glasses.

It didn't matter that María de las Nieves was not in the least interested in him. If you are going to live in an imaginary world, Mack told himself, then you have to inhabit it all the way, until you make it real to yourself, or else surrender it to oblivion. You have to prepare yourself for the moment when the right words will be spoken, and everything might change. You have to search for those words beforehand, and keep them ready in your heart's pocket. You don't know when the moment will come, but you have to anticipate it always, and guide it toward you. Maybe Mack, in the haunted frustration of this long and tragically aborted Return, really was going a little-little mad. But in his strategies, he did not lack all good sense. He knew from the bootblacks in the Parque de la Concordia that for a while following their abrupt encounter there, María de las Nieves had avoided the reading room kiosk. So as not to run into him again, he suspected, with a pang of self-pity. What other reason could she have for avoiding the reading room, if before she had come almost daily? Then he'd learned from the bootblacks that she was again going to the reading room kiosk, but that now she always made her little servant sit inside with her. It would be an impertinence, and most undignified, Mack understood, to ambush María de las Nieves there again. So, while his frustration over not encountering her anywhere else gnawed at his patience and sense of not-very-well-being, he avoided the reading room in the Parque de la Concordia.

That last morning when he'd seen her there, María de las Nieves had fled with a page torn from *El Progreso;* later that same day, at the Immigration Society, Mack had examined an intact copy, and found the article about José Martí and the poetry tertulia, and the little announcement about the composition class. That art which so elevates the merit of women. He'd puzzled over her reasons for so frantically and furtively making off with that page of the newspaper. Well, because of the Cuban, obviously. But why covet this particular article? Was it just the mention of his name, or was it the announcement of the evening class? Mack guessed it was the latter, and then he learned from Don José Pryzpyz that she was indeed enrolled. "María de las Nieves," the Hebrew umbrella mender informed him, "has a deep appreciation for poetry and literature, learned in the convent. She always carries a book in her purse, you know, Mack. And if you ask her what she does with her nights, or on any Sunday, she is more likely to tell you that she has been reading than anything else, and that the dawn often surprises her deep in the reading of some book."

Mack had answered, "Apart from going to church, and the cockfights and bullfights, I can't imagine what else a proper young woman, living here without any family, can find to do on a Sunday, Don José. It's not as if she can go to the Bola de Oro baths and stand around in lukewarm water, smoking a cigar and conversing with the other gentlemen about the cockfights."

He knew that around the capital young José Martí was now commonly referred to as "Dr. Torrente," often in a tone of respectful affection but sometimes derisively. In the Café de Paris, Martí was often talked about; he was in *la boca de la gente*. Yankees were universally indifferent to the topic of the Cuban, of course, but Spaniards, for example, were not; and *chapines*, as countrymen were called here, seemed especially fixated. Often they were young men of the freethinking sort who had been to meetings and parties with Dr. Torrente, to recitals of poetry and oratory, or who had attended his lectures as students. Señor Martí was lecturing, Mack half understood, in a number of different subjects at the university, but he was also teaching in the new Normal School, whose director was another Cuban exile, an eminent educator recruited from New York by the Liberal government. All that, and an evening class in composition for young ladies. How could such a young man—a chunk of his youth lost to prison— have already learned enough to teach so many different courses, and still have time leftover to make himself the subject of so much awed and jealous conversation about everything else he did? Martí had even met with the President General, and with his most important government ministers, and now he'd been entrusted with writing new legal codes, or something of similarly grave importance, and he'd also been commissioned to compose a patriotic verse play about the Indios, and he was also starting a literary journal called *The Future*. So, as anyone who'd witnessed his debut at Chafandín's fantasy party could easily have predicted, the Cuban was enjoying a great success—which did not in the least trouble Mack; on the contrary, the higher the Cuban rose, the less likely he was to ever get in Mack's way.

It was said that the Cuban was engaged to a wealthy Cuban woman who was awaiting him in Mexico, and that at the end of the year he was returning there to wed. But that was still months away, plenty of time left for Dr. Torrente to embroil himself in a scandal that would lower him before even the most worshipful eyes. The gossip attaching itself to the Cuban's name was of the sort one always heard in the Café de Paris, which was, after all, a brothel, and even if it was a first-class brothel, you couldn't expect the men playing dice at the bar to actually spend their nights in informed argument over the new legal code, or thinking up clever verses for a patriotic ode to the Indios. Mack wasn't particularly surprised by the gossip he heard there about Martí, except that it was gossip to which someone now and then added a strikingly sneering or reproachful comment; it was not every day that men in a brothel would express such moral indignation over another young man's romantic escapades! But the Cuban was not supposed to be ordinary in any way. Apparently he generally carried on and presented himself as a man of superior morality; at least that was how he struck many people. Have you ever heard Dr. Torrente speak? went a typical tirade at the crowded brothel bar. Why, sometimes he sounds like one of our own proudly atheistic new materialists, though one who speaks with the voice of Orpheus! And then the next time your hear him, he sounds like a priest who wants to be an ascetic saint, talking of purity and sacrifice and all of that. I have actually heard Martí proclaim during a lecture: I know the soul exists because I know I have one, I feel it. He feels his soul, but he is just as adamant that it is the Church that has most held our societies back, that before the Liberals, this city was only a warehouse of monks and nuns, and that the priesthood is immorality incarnate. And so he applauds every measure that this government takes, as if we are living in a revolution as profound as that of France or the United States of America. And don't let him get started on the subject of la madre patria and Cuba, whatever you do! —Don't let him get started? Ja! Now that's impossible! —But he'll make you weep for that solitary star as if were your own!—It was as if whenever the voluble Cuban's name came up in the Café de Paris, the men sounded womanly and in love, or else their voices were thick with envy and malice.

So what if Dr. Torrente was said to be conducting at least two love affairs—anyone could name any number of respectable men said to be carrying on more than that number at the same time, and you could put old Chafandín's name at the very top of that list! But General García Granados's adolescent daughter was one of the women the Cuban was said to be conducting a love affair with—that also came as little surprise to Mack—and another was said to be the wife of a respected Liberal magistrate. But what else can he do? protested the Cuban's defenders. Damas and doncellas throw themselves at Pepe Martí! A hot-blooded young man, from the hedonistic city of La Habana, enjoying his last months of freedom before marriage! —But a virginal niña from a family of the very highest social rank, no matter how libertine the reputation of her household, and also a respected magistrate's wife—who dares seduce women like that?!

Only a shameless and amoral interloper, lacking all respect and under-standing of our ways! —Yet Chafandín and Martí play chess together nearly every day! —A poet should not be a devourer, but among the devoured; the other night I heard Martí speak those very words. Don't you see? Martí is no crass seducer, he is among the devoured! And Doña Carlota Marcorís, moving in to shepherd the men's attention toward her idle prostitutes, singing out, Gentleman and gossip, two things no first-class House of Tol-erance can do without, but there are other things it cannot do without! —Such as Colonel Pratt! an anonymous voice impertinently called out. Doña Carlota's monopoly on licensed brothels was protected by Colonel Pratt, the new police chief from New York, who had any of her competitors arrested and ordered his police—in their new uniforms of navy blue frock coats with brass buttons and celluloid collars and white gloves—to hunt down any girl who escaped from any of her houses and drag her back to Doña Carlota. *Rosefingers,* that was what people now called the police, their white gloves fragrant and stained with the rouge and cheap perfume of captured runaway whores. Colonel Pratt was building himself a home in the center of the city, on land that had once been part of the orchard of the Convent de la Concepción, neighbor to the magnificent mansion already raised on another portion of that land by the Minister of War.

And who would ever have imagined men in a brothel actually pronounc-ing, and with such malevolent conviction, such phrases as *class in literary composition for women* and *Academia de Niñas de Centroamérica?* It turned out that María García Granados was a student in that class along with María de las Nieves; according to the gossiping caballeros the girls' academy was one of the main stages upon which the scandal was being played. María de las Nieves could moon over the learned Cuban all she wanted—Mack had nothing to fear from that quarter!

One afternoon, when the rainy season had begun and he was in an espe-cially gloomy mood, and had been out walking in his India-rubber poncho with a secondhand umbrella purchased from Don José, his high-crowned black fedora pulled down low over his eyes, indifferent to the crashing downpour, Mack found himself crossing the picturesque but nearly flooded Parque de la Concordia, with its Parisian-style kiosks and gardens and drowning clipped-wing tropical fowl, and he stared across the street at the British Legation, sullenly imagining her sitting inside with the portly First

Secretary, giggling together like cozy lovers and eating British crackers from one of those tin boxes emblazoned with an image of the dour Queen. Seized by a morbid nostalgia, like a war veteran who can't help but return to the sight of a crushing defeat, Mack allowed his sloshing steps to lead him toward the reading room kiosk, his thoughts formulating, as if for the understanding of a dull but questioning student, his own intention to just sit inside it for a while, because that was the last place he'd spoken to her, nearly two months ago, and today he just wanted to sit there. He closed his umbrella, stepped through the door and there she was, seated at one of the writing desks, María de las Nieves, with her little servant in a chair pulled up alongside, both wrapped in black cloaks, reading a newspaper together. The servant, lifting her sharp gaze, instantly recognized him. He had time for one fast decision, only *one*—and that was to speak in Spanish, in the politest national manner.

"Excuse me, Señoritas," Mack calmly proceeded. "I thought this reading room would be empty. With your kind permission, if you will be so fine, I am going to sit here a little-little-while and read the little-newspaper, until the little-rain passes."

María de las Nieves, glancing up indifferently, did not recognize him, or gave no sign that she did. Her servant said, "It is not a little rain, Señor. It is practically a hurricane." María de las Nieves sighed in annoyance and said, "María, ya," and then, as Mack averted his face, staring down at the ground, she politely answered, "Of course, Señor. Very amiable, thank you. We understand."

And Mack said, "Thank you, Señoritas. Very amiable as well, and also, so fine. Thank you." He stepped out of the puddle forming around his feet, placed his umbrella in the stand next to the one that was already there (bright blue silk, a whalebone handle with inlaid silver sunflower, the birthday gift its craftsman, Don José, had proudly described to him), and he strode to the other writing desk, pulled out the chair, sat, opened a newspaper, stared at it, not even daring to remove his hat, and pictured himself as a muscular racing horse with a wildly beating heart being perfectly restrained at the starting gate by a most able jockey. Mack remained in that position for an eternity, without reading a word of the newspaper, while he rehearsed his conversation, which he knew might be the last he would ever have with her if it was not effective.

Without any word of introduction or explanation, María de las Nieves, in a dramatic whisper, began reading aloud to her servant: "The correspondent of the French Havre agency in Saratoff, Russia, reports that there, in the past year, wolves have devoured thirty-seven thousand sheep, eleven thousand horses, ten thousand oxen and cows, five thousand pigs, and eighteen thousand barnyard birds. Sixty-eight people have been attacked, twelve of them killed, and three eaten. Doesn't it appear humorous to our readers that Europeans think Central America is savage?—*ja.*"

The pretty servant inhaled in noisy horror, exhaled a "Dios mí-í-í-o!" and said something in an Indian language, which made María de las Nieves quietly giggle.

Mack now removed his hat and said, "The telegraph and the modern newspaper have made the world so much smaller. It is as if the world is now one great city. Señoritas, the newspaper makes us all citizens of the country called Progress." He nodded, firmly and sagely, and added, "Wherever newspapers are published, people now live in continuous discussion of issues great and small, at least as compared to before—that is even true of this Republic."

María de las Nieves looked up at him, and though this was the first time her delightful glower had ever been so intently aimed his way, Mack did not quail beneath it, but steadily observed the series of subtle shifts and transitions in her expression. If her facial features—her tiny, flared nose—were not so delicate, perhaps her astonishment and dismay would have seemed more daunting. Whatever thoughts were passing through her mind as she studied him, he would not assume they were terrible; he would not assume—

"Why do you speak English?" she finally asked. "And with that accent?"

These were more or less the words he had foreseen, and he had his answer ready: "I grew up in New York City. Where did you learn *your* English, Señorita Moran?"

She waited, as if doing some rehearsing of her own, before answering in carefully enunciated English: "Because my father was an American, from New York also, and I learned to speak English from him on our coffee farm, before he died. And I was cared for by a nanny from British Honduras, and later, in the convent, I had a teacher who was also from New York. So I've always been able to practice my English. Now I work at the British Legation, which I believe you already know."

"Yes, at General García Granados's fantasy party, it was mentioned, of course. You were also born in New York?"

"No. I was born in the Yucatán. My father managed a henequen estate there."

"In New York," he said, "I was a clerk in the coffee-trading company owned by Mr. Jacobo Baiz, who is now this government's consul in that city. I was given the great opportunity to work for him because of a connection of family to Don Sínforoso Revolorio, who for many years was the Conservative regime's Chargé de Affaires in the United States. So I also am familiar with the atmosphere of diplomacy." He silently counted to five, then added, "My mother was his cook. Don Sínforoso saw to it that I received the same education as any American boy. You said, I remember, that you also lived on a cochineal estate in Amatitlán, which your father also managed."

"Yes, of course," she said quietly, glancing out the door at the vapory rain. "María, we should be off now. "

"But we only have one umbrella, Doña Nievecitas."

"You are welcome to borrow my umbrella," said Mack. "Recently repaired by my great friend Don José Pryzpyz." That was too much, and his smile was too broad—his first mistake, but he quickly reestablished his air of thoughtful reserve. "You know, I recently went out to Amatitlán, to see, for my own curiosity, the old cochineal estates. Have you been back there?"

"No, Señor."

"It was a very interesting trip. You can learn a lot by studying the ruins of an old trade, just as you can learn worthy lessons about our people today by studying the much more ancient ruins left by our American ancestors. Don't you think that is true? But I am not so interested in antiquities, oh, not really; I am interested in modern business. Extraordinary, though, what a delicate and complex enterprise cochineal farming is, Señorita Moran."

"I really don't remember anything about it, Señor." She shifted in her chair as if preparing herself to go. "I was a very small child."

"Well, no doubt you would have been proud of your father's mastery of cochineal farming. There are still a few of the old plantations hanging on now. They sell most of their harvest to the Indios, who use it to dye their wool. But the highest-quality insects are still bought by the Vatican. The beautiful scarlet of Cardinals' caps, that still comes from our Central American cochineal. Also it is used to color some powders that women use on their faces; I'm sure you could tell me which ones—" He waited, and when it was clear she was not going to tell him which ones, he continued: "If you went out to Amatitlán, Señorita Moran, I'm sure any of the remaining farmers would happily give you a tour. Who knows, maybe some of them even remember your father, and would be happy to share some anecdotes. I stayed two days, and learned so much from them. I'd wager I even saw the farm, or the ruins of the farm, that you were born on."

"Doña Nievecitas was born in the Yucatán," interrupted the little servant.

"Of course. Pardon me. I meant where you spent some of your earliest years, Señorita. Was it by the lake, do you know?" In truth, nobody had spoken well of Timothy Moran, and if there was unfairness in that, it was only to the degree that the circumstances surrounding his hurried departure from Amatitlán had obliterated any positive memories of the man they had known before.

The rain kept up its steady clatter on the kiosk's conical roof and the mud and paving outside. María de las Nieves and María Chon sat stiffly shoulder to shoulder listening to Mack as he began to expound on cochineal, down to the most arcane details of the obscure and vanishing trade. A seemingly incautious strategy, but he knew what he was doing. Mack was showing her some of the very best traits to be found in the temperament and ambitions of the northern Yankee (traits, he thought, she might even be telling herself her father must have possessed). He was putting on display some of the purposeful, stolid, even heroically tedious energy indispensable in any man who is really going to found and maintain a business capable of lifting himself and a bride up from low origins into a situation of secure prosperity. This was a long-planned tactical conversation that Mack was now embarked on—and if some day María de las Nieves also realized how carefully discreet he'd been concerning his secret information about her mother and disgraceful father, all the better.

"Amatitlán has the perfect climate and soil for cochineal," he told her. In Amatitlán, there were two harvests a year, between the end of the rainy season in October and its beginning in May, whereas the towns just on the other side of the volcano and hills produced only one. "Do you know, Señorita Moran, that in some parts of Lake Amatitlán the pumice stones lie so densely upon the water that they form a floating peninsula that you can actually walk out upon . . . ?" And that for miles around on the volcanic side of the lake, all one needed to do was dig down a foot or so into the black soil to find water boiling as if in a pot, heated by the volcano's subterranean fires and gasses. Did she realize that it had only been seven years since coffee had first leapt ahead of cochineal as the country's leading money earner? And that just one year later, coffee earnings had doubled insect earnings! And now there were only those few plantations left, and many ghostly ruins looking a century old, not just seven years. On the other side of the world, a synthetic chemical dye had been invented, and over here, just like that, so many fortunes, and a whole way of life, had collapsed. The lakeside town, which in its glory attracted from all over Central America and the world the parasitical refuse that is always drawn to a scene of prosperity, was now a sad place of abandoned cantinas and billiards halls, with just a few old loafers hanging about (and addled, diseased old whores). Mack told María de las Nieves and her servant how he'd ridden past league after league of the old farms, the rotted and petrified-looking carcasses of the bug-breeding cactuses still standing in their tidy rows, and the ruins of those unusual adobe sheds, long and so narrow—a yard or so wide—in which cactus leaves covered with breeding insects were hung up every winter, and in so many of the old yards he'd seen the cracked, crumbling domed ovens, some overgrown with jungle, in which the insects had been baked before being sifted and cleaned and packed into heavy bales, wrapped in oxhide and shipped to Europe.

So it was an astonishment to the eye to suddenly come upon a plantation of live cactus, of freshest light green hue, and other cactus, those completely covered with insects, looking silver-plated in the sun, and to see the Indias standing and bending over in the rows, touching the cactus with thin pieces of cane, as if painting some intricate design upon them, but actually plucking the insects off one by one and dropping them into the cane baskets cradled under their other arms. Mack had stood and watched, transfixed by that scene of Oriental delicacy and calm. (He did not tell María de las Nieves that he'd stood there imagining that this was how the Yankee Timothy Moran must have first spotted Sarita Coyoy, still a girl herself, hired to pluck bugs from cactus in the cochineal farm he was managing.)

"Such a complex, fragile, and ancient trade, Señorita Moran! Employing curious little implements—our ancestors who, thousands of years ago, invented the art of making dye from cultivated insects must have used those very same tools!—all soon to be obsolete, the little sticks of cane, and those little boxes, made of palm bark, the four corners of each folded in and pinned with a thorn—*cartuchos,* they are called. Each little cartucho holds a hundred or so insects. And every October, these cartuchos are supposed to be fastened one to a cactus leaf, and do you know that within hours that leaf will be covered with the tiny insects that crawl out of the cartucho? And that the insects breed at such a rate that if the cartucho is not removed in time, the overpopulated leaf will not be able to nourish them all, resulting in an inferior dye bug. But if the weather is cold and windy, the insects will be reluctant to crawl out of their cartucho, huddling inside, or else they will be blown away as they do emerge, and if there is an unseasonable rain, the insects drown, and the crop is ruined. But if the weather cooperates, the cartucho can be moved to ten or twelve different leaves before the mothers inside are finally exhausted, and then the boxes are shaken out, and those prized mother insects are packed into the cane trays and baked in the ovens, and this results in the so-called black cochineal, which produces the reddest dye, the one Cardinals' silk caps get their scarlet color from, and fetches the highest price. The insects of the regular harvests result in the ordinary cochineal, which produces the more subdued red of, for example, those rough woolen blankets our Indios make. Cochineal, you know, is good for dyeing wool, or also silk, but not for cotton. Before those ordinary bugs can be harvested from the leaves, eighty days or so have to pass, but you would be surprised, Señorita Moran, at how eventful and suspenseful those eighty days can be. Consider just the short lives of the male insects. After two weeks or so, if I remember correctly, the males begin to grow a downy covering, and weave a thread from which they dangle from the cactus—so that the cactus looks covered by an artificial snow, like a Christmas decoration in the window of a New York department store. Then those tiny male flies hatch, and fly right back to the leaf to impregnate the females, and as soon as they've finished the job, they fall off and die. But any unexpected rain will wash all the males off of those leaves, leaving the female insects without any chance of finding mates and the crop ruined . . . There are ants that attack the cactus at the roots, and must be poisoned, and many other predators that Indian women used to be hired to pluck from the plants by hand—. Why, I haven't even started on the methods of baking the insects. If I get started on that—"

"Oh, yes, I can imagine," said María de las Nieves, but now, for the first time since he'd begun to speak, she finally smiled, not a warm smile, but a bemused and ever so slightly condescending one. "Is all of this meant to be interpreted as metaphorical, Señor?"

"Perdón, Señorita?"

"In the farming of these bichos, you find a sort of fable or moral or poetical meaning?"

"I am interested in the details of the business. You see, every business is made up of such a multitude of details, Señorita Moran, and it's good practice to memorize them. It's good mental practice for the day in which you'll have a business of your own to manage. But—it's a story you want?" This was unforeseen, that she would ask for a story, and ignoring her softly uttered, "Oh no, Señor, but thank you," he stared down into the drenched hat upturned on his lap, as if the story he'd once heard but was not sure that he could exactly recollect would now spell itself out there. "This country produced the finest cochineal insects in the world," he said adamantly, in not quite a storytelling tone. "And it was illegal to take any of those insects out of the country alive. But once a traveling British textile merchant stole a little box of finest-quality bugs. The Army was called out, and the official border crossings were all ordered closed, and all over the country, every traveling foreigner was stopped, his luggage emptied out, and his clothing stripped so that he could be searched. Well, the scallywag eluded arrest and slipped out anyway, and before long the British were raising cochineal in Gibraltar."

"They are ruthless, aren't they, the British," she laughed. "I know a story something like that. You're aware of the famous statue of La Virgen de Dolores de Manchén, here in our Church of San Sebastián? Apparently, some British travelers once tried to steal that too. Yes, they really did! And just as in your story, the Army was ordered to catch them. Except this time the villains were captured, and executed, and the statue was restored to its place. I heard this story from my teacher, who is also a poet, just the other evening."

"You are devoted to La Virgen de Dolores?" Mack asked, surprised by this note of religious fanaticism. "Or is it only this statue you are particularly devoted to?"

"Oh no no, that is, not in the old-fashioned way," she answered, stiffening slightly. "But that statue is considered to be a masterpiece of the old colonial religious art. My teacher, in fact, asked that we all go and look at it, but not for religious reasons. He says such statues really do possess a soul, put there, inside the wood, by the intensity of the religious faith and love of the artist who made them. The maestro says you can look at a statue and tell if it has a soul or not, and thereby know if that artist was a person of true faith or not. And that all art, even modern poetry, must have such a quality in order to be beautiful."

"Only Catholics can make art?" asked Mack, pitching his voice skeptical and strong. "What about people of other religions? Do those simple wooden statues the Indios make also have souls?"

"Oh no, he doesn't mean it like that at all. He means—" She paused, lightly scratched an itch on her brow, smiling as if to herself, and glanced again out the door at the dwindling rain and the gray air filling with mist. "Well, thank you, Señor Chinchilla, for your most interesting conversation. I'm glad I have a better idea now of what my father used to do."

"The pleasure has been all mine, Señorita Moran," said Mack, rising, hat over chest.

The servant, María Chon, was still staring at Mack with her mouth agape and an expression of perplexed alarm in her eyes. "Adiós, Señor" was all she said, as she also stood up, pulling her black cloak tightly around her. But before exiting, she stopped and turned and her hand emerged from the cloak like a beggar's, except when she opened her palm, it was to show Mack the little cri-cri he'd given her so many weeks before, and just as quickly she withdrew it, and followed María de las Nieves out the door.

Mack remained seated for a long time, trying to decide how he'd fared and how he should feel, and considering what he'd learned about María de las Nieves. Had he succeeded well enough to ensure that she would welcome another conversation the next time he saw her? A soaked park duck was standing in the door of the reading room as if undecided whether or not to enter. "So, duck," asked Mack, "did you see her expression when she walked out of here? How was it, Señor Duck?"

Well, he'd managed an honorable showing during that extremely per-ilous conversation about art. She was certainly taken with her "teacher," but that did not surprise him. And she seemed to have no idea that she had not been born in the Yucatán, but right here, in Amatitlán. At least according to what Don Juan Aparicio had claimed to have only recently learned about her after so many years of believing otherwise. Did it mat-ter? Did a person need to know where she had been born? Was it better *not* to know that your father was a scoundrel? Could Mack even say for sure that he knew where he'd been born, and of what father? And he remembered that sweltering summer night when Don Juan Aparicio had told his story, the windows thrown open to the muffled evening roar and strong "perfume" of the harbor, the constant near and distant racket of ships' horns, whistles, bells, gulls cawing. By then, in his two years of living in New York, Don Juan had picked up something of the showy Yankee way of telling a story, hand in his watch pocket, waving his cigar in the air, tilting so far back in his chair that just a little more and he would surely tumble backward, and he was well into his story about the little half-Yankee wild girl in the forest—how, having heard rumors from his Indio workers about the strange female trio living in the forest, he'd gone and found them: the young girl, her widowed Indian mother, the black English-speaking servant, and the trunk filled with English and American magazines the Yankee had left behind, and the buried bottles of whiskey, and the notebook in which Timothy Moran had scrawled the Latin names of a few orchids and nothing else—and so on, et cetera and et cetera—captivating Salomón and Mack with the story of María de las Nieves/Sor San Jorge, and what Don Juan Aparicio had always believed the histories and circumstances of the girl and her mother to have been. Imagine his surprise, then, when the black Belizean maid, Lucy Turner, whom he'd brought to be his domestic servant in New York, not only to have a familiar face from home around but because she spoke English, had just the other day told him the apparently true story of Timothy Moran and Sarita Coyoy. In all her years of working for the Aparicios in Los Altos, Lucy had kept her silence. Well, yes, Señores, during all those years, Lucy and he had never had a long conversation of any kind, and certainly not one in English. Well, before coming to live in New York, his English hadn't been nearly fluent enough to sustain such a conversation with Lucy, even if he'd been so disposed. Then, just the other day, she'd come into the parlor, set down his tray with his evening drink of hot chocolate, a bottle of brandy and a cigar also upon it, and just like that, that woman of ferocious demeanor and prim manner had started in: Don Señor Aparicio, I have something I wait all these many years to tell, and now my conscience needs to tell . . . And there in Jacobo Baiz's office, Don Juan retold the black servant's story: Sarita Coyoy and her daughter were not from the Yucatán at all. None of them, not Sarita, not herself, and as far as Lucy Turner knew, not even Mr. Moran or his wife, Elsa, had ever even been to the Yucatán! Lucy herself had come to Amatitlán directly from British Honduras, as so many had during the years of the cochineal boom, in search of work, which, of course, she'd found with the Morans, who needed an English-speaking servant. So Sarita Coyoy was a native of Amatitlán, not the Yucatán. Just a local Indian girl (Juan Aparicio had elaborated) and, like most from that area, probably a bit of a zamba descended from the African slaves the Jesuits had kept on their old sugar plantations there, and who'd long ago disappeared as a separate race, having so mixed with Indios. "Of course," added Don Juan Aparicio, "the habit of San Ignacio has never been an impenetrable armor against the arrows of Cupid, and so they too figure into the obscure ancestral origins of the unusual Indios of Amatitlán, who tend to be taller and of a darker complexion, or else whiter and with a reputation for greater—" (with an alert glance directed at Mack, Don Juan decided not to finish his sentence). So Timothy Moran had fallen in love with an Indita who worked on the cochineal plantation he was managing, who turned out to be Sarita Coyoy, over whom Señor Moran lost his head and heart and even, one could say, eventually his life, though the mule that kicked him in the stomach was hardly free of blame. By his scandalous behavior in Amatitlán, Timothy Moran had turned his wife, Elsa, into the subject of awful ridicule and humiliation. Having abandoned her for the India in the most public way, he was spied going about everywhere with his pretty little aborigine, who was soon pregnant. Just days after the infant girl was born, Mrs. Elsa Moran committed suicide by throwing herself into a steamy well of boiling water deep down in the volcanic earth. The mood in the town turned violently against Mr. Moran. Many among the white foreigners and criollos vowed to kill him, in order to make an example of him. So Timothy Moran and his new little family fled, not immediately into the mountains but to Mazatenango, where for some two years Moran managed a sugar plantation, telling his story about the Yucatán until the truth caught up with him and then he did flee into the mountains, where it was true that he'd intended to forge a new start as a coffee farmer. Lucy went too, because she'd become attached to the baby girl and even to Sarita Coyoy, who'd never asked Timothy Moran to become so recklessly passionate over her and had lacked the guile to resist; also because the servant had no better option. All that time, for years, Don Juan Aparicio had believed that María de las Nieves's father had been an honorable if rustic Yankee adventurer-entrepreneur who'd sensibly fled the savage Indian uprising in the Yucatán, bringing his young Yucatec Maya wife and daughter with him. Sarita Coyoy liked to make a vain show of how she was such a civilized India that she couldn't even speak her native language, only Spanish. But the Indios of Amatitlán, he explained, tended to be Spanish speakers anyway, after so many long years of living among Jesuits and cochineal farmers. Why should Juan Aparicio have suspected anything? Now that he knew the truth, Don Juan rhetorically asked his listeners in Mr. Baiz's office, what should he do about it? Should he tell his own wife and children? And what about poor María de las Nieves? Was he under any obligation to tell her? Well, my good fellows, he had decided that he was not.

Juan Aparicio knew that his wife had already expelled Sarita Coyoy from her home—for other reasons, which he did not go into in Don Jacobo's office—and he knew that she had a new "husband," a prosperous Indio sheep farmer, for some of our Indios do grow wealthy, he said, and follow a way of life somewhere between a semicivilized village one and that of a stable artisan in the city. But, Don Juan had told them, he had not embarked on this story for the purpose of mortifying his listeners, though of course he himself had been somewhat mortified upon hearing it, given his long relationship to those involved. "Perhaps a story like this one," said La Primera Dama's father, "should be shared simply because it is so curious, that is all." And with a laconic flourish of his cigar, he'd added, "Simply because it is so curious, and leaves us with a bit of a moral dilemma to ponder. " Well, if so, Salomón and Mack were gratified and willing ponderers that night.

THERE WERE REASONS, however, for Sarita Coyoy's expulsion from the Aparicio home that the two boys could never, at least not then, have guessed at. These were somewhat alluded to many years later, aboard the California-bound steamship the *Golden Rose,* as Paquita and María de las Nieves again sat up talking in the presidential widow's stateroom a few nights into the voyage. María de las Nieves, that night, for the first time ever, bluntly asked Paquita why her mother had been forced to leave the Aparicio family household.

It so happened that Paquita had, for years, suspected, if not quite assumed, that her father had taken Sarita Coyoy as a lover. That last time when she'd come home from the convent for Christmas, having decided to marry, her mother had informed her that in New York Paquita's father had required a servant who spoke English, who understood him, who knew something about his likes and dislikes, and that of course for those reasons he'd requested that Lucy Turner come to work for him in New York; but that then Sarita Coyoy had raised a terrible fuss, insisting that she, as the widow of a Yankee from New York, was the one who deserved to go, despite the fact that her English was nearly nonexistent, and soon afterward, in her own offended jealousy and pride, Sarita Coyoy had renounced her privileged situation of a room all her own over the stables in the servants' quarters, and her job as an inside servant with such trifling duties that she was more like a dependant but eternal guest of the house, in order to cohabit with an Indio sheep farmer in Barrio Siete Orejas. Later Paquita learned from the household's other servants that it was her mother, Doña Francisca, who'd insisted that it be Lucy and not Sarita Coyoy who should go to New York; and about how bitterly and furiously Sarita had protested that El Patrón had promised that *she* would be the one to come and work for him there, complaining to and even berating the other servants as if it were somehow in their power to reverse the great injustice. Sarita Coyoy was only fifteen years older than her daughter. She was still, after all, the same youthfully limber, sumptuous-lipped, siren-eyed Yucateca who, not so very long ago, had so enthralled Timothy Moran with her saucy yet improbably ladylike and self-assured ways.

"The truth is, I really don't know very much about it at all," Paquita finally answered in a placid tone. "I thought your mother left because she'd taken up with that sheep farmer."

María de las Nieves sat pensively fanning herself a moment, before finally answering with the heavy sigh of a universal daughter: "Ayyy pobre Mamá."

# Chapter 4

he former Primera Dama, being so recently widowed, didn't think it proper that she appear in any of the ship's public rooms at night, and María de las Nieves was also in a reclusive mood. Her presence on board had awakened the curiosity of the other passengers, especially those among the late dictator's fleeing entourage—women turning to whisper behind their fans, eyes following her with seasick stares; she wasn't going to answer any of their questions, she wasn't going to let them know anything about herself and Mathilde! During the day the two young mothers did escape the inferno of the cabins to stroll around the shaded promenade, and took their meals with the other first-class passengers, and played with the children on the hurricane deck when the sun was not too harsh; like two sisters who in an emergency know how to put aside lifelong differences, Paquita and María de las Nieves strolled, sat, dined, and played together. On board the steamship the *Golden Rose,* their childhood closeness had been reestablished, if not entirely their trust and affection, never a simple matter anyway. Nightly they sequestered themselves in Paquita's stateroom to converse and sip brandy. Afterward María de las Nieves would go to her own cabin and read by candlelight until, instead of going to bed, in a state of restlessness that not even the hours-old effects of the brandy could dull, she climbed the stairs from the promenade to the hurricane deck and nervously walked out under the stars amid the polyglot rabble camped out there, following a path that kept her at a small distance from the men gathered along the rail and the interspersed rows of sprawled bodies, many asleep, just inside. Amid a circle of red-eyed Mexican stokers and sailors staring up from their game of dice as she passed, or lounging against the rail or a mast, were those eyes that always found hers, like the eyes of a nocturnal jungle animal drawn to the edge of the same firelit clearing every night. She instantly looked away every time. She circled the hurricane deck, apprehension coursing through her limbs, smoking her cigarrito, never allowing herself to pause or linger, ignoring any and all voices murmuring or calling to her from the darkness, until she was back at the same stairwell she'd climbed up through, and then she hurried down its slippery steps, always with that same mixture of relief and embarrassment. Yet she looked forward to this final part of the day, her nightly, nearly illicit promenade around the hurricane deck, most of all; also to her reading, and to her conversations with Paquita. She was enjoying her first ocean voyage, she couldn't deny it, though every morning she worried that she was also picking up a dangerous habit of brandy drinking. On land, that would have to immediately stop. Or once they were settled in New York.

In Acapulco they had the opportunity to go ashore and walk about the hilly town and observe the scandal of the dark-skinned pretty girls in their shockingly scant but blazingly white dresses who sold necklaces of pink seashells on the beach. Those unabashed Mexican girls made directly for the male passengers and ship's officers, Yankee and European, who all seemed to shed in an instant the formality and constraint that had so far guided their shipboard behavior, quickly falling into openly flirtatious relations, some even forming small strolling parties with their new companions, and even the Central American passengers agreed at the end of the day that the seashell necklaces many of the men brought back were exceptionally artful; though in their own countries, even to such an experienced world traveler as Paquita, seashells were still considered as unlucky as anything, and it seemed insanity to bring articles of such ill omen aboard a ship that was still eight days from San Francisco.

Two nights later, when they were again conversing over brandy in her stateroom, Paquita broke a lull by remarking that María de las Nieves had never spoken any opinion of the Pinkerton's National Detective Agency report on Martí's activities in New York City, which, four years earlier, she'd procured there from her aristocratic friend the Spanish Consul, and then given to her.

It was true, María de las Nieves had never acknowledged that perverse "gift," delivered into her own hands by a servant from the Presidential Mansion. When she came to the door that evening and found the mandadera from her old convent standing there with a black shawl over her head, her first terrified instinct had been to run back inside and hide.

Then she'd recognized the impossible lattice-toothed grin and remembered who was currently employing Josefa Socorro, and embraced the servant with feigned delight, and new suspicion and fear. But later, reading it, she'd been swiftly overtaken by a new anxiety. What was she to do with this poisonous document, after all? It narrated events already more than a year old; and Martí and his Cuban comrades had apparently discovered that they were being spied upon and infiltrated, and then the Pinkerton operatives' surveillance, and the narration, had abruptly ended. María de las Nieves had done the only honorable thing: she'd mailed it to Martí, at the address of the boardinghouse in New York. When several months had passed and she still hadn't received any letter of acknowledgment, she wondered if the package had gone awry, as mail carried to and from her country by the Pacific Mail so frequently and notoriously did: by now the package and its contents might be just a lump of sodden pulp, she'd imagined, half-devoured by rats and sea worms, in the hold of a steamship diverted to the China route, or in some neglected corner of a Panama warehouse. Then she began to fret that it had fallen into the wrong hands, and that by her good intentions she'd only caused her old teacher and friend harm or distress. Fifteen months after she'd mailed it, she received notification that a package from the United States owing postage fees was waiting for her at the postal office. She and her daughter were then in their time of deepest poverty, and several weeks passed before she could finally afford to take possession of the mysterious brown paper parcel without a return address. Inside was the package she'd addressed to Mr. José Martí, in the same now dampness-stained heavy butcher paper and twine she'd originally wrapped it in, upon which an anonymous hand had scrawled in pencil that no such person resided at that address.

María de las Nieves had to be careful how she answered now: she took a slow drink of brandy while trying to mask her anxiety by training on Paquita a long gaze that she hoped would seem to convey an undeceived bemusement—though she had no idea what it was she was pretending to be undeceived by—and also a touch of moral condescension.

"Yes, that," she finally said. "What do you suppose I thought?"

Paquita impatiently raked fingers through her loosened hair, lifted her chin, and said, "You must admit it made for a wicked comedy. And I thought it would do you good to read it, in your circumstances, at that time—*usté sabe.*"

"I see. We'd spoken only once or twice in nearly five years, but you considered yourself knowledgeable about my circumstances."

"Ayyy Nievecitas, every day I thought of you. I worried about you, always, I prayed for you—"

"Why pray for me, Paquita, if I no longer prayed at all?"

"Who has ever heard of anything more puerile or commonplace than deciding to become an atheist because you no longer believe in the literalness of the Immaculate Conception. Sometimes, María de las Nieves, you sound like a drunken schoolteacher who has read a little Renan. Weren't you going to become a Protestant?"

"I tried a bit, yes." She laughed despite herself. "But no, nothing happened."

"The Reverend Hill, the gringo, you didn't like him?"

"He was very disdainful of Catholics, and of nearly everyone else too. He seemed a courageous man, but no—" She shrugged. "No no no . . ."

"And the detective's report?"

"I admit that that night when it was delivered to me I began to read it but I don't think I even finished it. I put it away, and never looked at it again. But I read enough to understand why you'd sent it to me, and that did make me sad."

"Because there it all was, reclaritito"—very-little-little clearly—"no? He was exposed as he should have been when he was among us—"

"I thought it was sad that Maestro Martí's dignity and reputation were being violated by people of such preposterously low stature compared to his, by the lowest sort of spy, and that you thought a bath in that swamp would be helpful to me. Yes, Paquita, that made me sad."

"Ah, so it did not interest you to learn that there in Nueva York Martí was raising the same suspicions of irresponsible treatment of naive young women as he did before—including a woman whom he apparently left in the very same state as perhaps he did you, the owner of his boardinghouse no less, where he was living with his own wife and infant child and his landlady's husband, all under the same roof. *That* did not open your eyes?"

"That is a very liberal and pernicious interpretation of what that report contained, Doña Francisca Aparicio de Injusto. And if I remember correctly, I find it far-fetched to refer to any of the women mentioned there as *naive*. God knows, mi reina, you do have theories, about me, about everybody."

"Don Hipólito believed it," said Paquita, referring to her aristocratic friend the Spanish Consul General. "He had his reasons——"

"And I don't need to hear them," said María de las Nieves. "Señor Martí is not Mathilde's father, and it would be most unjust of you to ever plant such an idea in my daughter's mind. When the time comes for her to know, I will tell her myself who her father was. Someday it will be up to her alone to decide if she wants to share that information with her strange Tía Paquita. I have sworn to never tell anyone but Mathilde. So you still have a long wait until you'll even have a chance to get your fingers around that pearl which it appears you so covet."

"It's not easy to be a natural child, in any society."

"Yet the world is full of them. Including your own many stepchildren, some of whom are even older than you are."

Paquita laughed in soft surprise. "No one hid the identity of their father from *them*, Las Nievecitas. And Rufinito was very loving and generous." One of El Anticristo's natural sons, Venacio, a general, educated in French military academies, perished in the same military defeat as his father; another illegitimate son, by another mother, Antonio, a cadet at West Point Military Academy, was waiting for them in New York. Their father had told them that they would never inherit anything but the education he would provide them, and the honor of his name.

María de las Nieves drained her brandy with a restless swallow and reached for the crystal decanter, poured some into Paquita's snifter, refilled her own; the two women sat regarding each other in tense yet soft silence for a moment: it was like a stare between confused lovers that at any moment, out of baffled inarticulateness, could turn into laughter or tears.

"Sign your mansion in New York over to Mathilde and me and come to work as Mathilde's governess, and then I will tell you what you want to know."

Paquita smiled. "Of course, corazoncita. At your service."

"We can have a party to formally introduce Mathilde to your four hundred society friends, so that then they will forever after accept her. "

"Muy bien. Whatever you want, chula."

"But you are not well educated enough to be Mathilde's governess," said María de las Nieves. "You can give her lessons about society, I suppose."

This was said in a gentle enough manner that both giggled quietly, as if they were girls again, immersed in one of their very long games.

"I thought that report made it quite clear that Martí had impregnated his landlady," said Paquita. "So what if he did? Actually, I don't care if he did or if he didn't, you know, not anymore."

"Why is it you are always so skeptical of poor Martí, and never of the credibility or motives of a vulgar and pompous spy working for the Spanish, no less? An American conspiring against a cause that his own patriotic pride and honor should have led him to embrace—Cuban Independence from Spain, Paquita!"

"A detective, not a spy. An honorable profession, with its own code of honor. Like a priest's."

"Camarón—! A priest's, you said? A priest's code of honor?"

Paquita pertly nodded.

"You know, there really must be a God and He is totally crazy. Because look who He chooses as His new Defender of Religion! *Ea*, Paquita, you remained close to Canon Ángel Arroyo throughout all those years. Of course you did, pues sí, he used to visit you at school before you were wed, and bring you messages from your secret beloved, and then later Padre Ángel was always the priest closest to your husband, he even became a deputy of the National Congress, and your husband arranged for him to have a residence affixed to the Cathedral, a beautiful old house usually reserved for an important bishop, and everyone in the city knew that no matter what else was going on in the country, or no matter how hard your husband was making things for other priests, Padre Ángel remained very devoted to you, Paquita, visiting in the afternoons for coffee and cake. Yes, I know, later there were other priests who visited you, who came and confessed and prayed the rosaries and ate little cakes with you, everyone in the city knew about that, and they were grateful to you, for if not for your intercession your husband would have been even crueler to priests, to the Spanish-born ones especially, who certainly are detestable, but you've probably known Padre Ángel Arroyo as long and as well as anybody has, mi doñacita. So surely you heard the rumors that the housekeeper he lives with in that splendid house alongside the Cathedral is actually his lover, and not only that, that she is actually his half sister, by whom he has now had five children, and who live there too. Do you believe it, or is that just a rumor? You would never expose your own children to such a depraved beast by inviting him into your own home for coffee and cake if you believed it to be true, would you? Yet people spread such stories about your good friend Padre Ángel!"

"Then what happened with you and Martí that afternoon—that afternoon when you went walking by the Río de las Vacas?" Her black eyes shone coldly like a dog's in the dark.

María de las Nieves gazed back at Paquita, stunned; actually, she looked a little dizzy and confused, as if she was just coming to understand that a knife had been plunged into her belly, and that in just another second or two she would fall over—. She rose to go, her lips tensely curled on the verge of tears, but when she spoke she managed to master herself, and made her voice clear and haughty: "All these years you've been living in a Platonic cave, where the fabrications of spies and informers were the only reality you knew. Truly, poor little you. Well, now you'll find out."

She walked out of the stateroom and down the promenade leading to her cabin, the blood rushing inside her louder than the ocean and the wave-crushing wheel. In New York, I won't live with her, she told herself. I don't care what happens, I will not live there ... But what about Mathilde? Holding on to the rail with both hands, she gazed out into the floating ink of this moonless night and the sluggishly rumbling ocean ... from far beyond the black horizon, like a folded telegram passed from one heavily rising and collapsing wave to the next until at last it reached her, came the blunt message that of course she would not strike out on her own in New York. No, she would inhabit some little corner sewing room until she was an old angry mouse, and her daughter would grow melancholy, pretty, and so odd she would frighten men, and end up married to a stable steward or circus performer. *Noverim me, noverim te,* carajo! I am twenty-five, unmarried, with no money of my own, headed with my daughter to New York City, where no one, with the exception perhaps of Lucy Turner, knows or loves us. Who knows if Pepe Martí still lives there, or even cares anymore who I am?

Mathilde was asleep in her bunk behind the curtain when she let herself into the steamy cabin, and she moved quietly so as not to wake her, and sat in the armchair pulled up to the small desk, and reached under it for the satchel in which she kept stationery, newspaper clippings, and the pasteboard folder holding the Pinkerton detective report, which she'd been reading every night since the second night of the voyage. She put the folder down on the desk, patiently undid its ribbon, and sat silently in the darkness, until finally, striking a match, she lit the candle and moved it closer as she leaned over the report's 218 pages, copied entirely, mostly in brown ink, in a mostly minuscule and hard-to-read script, on unlined stationery, every page headed with the printed logo of a sedately staring eye and the slogan *We never sleep* and the words *Pinkerton's National* above, *Detective Agency* below. In the chaotic days leading up to her departure, she'd been unable to find any book in English that promised accurate descriptions of New York City. Then she'd had the idea that the detective's report must hold some clues about life there. (Though, had she not had that idea, it's hard to believe she would simply have left it behind.) But over the last few nights in her cabin the Yankee detective's methodical account of his and his fellow operatives' months of surveillance of José Martí had absorbed her in an unexpected manner: it had reimmersed her in the time, eight years before, when she'd known Martí, a time barely alluded to in the report. Of course it did cast a certain light upon Martí, and hold him up for scrutiny, and not impartially. But she knew how to read through the scrim of the detectives' prejudices. Now that she was headed to New York, she was reading the report in a new way; as if these pages had yet to be salted whenever she'd read them before, and now they were (ocean-air) salted and a new flavor seeped from them:

Miss Susan Paral, for example, had stepped into the leading role. She was not, of course, mentioned in any more pages now than before, yet over the last few nights María de las Nieves had become especially fixated by Miss Paral, the young gringa Pinkerton operative who came to the boardinghouse to take Spanish language lessons from Martí, which his wife, Carmen, often sat in on as well. That same New York City boardinghouse, owned by a Cuban couple, Manuel Mantilla and his wife, Carmita Miyares, at 51 East Twenty-ninth Street, where a Pinkerton operative, identified only by the initials *E.S.*, had taken a room as a boarder, passing himself off as a university student. E.S. was clearly the central figure of the espionage operation against Martí, and the report's main narrator.

*Gentlemen: My operative "E.S." reports the following relative to Mr. José Martí—.* The report commenced with those words, formally addressed, by Allan Pinkerton, to Spanish diplomatic officials, including Paquita's friend the Spanish Consul General.

Even strolling through the sinuous streets of Acapulco two days before with Mathilde, María de las Nieves had found herself inwardly dwelling upon the ambiguous but perilous adventures of Miss Susan Paral, hardly noticing any of the picturesque village's sights, until her dark, skinny sailor popped up again, tersely inviting them to dishes of flavored ice in a café he knew of near the market. He seemed younger, his eyes more tame by daylight than at night on the hurricane deck; she was older than he was, she was a little shocked to realize, *maybe* even a decade older. Pretending to not even recognize him at first, she refused his invitation, coolly and adamantly. She and Mathilde waited, idly circling, until the poor sailorcito was out of sight; and then they found the little café on their own. There, sitting over her plate of melted coconut ice, she forgot about Miss Paral and fell into that familiar spirit of sullen introspection which often seemed to rise from the bottom of her heart like a noxious tide, which meant that it also reliably receded, usually borne away on a series of long and oblivious sighs. And she apologized to Mathilde for not having heard her the first time she'd asked: "Mamá, is it true that the Negro waiters take our tablecloths to their beds at night to use as pillows, and put them back on the tables in the morning? That's what Elena says." Elena was the oldest of Paquita's daughters. María de las Nieves had also heard Paquita complain that the tablecloths grew dingier by the day. True, it was hardly a bright starchy tablecloth they'd breakfasted at that morning, but had it really been so much whiter on the first day of the voyage? "Of course they don't," she told her daughter, thinking that was better than answering truthfully: I hope not!

María de las Nieves had never actually read the Pinkerton manuscript straight through from beginning to end because its changeable handwriting—sometimes more composed, often appearing frantically rushed, or for

pages at a stretch growing ever more cramped and tiny, as if it too was trying to hide—made for an exhausting and obstacle-strewn terrain. Her
knowledge of the report's contents was derived from a constant perusal of
its most legible portions, from which, once she had those paragraphs nearly
memorized, she ventured out forward and backward: a mental map of her
sporadic reading of the report over the years would have depicted, instead
of any series of logical progressions, something like a dense pattern of over-
lapping spiderwebs, each spun out from its own middle. She didn't doubt
that there must still be gaps that she'd never actually read. Now in the
cabin she flipped quickly through pages until she found an entry on Miss
Paral and her Spanish classes, and slipped right back into E.S.'s despicable
narration, addressed to someone always referred to as "Sir Superintendent"
or simply "Sir," obviously his superior at the agency. Here on this page the
boardinghouse infiltrator wrote:

—Sir Superintendent, I suspect that Miss Paral is not being forthcom-
ing with me. Undeterred by Mr. Martí's difficulties in speaking the English
language, Miss Paral relates their conversations with too much enthusiasm,
even those parts which someday in the future, when she has calmed herself, I have no doubt she will recognize to have been claptrap. Sir, she is
even attempting to translate one of Mr. Martí's "poems," beneath the pre-
text of wishing to seem his eagerest student and more completely win his
confidence. Miss Paral repeats back to me his legends with too much exalted feeling, and her exaltation seems to grow by the week. Yesterday she
recounted for me a story he told about a Cuban rebel general who found a
white dove lying on the battlefield, stunned by artillery fire into uncon-
sciousness. The Cuban hero picked the dove up off the ground, wrapped
it in his monogrammed handkerchief, and dispatched a peasant boy to
recklessly and foolishly convey the catatonic bird (in autographed silk dia-
per!) through enemy lines in order to deliver it to his beloved and pregnant
wife, residing at an otherwise abandoned plantation house with some servants and the fugitive wives of other rebel officers. "Ain't that the most
romantic and gallant thing you did ever hear?" Miss Paral asked me, her
blue eyes glowing with misty rapture like blue harbor lights in a milky
morning fog. "Miss Paral," I told her, "amid this golden anthology of
Antillean heroism and gallantry we seem to be paying you to compile during your weekly Spanish lessons with Mr. Martí, have you not managed to

garner from our effusive subject even a few pebbles of actual information? Only all this frothy spray and spew? I dine with him several times a week, of course, in our little *pensione*, Miss Paral, and know that *Signore* Martí, though lately he is often a very brooding *cavaliere*, if sufficiently stoked by praise, admiration, attention, a few glasses of wine, or a little gin, will sometimes present a majestic but not exactly well-defended conversational *castello*, for he is hardly immune from making proud innuendo, I believe, regarding rebel conspiracies. However, I am not ideally constituted to make very sweet blue eyes in order to coerce from him a tale of his *own present heroism*, something risky and actual in which he himself is *currently engaged*, so that I might sigh over his bravery, or even find cause to consider our slight hero deserving of a secret little kiss of conspiratorial encouragement. What do you say, Miss Paral? I have heard from Martí's own lips that he considers you most lovely. I have heard him say that you, Miss Paral, have given him *a new idea of American beauty!*"

Sir Superintendent, continued E.S., our opinionated Cuban friend has even been shameless enough to inform me at table in front of his very own wife and the other Cuban boarders that he considers our Yankee women to be well formed and intelligent, though too excessively pragmatic, athletic, assertive, and wealth-obsessed to be considered truly beautiful, and blablabla regarding the tender virtues and volatile and seductive black eyes of the women of the tropics (though Mr. Martí's wife's eyes are an arresting hazel). That is, until he encountered the celestial gaze of Miss Paral. Mr. Martí believes Miss Paral to be the first true Southern Belle to have made his acquaintance. He states that he now better understands the chivalry and fanatic code of honor of our deservedly vanquished Confederate brethren, if they also believed they were defending their ideal femininity from a society capable of shaping such manly, materialistic women. Oh, Sir, what wouldn't I have given to have been able to reveal to our suave Caribbean insurrectionist that our cleverly cultivated flower is actually native to Schenectady, and a born actress indeed! At our most recent reunion, I did ask Miss Paral: "When Mr. Martí goes to meet steamships arriving from and headed back to Cuba at the docks, and boards and mingles with passengers and crewmen, and sometimes goes into their rooms and cabins, thus completely eluding our surveillance, who does he go to see? Does he go to trade messages? In what manner and what do they say? When he enters the hotels, Miss Paral, again often eluding our agents, to what purpose? Can't you find any of that out, Miss Paral?" She responded that Mr. Martí has told her that the way of life in our newer hotels is something that a Latin American would never be able to fathom. "That is a remarkable statement, Miss Paral," I retorted. "What is it that Mr. Martí cannot fathom?" She answered with what seemed to me a wicked little smile: "He construes our hotels to be monstrous edifices constructed solely to provide subterfuge for vice, and to destroy family life. Also, that our hotels engender a physical and spiritual sickliness by completely turning people away from the pleasures of the out-of-doors, of nature. Pepe has learned that there are even families who live in elegant hotels and never leave, taking all their meals, entertainment, and even exercise there, and this astonishes and dismays him." (Miss Paral maintains, Sir, that Mr. Martí insists she call him Pepe, pronounced *peh–peh*.) I said, "Well then, Miss Paral, why is it that Mr. Pepe is himself constantly scurrying in and out of hotels, and often escaping our surveillance in the process?" Sir, I am concerned about Miss Paral, and worry that she meets our Cubano in secret, perhaps even in such a hotel, or is hoping or planning to. I have written previously concerning the discord in Mr. Martí's marriage, which can only abet this situation. I would advise assigning agents to follow Miss Paral as well, but I fear that she would too quickly notice, and take her revenge upon our mistrust by betraying us to the subject of surveillance. I have also considered suspending her Spanish classes if, in two more weeks, her efforts still lack results; however, I fear the same reaction—

And María de las Nieves remembered Martí miming the invisible handkerchief-wrapped dove in his own hands while crossing with weightless strides the lecture salon at the Academia de Niñas de Centroamérica and telling them that same story (minus, of course, the operative's sour annotations), and just when he got to the part where the rebel general's gift was laid by the messenger into the pregnant young wife's hands, so did Martí, stopping before the seated María de García Granados, pretend to lay the hero's dove into her outstretched hands, and she, long-lashed eyes glistening with emotion, raised the invisible dove to her lips and kissed it, and the other students swooningly ayyyy'd and applauded.

*Actor and actress!* she'd silently seethed. Her convent-refined nose for humbug told her that they must have rehearsed the scene beforehand.

"WHEN YOU ARE ready to learn, María de las Nieves, your teacher shall appear," Don José Pryzpyz told her one afternoon when she was visiting him in his workroom. It was one of his Hebrew sayings. If a young Hebrew boy is predestined to learn the secrets of the sacred mystical texts, then, at the right moment, his teacher will appear. Don José was making a joke about teaching her how to work with caucho. "And what do those mystical texts contain, Don José?" she asked. The umbrella mender said that there were thousands upon thousands of such books, that libraries larger than Buckingham Palace had been built just to house the writings of the Jewish mystics, and that their every word was pure nonsense.

Don José continued with his lesson on the subtleties of vulcanization. He was teaching her how to make a pair of India-rubber boots from scratch, perfectly fitted to her own feet, his method based on that of the Amazon Indians, which he claimed to have improved. Already he'd sewn stockings from cut pieces of heavy drill, and stitched soft leather soles into their bottoms, and pulled them over wooden molds greased with coconut oil and soap, and now he was ready to begin brush-coating the boot-socks with layer after layer of the raw caucho sap already simmering in a large iron pot. It was better to add only ammonia to the milk at the start, Don José told her, because he'd learned from experience that India-rubber clothing articles which contained sulfur, especially in the tropical heat, gave off a stench of rotted eggs, the warmer the temperature, the more unpleasant. Smoking the boots with sulfur when they were hung to dry would sufficiently improve their durability, and wouldn't smell nearly as badly.

It had now been more than two years since the afternoon when Don José, seated in his front room, had glanced up and noticed the adolescent girl standing out on the sidewalk studying his window, in which nothing was displayed, and staring into his shop with a strikingly absorbed, even somewhat perturbed expression. It was November, the beginning of the dry season, and she was not carrying an umbrella or parasol. Though she was brown-complexioned, and wore a black shawl over her head, he knew that she was not a servant sent by her mistress to make a purchase or pick up a repair: her cream-colored dress was not a servant's dress, and her manner of studying his window was not a servant's manner. A young woman seeming so interested in his shop was a very novel occurrence. But what was she looking for? He was never really able to explain it to María de las Nieves (or to Mack) later on, but then and there he'd had the premonition that something unexpected and marvelous was about to occur, or even had already begun to, and he'd sat watching her through the window with such growing curiosity and suspense that he soon felt short of breath. It was as if she saw something in his window that no one else could see, he decided. As if only she could see that in his window there was displayed one of those nativity scenes that people here spread over their floors at Christmas, with tiny mechanical camels and donkeys moving their heads up and down, and such touches as an aeronaut's balloon attached to a wire endlessly circling like a clock hand, and one of the turbaned three kings leaning out of the basket with a telescope to spy the Holy Infant. Christmas was not very far off, after all. Maybe he should go out and say to the girl, So you like my nativity scene? and perhaps she would pick up on his game, and they would each describe what they could see, and in that magical way, a friendship would begin. But maybe it was inappropriate for him, a Jew, to be making up a game about an invisible nativity scene. Maybe she's illiterate and can't read the sign, he thought, and is wondering what is sold here. Yes, that's probably it, he told himself, feeling disappointed; he would go out and tell her about his business, and invite her in for tea. A sudden apprehension gripped him: what if her curiosity was related to his nighttime trade, what if she was standing outside trying to work up the courage to come inside to ask for a condom sheath? The possibility mortified him and he froze in his seat. Now he did not know what to do, whether to stay seated or go outside and speak with her. He felt deeply divided—one side wanting to make this sympathetic-looking girl's acquaintance and the other suspecting that she was brazenly depraved—and he felt his paralysis opening ever wider, a canyon swallowing him from within. Her expression had softened; she was looking into the window now as if her thoughts were somewhere else. She glanced hesitantly down the sidewalk, then in the other direction, and before he knew what, the door to his shop was opening and she was in the front room, staring with eyes of luminous mud as he sat in his chair like a lonely ticket seller, and she was explaining, in a polite and confident voice, that a little more than two years before, when she was a schoolgirl, she'd passed by this shop and seen a crowd of men gathered outside the window, and that she'd wondered ever since what was being displayed there that day, to have drawn such an eager crowd—

"Oh . . . two years? Oh, Señorita . . . Oh, I no remember . . . In my window?"

"It was causing such a sensation, Señor, anyone could see—do you prefer to speak English?"

"An umbrella was displayed there, perhaps?" (Gaping in astonishment at this persistent girl who'd just spoken to him in lightly accented English, clearly Indian-blooded though her appearance was also somewhat distinct, the hair visible under her shawl a dark reddish hue, her eyebrows black—)

". . ."

"Ah! Now I remember, Señorita!" And he darted into the back of his shop and came out carrying a doll he'd made out of umbrella spokes, a molded little ball of India rubber impaled upon its spoke-neck, clipped bits of broom straw stuck in for hair, the entire frail-looking apparatus painted yellow. During the dry season, work slowed, and out of boredom and inexplicable nostalgia, Don José had fashioned this yellow doll.

"It was my Strawman that caused the commotion that you witnessed!"

She seemed slightly disillusioned. No harm done, he'd somewhat guiltily told himself then and many times since; this was the kind of lie one told to a good girl. He offered her a glass of tea, and she ended up staying most of the afternoon, and ever since they had been bonded in close friendship. She is the sunshine of my life, Mack! Not until he was befriended by Mack Chinchilla did he have someone to confide such emotions to. Nobody else would have been the least interested.

Back then, María de las Nieves had only recently returned to the capital after living with her mother and the sheepherder in Los Altos, and with the money from the sale of her late father's land had bought her little house. During those first unforgettable weeks and months, she'd spent much of her time at home, savoring her freedom and solitude, reading books, devoting herself to whatever domestic improvements she was capable of herself, and only pretending that she could pass the next seventy years this way if she wished, knowing that soon she would need to find employment, or a husband. Or she went out and roamed the streets hour upon hour as if the city really was a grand metropolis of inexhaustible amusement, edification, and surprise—though always dreading crossing paths with some incognito nun from her old convent scurrying out on some errand from her clandestine nest. She still sometimes saw professional mourners going door to door begging for eggs, and if they were not collecting them to bring to nuns in hiding, then who for?

One drizzly afternoon during those same months, when she was out walking again, María de las Nieves came upon another mysterious crowd in the street, formed outside a house that turned out to be the United States Legation and drawn there by the sound of robust quarreling between the U.S. Minister Resident and his wife coming from behind the shuttered windows. Like that earlier crowd outside the umbrella mender's shop a few years before, this one would also have a profound repercussion upon her life. It so happened that hardly an afternoon passed without the rancorous domestic drama inside the diplomatic residence resuming, but because every shouted word and insult was in English, the almost daily audience in the street never could understand any of it. On the few occasions when Yankees or English pedestrians also stopped to listen—instead of hurrying past with very affronted and derisive expressions fixed on their faces—they never spoke Spanish well enough to translate or, if they did, were too proud to help. Though for as long as they did stay to listen, those English-speaking foreigners always became the new object of the crowd's riveted attention: if a foreigner let out a scandalized laugh over the last outburst of incomprehensible screeching from inside the legation, the crowd would imitate that laugh, or roll their eyes in disgust, or sadly shake their heads, if that was what the foreigner had done first. Discomfited at having so many eyes so raptly fixed upon them, their every grimace and gesture mimicked, these Yankees and Ingleses usually made a hasty retreat. That afternoon María de las Nieves witnessed just such an encounter between the crowd and a pair of rough-looking gringos, and felt so instantly provoked by their coarse disdain—*Mind your own business, you mob of dusky miscreants,* one drawled as they left—that she began translating out loud even before the men were out of earshot. The astonished gringos turned and scowled and before she'd even finished translating her first exchange of invective and abuse, the crowd had protectively closed around her. She didn't understand everything the battling couple was saying, of course, but it was hardly a drama by Shakespeare. Shawl over her head in the drizzle, hugged tightly around her, her face a picture of childish delight at having this chance to wield her rare gift and make herself the center of such excited attention, María de las Nieves had gone on translating, though without mimicking the infuriated, caustic, railing, accusing, snarling tones and inflections of the unhappy pair, speaking instead in a soft steady voice that made everybody push in closer to hear. No one, seeing María de las Nieves before actually hearing what she was saying that day, would ever have guessed the horrible words flowing from her lips: the U.S. Minister's wife's scalding rants of blame, his savaging slurs, some comical enough to elicit hoots and titters. It turned out that she wasn't even really his wife—*my so-called wife . . . yah, yer so-called wife, so what, but yeh lured me here anyway, din yeh, wid all dose pretty promises, moon and stars, lords n ladies, fancy diplomacy parties, yeh, and not even once . . . I should have left you in that harlot's nursery where I found . . . Aw shud up er I'll break yer jaw, yeh parched pea-testicled lil cowerd!*—cobardito de testiculos de chicharos resecaditos! And just as those shocking words were out of her mouth, María de las Nieves glimpsed, pausing on the sidewalk just beyond the crowd, two pedestrians, a beautifully dressed young woman on the arm of an elegant young man, sharing an umbrella of pearl-hued taffeta, the golden-faced woman looking directly at her with an expression of shocked reproach, and just as the man, with a haughty backward glance, took her by the arm and turned her away from the crowd and they resumed their stroll, María de las Nieves realized that that beautiful doncella was none other than Sor Gloria de los Ángeles, her former sister novice. As if both spellbound and humbled by this revelation of her own disgrace, she went on translating, but in a crushed voice, until the Yankee diplomatist's not-quite-wife collapsed into sobs, which there was no need to translate, for they sounded as if they were spurting from her soul like blood from a severed artery, rising ever higher from behind the ivy-draped walls of the legation, until a scarlet geyser of sobs had ascended into the gray sky, and then it subsided all at once, and a shadow like the shadow of death fell over the silenced crowd. By then María de las Nieves, head down so that nobody could see her devastated face, was already halfway down the block, heading home.

Months passed before she even allowed herself to walk down that street again. But among the crowd outside the U.S. Legation that afternoon was

Higinio Farfán, employed as a British Legation clerk and translator for seventeen years despite his rudimentary command of English, which instead of improving was actually deteriorating over time, along with his memory generally. Minister Gastreel had recently told Higinio Farfán more than once that the quality of his work was unacceptable. But the clerk did not forget María de las Nieves's performance: that very afternoon he'd paid a street urchin to follow her home in order to learn her address. An adolescent girl could not become an official British Legation clerk, of course. But what if her translating skills were perhaps unequaled among the not extremely well educated populace of the entire Republiquita? Couldn't she be hired in an unofficial capacity, like a servant with clerical duties, if, in exchange for the chance to employ her, the fiftyish Don Higinio was allowed to retain his job and dignity?

"In the illustrious annals of Isthmus diplomacy, Mr. Noah Cale's tenure here was that rare sordid episode," cracked Wellesley Bludyar, with a sheepish smile, sharing with María de las Nieves his own privileged knowledge of the shamed U.S. Minister. By then she'd already been working at the British Legation several months. Minister Cale, the smitten First Secretary told her, used to import furniture duty-free, claiming it was for his legation, which he would then resell at a hefty profit, and not only that, the Yankee Minister had once tried to prosecute a servant who'd fled his employ, charging that she'd stolen a mattress worth eight dollars. The frightened but incensed girl had gone to the Mayor to seek redress, telling him that she considered herself entitled to the mattress for ". . . for what she called . . . eh, sorry . . . rather what the Mayor later referred to as—" Bludyar paused in his narration, his eyes filling with blue panic. María de las Nieves lightly slapped at his lap with her hand and said, "Ya, Wellesley, tell me!" "Ahhh, yes, of course, sorry . . . for secret services, you see. In the end," Bludyar raced on, "the Mayor himself paid for the mattress and that put an end to the matter. And poor Cale was soon after recalled." Bludyar's blush went on deepening, like a boiling beet. "Never gave a single diplomatic dinner while he was here. Colonel Williamson, of course, his replacement, is entirely a gentleman, with a very charming and lovely wife, Margarita—from Cuba, Snows, did you know?"

Later her friend Vipulina Godoy, the former Sor Cayetano del Niño Salvadór del Mundo, the nun who escaped from Nuestra Señora de Belén simply by walking out the front door, told María de las Nieves that she must have been mistaken, that a year or so after the de-cloistering Sor Gloria de los Ángeles had fled her parents' home and rejoined Sor Gertrudis in her hidden convent. María de las Nieves admitted that it *was* possible she had been mistaken: a fleeting but provocative resemblance, perhaps. There she'd been, imagining herself as a sort of San Antonio de Padua preaching to the fish crowding close to shore in their eagerness to hear, dazzled heads and fins out of the water, and her guilty vision of Sor Gloria had dried up the sea.

"But where is she?" she'd asked Vipulina. "Where is their secret convent? Haven't you found out where yet?" María de las Nieves knew that one night Vipulina, in her aunt's house, where she was living, had received a surprise visit from Sor Gertrudis. The foreign nun had emerged from her hiding place, disguised in secular garb, only lowering the black veil rolled up beneath her hood once the door had been answered and she'd been recognized, to ask Vipulina if she'd at last repented of her sacrilegious ways and had rediscovered her vocation.

"Claro qué no, Las Nievecitas! And I don't think I want to know where it is." (Vipulina claimed that she'd answered her former Prioress with an even more vociferous *Claro qué no!*)

In eight more days, Don José told María de las Nieves, she would be able to wear her new India-rubber boots home. The boots were drying in the small patio behind the shop, over a smoky fire of dried baby corn husks and sulfur.

Don José's hair, mustache, and beard, a sheenless ash-brown, framed his head in such a way that he always looked like an otter just popped up from the water, with hungry, hopeful eyes, rims a livid pink, as if perpetually inflamed by the fumes of cooked caucho sap, ammonia, sulfur, soldered metals, and burning charcoal. Seated on his stool, crouched over his miniature blacksmith's forge, knees rising nearly as high as his shoulders on either side, beneath low rafters of dangling steel and whalebone umbrella spokes, surrounded by piled bolts and cut pieces of taffeta, silk, and other fabrics, bricks of raw caucho and vulcanized sheets, collapsible umbrella tubes, the stacked woods of varying qualities from which he cut and shaped umbrella handles and molds, Don José resembled one of his own peculiar umbrella-spoke dolls, a pagan giant blacksmith with umbrella-spoke limbs inside a mountain cave, turning out a new race of spoke-limbed creatures with India-rubber heads.

Three or four times a week María de las Nieves came in the afternoon and sat with the Polish-English-Hebrew umbrella mender, usually in his back workroom. Don José's was a winter trade, and during the dry season he had much free time; now, to keep his fingers busy, and more for María de las Nieves's amusement than his own, and also to provide a ready path out of any too prolonged silence that might occur, he made umbrella-spoke dolls. Lately he often attached strings to his creations too, and even walked them about the floor, but not very much, for it made them both feel silly and embarrassed. It was María de las Nieves's job to fashion heads out of caucho, wax, scraps of wood, pincushion-like balls of fabric, and also to sew costumes if she wished, and to name the creatures. The former novice nun was, of course, a deft sewer, but the puppets were not exceptionally artistic. Very few so far represented any improvement in craft or fancy over the Strawman, Don José's very first creation. He thought that, for Christmas, they would place a few in the window and see if they sold; if they did, they'd share the earnings. But he was resolutely against staging a puppet show, and was so uninterested in providing his creations with any kind of story that he never remembered the names María de las Nieves made up or the characters she sometimes improvised for them, which was surprising, because he usually doted on whatever she did.

"—But it is true, María de las Nieves, that when I was a child, I was delighted by puppet shows," Don José explained to her. "In particular I remember one, staged in a small theater gazebo which appeared one day in a park near my home in Manchester. An entire opera, Mozart's *Le Nozze di Figaro*, performed by very lifelike marionettes, not one higher than your knees, María de las Nieves, with an entire orchestra at the edge of the stage, all of the violinists bowing together, including one pretty young lad violinist, with golden curls, who kept turning his head to watch the opera and losing his place in the music, provoking the marionette conductor to lean over and smack that boy in the head with his baton! You ask how is that possible, a Mozart opera staged by puppets, but I saw it. You'll find it a little easier to believe when I tell you that the puppets did not sing, nor did the musicians actually make music. It was mostly silent. From somewhere unseen, a voice sang a few snatches of melody, but only now and then, accompanied by a lone fiddler."

After a moment María de las Nieves commented, "It would be effective to put on such a show at the new school for the deaf—I know they would enjoy it."

"Hehhehheh." The umbrella mender had a low, rumbling laugh. "Well, it was not entirely silent."

She raised the arm of the puppet she was costuming and said, "Off with her head!" Especially during the rainy season, when as soon as Don José finished repairing one umbrella he had to turn his attention to another, María de las Nieves often read out loud to him as he worked: *Alice in Wonderland* was a particular favorite.

"You could stage the story of Alice, Don José."

"I feel no need to, María de las Nieves. I enjoy the book, that is enough."

"For children who cannot read, or who are sick in hospital beds."

"Who cannot read," he snorted disdainfully.

"Or for Indian children."

"You would do them a greater favor scrubbing them for lice."

"I could translate it into Mam, Don José!"

"Hehhehhehheh."

"*Q'imila twi'!* That's 'off with her head' in Mam, Don José."

"What other book would you like to make into a puppet show, María de las Nieves."

"*Middlemarch.*"

They fell silent for a moment.

"Mrs. Gastreel lent it to me."

"I have not read that book."

A moment later, she remarked, in a low and portentous tone, "*The key to all mythologies.*"

The umbrella mender glanced at her as if waiting for her to elaborate, then returned to his puppet. And their silence returned.

"What are the people who study those Hebrew holy books like, Don José?" she finally asked.

"They become, it is said, radiant with wisdom and light, or they go completely mad. Not that anyone can tell the two apart."

"Have you ever seen such a person?"

"I've seen more than a few Hebrew madmen. How they got that way, I might have my opinions, but I'd rather not say."

"Maestro Martí is certainly radiant with wisdom and light, Don José."

"Did I tell you I sold Señor Martí a very sturdy used umbrella which I'd rebuilt?"

"Yes. He even knows about Hebrew religion, Don José. He told us that the Hebrew mystics have a belief that he likes very much, and that is that the power of the spoken word is such that it can awaken sleeping hearts and souls and allow you to converse with God."

"So, even the Hebrew mystics Señor Martí knows about! But your very learned friend is an atheist like you and I. That is his reputation, isn't it? I've heard it said that the Conservatives consider him the very devil in a twill frock coat. Well, I know from a very credible source that he is a Freemason."

"Sometimes I tell you things, Don José, that are not necessarily untruths—but in others moods, I might retract them. And the next day, I might change again."

"The secret of your religious vacillation is safe with me, María de las Nieves."

"The nuns believed the opposite, that silence and interior prayer are the best way to converse with God. Yet they wrote poetry in celebration of their silences, which was read out loud to the rest of us in order to help us find silence."

"We will have eternity to be silent."

And they fell silent again, until María de las Nieves said, "Those who speak badly about the Rosenthals, Don José, for selling flowers that one could always pick for free in the meadows outside the city before they opened their flower shop, have to admit that before people also preferred artificial flowers to natural ones. And now everybody wants beautiful and varied bouquets from the Rosenthals' shop in their homes. Because of the Rosenthals, people notice our country's floral abundance as never before."

"The Rosenthals would be delighted by your praise, María de las Nieves. I'd never thought of it, but I have no doubt that what you've perceived is true."

"And every patoja wants jasmine or a rose to wear behind her ear or in her dress. And in the newspaper it said that jasmine has become so popular that there is now a shortage, and young men have even been caught climbing over walls just to steal a blossoming branch from a stranger's garden. And there are even men who now wear flowers in their buttonholes every day, which they can also buy from the Rosenthals. And coffee trees, with their white flowers and red berries, are now considered the source of all our country's wealth."

"I see. And soon we will even be eating flowers. For dinner, the hostess will place a large vase arranged by the Rosenthals in the center of the table, and we will all lean in with our forks and knives or, better yet, like savages we will tear off blossoms with our hands . . . hehheh . . . and eat them with tortillas and a little salt."

"And Maestro Martí says that our poetry should find its inspiration in natural American beauty. He says Europe has its own character and poetry, but America is entirely different—a land of tender black-eyed women and white jasmine, is what he said, and that our poetry should be like that, and as fresh as our highland air, and, pues—he continued in that vein."

"Your Dr. Torrente has a gift for continuing in his veins."

"But don't you think it's significant, Don José, that the Rosenthals with their flower store and Senor Martí with his poetry take completely different routes to the same idea—. Now it is fashionable and modern for us to see ourselves reflected in our own flora. And nobody wants artificial flowers."

"That is progress, María de las Nieves. The future has certainly arrived. But the English have always had an appreciation for fresh flowers. What if it is more truly American to prefer artificial flowers? What we really need to do is convince the people of Europe that drinking one cup of coffee every ten minutes is essential to good health, and then this will be among the richest countries in the world!"

She wished she had black American eyes like María Chon's—. I'll bring a sprig of jasmine home to María Chon, she thought, and braid her hair into two tresses decorated with jasmine blossoms, and put carmine on her lips, and this evening we'll promenade together in the Parque de la Concordia.

"Maestro Martí," she said, "also says that one of the formulas of eloquence, not just in literary composition but in life, is that what comes from the heart goes to the heart."

"That seems very simple and wise, María de las Nieves, and I am sure it is applicable in no end of ways."

"And what comes from the soul goes to the soul."

"The soul, well—I don't dare to speculate about the soul."

"And he says that he didn't learn those things from reading, Don José, but from his own observations and experience."

"I WANT TO share with you what happened to me this evening on the walk from my home to this school, a walk I know I will remember for the rest of my life," José Martí, arms thrust back, fingers nervously entwined in the tails of his frock coat, told the twenty-three young women and adolescent girls enrolled in his class in Literary Composition for Women. "This evening, when I stepped out of my house and onto the avenue, I was instantly disoriented. It was as if the avenue outside my door had suddenly turned into a different one from the avenue always there before. Had my little house suddenly been dropped down in some other strange and splendid city? I gazed down the avenue, and it appeared to be twice as long as usual—from where I stood to the nearest corner was now twice as far as the last time I had stood there. And though everything around me had the absorbing aspect of the unfamiliar, I noticed that these were indeed the same buildings that had lined this block before. What made everything seem so unfamiliar, I realized, was the light. Could it be, dearest damas and niñas, that this evening this country experienced the most singular and beautiful sunset in our history? The supreme masterpiece of all sunsets in the history of the Americas? For the light seemed entirely animate. It seemed to have stepped out of the invisible jungle of the air to drink water from one of our fountains, and to taste the fruit of our gardens and orchards, and then to lie within the perfect symmetry of our long straight streets like a living thing biologically related to every other living being and thing that surrounds us—for there within that light, translucent and phosphorescent, were all the shades of green of our jungles and of our mountains and of the mosses covering our most ancient walls, and the reds, oranges, yellows, and all the other colors of our birds and flowers, a living sweet light exhaling the fragrance of our chaste white jasmine and of your own pure hearts and souls. And this light, like a metamorphosing angel taking the shape of the air, filled me with extraordinary bliss. I noticed something else as I walked, not only the light and the peculiar elongation of the avenue, which was perhaps an illusion of that light, but that the avenue, usually so busy at that hour, was empty. There was no one else out walking, no carriages, horses, or mules, no sad sturdy Indios bent beneath their heavy loads. The avenue was empty; not even I was there. As I went forward, I was aware of my own consciousness, yes, but I could not even hear my own footsteps or see my own shadow. It was as if I too had been absorbed into that beautiful living light. Of course that light was *good*—because of it, I felt filled with goodness and gratitude and love. One of the proofs of the imperfection of existence is that such moments of bliss are so rare—such moments when you feel yourself at one with nature. It was like that other late afternoon written about by the great New England poet Emerson, during which a man loses his sense of self and disappears into the world, transforms himself into the world on an afternoon so rare that he will remember it all his life. At such a moment, where should your footsteps carry you? You have to walk back into your old unhappy self, return to your former shape. Not even the greatest mystics just walk off into light forever, do they? Do they, Señorita Moran? They do not, true? If you are slowly falling back into the darkness of your former self even as you are still walking down the avenue of light, where should your footsteps lead? Shouldn't they lead you to whom you love? Let yourself be carried to the door of that place which, in all the world, is where you will most love and be loved. Arrive like a lost child who has finally found his way home and breaks into tears of happiness, anticipating his mother's embrace. Arrive like our old friend the soldier of liberty who in his rebel encampment received the message that his wife had given birth to a son, and so he mounted his horse, and rode through the night, behind enemy lines, to the ranchito where his beloved and the other rebel wives were living in hiding, and he stood outside the door and shouted: *Wake up, women, all of you, and come outside. Here at the door stands a man desperate to embrace his wife and know his son!* Where have my footsteps brought me? They have brought me here, to this classroom, where the white dove of purity, modesty, and love nests in all of your hearts, and the eagle of poetry and learning lifts our spirits and thoughts—"

Who did Martí look directly at then? Not at María de las Nieves, sitting alongside María García Granados that evening, sharing one of the double desks. He looked first, though his eyes did not linger, at the former president's daughter, and then quickly around at the flushed faces of all his enraptured niñas and damas:

"They have brought me here to my students in the Academia de Niñas de Centroamérica."

Maestro Martí's evening class in Literary Composition for Women was held in the school's main lecture salon and auditorium. In one corner of the room, upon a painted plaster pedestal representing the Island of Cuba as a wave-lapped rocky crag, stood a female mannequin dressed in white tunic and purple sash, the soft red Phrygian cap of revolution upon her head, her extended arm holding out the rebel flag of the Solitary Star, and at her feet, amid the broken chains of slavery, three nearly naked plaster Africans raising their arms in gratitude to the female symbol of Cuban liberty. Red-and-blue bunting framed the small stage behind the lectern, and prints of Cuban revolutionary heroes and of Cuban scenes decorated the walls. The school's director was Margarita Izaguirre; her eminent brother, José María Izaguirre, directed the Normal School; their sister Clara and their three young nieces, Clemencia, Catalina, and Lucía, also taught at the Academia. The Izaguirres were like a dazzling circus family of exiled Cuban independistas and educators. During the day the Academia's young school-girls, drawn from the city's most elite families, heard a steady stream of exalted talk about Cuba. Of course the students in Martí's evening class also heard a great deal about Cuba. The incessant glorification of Cuba and Cubans and all things Cuban in the new progressive schools did eventually irritate people: parents, friends of parents, acquaintances of friends of parents, Liberals and Conservatives alike, until even illiterate muleteers were indignant about all the talk of Cuba in the schools. When, before long, anonymous pamphlets filled with cruel sarcasm and ridicule, much of it singling out young "Dr. Torrente," began to circulate throughout the city, was there anyone so innocent of the situation in the schools as to actually be surprised?

MAESTRO MARTÍ ALSO had a passion for reading newspapers, and occasionally coincided with María de las Nieves and María Chon in the reading room kiosk in the Parque de la Concordia. There, and whenever they spoke just after or before class, or ran into each other at some other public literary function or lecture, Martí often wanted to converse with María de las Nieves about one or the other of two subjects: nuns, especially the poetry and writing of nuns, and the life and customs of the Indians. She'd never before met anyone so persistently curious about those two seemingly unrelated subjects. She was grateful for any attention she received from her teacher, of course. According to Martí, the lively simplicity of convent writing had kept the Spanish language alive during the more than two centuries that learned men had been suffocating it with ornate rhetoric and moribund forms. About nuns and their writing she had plenty to say, of course.

Once, as Martí stood outside the door to the lecture salon before class, he'd greeted her as she came down the corridor by holding out his hands and reciting an irreverent quatrain by the immortal Lope de Vega (whose most beloved daughter had also been a poetess-nun) that asks a convent-bound "María" why she had to marry God; did He make her so lovely only to anger all those from whose eyes she would now be hidden? Why had Maestro Martí ambushed her with such a poem? All the other students gathered there had waited to see how she would reply; it had seemed a kind of test, not just of her cleverness but of her ability to calmly absorb what a vain, easily deluded girl might construe as a flirtation poorly disguised as the enthusiastic literary banter of her teacher. After Sor Gertrudis's novice classes and then Minister Gastreel's often peremptory manner, María de las Nieves was certainly accustomed to being put on the spot. But she hadn't known what to say; for an instant her mind had gone blank—but thankfully she hadn't needed words of her own that day, because another lightly blasphemous poem had quickly come to her, and before she could think anymore it was dancing from her lips: *But, God, I am not like the branch of an oak tree, always tranquil / I am not like sandalwood that I*

*never change my smell. / I do not love the immutable, such as the enormous boulder in*
*the path, / or the eternal silence, or infinity.*

And Martí had smiled, not with surprise, she'd thought, but as if this
was exactly what he'd hoped for, and when he'd applauded, so had the
other girls, and she'd tried to carry herself as if really it was no great thing.
She'd had more poetic education than most of the others, because of the
convent, and Maestro Martí knew that, and that was all. Only María García
Granados, having grown up in a home always visited by poets and with
Central America's most celebrated female poet among her ancestors, might
know more, or as much.

"I'm sure that someday soon you will be starting your own family, María
de las Nieves, with a husband, and children. But what can it be like for a
former nun to marry?" Martí asked her at the reading room kiosk one day,
perhaps teasing her a little. "To devote a love formerly promised to God to
a man whom you will not, or at least should not, pray to?"

"I'm in no hurry for that, Maestro," she answered confidently. "From
what I've been able to observe, I think being married to God must be easy
compared to being married to a man."

Talking about the ways and customs of the aboriginal people, on the
other hand, always made her feel tongue-tied and remote, though for Martí
she always did make an effort. Not surprisingly, María Chon was more
knowledgeable than she was. One memorable afternoon, when Martí encountered María de las Nieves and her servant together in the reading
room kiosk, he kept them talking there mainly about the Indios for hours.
Martí addressed her and María Chon with such natural civility and equal
deference that neither even noticed the breach of formality, and ended up
conversing with Martí as two inseparable friends, rather than as employer
and servant (employer and servant who were, in fact, inseparable if often
tempestuous friends). María Chon's knowledge of Indian practices and
beliefs was hardly encyclopedic, however; in fact Martí seemed to know
much more than she did—though his knowledge was mostly learned from
books—and he ended up doing almost all the talking, sharing with them
some of what he'd discovered a few months before, during his intensive
week of investigation and study in preparation for the patriotic play on
native themes he'd been commissioned to write by the Supreme Government for a student production at the Normal School. Dr. Maríano Padilla,

who owned the best library of rare American books in the entire Isthmus, had allowed Martí to study his rare manuscript copy of the Popul Vuh, the sacred bible of the Quiché Maya, with Fray Ximénez's sixteenth-century translation, the very same manuscript the bibliophile had lent to the Abbé Brasseur de Bourbourg and upon which the pioneering cleric had based his French translation, published in Paris twenty years before, a copy of which Dr. Padilla had also given to Martí. So now Martí had read the Popul Vuh in antiquated Spanish and modern French, and said he had not been so transported by a work of poetry since reading Byron as a schoolboy. "It is our own brilliant indigenous *Iliad*!" he exclaimed to María de las Nieves and María Chon in the reading room kiosk; they both tried to at least look as if such a pronouncement excited them also, though María de las Nieves had not yet read the *Iliad*, and María Chon had never heard of it.

Martí went on describing what he'd learned about the Indios, eyes dreamy and smoldering, his soft swept-back curls swaying atop his head like innumerable just awakening cats. Listening to Martí always caused a suspenseful knot of excitement to form in María de las Nieves's stomach. It was as if his thoughts and learning were carried forward by an endless magical army of words one could almost see, column after column marching across the wide plain behind his forehead to some impossibly gentle yet percussive rhythm and leaping from his lips. She wondered what it was all for and if it would ever stop and did not want it to stop, though sometimes her attention, exhausted, wandered off to sit in the shade. Martí wanted to know about everything, had questions about everything: Did they understand the Mayan calendar, the 260-day year in which every day was itself a god, with a name such as 8 Monkey, and attributes and auguries residing within that name? Sí pues, María Chon had heard of that. But only certain men understood that kind of thing, she said; you had to look for them in the forest, and bring gifts. Did María Chon feel that she lived among gods and spirits, and that they were all around her? Could she name them? Yes, they hid all around, María Chon admitted, though not here in Tuj Sib, which was the Indio name for the capital, she told him, showing off, for she never said Tuj Sib around María de las Nieves. They were not here in Tuj Sib, and she had forgotten their names. And with a slight scowl, María Chon abruptly added, "Señor, I only pray to God and the Virgin!"

But in the end, María de las Nieves had to admit that she really didn't like talking about what the Indios believed. She felt no admiration for the primitive way of life from which her own mother had come and to which she'd embarrassingly returned. And so it wasn't just María Chon monopolizing Martí's attention that was irritating her. After a while her sluggish reluctance to listen anymore won out, and like any student or novice nun more interested in her own thoughts than whatever is being droned on about in class, she stared out through the kiosk's door, and watched the people strolling through the park, and wondered why though some men walked with a confident gait, you could tell that they were not confident at all. How could she feel so certain that she liked that man but didn't like another simply because of how each walked? That one, walking energetically on the balls of his feet, his arms swinging too loosely, would fill you with dreariness whenever he spoke, but that one, plodding heavily along, hips wider than his shoulders, big ears a translucent pink in the sun, dimples like deep thumbprints, definitely knew how to make any girl smile . . . she deserved to be proven completely wrong of course . . .

Martí was saying that he did not agree with the famous archeologist Dr. Le Plongeon, the self-proclaimed discoverer of the ruins at Chichén Itzá, whom he'd actually encountered and spoken to in Isla Mujeres on his original journey here just months before, and who believed the pyramids in the Central American jungles to be the work of ancient Egyptians and Babylonians.

"Your ancestors alone are responsible for that glorious civilization," Martí announced to María de las Nieves and María Chon. "Wouldn't you like to see those ruins one day?"

"I would rather see the pyramids in Egypt," María de las Nieves answered. It was true, she would like to see Egypt. "But no—." Now she was flustered. She'd retract. "No, that's not true," she blurted. "I think I would rather see our pyramids in the jungle."

"I don't want to see ruins anywhere," offered María Chon, "and never in the jungle—too hot and too many snakes! I want to go live in New York or Paris with Doñacita las Nieves."

For a brief moment Martí seemed bewildered; then he let out one of his high bleating laughs. Perhaps one day, he told them, if Dr. Le Plongeon had his way, they would be able to see such ruins after all. Dr. Le Plongeon was busily promoting his controversial plan to purchase and transport Chichén Itzá stone by stone to the United States and reassemble it there.

Often when Martí saw Indios walking in the streets he fell silent and watched, his expression grave and thoughtful. Another time, when they had gone to stand outside the kiosk in the shade for a while, a line of Indias had crossed the park, the mother first, her daughters in descending order of height behind her, all dressed exactly alike, in richly embroidered purples and blues, wearing necklaces of scarlet beads and silver, hair wound with scarlet ribbons, and Martí had removed his hat and slightly bowed to them and proclaimed: *"La grande dame, et les petites dames."*

"We made the Indios what they are today, María de las Nieves," Martí told her later that afternoon. "But only the Indio can save us. Only the Indios can save America." And for a long while he elaborated on what he meant, speaking movingly but calmly about the sleeping potential and tragic histories of both the Indios and the Americas, until, with impassioned eyes and tender vehemence, he added, "And you represent the new American intelligence, María de las Nieves. You will be a mother of our new America." She stubbornly replied that unfortunately hers was an example of a very old form of intelligence, for she'd been educated by nuns in a convent. Martí looked at her then with an expression of concern, a little saddened, perhaps, or even apologetic. "But even in our convents," he said gently, "the new rises from the old, María de las Nieves. Wasn't a nun's convent in Mexico a cradle of our new American poetry?"

Martí was optimistic about the Liberals' programs for the Indios. Great changes were occurring in their little country, which might turn out to be exemplary for all the young American republics. True, the Indios were now required by law to provide manual labor on the new coffee plantations on demand, but in the long run even that draconian measure could be a good thing, if it inculcated modern work habits and virtues. Similar praise might be rendered to the policy of expropriating the Indios' fallow ancestral lands and putting these into the ardent hands of young coffee pioneers, who created wealth and employment. Whenever the Supreme President General of the Republic went up into the mountains, didn't he come back with poor, barefoot young Indio men, and send them back a year or two later as schoolteachers? Wasn't it popular education that saved France? That allowed France to finally triumph over the forces of reaction and nostalgia!

In the reading room that afternoon, Martí exulted: "And more than once I've been told by young men of this government that in Sacatepéquez there is an Indio Jefe who reads newspapers, and is fluent in French, and has been building schools in the clean, well-managed villages and hamlets under his jurisdiction, where he doesn't just teach students to read and count, but instills modern virtues!"

That evening, after they had said good-bye to Martí and were walking home in still overwhelmed silence, María Chon blurted:

"Este Cubanito, el pobre, como lo engañan—what lies they tell him!"

AT THE ACADEMIA de Niñas, a special fiesta was being planned in honor of the ninth anniversary of a rebel battle victory over Spanish troops in Cuba. Schoolchildren would stage patriotic plays, and the Izaguirres, with the help of some of the older girls, would decorate the school to look like a Camagüey sugar plantation house during a harvest festival, and prepare a feast of Cuban dishes and treats; a pig would even be roasted over a pit in the garden. Martí chose María García Granados to recite a patriotic poem composed for the occasion by their Cuban friend the Bayamés Bard. Several times a week Martí and Chafandín's daughter met at the school before the composition class to rehearse. On one of those late afternoons— prettily lit by an ordinary sunset—María de las Nieves, wearing a new hat of cream-colored straw trailing long yellow ribbons, her stomach a basket of excited nerves, arrived at the school earlier than perhaps she meant to. She was waiting outside the lecture salon when she heard a young woman's delicate and melodic voice floating through the empty corridor: the cadences were those of a poem, but she could make out only a few words— *Cuba . . . virginal . . . universal . . . Cuba . . . paradise . . . freedom . . . love . . .* Then the recitation was finished, and María de las Nieves stood in the corridor listening to the silence, holding her breath, straining to hear any sound from either one of them. That silence did turn animate: an invisible crocodile stealthily crawling down the corridor with death on its breath. Jealousy, self-pity, the lid on a box filled with the dark cold air of heartbreak just creaking open—. She quickly retreated, went out of the school onto the Calle de San Augustín, and slowly circled the block thinking that maybe she would just go home. She arrived back at the school ten minutes after the class had begun: Maestro Martí was in raptures over a poem by Hugo, "Tristesse d'Olympo," a poem which laments that the happy moments of life cannot be eternal. She sat in a chair against the rear wall with her hat in her lap. At the end of class Martí called to her as she was headed out the door, asking her to please wait. What did he want? Was he going to invite her to recite a patriotic poem too? She waited warily for Martí to finish speaking to the other students, who always gathered around him after class. She felt a touch on her sleeve and turned to find María García Granados standing there, and they exchanged the usual polite words and smiles of salutation. In her smile she saw his smile, his lips invisibly pressed to her lips. María de las Nieves immediately blushed, as much from a sudden impression of the other girl's beauty and grace as from embarrassment at her own jealously. But María García Granados's beauty puzzled her, for it was not that she was so exceptionally fine-featured—her nose was a bit too long, slightly bulbed, and her ears were big and droopy— but her long-lashed, intelligent eyes seemed to bathe you in a warm light of affectionate kindness, and her lips had the color and velvety softness of a dark pink rose, and she had undulant black hair worn in two loose plaits flowing down to her waist, and her flawless skin was pale but it was a paleness of so many gradations that every time you looked it was different, as if its temperature rose or fell with her every inner thought or emotion, and her blood was a nearly phantom nimble cavalry of the most superior horses and officers, silently riding this way and that way throughout her veins and fanning out over her skin, always knowing exactly where to go and where to hide in order to mesmerize, ambush, bewitch, and arouse desire. Even though we're the same age, thought María de las Nieves, her beauty and charm is womanly and girlish at the same time. She always has delicate violet shadows under eyes, because her father has guests over for gambling games and parties nearly every night and she stays up so late, and she plays Chopin nocturnes on the piano for them while the men savor their last brandies and cigars, and everyone says that her fingers caress the keys with an exquisite expressiveness unmatched by any other female pianist in all Central America. Her perfectly fitting burgundy dress, with black-lace-trimmed low collar and ruffled sleeves, was, of course, from Paris. "Just last night my mother was asking about you," said María García Granados. "And

I told her you are the student Pepe holds in the highest regard," and in her small, sweet voice, she added, "Well, it's true, Las Nievecitas." María de las Nieves stood dumbfounded for a moment, not having any idea what to say, and when she finally answered, "Pues, gracias, María," her voice was nearly inaudible, and she only wanted to escape. And the other girl said, "My mother wondered why we haven't seen you lately." And María de las Nieves answered in the most absurdly solemn tone, "I don't know why, María. I'll be happy to see her whenever she wants."

And then Martí was walking toward them, his eyes ablaze like a happy demon's, and holding out a book with a pale paper jacket and red print, which he put into María de las Nieves's astonished hands, telling her that he'd found this recently published translation of Sainte-Beuve's *Portraits of Celebrated Women,* and had thought immediately of her, and he complimented her on her new hat. She said thank you and gaped at the book in her hands; hers was partly the paralyzed shyness of someone un- used to receiving gifts and whose first reaction is to feel it as the most monumental occasion, before plummeting into insecure confusion over what the gift's meaning might actually be. She felt María García Granados's warm touch on her arm again, and heard her say, "Pepe gave a copy in French to my mother, and she is adoring it. I'm reading it next. We'll have to have conversations about it, Las Nievecitas, the three of us—or the four of us," and she smiled at Martí. Outside, two servants from the García Granados household were waiting to escort the former President's daughter home, and Martí, who lived only a block farther on, would accompany them, and María de las Nieves, with effusive good-byes, turned homeward after a few blocks, clutching the book, laid atop her com- position book, over her chest.

Only when she got home did she realize that he had inscribed it: For my celebrated student María de las Nieves, whom the future also celebrates. Your fraternal friend, your Pepe Martí.

After dinner—rice, beans, tortillas, a bit of leftover boiled vegetables and mutton, hot chocolate—she sat at the cleared dining table by lamplight cutting open the book's folded pages with a pair of scissors, smoking a cigarrito, while María Chon, also smoking, sat and watched. Amada Gómez, the melancholy boarder, was at the table too, immersed in her paid sewing. María Chon seemed to comprehend the gift's significance; a look of reverence was fixed on her face, and she was unusually quiet. When she was finished, María de las Nieves carried the book and the lamp into her bedroom and lay fully clothed on her bed and began to read. The first faint light of dawn in her window surprised her while she was deep into the chapter about Madame Roland. Who, then, was the object of that late, unique, heartrending passion? she read. A prejudiced public has named Barbaroux, but there is no proof that it was he. A sacred veil will continue to hide this latest storm, which gathered and passed in silence over her mighty spirit when death was near—

Weary from holding the book up in the air, María de las Nieves set it aside on the bed and stared at the ceiling. *A sacred veil* . . . Three years ago, at this hour, having just pulled on her own veil, she would have been bent over her Meditation Points in her cell. Now, before sleep, she was reading about a French heroine of the century past who'd also spent a part of her childhood in a convent, who forever after cherished austerity, yet who as a married woman and mother fell in love more than once, became an influential radical politician and finally a revolutionary martyr, a profuse writer as well, one who knew how to judge and manipulate men and even influenced the course of actual events in bloody France. Had Madame Roland been a man, Sainte-Beuve even claimed, she could have been the savior of her land! So far the author had barely mentioned her husband, Monsieur Roland, except to state that he was an inspector of manufactures, devoted to industrial and economic studies, whose intellect Madame Roland enlivened with her own readings in philosophy and poetry, and that he was the lesser politician of the two.

María de las Nieves took up her book again, and read: We do not find her, at fifteen, completely enamored of any but M. De Guibert. Her feeling is the very opposite of infatuation—. But who was M. De Guibert? A teacher? And what about Madame Roland's husband? Why didn't Sainte-Beuve tell about their courtship? Obviously, this was one of those authors who considered it mediocre to answer any of a reader's most obvious questions. She put the book down again. Maybe she would never learn how Madame Roland had fallen in love with her husband, or even how she had died . . . She was going to be useless at the legation in the morning. She got up from her bed, closed the shutters, and flopped down again, too tired even to undress. *The very opposite of infatuation*, she silently and gravely repeated, more than once, as if the phrase was imbued with a secret power that might help her.

She woke soon after drenched in sweat inside her clothes and feeling as if some animal with coarse claws had been trying to dig its way out of her insides: finally exhausted, the animal seemed to have curled up into a heavy ball of wet fur and gone to sleep. Without saying his name or even visualizing his face, she knew that he was the cause of this raw ache and leaden sorrow inside her.

All the next day at the legation she felt slightly feverish, her breath and eyes hot and acrid. She felt deeply frightened in a way that she hadn't since those ghastly days of her first menstruation in the convent. Mrs. Gastreel must have noticed because she brought her a pot of chamomile tea, a slice of angel cake, and a small pitcher of thick cream. Pay attention to reason like Madame Roland, she commanded herself. I will love Wellesley Bludyar to the end of my days, if he will have me. Over and over she silently chanted that she loved Wellesley Bludyar, and grew ever more miserable. When she caught the First Secretary's eye as he was heading into Minister Gastreel's office, she made herself smile at him as she hadn't in weeks. Desperate for a cigarrito—she was not permitted to smoke in the legation—she ate her cake in three bites.

Wellesley Bludyar was euphoric. But inside the office he found Minister Gastreel impatiently waiting to dictate a letter to Lord Derby. While Wellesley sat at his desk copying, the British Minister improvised his dispatch to the Foreign Secretary in London, regarding German ambitions in Central America, from notes he'd hurriedly scrawled following a diplomatic dinner at the Mexican Legation the previous evening. Suddenly the image of María de las Nieves's shatteringly false smile and desperate eyes came back to Wellesley Bludyar, and an all too familiar bleak wind gusted through his heart. She is trying to make herself love me and cannot, he told himself. She knows she should. She feels more indifference than she can even bear to admit. A feeling of doomed dramatic bitterness overtook the First Secretary. Perhaps he'd never felt so closely bonded to her as he did now, though it was not requited love that bonded them but his desperate imagination: so piercingly could he imagine his lips on her skin, tasting her faint flavor of old lemon rind, his nose against her hair and nuzzling behind her ear, that it really was as if his lips and nose were in those very places, and because he understood now that they would never be there, he also understood that he would never be able to forget what it had been like . . . And now he had lost his place in the dispatch . . . "The German designs on the Isthmus," Minister Gastreel droned, "covertly evolved by Prussia and the Hansa cities over decades, are, under Bismarck's Empire, coming to fruition . . ." I should try to convince her to become my wife anyway, he thought; what's there to lose? He laid down his pen and looked up with a baleful expression at Minister Gastreel, who was improvising a description of the disagreeable personality and dangerous abilities of the German Empire's haughty new Chargé d'Affairs—

"I am most sorry, Your Excellency," said Wellesley Bludyar. "I was suddenly feeling a bit indisposed, and have lost my place."

Minister Gastreel's steely eyes slowly registered that perhaps some crucial portion of his diplomatic intelligence had been lost forever; he asked the First Secretary to read back the last words he'd copied.

"In this Republic alone Germans currently own thirty-seven merchant houses, 12.8 square kilometers of sugar plantations, and 15.3 million coffee bushes . . . And there I lost my place, Your Excellency, at the number of coffee bushes owned by Germans"—and he looked up to receive Minister Gastreel's infuriated glare.

"Perhaps, Mr. Bludyar," said Minister Gastreel, "your responsibilities should also be delegated to Señorita Moran." Higinio Farfán, the legation clerk, watching from his desk in a corner of the room with an expression of being much too satisfied at the First Secretary's disgrace, turned back to his habitual idleness.

"I have no doubt Señorita Moran would perform them better, sir."

Could it be that Minister Gastreel noticed his young First Secretary's unhappiness and decided to spare him any further humiliation? His wife, after all, was Wellesley Bludyar's increasingly exasperated confidante; it confounded her that Wellesley continued to be so pathetically in love with the legation's unofficial translator, who—amusing and clever and useful to her husband as "Snows" undoubtedly was—was also, after all, no more than what she was. It hardly needed saying that if Wellesley were to marry her, his diplomatic career would be ruined. María de las Nieves's apparent rejection of Wellesley was, she'd quipped to her husband, certainly proof of God's continuing benevolence toward the British. Proof also, if any was needed, of the mestiza girl's farcical social ignorance—if it was not in fact some incomprehensible and poisonously effective Latin female strategy for seducing poor Bludyar by slowly eroding his manliness and spirit so that he wouldn't be able to regain his senses before she entrapped him forever, and turned Bludyar into just another of those expatriates slowly addling themselves with cheap aguardiente amid a domestic quagmire of half-breed offspring. Perhaps this was the moment when Minister Gastreel decided to heed his wife's advice that what Wellesley Bludyar needed was to be sent on a long and arduous foreign assignment. The legation would certainly be left direly understaffed, though it was probably true that María de las Nieves was by now perfectly capable of performing much of the First Secretary's work. The Minister Resident's duty to the Queen was not to coddle Wellesley Bludyar for his mediocre clerical skills but to give his young apprentice a last opportunity to harden himself, to lose his callow sentimentality. Otherwise he was a danger to the Foreign Office, and thus to Britain, and thereby not much better than a traitor.

"Oh well," said Minister Gastreel, giving the notes in his hand a light shake, "what I'd dictated so far was not entirely spontaneous. Only if you feel up to it, Bludyar, let's begin again, shall we?"

Outside, still in her usual seat in the corridor alongside the courtyard garden, María de las Nieves had pulled *Portraits of Celebrated Women* from her purse. It turned out that the book had a second chapter devoted to Madame Roland! If the perfect moral creature is ever to be formed within us, she read, it is formed early. Sainte-Beuve, in that chapter, expressed his terrifying theory that a person reaches a peak of moral completeness, integrity, and grace by twenty, which over subsequent years slowly deteriorates or even *ceases to be*. Meanwhile a person goes on living around his or her ruined or even evaporated core, *at best* merely mimicking the moral excellence and heroism of vanished youth!

She read: We are fortunate, therefore, whenever we can discover an original likeness of those who are foreordained to fame; when some unforeseen chance reveals them to us exactly as they were at the chosen and unique moment, at their blossoming, *their hour of beauty*.

Sainte-Beuve had been inspired to write this second chapter by the recent publication in France of a volume of correspondence between the girl Madame Roland—she was then Mademoiselle Phlipon—and two young sisters, students also, whom she'd met in her convent school. The first letter was written by Madame Roland when she was seventeen, the same age María de las Nieves was now; the last, dated eight years later, announced her impending marriage to Monsieur Roland.

So, according to Sainte-Beuve, María de las Nieves was now nearly as good as she was ever going to be, and was approaching her own *hour of beauty*. And if María García Granados was indeed more beautiful than her in all respects, as anyone with eyes, ears, and a brain in their head would doubtlessly agree, then that distance between them must be as eternally set as that between planets and could not be overcome in the little time that she had left, before her *hour* struck, no matter how diligently she tried to cultivate herself . . . Yes, but what if her own inner core deteriorated more slowly than the other girl's? What if her inner core, or a healthy portion of it, was still there when María García Granados's was almost eroded, or had even ceased to be? Sainte-Beuve hadn't allowed for or explored such a possibility in his theory.

Nor had he even informed his readers how Madame Roland had died; nor, apparently, was he going to. Of course it must be common knowledge to readers in France. While writing, Sainte-Beuve wouldn't have been thinking of young Central American readers who'd never even heard of his heroine. María de las Nieves read on, intrigued to find the life and intimate writings of a girl her own age so pored over by a secular writer instead of a religious one. And she read with a peculiar confidence, a near certainty that she would find her own dilemmas at least interestingly addressed here, for all the signs were there: the young Madame Roland also had her struggles with religion, and the usual difficulties over vanity; reading was her passion too, she worried about the reader's self-flattering deceptions, and she thought deeply about how to master this problem of perhaps loving books too much. Then, full of confusion, she entered "the age of emotion," and likened her first suitors to a swarm of bees buzzing about an opening flower—here Sainte-Beuve's prose grew excited, and María de las Nieves could almost feel the quickened words rushing beneath her fingertips. Now she was reading with her mind and heart opened wide, silently waiting for answers, for help. While she could hardly claim a swarm of "suitors," it did seem like good advice to maintain a satirical attitude toward those she did seem to have (there were only Wellesley Bludyar and

"Don Cochinilla," as María Chon had taken to calling poor Señor Chinchilla.) The girl Madame Roland (Mademoiselle Phlipon) wrote: *My sentiments strike me as very odd. What can be stranger than for me to hate anyone because he loves me, and from the moment I try to love him?*

Most girls still go to the Shrine of San Antonio to seek help in matters of love, thought María de las Nieves. But not me. With the back of her hand she shooed bees from the little pitcher of cream and read about young Mademoiselle Phlipon's involvement with a man named La Blancherie. The girl Madame Roland prepared to finish him off as she usually did her suitors, rhetorically declaring, *Let us settle the claims of this individual,* but instead of burying him with ridicule, she found herself confronting, for the first time in her life, feelings of love. And better proof could not be furnished if required, wrote Sainte-Beuve, that there is nothing in love save what we put into it, and that the object of the flame counts for almost nothing. La Blancherie was a writer of twaddle!

She held the book open on her lap and sat pondering the truthfulness of what she'd just read. Surely José Martí was no La Blancherie, and so no sensible comparison could be made. In another three weeks, the composition class would end; a few weeks later, Martí would be leaving for Mexico, to marry his fiancée; or else the unthinkable would happen, and he would succumb to his love for María García Granados and stay. That did not even have to be spoken. Everyone knew that. Everyone in her composition class was aware of that, everybody in the circle of those students' close relations and friends, all the Cuban exiles and their closest friends, every poet in the Literary Society of "the Future"; weren't they all waiting to see now what was going to happen?

Only when the girl Madame Roland ran into La Blancherie in the Luxembourg Gardens wearing a feather in his hat did disillusionment finally begin to set in—. Pues, there it was, so Martí was no La Blancherie; if it had been her fate to choose a La Blancherie to be her first beloved, she would have fallen for José Joaquín Palma, the Bayamés Bard, who always wore a long feather in his hat (and, at least in her opinion, was a writer of twaddle). But the conceited Bayamés Bard had never paid the slightest attention to her; he too was notoriously smitten by María García Granados. If the Bayamés Bard had made himself her suitor, might she have been blinded by "the Blond Arab's" famous beauty—his thick golden beard, his proud Assyrian nose—despite the feather in his hat? And then would she ever have seen through him? But nothing seemed as ludicrous or unlikely as the image of herself held amorously in the arms of the Bayamés Bard. Why couldn't she accept in her heart that being loved by Pepe Martí was just as unlikely? That Martí was *good* (if a bit gullible) made it *no more likely*. It was she who deserved to be ridiculed. There, María de las Nieves, a bit of reason and clarity at last!

Later in the correspondence, a Monsieur Roland began to appear: an austere man who inspired considerable awe at first, though his solemnity also made him a figure of fun. But here Sainte-Beuve changed the subject, suddenly leaping ahead twenty years in his narration: Madame Roland is in prison awaiting the scaffold and the older of the two sister-correspondents hastens to her and offers to switch clothes with her so she can escape and Madame Roland replies, "But they would kill you, my dear Henriette," and will not consent.

Then, just like that, Sainte-Beuve went back to the early days of Monsieur Roland's courtship: The two converse about everything. They argue. Four or five years go by. She reads Plutarch, Seneca, Homer; of course, Rousseau. Atheism was a product of the eighteenth century; atheists inspire horror, fascination, respect; the best men seem to be atheists—. Does La Pequeña Paris de Centroamérica run one hundred years behind the real Paris in all things?

"Snows? Sorry to disturb—. Mrs. Gastreel needs you to translate. The wives of the Minister of Works and the Minister of War have to come to pay a visit, and are waiting . . . but Snows?"

"Yes, Wellesley?" (Looking up from her book, observing him as if through the wrong end of a telescope, she warily reflected that on a normal day the arrival of these señoras would have inspired at least a few words of comic derision from Wellesley—)

"I am asking permission to call on you at home."

" . . . "

"*Your* permission, to call on *you* at home," he nearly whispered.

"Oh . . . Pues, está bien . . . Of course, Wellesley!" (Though she still pronounced it *Gueyeslee*.) She smiled up at him. (*Now let us settle the claims of this individual* . . .)

"When would be a good evening, Snows?"

They agreed that Thursday evening, when she had no class, would be a good evening.

"Just between you and me, Snows. Confidential. You know, here. Minister Gastreel and, especially, the Chiefess."

"Oh, yes."

". . . Good book, is it?"

"Very. Yes. Then I should go now to Mrs. Gastreel . . ."

As she walked into the house, she thought: To anyone looking at me right now, I would appear to be the same María de las Nieves as yesterday. How absurd! But it's as if from the moment Maestro Martí put that book in my hands, I've crossed into a whole other life . . .

That night at dinner, Amada Gómez, her widowed boarder, said that a person could fall in love only once. María Chon asked, "Is that true, Doñacita?" And María de las Nieves sensibly answered, "Amada only ever loved her husband, María. You know that."

But what if she was in love with Maestro Martí with no hope of that love being requited, and it was the only love she would ever know?

It was as if María Chon read her thoughts: "Doña las Nieves, if that Cubanito won't marry you, you know Don Cochinilla will."

She resolved from now on to simply ignore the mediocre and insolent remarks of her mediocre and insolent servant.

"I still prefer Don Cochinilla to the Chino Gringo," persisted María Chon.

"So many suitors, María de las Nieves," clucked Amada, though no smile creased her complexion of sad, yellowing velvet.

"They're not suitors until they come to call on her *en casa*," said María Chon, repeating the very definition María de las Nieves had supplied for her some weeks before. "But how is anyone going to ask permission to call if she will not go and sit in the window like a decent young dama?"

"Why don't you go and sit in the window with a pair of donkey ears on your head and a For Sale sign hung around your neck."

"Uy uy uy! Pues I'll marry Don Cochinilla if you won't."

"And together the two of you will lift the art of matrimonial conversation to heights never before imagined."

She changed the subject, coldly telling them her news: a man had asked permission to call on her next Thursday evening. Would Amada do her the favor of chaperoning? She refused to let María Chon know who it was.

Undaunted, María Chon said, "An honest girl never lets a man know she likes him until she has received from him so many proofs of his respect that she can be sure he doesn't want her only to be his toy." Obviously she'd heard that somewhere, or read it in a newspaper, but what struck María de las Nieves was that she'd memorized it. Was María Chon also entering *the age of emotions*? But look, she's drawn to formulas of goodness! At a time when moral fashions are going in another direction entirely—at least according to the social commentary of Juslongo Orsini in the weekly newspaper of La Sociedad Económica. As she was leaving the room something in Amada Gómez's placidly satisfied expression caused another scenario to occur: Amada and María Chon had been gossiping about her. *Why did she buy a new hat?* she imagined Amada saying in a tone of stingy reprobation. (*What a gay little hat!* Amada, that hypocrite, had said the very day she'd bought it. *And who is it meant to charm?*) As if she would ever allow herself to be someone's toy! So those pious words had been spoken by Amada first, directed at herself, and now María Chon had slyly repeated them. There was as much intrigue in her little house as in the convent!

Deep in the night, she woke again and lay awake in the dark, unable to regain her sleep, feeling crushed against her mattress by the weight of a doomed and pointless love. It happened again the next night, and the night after. Every night at the same hour, like clockwork, her eyes opened upon a ghastly theater in which she watched Martí and María García Granados in the roles of happy lovers while she wasted away in the shadows, shrinking, pale, and unnoticed, or Martí answering her ardent confessions with indifference or disgusted bewilderment, and other scenes that grew more humiliating and lurid with each passing night. She felt trapped inside a body grown heavy and wild with despair and fear. One night she dreamt that she was lying in a bed of corn husks weeping in a way that was not her own quiet weeping but with the keening wails of a heartbroken India, and when she woke, she found herself tightly curled up and squeezed into a corner of the bed against the wall, cheeks sticky with dried tears and as grimy as if a wind had been blowing sand and dirt through her bedroom all night.

When she learned that La Primera Dama of the Republic was to be the guest of honor at the Cuban fiesta at which María García Granados was going to recite the Bayamés Bard's patriotic poem, she decided to stay home.

In three days it would be Thursday, the evening Wellesley Bludyar was going to call. If she was going to have callers, she decided, she needed an album for them to write in. She knew from the gossip of the girls in her composition class that Martí had once remained in the García Granados's garden until long after even Chafandín had gone to bed, laboring over a poem in María's album that ended up filling many pages, and that before letting himself out of the house at dawn, he'd stopped into the kitchen and left the album with one of the servants, asking that it be served to its owner with her breakfast, with a sprig of lilac marking the page where his poem began. So Wellesley Bludyar would be the first to write in her own album; well, they didn't all have to be poets. She went to Emilio Goubaud's book and stationery shop, where, because for once she was actually purchasing something—and not some inexpensive trifle!—she felt free to ask the clerk behind the counter to show her nearly their entire inventory of European stationery, writing and desk utensils, and even imported cigarette papers, and she stayed for two hours, raptly inspecting every item. The album she bought had deep purple pasteboard covers, tied with a black satin ribbon, and ivory-hued German paper, and she even bought a single sheet of Spanish deerskin stationery to keep pressed between the pages—it exactly resembled a thin, crisp, tawny sheet of writing paper, though when rubbed between her fingers, it had the feel of finest chamois leather. Her new hat, the album, the special sheet of paper—she'd even tried to bargain with the clerk over the colored pencils that came in a prettily enameled box from Macao; she was spending far too freely, and for the first time since she'd been hired at the legation, she was going to fall short of her month's expenses.

María de las Nieves's savings were deposited with Padre Lactancio Rascón, her old chaplain and Confessor in the convent; and so she went to see him in his parish house, in Jocotenango, the venerable Indian barrio at the far northern end of the city, to ask for a little of her own money. Padre Lactancio greeted her in what was now his usual manner, with mordant self-satire and irrepressible affection: "Our Señor truly is forgiving, if He brings Our Niña of Wool to Jocotenango." But he was clearly in low spirits, and looked shrunken inside his dingy cassock, and was convalescing

from a recent illness that had left his haggard face resembling a smudged
charcoal sketch. He sat upon a small wooden bench, and she in a hard
wooden chair, in his plain little sitting room. In one hand the priest held
a dirty-looking ball of wax; throughout their conversation he kept hoisting
one leg or the other over the opposite knee, as if he only wanted her to
notice the tattered soles of his shoes, but then he rolled the ball of wax
against his black stockings, picking up fleas. (As soon as she got home, she
would bathe in hot water, and give all her clothing to María Chon to laun-
der.) Padre Lactancio's gloomy little church served a poor Indian parish—
the former nuns' chaplain was scandalized and helpless before the
superstitious manner of their worshipping. The Indios seemed to observe
a religious calendar, he drily complained, which did not exactly correspond
to that of the Roman breviary. Not one of his parishioners could understand a single word of the Latin Mass. He now owned only one suit of
secular clothing, the priest told her, which he was required by law to wear
if he wanted to go out into the street on his own, and his sole top hat was
made of painted cardboard. A few pennies here and there for a funeral, a
baptism was all he earned from his parishioners. Of course he no longer had
nuns to prepare his meals, only one undeniably kind and loyal Indian servant, who, he whispered crankily when she was out of the room, lacked all
skills. The only meat he ever ate was chicken, once a week at most. Even
baked bread was a luxury. He lived like a Franciscan missionary friar of
centuries before—there were days he ate nothing but fruit picked for him
from local trees. Padre Lactancio's eyes were lusterless whenever he
looked at her now; their old wicked and lingering lights had been doused
and replaced by a befuddled inkiness—eyes that could deceive you into
thinking it was simple and naive human goodness that lay in ruins inside
him. Of course María de las Nieves knew her old Confessor better than
that. But for all his faults, she considered him a dependable friend and one
of her only human connections to her past, and this visit filled her with a
confusing nostalgia. She sensed that Padre Lactancio was a deeply de-
feated man who now took little solace or instruction, if any, from God. But
wasn't it hypocrisy, or at least wrong, for her to wish for the priest to again
be as he'd been in the past? Shouldn't she be glad that she no longer had
to be wary of his timid lechery? And why should she want him to believe
in God and the divine Catholic priesthood if she no longer did? Not in the

latter, certainly. Yet it made her sad to find him so changed. Padre Lactancio went into his sacristy to retrieve her money, and was gone for a long time, and when he came back his expression was so unhappy she thought he must be acting, and she felt a sickening jolt of suspicion—but then she saw that he was carrying the money she'd asked for and a piece of weathered paper on which he kept a careful account of the balance left under his safekeeping. Padre Lactancio didn't even ask her, as he had during every one of her previous visits, if she wished to confess.

Later María de las Nieves guiltily admitted to herself that no matter how cynical and embittered he became, Padre Lactancio would never steal from her. She'd been advised by Wellesley Bludyar that it wouldn't be prudent to keep her small savings with the new government bank anyway: he was sure that certain officials were helping themselves to whatever was there, and that soon all its investors would discover that they had been defrauded.

FROM THE NEWSPAPER, María de las Nieves, in a lightly satiric tone, read out loud: "Haven't you seen, reader, a young girl seated in her window contemplating the sky with an expression of melancholy ecstasy? Well, she is a *romantica*, nowadays a type disgracefully abounding. Her motive is to make herself interesting to the eyes of those gallants who can't resist trying to win the attention of such a creature, so rarefied and strange in all her acts and actions. Of course she is beautiful, so beautiful, so pale, so sad, usually dressed in white. What a spiritual woman she is, how well her pale pallor suits her . . . though of course it's been acquired through the constant use of vinegar. When la romantica falls in love, she wants all her amorous trysts to take place in the clear moonlight of the Necropolis."

María Chon, seated alongside her in the reading room kiosk, asked where Necropolis was, and when she told her that it was a word for cemetery, María Chon reached out and stroked her arm so gently that a shudder swept over her skin. María de las Nieves wanted to protest: But this has absolutely nothing to do with me, idiota, and María Chon's eyes, two radiant black sunrises, were fixed on her lips' brief silent struggle to speak those words, and she decided to just let it pass and say nothing; she stared down at the page of newsprint until she felt María Chon's tentative touch on her arm again, and heard her say, "Let's read about something else, mi Doñacita," and then her servant turned the page, and began to read aloud (though haltingly) from the newspaper's column of anonymous personal messages: "Pablito, I like you like that: last night at the theater you really shined. Let's see, picaronazo: that business of arriving at nine-thirty, coming serenely down the aisle coughing loudly into your hand and tossing enchanting looks toward the boxes, that made a good impression, chico, keep it up and soon you'll be the one all the beauties desire, but allow me to give you a bit of advice: try not to sigh in that bestial way of yours, an elderly man in a seat near yours complained bitterly during intermission that with just one exhalation you left him constipated." María Chon laughed riotously, and twice repeated the old man's insulting complaint.

Perhaps it was just as well, thought María de las Nieves, that she'd never yet been invited to the opera. *What a sweet hat, which you've now premiered twice, at the Academia de Niñas, and at the opera. Are you going to wear it Thursday night too?* Imagine coming upon that in a newspaper! Every year the government paid to install a European opera company in the National Theater for several months. According to Mrs. Gastreel, it was now considered "quite the proper thing here" to ostentatiously train one's opera glasses on La Primera Dama's box in order to "admire her beauty and wardrobe and the several layers of glittering diamonds with which she festoons herself."

On the Thursday evening that Wellesley Bludyar was to call on María de las Nieves at home, he never arrived. She waited with Amada Gómez and María Chon until midnight, when they finally devoured the imported delicacies—canned asparagus, sardines in olive oil, Swiss cheese, a small piece of English ham, and soda crackers—she'd splurged on for the visit. She went to bed carrying her still-spotless album under one arm. There would be a reasonable explanation, she was sure; she did not entirely discount the possibility that Wellesley had simply lost his nerve. She fell quickly into an untroubled sleep, and woke at the usual predawn hour to face the punishing consequences of her misplaced love.

The next morning at the legation she learned that the First Secretary had been dispatched the previous day on a mission so secret that he had not even been permitted to say good-bye to "his friends." Minister

Gastreel told her, "Mr. Bludyar might be away as many as six months, Señorita Moran, or even longer, I'm afraid," this last spoken with raised brows and a softly drawled, obviously insinuating or probing emphasis, and she felt a peculiar hostility surging inside herself under his assessing gaze, though she managed to maintain her own composed expression. In the meanwhile, the Minister Resident asked her, would she be willing to assume some of the First Secretary's duties, such as copying letters to the Foreign Office? He could offer only a slight escalation in wages. But before she said yes, Minister Gastreel needed to prepare her for the graver implications of accepting: she was not only going to be receiving an education in the realities of international politics and trade usually available only to the young gentlemen of the British Foreign Office, but merely by copying letters and dispatches she would frequently be coming into contact with highly confidential information. Minister Gastreel, of course, harbored no doubts about her trustworthiness, but he did want to be sure that she understood the discretion that would be required. Her position at the British Legation would still be an unofficial one, but the only other female in the country with a more delicate political employment was the telegraph operator in charge of the government's exclusive wire at the National Palace. Dolores Alarcón was only two years older than María de las Nieves, but at the Sociedad Económica's school for telegraph operators she'd so far surpassed the other students in intelligence and digital nimbleness that upon her graduation the government's Superintendent General of Telegraphs, the capable Canadian Stanley McNider, had immediately hired her. Now she was engaged to be married to Mr. McNider, though he was a quarter of a century her elder.

When María de las Nieves returned home that evening she found an envelope, bearing the British Legation's seal, waiting. Inside was a fragrant letter from Wellesley Bludyar explaining that he'd been unexpectedly sent on a mission, and expressing his "most heartfelt regrets." He promised to call as soon as he returned. The envelope was filled with downy white jasmine petals. She put the letter back into the envelope and placed it inside her album, and there it remains, over a century later; the petals, of course, long since turned to odorless jasmine dust.

# Chapter 5

$\mathcal{I}$ t is also true that when you went to Europe you had a pregnant don-key brought on board your steamship so that if your midwife's breasts ran dry, you could feed your baby donkey milk? And that was because your hus-band didn't want you nursing from your own breasts like an Indian?"

Paquita had apologized to María de las Nieves for their argument of the previous evening. They had embraced, and kissed each other's cheeks.

"But how did you know about that?"

"Paquita, it was the kind of story anyone could hear in the market. My servant told me." It was one of the more sympathetic stories that circu-lated there about La Primera Dama.

"Yes, it's true," said Paquita cheerfully. "And one night during that voy-age, Rufino came back into our stateroom carrying a glass of milk he'd just gotten from that donkey. It wasn't for my baby, though; he said he wanted to drink it himself. He wanted to show off, you know, that even though we were sailing to Paris, he was still the rough rural man. I said, That's milk from the kitchen. Give me a taste, Rufinito, so that I can see if you are telling the truth. María de las Nieves and I used to drink donkey milk when we were chiquillas on my father's farm, so I know the taste. But no, he would not share it, he said he was not going to make love to a woman with donkey milk on her breath, and he drank it all down."

Paquita had a sarcastic glitter in her eye that suddenly warmed María de las Nieves, and made her laugh.

"So tell me, Paquita mía. Tell me, at last, what is it that your spy—it was a spy, wasn't it?—saw take place that day, between Martí and me. Vamos, it was all a long time ago, querida, after all."

"No no no. If I tell you, you're just going to storm out again. I've been thinking about what you said to me the other night, mis Nievecitas, and I've decided that all your accusations were true—yes, all of them. You believe that I was corrupted by my husband's power, that I relied on his spies, and I cannot deny that. So yes, you've hurt me, but you've also made me see what even my own mother and every priest I've ever known have wanted to hide from me. Claro, I did have an excuse. After all, there *was* a conspiracy, María de las Nieves, to murder not only my husband but also myself and our children as we slept in our beds. After that conspiracy was exposed, I changed; I suspected, feared, and hated everybody and felt I had the right to tear the roof off every single house and look inside and tell anybody what I saw. So much power was, I agree, as you say, deranging. The world lost all harmony for me. And the only way I could restore it a little-little was by leaving the country, and spending more and more time in New York and Europe."

"Your husband used that conspiracy to imprison and murder and torture anyone he or his friends didn't like. But that's not what you mean by lost harmony."

"And I felt he was justified. I know now that he went too far."

"Too far. Pues sí." They fell silent; she remembered poor Higinio Farfán—. "Where were Pepe Martí and I, exactly, when your spy . . . spied us."

"He followed you out past the San Juan de Dios Hospital pasture, and down into the valley, almost to the River of the Cows. There, in a little cuenca, a hollow at the foot of a cliff, you stopped."

"You remember what happened better than I do."

"I doubt that. And something else. It was the day that aeronaut went up in his balloon with the puppy. Wasn't it the same day?"

"I didn't see anybody following us."

"Of course not, Las Nievecitas, he was a spy."

THE CELEBRATED MEXICAN aeronaut José Flores, conqueror of the far loftier Andean skies of Quito and Cuzco, had been the first to go up in a hot-air balloon over their city twenty years before; also the last. Had he succeeded that day, a modest chapter would have been added to El Gran Flores's hemispheric legend, but he would have won unambiguous glory and a lasting place in the history of the capital. His triumph would have shown the Conservative Citadel's population that, despite their little country's suffocating backwardness and sullen xenophobia, they too could partake of the era's worldly marvels. The image of that potato-hued balloon floating in a radiant sky high above the bell towers and domes of their thirty-eight churches and monasteries might even, over time, have come to seem emblematic of the moment when the city began to change, opening to the future like a flower startled out of its timidity. Instead the famous Mexican aeronaut flew his balloon directly into nightmares and shuddering memories and stayed there, endlessly reenacting his catastrophe in a cloudless blue sky where it hadn't rained for twenty years.

At the top of Señor Flores's ascent that day—when he seemed to have attained an altitude as high as the peak of the horizon's highest volcano, where no known mortal had ever set foot—the basket he was riding in caught fire. Down in the city, across the plain, throughout the valley, and in Indian villages nestled in the surrounding hills and mountain slopes, all eyes were fixed in horror on the angry ball of fire in the middle of the sky, and on the slowly sagging belly of the balloon above. Finally the balloon collapsed, drifting sideways for a moment like a galleon in flames, and then the entire conflagration plummeted to earth, and the shocked empty sky was left holding only a few black ribbons of smoke, and a wailing made of thousands of human cries went swirling like a wild windstorm throughout the city, innumerable small twisters of hysteria and fear charging down every street. Mandaderas emerged from every convent, carrying trays and pitchers of chamomile and rue tea to calm peoples' nerves, most rushing toward the bullfighting arena and its plaza, where the greatest number of people were gathered. The burning balloon crashed in a cornfield outside the Indian pueblo of San Pedro de las Huertas on the southern plain, and later all that was found of the famous aeronaut amid the blackened, smoldering, astonishingly reduced wreckage were carbonized bones and teeth.

In the dogmatic spirit of those times, the balloonist's tragedy was widely interpreted, especially from the pulpits, as divine castigation: the population's blind enthusiasm over El Gran Flores's vainglorious defiance of earthbound humility had been repaid with a spectacle of gruesome death that scattered ashes over all their mortal souls, and darkened every individual conscience. Even the city's monjitas, it was whispered, had abandoned their prayer choirs and run out into their convent orchards to watch the historic ascent. After that the city lost all appetite for hot-air balloon flights. But these were new times, and in honor of the Supreme President of the Liberal Republic's birthday, another aeronaut, also Mexican, though a far more obscure figure than his doomed predecessor of two decades before, Juan Rios from the small port city of Tampico, came to the capital to perform a balloon ascent that nearly anywhere else in the civilized (or even "semicivilized") world would be regarded as little better than a second-rate circus act. However, the resourceful Tampiqueño's flight would not lack novelty: at the peak of his ascent he was going to drop a puppy in a silk parachute from his basket.

That same Sunday, as they had for three successive Sundays, since the drizzly petering of October's last rains, the Central American Baseball Club, playing their inaugural season, had gathered for their weekly doubleheader in the pasture behind the San Juan de Dios Hospital. It was a much less popular thoroughfare for strollers, picnickers, and kite fliers than the Cerrito del Carmen, or the meadows of El Calvario, or the Plaza de Toros, or the increasingly fashionable, if always sandy and dusty lot where the train station was going to be. In the pasture behind the hospital—disregarding the unavoidable intrusion of wandering livestock, stray burros, and dogs —aimless Sunday drunkards stumbling across the outfield were the only regular nuisances, and were easily chased away with vehement shouts and gestures. A majority of the ballplayers were Yankees working on the railroad, and others were young merchants or commercial clerks, and there were even a few would-be coffee planters and entrepreneurs; Captain Warren Morrissey, a veteran of the Indian wars in the Western Territories and an Attaché at the U.S. Legation under Colonel Williamson, and Lieutenant "Googey" Burns, Police Chief Colonel Pratt's assistant, also came out to play. The railroad company provided bats and balls, and gloves on loan; uniforms were promised for the second season. The Baseball Club was made up of two teams whose rivalry was growing more passionate and testy by the week, and who called themselves the Western Bald Eagles and the Broadway Boiled Oysters. The Boiled Oysters' star player, as pitcher and shortstop, was the taciturn Yankee Indio Mack Chinchilla, First Secretary of the Immigration Society, who'd formerly played infield in the New York trade league for a team representing the lower Manhattan coffee and tea traders. Setting out for Central America from New York, Mack had even packed his baseball glove, but lost it with his pack mule in that rushing river during his perilous journey to Cuyopilín.

It was the fifth inning and Mack, who'd hit a rare home run and was pitching commandingly, had led the Boiled Oysters to a six to three advantage. When it was his team's turn to bat, Mack stood off to the side, stonily aloof from his eastern teammates, who ignored him in return, though they knew they could not win without him. Indeed, the only player Mack genuinely liked happened to play for the West, "Wild Bibby" Lowenthal of the family that owned the California General Store, and a regular at the Café de Paris, where he was a generous and garrulous favorite of all the señoritas, so it was not just because Wild Bibby was a Hebrew that Mack liked him. On his own team he had Gabriel Sugarman, a Yale-educated railroad engineer and a conceited snob; in fact, Mack wished Sugarman would join the Bald Eagles so that he could pitch the ball at his head. In the distance the grassy slopes of the hill topped by the Church of the Carmen swarmed with bright colors, women's dresses, hats, parasols, amid which, looking like ants struggling through the ruins of a lavish cake, strolled men dressed in black. Any of those tiny flashes of color, thought Mack, could be María de las Nieves, in her pretty new hat.

Mack was back out on the mound when he heard a distant roar from the Plaza de Toros, and the tinny strains of Colonel Dressner's military band striking up again, and knew the aeronaut must have just lifted off from the bullring, the same spot where El Gran Flores had begun his doomed flight on another sunny afternoon twenty years before. The batter, Captain Morrissey, lifted his eyes to watch but did not step back from the plate, and Mack hurled a hard straight strike; it should have been strike two, but the umpire wasn't watching either, his beefy, walrus-mustached face lifted toward the horizon. Mack shouted, "Two strikes!" and turned and saw the canary yellow globe like an enormous trembling egg yolk slowly rising into view over low rooftops and luxuriant trees alongside the hill of the Church of the Calvario. Who among the Yankee ballplayers cared enough about a balloon flight to justify suspending the game? Only a few. But everyone wanted to see the parachuting dog. Still, the balloon had a long way to go to reach the top of the sky. And the game resumed with a ferocious argument between both teams about whether the second strike Mack had thrown to Captain Morrissey should count. The umpire was the Chief of Police, Colonel Pratt, whose status was portrayed as a guarantee of impartiality but who usually sided with the Boiled Oysters; this time he ruled against them. With a two-and-two count, Mack's roundhouse curve broke so spectacularly in front of Captain Morrissey's face that he had to jerk his head back to save his nose, while the ball finished its twirling plunge, just nipping the rear outside corner of the plate at the level of the batter's knees—at least according to umpire Colonel Pratt, who called strike three. It would be preposterous to suggest that the former New York City police officer had anything against former U.S. Cavalry Indian fighters; on the contrary. But Captain Morrissey had no doubt that the Indio on the mound had just tried to hit his nose, and he ambled out toward Mack, rolling up his sleeves, preparing for a fistfight. There were several of these brawls every game, and all the other ballplayers launched into them with such relish that they were the only aspect of the Yankee sport that local newspaper chronicles ever mentioned. Now, at the bottom of the brutal and struggling pile, Mack had his teeth clamped around the meatiest portion of a hairy hand, and biting down all the harder helped him endure the pain from the knee pounding into his kidney; wet mustache and tobacco-redolent lips were pressed against his ear, cursing his race, and then he felt teeth tearing with a rabid dog's fury into the soft cartilaginous flesh; but Mack had a thumb pressed against Captain Morrissey's eye, and was pushing so hard he half-expected to pop all the way through and be able to pull it back coated in the slime of a blue iris; the taste and smell of blood, sweat, dirt, saliva, grass filled his mouth and nostrils; the hatred he felt was joy; he knew that his vicious need to tear them apart and be torn apart was love, freedom, and an American way of allowing flawed and wounded men to walk off the field radiant and whole; such exertion felt good everywhere, in body and spirit, in his humming blood and marrow. It was remarkable how rarely anyone was actually kicked or punched in the testicles; they were gentlemen too, and knew that mainly Frenchmen and Spaniards fought like that. He felt the heaving, crushing swarm of muscle and bone beginning to lighten as ballplayers freed themselves from the pile, scrambling to their feet, and then, at the bottom, Mack and the proud former despoiler of the Cheyenne could finally let go of each other, and Mack, lying on his back, panting and groaning alongside his also panting and groaning nemesis, looked up and saw the yellow balloon in the middle of the sky and the parachute like a lacy doily drifting downward over the dark speck it was slowly guiding toward earth.

A very pretty noise arose from the city: so many happy and excited cries sounding all together like an enormous school just set free for the summer vacation. There were also the explosions, pops, and sizzles of fireworks and rockets. Mack, on his feet, wiping salty blood from his lips-ear-nose, imagined María de las Nieves and her imp of a servant smiling up into the sky and rushing around with the crowd trying to guess where the puppy would land. He hadn't spoken to her since their conversation about cochineal in the reading room kiosk. But everything he did, he did for her, including winning this ball game, because nothing was too trivial not to summon his best effort, and if in every single thing he did he only gave his best, it would be like living in a state of perpetual readiness for their next encounter. Whoever reached the puppy first would be allowed to keep it. He hoped it would be María de las Nieves, if she indeed wanted a puppy. And then he hoped not, because that would attract too much attention to her, she would have a moment of celebrity, and new gallants who'd never noticed her before would be inspired to compete for her heart. You call that giving your best, Mack, such weak-livered thoughts? He said a little prayer for the puppy to land unharmed and as near to her as she wished.

The ballplayers watched the slow descent of the dog in its parachute until it disappeared from sight behind distant treetops. Mack guessed the dog had landed somewhere in El Sagrario, one of the older barrios. They heard a brief rowdy faraway clamor, and then relative silence. The silence lasted too long. Much too long . . . Poor little country, no luck at all, nothing ever goes right.

Play ball! They had this game to finish and then another one to get through. The men went listlessly, anticlimactically, back to their positions. The new batter was some wiry dimwit hillbilly, probably a fugitive from jail; just looking at his narrow hungry conniving face filled Mack with ennui, and he wound up for the pitch—and stopped and turned around as soon as he heard the cheer rising—and the cheering seemed to float in the air above the city like something that could almost be seen, like an enormous soap bubble, but one made of some translucent material more resilient than soapy water, holding and prolonging all those cheering voices and festive exhalations inside its buoyant sphere. It was an impression that stayed with Mack for many years.

The puppy had landed in the garden of Doña Rebeca Zazúeta, an elderly widow. She hadn't realized it until alerted by the commotion outside her home; then it had taken a while for her and her servant to find and disentangle the animal from its parachute and bring it to the street door— that was the story that would appear in the newspaper the next day. The Indian servant held the puppy up for the crowd, took its paw in her hand and made it wave, and Doña Rebeca thanked El Señor Presidente and our Señor in heaven for having sent her this miraculous gift to lighten her widow's solitude, and the two women quickly went back inside with the dog and shut the door.

And then Doña Rebeca and the servant hurried with their prize back through the gloomy house decorated with old-fashioned religious statuary and paintings and out into the garden, frantically exclaiming, *Dios mío Dios mío!*—for what if they had taken longer to find the dog, and excited boys had scaled the walls into the yard? What if the crowd had demanded to see the exact spot where the *chucho* had landed? Doña Rebecca's husband had died thirteen years before, and after that the stable and chicken coop in the garden had quickly fallen into disuse, and it was there, more than a year before, that Madre Sor Gertrudis de la Sangre Divina had established her secret convent, along with nine of her former nuns. According to Padre Bruno's account of the episode in *La Monjita Inglesa*, his *vida* of the Yonkers-born Sor Gertrudis, the nuns had been in their makeshift little choir inside the stable quietly singing Nonne when they'd been distracted by the simultaneous eruption of shouting in the street outside, and then they'd heard, from very nearby, the squeals and whines of what sounded like an enormous mouse. They'd filed outside to discover its source, and had been confronted by the mystifying sight of someone's whitish bed linens dropped in a spread-out pile directly in front of the stable, and underneath it all, squealing and whining, moving around, some live thing. The nuns had still been standing there, in paralyzed confusion, when the servant, trailed by Doña Rebeca, had burst into the garden clamoring about a chucho dropped from the sky and that they had to find it and bring it outside, there was not a second to spare! Servants and sprightlier nuns had waded into the mass of fabric and strings and quickly uncovered the puppy. Sor Inés had cradled it in her arms while Sor Trinidad undid its little harness.

"Oh, daughters, look what God sends us!" And all had obediently turned their eyes from the dog to Madre Sor Gertrudis. "This puppy has black head and brown body, exactly like the habits of our Order!" The Yonkers-born Prioress had sprinkled Holy Water on the furry black head and made the sign of the cross, and in response, the puppy had only tried to lick her hand—so it was not a trick of the devil! Then Doña Rebeca and her servant had rushed the puppy away from them. And Madre Sor Gertrudis and her nuns, dressed in full habits, nine in black veils and one in the white veil of a novice, had dropped to their knees in front of the stable to pray that their convent would not be discovered. Those prayers had been answered: pious widow and servant had soon returned with the puppy.

Still, this apparent Miracle of the Puppy in the Garden posed questions, and the Madre Priora now had nowhere to turn for guidance other than her own prayers and meditations: Was this a sign that their Señor wished them to continue in their clandestine holy life here in the widow's stable, or was there some other message? What about their Constitution's rule against handling and petting animals? Wasn't it sinful to pass the puppy around as they were doing, some of the Sisters burying their noses in its soft fur? But if this truly was a holy creature, more angel than beast, then shouldn't it be loved as if they had received it directly from the hands of El Pobrecito de Assís—and that was the holy name Sor Gertrudis now chose for their little baby bear–like dog. The Yankee Prioress ordered that a simple feast of gratitude should be prepared. This day, she told her nuns, the most joyous of their long exile, would always remain a blessed anniversary in their religious lives, and perhaps someday would be celebrated throughout their Order.

Seventeen months had passed since Sor Gertrudis had first begun to venture out from her initial hiding place in the mansion of Don Valentín Lechuga's twin sisters, dressed in secular garb, to visit her former Daughters and Sisters in religion in the homes to which they had dispersed throughout the city. Those reconnaissance missions into *el siglo* had filled her with a new sense of urgency and resolve: some of her former nuns, especially the younger ones, seemed to have lost their vocations during their time back in the world, and two had already married, but others were suffering over their forced separation from the monastic life. Historians have recorded (but not Padre Bruno) that following the closing of the convents, many former nuns did join themselves to mortal husbands, and that a startling number of these young and not so young bridegrooms were active Liberals, or hailed from prominent Liberal families; some were even lowly soldiers. María de las Nieves, of course, had not been among those to receive a surprise visit from Madre Sor Gertrudis, but Sor Gloria de los Ángeles had been. According to Padre Bruno, not an infallible historian, soon after that visit Sor Gloria decided to rejoin her Prioress in the religious life, in defiance of the Ecclesiastical Governor's edict that novices were to be severed from their vows, there no longer being any legal means for them to make their full professions.

A wall of vertical pine planks, built by the clandestine nuns themselves, divided the stable in Doña Rebeca's garden: on one side was the oratory and little chorus; on the other the kitchen, a communal room, and a cramped warren of tiny cells. They repaired the old cistern, though daily Doña Rebeca's servant also brought several pails of water from the public fountains; a vegetable garden was planted. Nevertheless, there was often not enough to eat. The nuns were dependent on the charity of the widow Zazúeta, who since her husband's death had grown poorer every year. As the need arose, she'd even begun selling pieces from her collection of colonial religious art, a situation made even more trying when she discovered that almost every potential buyer she encountered was determined to cheat her. One afternoon, soon after the arrival of El Pobrecito, Doña Rebeca returned home with her usual fraught melancholy replaced by an air of girlish happiness, even though she was still carrying the same statue, one of her most beloved treasures, with which she'd left the house that morning, headed to the university, hoping to find there some honest professor with sufficient appreciation of religious art to pay the modest price she was asking. Later that afternoon, when it was finally the nuns' recreation hour, Doña Rebeca hurried out to the garden to tell them what had happened, and to present them with the precious statue: a seventeenth-century polychromatic one of La Virgen del Carmen, with a face of such beauty and purity that it could have been painted by Fray Angelico, glass eyes shining with a jubilant candor that made one smile shyly in return, and flowing robes carved by such a light and graceful hand that she really did seem on the verge of floating off on a gentle breeze. So had her Virgen del Carmen been described and praised by the young professor she'd encountered at the university that morning, and who had offered to buy it. The professor was a Cuban, and he'd spoken so kindly and eloquently about her statue, like a brilliant young Jesuit, that it was hard to believe him when he confessed that he hadn't even attended Mass since childhood, that he was merely an admirer of colonial religious art. Her Virgen del Carmen, the Cuban had assured her, possessed a lovely soul, which anyone with a soul of their own should be able to see. "I don't think you should sell this, Señora," he'd told her. Yes, she'd silently admitted, her eyes filming, it broke her heart to sell this most beautiful statue, in which she did sense the presence of the divine and its correspondence with her own immortal soul; but it also filled her with joy to make such a sacrifice for God, and for His Sacred Brides who lived in her garden, who hadn't even had hot chocolate in weeks. Unable to reveal any of that to the young professor, she'd answered him with downcast eyes. So the Cuban had paid her, somewhat less, it was true, than the price she'd sought. But then he'd confided that he really had no adequate place to display the statue, and asked her to hold it for him—in a few months he would be married, and expected to move into a larger house, and then he would surprise his wife with the statue, and, of course, pay the rest of what he owed. "Mis queridas," Doña Rebeca told the nuns, "our Virgencita, who weighed so heavy in my arms when I left the house this morning, practically carried me home herself." For now, she told them, this Most Holy Virgen del Carmen would live here with them in their hidden garden and cloister. Perhaps now some priest would be courageous enough to come to the stable in secret to confess the nuns or to say Mass; though none did. Even Padre Lactancio, their former chaplain, refused, claiming that he didn't want to risk exposing the Sisters to discovery. At carefully varied hours nuns went on slipping out of the house, in secular clothes, shawls over their heads, headed to different churches in diverse barrios to hide themselves among the regular worshippers.

A Western Bald Eagle was standing at second base and Mack had turned to check the runner when at the far edge of the pasture he saw a couple walking out of the city and toward the river valley and ravines beyond. The

woman wore a hat trailing long yellow ribbons, he was sure of it even at this
distance, and he could see the faraway cinnamon blur of her face. The
black-clad man beside her had a quick light stride; he resembled a typo-
graphically wispy question mark in a hurry. Even from here, thought Mack,
you can see his mouth yapping—though really he couldn't. Mack sighed in
angry disgust, not with her, or even himself, but in weary protest against
his life's overall and seemingly relentless design. Then he reminded himself: teacher and student, out walking, discussing poetry and literary composition for ladies—the new freethinkers' permissive manner of friendship
between the sexes, sure—so it did not *necessarily* mean—. To what conclu-
sions might Martí have leapt had he chanced upon Mack and María de las
Nieves conversing about cochineal in the reading room kiosk? Yes, Mack,
but there she'd been accompanied by her servant. Where was her usually
inseparable little servant now? Colonel Pratt and the other ballplayers
were shouting at him, caustically and intolerantly, as if Mack was *always*
doing this, holding up ball games for a moment of anxious romantic introspection. He turned and flung the ball—three feet outside the plate—and
gestured impatiently for his sprawled catcher to return it. Then he took his
time stomping around the mound as he might have if the bases were
loaded and he needed to regain his composure, but he only wanted to
watch as the couple disappeared from sight behind a hedgerow of small
pines abutting a cornfield—but look now: back at the other end of the
pasture, here she comes, chasing after them, the servant!—"What's a mad-
der wid you, Mack you! Throw da damn ball!"—but wait, no, that's not the
servant, it's a small masculine figure, in a beige hat with a floppy brim and
a high crown like an enormous crooked thumb, but headed in the same
direction. Mack turned and pitched to Giuseppe Centola, a sad-eyed swarthy bison with a long black beard, and the muscular railroad worker slugged
the ball harder and farther than anyone in the three-week history of the
Central American Baseball Club ever had, and the outfielders went running toward where the ball landed and disappeared into the high grass of
the pasture, which was also toward the small fellow in the cumbersome-
looking hat, who, as if frightened that he was indeed the target of the
Yankee stampede, took off in a short-legged scamper, headed for the
same hedgerow María de las Nieves and Dr. Torrente had just disappeared behind . . .

And now the score was six to five. Baseball always gives you one last chance to win. And everyone wants to be *campeón!* Mack didn't allow another hit after that, pitching with unyielding concentration, stamina, control, fury. "Everyone wants to be *campeón!*" he snorted disdainfully when the game was won. The conceited Sugarman mystifyingly replied, "*Qu'est-ce que c'est*, Mack? Everyone wants to be a mushroom?" and then laughed arrogantly to himself, for no one else understood the remark either. In the second game Mack played shortstop, made no errors, and reached base every time he came to bat, but the Broadway Boiled Oysters lost nineteen to twelve. There were two more brawls, each more savage than the first.

SOON AFTER LEAVING Mexico City, at the start of his roundabout three-month journey to Central America, José Martí had written from the port of Veracruz to his closest friend in Mexico, Manuel Mercado—the beginning of a lifelong correspondence eventually published as a sole volume—informing him that he was about to board a French packet steamer to Havana and that he was traveling, with apparently falsified documentation, under the name Julián Pérez—*my two middle names*, wrote Martí, *by which it seems I betray myself less: it's always better, even in grave circumstances, to be the least hypocritical possible. Undoubtedly you know by now, because you have the right to know everything that is mine, what a battle was waged that final night to stop me from undertaking this trip.* His fiancée's father, Francisco Zayas Bazán, had even offered to pay for Martí's impoverished parents and sisters to move back to Cuba from Mexico on their own if it would keep him from returning to the dangerous island. *That money is useless,* wrote Martí to his Mexican friend, *being that it belongs to Zayas: to you I don't need to explain any further.* Carmen Zayas's wealthy Cuban father suspected that the beguiling young exile was more interested in his wealth than in his daughter; Martí must have regarded his offer as a trap. He needed to prove that he could provide for Carmen, as well as for himself, without her father's help: he'd planned from the start to stay in Cuba only long enough to quietly arrange for his family's return, while also taking advantage of the opportunity, after so much time away, to assess the island's political situation firsthand. Then he would continue on to Central America, where his connections among the Liberals had assured him that university professorships were easily had. But in a series of letters written during that short stay in Havana, Martí had actually vacillated about whether or not to go to Central America after all: maybe he wouldn't be able to make enough money there, and in the end it would all be a gigantic waste of effort and time; and he was feeling anxious about Carmen, about the effects of their separation on their relationship, and even about the nature of her love for him. Having received a worrisome letter from his fiancée, Martí wrote to his friend in Mexico: *To believe without faith is a grave error, but it is even worse to love without faith. I believe in my Carmen, absolutely. I believe her capable of error, not of a disaffection which I do not deserve. You go see her, go see her between three and five in the afternoon and investigate the cause of these afflictions in her spirit.*

Martí clearly wanted to hurry back to Mexico City but was also worried that people would think him weak and lacking in character if he reversed himself; apparently Carmen had responded in that very manner to the suggestion of his premature return. Torturing himself over that perception, Martí launched a new round of letters denouncing himself for having vacillated but also trying to account for those vacillations in the best possible light: *If my thoughts of returning to Mexico hadn't been born of the absolute certainty that my life is already intimately attached to that of Carmen's, I would be ashamed of those apparently cowardly thoughts.* Finally he'd traveled on to the mountain city where his two unforeseen "niñas" of destiny were waiting: María García Granados and María de las Nieves Moran.

*I come filled with love for this land and these people,* Martí wrote to his Mexican friend in his first letter from La Pequeña Paris de Centroamérica, *and if my love for them doesn't overflow from me, it's so they won't take it for servility and flattery. If there are not many developed minds here, I have come to animate them, not to shame or wound them. Here, at last, the new is loved, and the saving spirit of inquiry begins to spread among young men. Without a literary circle, without the habit of the higher things, although with energy and desire for all of them, without newspapers—I have to be very prudent with my judgments here so that they won't appear arrogant. In this way my civility and fears shield my inner fires. These precautions haven't been enough to prevent my name from already being on the tongues of people* [en la boca de la gente] *to whom in a certain way I've exhibited myself, praised by some, and even effusively praised, repeated out of curiosity by the rest, and—I'd rather not know about it—perhaps perceived as an obstacle by a few.* He'd also rented a modest, well-situated house, just around the corner from the García Granados mansion, which he thought would satisfy Carmen's necessities when she at last joined him there as his wife.

Martí's early optimism seems to have been sincere: in a notebook he wrote that the country's secret charm was that it was severe without being sad, disdainful but never irritating, noisy but not riotous, agitated yet tireless: *Her party dress never gets wrinkled.* Yet his letters from that country would end fifteen months later with some of the bitterest words and harshest judgments to be found in all his writings; not even five months had passed before some of those notes were being sounded: *The absolute lack of nobility, of energy and freedom which, debasing the characters of the rest, disgust and irritate; this cement of foam upon which fortune, distancing me from men, obligates me to build my home, all this maintains my spirit in grave and sickly occupation, which for being mine, increases and exalts these same sufferings. Give life to America, revive the ancient, fortify and reveal the new; pour out my excess of love, write about grave subjects in Paris, employ my intelligence on great subjects without prejudice or preconceptions, make a great home in the soul for the voluntary martyr who comes to live in it, these are the grave tasks I have given my pen.—The mail is leaving, I'll sign off here. My Carmen hasn't received letters, which unnerves me.* (Complaints about the postal services are common to nearly all Central American correspondence of that epoch, from foreigners especially, including that of the Gastreels and other legations.) Announcing to his friend that he was writing a short book in praise of the little-known country's riches and virtues, he added: *This land is cruel, right now men in chains walk past my window. I'll liberate them!*

After the New Year, following his wedding in Mexico, when Martí would return accompanied by his wife, Carmen, he would also resume his correspondence with Manuel Mercado: *I am going to publish a journal here in which I will have to greatly disfigure myself in order to stoop to the common level. Here, out of inexplicable jealousy, the Rector of the University, a little man in body and soul, to whom I've done no greater wrong than praise in a lecture of mine a lecture of his which did not merit praise, has left me with a platonic course in History of Philosophy. I give a free class in philosophy, but my pay is the gratitude of my students. On my birthday the poor things gave me a pretty watch-chain.*

*You know the good intentions with which I came to this land,* Martí would write in his next letter to his Mexican friend. *It is true that there was an absolute discordance between their brutal ways and my free soul; it is true that I poeticized them to myself to be able to live among them; but these secrets have never left my soul. Have they read them in my eyes? Have they penetrated my caution? Poor Carmen! She has paid the price for my having learned a great lesson: if you have a little light inside yourself, you can't live where tyrants rule. Looking at my poor Carmen, my eyes fill with tears, and it is difficult for me to contain my bitterness. Among these men of extraordinary pettiness, any semblance of vigor, personality, austerity, energy, appears criminal. I've awoken unjustified fears, tenacious opposition, incredible persecution.*

None of the letters Martí wrote to Carmen while she was in Mexico City awaiting their wedding survive; nor do any of hers to him. We do know how preoccupied Martí was with María de García Granados, his "niña," his *palm tree made of light,* throughout many of those same months; we know that with certainty if we also believe there are literal biographical truths about Martí's life to be garnered from his poetry, including the poems written during his more than a year in Central America, in María García Granados's album in particular. Whatever actually occurred between Martí and the former President's tragic daughter, there is plenty of evidence to conclude that it was one of the most important emotional episodes of his life. Yet in none of his letters, not even in those to his closest friend in Mexico (who had *the right to know everything*) does Martí even once allude to María García Granados, or to her subsequent death, though he would attend her thronged funeral and years later place her white coffin at the center of his remorseful and most famous love poem; nor does he refer to any other woman he met there. Though to this very day, more than a century later, any visitor to that capital can meet, for example, elderly men who claim that their grandmothers knew Martí—I am not referring to ancient shoeshine boys or taxi drivers or retired dipsomaniacal schoolteachers or corrupt courthouse lawyers or resentful bureaucrats and clerks, but to true national eminences, men of untarnished reputations, of long memories and sometimes long learning, regularly cited and interviewed in newspapers regarding the latest local and even international matters, who only go out in public wearing a dark suit, tie, hat, and (often) dark glasses or else, in the most informal circumstances, a crisp guayabera—men, in others words, whose words are not taken lightly or skeptically, and who will tell you, without being able to offer any more evidence than that they heard it from their own abuela's lips, that Martí's time in La Pequeña Paris, especially in the months before his marriage, was most sexually active, for women there, in that small society just awakening to new ways, had never met anyone like the twenty-four-year-old Cuban, who, no matter how much he filled his notebooks and poetry with anguished sublimations of spiritual love over physical pleasure, possessed an irrepressible Caribbean sensuality despite himself, so opposite the generally repressed Spanish-Indian ways of that rainy mountain citadel, and of course a mesmerizing poet's idealism and charisma all his own. Martí was simply unable to resist all the female love and temptation thrown his way, at least according to the century-old gossip about the Cuban Apostle's secret love life, which, no matter how baseless, is still fragrant like the jasmine in the moonlit gardens where he quickened so many hearts and pulses in that city where his name remains in *la boca de la gente* to this day, and where one can encounter people even now who claim to have actually met, or to know of, the descendants of his love child with María García Granados (according to the almost certainly false romantic legend that she died in secret childbirth). Even in the volumes that collect Martí's diaries, notebooks, and loose papers, published years after his own death, a reader will mainly find seemingly coded or elusive yet disquietingly obsessive allusions to that tragic affair: "la niña's" name written on the back of a letter years later, her memory elsewhere evoked in nostalgic, remorseful, longing, and oblique jottings (and at least one exception: a fairly overt emotional confession written in his own hand). Good men marry young, Martí once wrote, and of course he did marry young, although we also know what a bitter disaster his marriage to Carmen Zayas—who did not want a revolutionary-hero-martyr-poet-saint for a husband after all—turned out to be.

Thirteen years after María García Granados's death, in New York City, when the Cuban Apostle was almost single-handedly organizing the revolution against Spanish rule in Cuba, he would write his poem about the niña *who died of love*, and confess that hers was the face he'd loved more than any other, in a collection of poetry that he would recite to his friends, and give to his wife, and soon after publish. Later he would tell a friend that twice in his life he'd seen the soul escape a body through a person's mouth, once while imprisoned in Cuba when he saw an old man whipped to death, and the second time, when he told María García Granados that he was going back to Mexico to wed Carmen. He would repeat that confession, more tersely, in another verse published in that same volume: *Quick, like a reflection, / twice*

*I saw the soul, twice: / once when the poor old man died. / And when she told me good-bye . . .* But there is no authoritative account of what really occurred between the two to be found anywhere, nor, barring the discovery of some long-lost or suppressed memoir or diary, will there ever be.

*Even a diary can be a spy,* Martí once wrote in another context, and that attitude, regarding the details of any personal as well as political intrigues, does seem to have guided his general approach to such writings; though sometimes he is tantalizingly allusive in those writings, often seeming to be flirting and teetering along the edges of an epic confession.

*Posterity,* wrote the son of Martí's close friend and literary executor, Gonzalo Quesada y Aróstegui, *will not be able to discover the names of all the women who touched the life of the Apostle.*

This much is known: after Martí's death, this note, scrawled in pencil on a pamphlet, was found among his papers: *When I married Carmen, more than out of the love I felt, out of gratitude for that which she apparently had for me, and out of a certain gentlemanly obligation which excited my alarming and punctilious imagination, I felt as if I were going to a sacrifice; which I'd accepted, not knowing true love; because I believed that one day that would come; I had a dawning of true love, after meeting my wife; in Central America, but I suffocated it in the belief of what I owed to the woman who had given me the gifts of her love in advance.*

In the "Diary of a Soldier" written by Martí's lifelong friend Fermín Valdéz Domínguez, which for decades has been suppressed in the Cuban state archives, apparently because of its disparaging observations about some rebel military heroes, there is a passage that today only a small number of people can claim to have actually read: there Domínguez is said to have written that Martí once confided to him that Carmen was no longer a virgin when they married—"a gift of love" hardly to be taken lightly, of course, in that era (or in any other! Though—etc.)—Martí suffocated his love for María García Granados because of what he felt he owed his fiancée, who had made love to him in Mexico before they were married, before he'd left for Central America.

*Women mistakenly believe, and men also believe,* Martí wrote in his notebook not long after, *that once the great prize has been given, the prize of the body, the earthshaking kiss, that everything has been given, and everything has been attained. Oh! No! The soul is spirit, and it escapes through the flesh's netting . . .*

"And if a bird lands on my shoulder . . ." Martí once confided, or confessed, to a younger friend seeking his advice on the subject of transient loves, his voice suggestively trailing off. We can find allusions, or the suspicion of such, to María de las Nieves Moran sprinkled throughout Martí's writings, in his poetry, and even in some of the anecdotal accounts left by those who knew him. She was not his most important relationship in Central America, nor was she later on in New York; of course he mattered a great deal to her. As usual, Martí left no overt autobiographical record of his thoughts or feelings about this other niña—no other uncharacteristically indiscreet jotting on the back of a pamphlet has turned up. But he did sometimes refer to María de las Nieves as his little bird—as his "pajarita," not his "niña."

> *La pajarita builds her nest of fleece—*
> *and then she has to flee her itchy nest.*
> *Why fly to the wool tree, not the flannel shrub, to rest?*
> *Why her lanate loves, and not the soft white down of geese?*

That bit of spontaneous light verse, which Martí later wrote for María de las Nieves, does indicate that, at least eventually, she confided rather intimate matters to him. María de las Nieves, to the end of her days, would remain guarded about her relationship to the Cuban revolutionary hero and martyr. But even some of the anecdotes María de las Nieves did like to share couldn't help but leave the impression of an at least ambiguous closeness; for example, that Martí, while fingering the long yellow ribbons of her hat, had once told her: A hat that's been riding atop a señorita's head for even an hour can tell us mischievous things about her. Question the hat; it might respond: Well, perhaps the señorita noticed and perhaps she didn't, but back there in the crowd there was a caballero who lifted these ribbons to his lips and gave them a deeply affectionate, I'd even say a worshipful, kiss. But if you ask the hat who that bold gentleman was, the poor hat can't answer. A hat knows no name but that of its mistress!

WHO LIFTED THE ribbons of María de las Nieves's hat to his lips? And where? Amid which crowd? Did it happen on the day of the balloon and the parachuted puppy? Did Martí actually see somebody give her ribbons a furtive kiss, or was he referring to himself? It couldn't have been Mack Chinchilla, for he was playing baseball, and Wellesley Bludyar was out of the country on a secret diplomatic mission. Was there another suitor? Was it some other day?

That Sunday afternoon Martí ran into María de las Nieves on the Calle Real, just as she was coming out from the arcade of shops along the south side of the Plaza Mayor. It took her a few seconds to collect herself: it was as if suddenly there were two Martís, the one who lived inside her, imprisoned inside her unhappy fixation, and this one who'd just stepped into her path, dressed as always in black, smiling warmly and greeting her. Because María de las Nieves was always imagining scenes between them that began with just such a chance encounter in the street, she also felt as if she'd intuitively sensed she was going to run into him just before it happened— as much as surprise, what she felt was delight in the powerful magic of her own intuition. That a love as secretive and frustrated as hers always attributes a nearly mystical significance to such mundanely coincidental encounters did not occur to her (nor would it until many years later). And where was she headed? Martí wanted to know. She confessed that she hadn't quite decided where, someplace with a good vantage point from which to watch the balloon, she supposed. And where was la señorita María Chon? Martí asked; didn't she want to see the balloonist too? María Chon had gone home to visit her family—they were now living near Zunil, she told him. But María Chon would certainly be sorry to have missed the balloon, she said, especially when she heard about the parachuting chuchito; hopefully it would land safely, it would be terrible if anything went wrong, she was sure he'd heard the story about what had happened the last time a balloon had gone up over the capital. Yes, he had, said Martí. He'd spoken to many people who had witnessed the horrifying incineration in the sky as children and remained haunted by it. Hopefully today's flight, and a successful landing by the parachuted puppy, would ease the apparently communal burden of that terrible memory.

"People used to believe," said María de las Nieves, "that if you heard a dog barking in the sky, that meant a new outbreak of cholera was coming, or some other apocalyptic catastrophe."

"That is an old Indian myth?"

"An old nuns' superstition. I heard it in the convent."

And like that, they fell into conversation, and she soon forgot all about the balloon; he'd witnessed many, dozens, of such ascents, in La Habana, in Spain; in Madrid there were days when the sky was so full of balloons it was like looking up into a celestial pear tree—

There was a famous French aeronaut named Nadar, Martí told her. One of the singular characters of Paris. A friend of Baudelaire's, of Hugo's. A pioneer of the art of photography as well, the first to take photographs from the air. About fifteen years before, Nadar had gone up in his famous balloon, which bore the name *Le Géant*, on what was intended to be a flight of world-record duration; his wife and a friend or two were accompanying him as passengers, and also a dog. The party took off in *Le Géant* from Paris in the morning, and all day they floated over France, caught in a strong and steady eastern wind, and then it was dark, they were lost, and their watches told them it was midnight. Far ahead of the balloon's relentless path, and far below, Nadar saw lights, and he brought the balloon down as low as it was safe to, and discovered that they were the lights of a train station.

"And as the balloon passed over," said Martí, "the great aeronaut shouted down: *Ou est-ce que nous sommes?* And from below came the reply, shouted back by one of the station workers: *C'est Erquelinnes* . . . Erquelinnes? Erquelinnes is in Belgium, on the border. And a little Belgian man in a uniform ran out of the station shouting up at the balloon as it floated away: *Arrêtez! Arrêtez!* The passengers must disembark for their customs inspection!"

Martí almost never told a story simply because he thought it was funny. Had he now? Just to make her laugh? She laughed, her usually murky eyes undoubtedly glowing with a girlish adoration that he couldn't have helped but notice.

"And *Le Géant* floated away into the night," Martí went on. "At the train station, even when they could no longer see the balloon, they could still hear *le chien* barking in the sky. The next day, near Hannover, the balloon crashed, and all the passengers were seriously hurt and had to be hospitalized, Monsiuer Nadar with two broken legs, and his wife with injuries even more severe."

"And the chucho?"

Martí didn't know what had happened to the dog. He did know that later *Le Géant* had been put on display in the Crystal Palace in London;

such was the balloon's fame that day after day crowds had paid money just
to see it.

They were ambling toward the city's eastern outskirts, and Martí said
the pasture behind the San Juan de Dios Hospital might offer a good vantage from which to see the balloon. But they did not reach it in time;
alerted by the happy roar rising from the city, they stopped in the street
and looked up over the line of trees and churches and briefly watched the
puppy's descent in a parachute and the canary yellow balloon hovering far
above it in the limpid blue sky. They resumed their walk, and did not even
notice the baseball game at the opposite end of the pasture whose margin
they soon after traversed. Was Martí putting María de las Nieves's reputation at risk by drawing her, alone with him, into this Sunday afternoon
stroll? He would have been, had María de las Nieves been María García
Granados; had she belonged to a social class that at birth bestowed a pris-
tine reputation on its females like a second soul, societal rather than divine. Martí must have been aware of that: as if lending María de las Nieves
the secondhand but unsullied reputation of a girl situated somewhere
between María García Granados and the lower regions where virtue was
not actually required of a girl, he expressed regret that María Chon was
away. María de las Nieves silently noted the remark as a kind but superfluous courtesy.

But then Martí asked if she expected María Chon back by the next
weekend. María de las Nieves answered that she did not expect her to
have returned by then. Martí said that he was sorry to hear that, and now
she glanced at him in puzzlement, while he tranquilly elaborated that
lately he'd been thinking about that Jefe Indio in Sacatepéquez whom
some of his Liberal friends had told him about, who spoke French, read
newspapers, built schools, instilled virtues. Martí said that he was writing
a little book, which he planned to publish in Mexico, to awaken readers to
the qualities and riches of her little country. Wouldn't a word portrait of
that Jefe Indio be a perfect advertisement for such an important aspect of
the country's current transformation—the advancement of the Indian?
Sacatepéquez was not so far. If one left by stagecoach at dawn, perhaps
rented horses once there, and had luck finding the Jefe Indio—such a
señor could hardly be anything but well known—one might even be able
to return late that same night. Or better yet, why not stay over, rent re-

spectable rooms in Antigua, the old earthquake-destroyed capital, and linger the next morning to tour the reputedly magnificent ruins of the old baroque convents and churches. And it would be prudent, Martí told her, perhaps even necessary, to travel with a translator, if he was going to be venturing into the villages. He knew, of course, that María de las Nieves spoke an Indian language, and that she was a translator by profession. He would be happy to hire her. He couldn't imagine a better companion for such an expedition. But he also understood that it would seem inappropriate for her to undertake such a journey in his company if she were not at least accompanied by her servant, la señorita María Chon. Unfortunately, he was impatient to make the trip, and was even thinking of going the next weekend; he had so little time left to finish his book before his return to Mexico.

"Pues sí, of course, one couldn't go without María Chon," she replied in a faraway voice, for María de las Nieves still was not quite able to comprehend this incredible invitation: he wanted her to go with him to Sacatepéquez, but only if she was accompanied by her servant, was that really it?

Was there anybody else who might chaperone?—Amada Gómez, her boarder—a disagreeable option. Vipulina? she wondered. Would Vipulina's aunt allow it? Would Vipulina even want to go to Sacatepéquez with her and Martí?

"At any rate, I speak Mam. In Sacatepéquez they mainly speak . . . Cakchiquel, no?"

"Are they similar?"

"I might be able to understand, and make you understood. At least until we find your Jefe Indio—well, then we can all speak French."

He nodded in assent, as if he thought she'd meant her last remark seriously, and that it hardly needed to be said. Clearly his intentions were purely professional and intellectual; it was all in service of his book. He was insisting that she be accompanied by a chaperone. Or was he waiting for her to say she would go without a chaperone? So, was this the sort of moment she'd been obsessively dreaming about, suddenly enveloping her in a plausible scenario that must be one of the few she hadn't imagined? She was filled with the most extraordinary confusion, excitement, fear: a dense flock of mixed-up birds inside her.

While she was sorting through these thoughts and feelings, even asking herself what young Madame Roland might have done in her place, María de las Nieves's footsteps propelled her ahead of Martí. It would be wonderful to be able to report that Martí adjusted his own pace to follow quietly behind, that it was here that he lifted the trailing yellow ribbons of her hat to his lips. But he didn't. Or if he did, María de las Nieves never noticed.

But now Martí again drew alongside her, and began telling her about a treatise he'd recently read by an American archaeologist and linguist regarding the conception of love in the Native American languages. Shouldn't a people's vocabulary of love, asked Martí, reveal much about their inmost heart? For example, he told her, in the European languages there were words for many kinds and degrees of love, but no longer words solely to express a love of the gods, such as the American languages still possessed. Apparently the North American Indian tribes had impressively varied concepts of love. But the Nahuatl-speaking Aztecs, he said, though a more advanced culture, had had an astonishingly impoverished vocabulary of love. The Aztecs had only one basic word to express every variety of the emotion, from human to divine, chaste to carnal, and as they walked along the northern border of the pasture behind the San Juan de Dios Hospital, the amazing Martí even pronounced the word, *tlazóltl*—and not only that, he told her, but that word shared the same verbal root as several other verbs, such as the one meaning *to wear out an old garment*, and all those words were descended from the Nahuatl word *zo*, essentially a sharp, pointed instrument used to puncture objects and flesh. And so, María de las Nieves, Martí told her, those ancient Mexican Indians apparently had verbs for *to puncture* and *to draw blood* long before they had any word for love, and this, at least in that American scientist's opinion, told ominously against their culture. But the ancient Aztecs produced no Popul Vuh. They left no *Annals of the Cakchiquels*. And in the language of the ancient Maya of the Yucatán—

"My mother was a Maya from the Yucatán," María de las Nieves interrupted, "though not an ancient one." For he was confusing and making her nervous with all this talk of love and she had to put a stop to it right now and study his words in her mind. Was he really only offering her a lesson about the Indian languages?

Martí already knew that her mother was originally from the Yucatán; she'd told him during their conversations in the reading room kiosk. Though Martí politely said, "Yes, of course, she is from the Yucatán, I had forgotten." Pues sí, her mother had met her Yankee father in the Yucatán, she said, and they had married, and then they had come here. And they walked in silence, as if Martí was giving her the chance to say something more about her parents if she wished, which she did not.

"Can you speak Yucatec Maya too, then?" Martí asked. She answered no, that her mother had always preferred speaking in Spanish. The language of the Maya of the Yucatán, he then told her, was notably rich in concepts of love.

"But what is most fascinating, María de las Nieves, is that in that ancient language, all their many words for love shared the same root—*ya*—as their words for pain, suffering, wounds, and misery. It is as if the ancient Maya, who lived so closely to nature, developed the same romantic ideas about the relationship between love and suffering as, so many centuries later, did the poets of Paris and London."

"Ay *sí!* People suffer too much over all of that, don't they? *Bastante!*" She turned her head to the side, briefly closing her eyes in mortified self-reproach.

Martí repeated, "Yes, bastante"—a word meaning both *quite a lot* and *more than enough*—his gaze coasting over the ground; he hadn't noticed her embarrassment. He must be thinking of María García Granados, she suddenly thought. And now, when he looked back at her, she sensed, like a shadow rising inside of him, that María García Granados was about to darken her day, that he was on the verge of confiding his feelings for the other girl to her, and silently she begged him not to; but instead he told her that in the Quiché and Cakchiquel dialects *logoh* was the word for love, and that in both it also meant to buy.

"But that is not as ominous in its implications as it sounds, María de las Nieves," said Martí, "for such words derive from the worthy sentiment *to value highly*. Doesn't the word *carus*, the *ipsum verbum amoris*, as Cicero called it, mean both expensive and beloved? The English, of course, say *dear*, which can sound very tender, but also so distressed and pecuniary. How do you say *love* in Mam?"

"*Laaqjil,*" she answered.

They had turned the corner of a row of small pines and were on an old cow and mule-train path descending between a cafetal, with coffee shrubs shaded by banana trees, and a steep dirt slope from which swallows were darting and swooping. The dirt path wound gently down to a river valley running through the deep ravines of the mountain plateau. It was one of those late October afternoons when the temperature and even fragrance of the air seemed to belong to a climate of apples and pumpkins, rather than to one of coffee and bananas.

"But, Pepe, are you sure that Jefe Indio really exists?" she asked.

She could see that her question had surprised him, and she hoped that he was not offended.

Finally Martí answered, "He should exist. It would be good to find him. But I do realize, María de las Nieves, that he may not exist. Do you think that he exists?"

"I do not think that he does," she said. "Pepe, listen to what I have to say, please—" María de las Nieves felt emotion, conviction, and clarity surging together in such unfamiliar concert that she was afraid she wasn't going to be able to finish what she wanted to say before it all left her; and if it did leave her, she knew she'd end up in tears. "I don't know if you already know about this or not, but last weekend, Pepe, our President General and his wife gave an afternoon garden party for members of his government, of the parliament, and many other supposedly distinguished and wealthy people of this city, many formerly allied with the old regime— people who were very eager for the restoration of their old elite status, which this very coveted invitation apparently symbolized. As the party was ending the servants suddenly came out of the kitchen and into the garden, all carrying silver trays piled with fish—a large catch of still edible fish, supposedly sent as a gift from the Jefe Político of Puerto San José. How could El Señor Presidente and his family eat so many fish? The fish had to be given away before they spoiled. And so all the men and women, all of them dressed in their very best outfits, wearing their finest kid-leather and ostrich-skin gloves, had no choice but to take a smelly fish from a tray with their own hands, and carry it out through the gates, to the street, and into their carriages, because no one dared to just leave a fish lying there in the street. This entire escapade was apparently conceived and staged just for the amusement of La Primera Dama. Supposedly Doña Francisca, as she stood there saying good-bye to her humiliated and obsequious guests, couldn't stop giggling like a naughty little schoolgirl. These are the quality of people, Pepe, who see that you have a noble and good heart, and that you so want to believe the best of their glorious Liberal Revolution, and that you envision great things that their minds and hearts are too small and corrupted to hold, and so they tease you and laugh at you behind your back by making up some story about a Jefe Indio who speaks French. Running off to Sacatepéquez in search of him is just what they expect you to do. Thank God they didn't tell you he lives all the way up there in Huehuetenango!"

Martí walked with his head down, his stride lengthening until, realizing he was leaving her behind, he turned to wait. And María de las Nieves, coming toward him, must have looked a little abashed and frightened, wondering if she'd gone too far and if that was a critical look flashing in his eyes. But Martí was probably moved by María de las Nieves's speech, and impressed by what it revealed about her character, if also a little taken aback by her vehemence and embarrassed by what her passionate words had too plainly exposed about him. For all the seeming gentleness of his character, Martí did not take mockery or disrespect lightly. He was destined, after all, to become an indefatigable revolutionary leader, strategist, and warrior, a frock-coated summoner of young men to warfare and death, a lover of life and of death who would finally choose the latter—who almost two decades later would disappear into the paradigmatic martyrdom that would transform his entire life into an enormous heroic statue, one whose shadow still falls everywhere. Of course María de las Nieves could not yet have foreseen any of that—that his destiny as a ubiquitous statue would with every passing year petrify a bit more of her own life, trapping love and the memory of love inside its airless air, turning even her own tongue and memory to dutiful marble and bronze. (Perhaps posterity will never be able to discover the names of all the women's hearts melted down to help make that statue, though María de las Nieves's heart was certainly one of those, and it was willing.)

What María de las Nieves undeniably witnessed that day, in Martí's eyes and pallor, was the flare of his recognition that he had enemies, causing him hot anger and pain, his eyebrows and mustache suddenly standing out in his face like lightning-illuminated owls flying through white night. The world must have seemed suddenly different to him—though it wasn't knowledge he couldn't absorb. Because within moments he composed himself, and seemed even more tranquil than before, and in his eyes there was a soft new glitter: of fondness, of surprised tenderness, an open and dazzling look that fell over María de las Nieves like a soft net.

Now they could hear the rushing river nearby, but they could not see it. They were standing in a grassy declension lower than the riverbank, just off the dirt path, in a hollow beneath the cliff wall. And there was a faint but delicious tang of freshly dug earth in the air—as if the approach of evening caused the earth to release its flavors into the cooling air, as is the case with certain flowering plants, such as nightshade or the cactus called Reina de la Noche, which opens its sweet white blossoms only in the dark. The fading afternoon seemed to have a similar affect on María de las Nieves: in the powdery glow of her smooth cinnamon skin, in the softness at the base of her neck and just over her lips, there was a desirability that perhaps Martí hadn't noticed before, which he now felt inside his mouth like a thirst pang. Martí was looking down into her slightly upturned face, soft strands of her hair quivering over her forehead and vivid black brows and falling away from her cheeks—sweet-looking young lips, and the dark wet gap between her teeth. How could he not have felt carried away by eyes so luminous with emotion, eyes welling with a still innocent girl's sense of the astounding momentousness of her unprecedented moment? Her invisible future hovered over her like a sad little canopy, held up by four shaky sticks . . . He would not give in. He was soon to be married.

"María de las Nieves, what you say is probably true," said Martí quietly. "I am moved by your honesty, and the high regard you seem to have for me. But I will go and search for that Jefe Indio. For his sake, I am willing to be made a fool of."

"Pepe, I'll go with you—"

Just like that, their lips touched, and his arms enfolded her small, weightless waist—yes, before she could even finish what she was saying. So it was then that it happened, that incredible kiss, which from now on would accompany her on her lifelong journey. And maybe the sun dropped beneath the high wall of the ravine far above, and the light in the valley darkened—that falling evening shadow which in his poetry Martí would inevitably evoke as the passing overhead of an enormous wing.

And she quietly stammered that she loved him. "I love you, Pepe." She gasped, and took a breath, and said that she knew he was promised in marriage and that she shouldn't be speaking as she was, and that she expected and asked for nothing, that it made her happy just to have spoken the truth, and that she would forever remember this walk and this kiss as the happiest moment of her life so far.

Is that really what happened, there in the *cuenca,* in the river valley, between María de las Nieves and Martí? In the volume of Martí's *Collected Works* that compiles random writings, including hundreds of apparently stray bursts of scrawled introspection found among the papers gathered from his Front Street office in New York City after his death, the reader finds this:

*From this world I don't want any more than my duty, my friends, and my children, and the memory of the fugitive hours in which I've been loved. Not long loves, with selfish interests and enervation: but the tree covered with unexpectedly blossoming flowers as evening falls, or a timid confession in the valley in the shadow of a wing, during a burning kiss; and when Car. seeing me arrive sick, set the candle on the floor.*

*in the cuenca,*

*in the hueco* . . . alongside that word for hollow, Martí drew a picture of a wing.

Of course some of that almost exactly echoes the language and imagery of the famous poem about María García Granados, which begins: *A la sombra de una ala... By the shadow of a wing, I want to tell this story in full flower . . .* But the kiss in that poem is a good-bye kiss, and it is not the kiss but her *frente,* her brow, or her face, that is described as being like red-hot bronze—evoking fever as much as passion—though the poet also declares that *frente* to be the one he has loved more than any other in his life (*la frente / Que más he amado en mi vida!*). Would a confession of love from María García Granados, whom Martí saw daily in her father's house, whose album he filled with love poetry, have been so unexpected that he would have compared it to a tree covered with unexpectedly blossoming flowers as evening falls? Perhaps. A timid confession of love in winglike shadow—that could be María de las Nieves too, or both of those niñas. The placement of the word *or* suggests two separate yet perhaps similar episodes: the metaphoric unexpectedly flowering tree *or* the burning kiss in the shadow of a wing. Was the kiss between María de las Nieves and Martí really a burning kiss, or was it briefer and more fumbling? Maybe Martí synthesized details, sensations, memories, imagery from analogous episodes in his famous poem. Is it possible that Martí shared burning kisses and received timid confessions of love from both María las Nieves and María García Granados? Of course it is.

But which "Car." sets the candle on the floor? Carmen Zayas Bazán or Carmita Miyares de Mantilla, the owner of the boardinghouse in New York City where Martí would rent rooms, and who would later become his lover? The fact that in his nostalgic scribbling Martí was recalling *fugitive hours* of love makes it fairly obvious that he was not referring to his wife.

All first kisses plant the possibility of more to come; that possibility remained long after Martí, that afternoon in the river valley, said, "Of course you are right, María de las Nieves, I am about to be married. But your declaration of love is a surprise gift that I will always treasure, and which I will try to be worthy of in the most fraternal way. Someday soon I'm sure somebody will speak to you as bravely and beautifully as you just have to me, and then you'll understand how moved and grateful I am. And I hope that you, in return, will be able to speak to him as you have to me. That really will be the happiest day of your life, María de las Nieves."

If María de las Nieves had not declared her love, maybe they would have gone on kissing. But she had, and so that moment of spontaneous passion had subsided. It must have been confusing enough for Martí to carry his loves for both his fiancée and María García Granados around inside him: he must already have felt as if he was going around with two constantly riled stomachs; he certainly didn't need a third.

Another Cuban who was a frequent visitor to the festive García Granados household later recalled seeing Martí and María García Granados seated at the same table, oblivious of all that was going on around them, sunk into the silent misery of their obvious love.

"—HE SAID THAT he saw you and Pepe Martí kiss. That's all. Obviously I wouldn't have forgotten if he'd reported anything else."

"And you never wanted to kiss Martí, Paquita?" María de las Nieves challenged.

"I'm sure you remember, Las Nievecitas, what my husband did to that poor young man who was director of our orchestral society, just because I used to laugh at his jokes and let him flirt a bit, and because he always sent me flowers on the morning of the day our society was going to meet. No wife could have been more faithful than I, María de las Nieves." And there was something bold and hard in Paquita's eyes that said: Don't think it's such a simple matter to judge my life. Don't think I'm not aware of its every sinister nuance. My life might have happened anywhere where men love unrestrained power, so it could have happened anywhere.

Yes, María de las Nieves had heard those rumors: that in the dreaded dungeon of the Guardia de Honor, commanded by General Sixto Pérez, the most notoriously sadistic of El Anticristo's executioners, the young man had endured "the punishment of Abelard," along with the usual floggings with long elastic sticks cut from quince tree branches, like magic wands for lacerating the flesh, every flick leaving a vivid blue stripe that slowly turns scarlet. From the barracks of the Guardia de Honor he was taken to the Presidential Mansion for an audience with the President General. Paquita, upon seeing the prisoner being led across her patio, his bare back red and pulpy as a split-open pomegranate, was said to have fainted. Her husband, in a gesture of respect to the young man's illustrious family, freed him, and as soon as he'd sufficiently regained his health, he fled the country; it was soon reported that he had entered a seminary in Spain. (Many years later, in fact, when relations with the Church had been repaired, Paquita's former admirer would return to the country as its new Archbishop, a plump prelate of such gentle character and manners—most deceptively gentle, many would say—that his nickname among the populace would be Sor Turtledove.)

"Is it true that you fainted when you saw him, Paquita?"

"Yes, Las Nievecitas, that is true."

IN SEPTEMBER, ON the country's Independence Day, in the faraway mountains of El Quiché, a thousand Indio campesinos had marched from their villages to the Jefe Politico's headquarters in the departmental capital of Santa Cruz to protest the forced labor drafts that sent Indios, often at the local Jefe Politico's whim, to work on the coffee plantations, or to build roads or to serve as beast-of-burden mozos, for almost no pay. Order was swiftly reestablished, hundreds were imprisoned, the Jefe Politico telegraphed the Supreme Government that the Indios of El Quiché had declared themselves the enemies of Progress and were in a state of war. Soon after, the President General appeared on the scene. Forty Indians, chosen at random among those arrested, were to be identified as the rebellion's leaders and executed. In the abandoned church at San Pedro Jocopilas, where he and his officers were camped, Paquita's husband was breakfasting alone in the rectory when a young Spanish priest entered unannounced, fell to his knees, and pleaded for the lives of the condemned prisoners. It so happened that the priest was also the owner of a coffee farm: the Jefe Politico was always drafting the priest's laborers and sending them to work on other plantations, but his workers were loyal, he paid them fairly and offered masses and free baptisms. The rebellion had originated, the priest bravely confessed, among the Indians who worked on his farm. Rufino the Just berated him with the coarsest language, but that outburst was insufficient to expel his rage, so he began pummeling the priest's head with his fists. Just then his military waiter came in carrying a tray holding a pitcher of fresh coffee and a basket of warm tortillas. He saw that the priest's arms were raised, pushing against the President General's chest, or reaching for his neck; perhaps he was just trying to ward off blows. The waiter set down the tray, pulled out his pistol, and shot the priest, who fell wounded to the floor, and then the waiter fired the fatal bullet. Other officers and aides-de-camp rushed in. Though it was never included in any official version of the Spanish priest's death, it was widely whispered later that a frenzy had overtaken them all, that the President General and his officers had all stood around the corpse kicking and stomping the body with such force that the priest's intestines began to spill from his mouth.

In the faraway city, it was always hard to know the truth of what happened in the mountainous Indian departments. The waiter, proclaimed a national hero for having curtailed the crazed pistol-wielding Spanish priest's murderous attack on the President, was brought to the capital from his rural garrison and installed as a steward in the Presidential Mansion.

He began to drink heavily; he could not hold his tongue about what had really happened in the rectory in San Pedro Jocopilas, especially when in the presence of La Primera Dama's pretty servant Modesta Sabal. His groping attentions and grotesque confidences apparently deeply distressed the devout Modesta, for one morning she disappeared, and later it was rumored that she'd fled to the Monjita Inglesa's clandestine convent somewhere in the city—which Padre Bruno, writing fifty years later, did not confirm, which is not surprising as in his book he paid little attention to the comings and goings of servants, and even less to their names. La Primera Dama discovered soon after that jewelry and precious gems were missing from her dressing room. The heroic waiter, accused of being the thief, was sent to the dungeon prison commanded by General Sixto Perez in the barracks of the Presidential Honor Guard, and was never seen or heard from again.

Just days after the successful balloon ascent and puppy drop, during the first week of November, the city's happy afterglow—a faint yet poignant echo of the citywide joy that had followed such long-ago events as Pope Pío IX's declaration of the Immaculate Conception as church dogma; and the procession of Serapio Cruz's severed head—was shattered by the dramatic exposure of a shadowy conspiracy known as the Homicidal Fraternity of the Black Rosary and its averted plot to murder the President General, his wife, and their children as they slept on the Night of All Souls. The plotters, it was said, had drawn lots to decide who would have the honor of murdering La Primera Dama in her bed. The public executions in the Central Plaza of arrested conspirators began almost immediately: seventeen men, including the plot's accused leaders, a Polish-mercenary colonel who commanded an artillery battalion, a general, and a priest, faced the firing squads over two days. The plaza had been sealed off from normal traffic, and the surrounding streets, sidewalks, and arcades were filled with spectators. Many came out of morbid curiosity, or watched helplessly in taciturn horror and pity, though the Liberals' most ardent supporters cheered as the groups of condemned and bloodied prisoners, some needing to be carried on stretchers, were brought out from the Palace of Government and led to the row of chairs in the middle of the plaza, in front of the fountain with the riderless equestrian statue in its center (King Carlos III having been violently toppled from his mount in the year of Independence from Spain.) Bringing up the rear of the grim procession was the parliamentary deputy and priest, Canon Ángel Arroyo, purple socks flashing beneath his cassock, there to give the prisoners their last rites. Facing the plaza, in the Presidential Mansion, from a window balcony decorated like a gala opera box, the President General, cigar in mouth, accompanied by the again pregnant, adolescent Primera Dama and select government eminences, observed the meting out of justice; after each volley of rifle fire, as the dead tumbled off the chairs and slid to the ground, the men stood and applauded. In a letter to Lord Derby at the Foreign Office a few days later, María de las Nieves would copy down Minister Gastreel's dictated opinion that at least two or three of the executed men were innocent: "Though it is difficult to ascertain the full facts," he added, "in a land where for the populace it is such a danger to even inquire about them." There were many versions and rumors about how the murders and seizure of the government were to have been carried out, and of how many conspirators the plot actually involved, and of how it had actually come to be discovered and prevented. Soon it was obvious that from now on anyone might be suspected, accused, or arrested for having belonged to or abetted the conspiracy of the the Homicidal Fraternity of the Black Rosary.

As had occurred before during such moments of national crisis, patriotic exaltation combined with centuries of racial humiliation to feed fantasies of vengeance against white foreigners. Mr. Gabriel Sugarman, a civil engineer working for the railroad, coming upon a mob taunting the children of the German Minister, attempted to offer them his protection and was attacked by military officers, who struck him with rifle butts and knocked him to the ground before leading him away to prison. The members of several legations were detained, brashly charged with having conspired with the plotters, and just as swiftly freed, before any diplomatic minister even had the chance to utter the threat of gunboats and reparations.

Only poor Higinio Farfán, the British Legation clerk and official translator, was arrested and, not being a true Inglés, kept overnight in General Pérez's prison. Minister Gastreel did not learn of it until the next afternoon, when Señora Farfán arrived at the legation with the news, the first time anyone there had ever seen the much younger wife of the clerk and official translator. She was an astonishingly delicate and pretty woman, dressed in muted pink calico and a shawl of white wool, with a walnut complexion and swirling ebony hair, which she was continuously brushing back from her evergreen eyes with a fetching gesture of her hand. Yet she was not much taller than the five-year-old daughter accompanying her. Señora Farfán remained so impressively composed that María de las Nieves, who never left her side, felt as if she, not the anxious wife, was the one being soothed. Over several pots of tea and sweet English butter crackers, Señora Farfán made small talk that, despite the terrifying gravity of the situation and its only being small talk, revealed a sparkling intelligence and spirit throughout. María de las Nieves even found herself trying to imitate the clerk's wife's manners and tone, the genuine poise that made her courage seem as natural as water and light; she had the yearning but excited epiphany that she'd discovered a model for the kind of woman she wanted to be. "Yes, this is my only daughter," said Señora Farfán. "Like Our Queen of Heaven, I've only given birth once. But every mother stands upon the moon, is robed in the sun, and has the twelve stars of the Apocalypse over her head." How did she make such blasphemous words come out sounding like a spontaneous embodiment of modesty and charm? What kind of noble heart must lurk inside Higinio Farfán, that he'd managed to win his diminutive but spectacular wife?— the legation clerk's personality was as glittering as ashen charcoal. But when Mrs. Gastreel came to tell them that the clerk and Minister Gastreel had returned, Señora Farfán immediately sprang from the table and, trailed by her little daughter, ran toward the vestibule, and all the sobs that had been gestating inside her came bursting out even before she reached her pulverized husband. It was certainly not wrong of Señora Farfán to become so emotional, María de las Nieves knew, but still, she was stupefied, and felt humiliated for her. Anyone could see by the expression on the Gastreels' faces that they considered that prolonged noisy flood to be excessive, even vulgar, and she felt desperate to tell them how badly they were misjudging Señora Farfán. She remembered Madame Roland and the writer of twaddle, and Sainte-Beuve's dictum that the object of a great woman's love counted for almost nothing. Maybe this was proof, staged before her eyes, as the lessons and miracles of the Bible so rarely were. But didn't it ever happen the other way around: that a young man anyone could see was destined for greatness fell blindly for a young woman everyone else would think was far beneath him?

Later Minister Gastreel dictated a detailed account of the episode to María de las Nieves, which she transcribed into a dispatch to Lord Derby in the Foreign Office. "I have the honor to inform Your Excellency," dictated the Minister Resident, "that this has been a most rare and satisfying instance of diplomacy, all the more so considering the country in which it has occurred." It was true that as soon as he'd learned of the arrest and detention from Señora Farfán, the British Minister had followed a decisive course: after instructing Don Lico, the concierge, to send his carriage to the Presidential Mansion as soon as it could be readied, he'd donned his top hat, spoken reassuringly to the clerk's wife, said a cheerful good-bye to his pregnant wife, and headed off alone on foot toward the dictator's residence, eight blocks away, opposite a corner of the Central Plaza. Pushing his way through the milling crowd of Indian beggars and supplicants outside, Minister Gastreel refused to state the purpose of his visit to the soldiers and officers at the front gates, nor would he agree to wait for an appointment. It was urgent that he speak in private to the President General, he would offer no more explanation, and he purposefully strode forward, defying them to prevent him from entering. Inside, in the vast interior courtyard, he saw a low wooden platform, recently erected, upon which a man lay prostrate, tied down by the ankles and wrists, with four soldiers standing over him, two on each side, each with an arm moving tirelessly up and down—that transparent blur of wings seemingly affixed to the prisoner's muscular back was caused by the quince switches flashing up and down in the soldiers' hands. The prisoner had a Herculean physique, he was certainly not Higinio Farfán, but Minister Gastreel was determined to confront the soldiers with their brutality; he stopped and in his most stentorian voice, asked if the prisoner was the British Legation clerk. The soldiers did halt the lashing, but only to stare back at the Englishman, until one, in a raised but neutral voice, replied that it was not the clerk. Minister Gastreel retorted, "Then who is this man? I demand to know his name," and the soldiers looked at him blankly, until his exasperated voice boomed out again: "Do you even know your prisoner's name?" One of the young officers escorting the Minister toward the President

General's office then interjected in a solemnly hushed tone, as if he'd just been asked a question in church: "Señor Ministro, with all respect, the prisoner is not Señor Farfán." No sooner had Minister Gastreel turned away than the soldiers on the platform went back to flogging the prisoner, who was enduring his torture in uncanny silence, perhaps because he was already unconscious—the switches striking his flesh made a familiar sound, which the Minister would be unable to identify until several hours later when, as he lay awake in bed replaying the day's events in his mind, it would come to him: the quick, ticking splatter of icy rain against slush on an otherwise silent winter night.

The courtyard was filled with the songs of caged canaries and finches too, but the bleating of a sheep surprised him, and in the twilight it took him a moment to pick out the murky hues of several ragged sheep grazing in the grass between paved paths. There was also a milk cow in the courtyard, and a saddled pale horse tethered to a cypress tree, and a fawn, and an emerald-beaked toucan on a hanging swing, and, crouched in a flower bed, a pair of small creatures that the Minister could not identify, with long rabbit ears and long monkey tails and large somber eyes; and from beneath the shadowy eaves of one of the long verandahs came the obscene shriek of a parrot—he detested those birds, their squalid ambience of rotted fruit rinds and inanity. *A tropical tyrant's menagerie*— those very words, Minister Gastreel told María de las Nieves later as he dictated his dispatch, actually formed silently on his lips. Someday it might serve as the title for a memoir of his diplomatic service here. And he felt a stab of longing to be home in Yorkshire, all of this finally behind him, writing that memoir in his study; and he braced himself for his encounter with the dictator.

"It is completely contrary to the rules of international law and diplomacy for the employee of a diplomatic legation to be arrested without the express permission of the representing Minister—in this unfortunate case, of course, that being myself," Minister Gastreel wasted no time in explaining to the President General in his office, which had a cluttered mercantile air: against the wall, in every corner, were stacked fragrant sacks of coffee beans from all of his plantations. Rufino the Just reclined against the arm of a hide-draped sofa, his knees drawn up so that his feet, in ankle-high kid-leather boots, rested atop the sofa, his thick black leather whip propped atop one of those knees. Two facing rows of straight-backed chairs were arranged at right angles from each end of the sofa. In his dictated dispatch to Lord Derby, Minister Gastreel would recount how very tempted he'd been to choose a chair perpendicular to the end of the sofa that the President General was leaning back against, so that the tyrant would be forced to twist himself around and look over his shoulder when he spoke. Though that, Minister Gastreel admitted, would have been a very trivial provocation. He chose a chair facing the lounging President. The whip resting on his knee, fashioned from the member of a once prized bull, was an important symbol of the dictator's legend. Of course, rather than impressing Minister Gastreel in any way, the brazenly displayed whip only confirmed his most contemptuous prejudice—though Rufino the Just would have understood and anticipated that, just as he understood that Her Majesty's Foreign Office had always favored the Conservatives and was always working to undermine him, here and in London, throughout the Isthmus, everywhere. The British Minister's taut facial expression of just perceptible repugnance probably even caused Rufino the Just a gratifying inward shiver of violent vindication: he was right to despise the British most of all. He got up from the sofa and came and sat, whip across lap, alongside Minister Gastreel, and at that close distance stared sedately into his eyes. Would the translator be handed over then, the dictator asked, once a request for the British Legation clerk's arrest was properly submitted?

Minister Gastreel declined to provide an answer, nor did he even inquire what the charges against Higinio Farfán might be; he simply repeated that any such demand would have to be formally submitted to the British Legation by the Supreme Government's Foreign Minister.

The two men sat in loathing silence until Higinio Farfán, missing his coat and his shirt, arms drawn back and tied at the elbows, his soft hairless torso slick with blood and covered with welts that resembled long lizards' tails and pulchritudinous mouths, was finally led into the office. Without offering any apology, the President General rose to go. But Minister Gastreel requested that he order his soldiers to untie their prisoner, and to bring an officer's cape so that the clerk could cover himself. The Señor Presidente tersely complied, said good-bye like a Yankee with a firm handshake and brisk clap on the arm, and exited with a relaxed air, no doubt looking forward to the imminent consolation of the affection of his children and the embraces of his lovely young wife. And Minister Gastreel escorted Higinio Farfán, gingerly wrapped in the cape, both his thumbs hooked under its collar so that it hung down his back without touching it, out to the waiting carriage, where the clerk, worried that he would stain the interior's upholstery with his blood, offered to sit alongside the driver. The Minister insisted that he climb inside. They rode back to the legation in separate silences, though the clerk sporadically groaned as the carriage rocked over the drastic paving. The leather curtains had been drawn to shield the clerk from public view, but Minister Gastreel lowered his eye to the spy hole and saw a lamplighter lifting his flame to a tallow lamp, and thought that the lamplighter resembled a torch-bearing monk lighting candles in the murky corridor of a ghostly monastery. Every other city in the world that regards itself as hospitable to progress entered the century of gaslight decades ago, he reflected. Why does anybody care what happens here? Why lift a finger, if Yankee dominance over the Isthmus's affairs seems so inevitable in the end? Because diplomacy, Señorita Moran, for all its pragmatic skepticism, is finally an ever hopeful occupation; in that respect, all powerful countries are alike, for with the power to right wrongs comes the responsibility to do so, and in nearly every noteworthy circumstance that arises, doing good is usually at least an option. Also, this region still imports more products from Great Britain than from any other country, though the Germans are gaining, and the Americans loom everywhere. Minister Gastreel was certain that his successful effort to free the legation clerk had indeed served the good and universal purpose of power, and no other.

But Higinio Farfán's gratitude evaporated quickly; with every passing day, he grew more sullen and brooding. María de las Nieves assumed, at first, that he was just worried about what Minister Gastreel would decide to do if a request for the permission to arrest him was formally submitted by the Foreign Minister. "The Minister has never even asked me if I had anything to do with the conspiracy or not," complained the clerk. "Of course I did not!" She knew he had no cause for worry, that Minister Gastreel, on principal, would never allow El Anticristo's government to savor any victory, not even one of law and protocol. And she tried to reassure the clerk of that when he asked if he could speak to her in private: "I think I know what is worrying you, Don Higinio," she began. But it turned out that he had something else on his mind, and wanted her "considered opinion, Señorita, since I know el Señor Ministro seems to take whatever you say into account." Didn't she think it was unjust that Minister Gastreel had not demanded that reparations be paid to him, as he had following the arrest and flogging of Consul Magee, who, pues fíjase, had been treated no worse, and was now wealthy? With a sense of wounded surprise, María de las Nieves realized that his question made her uneasy. "Let me meditate on this, and then I will tell you," she told the clerk to whom she owed her job, whose heavily sagging, sad-eyed face was still black and purple with bruises. For several days and nights she did worry over his question, and always came to the same conclusion: If she were to ask Minister Gastreel why he had not insisted that reparations be paid to Higinio Farfán, as they had been to Consul Magee, it would be received as an unsubtle and even insubordinate critique of his handling of the affair, of which he was so proud—and she would probably, no, she would certainly lose her position. Was the wonderful Señora Farfán actually encouraging her husband in his bitter indignation? Maybe she didn't even know about it. María de las Nieves began to resent the self-pitying clerk, and tried to avoid having any further conversation with him. Why couldn't he speak for himself? Why should she say anything, if doing so only meant that they would both lose their employment? How tedious and ordinary her life would become without her job at the legation! But Higinio Farfán had revealed her to herself as just another female coward and hypocrite, and whenever she met his eyes, she glared, and spent the rest of the day in turmoil and silently seething against him. Now, when she woke in the deep hours of the night, she tossed and turned in her bed between two bonfires of unhappiness, between the impossible ghost of a kiss and shame that only mocked her with how unworthy of that kiss she really was, because she knew that he demanded virtue and self-sacrifice of himself in all that he did, and would expect the same of any woman he loved.

At least the oppressive shadow looming over the end of her class in Literary Composition for Women had been dispelled by the exposure of the Homicidal Fraternity of the Black Rosary. On the evening of their last class, Maestro Martí had earlier announced, they were going to have a fiesta, and he would select the best final compositions so that their authors could recite them before the invited guests, which would include that unfailing patroness of female education and the arts, La Primera Dama. But now La Primera Dama appeared only at executions, and their graduation party was going to be a much more muted ceremony. For those final compositions, Martí had assigned a topic: they were to compose a letter to a hypothetical daughter on the eve of her *quinceañera*, advising her on what to look and hope for, what to demand and expect from a future husband. Though most of the students, Martí acknowledged, were of an age when they were still in need of such guidance themselves, they would nevertheless profit from this written attempt to project their own purity and innocence into imaginary older, more experienced, and wiser selves. Someday, said Martí, they might all need to offer a fifteen-year-old daughter such advice, and poetry was rarely both so beautiful and consequent as such a letter from a mother to a daughter could be. They were to write from their own hearts, and in their own words. He reminded them again of the example of Victor Hugo, who only by tinkering with the metric scheme of the classical alexandrine—an accent shifted from the usual syllable to an unexpected one, or a pause, the briefest intake of breath, hopped from one side of a syllable to the other—had introduced the French to the tumults of the intimate self and to the lonely responsibilities and deceptions of history. "Isn't it true, mis niñas," said Martí, "that in our just awakening Americas, we've also spent centuries shut out of our own selves, terrified of and deaf to the true sound of our own voices? Our own Spanish hendecasyllables have been asleep beneath our warm humid earth for centuries, pale and silent, wings folded, waiting for the call of your gentle and honest voices."

That final composition should have been an opportunity for María de las Nieves to deploy skills in which she was sure to triumph over all her classmates, even María García Granados. She did have a boldly Hugoesque idea: she would take the form of an autobiographical nun's *vida*, a genre she knew Martí had an enthusiasm for, and apply it to her own journey through life, but address it to an imaginary daughter instead of to a Confessor, culminating in a description of a husband who would share many worldly traits with her composition class teacher. Nevertheless, when she sat down to write, she discovered a stubborn spirit of self-denigration waiting to ambush her at every turn. She was unable to drive her recent moral failure in the case of Higinio Farfán from her mind, and then a hundred other things she only felt guilty or embarrassed or confused about and which rarely troubled her by day. The hours struggled by like a routed army in retreat, and the night slowly assumed the blurred, feverish atmosphere of anxious insomnia, her head filling with acrid vapors that burned her eyes from the inside. Even the trauma of Madre Sor Gertrudis's betrayal was resurrected, and then no matter how hard she tried to think about something else, she couldn't. How could you have, Nana? How could you have left me in a punishment cell, at the mercy of soldiers? She ended up running out of paper, and nearly of ink, and finally, exhausted and demoralized, she went to bed and quietly cried herself to sleep with her face to the wall.

When she tried again the next night, the results were no better; in the morning she didn't go into the legation, sending María Chon with a note explaining that she'd caught a chill and was ill. She stayed in her bed, recovering from her futile night battles, depressed and dozing, through most of the day. That night, after a hot water bath in the zinc tub in a covered nook of her little patio, she sat at her table, a blanket wrapped around her shoulders, with a cup of beef tea and some toasted tortillas and wrote Martí a letter that in the end left her feeling so drained and shamed by its sentimental excesses and confused confessions that her having put it away and saved it seems a small miracle now; indeed it was the most lucid piece of writing she'd yet managed. (Sixteen years later she copied entire paragraphs from it for the letter she did actually write to her daughter, Mathilde, on her fifteenth birthday.)

But she still didn't have anything to hand in to Maestro Martí. And she'd run out of paper again. She was about to commit the sacrilege of tearing a page from her still spotless album when she remembered the sheet of deerskin writing paper she kept there. She spread the tawny sheet, which had something of the texture of a cured giant moth wing, carefully before her, and plunged in, the steel tip of her pen softly squeaking, the ink bleeding into the sheet of paper-thin chamois more than it would have into ordinary paper, and she didn't allow herself to stop and examine what she'd written until she'd finished. —Esteemed Señor Maestro Martí, I don't know what I think about love, and have no advice to offer anybody. Every new book I open, I say to it, I am reading you because I don't know *camarón*, and maybe you have something to show me. I think the best I would be able to do now would be to imitate with my own false words what others before me have originally written with true feeling and understanding. Please ask me again in five years what I know about love. I don't like false poetry or just making up stories, and dearest Maestro Martí, neither do you ... In the end, she was spared a decision about whether or not to submit the unremarkable outburst because their final classes were canceled. A new round of arrests and executions had created a turbulent climate requiring well-bred and respectable damitas and doncellas to stay indoors.

Nine days after the exposure of the murderous conspiracy, Paquita left the country with her children, traveling for the first time without her husband to New York. Six weeks later, screams could still be heard coming from the Presidential Mansion at all hours; it was said that Rufino the Just, whip in hand, often presided over the interrogations himself. The city's prisons were full. There was no official place of employment, or any organization or club or school that did not feel obligated, in the immediate aftermath of the first arrests and for weeks after, to publish, in the government gazette and other newspapers, congratulatory messages to the President and his family, and denunciations of the condemned conspirators of the Black Rosary. But one such notice, published by the Cuban-dominated faculty of the Normal School, was noticeably more poetic than others: *Señor, comply with your benign duty: the daggers of men can never reach the heart that does good. The partisans of the shadows and the heroes of poison and superstition flee from the partisan of free men and of education and learning ... And if in the shadows they sharpen their daggers, don't be alarmed, Señor, because in the schools they train consciences. Those you have educated will be your soldiers.*

The Izaguirres asked him to write it, and what could he do? It was not as if the Cuban director of the school and his brother hadn't contributed their own ideas about what the notice should say. Any message less ardent or felicitous might have brought repercussions, and he was the one who knew how to transform obligatory sentiments into stirring metaphors of honor. Martí would write and publish thousands upon thousands of pages of prose in his life, but perhaps none were triter or filled him with more embarrassment than those; though not shame, because the heart of a man who does good *should* be safe from the daggers of men ...

But his heart was good, and it wasn't safe. It had never been more vulnerable, or more filled with lonely doubt and foreboding. He was struggling with feelings he could not allow himself to confess to anybody, not even to his closest friend in Mexico, for how could he be the one to bring such dishonor into the world? It is better to suffer dishonor alone and in silence, rather than to publicly bring it upon others as well as upon your self. Silence can console the heart and soul, it can even preserve or heal a love; it is not, of course, always the opposite of courage. But can silence ever console a city or a nation? Not when it is made of fear, lies, guilt, shame, cowardice, hypocrisy, and death. Martí never went to Sacatepéquez to look for the Jefe Indio who spoke French. It wasn't only that the city and the countryside seemed too grim and dangerous for such an excursion: he knew now that such an incarnation of an exemplary modern Indio could not exist here, and that if he did, he did not want to have to justify him. About some matters, he was still free to change his mind, to have a *change of heart*—. He was preparing to go to Mexico to marry his fiancée, and he felt as if he were going to a sacrifice.

Before leaving, he said good-bye to María García Granados, a visit now immortalized, of course, in one of the most famous poems ever written in Hispanic America, for it was then that she gave him the scented silk pillow she'd embroidered, saying, "Take it, Pepe, it brings luck." And she retreated into her house to await his return. Perhaps he would have a change of heart. The fragrant pillow, salty with her tears, would perhaps work its spell, and he would reach Mexico City and realize his mistake— or turn around even before he reached it—and rush back to his niña!

How many other women were waiting for Martí to come and say good-bye? Was the magistrate's wife Mack Chinchilla had heard spoken of in the Café de Paris waiting? The other women the city's eminent but sentimental old men still speak of to this day? Without doubt, at least one was waiting. Martí, who'd never called on her at home, did not make a special visit to say good-bye to María de las Nieves now; after all, he planned to return, after the New Year, with his wife, and resume his teaching. Perhaps he would remain in the little country for the rest of his life, and peacefully raise his family there; Cuba would liberate herself without him or would never liberate herself, and someday they would be old friends who ran into each other in the street, fussing over each other with childish affection: Ay Doña Mariquita de las Nieves, now your hair really is snowy, but your eyes are the same eyes that took my breath away when you were seventeen. Ay Don Pepe Torrente, so exagerado, just the same as back then!

At the end of November, only days before he was to leave for Mexico, María de las Nieves encountered Martí in the street, and wished him a safe journey and the happiest of wedding days; she knew she'd spoken well (with the cheerful womanly poise of Señora Farfan) and that she'd sounded affectionate and sincere. When he thanked her his eyes had an even fonder shine than usual, and she could tell he was making sure to hold her gaze longer, more pointedly, than was usual also, and she felt a little shiver of excitement, and her relieved heart danced a little with happiness and pride. Then he took off his black felt hat and slightly bowed his curly head to her. Was there anything more that he should or could say? His hat was atop his head again, and the air became a transparent hourglass through which the very last grains of sand were tumbling. There was nothing left now but to punctuate this sweetly poignant and successful goodbye by simply smiling and pronouncing, one last time, the word *good-bye.* "And I hope you will call on me as soon as you return, Pepe," she added helplessly. "I do look forward to meeting your wife. And you still have to write something in my album. It's waiting for you, and I won't let anybody else besmirch it until you have." As soon as she finished speaking those words she was convinced that she would never see him again, and that her last memory of Pepe Martí would always be of his embarrassment, the sting of his disconcerted eyes, his final polite but hurried good-bye, erasing all the warmth that had come before. She walked home, with erect posture and, of course, on her feet, though inside she felt as if she were walking on the bloody knees of a humiliated penitent.

FROM APRIL TO August of 1880 the Pinkerton's National Detective Agency operative known as "E.S." lived in the same New York City boardinghouse with José Martí, his wife, and year-old child, pretending to be Martí's friend while spying on him, on his political activities and friendships, his disappointing marriage. The operative even intruded into the Martís' rooms when they were out, and went through his writings, and sometimes risked smuggling one of Martí's notebooks back into his own quarters. He copied down even Martí's most trivial and private personal jottings almost indiscriminately—because E.S., though trained in the decipherment of even the most difficult handwriting, did not understand Spanish—in the hopes of turning up something that might provide the detectives with a new advantage once the words had been translated in the Pinkerton office; also so that Spain, the agency's client, would receive the fullest portrait of her Cuban adversaries in exile—

María de las Nieves, seated at her cabin table in a nimbus of candlelight aboard the *Golden Rose* as it chugged up the night-darkened coast of Baja California, was again immersed in the Pinkerton report. She reflected: It's almost as if poor Pepe is aware of being trapped in this diabolical report the Yankees detectives are spinning around him, but as in a nightmare he is helpless to do anything about it or even to voice a word of protest. No wonder he seems so unhappy, so frustrated and vulnerable. All this occurred five years ago, she thought, when Mathilde was nearly two, almost the same age as Pepe's son; a sad, bitter epoch in my own life too. Though she hadn't had detectives trailing her, she'd also learned what it was like to feel betrayed, spied on from every side, and even scorned by those she'd considered her friends.

According to the report, there were twenty-five detectives from the agency trailing the Cubans in New York, and seven of those, including E.S., were assigned to Martí alone, who barely knew his way around the metropolis, where he'd arrived only in January. Though even before that first month was out, Martí had already given a speech in a public hall, where he'd mesmerized the packed audience of Cuban exiles, the usually politically aloof "aristocrats" and proud veterans of the Ten Years' War sitting in the front rows, and the black cigar-factory workers crowding the back, stunning them with unprecedented epiphanies of their common condition as denigrated Cubans far from home in the land of the disdainful Yankee, rousing them to embrace their common cause. (It was this speech, María de las Nieves knew from the report, that had first alerted Spain to Martí in New York.) So "Dr. Torrente" had again landed with a great splash in a new city. He was even named Interim President of the Cuban Revolutionary Committee in New York in place of General Calixto García—who, rather than be captured alive by Spanish troops during doomed fighting in Cuba years before, had put a gun under his chin and fired, but the bullet came out through the middle of his forehead without killing him, leaving him with a scar that made it look as if a tiny comet had smashed into his brow. In March General García had sailed under cover of night from New Jersey aboard the schooner *Hattie Haskell* with a handful of rebel expeditionaries and a cargo of weapons, purchased with funds raised by the Cuban Revolutionary Committee, headed to Cuba to reignite the insurrection, dormant since the end of the War of Ten Years and the treacherous pact of Zanjón (the Pinkertons now knew everything, and consequently, so did Spain). The legendary warrior's successor, the Revolutionary Committee's young Interim President, had just published his first piece of art criticism in the New York cultural weekly the *Hour;* one of his fellow Cuban boarders, an artist and illustrator, had introduced him there. He had no other reliable income, and a wife and baby son to support, and that young wife disdained the circumstances in which they were living and all his reasons for imposing such a life upon her; a woman raised to live in sumptuousness and glamour residing in a humble boardinghouse in a city of sumptuousness and glamour where now she couldn't even afford to buy a new dress. She'd imagined it impossible for Pepe to do worse than he already had when he'd brought her to live in La Pequeña Paris at just the moment when he was becoming a pariah in that savage little city. But New York was even worse, because at least in La Pequeña Paris Pepe had rented his own house, and provided a steady if minuscule income, and life was so much more affordable, though, to her, it had seemed no less bewildering, tense, or ominous. At least, thought María de las Nieves, that must have been Carmen Zayas's perception. Actually Martí's pretty wife, the few times she'd encountered her, had impressed her as being haughty, polite, conspicuously neat, intelligent though not keenly so, jealous, moody, easily bored, high-strung, more remote than actually unfriendly, all these traits softened by a sensuous air of Antillean grace and well-bred courtesy. María de las Nieves couldn't help but pity Carmen Zayas for having attached herself to an extraordinary man of perilous destiny whom she clearly did not understand and whose eyes in turn did not look upon his wife—as more than a few had already observed—with the same love with which they sometimes shone on *at least one other.*

Yes, back then both Pepe and his wife had reasons to feel disillusioned, thought María de las Nieves, but now that was all some time ago, and maybe they are happier now. Though Cuba, of course, is still under the rule of Spain. The military expeditions of 1880 having failed—quickly surrounded, General Calixto García had been forced to surrender—Martí renounced his leadership of the Cuban Revolutionary Committee that June, even before he and his Cuban coconspirators realized that they were being spied on by the Pinkertons. In the ensuing five years there had been little news in the newspapers of renewed warfare in Cuba. So Pepe's life must be quieter now too, she thought, and maybe he has repaired relations with his wife, and they've had more children, and the noble manner in which he has endured his defeats has softened her heart and she can finally love him as he deserves, and perhaps he is earning money from his journalism and other writings and now provides for his wife at least the respectability she craves, or maybe her father, despite being a Spanish loyalist, has overcome his loathing of his son-in-law enough to finally send money. Though I can't imagine Pepe satisfying his wife's persistent desire that they return to Cuba to live under Spanish rule and that he peacefully practice law and write his poems there and renounce all insurrectionary conspiring—but who knows? Anything is possible. This report, after all, opens a very biased window on only four months of his life! But even taking into account E.S.'s prejudices and motives, one has to admit that this is a gloomy, brooding, and even infirm José Martí, who only seems to brighten in the presence of his little son, or that hearty Carmita Miyares de Mantilla, who owns *el boarding* with her husband, who is also ailing, or when Miss Susan Paral comes for her Spanish lesson. Sometimes at their dinner table, drinking the wine provided by the treacherous E.S., Pepe does become intellectually and verbally excited in the familiar way. But the Martís' marriage, as depicted here, could hardly seem more anxious and bleak:

*One hundred daggers in my chest could not cause me the pain this first letter has caused me,* María de las Nieves read now, in a section of the report in which E.S. presented and commented on writings that he'd copied from Martí's private notebooks. *Blind! She is blind to me! I have gone this night to see Faust. La Nilsson is the attraction. With these eyes devoured by the tears which I can no longer weep, I couldn't see her well, so I concentrated on listening. What cadences, what a manner of finishing, the last pure note descending into a teardrop. Her sobs rip open the breast. La Nilsson has no rival!* From here on, wrote E.S., Mr. Martí continues on at length about La Nilsson's performance at the opera and her method of singing, words which I did originally attempt to transcribe without comprehending their meaning, but which, now that they have been translated, I do not include here, assessing them to be superfluous to the requirements of this office report. Only when Mr. Martí has finished his eulogy of the great diva's talent does he again strike the maudlin note of personal anguish with which his diary entry begins: *As for her face and figure, what eyes did I have to see her with, if my own are too weak even to be able to see these creatures which I carry in my own heart?* I have since heard Mr. Martí make a reference to the time when he saw La Nilsson perform in *Faust*, continued E.S, so I can affirm that the Martís' marital strife predates their unhappy Gotham reunion. It is also a good example of the subject's emotional volubility. What sort of man confides to his diary in one breath that a letter from his wife, mother of his only child, has caused him more pain than *a hundred daggers* and that he cannot even see La Nilsson for the tears in his eyes, yet with his next breath embarks on pages of highly detailed opera critique? Is this a sincere man or a superficial one, easily enthused and overwrought in the characteristic manner of the Latin temperament?

The notebooks are also interesting, I should add and can hardly overstate, Sir Superintendent, for the many morbid meditations on death, martyrdom, sacrifice, duty, and so forth which their pages contain. There is also a very great deal of literary pontification, page upon page upon page, and poems. The subject writes poetry, often deep into the night. There are several more scribbled outbursts against his wife. In one Mr. Martí laments a solitary and fateful night, solitary though he is in bed conversing with his partner. Why so fateful? Because he finds her so indifferent, her spirit apparently not at all kindred to his own when, as they lie together, he speaks to her of a book just begun, of *the union of all our peoples,* of his misunderstood ideas, his pain at the misery endured by others—Mr. Martí, I presume, is referring to the usual anonymous masses who darken the globe. He also seems to criticize his wife's apparent overvaluing of domestic well-being and her inability to *laugh at poverty.* On the notebook's next page he writes: *What do you want, my wife? That I do the work that should win me applause on earth, or that I live, eaten up with rancor, without applause*—and he briefly continues on in this vainglorious manner, though with some rather esoteric turns of phrase and poetry which baffled even our office translator, Mrs. Dominga Hurley, though this outburst is also interesting because in it the subject comes as near as he ever does, in the private writings I have scrutinized, to confiding subversive ideas and ambitions. (For all I know he may also do so in his poetry, most of which is of the unintelligibly tormented strain, according to Mrs. Hurley, though she also says there are one or two very pretty ones about his baby son, "Pepito," and the happiness and pride the subject finds in fatherhood.) He obviously guards himself against writing down any details of his insurrectionary activity, though he does not protect his emotional existence in the same way; no, this he rather lays bare. I draw your attention, Sir Superintendent, to this diary entry, a copy of which I've also passed on to Miss Susan Paral, who should certainly profit by the insight it provides into Mr. Martí's current emotional state, and the shameless versatility of his justifications of romantic conquest: *It almost always happens that relations which began in love end by having no mutual bond other than duty. Is it that the satisfaction of love kills love? No! It's that love is avaricious, insatiable, active: it is a great restless force, and it requires great daily nourishment, and it is the only appetite that is never sated—only incessant, tender, visible, and tangible solicitude can nourish it. A fresh kiss smoothes the brow which cannot be smoothed by the fading heat of very loving kisses already given. Neither lover can allow a lack of frequent mutual solicitudes to cause the always ardent soul to feel that need for nourishment, and to feel pushed to search for it, or disposed to accept it, should life by chance offer it. The amorous attentions one bestows build up resistance in the beloved's soul against the invasion of an alien love. Intelligent compensation, delicious prize, such sweet work! By giving happiness to another, we construct our own. You can live without bread—but without love, no! Never squander an opportunity to console a sadness, to caress a gloomy brow, to ignite a languid gaze, to reach out a hand hot with love. Perpetual work, work of every instant, is tenderness. But without it, the unsatisfied love will search for employment! There is one word which sums up this entire tactic of love:* dewdrop. *Always there should be a fresh pearl quivering on the green leaf. A word in our ear, a stirring look in our eye, a humid kiss—. If you don't love like that, you will never be loved. You will fall and fall again and cry out in desperation and lose yourself in black abysses, and die alone. Love is a wild beast that needs to be fed anew every day.*

Dewdrop! Qué bonito, thought María de las Nieves, except I despise such romantic prattle; he sounds like a Novice Mistress exhorting her novices on how to daily renew their love for the Divine Husband. Yet here she sits with a lump in her throat, eyes welling. If love is a wild beast that

needs to be fed every day, she thought, mine starved to death a long time
ago. Then María de las Nieves sat motionlessly at the little table in her
cabin for a long while, worrying over this problem that self-pity had led her
to: Could it really be true that for rest of her life she was going to be like
an old maid in an English novel? But she couldn't bare to think about it
anymore, and the candle was sputtering, and she twisted in her chair as
if about to lift herself up from it and begin undressing for bed because
she was too tired and depressed even to take her walk on the hurricane
deck, but then she slumped forward on her elbows over the report again
and read there what E.S. described as another of Mr. Martí's most recent
diary entries:

*Love: renews. I feel, while loving, a generous forgetfulness, a fortifying hope. A
woman said to me, "This is my second youth."* I do not know, wrote E.S., to which
woman Mr. Martí refers, though she is not, as far as I know, not *yet*, our
Miss Susan Paral. I will add, Sir, that for reasons that must now seem
evident, I believe that Miss Paral should be encouraged to play upon Mr.
Martí's emotions without limits, though she should also be closely watched
by us, and regularly interrogated. E.S. next recounted a conversation between himself and Miss Paral that occurred in some location where they
had met to share information and elaborate a course of action: Miss Paral,
wrote the operative, remains infatuated with the subject of our surveillance, to such a degree that the purpose of her mission often seems to slip
her mind. But I forget too easily that Miss Paral is a born actress, if one can
actually be born to such a thing. Therefore I don't worry very much about
her anymore, and I do believe that in the end we will be able to count on
her. *"Como estar usted hoy, Señorita Paral?"* I asked. "As our Spanish clients
are paying for your lessons, I am sure they would be indignant to learn that
our bothersome curiosity regarding your teacher's clandestine activities is
interfering, alas, with your mastering of the mother tongue. You must advance in your Spanish, Miss Paral!" Miss Susan was, that day, radiantly
delighted with a poem Mr. Martí had recited for her at their last lesson,
one not his own but by the notorious Whitman, which contains a brief stanza
which I did manage to copy down while cackling as if I shared Miss Paral's
excitement over its overt rhetorical promise. The poem, Sir Superintendent, which so bewitched our enchantress-scholar evokes sleepers lying
unclothed hand in hand in a chain encircling the globe, promiscuously

intermingling peoples of all nations, races, persuasions, and occupations, and includes this phrase, which I induced Miss Paral to repeat several times until I had written it down exactly: *The scholar kisses the teacher, the teacher kisses the scholar, the wrong'd is made right*—my idea being to implicate her, to make it clear to her that she herself had now told me what to expect. With a very grave countenance on my face (for I too can act) I copied down this line of poetry, converting it before her eyes from literary coquetry to solemn contract. Then I put on my hat, and before getting up to go, weightily sighed, and said, "Very appropriate words, Miss Paral. *The wrong'd is made right.* Ours is sometimes an unseemly business, but in the end we must have faith that though the likes of you and I are dispensable operatives who perhaps cannot see very far into the greater design of those we are serving, we serve the right, and not ever the wrong. Otherwise, Mr. Pinkerton's National Detective Agency would certainly not enjoy the matchless reputation that it does." Miss Paral replied, "And that good end is the maintaining of Spanish rule over Cuba? Or is it maintaining it long enough until that whole island should rot, and then we can pick it up and put it in our pocket like a fallen fruit." I answered, "Who do you refer to, Miss Paral? What would Mr. Pinkerton or the agency want with Cuba? As I've just said, we are loyal agents who cannot see very far. But directly in front of us and under our noses, there is just now a great deal that we can see, don't you agree?"

# Chapter 6

"Have you seen Señor Triple-Jota's window, Don José?" María de las Nieves asked one afternoon at the beginning of February, in the umbrella mender's workroom. The Yankee photographer's actual name, J. J. Jump, was by no means easy even for María de las Nieves to pronounce. Don José was teaching her how to keep business accounts—his ragged copy of Friar Luca Pacioli's fifteenth-century classic, *Treatise on Double-Entry Bookkeeping,* lay open atop the table between them—and they were drinking tea. "My portrait is displayed there," she added cheerlessly. "Number eight."

"But that is wonderful, María de las Nieves!" Of course her portrait had never been displayed in the photographer's window before, and now there she was, in J. J. Jump's monthly ranking of "Our Most Popular Beauties," not even ninth or tenth, but the eighth most sold print in January. The umbrella mender's strained smile betrayed that he was puzzled too. On the first business day of every month, Señor Jump displayed the previous month's ten most sold portraits, pinned to a black-velvet-covered board in his window.

"Does this mean you are going to be displayed at the International Exhibition?" A selection of the New Jersey native's photographic portraits of the capital's women was going to be featured in the country's exhibit at the International Exhibition soon to open in Paris. "Imagine, María de las Nieves, the royalty of Europe pausing to inspect our little Republic's exhibit, and while sampling a cup of our finest national coffee, gazing upon your—"

"I just want to know who has been buying my portrait," she implored. "He sold two! Who has bought them? And why?" Wellesley Bludyar had been away on his secret mission for months. And how likely was it that Pepe Martí had gone into J. J. Jump's photography studio to buy her portrait sometime during the last two weeks of January, just after his return from Mexico with his new wife?

"I see . . . I can assure you . . . María de las Nieves, I do not know if I regret to say, or if I am happy to say, that I have not bought one." Don José frowned and his face looked as if it were being steamed.

"Oh, Don José, I didn't suspect you." Now she felt flustered. "Of course I would be relieved to find out it was you."

"Surely, if you are number eight, María de las Nieves, more than two of your photographs have been sold."

"No. Only two." She blinked as if sand had blown into her eyes, and said, "January is the worst month for business." Nine and ten, she explained, hadn't sold even one, but were chosen based on the number sold in December. The top three or four, J. J. Jump had told her, always sold many times more than all the rest combined. She didn't need to add that for nearly forty consecutive months, La Primera Dama had held the first rank.

"But why are you not happy, María de las Nieves?" asked Don José. "Surely J.J. is a good enough friend to let you know who your secret admirers are?"

"No, Don José. Of course he will not."

When, three years before, J. J. Jump had started making extra prints from the negatives of his female customers' portraits and offering them for sale, he'd also guaranteed never to reveal the identity of his purchasers, only to keep a monthly tally. In return, he charged his female customers less for portraits and calling cards than his rivals did. Printed announcements and handbills had explained that the sole inspiration behind this latest Yankee innovation was one foreigner's discovery of the unparalleled loveliness of the country's women, and his respectful desire to celebrate it. Before long there was not a self-regarding dama or doncella who hadn't come into J. J. Jump's studio to be photographed, and some came nearly every month; there was barely a male of even modest means, whether married or not, who hadn't stopped in to pore through the print-stocked bins in search of an image to honor or adore.

Strapping, broad-shouldered J. J. Jump looked more like a logger or railroad foreman than a man with an indoor trade, and certainly didn't dress like one growing wealthy from it. He had eyes like bright blue rays, a bushy beard the golden hue of well-roasted potatoes, and a robust complexion despite so much time spent in the dark with his strong-smelling chemicals and negative plates—he'd recently taken on a young assistant, sallow Hernán Pedroso, to do much of that work. Always wearing a gigantic brown double-breasted overcoat with rolled-up sleeves, no matter what the weather, heavy black boots, and a peculiarly ostentatious stovepipe hat, towering J. J. Jump loved to meander the streets, searching markets, stopping at laundry fountains, always looking for pretty mengalas to invite back to his studio to have their portraits taken for free. His friendly, peaceful character seemed to belie any vice at the heart of his obsession; as far as is known, he never set foot in even the most pretentious of Doña Carlota's bordellos. Though the majority of his customers clearly regarded a light complexion as an essential component of feminine beauty, J. J. Jump made no secret of his own preference for mestizas, mulattas, even pure Indias. Whenever he claimed Central American women capable of a beauty far surpassing any he'd seen anywhere else, many of his listeners assumed it was just a questionable business ploy. "It is the moreno tint," J. J. Jump enjoyed explaining like an earnest connoisseur, "and a nobleness of expression coming from the blending of these ancient and passionate races which I find so superior to the regular features at home." But he'd never been known to show a romantic interest in any woman, regardless of tint. One day he finally did, with a curvaceous, lightning-eyed girl named Margarita Jiménez, the sixteen-year-old daughter of an ordinary butcher in the market. She was certainly pretty, and probably a virgin, but J. J. Jump's choice of a wife was controversial: was this what he'd so publicly and patiently been searching their city for, a mengalita like any other? It didn't seem fair to the so many other marriageable, no less deserving girls of the popular classes whom the Yankee photographer had passed over. Though born a Methodist, J. J. Jump married the butcher's daughter in a Catholic Church wedding. The mood of resentment hardened against the Yankee photographer, the entire city seemed to have turned coldly against him. J. J. Jump continued selling portrait prints, but for a while his trade was nearly as furtive as Don José's nighttime one, and the unveiling of a new month's rankings was met with nearly universal indifference rather than the former clamor of debate and celebration. Then it was announced that one hundred of J. J. Jump's portraits of "Our Most Popular Beauties" would be displayed at the International

Exhibition in Paris, and all his popularity flooded back. (Over the next two decades J. J. Jump and Margarita Jiménez, who was almost never seen at the studio, would produce a child almost every year, all but two of whom survived into adulthood; to this day the couple's descendants abound in that city, though the surname Jump is no longer associated with either photography or wealth.)

María de las Nieves had befriended J. J. Jump in much the same way she had other merchants, lingering for hours in the reception room of his studio, seemingly absorbed in every detail of his business. There were merchants who would have been exasperated by her patient inquisitiveness, especially when they realized she was unlikely to spend money, but her instincts, honed by her character of a lonely wanderer and an idiosyncratic exactingness, always guided her toward those who would delight in her curiosity, or at least be kind. Meanwhile the ordinary shopper, less discerning, less vulnerable, found unpleasant and treacherous encounters with the city's merchants impossible to avoid. María de las Nieves never tired of looking through Señor Jump's ever-changing stock of hand-colored postcards, *cartes-de-visite*, seasonal cards, stereoscopic scenes, and fantastic paper theaters, or the collection of costumes kept in three cedar armoires in the dressing room behind the partially glass-roofed photography studio, where a wide selection of painted backdrops and props was also stored. The Emperor and Empress of Japan, a Moth Man or a Butterfly Lady, San Francisco de Assís or Santa Rosa de Lima, a Conquistador, Queen Isabella, a Maharajah, a Bedouin, Tío Sam, a harlequin, a striped tiger or a polar bear, even the typical dress of all the country's Indian tribes, these and many more costumes were available for customers to pose in.

When J. J. Jump received a new collection of stereographs, María de las Nieves was often the first to view them; in exchange, she catalogued the cards in Spanish. A new shipment had recently arrived from San Francisco, in undamaged and dry condition, and she spent that Saturday afternoon on a stool at the counter before the mounted stereoscope, pulling the twin-image prints from their wax-treated envelopes, sliding them into the viewing tray, and staring into the eyeholes, where the two matching images were converted into a single one in the viewer's brain, as if seen through binoculars, with an astonishingly realistic illusion of depth and space— such was the optical explanation of what still seemed more like a magical invention. Only the movement, color, and noise of life was missing from these three-dimensional scenes, but those she could supply herself; it wasn't so different from what happened when she immersed herself in foreign newspapers in the reading room kiosk, where through concentrated daydreaming snippets of faraway news and information could finally seem infused by some actual light of the whole place: a fragile and fleeting illusion, always, but delicious whenever it occurred. Traveling foreign photographers occasionally visited the city, one saw them bent under the black curtains of their tripod box cameras on the grassy slopes of El Cerrito, and J. J. Jump, who liked to go out to meet them, said that some did use stereographic cameras. So perhaps in Paris, at this very second, a girl like herself was seated at a stereoscope studying images of this city and imagining what it would be like to live in La Pequeña Paris. Maybe she even saw herself retreating into a photography studio to escape into some other part of the world via stereoscope. In this new batch many of the stereographs were of the American West. "Chief Red Cloud"—a wonderful name, she thought; without a doubt people would respect our Indios more if they still used such names. She numbered the envelope and carefully printed *Jefe Nube Rojo* next to the corresponding number in the ledger. Half-naked, long-haired "Braves," lean and muscular, with handsome, manly faces, carrying rifles, each wearing an erect feather atop his head; serious and formidable men, despite the feathers, wearing their nakedness like Greek statues do—*Bravos con rifles,* she entered in the ledger. Nobody ever refers to our Indios, she thought, as Bravos. Pues, Pepe Martí would, I suppose. Instead of trudging along under huge loads like our Indios, the Bravos ride stallions, hunt buffalo, and roam their vast rugged terrain relentlessly waging war. A series of pictures of railroad bridges—this one darkly silhouetted against a pale sky, spanning a vast gorge, a bridge as delicate looking as an intricate mesh of toothpicks, yet there was a massive black locomotive pulling an endless line of cars across it. She picked up an envelope labeled *Cañon de Chelle, New Mexico,* which provoked an odd sensation of surprised recognition, as if she'd forgotten that New Mexico actually existed and could be visited by means much more ordinary than those employed by her old heroine, Sor María de Agreda. She fitted the card into the holder, pressed her eyes to the stereoscope, and stared into an enormous stone canyon. Above the canyon floor, within a wide niche in the massive cliff, were some adobe dwellings, crude and rectangular; they looked abandoned and as if they'd been nibbled at along their corners and seams and were now slowly crumbling. Maybe Indians lived there, she thought, in the time of Sor María. A spectacular light poured into the canyon in slanting silvery bands that flaringly illuminated every stratum of the cliff, every little pock in the facades of the old mud dwellings. María de las Nieves tried to imagine the beautiful adolescent Agreda nun, rosy-cheeked, dressed in blue like the Virgin, softly descending on a ray of silvery light to catechize the Indians who lived in the village at the cliff bottom. During her year in the convent she'd been well trained in deep meditation and spiritual visualizing. Now she stared into that light until she was almost convinced that it was on the verge of transforming into Sor María herself—like cloud-forest air so heavily saturated with humidity that a sudden noise, even a clap of the hands or a loud sneeze, can be enough to nudge it into rain. But without the daily practice of disciplined prayer it was impossible to cast such a spell. Instead, something about the state of those mud buildings provoked a sense of disillusion. Why were they empty ruins? What had happened to the Indians catechized by Sor María? When the convents were closed, she'd been left behind in a punishment cell with Sor María's "autobiography" of the Holy Virgin, in which it was revealed that God, preparing the young Virgin for marriage, had filled her with knowledge and power, wanting His wife to be His equal. María de las Nieves fell into a melancholy and banal reverie over that memory and the passage of time—did it seem like a long time ago, or a short time? Then she felt stirred in a deeper way. She thought about Martí, and the way his loquacity ran on and on inside of her: phrases he'd spoken, ideas he'd taught, his conversation, which she replayed inside herself, and meditated on, and tried to make her own; even the way she tried to seek out and read any book he'd mentioned. She'd been at this hopeless romantic-pedagogical task for months now and the river of his words was finally running dry. Since his return from Mexico, he'd avoided the reading room kiosk in the park. He had not taught her anything new since the end of her composition class. She felt a surge of indignation, and thought, Now I'm like one of those abandoned Indian ruins; I might as well be crumbling into dirt. But that's a frivolous comparison, admit it, María de las Nieves; he never promised you anything that he hasn't given you, and you're still too young to be a ruin. She felt resignation come into her, settling into her bones like the onset of a mild fever. For a long while she sat on the high stool leaning into the stereoscope, one hand lifted to its handle, looking like a stargazer who has fallen into a star-wandering trance at her telescope, or else asleep. J. J. Jump had to repeat her name three times, "—to call you back to earth."

J. J. Jump often offered to photograph María de las Nieves at no cost. More than once, of course, she'd accepted, though it sometimes bored her to have to hold a pose over and over, like a barely breathing statue, especially when she began to suspect that he invited her only so that Hernán Pedroso could practice making portraits, sessions that usually ended with her feeling headachy and listless from the chemical ether fumes. One day J. J. Jump asked if she would pose with María Chon, both dressed up in Indio traje, for a series of photographs he hoped to include, as "national types," in his display at the International Exhibition in Paris. Her quick refusal embarrassed J. J. Jump, and he stammered an apology; afterward, for more than a week, she couldn't overcome her reluctance to drop in on Señor Jump even to say hello. There was not a costume in his studio, however, that María Chon was not delighted to don for the Yankee photographer and his assistant. Now her servant went to the photography studio by herself, and lately seemed to have become Señor Jump's favorite model. Was the Yankee photographer contriving to encourage a marriage courtship between Hernán Pedroso and María Chon? Though he'd never given any overt indication of any such ambition, María de las Nieves's intuition and reading of small signs told her that it was so. Because Hernán was receiving the training of a true apprentice, it would be a good match for María Chon, certainly better than seeing her married off to a soldier or some low sort of artisan, which was not to say that el Pedroso would not be lucky to have her Mariquita, though the pretty little demon would definitely end up trampling all over him; despite his gift for retouching and coloring photographs with crayon and Chinese inks, Hernán did seem lacking in the purposefulness and vitality of character that he would need if he was really going to establish himself as a photographer on his own one day—; why was all of this making her feel so irritated? A short while later María de las Nieves was unable to resist remarking to her servant how odd she found it that she, so rarely photographed, had this month ascended into "Our Most Popular Beauties," whereas María Chon, of whom Señor Jump and his assistant had made hundreds of portraits, never had. "Envy is the opposite of a sundial, Doñacita. It only casts its shadow in the dark" had been her maddening reply—

"Don José, I think you might be able to confirm for me the identity of at least one of the purchasers of my portrait," she said flatly. "Your friend from New York, pues. The First Secretary of the Immigration Society."

He looked at her so unhappily she felt a guilty stab of pity—whether on behalf of Don José or "Don Cochinilla" or both, she didn't know.

"Yes, all right, María de las Nieves, I will try to find out," Don José finally answered. "But if it does turns out that Mack Chinchilla bought one, I hope you will keep that secret. Mack is a good boy, and has only the finest intentions, and I know you would take no pleasure in humiliating him."

"I can't think of him as a boy, Don José," she answered. Of course she had no desire to cause his friend any discomfort, she told him; it was just that not knowing who'd bought her portraits was robbing her of all inner peace.

But Mack Chinchilla insisted, with earnest shrugs and tosses of his head, that it had never even occurred to him to purchase a portrait of María de las Nieves at J. J. Jump's studio; that was the sort of thing all those awful Don Juanes and frippery dandies did, and anyway, he was not one to waste his money like that; it would be like buying a pill just to give himself a case of demoralization. "—But why, Don José? Did she say she suspects me?"

"No, of course she did not," replied the umbrella mender.

"Oh, pshaw! Then why else do you ask me?"

"Yes, of course, Mack. I see no way to disguise it. Right you are. But it will be our secret that I've told you, won't it be? On your oath?"

"On my oath. And so long as we're taking oaths, Don José—all right then, I did purchase a portrait. In a moment of weakness. What of it?" Mack's eyes brightened, and he wore an exultant grin. "But who bought the other one? Who is my rival, Don José? Not the matrimonial Cubano, eh? Not the banished portly diplomatist. I'm very encouraged that she immediately suspected me, Don José, and asked you to inquire about it."

"I won't say that what you wish for is impossible, Mack, since it seems that no one, perhaps not even María de las Nieves herself, will ever be able to dissuade you. But give the young lady time, a good amount of time. She is a bit overwrought these days. A bit"—and the umbrella mender rapidly rubbed his fingertips against his thumb, a pained expression on his face, teeth gritted—"like *this*. In some sort of tetchy turmoil, I think. But I cannot really say why, Mack."

The Immigration Society's one-room office was located in La Sociedad Económica's sprawling single-story mansion, which also housed the school for telegraph operators, the new Meteorology and Astronomy Observatory, the Museum of Natural History and Archaeology, the headquarters for the country's preparations for the International Exhibition in Paris, a drawing academy and art collection, a members' library and reading room, the weekly newspaper's editorial office, and other forward-looking enterprises, partially funded by the Supreme Government through a mandatory tax on every game of billiards played in public rooms across the country. Mack Chinchilla handled nearly all of the Immigration Society's day-to-day business by himself now. Though his jefe, Don Octaviano Mencos Boné, chaired the meetings of the Board of Directors, where the most crucial matters were decided, he only occasionally came to the office. For many of the past months, Don Octaviano had been traveling abroad on Immigration Society business, opening an agency in San Francisco and establishing ties to emigration agents, consular officials, and colonization societies in Europe.

One evening not quite two weeks after his conversation with Don José regarding the photographs, Mack, wearing a new Western Stetson purchased at his friend "Wild Bibby" Lowenthal's California General Store, stiff leather portfolio cradled under his arm, left the Immigration Society two or three hours earlier than usual; he was resolved to walk directly to María de las Nieves's house. His urgent purpose, he was convinced, excused the extreme impertinence of turning up uninvited at her door. María de las Nieves only had to give him the chance to explain himself and she would understand why he was asking for her help, with no other motive than advancing a just and good cause. He would arrive without flowers or any even modest gift; she would not hear or witness one thing that could make her doubt that his mission was other than what he said. When, that afternoon, while sitting at his desk feeling crushed by his honestly assumed responsibility, despairing over his inability to set down in persuasive writing what he knew in his heart and mind to be right—he lacked the education, the mastered intellectual skills—when he'd finally accepted that he wouldn't be able to write his report on the Hebrews, due at the next meeting of the Immigration Society's Board of Directors, without some, no, without a great deal of help, at that same moment he'd also thought of María de las Nieves. He knew that she would sympathize, and could help him write the report, if she wanted to. So he'd discovered a reason to call on María de las Nieves that paid honest homage to what she must consider most superior in herself, which in turn would allow her to see *him* as a disinterested man fighting to do good, yet one humble enough to ask a woman for her help. That was true enough. The elevated character of this accidental courtship strategy stunned Mack. Doubtlessly there were men—true gentlemen—who knew to behave this way without having to undergo such churning premeditation first. But now that Mack had discovered and memorized this formula on his own, he would not forget it, and knew that he'd been improved.

Though it was just a little past six, darkness was falling, and an orange quarter moon already hung low in the southern sky. María de las Nieves lived at the city center's outer edge, on a callejón with no lighting and extremely irregular paving but lined with small, squat, solidly built houses at least a half century old. Venerable trees rose from the inner gardens of at least some of the houses, with evening birds and squirrels chattering and rustling in their darkened foliage, sending detritus, twigs, pinecones pattering off the tiled roofs. Bats flashed past the orange gash of moon. The little side street might have been a lane of cottages in a deep wood, except for the clattering evening traffic of wheels and the hooves of domesticated beasts on the avenue just behind. A perpetually gritty and excrement-scented dry-season haze hung in the air. There were still many pedestrians out at this hour, returning from employment, school, social visits, evening Masses, the countless errands and digressions of city life. The houses were unnumbered, but he knew hers was near the end, the fourth on the left—this one, with three barred windows facing the street, shutters cracked open. The sole window to the left of the front door was dark, but from the two on the other side came the serene glow of lamplight. Gathering himself there, Mack had the nervous idea that the light was animate, radiating out into the dark just to peer into his purpose and thoughts and report back to its mistress. He would have to state the reason for his visit clearly and quickly. His excitement felt like tensed barrel slats inside his stomach. He reached for the iron knocker, which was in the shape of a downward-leaping rabbit or hare—you clasped both ears with one hand, thumped its outstretched paws against the door. She must, he thought, especially prize this unusual door knocker. Had he knocked loudly enough? Then on the other side of the door a voice sharply demanded *"Quién?"* He sternly answered, "Soy Marco Aurelio Chinchilla"— sounding, he worried, too much like a policeman. A shutter to his right banged open, and her servant poked her head out inside the iron grille cage and exclaimed, "It can't be!" and withdrew back inside, and a moment later the door was flung open, and now there she was, looking up at him with her happy black eyes, "Don Cochinilla! What a miracle—" but then the mercurial girl's expression fell away like a mask, and in an anxious near whisper she asked how she might serve him. He needed to speak with la Señorita Moran about a very urgent matter, said Mack. María Chon stared as if that was the last thing she'd expected him to say—then she gasped and asked, "Is something the matter with Don José?" He told her that Don José was well. She smiled prettily and said, "Un momentito," but added, with a quick roll of her eyes, "You know how she is—pues, maybe you do," and shut the door. From inside he heard María Chon trilling-calling, "Mi Reina Victoria! Mi Excelencia! You will never guess—" and a gay screech of laughter.

It turned into a wait, which was not discouraging. He heard the hooting of an owl somewhere near. Recently in his hotel room he'd dreamed that his old friend Salomón Nahón was sitting on the edge of his bed, hands folded on his lap: it was Salomón, but where his face should have been there was only a shadowy void. The door finally opened and María Chon, smiling, said, "Pase, pues," and, forgetting himself, he responded, as he stepped through the door, with a smile of his own.

There was María de las Nieves, standing several feet back from the door, regarding him in a way that, though unalarmed, was definitely wary, and he wished furiously that her first sight hadn't been of his silly grin. He removed his hat, held it over his chest, and—but just seeing her like this, so suddenly near, caught at his heart—launched into his formulaic recitation of formal apologies, though forgoing the usual lavishing of diminutives and superlatives required by local decorum. (That is the genius of this ritual, Mack wrote later in his diary, "The Return." It gives a man all the extra time he needs to settle his nerves before he has to speak with his own mind.) She wasn't dressed in one of the refitted European dresses she wore to the legation, but had on a loose white blouse that left her forearms bare, and a dark blue skirt without plaits or frills, and a rose-colored silken shawl, which she hugged around her, and her hair was worn in two limp braids tied with velvet ribbons, tucked behind her ears—she was dressed, in fact, not too differently from her servant, he thought, minus Indian embellishments and adornments.

"—However, Señorita Moran, this is not a social call, as I'm sure you've already deduced," said Mack. "I've come to ask for your help in opposing an act of execrable prejudice, one that is likely to happen at the next meeting of the Immigration Society's Board of Directors—unless we succeed in preventing it."

But that lofty-sounding declaration was not enough to win him an invitation to come inside: María de las Nieves's expression was practically unchanged. She was waiting, apparently, for him to explain exactly what he meant *by that.* Inside the entrance there was no vestibule, only a straw mat, a glazed umbrella urn, a rack for hats and coats next to the door, and he stood facing her little parlor, which seemed also to be her dining room, lit by a kerosene lamp on a table at the back, with a candelabra lamp on a side table. A mature woman sat in a wicker rocking chair, ostentatiously busy at her sewing. There were a few more furniture items, including a small sofa, in a shadowy front corner of the room, and some decorations; at the back, draped by a curtain, was a door certainly leading to the rest of the little house and garden patio. Mack smelled vague odors of cat urine and chicken coop, and thought that she must keep egg-laying hens out there.

"At the meetings of the Immigration Society's Board of Directors," he explained further, "the members always like to have reports on the different nationalities and races, on their suitability as immigrants. Sometimes there is just one speaker, who is supposed to state the pros and cons as he has studied them. But generally the men like a debate: someone to argue in favor, and someone against. Then they discuss it among themselves, and decide whether or not that nationality, or race, should be encouraged by the Society to emigrate here, or be discouraged, or even kept out—" At the next meeting, Mack explained, the Board would be taking up the matter of Hebrew immigration. Don Señor Casimir van der Putte, a member of the Board and an importer of German machinery, originally from Hamburg, would be arguing against the Hebrews. Initially, "El Hamburgués," as he was generally referred to by at least the criollo members of the Board, had been scheduled to give the report unopposed, though he'd already uttered many opinions that left no doubt that he was against allowing any more Hebrews into the country. No other member of the Board had volunteered to take up the Hebrews' defense, mainly because—so believed Mack, at least—El Hamburgués's vehement conviction and eloquence so intimidated them.

"Though I am only the First Secretary and not a member of the Board, I spoke up, Señorita Moran," said Mack. "I felt that I had to. I'm from New York, and I've lived among the Hebrews there, and was even employed as a young fellow by the Supreme Government's consul in New York, Mr. Jacobo Baiz. For all those reasons and more, I told the Señores of the Board, I believed myself qualified to give the report on behalf of the Hebrews. I volunteered to do so, and the Board did charge me with the assignment—" But writing the report, he told María de las Nieves, turned out to be easier promised than done. He had little preparation for such an endeavor. All week he'd been struggling over it. Every day El Hamburgués sent a young German clerk to La Sociedad's library to research historical and scientific evidence in support of his opposition to the Hebrews. But Mack had immersed himself in the library too and, in order to better prepare his arguments, had looked into many of the same books that El Hamburgués's clerk was studying. Mack at least had the advantage of being able to stay on in the library long after the closing hour, while the clerk could not. Almost all of those books were from Spain, he explained, and all were filled with hateful calumnies, many of which he knew to be the same defamations hurled against the Chosen People since medieval times, and which would be laughed at in a modern American metropolis like New York, where immigrants from every race and nation were forced to live in close proximity and could see for themselves how preposterous so many of the more extreme European prejudices were. "But I do not know how to set down my arguments in writing, Señorita María de las Nieves, and the intellectual tone, I admit, is not accessible to me. It turns out that I can't just sit there and write more than a few lines at a time. And my own strong feelings make everything I do write sound like shouting. I know that what

I've written so far will not move the heart of anyone on the Board who is ready to oppose the Hebrews. Even our one Englishman, the coffee planter Mr. Smith, seems to be on the side of El Hamburgués, and that is disappointing, because England supposedly has a good reputation in this regard. Even Queen Victoria, I have read, endorses the belief that the English are partly descended from the ancient Israelites."

Now Mack had told her what it was all about. He'd spoken as well as he could, or ever had. What more did she need to hear? With his hat still pressed to his chest, he hurled a bold look back into María de las Nieves's swampy gaze.

María de las Nieves, seeming at least slightly flustered, asked, "But why do you come to me, Señor Chinchilla?" María Chon was in flagrant gape beside her.

"Because you are the good friend of my good friend, the Hebrew umbrella mender Don José Pryzpyz," said Mack (he'd prepared an answer for this very question). "And because you studied composition at the Academia de Niñas de Centroamérica with the esteemed young Cuban Señor José Martí, who in turn regards you as a favored student and friend. Don José says that you love reading, and that you've had the habit of study since your days in the convent. You are employed at the British Legation, where your writing and language abilities are so valued. And because you were once a nun, it is obvious, at least to me it is obvious, Señorita María de las Nieves, that Christian charity still lives in your heart."

Rather than giving any sign of being moved by these words, María de las Nieves seemed to have been sent by them into some remote corner of her thoughts; seconds later, she looked as if she was about to ask an urgent question of her own, but one that she found difficult to phrase, her lips silently contracting, her eyebrows drawing together. Finally, seeming to have lost or relinquished her struggle, she said, "Bueno," and that she felt honored by his kind words, though she also thought he had an exaggerated idea of her abilities. Of course, she would do anything to help Don José. If the Immigration Society were to decide against the Hebrews, would their friend be at any risk?

"I don't know," said Mack. "But you've experienced firsthand, I know, the violence with which this government acts on its prejudices."

She looked confused. "How do you mean?"

"Well, the closing of the convents."

"Oh!" She released a girlish giggle. "Yes, I suppose that is true." She asked him when he needed to give his presentation, and he told her: "To-morrow. At eight in the evening." She expressed surprise that there was so little time. Mack said he wouldn't even have considered asking her if he'd had anyone else to turn to. "I did think of going to Señor Martí," he added insincerely, "but—"

"But he would win your argument for you, and just like *that!*" She snapped her fingers so sharply it was as if a little pistol had fired. "I'm sure he'd regard it an honor and a duty to help you—intolerance has no greater enemy! Truthfully, you should go to him, Señor Chinchilla. Oh, right now, before the hour is too late! Do you have his address—"

"I've never even met the Cuban maestro!"

"I can write you a note of introduction"—she was already turning from the doorway. Mack desperately repeated, "But I've never met him." María Chon, he noticed, was observing this scene with a look of archest mirth. He added, "And he's just married. He and his wife might not even be receiving visitors. And what if they are not at home? There's no time. I wish I'd thought of it sooner, Señorita Moran. I would gladly take your advice!"

Shawl-draped arms crossed, she regarded him now with studious skepticism. "Vaya, Señor Chinchilla," she said finally, and gestured—a little haughtily, her shawl moving like a wing—toward the hat-and-coat rack. "We are going to give it a try." Mack hung up his hat and followed her into the little sala, to the rectangular pine table where she said they could work. She introduced Mack to Doña Amada, her boarder. When Doña Amada looked up from her sewing, she trained on him the fierce stare of a bird of prey. María de las Nieves said, "We'll need writing implements, no?" She left Mack and the two other women alone in the room. Along with the burning lamp, there was a vase holding white camellias on the table. In one corner of the room, upon a small table, was an austere little shrine to the Virgin: a delicately painted but antique-looking wooden statue, somewhat rustic in the Indian manner; a single lit votive candle infused the Virgin's cloudy glass eyes with a muted glow. Remembering their last conversation in the reading room kiosk concerning the Cuban's ideas about religious statuary, Mack reflected: she thinks this simple statue possesses a soul, put there by the honest faith of whoever made it.

"Did you see la Doñacita's picture in Señor Jump's window, Señor Chinchilla?" asked María Chon, seated now at one end of the table. "She is number eight this month." The boarder again stared at Mack, who felt now as if his face was being hotly magnified inside a gaslit crystal ball.

"I did," he answered. "When Don José told me about it, I went to see Señorita's Moran's portrait. Very fine."

"But you bought one of her portraits, no?"

He felt bewildered—he'd judged María Chon an ally. He answered: "Doesn't J. J. Jump say that the integrity of his game depends on keeping secret the names of his customers?" Amada Gómez gave a sharp bark of disagreeable laughter. María Chon said, "She only sold two, tu sabes. Who do you suppose bought the other one?" With her happy eyes flashing maliciously, she answered herself in a loud whisper: "Don José!" Amada Gómez murmured, "Imp. Uyyyy."

When María de las Nieves returned, she set her writing items—pen, inkwell, blotting pad, sheaf of paper—on the table one at a time, slid the lamp to one side, the vase to the other, and sat down across from Mack. Then, as if the little trip had tired her, she leaned back in her chair and yawned deeply, holding a corner of her shawl over her mouth; with her head hanging far back, she gazed up at the whitewashed ceiling for such a long time that Mack felt the stirrings of distress, until her hand and shawl fell away from her mouth, allowing him a glimpse of the soft underside of her tawny chin and the thin, stretched muscles of her neck; she rocked forward again and, looking at him, said serenely, "Perdón." Mack, in a reawakened state of disbelief at finding himself in such close proximity to his beloved, mesmerized by her every tiny gesture, mumbled, "Not at all." "María," said María de las Nieves, "will you go and make some hot chocolate? Señor Chinchilla, how do you like your chocolate? Thick or frothy?" "Thick," Mack ventured. María Chon wrinkled her nose in disapproval. "Very sweet, or not?" Mack had never before been so thoroughly interrogated about his hot chocolate preferences, and asked María de las Nieves how she preferred hers. "Barely sweetened," she said, "and not too thick." "I'll take it like that too," he said. He added that she should feel free to call him Mack.

"And a pitcher of water and some cups, María, favorcito," said María de las Nieves.

"Síííí, mi reina," answered María Chon, getting up from the table with her own show of exhaustion.

When she was gone, Mack remarked, "You treat your servant, and tolerate her, as if she were your mischievous little sister."

"What you've heard is angel talk compared to our usual dialogue," said María de las Nieves, with a note of pride. "I've known María Chon and her family almost all my life. We grew up near each other, in the mountains. Her family, her tío especially, helped us survive after my father died. So this business of her being my servant can seem make-believe to both of us, and sometimes we forget to stay in our roles. Many nights here, you know, it's just the three of us, sitting around this table, rolling cigarettes to help meet the expenses of the house. Yes, that's what we do. I don't tell you that to find sympathy, of course not, that's just the way it is here, as in many other houses where only women live, you know, or perhaps you don't know. If it weren't for my father's land—" She decided not to finish. "But la María Chon is completely irrepressible. Most of all this is a house of crazy women, Señor Mack Chinchilla. Three crazy *Indias* live here, do you know? María Chon is the beautiful one, and we—we live vicariously through the adventures of our beautiful Indita, don't we, Doña Amada? María Chon has by far the best prospects of the three of us, doesn't she, Doña Amada?" And María de las Nieves covered the lower half of her face with her shawl, giggling so deeply that her shoulders shook, while Amada Gómez clucked her quiet and complicit laughter, and wagged her head as if this really was quite scandalous after all. Mack felt discouraged by this unforeseen and wild turn in the conversation, and made an effort, as if tightening a tourniquet within, to stop himself from indignantly protesting that of course his beloved had prospects—

"Don't you find María Chon pretty, Señor Mack?" María de las Nieves was coquettishly asking. "Very very pretty?" It was true, he'd never before been inside a house where only women lived, not counting bordellos, though in those they also enjoyed flummoxing a man like this, and rarely succeeded so well! He blurted: "But so are you, Señorita María de las Nieves . . . And you too, Doña Amada."

"Ahh" was María de las Nieves's almost desultory response, as if he'd somehow failed her test. "Gracias, pues, *Meester* Mack." And now she leaned forward, her elbows on the table, smiled primly, and said, "Let's get to work, no? I'm a little bit aware, you know, of what your Immigration Society does, because of some of the correspondence that comes through the legation. I know that you petitioned—twice, I think it was, no?—to have this country added to the list of those, so far including only France and Holland, permitted by the British Parliament to import English Indians to their territories. Both times, you were refused. I also know that you turned down the petition of a group of would-be colonists from Ireland who wanted a land grant for a farming colony. So I think this is very odd. Why do you request Indians from India, and turn down the White Indians—as Minister Gastreel calls them—of Ireland?"

"First of all, I did not refuse, or request, anybody," said Mack, his smile turning to chalk in his mouth. As First Secretary, he had nothing to do with such decisions. He might not agree with them, he said, but nobody had ever asked his opinion. Those decisions were made by the Board of Directors, who would next take up the question of the Hebrews; now, for the first time, he would have a chance to influence one of those decisions. The Board, explained Mack, had ten members, all prominent men, half of them foreign-born, such as El Hamburgués, and half criollos, such as Don Octaviano. While these two sides had their disagreements, both agreed that the main mission of the Society was the moral and material improvement of the Indian, and thus of the nation, by inserting exemplary foreign immigrants, Europeans especially, in their midst. That was why the Supreme Government had informally agreed to commit ten percent of all uncultivated land in the country to the Immigration Society for distribution. Originally the ideal had been to place a farming colony of Europeans in every Indian department. (The criollos preferred a lower class of white immigrant more inclined to interbreed with the Indians; the foreign-born members of the Board refused to adopt the promotion of miscegenation as an official policy—but Mack, sensing that María de las Nieves was likely to be made uncomfortable by it, withheld that information.) Of course, the Board understood that not all Europeans were suitable for life in this country, as evidenced by the tragic examples of the first immigrant colonies decades before, such as the Belgians, so quickly decimated by illness, starvation, and despair. And often the most suitable Europeans had no desire to come here anyway, for as Don Octaviano had discovered on his trips abroad, ideas about Central America were regularly propagated in Europe that would be unforgivable—Mack quoted his jefe's exact words—*even if they were aimed at countries where the light of civilization has never shone!* (And now María Chon came in with a tray of hot chocolates, served in cups fashioned from jicara gourds; seeing Mack so well launched and holding María de las Nieves's attention, she set the cups in their holders down on the table, and quietly went out again.) The Board, Mack pressed on, considered it a law of nature that Europeans could thrive in the tropics only at elevations of twenty-five hundred feet or higher, and that was why the Immigration Society had petitioned for English Indians, to insert them as agricultural workers in the hot zones, believing them to be more persevering and intelligent, said Mack stonily, than our Indios, and also less likely to rob. And how, María de las Nieves interrupted, did they know that the English Indians were more intelligent, and less likely to rob? Had any member of the Board ever been to India? No, answered Mack, not one had been to India. They had also considered importing workers from the Celestial Empire, he continued, but Don Señor Sanservain, the Californian wine grower who'd received an enormous land grant in Verapaz, had given a report on the immorality of the Chinese coolies in California, which so far none had been able to refute. The emancipated Negro of the American South was rejected for similar reasons, though an obviously biased source, not a member of the Board, Mr. Doveton, a Confederate diplomat in Mexico during the War of Secession and now resident in this country, had been invited to give that report. In the higher altitudes the Immigration Society, especially the foreign members, favored settling immigrants who were already in a position to raise a coffee plantation of their own. But smaller agriculturists were also much in demand, to provide food, increase the variety of vegetables grown, and invigorate by example the Indio's monotonous concept (corn, frijoles, chilies) of garden produce. (María Chon came back carrying the water pitcher and glasses, and unobtrusively took a seat at the end of the table.)

"—Onions are easily grown here," said Mack, "but nobody thinks of eating them. So that even when those who most admire Paris as the beacon of everything excellent and modern in the world travel there, such as Don Octaviano recently did, and discover that every little restaurant now advertises onion soup, that even the most fashionable and wealthy Parisians consume onion soup the way our Indios do beans, then even the jefe of our Immigration Society is stupefied, and when he comes home and recounts his discovery, at first they think Don Octaviano is just having a joke at their expense!" For a good while longer Mack went on in this way, relaxing now into his mastery of Immigration Society detail, encouraged by the keen attention with which María de las Nieves was listening; she was admiring, he hoped, the quietly sardonic and democratic American spirit underlying his exposition. Even María Chon seemed relatively absorbed, though Doña Amada had dozed in her chair, not stirring even when her brass thimble slid off her finger and rolled across the floor.

Don Señor Smith, the Englishman, Mack told them, had begun his notorious presentation by shrewdly acknowledging that the Irish have good qualities—the majority of the Board, digressed Mack, even the Freemasons among them, still favored Catholics over immigrants of any other persuasion, and became defensive when any aspect of Catholicism other than priests came in for rough criticism (and now a gray cat crept into the room and leapt up onto María de las Nieves's lap, and she softly cried out and pushed it onto the floor, though María Chon quickly scooped up the cat and, cooing, "Mishi-mishi," sat down cradling it in her arms). But the Irish are a restless people, Mr. Smith had then argued, inclined to alcoholism, with a pronounced liking for savage brawling and, most worrisomely, addicted to clannish political intrigue and secret societies, all in all a poor example to place before the inert Indio. The Supreme Government and the Immigration Society were fixated on the idea that the eventual canal through Nicaragua would focus the eyes of the world on the Isthmus. By prudent immigration policies, as Don Octaviano liked to phrase it, Central America would have a singular opportunity to foment a new race of American Giants. But that global attention would also attract all manner of dangerous political designs and peoples. The streets of Berlin were now overflowing with unemployed and homeless Germans, and the new *Kaiserreich* encouraged them to go abroad. What this country didn't need were desperate urban immigrants without skills or education or talent, or the socialists, anarchists, and nihilists abounding in all the wretched industrial cities of Europe—

"Germany," María de las Nieves interjected, "also preoccupies Minister Gastreel. Instead of colonizing Central America through military imperial aggression, he says that the Germans are gaining commercial supremacy through the emigration of their merchants and farmers. Already only the

British sell more of their products here. And Germans do not become se-
duced by Central American culture; they remain loyal only to Germany.
But should Central Americans begin to imitate the German culture, says
Minister Gastreel, as they once did Spain's, and now love to copy the
French, then the Isthmus will eventually become absorbed into the new
German Empire in a way that entirely circumvents the Americans' Monroe
Doctrine. It might even be the Germans who end up with the canal."

Mack could not help but marvel at the special excitement with which
María de las Nieves discussed foreign affairs. He said a bit shyly: "I've
never heard that explanation. What do the British plan to do? And what do
the Americans say?"

"Though the Krupp cannon must be our Supreme Government's favorite product in all the world, Central Americans are unlikely to begin dressing up in lederhosen; that, at least, is Minister Gastreel's opinion. But I've
said more than I should have already, Señor Chinchilla."

"The Germans also do well in New York," said Mack. "There they do
not resist becoming Americans, though they do not give up many of their
old ways."

"My father was a New York Irishman," said María de las Nieves. ". . . Pues,
of some sort or another."

Mack would repress his feelings about the Irish of New York. "The Irish
incarnate the cheerful and hearty democratic spirit of our greatest American city."

"I so want to go to New York City someday. Maybe that is my destiny,
eh Mariquita?" she said, turning to her servant, who was absorbed in playing with the cat in her lap. "To find an Irish husband like my own papá."

There is not one of them who will mistake you for a daughter of Erin,
thought Mack jealously; they'll be more likely to call you an African monkey. Though in the little upturned nose, the jaunty elasticity of her lips,
and even the perky ears, he thought, one might divine a trace of Irish an-
cestry, if tipped off to it before.

"We'll get there someday, Doñacita," said María Chon, in a tone implying she'd heard the wish expressed many times before. Mack agreed that
they would.

"But what are we going to do about the Hebrews?" asked María de las
Nieves. "I'm not hopeful now. With the exception of the English Indians,

it seems that your Immigration Society doesn't want anyone to come here."

"Ha-hah!" laughed Mack, too raucously—Doña Amada woke up and peered at him in sorrowful disbelief. He laid his leather portfolio upon the table, unfastened and opened it, brought out a small bottle with a plainly printed paper label, and handed it to María de las Nieves. "This is Florida Water from Don Simón Goldemberg's pharmacy, Señorita María de las Nieves. He was recently in Paris, to study clean bottling. Don Simón is the first to bring sanitary bottling to this country. In Paris he also became an agent of the House of Bary, which makes this first-class Florida Water. At the opera the other night, Don Simón was giving out these samples so that people could compare his Florida Water to the many fakes now being sold here. I was there because Don Octaviano had invited me to join his family in their box. Please take it, Señorita María de las Nieves—well, I have no use for it."

María de las Nieves picked up the bottle, looked at María Chon, gave a little shrug, unstopped the bottle, sniffed it, and then passed it to María Chon.

Mack made a show of perusing the notes he'd copied from books in La Sociedad Económica's library. Much of what he'd read in those books could not even be repeated in front of a lady. He wondered if El Hamburgués would dare to inform the Board that, according to the wisdom of Europe, Hebrew men menstruate, grow female breasts, and rarely stop masturbating, and the women are given to nymphomania. Mack repeated for María de las Nieves those calumnies that he thought she could withstand listening to, many of them of a more or less familiar nature, even, or perhaps certainly, to a girl raised in a convent. (Though they almost never meant it as praise, Mack rather enjoyed the scholars who wrote about the common traits shared by the Hebrews and the uncivilized Indians of the Americas—the shapes of skulls, noses, droopy ears; the sacrifice of chickens; lunar calendars; supernatural demon worship; hieroglyph-like writing; guttural pronunciation and the typical male's too vehement manner of speaking; cruel justice; the separation of male and female in rites and worship; general lasciviousness; the female love of gaudy adornments and oily unguents; excessive washing—and argued that it was obvious that the Indians and the Lost Tribes of Israel were one and the same.)

Then Mack launched into his story about his life growing up in New York, his apprenticeship with Mr. Jacobo Baiz, his eventual rise from office boy to clerk with fine prospects, and about his great friend Salomón Nahón—he didn't mention Reyna Salom, though. Noticing that María de las Nieves grew pensive just at the mention of Don Juan Aparicio and his purchase of Jacobo Baiz's firm, he moved on to a lively account of the Oriental Hebrew cafés in New York and some of the colorful characters he and Salomón had met and caroused with in that world. And then he told her the story of his return to this unknown country of his birth, his adventurous journey across it to Cuyopilín, to the homestead of the brothers Nahón, and Salomón's tragic end. María de las Nieves seemed affected by Mack's story. Slowly shaking her head in disbelief, she quietly said, "How can such things happen? Those poor brothers. And how sad for you, Señor Chinchilla, to have traveled all that way, only to find your friend murdered." When María Chon said that he must want to find out who had killed Salomón and avenge him, Mack said that of course he would never leave this country until he'd done that very thing.

"—The argument that the Hebrews of the Diaspora have proven that they can adapt to any environment would usually count in their favor with the Board," said Mack. "But El Hamburgués is sure to point out that they are often accused of blending in too well and of coming to resemble, on the outside, whoever they've come to live among—even Indios. In Cuyopilín, Salomón Nahón did become a little bit of a wild Indio, but that was a good thing!"

María de las Nieves ended up writing Mack's entire report herself—that is, at first she relied on Mack's notes and suggestions, but soon she was ignoring these, and relying on her own memory and knowledge, especially of the Old Testament. Mack, in the rarest state of bliss he'd ever known, sat watching her bent in concentration over her writing, her braids slightly swinging with the movement of her hand and the pen whispering and squeaking across the pages, listened to her exhaling through her nose, her soft outbursts of exasperation, the wet tapping of her tongue against the back of her teeth, as if counting off syllables. The sweet smell of Florida Water suffused the air. Doña Amada had finally gone to her bed; María Chon was asleep, head in folded arms atop the table. Mack felt as if he were married, that as soon as María de las Nieves was finished, he would fold his arms around her, and lead her adoringly to their bed. He marveled at this vision, which now seemed attainable. Why couldn't this illusion of being married, *from this moment on*, be the reality? He imagined their little daughter, curled up in a chair and hugging a cat, saying "mishi-mishi" like María Chon. Even imaginary happiness, he thought, is happiness.

As in many older houses in this city, the ceiling in the parlor was not a real one, but was made of wide sheets of canvas, stiffened by whitewash, laid over the tops of the walls. It resembled a plaster ceiling but wouldn't collapse on people's heads in an earthquake. Above it was the roof of planks, pitch, and tiles to keep out the rain. Whenever the wind gusted, the decorative false ceiling shivered and rattled, and the reflection of the light from the lamp shimmered upon it like rays of silvery sunlight spreading inside a cloud.

When María de las Nieves was finished, she read what she'd written out loud. It struck Mack as luminously well reasoned, filled with feminine feeling yet irrefutable argument, and as well aimed as if she'd been studying her adversaries all her life. She ended with a paragraph devoted to the virtues of the Hebrew Heroines of the Old Testament, the purity of Sara, the beauty of Rebecca, the sweet piety of Esther, the humility of Raquel, the saintliness of Ruth, the fierce heroism of Judith, the chastity of Susana, virtues that pointed to and finally found their perfect combined expression in the Most Holy Virgin, blessed Mother of God, sweet Mother of Our Americas . . . et cetera.

SIX MONTHS LATER, when Mack Chinchilla found himself fighting alongside the remnants of the doomed Indian rebels under the command of the *chuchkajawib* shaman Juan Diego Paclom in the War of the Caves, he asked himself: Would that night when María de las Nieves wrote the report while he sat worshipfully at her side be worth dwelling upon *right now* if it had only been an isolated occasion, floated away in time—rather than a memory connecting him to who, and where, he was today? That evening, as Mack crouched before the mouth of a high mountain cave overlooking the vast mountain valley alongside Don Juan Diego as he prepared a ritual involving the burning of pieces of paper smeared with caucho, the "mother-father" shaman-priest surprised him with a remark about memory: pulling at a clump of India rubber, stretching it between his fingers and letting it snap back into place, the *chuchkajawib* said, "Caucho remembers. Caucho is memory. It remembers where it was before, Don Mack." That was all, but Mack had never thought of memory in that way, and almost instantly he recalled the night when María de las Nieves wrote the defense of the Hebrews, which was still his happiest and most hopeful memory, though in reality it would seem to have led to nothing but disillusion. Was he wrong to remember that night so fondly then? Was it proof of flawed memory and vain fatuity? He tried to conceive of that night as pulled elastically far away from him in time like a piece of stretched caucho, and now, through memory, instead of breaking off, snapped right back into him, restoring him to an original shape, making him whole. Yes, he thought, that's right, it's not just a memory that I was separated from back there, and might as well have lost. It's a part of how I got here. Mack, the ever hopeful American lover, Mack, the doomed American warrior, both fused inside the same elastic caucho-man!

THAT NIGHT, WHEN María de las Nieves had finished reading out her defense of the Hebrews, and Mack had finished profusely thanking and praising her, he should, without delay, have said good night and departed.

"You are very devoted to the Most Holy Virgin after all, aren't you," he said instead, hoping to prolong the night a bit longer. "Like my mother is."

"Señor Mack," María de las Nieves said quietly. "I have a platonic love for the Virgin. I can't explain it any better than that."

But she made no move to rise from her chair, or to disturb the sleeping María Chon. Instead she leaned across the table to light a cigarette from the lamp, and sat back savoring it, seeming a little bit oblivious of him now—though not at all signaling that he had to go away; in fact, he sensed her reticence colluding with the idea that he should stay. Still, Mack kept quiet, as if not wanting to remind her of his presence. Then she slowly exhaled her smoke while looking directly at him, with that now familiar expression of seeming as if she wanted to say something else, which probably she would not. She reached for the pitcher of water and poured some into her ceramic cup, and asked Mack if he wanted some, and he held his cup out, and she refilled it. "Do you like working for the Immigration Society?" she asked. He answered that often, of course, he found it disagreeable, and that he certainly hadn't come to this country with any notion of seeking such a sedentary job; though were he only to judge the men of the Board from a moral point of view, he would also make himself deaf to all that there was to learn from them, for they were all men who, in this country and elsewhere, had succeeded in agriculture and commerce. Every day Mack spent among such men, in his office and in the environment of La Sociedad Económica, he learned some new thing about the march of scientific or industrial progress in the world, or about the ever expanding economic opportunities in this country, for though few now could afford to start a coffee plantation on their own, many other paths to wealth were being pioneered. There were now individuals in this country cultivating silkworms with success, and planting olive trees and making olive oil, and mining alum nitrate, and growing and producing opium of the highest quality, and La Sociedad Económica, whose slogan was *Science is not truly useful until it has been vulgarized,* aided, monitored, studied, and issued reports on all such efforts. It was ironic that in this country, to which he'd come with the plan of quickly establishing himself in coffee farming alongside his friend Salomón Nahón, Mack had instead discovered what the early need to hold employment and learn an occupation in New York had denied him: the environment of a college, one where only useful subjects were taught. He was no less determined to *get somewhere in life* than he'd ever been, Mack told María de las Nieves, and he was sure this period of learning and study would help him *get there* someday soon. But what about her, Mack asked; did she like working at the British Legation? She answered, "Yes." But it was a yes that trailed a sense of much left unsaid. This time, he thought, her reticence *was* a signal that it was time for him to go. But they went on conversing about what each had recently been reading in the newspapers. Then, as if they were again at the beginning of the evening and just conversing "to break the ice," they discussed the dry-season climate, and its dire effects on the air and the water brought to the city via its century-old aqueducts. Mack joked, "Every day in this city we each swallow enough sand and grit to make an adobe brick." If she watered white camellias like these on her table even with water run through a pumice-stone filter,

Mack told her, the petals, when they dried, would be stained; to illustrate, he dipped his fingers into his cup, sprinkled water onto her camellias, and said, "You'll see tomorrow, those white petals will be stained. What do you think this water does to our insides?" María de las Nieves said, "It stains our insides also, I imagine. But the insides of our stomachs are not as white as camellias, and even if they are, nobody will ever notice," and she added with a wry tone: "After all, our stomachs are not our souls." Though she did have a cistern for collecting rainwater in her garden, she told him; at this time of year, of course, it was dry. Did she also keep hens in her garden? asked Mack. "Despite this Florida Water, you can still smell my hens?" A little, he laughed, yes. He thought: It can't be possible for a man to feel more love than I do now. But she did not invite him to see her garden. Only a minute or two later he was standing just outside her door, saying good-bye. Before she closed it he hastily added that he would come again to tell her how their defense of the Hebrews was received. She said yes, of course, and smiled: "But only if the news is good!" A bakery he passed on his way home had hung out its red lantern, and he went in and bought a warm French roll, fresh from the oven. Outside he tore with his teeth through the crunchy crust, into the feathery steam of mildly sour bread, and paused to self-consciously savor this moment of happiness, beneath the stars, in the deserted rutted avenue glowing with orange moonlight. A dreadful intuition reversed the current of his reverie, like a terrible giant picking up a river in his arms and hurling it back down, causing it to flow backward. Mack stood in the street and faced this enemy intuition with a defiant inner gaze. Well, we'll see; I'll know soon enough whether she cares for me at all or not. Anyway, he thought, resuming the walk back to his hotel, carrying the roll in his hand, the stomach's insides are not so hidden, no, not anymore: in Paris, he'd recently read in a newspaper, a genius surgeon had boldly sliced a patient's stomach open in order to remove a copper fork that the young man had accidentally swallowed months before and that had finally brought him to the verge of death, and the fork had come out completely blackened by gastric acids, and the surgeon had then stitched the patient's stomach closed again, saving his life. María de las Nieves, the inside of the stomach is black as pitch—!

At the meeting of the Immigration Society the next evening the Board was so moved and persuaded by María de las Nieves's report, read out loud by Mack, that in the end they voted to neither encourage nor discourage Hebrew immigration. When Mack returned to her house the evening after to deliver the good news, María Chon answered the door, and though the pretty little servant's manner was cheerful, she told him that María de las Nieves was out but that she would give her his message; then the door closed.

But that did not mean that Mack had not established enough of a relationship with María de las Nieves to commence a formal courtship. Who else should he have invited to the opera benefit two weeks later, cosponsored by the Immigration Society and the Friends of Italy, on behalf of the more than two hundred penniless Italians stranded on the Atlantic coast? Only days after Mack delivered María de las Nieves's report, the Minister of Works received a telegram from the port commander at Santo Tomás notifying him that 243 Italians had been put ashore by a French ship captain and abandoned without food or resources. It was the same part of the coast where, three decades earlier, the first Belgian colony had met catastrophe. The Italians had sailed from Marseille six weeks earlier, bound for Venezuela, where supposedly land and provisions for a farming colony awaited, but when they arrived, the Venezuelan authorities claimed no knowledge of them, and refused to pay the French ship captain money owed under the contract he'd signed with their government's consul in Marseille, and so he'd indignantly sailed away. Having finally deposited his human cargo at that isolated Central American harbor—he told them they were in Louisiana—the Frenchman escaped in his ship under cover of darkness, taking one of the Italians' adolescent daughters with him. The Supreme Government placed the Immigration Society in charge of the emergency, and Don Octaviano placed Mack in charge. Mack was not to have a moment of peace or rest for the next six months. Already some of the Italians had fallen ill with tropical fevers and dehydration; many had gorged on unripe guavas, mangoes, and other unfamiliar fruits and vegetables as soon as they were ashore, and were immobilized with stomach pains. The opera benefit was to raise money to transport the castaways inland to the capital, and help provide for them once they arrived. The touring Italian Lyric Opera Company, then in residence at the National Theater, agreed to donate the night's receipts on behalf of their destitute countrymen. So Mack had invited

María de las Nieves to the opera. And she'd been happy to go! So happy that when he'd sent a messenger boy to the British Legation with the embossed invitation, that boy had returned with her answer the same afternoon.

It was María de las Nieves's first opera; the first time also that Mack, by his sudden ascension to a weighty position in the Immigration Society, had ever been in the position to invite anyone to sit in an opera box—the Box of Honor, no less! And she was the very picture of excitement, at least through the evening's early stages. When he transported her in a hired coach to the National Theater, the neoclassical edifice's handsome white facade illuminated by blazing torches that night, and led her up the stairs and to the Box of Honor—her hands in kid gloves loaned to her by Mrs. Gastreel, one resting expertly-lightly on his own arm, the other carrying her fan—María de las Nieves seemed to Mack like a girl living out a fantasy, one of those bookish fantasies in which a heretofore anonymous heroine is placed before society for the first time, and sets hearts and imaginations aflame with her fresh and innocent beauty. He'd never seen her with her hair up before. Her curving, dusky nape, the broad Indian-shape of her skull, these he tenderly noted. Her thin neck and delicately jutting ears were like an underwater flower he was swimming toward (but would never reach). Mack took deep proprietary inhalations of the sweet fragrance of Don Simón Goldemberg's Florida Water. The "Box of Honor" was actually La Primera Dama's box, but as she was still in New York with her children, recovering from the shock of the Homicidal Fraternity of the Black Rosary, and her husband did not enjoy opera or care for these events, it had been donated to the Immigration Society and the Friends of Italy for the benefit. Then came the electrifying moment when María de las Nieves's lips nearly brushed Mack's ear: her words and damp breath roaring inside his ear as she swayed closer to him than she ever had before to whisper, "This is an ironic moment, my finding myself here, in Doña Francisca's box. We have a secret history, she and I, you know. If she'd been here, I would never have come," and then she swayed away. She disappeared a long while into the First Lady's toilette, and when she came back, Mack asked, "How did you enjoy the toilette?" and she answered, "I've read about such luxury in books, Señor Chinchilla, but to actually see it leaves me speechless!" A playful note of insincerity in her words puzzled him, for he didn't doubt the truth of her answer—where else would she have seen a more elegant toilette?

The benefit commenced with speeches from the stage. Don Octaviano Mencos Boné introduced the Foreign Minister, who resembled a fat pink-cheeked boy in a gray wig and false goatee, and orated in a piercing shriek, waving his arms and bouncing on the balls of his feet: The rescue of the Italians from the greed and perfidy of the French sea captain and Venezuelan immigration authorities, went the Foreign Minister's speech, presented an unprecedented historical opportunity, for once the news spread that the Italians were happily and productively settled here, their little country's name would be known and admired throughout Europe. And the national march to prosperity would so accelerate that soon their sister Central American republics would beg the President General to undertake the glorious dream of an Isthmus united under his rule into a single republic that no other nation in the world would be able to call *small!* The speech won a rousing ovation. Though it was not known outside the Immigration Society, the burden of achieving that vision now rested almost solely on Mack Chinchilla's shoulders. He was the one departing at dawn on a long journey by horseback and riverboat to the coast to oversee the rescue of the Italians. It was going to be no easy logistical task, to lead 243 Italians through tropical wilds and desert and over mountains, all the way back to the capital. He leaned closer to María de las Nieves and told her about that, and she listened, an honest sweetness filling her eyes. She said, "You should feel proud, Señor Chinchilla, that they chose you for such a responsibility. I know their trust is well placed." What could he say to that which would not sound boastful, or falsely humble? At last he was beginning to resemble in the world the man he carried within, this man he knew better than any other. Already, no matter what else ensued, wasn't this night a triumph? He looked speechlessly into María de las Nieves's eyes, as if dumbfounded by her regard, and she smiled, her teeth flecked with the scarlet rouge on her lips, and he thanked her with a solemn nod, briefly lowering his eyes to the smooth nakedness of her shoulders, upper chest, and collarbones, bared by the low neck of her crimson gown, with no more jewelry than a simple silver-and-bead necklace with a medallion of the Virgin dangled into the shadow inside her slight yet pert cleavage. In the golden light of the theater's gas-burning lamps, María de las Nieves's skin radiated the indescribable freshness and suppleness of her youth. Mack felt a bewildered ache deep inside his entrails. Right here under your scientific nose, he thought, is the difference between the flesh of a young virgin beauty and of a brothel beauty, for the latter's skin, no matter how soft and delicious, is tinted by an *invisible residue,* and can no longer startle the air. María de las Nieves pulled her black lace shawl more closely around her, and turned in her seat to look again toward the stage. The chandelier over the auditorium was arranged into a large basket of flowers (donated by the florists Rosenthal). Now one of the women in the Box of Honor was to cut the ceremonial cord leading from the rail to the chandelier with the special dagger, emeralds and rubies flashing in its golden hilt, presented by the young officer in dress uniform who'd stepped into their box. But the officer unsheathed the dagger too abruptly, or maybe it was his facial expression: everybody in the Box of Honor, even Mack, flinched and drew back, as if he were an emissary of the Homicidal Fraternity of the Black Rosary. Despite her father's prodding, the obese twelve-year-old daughter of the Duc de Licignano, the Italian Chargé d'Affaires and Friend of Italy, sank even deeper into her chair, and refused to take the dagger. Don Octaviano's wife, Doña Eleuteria, a frail, quavering woman, protested that she wasn't strong enough to wield the dagger on her own, perhaps with His Excellency Il Duce's help—. But Mack was simultaneously on his feet, guiding the soldier toward María de las Nieves, insisting that the honor be hers. So María de las Nieves stood at the rail with the dagger in her gloved hand, all eyes inside the theater upon her—in her refitted rented gown and inconspicuous décolletage, no one would confuse her with the mysterious alabaster ingénue of a magical society tale. As she struggled to slice the rope, some derisive whistles and drunken sarcastic shouts did rise from the male audience in the floor seats, but finally she succeeded in severing it, and dozens of bouquets of flowers sped down the wires leading from the chandelier to every box in the balconies; to general applause, the orchestra began to play.

María de las Nieves's mood grew subdued, and soon it was clear to Mack that she had fallen into a sulk. From their box, he noticed, his beloved had a clear view of the Normal School's box, where the newlywed José Martí and his young wife were sitting; looking in the other direction, she could see the box where María García Granados sat with her mother and some of her sisters and male cousins in military uniforms. María de las Nieves could see Martí glancing toward María García Granados, and María García Granados glancing toward the Martís. All in all, a heart-sinking silent opera, Mack reflected. Months later, when he learned that María García Granados had died of illness at home in her bed, he briefly applied hindsight to his recalled image of the wanly pretty girl in her perfect Parisian gown, her elegant composure, who never hid her face behind her fan. Come now, Mack, you can't honestly pretend death had a role in that scene, standing watch behind her like a pertinacious death owl in hussar's uniform. At most she struck you as being in need of some regular dosage of Lydia Pinkham's Vegetable Compound. But the poorly nourished and melancholy look was fashionable; girls of that age consciously did things to themselves to acquire it. Here was the only aspect of the submerged drama that he indisputably remembered: both María García Granados and María de las Nieves were clearly a bit depressed and jealous to see Dr. Torrente sitting there with the impressive female who was now his wife. María de las Nieves didn't look at Mack again in that keen sweet way she had just moments before, when she'd praised him for being chosen Moses of the Italians. The opera was *La Sonnambula*. He did not want to leave her side even at intermission, in case she should suddenly revive, though Don Octaviano, who alternated cigars with medicated asthma cigarettes, invited him out for a smoke. The former Confederate diplomatist Mr. Doveton then invaded their box and boldly and mystifyingly directed some of his suave wicked flattery at her—. There really is nothing more about this evening that Mack, in his mountain cave, would like to recall right now.

THE REFORM SCHOOL for girls in the former convent of Santa Catarina, purged of its young female inmates (a number released into the care of Doña Carlota Marcoris, others transferred to the women's prison in the former Carmelite convent), was the Italians' first home. Eleven did not survive those first weeks on the coast, followed by the hard inland journey on which Mack led them. (Mack liked to say that riding horses had finally become as natural to him as walking.) Now that they were in the capital, Don Simón Goldemberg had offered two months' worth of free medications, and a military surgeon was assigned to care for the unlucky immigrants. An elderly Italian priest, Padre Perroni, visited every day and acted as translator. Don José Pryzpyz, in anticipation of the rainy season, donated umbrellas and waterproofed capes. But when the Italians complained about the gloomy atmosphere of the former convent, they were moved to La Sociedad Económica's School of Agriculture, situated on an old farm confiscated from the Jesuits at the edge of the capital; the students' vacation was indefinitely extended for the emergency. A few of the heartier Italians, including some comely young married couples, were quickly offered work by plantation owners and taken away; later it was rumored that Mack Chinchilla had profited from this human trade, though of course he had not.

In the city it became a fashionable weekend outing to go out to the School of Agriculture to see the Italians. Bringing old clothes and food for the refugees provided an excuse to stay and gape. Soon there were even a few Italian peasant girls dressed in secondhand gowns from the Parisian House of Worth; others wore the bright rebozos and blouses of traditional mengalas. Even poor people came, whole families setting out early in the morning on foot, bearing some rustic native dish with which to feed the accidental immigrants: pipian, spicy chojín, tamales, chuchitos, pots of simple black beans with moist white cheese, candied fruit, and slabs of brown sugar. Mack felt like the operator of a curious human zoo displaying "Italians"—nearly half of the refugees were Tyrolese, the rest from around Genoa—many with yellow hair and blue eyes, and so ragged and dependent, with such perpetually frightened, disoriented, and dirty visages, it was if they *wanted* to inspire pity and condescension. Despite their poverty and dejection, some of the young men and women were exceptionally beautiful, with gazes that floated across the air like languid birds of iridescent plumage. Whenever the Italians made music with their accordions and string instruments, the audiences gratefully applauded. Opera was such a passion in the capital that even poor people knew the melodies of famous arias; those who learned them by standing outside the doors of the National Theater on nights when the Italian Lyric Opera Company performed brought the contagious tunes home and to work, and from there they spread everywhere, so that whenever one of the Italians erupted into one of those songs, many of the spectators immediately joined in. At first the

Italians were astonished by the unlikely chorus and enjoyed singing back and forth, the Italians testing their audience's knowledge of opera songs and sometimes the other way around; it became one more attraction of Mack's popular zoo. But then the Italians, with no explanation, turned against this game, and refused to sing aloud for their public, and countered every request with sullen stares or indifference.

One Sunday Mack invited María de las Nieves out to the School of Agriculture, and dispatched the carriage he now had at his disposal to bring her. She arrived with María Chon. She seemed oblivious of Mack's newfound celebrity as overseer of the Italians. Did she even notice that the Italians called him *Il Capo?* It was obvious she was interested only in seeing the Italians. No memorable look, slyly coquettish word, or even meaningful silence was sent Mack's way. In fact, she doted on her servant. The two stood close together like an image of the Visitation, their heads nearly touching and turning in unison as they watched a certain bronze Italian buck, who wore a golden earring and did not seem less manly for it, stride past. Mack heard María Chon say, "Qué mangazo!" and then María de las Nieves: "Uyyy sí, qué mangazo!" What a big handsome mango! Cheerfully, without sarcasm, and followed by a spurt of complicit giggling—over that strutting, idle clodhopper! Mack felt a stab of grief; indignation blurred his vision. He forced a distant demeanor, but María de las Nieves did not seem to notice this either, because a wasp stung María Chon on the forehead, and María de las Nieves's reaction was extraordinary, as if some wild maternal instinct had awakened in her: she chased the wasp down and clapped it dead between her hands, and then, looking into her hands, scolded, "Barbarous insect!" and shook the mashed wasp off her fingers. People were staring, including a group of young women her own age, all wearing dresses of rich silk and elaborate hats and carrying parasols. Ignoring them, she turned and went swiftly back to wincing, sniffling María Chon and held her in a tight embrace. With an embarrassed, emotional-sounding little laugh, she said, "Maybe I am just a savage, but by what law of nature is that small ugly bicho allowed to hurt my Maricusa?" and she ordered Mack to bring medicine and a cloth dipped in cold water and a limón to hold over the swelling mound on the girl's forehead. Soon after, the two young women climbed back into the carriage and returned to the city. A few months later, when the first rumors of María de las Nieves's disgrace reached him, Mack remembered her exclamation over the handsome Italian, and realized that he'd indeed witnessed an early manifestation of her baffling transformation. Then he thought, No, Mack, you can't justify such a claim by the ruse of hindsight; for all you know she's long been in the habit of exclaiming over handsome men, like any other frivolous girl, and you'd never been in the spot to notice. And admit it, disturbing as it was, her killing that wasp also displayed something fine.

Before long the "shocking indolence" of the Italians had become the number one topic of conversation in the capital. No other aspect of the Italians was even commented on anymore, the Immigration Society Board members complained to Mack, as if he bore the responsibility for their guests' low morale and disappointing lethargy. Why couldn't the Italians show some sign of initiative, gratitude, or optimism? They seemed to grow more morose and quarrelsome by the day. They seemed willing to just live on handouts forever. They didn't seem to want to do anything but lie about in the sun, gorging on the perpetual parade of donated food. No wonder they were always falling sick! It was true that despite Don Simón Goldemberg's medicines, few had managed to stay healthy, and the many who'd fallen ill, with stomach disorders and recurrent fevers especially, had been slow to recover. It didn't help that the sole food the Italians regularly prepared among themselves—those stringy white *maccheronis*—so resembled the tapeworms infesting many of their bellies. Mack became indignant when he learned that a rumor was spreading through the ignorant city that the voracious Italians were eating the very tapeworms expelled by Don Simón's purgatives. He had to admit that even news of the death of Pope Pío IX had done nothing to stir the Italians from their slothful apathy. Yet they were as superstitious as Indios! Hearing the Jesuits' old parrots pronouncing the Ora Pro Nobis and Ave María in the branches of the farm's avocado trees, the Italians became hysterical, taking it as a sign that Satan had a hand in their misfortune after all; Padre Perroni did little to calm them. Why couldn't they regard parrots praying in Latin, proposed Mack, as a sign of miraculous blessing? Padre Perroni answered as if it were obvious: the Holy Spirit never communicated through parrots, for who could have faith in anything spoken by a creature so cunningly adept at counterfeiting voices?

Mack, on his journey to and from the coast, had actually been infected with tapeworms and several other lingering tropical ailments. He'd never been so thin, pale, and haggard. His fingers were covered with tiny sores from a nervous outbreak of eczema. Fungus infested his feet, crotch, and underarms. He felt plagued by lethargy, just when he could least afford even a minute of laziness. He had no time to indulge or contemplate his sorrow over his failed courtship of María de las Nieves, but felt the ache inside him like constant cold wet weather in his bones. Most nights Mack slept in a hammock strung up inside his office at the School of Agriculture. In the evenings, when the visitors had all left, he could hear the Italians, decamped in the other schoolrooms, in hammocks around the verandah, even in their beds of piled hay in the stables, crying out in pain over their illnesses and in histrionic lament; how bitterly they argued among themselves, or cursed God or the French sea captain; how dolefully they sighed!

The negative impression the Italians were causing was a source of mounting anxiety for Mack. Sooner or later, he knew, these complaints, if not reversed, could rebound dangerously against their "Capo." Tirelessly he defended his immigrants with stories about the vitality and work ethic of the Italians of New York. But he was desperate for some sign from his Italians that they might rally. Force was justified to put the Indio to work, the Liberals believed, but no one was ready to apply the same tenet to the Italians. There was only one solution, the Board decided: without delay, the Italians had to be set up in a farming colony. Once the Italians had land of their own to farm, surely they would rise to the challenge. Then the country—so went the Immigration Society's optimistic public line—would at last be rewarded with the promised example of European industriousness and domestic pride. If the Immigration Society was unable to deliver on such a promise, what was their reason for being? Influential Board members persuaded the Supreme Government that the country's credibility as a destination for immigrants was at stake, and to enact a new penny tax on every bottle of aguardiente distilled in the country to take care of the Italians until their farming colony was self-sufficient. Two farms on the plain outside the city were purchased with the Society's own funds. Once the Italians were earning money by selling an unprecedented variety of garden produce to the city, the Immigration Society would be reimbursed. In the meantime they only had to promise not to abandon or run away from the colony farms, on pain of imprisonment.

In all but official title, Mack was the administrator of both farms. He was so immersed in this work that he barely paused to reflect on the news that in the capital the teenaged daughter of the former president, General García Granados, had died of raging fever and consumption, though when later he heard the funeral bells tolling from across the plain, he stopped to say a silent and respectful good-bye to the girl who'd left such a vivid image and trail of sentimental gossip in his mind. Mack could not build every Italian family's house by himself; Il Capo could not plow, sow, and farm every family's parcel of land! After two months on the farms, most of the Italians were still living in stables, suffering from their manifold diarrheas and other afflictions, and were rarely able to muster more than a few men at a time to work on raising their cabins. It was widely noticed and remarked that Italians could not cut lumber any quicker than the Indios could. Nor did they plant corn any quicker than the Indios. Just like the Indios, they burned away the stubble of the previous year's crop and planted a new one in the scorched earth. The Italians preferred to plow by night, but this had more to do with staying out of the sun and certain superstitions about moonlight than modern agricultural knowledge, and they didn't plow any quicker than native laborers did either. The seeds they'd brought from Italy held promise, but months after the first plantings, few had sprouted. When some previously unknown varieties of beans were spotted growing on their beanpoles, the Immigration Society saw to it that this good news was widely trumpeted. But it was not enough. The rains were beginning. Tuberculosis and anemia were spreading, especially among their children; every week saw at least one funeral. Among the Italians, a belief now spread that Mack had the Evil Eye. Now nobody wanted to look Mack in the eye, nobody could comfortably or obliviously return his gaze, and so every attempted conversation became a torturous repetition of colliding and ricocheting glances and increasing nervous strain, of stares aimed hard at the air and into the ground. This development thoroughly poisoned Mack's existence and deepened his sense of lonely doom.

Because bread alleviates suffering but does not cure it, and their treasury was nearly depleted, the Immigration Society Board decided, over Mack's exhausted protests, to stop provisioning the Italians. Faced with starvation, went the Board's sneering reasoning, perhaps they would finally begin to labor as hard and as resourcefully as the Italian immigrants of New York. The Italians began to flee instead, escaping into the city and the countryside, into their diverse and mostly futile destinies. Mack was dismissed from his post and from the Immigration Society too.

THAT END WAS the beginning of this end: the War of the Caves and this Indian rebel headquarters in a mountain cave, where Mack now stood at its entrance musing on memory and caucho and watching the *chuchkajawib* Juan Diego Paclom crouched by the small fire, mumbling-chanting prayers, lifting caucho-smeared pieces of burning paper to his lips and blowing puffs of acrid smoke into the air, each black puff of caucho smoke floating off mysteriously spherical and whole over the valley.

And so, María de Las Nieves, after all those months of studying science and progress at La Sociedad Económica—thought Mack, as if silently composing a letter to her—I've ended up back in the Dark Ages, surrounded by Don Juan Diego's Indio-Christian hocus-pocus, and also by the Hebrew-Indio hocus-pocus of Rubén Abensur, the Hebrew teacher from Tangier brought by the Nahóns to teach in their school in Cuyopilín. The lunatic hallucinations of their New American Religion of Perpetual Resurrection, which they devise together, at least helps them ignore death and pass the time, and also heartens the remaining young warriors in our little rebel encampment. With mystical smoke puffs we signal to our enemies that we are not afraid of the deaths from which we, with the immortal breaths and secret names of the ancestors inside us, Perpetually Resurrect ourselves. Maybe this mystical show does succeed in frightening the government troops a little bit, especially the ignorant conscripts, making their officers reluctant to lead them into this valley, where we are apparently trapped. We can see the smoke of burning Indian villages rising from behind the mountain ridges all around us, we hear the crack of rifles, and feel the explosions of their artillery thudding through the earth, as if on the other side they are firing directly into the mountains with the intention of smashing through them . . .

Within days of the Italian colony's humiliating finale Mack had left the city, headed back to Cuyopilín atop another hired horse, only to discover, when he arrived, that the Nahóns were gone. As León had predicted the year before, the brothers had been driven out of business by Germans and had abandoned the accursed little country, Fortunato back to Tangier, Moisés to San Francisco, and brave León to El Salvador, where he'd bought a small cattle ranch and was breeding mules and acting as father to Salomón's natural son Máximo. The cause of Salomón's murder and the identity of his murderers remained a mystery, though surely León would keep the dream of vengeance alive, and plant it in the heart of little Máximo. The stone Mack had placed atop Salomón's gravestone the year before was still there, like a lump of hardened bread left untouched by birds. The Nahón homestead was collapsing into jungly ruin. But the Hebrew schoolteacher from Tangier, Rubén Abensur, and his wife, the India Felipa, were still living there. The pair had become the leaders of the largely Pipil Indian lowland village, whose population included so many natural offspring of the Nahóns, and where many of the women still went bare-breasted. Abensur had the paradoxical face of an ostrich, that profoundly dizzy glare and slight smile of ill-humored tenderness; but he was wiry in his body, and moved without clumsiness. He dressed in white cotton, with a floppy straw hat, and was much taller than Felipa, who had the fastidious, brusquely kindhearted manner of an Indian matron such as Mack's own mamá. She was obviously loyal to Rubén, yet seemed immune to his new revolutionary-mystical zeal.

It took Rubén Abensur little time to persuade Mack to join a plot to deliver arms to the Indian rebels opposing the Supreme Government and the new coffee oligarchy. Holed up in the mountains to the east, they were fighting under the loose command of a mysterious criollo plantation owner turned Christian-Mayan mystic whose nom de guerre was Juan Rubio. Rubén Abensur had never met this Juan Rubio—nor would he, or Mack, ever—but the Hebrew teacher from Tangier seemed the type who had always dreamed of a heroic fate and, finding himself with little to lose, had begun conspiring with the rebels in the doomed uprising now known to history as the War of the Caves.

At Rubén Abensur's behest, Mack had agreed to smuggle rifles from the coast to the mountain caves for money—he'd never sought any more involvement in the uprising than that. When he went to the port of Champerico to negotiate his price, his contact turned out to be the former

Confederate diplomat Mr. Doveton, now a confidential agent of the British. Three nights later a first shipment of Winchester rifles was rowed ashore under cover of night in a skiff commanded by the sun-burnished, slimmed young First Secretary of the British Legation, blue-eyed Wellesley Bludyar, who enveloped Mack in a hearty two-handed back-slapping embrace like a true Centroaméricano, and said, "Hello, you old avocado you." Later that night, as they shared a bottle of Nicaraguan rum by the dim light of a shaded kerosene lamp inside a cloud of insects, Bludyar slurred, "So what about Mary of the Snows, anyway? Just got a letter from the Chiefess telling me she's been *fixed*, as the muchachos like to say around here, though Snows apparently still thinks the Gastreels haven't noticed. I don't know the truth of it, do you? I'll tell you what, Mack, she could have ten bastards and I'd still marry her. Don't care who the father is either. When all of this is done, I mean to go back and tell her exactly that, too. But listen to me, why am I talking like this? This isn't me, Mack, or is it now?" The blond diplomatist–secret agent sat back with a brooding frown. "In Roatán a while back," he finally went on, "I became a bit too friendly with an Anglican Reverend and his family. And do you know what the Reverend told me? He judged me harshly, Mack, saying that I'd made all the Central American vices my own, and taken none of the virtues. Drink, lechery, conspiracy, mendacity, this so-called *machismo*. All right, then. So you tell me, Mack, what are the virtues?"

"Knowing how to watch your mouth," growled Mack, mastering himself though he felt turned inside out by Bludyar's vile revelation, which still hovered over him like a giant invisible horsefly getting ready to take another savage bite. "Respect and reserve toward a deserving lady . . . *Ehh* . . . You've probably noticed how the poor will share whatever they have with a stranger. Great and stoic endurance. Those are some of the virtues of the virtuous here. There must be more."

No surprise then, that in the widened, deepened, fortified cave where the Indian rebel leader and *chuchkajawib* Juan Diego Paclom had his headquarters, Mack was received as an Emissary of Her Majesty the Queen of England, and called, despite his own aboriginal features, "Don Mister Lord Englishman Jefe." Mack had arrived with an old Nahón peddler's cart filled with rifles, hauled up the mountain by the rebels that night. A shrine in their cave headquarters featured a portrait of Queen Victoria. Against the mountain cold, the doe-eyed youngish *chuchkajawib* wore a serape of heavy black wool, belted at the waist, and wrapped around his head a sort of piratical kerchief of the same material. "I know that your Queen speaks to God," he said to Mack, "but do you?" Mack admitted that he did not. Rubén Abensur interjected, "Mack is a messenger, Don Juan Diego, of the Empress of the Indians and Prime Minister Disraeli." He'd already informed Mack that the *chuchkajawib* and his followers believed that Queen Victoria had formed an alliance with the Indians to drive the Spanish speakers and all foreigners but the English from the country. The *chuchkajawib* thought all English speakers belonged to the British Queen's Empire. High on the mountainside, the rebels had a camp in a little wooded ravine directly beneath the cave, and there Mack had seen the tatterdemalion warriors hardening wooden clubs and the tips of long wooden lances over fires, and others sharpening their machetes, and sitting on the ground fashioning crude bullets for their old muzzle-loading rifles from thick pieces of telegraph wire cut down by rebel marauders; a small contingent of women was busy at the usual domestic chores. The rebels had last engaged government troops three weeks before, and in that battle had lost nearly half their men.

The next day three monstrous-looking individuals arrived at the rebel camp. Their skin was like white elephant hide, they wore only loincloths despite the chill mountain air, and carried old rifles and machetes. But their skins peeled off: they were made of caucho sap, which the three Indios had collected from wild India-rubber trees in the lowland forests and smeared on their bodies and allowed to harden; so worn, the sacred substance was delivered to the cave.

A crucified Jesucristo, painstakingly fashioned from inflated intestines and bladders, was displayed against a wall of the cave. Scattered over the floor beneath this garish and seemingly pagan Crucifixion were smaller examples of these air-filled idols, in human and animal form. Studying the nearly translucent, blood-speckled inflated limbs of this unique sculpture of the Savior, Mack had the terrifying intuition that they were made from the entrails of a captured enemy soldier, or even a German plantation owner. He was relieved when Rubén Abensur told him that of course they were not, that only animal entrails were used. For the Crucifixion a peccary's intestines and bladder had been used, inflated with "the breath of the ancestors," and artfully twisted and tied together with some plant thread by the *chuchkajawib*.

Later, amid acrid black clouds of burning caucho, the Perpetually Risen Jesucristo-Father was floated into a steady wind blowing out over the vast valley; also some of the smaller figures, called Little Romans, Little Germans, and Little Hebrews, and others representing guardian ancestor-spirit animals, such as jaguars and eagles. It was wondrous to see how the air currents, as if obeying the *chuchkajawib*, seemed to form and prolong a trail of black smoke, over which the airborne Crucifixion and parade of tiny grotesques traveled into the extinguishing evening light toward the colorful Pacific sunset, beyond the blackening mountains and valleys.

"They travel the umbilical road joining the Underworld to the Celestial region," explained Rubén Abensur, and then he intoned: *"Many of those who sleep in Earth's dust shall awake."*

Hopefully, thought Mack, this strange spectacle fills our enemies with unease; it would me. Though, of course, however arresting these rites were to witness, he regarded them with total skepticism. Rubén Abensur's own excited religious speculations, which he claimed aspired to a "spherical synthesis" of certain strains of Hebrew, Mayan, and Christian mysticism, might be deranged or brilliant, but Mack doubted they would ever have any theological importance for anyone outside this cave. Abensur was another of those who believed that the Maya were descended from the Lost Tribes. The native religion they'd evolved over centuries of wandering in the American wilderness and eventual settlement in Mesoamérica, the Hebrew teacher from Tangier explained, still held many echoes of the original one brought from the Holy Land. The Spaniards had conquered the Indians but had not, of course, vanquished their religion. Instead, the Indians had adapted Christianity as a system of symbols and rites within which to hide their own beliefs—just as one might revere an image made of intestines, elucidated Rubén Abensur, not necessarily for the image itself but because it has been inflated with the breath of the Nantat, the ancestors, the true makers, who fill the *chuchkajawib*'s own lungs and guide his hands as he inflates, twists, and ties—thus it was not mere idolatry. What if some of these Christian influences could be lessened or even removed or at least also balanced with Hebraic ones? The Christians situated God in the sky, but they confused earth and everything earthly with the

Devil—the Hebrew mystic did not. The God and gods of the Indios were inseparable from their land, but now that they were losing that land, they would need a portable God to survive.

"Our new synthesis might take centuries to develop, Mack," said Rubén Abensur, "or perhaps our God will suddenly part the seas of our confusion and ignorance and show us the quickest way. The Indios place their great Tree of Creation in the Milky Way, its roots in the Underworld and in ritual, but where should they look for the Tree of Knowledge? In the symbolism of some of our Hebrew folk traditions, as in the Sayings of the Fathers, the parrot denotes purity, the pelican love, the hawk alert senses, the leopard strength, and so on. Don Juan Diego, of course, has his own way of revering and summoning the animal spirits. Mack, I feel that Don Juan Diego and I are discovering our new language by recovering lost ones. In the old days, from Poland to Africa, before most turned their backs on the mystic ways, rabbis worked wonders too, just as the *chuchkajawib* does now."

After a long silence, during which the Hebrew teacher stared off as if he was finishing his monologue in silence, Mack finally asked, "The Hebrews consider the parrot a symbol of purity, Don Rubén? Why?"

For once, Rubén Abensur did not have a ready answer. "Because parrots faithfully repeat what they hear, never altering any word or letter," he said hesitantly. "Or perhaps there is some other reason . . . which I have forgotten."

Mack was a good listener. In even these streams of baffling nonsense, he fished for anything sensible, anything he might be able to use. Rubén Abensur, in the adventurous spirit of the era, was a democratic innovator, a decentralizer of religions. But his fanatical talk was also like a ghostly mockery of what Mack truly valued. Mack, a temperate Roman Catholic, was a seeker, but not a religious seeker. Where, for example, in all this madness was a lurking epiphany that might lead to a discovery of *petroleum jelly!* Mack accidentally stepped on some smaller-than-usual figurine fashioned from the inflated intestines of some also tiny animal, and it exploded beneath his boot like a steam-filled sausage, making a popping sound.

"It could be," Rubén Abensur abruptly added with a resigned shrug, "that our peoples have different ideas of righteousness."

The next day Don Juan Diego Paclom led Mack through the network of caves and tunnels to the heart of the sacred mountain. For much of the way, the two men snaked forward on their bellies, pulling themselves along on their elbows, through long, pitch-dark tunnels of rock and clay. The smoke of smoldering copal incense, flowing backward from the censer that the *chuchkajawib* carried aloft by cords wound around one fist, burned in Mack's eyes. They were also bringing food in sacks tied to the back of their belts, slung over their shoulders. Was the food destined for some ritual, or was the *chuchkajawib* intending a long stay? Mack didn't know. Finally he spied a reddish glow, far away in the narrow end of the tunnel they were crawling through—a faint glow that looked as if it might be radiating upward from some even deeper well or pit of bubbling lava within the mountain. That must be it, he reasoned, the sacred shrine at the Mouth to the Underworld. When they reached the end of the tunnel and were about to emerge into that mysterious dark red light, the *chuchkajawib* stopped to light more incense and to chant incantations. Mack, flattened behind him, was waiting with mounting impatience when he heard a groan deep in the earth, a rumbling that spread through the mountain in every direction as if Mack himself was its source; he felt the stony earth beneath him buck, as if somehow giving a hard kick, then actually wobble like a very thick pudding—loose stones rattled down the tunnel. Mack's terror and claustrophobia were absolute. It was an earthquake, and this was where he was going to die, deep inside the sacred mountain. He clung to the earth like a tiny wet feather. But the tremor passed. Maybe somewhere behind the tunnel had collapsed, and they were trapped, and death was only going to find them more slowly. But Don Juan Diego didn't give the least sign of being concerned. When the *chuchkajawib* was finished with his rite, he went forward out of the tunnel like a popped cork, and Mack followed unsteadily, clambering to his feet inside the mysteriously illuminated chamber. His clothes were drenched in perspiration, and he was gasping for air. The source of the reddish light, he saw now, was a crimson glass kerosene lamp in the shape of the Sacred Heart. Don Juan Diego was lighting candles. The usual small pagan statues and stone idols surrounded them, but there was one that surprised Mack: a large statue of a nun, not an Indian statue but one in the style of the Catholic Church—he had no idea which nun saint it represented, but he silently prayed, Madrecita, please stop the tremors, keep the tunnel open, please get me out of here alive, so that from now on I can live only by the Savior's example . . . Behind the statue was the airy blackness of another narrow cave opening: the Mouth to the Underworld, its earthen lip strewn with evergreen boughs and withered fruits and flowers.

"This is the convent, Don Señor Mack," said Don Juan Diego, his eyes shining with a trusting candor. "And that woman, do you know who she is?" He gestured toward the nun statue, but then, noticing Mack's shaken state, he laughed. "Are you afraid, Don Señor Mack?"

"That was an earthquake, no?" croaked Mack.

"Down here below, there are many earthquakes," the *chuchkajawib* matter-of-factly answered. "This is where the Nantat, our ancestors, live, and our sisters also." Returning his attention to the statue, he said, "This is María Candalyax. She is the Spirit Wife. Or else she is the Santa Virgen María. Those are some of her names. She wove the night stars on her loom. Sometimes she is a bad woman. She steals men from their wives, she seduced Juan the Baptist and drove him mad—isn't that true, Madrecita? She came to hide here after the bad government closed down the house in the city where she lived with her sisters. When Madrecita María is living with her sisters she is good, sí pues, but when she escapes, the problems come." The *chuchkajawib* bowed stiffly toward the statue and said, "Hola, Madrecita. This is Don Señor Mack Englishman Jefe, sent by the Queen Victoria to help us in our war." He turned toward the cave opening behind her and loudly clucked out some words in his Indian language. Presently Mack heard a stirring inside that darkness, and a soft whispery sound, and the faintest thump of footsteps approaching over hard earth. Five human figures appeared, draped entirely in black. They stood inside the little opening to the Underworld, the lip of which came up to their waists. Two carried long, slightly bent tapers. Only their hands were visible, and they were not the hands of men. They were dressed, Mack realized with a wave of renewed unease, in shapeless black robes resembling the habits of nuns, with black veils hiding their faces. They spoke nearly in unison, with the soft voices of timid women: "Buenas noches, Don Señor Padre Chuchkajawib Juan Diego. At your service."

These were the monjitas, Juan Diego Paclom explained to Mack, who married the spirit *chuchkajawibs* among the ancestors: "Night and day, they pray for us. Their prayers keep us safe—though not always, pues no . . . We've brought you food, mis hermanitas." The black robes were made of wool, the veils of a lighter fabric; each wore a long black scapular draped over her shoulders, with familiar Indian symbols embroidered in red and yellow thread. Elsewhere throughout these mountains, undoubtedly at that very moment, shaman-priests in caves and at other sacred sights were gravely performing their native religious rites according to orthodox custom; even Mack might have found it fascinating to observe any of those. If he were to survive and report what he was witnessing here to a newspaper, it would be as factual as anything ever printed; but would anybody believe it? Was he coming to the end of his nerves and all sound sense? Chills were climbing up his arms and the back of his neck and over his scalp. These fraudulent nuns had brought back a memory. Before, bemused disbelief and lonely, sentimental lust had filled that memory like all the light and shadow inside a single room; now he was propelled into another room, filled with something other than disbelief—not the opposite, not *belief,* but something else: in that former room, dingy and windowless, a creamy-skinned young whore, with eyebrows like golden wheat, and brunette hair that in this almost unanimously black-haired country was almost unanimously hailed as blond, and full pink lips, and honey-hued brown eyes, had told him that she was a nun too. Mack had never seen her before that night, but she claimed to have been working in the transient little bordello at the Hotel Imperio for more than a month (during that previous month, when he'd still, of course, been with the Italians, and was feeling depressed over his failed courtship of María de las Nieves, Mack hadn't been going out at night). The bordello at the Hotel Imperio, though operated with the collusion of Doña Carlota and Police Chief Pratt, was allegedly staffed by a group of "self-employed" Yankee women from San Francisco who were visiting the country for just a few months. But when Mack arrived, he found only this "blond" young "American girl" waiting on the red velvet couch. A mulatta from Belize sold a small selection of liquors from behind the tiny, deserted bar. They were the only people in the little upstairs parlor, to which Mack had been lured by lonely homesickness and a desire to fornicate in English; he'd learned from Mr. Doveton that professional prostitutes from the U.S.A. could be had there. This girl, however, made no attempt to speak English, and only the very subjective hue of her hair qualified her as a Yankee. Her sleepy-looking yet quietly fetching eyes, her easy smile, her obvious lusciousness, the pleasing gentleness of her young voice, the clotted bile of defeat and disillusion weighing inside him, all motivated Mack's offer to go with her to a room.

"You mean to say," asked Mack after her curious confidence, as she lay warm and naked in his arms, "that you were one of the monjitas expelled from the convents a few years ago?" When she'd told him that she was a nun, he'd immediately thought, of course, with a sad pang, of María de las Nieves.

"No, Mack," said the young whore, who called herself Conchita. "I mean that I'm still a cloistered monja now, a novice, actually. I live in a convent, a secret convent here in this city." And she smiled at him in a challenging way.

"Ha-*hah!*" he burst out, finding her assertion adorable, her lighthearted if bizarre playfulness the perfect solvent for his bitterness; yes, he was grateful and glad that he'd come here tonight. "You're funny, Conchita! And I suppose this place is the secret convent, and that only nuns are employed here."

"I knew you wouldn't believe me, Mack." Her voice was high and melodic, and on the verge of laughter. "No matter what I say, you still won't believe me. But I don't care!"

"Bueno," he said flatly. "So, you're a nun, you come here to work, and then you go back to your convent and repent. Right?" Mack had a crazy idea: maybe he could fall in love with this beautiful young woman, in whom some degree of innocence and playfulness remained so lively despite her denigrated existence. Was she that mythical being of brothel lore, a girl a man might want to free from here, marry, and take back to New York, where no one would ever know her past, where she would excel as a wife and mother—? Or else was she a sort of free-spirited nymphomaniac with a delusional mind, promising only inevitable despair and disgrace? She didn't seem newly driven into this sordid life, frightened and grieving. She seemed at peace, and anything but hardened. She unveiled her buoyant, custard-hued breasts with the air of a girl who likes to admire herself in a mirror, and even in her lovemaking, Conchita gave and took pleasure with a seemingly carefree delight, free of low lewdness, leaving him feeling more satisfied by the act of physical love than ever before; like many romantic bachelors, Mack had yet to make love to any woman who didn't sell her caresses. "Don't feel so bad, Conchita," Mack continued earnestly. "I know that repentance isn't a bad thing. But I'd bet you have less to repent of than most people do."

"The sacrament of penitence is a divine blessing, Mack, because it allows us to seek and work toward perfection and God," she said. "But it's not how you think. I don't go back and forth between here and the convent. I'm in both places at once." She smiled benignly. "Yes, that's right, now I'm here with you, but I'm also back in the convent, deep in prayer. The first corporeal me is back there, praying to our Virgencita del Carmen. Anyone seeing me only sees a novice deep in prayer."

"Hah," said Mack, caressing the back of her head, his fingers wound in her luxuriant hair. "All right, if you say so, mi amor. And right now I'm back in New York, a wealthy manufacturer living in his mansion with his beautiful wife who—by gosh, could it be you? Why—it *is* you, Conchita! Hahaha. You must go to confession, eh? What does your priest say about all of this?"

"Oh, Mack, the poor padre!" She giggled. "Once a week I leave our hiding place to walk to Jocotenango to see the same padre who used to confess me in the convent. But as soon as the padrecito sees me coming, he exclaims, Oh no, Sor Gloria, not again, I don't want to hear it, please go away! *Jijiji.* But he does accept my confession. The padre does believe now that our Señor in heaven understands how desperately we need money. The widow who takes care of us can no longer feed us. Someday, we will abandon this country, the arrangements are being made, but that too will require money. So God has graced me with the means of transporting myself by prayer to this place, where I can earn more money, more quickly, than any other way. Every morning I hand the money to our Madre Priora, who only once asked how I came by it, and now prays for me. Here is something else I'm going to tell you that I suppose you won't believe. In my true corporeal body, my virginity is still intact. Virgins are angels on earth, Mack, just as angels are virgins in heaven. Nevertheless, the padre says I have the seven demons inside of me, and will soon have to undergo exorcisms, as La Magdalena did."

"OK, you silly girl, that's enough," said Mack. "You're scaring me. I like you, Conchita, in a way that I've never liked anyone I've ever met in one of these places—not that I've frequented them so much, you know? Please, I don't want it to turn out that you really are crazy. All right? Promise me you're not crazy."

"No. Really, I'm not crazy. I promise, Mack." The phenomenon she was describing, she told him, was called mystical bilocation, and could be read about in many theological treatises and saints' lives: that of San Alfonso María de Ligorio, for example, who while he dozed in his chair in Arienzo was also in Rome saying final rites at the bedside of Pope Clemente XIV, there being no doubt that he was seen in both places at the same time. How did God divide the vital fluid of mortal life so that it could manifest in two places at once? Bilocation was a supernatural state, brought about by prayer, and an act of Divine Will by which God helped people who otherwise were prevented by earthly circumstances from bringing comfort or doing good, as was her own case.

"Basta, ya, I believe you, enough of this," laughed Mack. "Listen, I had a friend who used to be a novice nun too, right up until the day they closed the convents. María de las Nieves is her name."

Conchita sat up in bed; with her hand on his chest, she looked excitedly down at Mack through her falling hair. "Do you mean la Sorita San Jorge, Mack?" she exclaimed. "Of course I know her! We were novices in the convent together. If it's the same girl, then this really is a little miracle! How is she? Oh please tell me she's doing well. Is she married? Does she have children? I saw her once, you know, in the street, more than a year ago . . ."

Mack realized that Conchita really was a former nun who, falling into hard circumstances after the secularization, had turned to prostitution, hiding her shame inside an angelic delusion; poor deranged broken sweetheart. Guilt and self-loathing awoke inside him, bringing a taste of cold cigar ash to his tongue. He answered tersely that he didn't really know how María de las Nieves was doing, he hadn't seen her in a while, but no, she wasn't married. Had she really known her in the convent, he asked, betraying some impatience and mistrust, or was she just playing with him?

"Does your María de las Nieves always look like this?" The pretty young whore imitated a blankly fixated glower, and Mack laughed despite himself. "And is she very allergic to wool? And does she like to make herself sneeze with it?" "Eh? *Sneeze?* Cómo?" And she told Mack a story about

María de las Nieves's allergy to wool, and about her way of making herself sneeze with pieces of wool, and how this vice had led to her imprisonment in the convent—. "It's fun though, you know, that's the strange thing," said Conchita. "It would be very sinful for me to do it in the convent, but I can, claro, when I'm here." And she giggled again. "Pues, I'll show you. Right now, mi amorcito." At the foot of their narrow bed in the small lamp-lit room was a balled-up blanket of the type made by the Indios of Momostenango from sheep's wool, heavy, coarse, and hairy. Mack watched, a little alarmed, as the girl delicately probed the inside of her nostril with a single bristle of wool pulled from the blanket, while her body stretched as if reaching with every nerve for the spasm that finally came with her sneeze, and she fell back onto the bed laughing, a hand cupped over her nose. Mack, reinflamed, tried to climb on top of her, but she pushed against his chest with both hands, and twisted lithely out from under him.

"First you try it, Mack, you make yourself sneeze," she said. "It's dangerous, you know. After a while, you just can't stop doing it! You sneeze so much that you begin to smell something, like a gas leaking from your own brain, with a bit of a sulfur smell. You know what that is? It's the smell of Satan!"

Well, Mack would not do that. He would not grope for a little hair of wool in a blanket, and stick it up his nose—no, not even if she picked it for him. What? *No*, he refused. Even if she—. Hahaha. What, *you*—? OK, OK. But only once, Conchita! He watched her carefully combing over the blanket with her fingers until she found what she was looking for. Then it was not so bad, was it, to have her lying atop him, her breasts pressed against his chest, his hands clasping her round buttocks, her cheap-perfume-smelling hair coolly falling around him while her warm glowing face hovered over his, concentrating, and her hand, thumb and index finger pinching-twirling a sharp piece of wool, her pinkie out like a tiny wing, descending toward his nose—. Well. The little tickle, the gurgling singsong coming from her throat as she concentrated like an artist on her tickling, while he now also concentrated on slowly rubbing her down there, the warmth spreading through his face as she—*no!* Awful and unmanly! Limbs rigid with revulsion, he grabbed her wrist and shoved it aside. Smell of Satan indeed! Crazy putita! No more of that! Then he made her make love like a woman to a man (after agreeing to pay for another hour).

Maybe it was only the suggestion of wool, he thought, that connected this moment to that past one, as if by an invisible but bristling and numinous correspondence, annihilating time and space. He remembered María de las Nieves on the night of the opera, her fresh and radiant skin, her briefly adoring eyes, and the sacred sweetness of the emotion she'd aroused in him, which somewhere in this world must still exist, not just as memory but as pure emotion, like caucho sap mystically restored inside one secret, green tree hidden deep in the tropical forest and which someday, if he got out of here alive, he would go searching for. Mack was on the verge of tears. Was María de las Nieves really pregnant? By whom was she pregnant? Was there any hope that Bludyar's information was not true? Why should he hope? What, now, was the right thing to hope for?

A monjita who'd briefly disappeared back into the secret cloister at the Mouth to the Underworld now returned carrying in her hands a fleshy sphere, nearly translucent, tautly inflated—the bladder of some sort of animal, Mack deduced—which she lay into the open palms of Don Juan Diego Paclom. The *chuchkajawib* explained to Mack that this *globo* had been inflated with the breath of the Nantat, the ancestor spirits; he undid its knotted umbilical, swiftly brought it to his lips, and let it deflate into his own mouth and lungs. The symbolic meaning of this ritual struck Mack as being, for a change, overt.

Now he remembered how Conchita had lifted the India-rubber condom sheath to her lips and blown into it, slowly filling it with her breath, until suddenly it slipped from her grasp, briefly spurting forward into the air as it deflated and fell onto the bed.

# Chapter 7

𝒪n January, María García Granados had sent Martí a brief note: *It's been six days since your return, and you haven't come to see me. Why are you evading a visit? I have no resentment toward you, because you always spoke with sincerity to me of your moral situation of being promised to la señorita Zayas Bazán. I beg you to come quickly. Tu niña.*

Not one of the letters José Martí's fiancée sent him from Mexico during the previous year survives; undoubtedly hundreds, maybe even thousands of the letters he received during his lifetime have been lost. But Martí saved this desperate note, tucked inside the embroidered, scented pillow she'd given him just before he left for Mexico to be married. The note is often cited by the Cuban hero's hagiographers as proof that he maintained an honorably chaste relationship with "la niña" throughout— they were *just friends*—exonerating him of any culpability in her unhappy end; though he never exonerated himself, and gave perpetual life to his remorse in a poem. But go back and look at that note. Who or what is really there? Behind every phrase there is a shadow. *I beg you to come quickly.* Look at the one hundred and ninety-three lines of poetry Martí scrawled in María García Granados's album: *I love the beautiful disorder, so much more beautiful / since you, the splendid María / shook your hair down over your shoulders / the way a palm tree, throwing off its HOOD, would do it!*

After the newly wed Martí returned from Mexico, he stopped visiting the García Granados home; before he'd gone there almost daily to play chess with the former president, always anticipating the chance of some close conversation with his oldest daughter. General García Granados, who would also die of tuberculosis, only four months after his daughter, encountered Martí one afternoon at the Jocotenango fair, and invited him—with a gentle note of urgency and admonishment that was only to inflame Martí's fantastic remorse through the years—to bring his wife, Carmen, to the house to meet the family. Martí never went. He did have one last glimpse of María alive when, as he was walking past the García Granados home with his wife, a movement drew his eye toward the balcony of her room and he saw the Persian blinds in the window swaying as she withdrew.

He didn't visit or seek out María de las Nieves, either, during those first months after he'd returned married. Near the very end of his time there, though, he did finally come to see her, just when she'd never been so in need of such a visit in her life. Fourteen years later, Martí mailed María de las Nieves an inscribed copy of *Versos Sencillos,* and she read that poem about the niña who died of love, and her first visceral reaction was to feel taken aback by its strange impropriety, and then pity, for him and also for her late rival. She didn't immediately think about herself, didn't stop and reread the disconcertingly morbid poem to reawaken any echo of her former bathetic longing; her life had moved on, she was by then the harried mother of two children, and laying the slender volume on her lap, she forced herself to sit quietly and remember back to that time, which may not seem like such a long time, though just think of the difference between being a woman of thirty-one and a girl of seventeen. She remembered the opera benefit for the Italians and María García Granados's face in the dimly gaslit shadows of her box like a pale light that gives off no heat (was her illness really provoked by a broken heart? would she really have lived if Martí hadn't gone back to Mexico to fulfill his promise of marriage to the Cuban?) and Martí's nervous glances from within his box across the auditorium toward hers, and she remembered her own misery. Mack had had every right to detest her that night, sitting there sulking and blaming him for having made a spectacle of her too, when she'd leaned over the rail to cut the rope and heard those scattered drunken shouts and whistles of mockery. She who'd been courted by a blond British diplomatist; who'd held the secret of her kiss with the brilliant young Cuban who even at that moment, his beautiful new wife sitting beside him, was reawakening and fanning desire and jealousies throughout that rabid coliseum; she who had never before even been to an opera was *embarrassed* to be there with poor Mack Chinchilla. At intermission Mr. Doveton, the former Confederate envoy, stepped into the box and, steadily smiling down at her, asked grandly: "How did this young beauty become so brown?" and then winked at Mack and raised his glass of champagne to her and said, "From being so frequently toasted." Mack forced a chortle, and lamely bantered, "There is your chivalry of the Old South." She fumed, hating him. Not until they were in the carriage and the torturous night was nearly over did Mack say, "I'm sorry if Mr. Doveton's flattery offended you. I should have spoken with more sarcasm, at least. I think he is awful too, you know." Faced with her light shrug and continuing silence, Mack added, "When I introduced you it seemed as if he already knew your name." And she answered, "It didn't just seem. He spoke it even before you did." Mack stammered, "Yes he did, didn't he. How is that, I wonder." And she answered that she'd seen him come into the legation on a few occasions to meet with Minister Gastreel. After a moment Mack said, "The British took the side of the Confederacy during the war, so that is not surprising." And she withdrew into her silence for the rest of the ride home, knowing that she was tormenting Mack and telling herself that she did not care.

Soon after, María García Granados fell ill, and was confined to her bed. But people fell ill all the time; usually they recovered. Nobody sensed a Sainte-Bueve-like incipience hovering over her decline, preparing to record it for all time. Didn't she get better for a while? Didn't she at least go back to attending day classes at the Izaguirres' school? It wasn't until decades later, with the first publication and wide dissemination of Martí's *Collected Works*, that people in La Pequeña Paris realized that a poem connected them to the Cuban Apostle's immortal glory—that their proximity to the events narrated in that poem, mainly characterized by gossip, connected them, making even gossip seem like an extension of the poetic ecstasy in which they imagined the poem to have been written, for weren't such poems always written in such a state? And they began searching their faded memories for anything they could remember about the tragic idyll that had played itself out in the same schoolrooms, elegant parlors, and gardens they too had traversed in their youth. *I can only say that Martí was human*, more than one now wrote, forgivingly, and for posterity, with tolerant wisdom and hindsight, as if they had always known that the adolescent girl's having died of tuberculosis was a ruse and that the cause of her death was what the martyred hero had finally admitted it to be in his poem. One diplomat and writer, who did indeed attend the Cuban Izaguirres' progressive school at the same time as María, though he was twelve years younger, the equivalent of a kindergartner to her senior, wrote in a book published half a century later: *We, her schoolmates, saw how María García Granados languished in plain sight. She was never a noisy bell, but a tinkling chime of resonant crystal.* Despite their age difference, he was able to recall: *She knew about a lot of things, and referred to them gracefully. She relied more on narrative exposition than on analysis. Possibly her kindhearted ingenuousness extinguished her critical sense. Now she had completely changed: the little crystal bell no longer chimed. The schoolgirl was quiet and sad. I saw her once, at that time, at the edge of a pila, as the fountains from the colonial era found in every home were called. With a stem of roses she was stirring the water in which her large eyes were abstractly fixated, as if dwelling on that impossible ocean the beloved had placed between them. One day our schoolyard, always as noisy and cheerful as an aviary at the beginning of the day, was cold and silent. The older students were weeping, huddling together, speaking in low voices. We, the younger ones, began to understand. That day classes were suspended; we picked flowers for the compañera who would never return. One or two days later Martí came to the Izaguirres' school. The older muchachas, the deceased's schoolmates, as they had so many times before, crowded around. They sobbed, listening to him. He made as if to go; they tried to detain him. He, always so gallant and willing to bend over backward to comply, was now unable to. He'd come in search of something he was unable to find. When he left, he was paler than when he'd arrived, and the look of anguish in his expression had intensified. His recently founded home was not the proper place to unburden himself of his sorrow. On the contrary, there he had to conceal it, and build a little nest for it in his heart. He looked for his friend Palma. The Bayamés Bard lived in a pension owned by las señoras González*—there Palma recited the poetic elegy he'd just composed in honor of the dead girl while Martí *listened in ecstasy.*

Only a month or so before, at a Saturday program of lectures and recitals, a *sabatina*, held at the Instituto Nacional de Señoritas, that María de las Nieves, finally unable to resist this chance to tour the grounds of her old convent, had attended, she'd encountered Doña Cristina and asked after her eldest daughter. "María is still a little-little ill, la pobrecita," said Doña Cristina, her anxiety evident in her softening eyes and drawn expression. María de las Nieves expressed surprise; she'd thought María had recovered. Hadn't she gone back to school? (If María de las Nieves had been given the choice between her job at the legation or going to school, which would she have chosen? She would probably have answered school, without necessarily being truthful.) Doña Cristina said, "She did get well. But then she went bathing, and that same little-night, she fell ill again. That's why I so wanted to come this evening, María de las Nieves, to this edifice which in the time of our Madre Melchora was always a place to find consolation for any tribulation. Now, have you noticed? Even our Madrecita's peach tree is gone. And instead of her villancicos, we are going to hear a lecture about magnetic rocks, and witness the inauguration of the modern lavatory facilities, to the accompaniment of, no doubt, I'm sorry but not unafraid to say, an insipid speech by my successor . . . But as you well know, Madrecita had a biting sense of humor." Her successor? It dawned on María de las Nieves that Paquita was going to be there too. Should she flee? She would not! She made a mental note to herself to bring a box of candies to the García Granados house for María the next day. Doña Cristina had taken her hands in hers, and her expression had changed: "But you, María de las Nieves, how lovely you look, such a pretty light in your eyes, and that radiance in your cheeks. I have six daughters, you know, and not a little expertise in these matters. Mis Nievecitas, are you in love?" Oh yes! Yes, she was! But she answered, "Of course I am not, Doña Cristina!"

*Give me a thousand kisses, then a hundred; then another thousand, then a second hundred; after those, even a thousand more; then, a hundred—.* That is from a poem by the Roman Catallus, mi amor. Tomorrow I will see you, King of my Heart, King of my Everything. Tu niña. —That morning she'd sent María Chon to deliver that note, written on a sheet of German stationery, to Don Lico, the legation's concierge, on her way to the market.

Nowadays it seemed as if every other private thought she had brought a warm flush to her cheeks. Who couldn't see the inward dreaming in her eyes; or her wakening flashes of consternation and nervous glowers, as if worried that anyone could read her thoughts; or the furtive life in her lips, reliving pleasures, tiny nibbles, tastes of salt and honey, her lips pulled in, trying to hide what they knew, closing into a bud, as if in deep musing thought, and giving her away even more! María de las Nieves really was a woman now, an overjoyed member of the secretly sinning multitude, worried only about getting caught. What did she care about Paquita, or about her old convent, or about her sick friend, or even about Pepe Martí? Now here she was, in this same school hall where, as schoolgirls, she and Paquita had once undergone public examinations in front of an audience that had included President General García Granados and El Antricristo, sitting now alongside Doña Cristina, waiting for the current Primera Dama to make her entrance. She and Paquita hadn't exchanged a word in five years, since that day when she'd crossed from school to cloister—for five years she'd avoided any encounter where she and Paquita would be forced to speak to each other. She'd long ago stopped questioning why that should be so. Her resolve had become something deeper than habit, beyond conviction, hate, or love. But now she was excited to see her childhood companion, the despot's fertile young wife. Truly excited to see her! As if her own happiness and secret pride protected her from anyone who came into her orbit. Or else because her own sinning made her imagine that they now shared some cozily dissolute and tolerant bond.

La Primera Dama entered the hall, surrounded by soldiers, moving like a beautiful storm wrestled into fabulous fabrics and jewels. Paquita seemed taller than before, and her figure was astonishingly statuesque, more womanly but also more slender; captive electricity sizzled in her darkly shining eyes, in her opulent hair, beneath her blanched complexion. She looked so regal, so remote, so full of expensive female grandeur yet so airily light, cold, fragile, cultivated—; yet she radiated a lonely animal heat. Doña Cristina murmured, almost contritely, that Doña Francisca's long stay in New York seemed to have served her well. But the sight of her pierced María de las Nieves's heart in the most unexpected way. Just a moment ago, she'd been parading through her own sunny meadow, and now it was as if she'd tripped and fallen into a deep hole and everything was murky bewilderment. Poor Paquita. My poor darling. Why poor Paquita? She didn't know why. But she felt her chest cracking open with compassion. Did Paquita see her? Was she only averting her eyes from this corner of the hall because she'd already spotted her prestigious predecessor? La Primera Dama was offering words of welcome to the audience now. It couldn't be denied that she spoke with a rote charm. She'd prepared a little speech on the Spirit of the Age. "Now that the telegraph has united the world," said Paquita, "it is as if we all share the same intelligent brain. The brain of the modern world. Then it's good to remember that the first message sent by Señor Morse by telegraph from Washington to Baltimore was *What hath God wrought*—" In perfectly enunciated English she pronounced those words, which she then translated, and repeated in English: "What hath God wrought?" And she let the question hang—but was she actually going to attempt to answer it? "What hath God wrought," Paquita repeated, as if she were only giving an English lesson. Imperturbable, speaking with poised simplicity, Paquita went on: Once, this had been a convent school. Yes, a cave of dark ignorance, according to some. Now it was a school where young women were initiated into the world of modern things, of science and practical knowledge. But she herself had studied here, when it was a convent school—. Paquita's voice ever so slightly trembled. The nuns had made their share of mistakes, but she wasn't ashamed of the education she'd received here; she'd learned many useful things. Then it was good to remember Señor Morse's well-aimed question, with which he'd introduced the modern age. It was wrong to think such a question was not in keeping with the Spirit of the Age. It was a good question to ask oneself every single day, La Primera Dama told them, her voice rising on a surge of emotional conviction. Doña Cristina regarded María de las Nieves with a look of surprised sympathy, eyebrows raised and lips pursed. People are a mystery, said the look. But everything has an explanation too: "The assassination plot very much affected her, I think," the former Primera Dama whispered. The current one now rambled on a bit, mostly about the exemplary education women received in New York, which was where the school's director, Miss James, had been educated, and then Paquita introduced thin, tousled, fretfully chirpy Miss James, and to clattering applause took her seat in the center of the first row, two soldiers crouched on the floor in front of her feet, two in the seats directly behind her, others positioned around the edges of the audience. There were musical recitals, duets, trios; poetry recitals; a student read her winning essay on Padre Las Casas and the aborigines; there was a magic lantern show, with two schoolgirls taking turns explaining each image in each sequence: astronomical charts, African animals, London architecture, a tour of the Suez Canal . . . María de las Nieves, slouching deeper in her chair, swam back into her reveries, and a ditty she'd invented to go with her pleasure made her smile to herself, and maybe as she imagined singing the silly-scandalous words into his ear, they silently formed on her lips, or maybe her eyebrows only twitched up and down a little—but she sensed that she'd drawn Doña Cristina's attention and she looked sideways and stared into Doña Cristina's eyes for a moment as if in mutual alarm, though probably only María de las Nieves was alarmed, and finally the older women smiled gently, and gave her arm a little pat, and looked toward the front again, and

María de las Nieves sifted through the possible meanings she'd discerned in Doña Cristina's expression . . . flushed with shame, she vowed to stop thinking about him until . . . until, tomorrow . . . because this was how you became depraved . . . mental discipline, which you learned how to practice in this very building, María de las Nieves . . . Señor Gelabert of La Sociedad Económica was rising from his seat to give his talk, which would close the program, on magnetic energy and recent scientific experiments with magnets . . . Within a decade, the amateur geologist told them, man would be employing magnets to accurately predict earthquakes. No other part of the globe would benefit from this advance more than theirs. Imagine being able to know an hour or so in advance that an earthquake was imminent!

Where before in the Convent of Nuestra Señora de Belén a wall and locked door had separated the school from the cloister, there was now a wide passageway. (Another Suez Canal! Yes, it was a Century of Perforations! María de las Nieves's silent witticism made her face burn.) From the school, there was no longer a way into the church, the former choirs or crypt; the church was still standing but was entered now from the street. Even all the niches in the corridors had been filled in and plastered over and covered by the same white or pale green paint that coated every wall. Schoolbooks and stationery were now stored in the Chapel of Death. But the old dormitory was the new dormitory. And the towering amate and avocado trees in the old school yard were still the same, their dense shade still hiding decades of schoolgirls' whispered secrets.

"These lamps burn all the night," said Miss James, whose Spanish syntax made it impossible not to recall the far more robust Sor Gertrudis, "so no have sinister aspect the dark, and without feel afraid, little girls go any hour." They were being shown the new communal lavatory, which was entered through a grand pair of oaken doors, high and arched. "And is well ventilated, so no bad smell," said Miss James, pointing up at the high windows in the walls. "Windows in north, south, east, and west, open to all winds." María de las Nieves had decided that the lavatory must be an entirely new construction, but then she remembered that this had been the classroom of the free day school for poor girls; radically renovated, it looked as if even the roof had been raised. The latrine ran the length of the lavatory's northern wall, subdivided by private stalls, and now the Yankee school director was explaining how a strong current of water was piped along the bottom of the latrine and out into a small garden patio on the other side of the wall. Paquita, surrounded by her military guard, had departed right after Señor Gelabert's lecture, so that when María de las Nieves, standing alongside Doña Cristina, heard a voice whisper into her ear, "So *this* is what God hath wrought," she laughed, though quietly, and turned around to see who was being so amusingly irreverent about the Primera Dama's speech, and there was Paquita, her eyes happily gleaming.

They fell into an embrace, laughing, trading kisses on the cheeks, and looked at each other with astounded expressions, and embraced again, and gazed at each other some more, and María de las Nieves saw and felt Paquita's black eyes darting all over her face like a blind woman's tiny hands, wanting to touch every feature and measure them against her memories, and she knew that her own eyes were doing the same. "Ay, Las Nievecitas, I couldn't leave without talking to you." How astonishingly easy this was after all these years! "Without seeing the new latrines you mean!" But was it so easy? Here she is, she thought. This is *she*. She saw Paquita's anxious little lips, the voluble eyes, the pale worried forehead of she who in childhood had so feared but also loved her, like a true sister sometimes, or like her own extraordinary pet, brought back for her from some wild faraway place, a talking pet unlike anyone else's—English speaking!—but with a nasty little-little bite. Now here she is, thought María de las Nieves, trapped in her phantasmagoric womanhood and looking at me like a girl full of stupid delight to have recovered her lost pet. "Without seeing you and giving you a kiss, my darling friend, my darling sister, from now on we're going to be together again every day, María de las Nieves, promise me that's so," Paquita said, looking at her as if all the years had never happened and now it was her magical pet's turn to say something and she promised to laugh extra loud even if it wasn't amusing— "No, Paquita, no, we won't." "You can come with me everywhere, mis Nievecitas, to New York, to Paris." "No, Paquita, I can't." "I'll pay for everything, silly"—fury and confusion she was afraid she couldn't control rising inside her and she stepped back out of her embrace and said in an icy whisper: "After the way you and your family treated my mother, how do you even dare to speak to me, Doña Francisca!" The ridiculous melodrama of those words staggered her even as she spoke them and she saw Paquita pale and blinking and looking as wounded as ever and she fled, just like that, so fast no one had a chance to detain her or to say anything, taking deep breaths, out through the splendid doors into the cool night, thinking, I'm crazy. Who am I? Absurd! Why did I say that? I'm a horror!

THE *GOLDEN ROSE* had crossed into waters off the coast of the United States' territory of California and was now only four days from San Francisco. That evening, in the parlor of her stateroom suite, Paquita gave María de las Nieves a beautiful peignoir of richest white silk, and a flannel chemise with lace trimming to wear underneath, both packed in Parisian couture boxes with fine paper wrapping. She'd bought a peignoir for Mathilde too. She said she'd been saving these gifts for when they reached New York, but now that the nights at sea were growing chillier, she'd decided to give them to her. "A peignoir is for wearing in your private quarters at home," explained Paquita, "or while sitting at your toilette while having your hair done by your maid. Sometimes I don't take mine off for days."

María de las Nieves thought: I haven't had a maid since María Chon. "Try it on, chula," said Paquita. She took off her plain black dress and petticoats, draped them on a chair, put on the chemise and peignoir, and looked at herself in the standing oval mirror bolted to the floor. These were easily the most luxurious articles of clothing she'd ever worn, and they felt delicious against her skin. She thanked Paquita profusely, and said, "I think I'm going to become very friendly with flannel during the winters in New York. Mrs. Gastreel used to wear flannel undergarments even in the tropics. Her skin was sensitive, but not very. She could wear wool."

"Mrs. Gastreel," Paquita repeated enigmatically.

"You know, my former employer's wife. She used to believe red flannel was especially good for the skin and circulation. Imagine a woman like that holding such a superstition?"

"Oh, I remember Mrs. Gastreel too well. At the opera, whenever she would look at me through her opera glasses, she would make a face. And others began to watch her, anticipating that face, which would make them laugh, behind their fans of course. I suppose she was mocking my *ostentation*. I pretended not to notice."

"I'm sorry, Paquita, I shouldn't even have mentioned her," said María de las Nieves, contritely. "I don't think I've spoken her name in years," she lied. "She just popped into my mind—because of flannel."

"Heavy silk protects against the cold too," said Paquita. "And you can probably wear merino undergarments as long as you wear linen underneath those, like I do when it's especially cold. Don't worry, mis Nievecitas, I'll outfit you. I've been waging war against the New York winters for almost a decade and by now I could lead an army of tropical women against Moscow. They'd be very snug *and* beautifully dressed!" She laughed falsely and said: "Your jefa's disdain was also an extension of her husband's policies toward my Rufino, no? Or in her opinion I was just despicable. And *so*? She showed no mercy to you, though."

For a moment both women seemed to be listening only to the ticking of the bronze clock on the teak mantel, as if suddenly it had grown louder, which it had not.

"You would have heard, then, I suppose, Paquita," said María de las Nieves, "whatever it was that Mrs. Gastreel was saying about me."

"What she was saying about you? You mean when—" Paquita's gaze, suddenly as alert and predatory as a wild animal's, froze María de las Nieves.

María de las Nieves did not avert her eyes, and attempted a casual tone: "I imagine she said I was a whore and all that. Isn't that what you meant by no mercy?" But she realized she'd exposed herself, and was aghast at her blunder.

"So you want to know what Mrs. Gastreel was saying." And Paquita gasped, as if to denote dramatic surprise. Then her expression turned thoughtful.

María de las Nieves served herself more brandy and said, "I just thought it was the sort of thing your spies would have heard—her being the British Minister's wife, that's all. But you're right, it's better not to know. It was such a long time ago."

"Mrs. Gastreel knew your secret. That's it, no?"

"Obviously not. Oh Paquita, you are too ridiculous. Next you'll suggest that Minister Gastreel was my lover."

"But the Minister was not the only man at that legation."

"That is true, Paquita," said María de las Nieves.

"And the blond gordito had been sent away."

"That is also true."

"Of course Mrs. Gastreel had a hand in that too. She wanted—what was his name—?"

"Wellesley—"

"She wanted him separated from you. I'm sure you already knew that."

"*She* did? . . . Pues, no, fíjate. I didn't know that—" To learn this now, eight years later? "But how horrible, and—. This is horrendous, Paquita, the way you just come out with these things! It's demonic! How did you find that out?"

"In diplomatic circles, at least, it was common gossip. I'm amazed you say you didn't know." Paquita sat down in the armchair opposite María de las Nieves, sighed in frustration, and said, "Of course I'm sure the British had their own spies keeping an eye on you, just because you were employed there."

Looking askance, María de las Nieves found herself again in the mirror's golden oval: in her pink-trimmed white peignoir, the light-gilded snifter cradled in her hand, she looked almost like a woman of luxury in an illustration or painting. Seeing herself so transformed—after years of living and dressing like a penny-pinching widow or dingy bohemian—sent a strangely pleasurable but melancholy shiver through her.

"During one of our first nights of conversation you told me that you had spies inside the García Granados home."

"I didn't have spies, corazón, my husband did. Inside Chafandín's house? Of course he did. But mis Nievecitas, what's happening to you? Only a few days ago you were so disdainful of such morally tainted information. And now you can't stop trying to trick me into disclosures!"

"Cómo? Trick you?" She laughed despite herself. "I'm trying to trick you, Paquita?"

"I had offered to trade that information, no? So what are you telling me in exchange? Nothing. Then aren't you trying to trick me?"

"*Sanctus simplicitus* . . . Caramba!"

The ensuing silence turned out not to be a heavy storm cloud after all: Paquita reached out and grabbed both of María de las Nieves's wrists, gave each of her hands a quick kiss, and said, "About Dr. Torrente and Chafandín's daughter, I have to admit that the information that came from the servants inside that house was as mixed up and contradictory as the gossip outside. But I don't think she was pregnant when she died, pobrecita."

"No, I never believed that rumor either."

That night, after changing back into her dress, María de las Nieves took a walk around the lower deck with Mathilde, who insisted on promenading in her peignoir. Mathilde was becoming accustomed to sea travel, so much so that she'd finally submitted to taking a hot bath, her first in over a week, and in celebration had been invited to sit next to Captain Grandin in the dining saloon. The impressive Yankee captain, completely bald but with bristly brown eyebrows and a long mustache and a beard so brushed out it resembled dried sea moss, had told Mathilde that soon they would be seeing seals. Explaining seals to the exacting Mathile took some effort, but once Captain Grandin had succeeded it was as if the spark of life had been blown into his carefully sculpted clay and now Mathilde was carrying on as if all she'd ever wished for in life was to see seals and she kept imitating the captain's imitation, barking, flapping her arms together, pretending to snatch flying fish out of the air with her mouth. That evening, in hopes of diverting her from that increasingly irritating fixation, María de las Nieves bought sugar cubes and carrots from Mr. Wan—"Not *Juan*, Mamá, *Wan*"—a Chinese mess worker with a long pigtail who'd befriended Mathilde, and they walked all the way to the foredeck to feed the morsels to Relámpago, the late dictator's battle stallion. The night was a luminous indigo, a strong breeze at their backs pushing the black smoke from the funnel forward into the sky, where it hung before the nearly full silver moon like the trail of a vanished train. The tattered canopy over the horse's stall was briskly flapping in wayward gusts of wind, and feathers from the chicken roosts flurried about like snow. Relámpago stood facing the prow, white mane rising and falling like animate threads, one ear pointed forward, the other back. María de las Nieves noticed the horse's young Indian groom standing at stiff attention and his terrified stare, and then she looked toward the prow and saw the man jerkily aiming a pistol at the horse and clinging to the rail with his other hand, and she grabbed her daughter and swung her behind her skirts. The man was Colonel Quesada, the former Assistant Minister of War, whom she'd never spoken to before; his collar was undone, his long black coat fluttered around him, his hair was disheveled, he was wearing carpet slippers, his overwrought drunkenness gave his pampered chubby face an even more wicked aspect than usual, he was feral-eyed, and when he began to speak it was in a snarling masculine bellow: "He died in his own excrement, vos sabes! . . . He got down off this horse to make a shit . . . a perfect sniper shot, carajo! . . . Right under this son-of-a-whore horse's nose . . . this piece-of-shit historical horse who did nothing to stop it . . . Eh, isn't that true? Eh? . . . Isn't that why we're on this shitty ship, because of this shitty horse . . . Eh? . . . But now I am going to assassinate this hijodelagranputa historical horse!"

"Colonel Quesada," she called out. "Calm yourself! I have my daughter with me. Imagine what they'll do to you if you shoot that horse."

He stared at her, livid lip curled down, showing his lower teeth, looking like a stupefied goblin; but then he smiled slowly, an almost rakish leer: "That's Dr. Torrente's daughter, eh? Eh, stuck-up flaquita? Eh? Stuck-up but very tasty, eh? Venga—" She was already rushing her daughter back down the passageway when he roared after her: "I want to marry you! In New York, flaquita!" And she thought, Why? Why? Always the cretins who think they can talk to me that way! Who think I must be so easy to win!

MARÍA DE LAS NIEVES arrived at the legation one Monday morning and there he was, sitting in the corridor, at the same wicker table facing the garden where she and Wellesley had so often sat together whiling away the afternoons: an Indian-looking boy, taller, a little darker than most, dressed only in white cotton trousers and a collarless white shirt unbuttoned at the throat and worn leather boots, and without hat or coat. He turned his head and eyed her expressionlessly; a gaunt, serious visage, deep-set black eyes, the smooth skin of youth, straight black hair combed back from a high, oblong forehead. She thought he must be a new gardener, but also realized in that instant that that didn't seem quite right; but something menial. She didn't even think of saying hello. María de las Nieves went directly into the office she shared with Higinio Farfán, said good morning to the brooding clerk and to the servant Chinta, who was in the office mopping with a lack of energy that corresponded to her own phlegmatic mood. She still considered herself, in those days, the stoic prisoner of secret heartbreak and defeat. Unrequited love felt like another kind of lifelong vow. Now that it no longer hurt so much, it had only become even more tedious, a condition the recent attentions of Mack Chinchilla—currently immersed in his hapless Italians—had done little to alleviate. Even Don José seemed a bit bored by her lately. He'd told her he didn't want to hear another word about her plan to make her way to Cuba to enlist in the rebel cause.

Later she would be amazed that her first impression of him was so unremarkable. She would play with this as if with imaginary dolls, holding up one, her first impression, and then another, a later one—how different they were, yet they were the same person! One could waste many minutes on that silent game.

"Who is that muchacho sitting in the corridor, Don Higinio?" Higinio Farfán answered that he didn't know.

A little later she heard the pregnant Mrs. Gastreel cheerfully singsong a greeting in the corridor outside: "Good morning, Your Majesty," followed by her embarrassed titter. A flat American-sounding voice responded, "Mornin', ma'am."

María de las Nieves was in the middle of answering a letter to the butcher Henry Koch, who claimed the legation had neglected to pay its last six-month bill for meat. Minister Gastreel said the bill was outrageously inflated; that's why he refused to pay. It made no sense, of course, for Mrs. Gastreel to be addressing anybody in that way, never mind the muchacho she'd just seen sitting outside. Well, sometimes one imagines hearing things. But he'd answered, Mornin', ma'am. Not another Yankee Indio like Mack Chinchilla!

"Higinio," she said placidly. "Oíste?" He was at the window, staring out into the park. But the clerk said he hadn't heard anything.

When María de las Nieves went to the door and looked out into the corridor, the youth was no longer sitting there. The outer door to Minister Gastreel's office and library were closed—also unusual. Mrs. Gastreel was nowhere in sight either. She went back to her desk and tried to finish Minister Gastreel's condescending letter to the butcher. She got up again and walked all the way back to the kitchen, where she found Chinta talking to the cook and the other inside servant, the latter sitting on a stool and plucking the blue-hued turkey between her thighs. It was unusual enough for María de las Nieves to come into the kitchen, and that she did so now only to ask Chinta what had become of the muchacho she'd seen sitting in the corridor must have made it seem even odder. Chinta answered that she didn't know. Was it possible, María de las Nieves asked, that he was in the office with Minister Gastreel? La Chinta didn't know, though she allowed that it was possible. None of the servants could tell her anything about the mysterious muchacho. Later, when María de las Nieves left for lunch and the siesta hours, she asked Don Lico about the youth, and the concierge said that when he'd returned this morning from his Sunday off, the youth was there, and was apparently a guest of the legation, but he knew nothing else. When she returned, Higinio Farfán told her that Minister Gastreel had come in to say that the letter to the butcher was just right—"Blooody mind-ed," imitated Higinio, sounding like a morose cow—and that as there would be nothing else for her to do that afternoon, she was free to leave early; that was not unusual, yet instead of going to visit Don José or J. J. Jump, as she usually would have, she felt in a mood to be alone and went directly home.

The next morning, Tuesday, she didn't see him when she arrived, and told herself she might never see or even hear of the mysterious muchacho again. Seated at her desk she heard footsteps in the corridor, lighter than Minister Gastreel's; they were not Mrs. Gasteel's, nor those of a servant or a gardener, for it was not the whispering step of sandals or the slap of bare feet. When she went out to look, Minister Gastreel's outer door was again closed. That afternoon he called her into his office to dictate a routine letter regarding import duties; as she walked through his library and reception room, she saw no sign of the mysterious muchacho, or of anything else unusual. Later that day Mr. Doveton arrived, wearing a long salt-and-pepper coat, a high-domed, yellow-hued hat, and carrying a fat book under his arm. He tipped his gaudy hat to her and went into Minister Gastreel's library. The next morning, during her Spanish lesson with Mrs. Gastreel, she asked in English, "Who was that young gentleman I saw sitting in the corridor the day before yesterday?" "A gentleman, María de las Nieves?" the Chiefess answered, with what seemed sincere confusion. And now she did not dare to say, Well, an Indian boy, actually, whom you addressed as Your Majesty, and so she said, "I must be mistaken," and Mrs. Gastreel, for just an instant, looked at her peculiarly. Later, in her office, a strong intuition compelled her, for perhaps the tenth time in the past two hours, to get up from her desk and stand in the door, but she did not see him, and this time she continued down the corridor, headed toward the privies in the second patio at the back of the house. In the sparely furnished parlor she had to cross to reach the rear patio, she saw him: he was obviously just coming from that patio, headed back toward the front. He was dressed the same as the first time she'd seen him, only now he was wearing a derby hat, slightly pushed back atop his forehead in the jaunty manner, and he kept walking toward her with his humorous black eyes fastened directly on hers. In confusion she stopped. And he stopped also, only a few feet in front of her. His lips had a flagrant fleshiness; they looked almost pressed up against window glass. He smiled bemusedly, raising his eyebrows, but he didn't say anything and finally she realized that he wasn't going to, that it was as if he was playing some extraordinary game with her.

"How do you do," she said in English, determined to appear unfazed.

"Buenos días, Señorita," he answered, in the obsequious singsong of a servant. She saw the flashes of gold-capped teeth and of a teasing look in his eyes. He tipped his hat, bowed in a stiffly formal way, and walked on past her, toward the front patio.

She walked through the parlor and stepped into the rear patio and then turned back into the parlor in the hopes of crossing back in time to see if he was going into Minister Gastreel's library, and was shattered to find him still there, standing just inside the door as if waiting for her to reappear. He laughed rapturously, clapped his hands twice, and, with a satisfied grin, tipped his hat again, and turned and went out.

María de las Nieves was sure she'd never felt more humiliated or confused. She stood in that place for a long moment, trying to regain her composure, and then walked in a daze back toward her office, past Minister Gastreel's closed door. She sat down, stared at her desktop, folded her hands in her lap, and squeezed the knuckle of a thumb to make it hurt.

That afternoon, instead of going home for lunch and siesta or to visit Don José, she stayed in the park for all three hours, watching the legation through the doorway of the reading room kiosk. She saw Mr. Doveton leave and return an hour and a half later. And then two unusual-looking men arrived, and were admitted into the legation by Don Lico: a tall African in a denim jacket, wearing a forager's cap atop a flat cloud of frizzy orange-hued hair, and a natty little man, dressed all in black, wearing a pince-nez, and carrying a cane, who looked, at least from this distance, as if he might be an Indian also.

She returned to the legation a bit before four—it would not reopen until four-thirty—and without even stepping into her office went and stood outside the closed door to the library and was sure that she heard Minister Gastreel say, pitching his voice a bit above the rest, that a new crown, a sword and scepter also, were being procured from Spanish Town. She heard masculine murmurs of approval. When she left the legation that evening the men still had not come out. She described the scenes she'd witnessed so far, and the little she'd overheard, to Don José. Jamaica would be a likely enough place to procure royal regalia, the umbrella mender observed. As to any possible significance, he too was baffled.

Thursday passed in much the same way, with the strange clique again sequestered in the library. Daring to eavesdrop at the door once more, she recognized the same vain drawl with which Mr. Doveton had "toasted" her in the opera box so many weeks before now declaiming: ". . . O, that I were a mockery King of Snow, standing before the sun of Bolingbroke, to melt myself away in water drops . . ." Chinta stepped into the patio and she darted on, feeling ready to weep with frustration. (*King of Snow! Mockery King of Snow?*)

That afternoon, she returned from the siesta hours a little early and as if she'd been crossing the parlor from the front patio to the rear one and had suddenly tired, she sat down in one of the high-backed wooden chairs against the wall, and waited. It was as if she could hear her own nervous suspense whispering back at her from all the corners of the austere room, growing louder and louder. Though before much time had passed, Mr. Doveton entered, returning from the rear patio. She immediately wanted to flee, yet she remained seated, trying to think of a way to ask what he'd meant by King of Snow without giving herself away. "Good afternoon, Señorita Moran," he said in a gallant voice of soft surprise. "Come to have a quiet little read, have we?" He was not wearing his hat; his thin, longish, gray-yellow hair fell along the sides of his peach-hued pate in strange symmetry with his drooping, silky mustache. She lifted her hands to show him that she was not reading anything. "Oh, there now," he said, with a velvety chuckle, "I apologize for the presumption. I hope I am not disturbing you." And before she could think of anything polite to say, the very tall former Confederate diplomatist, seemingly in one long-limbed synchronized motion, had snatched a chair from against the wall, placed it closely beside her, and sat down. Looking straight ahead, he reached into his salt-and-pepper coat and withdrew from an inner pocket a simple envelope, which he then opened with an air of boyish reverence, his slightly trembling fingers pulling from it some sort of card, which he turned over and displayed. It was a photographic portrait of herself, taken by J. J. Jump.

After a long dazed moment, María de las Nieves raised her eyes from her own image and looked at him: his tightly compressed lips and baleful eyes gave him an expression of profound emotion. "I know, Señorita Moran," he began, "that I must not seem to you the suitor of your dreams, as every young woman has the right and every reason to dream for herself. But maybe you have dreams you are not even aware of yet, so committed are you to that special one, like someone who can only see one door in a great hall that is filled with doors . . ." And while she stared down at her own hands and lap, he went on, dropping his voice into a passionate whisper that she imagined she could feel uncomfortably heating the side of her face: he so admired her intelligence, her strong and cheerful spirit and charm, he even thought she was beautiful, yes beautiful, she seemed more beautiful to him every day, every time he took out this picture and looked at it, and he held the picture up for her, like a looking glass. She'd finally cajoled out of Don José that Mack Chinchilla had indeed purchased her portrait—now she knew where the other one had ended up and with that realization came the bleakest disillusionment. Everything he said and his manner of saying it only deepened her depression, which was beginning to feel unbearable. He would love and honor her, he would take her to the City of Mexico, make her the lady of a fine house there, or perhaps they could buy a coffee farm, or a hacienda, or perhaps she would like to live in the Caribbean, Cuba perhaps, or even Paris, why not my dear, you only have to say the word, and he would leave her a wealthy widow one day, he promised her that, she was still very young, and he approximately thirty years older, and he'd long vowed never under any circumstances to allow himself to last into a decrepit old age, she could be sure of his word, because as a gentleman of honor—. Perhaps because she sat paralyzed, distantly listening to his words as if they were the steady snipping of scissors dedicated to some task unrelated to her, he interpreted her passivity as something else entirely. She felt his large hand grip hers tightly and she looked up angrily and collided with his lips, pressed against hers like a smashed fruit from which his tongue emerged like a sickening fat worm, his hand clamped against the side of her face to prevent its turning and his teeth against her teeth, her scream like steam noiselessly escaping out the sides of her mouth—and she hurled herself forward onto the floor, and fell prostrate there, then got up quickly and went toward the door with both hands over her mouth and by the time she reached it she was sobbing, breathless, cringing sobs that seemed to plead please don't, as if she was more terrified by something about to happen than of what already had, and when she heard his adolescent braying at her back, "Oh, I am sorry! Oh Señorita Moran, I am so sorry! Please—" she broke into a little run, which in the corridor slowed to a brisk walk on pointy doe feet but nevertheless felt eternal, past the closed door of the library, back to her office, back to her little desk, where she sat crying into her hands while Higinio Farfán said her name, asked what had happened, and fell silent. It was the second time a man's lips had ever touched hers. Sour and unctuous old man! Was that really her fate? She'd marry that poor Mack Chinchilla first; he was a little coarse, but he was kind, he was purposeful, he looked at her so adoringly, he was *not old!* What ugliness, what horror, to think he'd just come from a visit to the privy and touched her with those hands! And took away Martí's kiss with his! Now her sobs were choking her, yet nobody came to her help or to see what the matter was, and she got up and without a word of explanation to the pathetic official legation translator she went out the door—only Don Lico cried out in surprise as she swept passed him out into the street: "Las Nievecitas, qué pasó?"

She did not go into the legation the next morning until nearly midday. One of the servants, María José, answered the door, and told her that everybody had departed not an hour earlier for a weekend in the countryside of Escuintla. They would be returning, said the soulful-eyed young servant, late Monday, or Tuesday, maybe Wednesday. Don Higinio had been sent home.

"Everybody? El joven, their guest, he went too?"

María José answered placidly that the youth had gone too. She didn't know if the other men had gone as well. When María de las Nieves asked if el Señor Ministro or la Señora had said anything about her not having come in that morning, she answered that she didn't know if they had or had not. "They only told me to give you the message that I've already given you," said María José, and she repeated the message about their having gone to the country, and when they would return. "Ah, bueno," said María de las Nieves, as if now she understood, and she thanked her, and turned—a wild hope seized her—and walked into the park to see if Martí was in the reading room kiosk. He was not, and she headed home. She spent the rest of the day and most of the next in her bedroom, on her bed, trying to read, but mostly submerged in seething introspection and torpor. Saturday night she roused herself and announced to María Chon that they were going to the countryside also. They would leave the very next morning, spend the day at a natural spring bath, and return that evening. Curative water boiling up from the earth, maybe that could scour the taste of Mr. Doveton's mouth from hers, if not the hateful memory. It was still dark when they left the house, headed to Doña Mariana Gutiérrez de Robles's stable and stagecoach depot. During the first bumpy leg of the trip, out of the barely stirring city, squeezed into a coach with seven other passengers, María de las Nieves and María Chon huddled inside their shawls, trying to doze against each other's jostled shoulders. The stagecoach was drawn by four strong but plodding horses that made the five-hour journey between the capital and Antigua, Sacatepéquez, nearly every day. Daylight slowly replaced darkness and María de las Nieves hugged the soundly sleeping servant and watched drowsily out the window, head bobbing to the monotonous bouncing of the coach on its cranky springs, as the volcanoes on the horizon slowly came into view in the sky. María Chon woke up and began making friends with the other passengers, who seemed delighted at the difference between her and her moodily silent traveling companion. Gradually the trees and vegetation alongside the road changed, enormous evergreens, giant pinecones lying in the road like spent artillery shells, cypress, poplars, nearly phosphorescent groves of mossy encinas—; those wiry bushes with flowers like tiny yellow arrows were a constant of the roadside landscape, but what were they called? A gritty powder, the perpetual cloud of fine volcanic dirt raised by the horses' hooves, had covered her and was making its way, inexorable as an infinite army of hungry ants, into her eyes, nostrils, mouth, ears, up her sleeves and skirts and down her collar, into her shoes, beneath her stockings and undergarments, coagulating with her sweat as the heat inside the coach rose until she felt entirely coated in a thin layer of moist, pungent plaster. She had no wish even to smoke, her mouth felt so caked with silt.

"It is going to be heavenly," she said to María Chon, "when we get to the baths and can wash all this off. Heavenly, no?"

"And for what, Doñacita," she answered, "if we're only going to get just as dirty on the way home?"

Meanwhile her spirit felt mired in a slow-moving sludge, which the novelty of traveling into the country had done nothing to dilute—; and those flaring yellow flowers? María de las Nieves turned from the window and asked María Chon: "What are those yellow flowers called?"

"Those yellow flowers? They're called pobrecitas," answered the servant.

"Really? Pobrecitas?"

"Sí pues."

"But why pobrecitas? Their color is so bright."

"Ah, who knows." (*Ah, saber.*)

She stared out the window again. A while later she turned back to María Chon and said, "You're just making that up, aren't you. You don't know what those flowers are called either."

"No, Doñacita. They're called pobrecitas."

"I don't believe you," she said. "María Chon, I always know when you're lying. You always make yourself look a little stupid when you lie. As if not lying and being stupid are the same."

María de las Nieves leaned forward and with exaggerated politeness asked the other passengers if they knew what the yellow flower was called, and they all eagerly admitted that they did not. One middle-aged woman in a begrimed bonnet did say that they bloomed for only a few weeks every year.

"But María Chon knows what they are called," María de las Nieves told the passengers. "Mariquita, tell them what those yellow flowers are called."

María Chon tersely complied: "Pobrecitas, pues."

"Ja. They are not. Pobrecita *tu*," said María de las Nieves.

The stagecoach came jerkily to a halt, as if sinking deep into the dirt; the driver yelled down that they were at the turnoff for the Free Spirit Baths. They were an hour and a half from Antigua and there would be other baths along the way but these, advised the stagecoach driver, who had an immaculately curled and dirt-encrusted mustache, were under new German ownership, and were said to be respectable and very clean. The two young women got out, the pointy-eared boy assistant handed down their belongings from the roof. María de las Nieves paid the driver a deposit to save two seats for them on the stage returning that evening. Next to the road a neatly hand-lettered sign, in Spanish and German, showed the way to "The Free Spirit Baths." Though she was a country girl, for a long time now she'd lived only in cities, and though this was hardly mountain wilderness or jungle, it had been years since she'd found herself in such a secluded place, headed down a forest path. Maybe we should have been less adventurous, she thought, and gone to baths closer to the capital. But this is Sacatepéquez, where Pepe and I were going to look for that French-speaking Jefe Indio; that's why I wanted to come. Well then, here you are, in Sacatepéquez at last. *And?* Did you expect to somehow pick up the trail of what might have been? To hear leaves whispering the words he might have spoken, his shadow suddenly appearing next to yours on the path? Is that what you expected? They walked a long time, at least half an hour, even longer; every time she was ready to turn back, they came upon another sign pointing the way to the baths. For a while the path's descent was steep and filled with loose stones, one of which rolled so sharply under her step that she turned her ankle, and they had to stop and wait until it stopped throbbing. María Chon, balancing the basket holding their few small bundles atop her head, unlit cigar between her lips, was surefooted as a mountain cat. Occasionally they came across donkey and horse excrement on the path; also that of deer and rabbit, and María Chon pointed out what she said was jabalí, or wild boar, droppings. If they came upon a pack, she warned, they had to climb into a tree as fast as they could, or else they would be charged and torn to shreds. But maybe María Chon was lying and they were the droppings of some other animal, or she was just wrong. Small lizards flashed across their path. They had to watch for poisonous snakes too. They heard a cow bell nearby and the crushing of brush but they could see no cow or any other domesticated beast through the trees. The path evened out, became less rocky, and tiny scarlet flowers sprouted from the packed earth, symmetrical petals facing up. This time María Chon admitted that she didn't know what these pretty flowers were called. "They're called Chinitas," said María de las Nieves challengingly. María Chon said, "I believe you, Doñacita las Nieves. And I believe you, though your face is a little bit stupid too." The forest thinned and soon they came into the warm open sunlight. The grass was yellowed, there was cactus, and a baby ceiba tree, its trunk a bright lime green, no taller than themselves, stood by the path. Up ahead, in the shade of a behemoth ceiba, was a little farmstead, with a thatched stone cottage and a wooden stable, and a bread oven and a water tank and barking yellow dogs and a round pen of woven sticks holding two white donkeys, and another holding pigs, and a stand of beehives, and a stream-fed little pond and ducks and geese and fruit trees, and well off to the side were the two adjacent low gray-black stone buildings of the Free Spirit Baths, each with a wooden portico draped with flowering vines.

One of the stone buildings held baths for men, the other for women. But they were the only two customers. The proprietors were a German, Don Ky, in his forties, and his Indian wife, Doña Rebeca, approximately ten years younger; she would attend to María de las Nieves and María Chon in the bath. Meanwhile, if they wished, her husband would prepare them a meal of roasted chicken, smoked ham and sausages, wild mushrooms, boiled and dressed potatoes, and an assortment of vegetable and fruit salads, as well as freshly baked bread, homemade cheese, pastries, and pitchers of sweetened rice water. The price of this feast was so astonishingly low, equal to that of a dozen oranges in the capital, that María de las Nieves responded with a panicked expression. But it was no trick, and Doña Rebeca's soft face and dark eyes exuded honesty and good humor. She was dressed in an embroidered huipil and corte and her long black hair was very lightly silver-streaked, tied with a bright ribbon just above the small of her back. Her husband was only an inch or two taller, with curly brown hair and a messy beard, a blunt-featured leathery face, and a gruffly amused demeanor; his belly was like that of a woman's in late pregnancy, hugely and spherically protruding, but otherwise he was brawny, with broad shoulders and large, gnarled hands. He wore striped Indian trousers with a belt of embroidered red cloth, and sandals—the first European María de las Nieves had ever seen wearing Indio attire—along with a loose white blouse. The couple had a son the same age as María de las Nieves, seventeen, who was in Germany studying.

There were four changing rooms around the women's bath. María de las Nieves took off her dirt-encrusted clothes, put on the white cloth robe Doña Rebeca had given her, and stepped into the chamber enclosing the large square bath. María Chon was already waiting there in her robe when she came out, staring uneasily at the water. A thin sulfurous mist lay over it, and though on its surface the water was placid and in its depths had an inviting gray-green translucence, from the bottom came a perpetual agitation, as if some invisible spirit was thrashingly drowning there, and tiny golden bubbles rose weakly toward the surface and vanished before breaking, as if afraid of letting out their secret. A very soft, frail sound rose from the water, with something of the tinkling, airy melancholy of marimba music coming from far away in the mountains on a windy day. Through an aperture high in the stone wall the nearly midday light was refracted down toward the water like a celestial ray of blessing. The melancholy sound, she realized, was just the overflow perpetually splashing through a wide slot at the top of one of the bath's walls. Water, contemplated like this, did possess a sinister quality. But water is the substance of life, she thought. If water is sinister, then so is life. Maybe that is the bubbles' secret: the essence of life is sinister, until—caramba!—transformed by the Divine Light!

"It's good for the skin," she blurted.

"Do you still want to go in there?" answered María Chon. "It's boiling. The truth is, I'm hungry, Doñacita. Why don't we just eat."

María de las Nieves, who'd visited the baths at Almolonga as recently as the year she'd lived with her mother and the sheep farmer in Los Altos, reminded María Chon that the water came from a natural hot spring deep in the earth and that it wasn't boiling, just hot, no hotter than a bath they might prepare in the zinc tub at home. "Vamos!" she announced, and she shrugged off her robe, and hung it from a peg in the wall. María Chon hesitated, her eyes furtively fixed with a look of surprise on María de las Nieves's nudity, and then she took off her robe, hung it up too, and the two girls looked at each other, startled to be so openly regarding each other's nakedness, but also astonished at the similarity of their physiques. María Chon's breasts were prouder looking; María de las Nieves's buttocks had a more pronounced curve; one girl was a coppery brown, the other cinnamon-hued; but their smooth bellies and navels looked interchangeable, as did their graceful upper arms and shoulders, and their collarbones, their slender thighs, the slight sturdy swell of their calves, the thin black triangle of hair, in these each girl was almost the exact copy of the other! María Chon giggled first, her black eyes impishly gleaming, and then María de las Nieves did too; probably both were blushing, and a little confused and disconcerted by this glimpse into an unexpectedly pleasing mirror. María de las Nieves got into the bath first, which came midway up her chest when she was standing. It was indeed hot, but also delicious, an immersion in a gently caressing substance weightier than ordinary water, rich with mineral aromas; it was easy to believe that it was salubrious. The water, the German had told them, contained sulfate of lime, carbonic acid, and muriate of something or other. Eventually each girl went to her own corner of the bath to soak in solitude, each wearing a distant but absorbed expression, as if listening to a barely audible opera performed by motes of light. Wash off of me, Mr. Doveton, sang a tempestuous diva mote, wash off of me, vile gringo viejo *pisgote*. María de las Nieves held her head under the water for as long as she could hold her breath several times in succession. A melancholy aria asked if all her recent unhappiness was punishment for having lost her fear of God. Later, as she lay floating on her back, staring into the ray of light, she found herself contemplating two images as if switching them back and forth in a stereoscope: the mysterious muchacho walking toward her in his jauntily worn derby hat, with his brash smile; the mysterious muchacho sitting in the corridor in the morning sunlight, anonymous and humble, as she'd first glimpsed him. Who are you? she asked one. Who are you? she asked the other.

After a while Doña Rebeca came in with another young, chubby-cheeked Indian woman, her assistant. They carried rolled-up mats of woven straw, and baskets. They came and went two or three more times, bringing in dry and leafy branches, and canvas pails of water. When the girls were summoned out, the two Indian women sponged their steaming skin with icy water; at first they could barely feel the water's coldness, but finally it made them shriek. Then they lay on their stomachs on the mats. Branches, first the scratchy ones, then the leafy ones, were vigorously scraped back and forth over their skin, up and down the length of their figures; not even the bottom of their feet were spared this invigorating treatment, which tickled at first and then became enjoyable. María de las Nieves felt so inebriated with pleasure that she barely noticed when Doña Rebeca began rolling her up inside a thick wool blanket that had been soaked in the hot water of the bath. The Indian woman vigorously massaged up and down her spine, rubbing and kneading her arms and legs through the hot blanket. Soon her skin felt as prickly as a cactus, but it was wonderful; she felt like a warmly purring cat rubbing against some rough but all-enveloping surface. The India's strong hands thumped up and down her body, pounding her buttocks, inside her thighs, up her spine again. The hands stopped moving, and a muffled voice told her to go ahead and sleep. She felt steamed into mush. Could she even wriggle her fingers and toes? She could. Slowly she rubbed her thighs together, squirming like a buried earthworm. She imagined herself with large womanly breasts, and that a man was caressing and sucking on them. Was that really herself, with such lush breasts, or was she dreaming that she was somebody else? And who was the man? He seemed not to matter. He mattered because he was loving her, but otherwise he was anonymous. Slowly and almost imperceptibly she squirmed inside the warm heavy wrapping of the soaked wool blanket, until that extraordinary warmth and sensation of bliss shuddered through her, and just went on and on, and she let out a shimmering sigh. Her limbs trembled and twitched, she could hear her heart pounding as if her own ear was pressed to her own chest, but gradually it quieted. A dream briefly glimmered through her sleep: Sor Gloria de los Ángeles, in her novice habit, on tiptoes, looking out a narrow window, saying, "They're all along the castle walls, wearing black masks and aiming their rifles at us," while she sat on the floor, feeling a deep contentment, and in a lazy voice she answered, "Tell them they can come in, Sor Gloria. We made enough arroz con leche for all of them." She wanted to go on sleeping embedded in this warmly buzzing mud for an eternity. She woke whimpering and frightened, her skin being torn apart by fire ants, and she called for help—

"You should have told me you were allergic to wool, niña!" Doña Rebeca scolded her. They were on the portico now, outside the bath. María Chon, in her cotton robe, was dozing in a hammock. María de las Nieves lay on a mat, her body slathered in sticky healing unguents, a linen sheet pulled up to her chin, watching hummingbirds flit in and out of the orange trumpet vines.

"It doesn't matter, Doña Rebeca," she said weakly. "That was like the dream of some miraculous journey that turns out to have been real."

"Yes, a journey!" repeated the Indian woman. "All too real, because look how you came back!" She lifted the blanket, and said, "But it's a little better. The welts are going down." Later, when Doña Rebeca finished washing her off, she ran split limes over her body, even the bottom of her feet, and it didn't sting at all.

To anyone who spoke English, of course, Doña Rebeca's husband's name was amusing, but the couple communicated almost exclusively in Spanish, with smatterings of Cakchiquel. It was late afternoon when they sat down at the long table under the ceiba tree, to the exorbitant meal Don Ky had prepared. Several of their Indian workers, including the woman who'd massaged María Chon, were at the table too. Don Ky said grace, in Spanish; his German accent was agreeable, lending his speech a somewhat musical solemnity. María de las Nieves had thought she wouldn't be hungry, but she ate voraciously; there was not a plate she didn't at least try. Even the lengthening of shadows, and the slow crawl of clouds into the afternoon sky, seemed to occur in a kind, tender, quietly rejoicing manner. The late-afternoon light and cooling temperatures woke up the fragrances of the landscape in a way that sharply reminded her of another time she'd been out-of-doors, feeling happy and dazzled by life, and she thought of her adventurous outing with Martí, recalled it, perhaps for the first time in a long while, without gloom, and felt the reassuring promise of his friendship in her heart. Don Ky spoke at length about the book he'd been working on for the last twelve years. His current chapter was about the similarities between Indian cosmology and deities and the angelology of Swedenborg, the Gnostics, and the Hebrew Cabbala. Though the Indians' beliefs were particular to their culture, said Don Ky, they were also universal to the enlightened human spirit, which always and everywhere seeks to comprehend and express the mysterious pulsations and emanations of the divine life within and all around us. Universality, opined their German host, was like a vessel in which the Indians would be able to preserve what remained of their threatened culture; he was writing his book to advance that cause. Whenever he had time to spare, he hiked into the mountains to visit Indian villages and learn about their beliefs; it was for this reason that he'd worked so hard to master Cakchiquel, and that was how he'd met Rebeca, whose father was a village wise man who knew many secrets. María de las Nieves was happy to listen and to pretend to listen to Don Ky, feeling too drowsy and sated to absorb much of it, even if it had been the sort of subject that interested her, which definitely it was not. She asked him if in his explorations he'd ever encountered or heard of a Jefe Indio who spoke French, built schools, read newspapers, and so on. "Ah, the Liberal paragon of the Indian chief!" The German's laugh was hearty but derisive; he was adamantly against the positivist materialism of the Liberals, which would be the cause of the Indians' forgetting who they were even more than they already had "—unless something is *done!* But no, I have not encountered or even heard of this worthy man, María de las Nieves." Don Ky, going around the table like a man on a proud horse, poured a silvery ribbon of schnapps into every cup of coffee. The color of the sky was fading to gray-blue, and the moon was visible like a filmy dot of evaporating meringue. Don Ky and his wife insisted that they stay over for the night. María Chon wanted to, but María de las Nieves said they should go. If the Gastreels and their guests returned from the country that night—she knew that was unlikely—she would have to work at the legation tomorrow. And this had been too special a day to spoil with an inferior copy. Nor could she be wrapped in wool again. And she was feeling restless. Anyway, they'd already paid for seats on the stagecoach. María Chon patted her elbow and joked about how *coda*, stingy, María de las Nieves really was. Don Ky and Doña Rebeca accompanied them all the way out to the road. They didn't have to wait very long before they spotted the coach's lantern approaching through the twilight. It was the same stagecoach but a different driver; the long and short of it was that María de las Nieves had to buy two new fares. Their good-byes were so effusive it could have been the parting of adoring relatives. The couple's son, Gunter, would soon be home for a long visit, Don Ky said with a meaningful squeeze of María de las Nieves's hands, which he'd taken in his own: they must come back and meet him. Of course, said María de las Nieves, she would be delighted! As the stagecoach got under way, she tried to imagine herself as Don Ky and Doña Rebeca's daughter-in-law: Would Gunter want to live the life of an educated rural mystic too? Could she grow to like that? What if he was very beautiful, with long golden hair? She and María Chon sat squeezed against the door—the coach was crowded, but the two took up only as much space as one normal-sized woman—and soon fell asleep in each other's arms. When María de las Nieves woke again it was damp and chilly and a heavy rain was thudding against the roof of the coach. Worried about catching colds from the dangerous air, she arranged their shawls over her and María Chon's heads, and they slept cheek to cheek, warm inside their improvised tent. They woke again to thunder and lightning. On the plain outside the capital the rain was heavier than before and so loaded with electricity that it fell with a strange luminescence, like long glass needles lit from within, and they passed a line of drenched mules and muleteers all glowing, even the mules, like archangels clothed in garments of light.

On Wednesday afternoon at the legation Chinta came to tell María de las Nieves that Minister Gastreel had asked for her in the library. The secretive clique had finally returned from Escuintla the previous night. She assumed that Mr. Doveton was with them, and knocking at the door, she felt misery and apprehension gripping her insides. But when she came into the library, Mr. Doveton wasn't there, nor were the other two strangers, the orange-haired African or the Indio who dressed like a dapper Londoner, and the mysterious muchacho was sitting down at the far end of the mahogany table, pushed back from it, a leg crossed over his knee and a look of boredom on his face. With a discordant sense of magnets repelling each other, his stare made her quickly look away, at Minister Gastreel. She labored through an exchange of formal greetings, inquiries about Mrs. Gastreel's health and if they had enjoyed their weekend, and Minister Gastreel enthusiastically answered that Mrs. Gastreel was very well and that indeed they had enjoyed their weekend, and he praised the natural abundance of the plantation they had stayed in near Escuintla, and the wonderful quality of the beef butchered from their host's cattle, and told her how they had even had some good luck catching fish and the most remarkable langostinos in the vigorous streams, which made one think of a tropical Scotland, and he asked if she had enjoyed her weekend, and she said that she'd gone to the country also, on Sunday, to the Free Spirit Baths, near Antigua, owned by a very kind couple, a German and his Indian wife, and yes, she had enjoyed herself very much. "The Free Spirit Baths," repeated Minister Gastreel in a tone of dry yet jovial incredulousness. "Were you required to manifest a free spirit while having your bath? And how does one do that?" She had to nip the inside of her cheek to keep from laughing and said, "The name refers to some mystical belief of the owners,

Your Excellency." She heard the mysterious muchacho's caustic snigger, but she would not look at him. "The Free Spirit Baths. By jiminy," scoffed the mysterious muchacho, but she still refused to even glance his way. Finally Minister Gastreel said:

"Señorita Moran, I want to introduce you to our guest, His Majesty William Charles Frederick, the King of Mosquitia. Young William is the exiled sovereign of the Mosquito nation, though he shall very soon be returning to reclaim his throne." He pronounced it *Moos*quitia and *Moos*quit*oo*. Now she had no choice but to look. The mysterious muchacho had stood up from his chair. He wore a pearl-gray silk vest over his white shirt, an undone tie, and his sleeves were rolled up, and a black frock coat was hung over the back of his chair. But this time when she met his gaze she felt unexpectedly exhilarated, and this caused her a small surge of panic. As if he was about to blurt something reassuring, his eyes widened and his lips parted.

"Your Majesty," said Minister Gastreel, "this is the young woman I know you've already heard some mention of, our legation's indispensable and somewhat confidential translator and interim secretary, Señorita María de las Nieves Moran. She also tutors Mrs. Gastreel in Spanish."

"How do you do," she said.

"How do you do, *Your Majesty*," Minister Gastreel corrected. Compliantly, she repeated the greeting.

"I'm delighted to see you again, Miss . . ." responded the mysterious muchacho; he looked stumped for a moment, and then he grinned widely, showing some gold-capped teeth, a few on the bottom, at least one on top.

"Miss Moran," said María de las Nieves. "Really, Your Majesty," said Minister Gastreel, with a hint of exasperation, "it is crucial that you improve your memory for names." And she said bluntly, "You speak English like an American." Now the mysterious muchacho, looking chastened, glanced at the diplomatist as if awaiting instruction. Minister Gastreel sighed and suggested they sit down.

"His Majesty speaks like an American because it was in the United States that he was, let us say, educated," said Minister Gastreel, "unlike many of his royal forebears, who were educated in England. The old Mosquito Kings, you know, could even read and quote Shakespeare and Byron and the like. It was one of the things they were known for, William's late

great-uncle, King George Augustus Frederick, especially. Royal legiti-
macy is not always so easily conferred—so we've been learning from
Mr. Doveton and our other guests this past week. Among the natives of the
Mosquitia, apparently, an ability to quote Shakespeare can only enhance
the perception of kingliness, because that is what the other great Mos-
quito kings of history and legend have done. But our good King William
can barely read, Señorita Moran, and Shakespeare is quite beyond him.
I don't pretend to be a literary man either. Mr. Doveton has been our
Shakespearian in residence. Would you like to give us a quote from *King
Richard II*, Your Majesty?"

"My rash fierce blaze of riot cannot last—but watch yer step, cause it
might last longer than yeh think." The muchacho did speak the words with
a swaggering enthusiasm, and let out a genuinely good-humored laugh
when he was finished.

Turning to María de las Nieves, Minister Gastreel remarked, "That
doesn't sound very Shakespearian, does it." He was clearly enjoying
himself.

"But it is, sir," insisted the mysterious muchacho. "Mr. Doveton and
I went over that one a great deal. I added the last part, is all. Which
Mr. Doveton said is a good thing, showing kingly gumption. Also there's a
place where King Richard says lions can tame leopards but can't change
their spots, and he said go ahead and change that to jaguar."

María de las Nieves couldn't help it, she laughed a little, and the hardly
less mysterious muchacho smiled at her appreciatively.

"And what was your opinion of the play, Your Majesty?" asked Minister
Gastreel.

"Well, there are no sword fights or battles. You could perform that one
with talking heads set on a table and not lose a thing, which Mr. Doveton
says is not true of the other plays we were going to study."

"His Majesty and Mr. Doveton were in deep exegesis of *King Richard II*
last week," said Minister Gastreel. "Apparently it addresses such matters
as royal succession, and what is a king, and, well, you know. Are you familiar with that play Señorita Moran?"

Something in the mysterious muchacho's last words regarding Mr. Doveton, echoed by Minister Gastreel's, caused her an unexpectedly buoyant
feeling. They spoke of him as if he was in the past. She took a chance:

"That's the one that mentions a King of Snow, isn't it? A mockery King of Snow, melting away?"

"I remember that part," said the youth.

"Very remarkable, Señorita Moran," said Minister Gastreel. "You never cease to amaze *me* at least. Is there a particular lesson you think our young monarch friend should take from that play?"

Now she was trapped; yet before she even had time to think of what else she might say, the words were flowing from her as if she'd just memorized them yesterday, as if they had been waiting within her all these years just to lead her through this particular gate, and into the astonished and dangerous esteem of the two men now listening: "Your Majesty, no man can truly be a King who is not ruler of himself, controlling and having complete mastery over his desires and passions. It is by crushing them and refusing to be ruled by them that a King's heart is put in the hand of the Lord. The hand of God is strong and presses hard, which is why God said, Whom I love, I correct."

The words came out just like that. It could never have occurred to either Minister Gastreel or the mysterious muchacho that they were the words of Sor María de Agreda, written to her infatuated admirer, the King of Spain, and not some artful paraphrasing of her near contemporary William Shakespeare.

"Whom I love I correct, yes, that is very good, very useful, and the religious tone is essential," Minister Gastreel said. "Our young King is indeed in need of some correction. Fortunately for us, there's still time, Señorita Moran—" The King's "regent," Wellesley Bludyar, Minister Gastreel now revealed, had in the past months made several trips to Greytown and to the Wanks River coast, laying the groundwork for the Mosquito monarch's return. The Mosquito King's Council was now assembling there—two members of which, Mr. Morgan and Dr. Slam, she might have glimpsed in the legation the previous week; they had departed that very morning, headed back to Greytown. Mr. Doveton would also eventually be making his way there. The regent, however, was still under the impression that the young monarch was rather more literate than he'd turned out to be. "Though young King William does have a credible air of kingly dignity, don't you agree, Señorita Moran?" asked Minster Gastreel. Obediently but neutrally, she assented. "I for one remain very confidant he can succeed," he said strongly.

"You know, he doesn't have to be an expert in Shakespeare. He'll have plausible reasons for having been educated in the United States instead of in England. But it is essential that His Majesty learn to *read*." He would also need to learn more about his kingdom, and the ways and traditions of his subjects. Mr. Doveton, said Minister Gastreel, was no longer available. María de las Nieves's assignment, he said, would be to teach the young King to read, assuming she had no objections. She answered matter-of-factly that she did not. Why should she? She had never objected to any other assignment.

For a moment the three sat in silence around the library table, as if something very grave had finally been resolved. Then Minister Gastreel said, "And, who can tell, Señorita Moran, maybe in time you will want to become the Mosquito Queen. Can you imagine such a destiny for yourself? Traveling to the Mosquitia as the new Queen of the Mosquitoes? It would be quite an adventure. Very well remunerated. The occasional trip to Europe, and so forth. And your friend Mr. Bludyar will be there, as regent."

These were perhaps the most bizarre words that anybody had ever, or would ever, speak to her. In retrospect they would loom ominously, casting a darkly illuminating light on what subsequently did occur. But Minister Gastreel had spoken in his exaggeratedly pompous tone, which meant his words were at least partly meant in fun, but as business too, letting her in, if she hadn't yet deduced it, on this deadly serious enterprise's masquerading aspect. With the shadow of Mr. Doveton seemingly lifted, she was in a receptive mood, and so the words struck her as no stranger than any other aspect of what was occurring, and even as a welcome acknowledgment of that strangeness in the form of a joke. She trusted Minister Gastreel, had even come to regard him in the light of a father, nearly. She looked from the diplomatist, with his compressed smile, his slightly flushing complexion, his alert steely eyes, to the mysterious muchacho, whose wet-looking mouth hung open, but then smiled shyly. He laughed, and she laughed a little too, as if at the preposterousness of it all, though it felt giddier and deeper than that. Only Minister Gastreel didn't laugh, watching them both, but especially María de las Nieves, yes, especially her, his merry gaze like dancing knives carving her up like a Christmas goose, or turkey, or duck, or capon, or whatever.

A secret and playful complicity had already formed, between her and the still mysterious muchacho. Nowadays they might even have felt ready to reach under the table and discreetly hold hands, so surely had they been set down that subterranean path toward at least a few moments of profound rapture, or many more. Already she felt less lonely; she felt accompanied in a way she hadn't before, though she hadn't quite realized that, and was still days from identifying why.

María de las Nieves knew, of course, about the old British protectorate in Mosquitia, on Nicaragua's Atlantic coast. She was vaguely cognizant that the British had exercised power there through succeeding generations of compliant Mosquito Indian kings. Minister Gastreel was now reviewing that history for her benefit. Presumably the mysterious muchacho had already had at least that drilled into him; the smoldering, fascinated stare with which he tortured her for the length of the lesson seemed to indicate that he felt little need to listen now. Earlier in the century the competition between Great Britain and the United States over influence in the Isthmus had grown so intense that it had more than once brought the two powers to the verge of war. After all, the emerging power had just usurped half of Mexico's territory—what was to keep it from sweeping down into Central America, where British influence, especially along the Atlantic coast, was entrenched? Those tensions were finally defused when the United States and Britain signed a treaty in which both renounced the goal of gaining exclusive control over any interoceanic route through Nicaragua. The mysterious muchacho had moved several chairs closer, as if to better listen to Minister Gastreel, but now he touched María de las Nieves's foot under the table with his, touched it firmly, and wrestled it back and forth a little, until she drew it back, realizing in terror that she had been letting him play with her foot. But that was only because she really was trying to listen, and hadn't understood what the youth was doing! —The United States regarded the British Mosquito protectorate as a violation of the spirit of their treaty, so Britain negotiated with Nicaragua a new status for the area: Nicaraguan sovereignty over Mosquitia was acknowledged, and in exchange the protectorate became a reservation, a self-governing, mostly autonomous entity to which the Nicaraguans had to pay a yearly annuity. But in the end the Nicaraguans had refused to uphold the treaty's terms, or even to recognize the Mosquito monarchy. With the waning of the California Gold Rush years, during which Nicaragua had provided the major transit route, followed by the Civil War, and the opening of the transcontinental railroad, United States interest in the country had drastically receded, but with President Grant's renewed interest in the Nicaraguan Canal, it had greatly revived. The British Foreign Office now perceived a U.S. inclination to act unilaterally regarding the canal, and to disregard their old treaty. Nicaragua, perceiving the same, also feared the United States. And so Nicaragua had agreed with Britain to finally resolve their disputes over the former Mosquito protectorate and their old treaty by placing these before Emperor Franz Josef for impartial arbitration. The outcome, Minister Gastreel already had been assured by the Foreign Office, would be a restoration of complete autonomy to the Mosquito authorities. Clearly this was the moment for the restoration of the old Mosquito monarchy, and of its traditional alliance with Britain, and renewed British authority throughout that coveted coast.

Minister Gastreel placed before the young pair a book, *Waikna; or Adventures on the Mosquito Shore,* by an American named Samuel A. Bard. It was more than twenty years out of date, he explained, and quite mocking of the British and the last young Mosquito King, George William Clarence. But the book did provide a detailed account of life and customs in the territory the mysterious muchacho was to rule, and came with sixty evocative illustrations. Bending over the seated couple, Minister Gastreel opened the book to a page with facing illustrations: a tiny human figure climbing the towering trunk of a coconut palm to fetch a coconut; three men in a canoe in a dense mangrove swamp, one aiming a spear, or perhaps a type of Amazonian blowgun, at the herons flying through the air. "You see," the Minister said, "it is a very watery region. Dr. Slam taught us how to catch crayfish from rivers in the Mosquito manner this weekend in Escuintla, didn't he, Your Majesty." The mysterious muchacho agreed, "Yes, he did." Minister Gastreel said, "Of course you'll probably want to be started on this right away. Well, why delay?"

María de las Nieves and the mysterious youth were left alone in the library, seated at the black mahogany table, the book closed before them. On the wall were framed prints of British racehorses.

"So you are not really the Mosquito King," she ventured after a moment of silence. "Is that right? You are being trained to imitate him as part of some intrigue."

"Sure," said the mysterious muchacho cheerfully. "That's right."

"Am I allowed to know your real name?"

"I guess not," he said. "What's your first name, Señorita Moran?"

"María de las Nieves," she said.

"Mary of the Snows," he translated, with a self-congratulating nod. "That's a very pretty name. What's it come from?"

"A miracle performed by the Holy Virgin. There was a very sinful pueblo in the desert, and she made it snow, to purify it."

"And did it work?"

"Of course."

"Hah. She ought to try that in San Francisco. It'd turn to whiskey, tobacco juice, and blood before it even landed." He chuckled.

"So you are not even originally from the Mosquitia?"

"Nope, from this country right here, I suppose, though my papers say I'm a Panamanian now. Though I don't know much about it." He told her some of what he knew about his own story: When he was a tiny child his grandmother, of whom he had no memory at all, had given him to an American ship captain in Puerto San José, Captain Ernest Buford, who raised him for a life at sea, starting as a cabin boy, which was how he learned to speak English, but Captain Buford died when he was eleven, and he stayed on in that life, and knew no other. He was a seaman assigned to the U.S. Pacific Mail steamer *Montana* when Mr. Bludyar found him in a Panama City sailors' saloon and began recruiting him to this new role. Heck, wasn't it going to be a grand escapade? And if he came through it all right, and took advantage of the opportunities sure to arise, he would be made wealthy. He was now sixteen.

"You are a year younger than me," she said, and added with a slight, crooked smile, "Your Majesty."

"Yes, Grandma, and you're the teacher."

She opened the book and told him to read out loud. He read slowly and haltingly and often with flawed comprehension; more than a year before, María Chon had been reading at about this level, though she'd since improved. It's not that he's not clever, she told herself; he's just never learned to read well at all. Sitting shoulder to shoulder in the library, they plunged into the book Minister Gastreel had assigned. On Thursday they worked for seven hours; on Friday, a little less. She came in on Saturday just to spend the long morning tutoring him. He read out loud, she corrected him, then they discussed what he'd read. The book described a bizarre and sometimes frightening world of primitive and often debauched Indians, wild jungles and labyrinthine swamps, piratical and murderous speculators and desperadoes, but it also held out the promise of all manner of adventure, which the mysterious muchacho, at least, seemed keen for. And they found much to joke and laugh over. Beneath his bravado, she thought, he was as sweet as green sugarcane, full of mirth and charm, and she was mesmerized by his boyish yet severe beauty. If he wasn't really the Mosquito King, then this was what that young king should look like, she thought—Wellesley had chosen well in at least that respect. All that Sunday she thought about nothing else but seeing him again on Monday. If she'd been able to look inside herself, at her own heart, the pumping organ hanging inside her chest would bear little resemblance to the one that had been there a week before. How would it be different? It would look like a floating, radiant, mystical fruit, the most perfectly ripened and delicious fruit ever! In a few months she would remember that pretty conceit, and think: I don't have the courage to look at what's inside there now.

On Monday he drawled, "Your laughter looks like it comes from yer ears, María Nieves," and he grabbed both her ears between his fingers, wiggled them up and down, and trilled a little sound with his tongue, as if ringing her ears like a little bell. Then he kissed her on the mouth. She knew she shouldn't kiss him back, that she should resist, but she let him kiss her, and soon his tongue was inside her mouth, and their tongues rolled together, and she felt herself melting, and his hands moving up and down her back, and up and down her ribs, and slowly circling her little breasts and closing over her little breasts and squeezing—he was a very forward muchacho, no doubt about that. When they finally stopped she gazed down at the book on the table, at its subtitle, *Adventures on the Mosquito Shore*, and thought, There I go. Who would ever have guessed I was going to end up Queen of the Mosquitoes?

Over the next six weeks, she would tutor him in his reading nearly every day. Soon, nothing else mattered but being with him. Almost daily now that moment came when they peeked out of the library to see if anyone was around, and realized they were alone. The legation would have closed for the day, sometimes hours before they'd broken off their lessons and kissing, or Minister and Mrs. Gastreel would have gone out to some official function or entertainment. Of course the servants soon caught on, but who cared about that? Who even cared about Higinio Farfán? She felt a little bad sometimes, thinking of what he must be telling his wife about her—and felt worse when Don Lico seemed embarrassed to meet her eye, and grew stiff and remote with her, and sometimes looked at her with a worried expression and seemed as if he wanted to say something, nervously licking his lower lip. But as soon as she and the mysterious muchacho were together again, who cared what anyone thought? You remember what it's like, no? Long ago or not so long ago? That vinegary taste of kissing always in the air, infusing it like the smell of melting April snow and thawing earth in a northern clime. And always sneaking into corners, sitting on his lap for hours, arms around his neck, kissing, giggling, whispering, mushymushy, so wet down there, so hard down there, oh, bursting—. Staying up late into the night, writing love letters, copying poems: Give me a thousand kisses . . . Tomorrow I shall see you, Your Majesty . . . Of course the mysterious muchacho had a real name, which he'd finally told her, and it probably wasn't a made-up name, though there is no way to be sure, and when she was alone with him she used that one too; he liked to call her Vieja, his Old Lady.

In the city it was so widely believed that girls grew up without any idea of nature that every year the three most elder nuns in the convent had come into the school to meet with the senior schoolgirls, to tell them what was going to happen when they were married. And every year the senior schoolgirls had listened to that committee of withered virgins tell them, from behind their lowered black veils, that they were to fornicate only to make babies, only on their backs and with their husbands atop them, never in any other position, for fornicating in lewd positions and for pleasure were the ways of animals and pagan Indios. And every year the senior girls told all the other girls, so that everybody in the school received this same secret knowledge year after year. And what had they all finally done with that knowledge? How did they store it and what did it change into until the time came when they were to make use of it? Had they really all nodded and thought to themselves: Yes, only with the husband on top, only to make babies, and never in any other position, never like those animals who do in the open what the pagan Indios must do hidden in the dark or deep in the forest? She was a country girl, and knew about animals, anyway. What was coming was inevitable; she foresaw that at least a week before it happened, and feared it only a little. Seventeen days after they had first kissed, the mysterious muchacho, after checking that no one else was about, locked the door and laid her out on the library table and undressed her with her help and they did it right there, with him on top, more or less, she joked later, as the nuns prescribed. It didn't hurt nearly as much as she'd thought it was supposed to. Love and pleasure began as the same thing for her, inseparable, him moving vigorously inside her, like the animals, but animals hid their pleasure, and did nothing to prolong it. After they were done that first time and he'd gone out to find a rag to clean the table and she was left alone in the library, dressing herself, looking at the spilled broth and cloudy smears left upon the polished surface of the table, she felt stricken and frightened by what she had just done, and began to cry a little. But when he came back in, as if instantly sensing her anxiety and humiliation and that maybe she was hating him, he embraced her, kissing and nibbling until she forgave him and kissed him back. After he'd cleaned up he put the sopping rag in his pocket and told her they would find a pretty spot to bury it, outside the city, and it would grow into a special tree. What kind of tree, mi amor? He didn't know what it was called, some tree with big red flowers, full of birds and monkeys and fruits, would that be all right? Walking home alone that evening she discovered her sinner's calm and poise: she enjoyed looking at the faces of those she passed, and imagining them looking at her, unable to see what she had just done, and understanding for the first time that particular form of freedom. Before long he even found occasions to bring her to his bedroom off the rear patio of the legation, which had earlier been Wellesley Bludyar's. Taking separate paths to their rendezvous points, they went for long walks outside the city, over the plains, through the valleys and ravines, where it was not hard to find secluded lovers' hideaways. She was prudent and never brought him home, not even when she knew that both María Chon and Amada Gómez were out. She had heard people describe the microscopic world inside a drop of water and felt as if they lived inside such a marvelous and secret world, invisible to all but themselves. Lying alone in her bed at night, she went over every inch of his body in her mind, especially his erect member, the smooth glossy brown of wet clay, the way it looked during all the stages of its perpetually resurrecting life. One night, while she was rehearsing the mysterious muchacho's nudity in the dark, she remembered the centuries-old story of Catalina de Puebla, the Malabar princess of a conquered kingdom, sold into slavery, purchased in Manila, and converted to Christianity by a Spanish ship captain who brought her home to Puebla, Mexico, and gave her to a priest to be his housekeeper. There she became renowned for her holiness, chastity, mortifications, miracles, and manner of sewing little glass mirrors into her skirts and blouses, which the young women of Puebla began to copy, and also for a holy vision she once had in which Jesucristo came to her naked, and she ordered Him to go away and come back with His clothes on if He wanted to speak to her, and He obeyed. It was no less credible than many other saints' visions but less agreeable to the Doctors of the Church, which was why "La China Poblana" had never been made a saint. María de las Nieves lay in her bed imagining a Jesucristo whose nakedness was the mysterious muchacho's nakedness, and thought, But she lied too; Catalina de Puebla didn't send Him away, she only said she did. (Decades later she confided a version of that memory to Paquita, by then twice widowed, religiously devout, and living in Europe, in a letter in which she came *only* that close to revealing the mysterious muchacho's identity to her lifelong friend-sister-adversary, destined never to know anything more about Mathilde's father than that María de las Nieves had once fantasized herself as Catalina de Puebla being visited by a Jesucristo with a body just like Mathilde's father's—.) The mysterious muchacho knew he was good-looking and that many found him winning; he was a love-hungry and expert boy who knew his way around cities and ports, and was precocious enough to have already learned how to recognize and act on the interest he aroused. A few older women and several poor girls, just ordinary niñas from squalid harbor barrios, not whores, he boasted, had been his teachers and first conquests. Sometimes he liked to make María de las Nieves wear the India-rubber rain boots Don José had made for her, and nothing else, when they made love; and then he pulled the boots off her and held them to his nose and inhaled their miry depths and told her it was her intimate smell multiplied and that he loved it more than any smell on earth and she protested that it was a horrible smell, rotten eggs and worse, and what was he, half pig? a cochinito boy raised by pigs?

From the start, it seems fairly clear, the Gastreels looked the other way. María de las Nieves was undeniably a capable girl; the Mosquito King was undeniably not capable in the same ways. Royally crowned or not, she could be extremely useful as his consort. She would watch out for him better than he could for himself. She would be his indispensable ally and aide. She would be his sixth, seventh, and eighth senses. They would have the power and resources of the British Empire behind them, but if reviving the Mosquito monarchy ever became a question of one individual's intelligence, covert guile, and tact, it was likely to be she who won the day. But what did María de las Nieves's devotion really mean to the mysterious muchacho? What conception did he have of the trials waiting ahead, and of how much he would need to rely on her? Unlike many of the other characters who've passed through this narrative, he left no written record of his thoughts, no letters, diplomatic correspondence, or diaries, few recollected or divulged conversations and confessions. Can we at least say that Mathilde was conceived in love? He did say that he was in love too. Over and over he told her he loved her. There was a little song María de las Nieves had made up and that she liked to sing softly and in four languages into his ear as they climbed toward their separate climaxes, especially when it seemed as if it was going to go on and on forever: *metelo sacalo / q'imitza" q'onkxa / stick it in pull it out / penetra extrahe id;* in Spanish, Mam, English, and Latin she would singsong it into his ear. *Shovel-nosed shark, / Grandmother, grandmother! / Shovel-nosed shark, / Grandmother!* That was his song for her. It came from the book; it was a Mosquito song.

They even practiced making crayfish traps the Mosquito way, as Dr. Slam had taught him that weekend in Escuintla. Observing the two kneeling in the patio garden one afternoon assembling the intricate traps, Mrs. Gastreel was reminded that they were still children, after all, and felt a pang of remorseful foreboding, which she cryptically confided to her personal diary. María de las Nieves and the mysterious muchacho took the traps down to the River of the Cows and caught a few frogs, and made love in a secluded wooded hollow beneath a cliff wall.

The mysterious muchacho really was reading more confidently, and now they were finally approaching the end of that book. They were reading about the *Sukia,* a haglike old sorceress who, according to the book's narrator, possessed more power over the Indians and Sambos of the Mosquito shore than any King or Chief. The grandfather of the present King had been killed on her order, yet that rustic sovereign had not dared to bring the *Sukia* to justice. Only the English, they read, frightened the *Sukia*. So much so that she finally fled, fearing that during the visit of some English vessel of war she would be blamed for the murder of two Englishmen who'd been slaughtered while turtling on the cays off the coast. Another reason for her departure, wrote the narrator, was the advent of a more powerful and less malignant *Sukia*, gifted with prophecy, knowledge of things past and to come, and who was beautiful and young and lived in a mysterious manner, far up the Cape River, among the mountains. Flames and the bullets of guns were impotent against the *Sukias!* Over the next few pages, the narrator described his encounter with the beautiful young *Sukia* known as the "Mother of the Tigers," who was less than twenty, tall, and perfectly formed, and wore a tiger skin, and gold bands around her forehead, arms, and ankles. There was a print in the book of the beautiful and bare-breasted sorceress in her scanty tiger skin, a tamed jaguar at her feet.

"By jiminy, my Queen," the forever mysterious muchacho playfully drawled, "what thinketh you about having that Mother of Tigers over some night for a banquet of crayfish, crab, and roast monkey." María de las Nieves didn't doubt that such terrifying episodes were now embedded in her destiny; according to the book, the Mosquitoes practiced polygamy too, and what was she going to do about that? "We'll have to get you a little tiger skin to wear," he chuckled, and he gave her a hard pinch on the rump, which made her scowl and pinch his cheek just as hard. The narrator continued, and the mysterious muchacho continued reading: "Whatever tone of lightness may run through this account of my adventures in the wilderness, those who know me will bear witness to my respect for those things which are in their nature sacred, or connected with the more mysterious elements of our existence . . ." The narrator wrote that, except for the somewhat melodramatic manner in which he'd been conducted up the mountain by the messenger of the *Sukia* to meet her, and the incident of the tamed tiger, nothing occurred during his visit that was visibly out of the ordinary. But he was puzzled and impressed by the relationship, the perfect understanding, that seemed to exist between his Indian guide, Antonio, and the *Sukia*. The narrator promised that the mystery of that

relationship would soon be revealed. He wrote that there has always existed a mysterious bond, or secret organization, among the ruling and
priestly classes of the semicivilized Indian nations of America, which all the
disasters to which they'd been subjected has not yet destroyed. *The aborigines of Mexico, Central America, and Peru are secretly united, and to this day are
bent on vengeance against their conquerors* . . . They were reaching the book's
closing pages, and she was reading now, by lamplight, at the library table,
while he listened with his head in her lap. Outside a steady evening rain
thrummed and splattered. The narrator was about to part with the loyal
Antonio, his guide; his adventures on the Mosquito shore were at an end.
It was night in the Bay of Honduras, and they were on a beach facing a
shadowy island. Approaching from behind, Antonio quietly laid his hand on
the narrator's shoulder. "I knew who it was," María de las Nieves read
aloud, "but I said nothing, for I hesitated to betray my emotion. He respected my silence and waited until my momentary weakness had passed
away, when I raised my head, and met his full and earnest gaze. His face
again glowed with that mysterious intelligence which I had remarked on
several previous occasions; but now his lips were unsealed, and he said:
This is a good place, my brother, to tell you the secret of my heart; for on
that dark island slumber the bones of our fathers—" Like the beautiful
*Sukia,* Antonio was descended from Baalam Votan, the Tiger-Heart, who'd
originally led the Mayas to the Yucatán, "—whose descendant I am, for am
I not Baalam, and is not this the Heart of the People?" And Antonio went
on to describe with reverence and fervor the golden age of the people of
the Yucatán, from whom María de las Nieves thought herself descended
too, and their war against the Spanish, and their defeat, and the dispersal
of the Holy Men, their wives, sons, and daughters, throughout Central
America, and their still burning vows of revenge, and Antonio now wore
around his own neck that same magical and sacred amulet, the Heart of the
People, which had instructed his glorious ancestor to lead his people to
war; and that, María de las Nieves read in amazement, was Antonio's destiny too. Wasn't it true that nearly twenty years ago, an Indian war had
driven her parents from the Yucatán? There was no part of her life that was
not already encoded in some book, she reflected. If she could find all the
right books, she might be able to decipher everything destined ever to
happen to her.

For the first time in many weeks, she thought of Martí, and felt swept by forgiveness and compassion and a kind of distant awe, as if he were already very far away from her life. She lowered her head and, with her lips against her young lover's ear, whispered, "We'll make war against Spain too, mi amor. We'll help my friend Martí liberate Cuba." She saw long canoes, filled with tireless Mosquito Indian paddlers and muscular spearmen, streaking like green lighting across the Caribbean!

One day a black-eyed Indian girl, perhaps the prettiest and sauciest the mysterious muchacho had ever encountered, with pretty milk teeth somehow immune to tobacco stains, brought a note for him to the legation from her mistress, in which she had written that she would not be able to see him that day or the next because she had to attend the wake and funeral of a friend who had died, a girl of seventeen just like herself. Imagine, mi Rey, having to die before ever having the chance to know what I now know! (Or did la niña have that chance?) Did the mysterious muchacho happen to be standing outside the legation talking with Don Lico when the pretty Indita approached with the note, which, as always, she handed to the concierge? Did she steal the muchacho's heart at first sight? Did she mean to? She was rarely anything but saucy, and India or not, you weren't likely to ever see a prettier girl in the streets of La Pequeña París, or even in all the world.

María de las Nieves still had her other duties at the legation, of course. Sometimes the mysterious muchacho went out into the city on his own. He had a normal young man's taste for billiards, and as long as he promised not to drink liquor or to reveal any information about himself, Minister Gastreel didn't object, and even gave him a little British Treasury money to spend. Although the actual date of their departure for Mosquitia seemed undetermined, or else was a closely held secret, she knew it must be approaching. Dr. Slam, a Mosquito Indian who'd studied medicine in Jamaica, had returned, with his pince-nez and silver-knobbed baton, and had taken a room in El Gran Hotel. The mysterious muchacho said that Dr. Slam knew that María de las Nieves was going to be Queen, but when she was introduced to him at the legation, she was referred to only as Miss Moran. As they had first done so many weeks before, the reduced trio of men enclosed themselves in the library. As she sat at her desk that day, tears welled into her eyes. She told herself it was nothing, but couldn't

quell her unease. She'd been feeling too emotional lately anyway; it was a
if her insides were made of still water into which any dropped grain of sand
caused absurdly expanding waves. The next morning, when she was giving
Mrs. Gastreel her Spanish lesson, the Chiefess broke wind, and though
they were sitting outside in the corridor by the patio, the smell filled her
nostrils as if there was no more air left in the world but that flatulence, and
a wave of nausea propelled her up from her chair with her hand over
her mouth, and she walked into the garden taking gulps of air, and when
she finally came back to the table, she apologetically explained, "I don't
know what is happening to me lately, I caught just a smell of those roses, and
it made me feel sick," and trying to compose herself, added, "A little like
Caterina de' Medici, no? She couldn't stand the smell of roses either—even
seeing a painting of roses would make her nauseous." But Mrs. Gastreel's
blue stare was cold and disdainful. "Yes, you do look a bit pale," the Chiefess
finally said. "Let's stop." That was their last Spanish lesson. At the legation one morning only days later, María de las Nieves learned that the
mysterious muchacho had departed for the Mosquitia with Dr. Slam the
previous night. Tersely, yet gently, Minister Gastreel said that the date
of the departure had been kept a secret until the last moment even from
His Majesty.

"So that, last evening, when we said good-bye, he did not yet know he
was leaving?" she asked vacantly.

"He did not yet know, Señorita Moran."

Then she dared to confront the Minister with what he had not alluded
to again since the day he'd suggested that she might want to be Queen:
"And I will soon be joining him there, Your Excellency?"

Minister Gastreel blinked once in surprise, and flushed so that the
creases in his rugged face seemed to fill with shadow, but he spoke
unflappably: "First we have to be certain that the crown, so to speak, fits,
and that his subjects accept His Majesty. Otherwise, you know, it could all
be quite unsafe."

"I could be a help to him in that," she said.

"Yes, Señorita Moran, I know that you could" was all that Minister
Gastreel would say. He turned gruffly away, leaving her by herself.

During the siesta break that day she sat smoking for a while in the reading room kiosk, until somebody else came in, and so she went out, and

walked the city streets in a teary daze until it was time to go back to the legation, where she passed the remainder of the afternoon in depressed suspense, waiting for any scrap of information to drop her way, like a miserable dog cringing under a miserly pauper's table. That evening, when she returned home, María Chon was out. Amada Gómez complained that when she'd come back from the dressmaker's for the siesta break, María Chon had been out then too, and had left no meal for her. There was no sign in the kitchen of any supper having been prepared for the evening either. They waited until nearly eleven, and then went into María Chon's room and discovered that most of her clothing, adornments, and odd possessions, even the cri-cri Mack Chinchilla had given her, were gone, and so was her small leather trunk, a gift from María de las Nieves so that she wouldn't always have to carry her belongings in a bundle on her back like a backward India. That morning, María Chon had walked her to the legation as always. So, instead of going on to the market, had she come right home and gathered up all her things?

The next morning María de las Nieves went to El Gran Hotel to inquire when Dr. Slam had departed, and the clerk told her that there had been no such person staying there, but when she described his appearance, he responded that in that case, she must be referring to Mr. Nelson, and that he'd left the hotel yesterday morning. A prying neighbor had once remarked to María de las Nieves that late one afternoon she'd seen a handsome young man courting her at her window—"eating iron" was the popular phrase she'd used, evoking the manner in which men pressed their faces to a window's iron bars to nibble at lips on the opposite side. María de las Nieves had stared at the busybody as if she must be a lunatic and said, "At *my* window? Then he was eating iron all by himself, I assure you." Later it had dawned on her that the young man in question must have been Hernán Pedroso, calling on María Chon. She would not have described Hernán Pedroso as handsome, but it was credible enough that someone else might. And so she'd asked María Chon if she had a suitor, and without hesitation María Chon had answered, with a dismissive snort, "Sí pues. Hernán Pedroso. But no, Doñacita, I don't think so," and María de las Nieves had mumbled a few words of empathy. Since the onset of her love she'd visited J. J. Jump's photo studio only once, and even her visits to Don José had grown infrequent, but she went to J. J. Jump's studio now

to ask young Pedroso if he'd ever stood outside her house speaking to María
Chon through the window, and he swore that he never had. "But did you
ever do anything else to make her think you were interested in her that way,
Hernán?" she asked. These questions obviously humiliated the sallow assistant, but he answered, "Yes, Señorita. I did. Here in the studio. And we went
for some walks. And I thought . . . I thought she cared for me, that she'd
given me proofs. But then . . . but, nooo." He fell silent and María de las
Nieves persisted, "But what happened, Hernán?" and he shrugged and said,
"She changed. What's it to me?" His eyes flashed with anger.

She stood in the sunny street outside feeling as if time itself had shattered into infinite pieces so that now this moment would never end. She
felt oddly transparent and lightened, as if even time had been drained from
her, though she was ambling into the outskirts of the city, headed vaguely
toward the Sierra de Canales and the River of the Cows. As she walked she
tried to review the evidence, her lips moving as if she was talking to herself, which she was, though silently. At home, she had been exceptionally
circumspect about her love; the mysterious muchacho's existence was an
important diplomatic secret, and it was obvious that neither María Chon
or Amada Gómez could be trusted with such information. Of course it was
not possible to hide all signs of the great transformation in her life, nor,
finally, had she even attempted to. She'd been aware of the strains her
behavior, the evidence of her happiness and of her secrecy, were causing
in her home: the air of resentment and curiosity, the stray comments over
her irregular hours, and Amada Gómez's increasingly frequent tight-lipped
stares of condemnation of what she couldn't even bring herself to acknowledge in words; and María Chon's excited, meddlesome, eager, teasing, and
even jealous inquiries and pestering. "Yes, I have a novio, now," she'd finally admitted to her servant and adored friend. "He's been staying at the
legation as a guest of the Gastreels. I can't tell you anything else right now,
Maricusa. Soon, mi corazón, soon I'll tell you, I promise." Wasn't that
enough? Wasn't it enough that eventually she'd even entrusted María
Chon with notes, addressed to Mr. W. C. F., which she was to bring to Don
Lico at the legation? She'd ascribed María Chon's wounded sulking and
resentful diffidence to her servant's forgivable immaturity and possessive
curiosity, which she truly had intended to address soon; she'd even spoken
to the mysterious muchacho about bringing María Chon with them to the

Mosquitia. And hadn't he looked her in the eye and answered, "The impostor King does not object to his impostor Queen choosing her impostor servants, my love."

She'd been going around feeling made of weeping water for weeks anyway. Even the odor of night flowers in her patio was now revolting to her. She wept, ate, vomited with nausea, wept, and vomited. Her blood had not come down when it was supposed to, she knew that, but she'd been trying not to think about that also; weeks had passed and now it had not come down again. Now she'd reached the River of the Cows. She sat down on the grassy bank and stared into the water frothing around the volcanic black stones. María Chon had run away with the mysterious muchacho and Dr. Slam to the Mosquitia. She had no proof that it was so, but she didn't doubt that such proof would soon appear. She was pregnant too. Of course she was. She'd known all along that she was going to get pregnant. She sat staring into the river until she noticed with surprise that it was growing dark.

At the legation she went about in a stoic torpor. She tried to rouse herself: the only way of finding out anything more was to stay here, performing her duties well enough. Very pregnant Mrs. Gastreel ignored her or else was sharp and rude, and no longer even offered her tea in the afternoons. It was as if she was acting the role of a diplomatist's wife who only now understood that the sly and clever little mestiza had stained the honor of her house. That was how Mrs. Gastreel acted, the hypocrite! Minister Gastreel, however, remained more or less himself, though he was rarely jovial. He also was nervously awaiting news from the Mosquitia. Sometimes she asked him, "Has there been any news, Your Excellency?" and he did not pretend that he did not know what she was referring to, but simply answered, "No, Señorita Moran. There has not been. It's still a little soon."

In that nightmarish manner another week dragged by, and then another, and part of another. The only reason she felt alive at all now was because of the new life growing inside of her, though she did her best to hide that. One afternoon Minister Gastreel summoned her to his office and handed her a telegram, and there she read: *WCF hung. Doveton Slam Morgan Others dead. Regent escaped to Jamaica.* Minister Gastreel said, "It's not clear who sent this telegram, Señorita Moran, so we'll have to wait for confirmation. I do find it very alarming, though, because they have the names, you see.

The Americans, I suspect. Sending the strongest possible message. Just brutal, they—. Of course, there will be repercussions—." The Minister made an effort to gather himself, closing his eyes; a moment later he opened them and, in a ghastly tone of strained optimism, said, "It does look as if dear Wellesley got away."

No mention of a yet to be coroneted queen, she thought. No mention of a dead María Chon. Others dead. Could Others even be a surname, Mr. Others? Would whoever had sent the telegram have just neglected to mention the fraudulent boy King's Indita novia? That was more than possible, she knew. But maybe the telegram isn't true, she told herself. That's what it is: *not true!* Three days later Minister Gastreel returned from a meeting at the United States Legation to which he'd been summoned by Colonel Williamson, the American Minister Resident, and once more called her into his office and invited her to sit down. Minister Gastreel's lips were pulled down at the corners, and his eyes had a myopic softness.

"Our worse fears have been realized, I'm afraid, Señorita Moran," he said, looking right at her. "Colonel Williamson has received the same information from his own consul in Greytown. He placed the blame on local property owners whose interests would be threatened by revived Mosquito control in the old protectorate—Nicaraguans, mainly, and *other* foreigners, he said." The U.S. Minister and Kentucky native, Minister Gastreel told her, had then spoken with regret concerning his former Confederate compatriot, Mr. Doveton, whose own philosophies and bitterness had resisted any healing of his severed patriotism, finally leading him to this sad and even treasonous end. The Minister continued: "Colonel Williamson then had the effrontery to say to me: I trust it was not the British who were encouraging this motley group in their pretensions, Sidney. I answered, Of course not, Colonel. And he said he hoped there would be no resulting ill will between us or between our two nations. But why on earth should there be? I answered. Oh, Señorita Moran, this is not a good moment, it is a very sad moment for us all. And, of course, I feel most directly responsible." His eyes seemed rimmed in blood.

She wept quietly while he sat silently across from her. Pride, shame, or something else prevented her from acknowledging her betrayed and usurped position by asking if he knew anything of the fate of María Chon. The next Monday morning Mrs. Gastreel met her at the legation door and told her she was being dismissed because of her immoral conduct. She said she was sure they both agreed there was no need to expound upon that conduct or its proof in any detail, and that it had been obvious to her for quite some time. The hugely pregnant Chiefess punctuated that argument with a curled gesture of her finger toward the small but noticeable swell of María de las Nieves's belly.

# Chapter 8

"In the Central Park, they raise a red ball high into the air so that the skaters will know when the lake has turned to ice," María de las Nieves told Mathilde aboard the *Golden Rose* one morning. "And because in New York everybody, but especially children, love to skate, that red ball is beloved." Though barely able to conceive of it herself, she had already done her best to explain ice skating to Mathilde. All over the city, she'd told her, children looked at the sky, climbed trees, leaned out high windows, sat on their parents' shoulders, just to see if the red ball was in the sky. "But Mathilde, your tía Paquita's house is just across the street from that park. So you'll always be the first to see the red ball."

"How do they raise it?"

". . . I don't know."

"Like a kite or a hot-air balloon?"

"I don't know, nena."

"What is the red ball made of?"

"Pues, I don't know."

"But why, Mamá, don't you know?"

"We can ask Paquita later. She, or Elena or Luz, or certainly Miss Pratt must know."

But she was fed up with asking Paquita questions about life in New York. Outdoor and indoor electric lighting, elevators, elevated trains, the telephone, ice-cream- and butter-making machines—Paquita found a malicious delight in overwhelming her with accounts of these inventions, some of which she even possessed in her own homes, and about which María de las Nieves could speak with little confidence, having only read about them in the newspapers.

"I've read in the newspapers that soon there will be ink pens that discharge electric currents into the arm to prevent fatigue no matter how much you write," María de las Nieves, fueled by a little too much brandy, had exclaimed earlier in the voyage. "Pues, without a doubt, I want one of those! And also"—she'd laughed, for she knew this at least sounded absurd—"electrical hats that will allow men to salute each other without having to use their hands. *Ad majoren industria gloriam*, no?"

"And what do you imagine such a device will look like?" mocked Paquita. "Really, Las Nievecitas."

In La Pequeña Paris, gas-lighting on the city's main thoroughfares had finally been installed, replacing the tallow lamps that had been standing since the capital's earliest days. Then, only months later, the first electric lights appeared, by the orange trees in the esplanade in front of the National Theater, six small glass globes dangling from a wire, electricity devouring the carbon rods inside, their glow penetrating the emerald darkness with such steady clarity and ineffable sweetness that just standing inside that soft sphere of light filled you with a hopeful glow of your own. No new electric lights had been added since, but the six little globes had instantly transformed the new gas lamps into dingily flickering relics.

Mathilde's question about how the red ball was raised brought back a memory of the mysterious muchacho. Of course María de las Nieves couldn't help but think of him every time she saw the young sailor on the hurricane deck, who seemed about the same age now as her lover had been back then, and so resembled him that he could be his ghost. One morning the mysterious muchacho had carried four carefully hollowed eggshells out of the legation kitchen and, going to a limón tree that grew in the patio garden, had shaken dew from the leaves into the openings in the bottom of each shell. Then he'd placed the eggshells on the rim of the fountain, in direct sunlight. A little later he'd called María de las Nieves out to see how the eggshells hovered in the air like tiny hot-air balloons. Well, three hovered; the fourth for some reason refused to rise. When she lightly touched one with her finger, it plummeted against the fountain rim and broke. Why dew inside, she asked, and not drops of ordinary water? It had to be dew, he answered, because it only worked with dew. Only with dew, mi amor? Qué bonito, and forgetting herself completely, there in the garden she'd kissed him.

Mathilde, ninety-five when I spoke to her, as long-lived and lucid as her mother is said to have been, told me that María de las Nieves never once in all her life revealed the mysterious muchacho's actual name. "As far as I know," said Mathilde, "or as far as we know—that is, I, and now you also—she never even wrote it down." William Charles Frederick was the name she referred to him by. Her mother had also never divulged to anyone, Mathilde told me, what exactly was discussed between her and José Martí when he came to visit her at home, just before he left the country for good, in July. By then María de las Nieves had secluded herself in the little house; Amada Goméz had moved out, María Chon was, of course, gone; and in a few more months, as the birth of Mathilde approached, her mother, Sarita Coyoy, would come from Los Altos to stay with her. María de las Nieves would only say, reiterated Mathilde, that the visit from Martí had saved her life.

"If you know anything about women from our part of the world," said Mathilde, black eyes gleaming in a deeply brown, wrinkled face, "then you know how melodramatic and proud they can be. It's no surprise that she kept her secrets so secret—a melodramatic silence that shouts to us from the grave: Look at me keeping my secrets!" Mathilde cackled affectionately, showing shiny, slightly yellowed teeth. She wore her gray hair in two girlish braids over her shoulders, each tied with a black velvet ribbon. She was thin and elongated-looking in a way that made her seem taller than she was, and remarkably limber, and I couldn't take my eyes off her slender hands, her fingers maybe the longest, most elegantly tapered I've ever seen, and though as wrinkled as you'd expect, still as nimble and expressive as they must have been when she was much younger. She played the piano, of course. Within three years of moving to New York, she'd won her first roller-skating competition. She learned to ice-skate too, but became, apparently, a girl dervish at roller-skating.

Though I should be used to it by now, I chafed a bit under Mathilde's condescension, for of course I understood, after so many months of "study," how women from that part of the world can be, even if I'm not from there myself.

"They must have talked a great deal, and she must have confided in him," I said. "You can tell that just from the little poem he wrote in her album."

"Yes. Why does the little bird fly to the wool tree and not the flannel bush?" Mathilde laughed gently. "It's a little poem, but it says everything!

Martí was the first to write in her album. The neighborhood gossips used those visits to start the rumors that José Martí was my father. Of course none of them knew anything at all about the mysterious muchacho, or about perfidious Albion's secret plot to advance their interests in the Isthmus."

"The evidence, what little there is, makes the Americans look like the perfidious ones," I said. "Murderous and ruthless, anyway. They wanted the canal all for themselves."

"Of course they did! Well, what was England doing, pretending it still had a future in that part of the world? They gave up after that, and well they should have. Went back to their Afghans and Zulus and Hindus and Chinitos, didn't they, where they still had something to offer—"

"Yes, all right," I said, knowing not to get into any of this with her. "Mathilde, you just said that Martí visited María de las Nieves at home more than once. Did you mean to?"

"Of course I did. There were two, maybe three visits. He was her friend, and he felt terrible for her."

"But you've always told me there was just one visit."

"There was the one that *saved her life.* Because of whatever he said. That was one visit!" She shook her long finger at me. "And one or maybe two more, during which whatever was said, joven, *didn't* save her life, though I'm sure much-amused her, and made her feel better, and took her mind off her sad situation, la pobrecita."

WITHIN A FEW months, though mourning and grief had hardly loosened their grip on her, María de las Nieves resumed some of her former routine, following her growing belly out into the city streets. Oh, my tiny baby, she had worried, you are going to have the most melancholy soul if your mami doesn't start getting out and about a bit. But even her friend Vipulina, still living with her religious aunt, and beginning to despair bitterly that she would never find a man to marry, was awkward and reticent around her. Even though it was no extraordinary scandal for a girl from her place in society to have ended up in her position, most people would feel bound to treat her disapprovingly, María de las Nieves knew. Still, people couldn't help being curious about the identity of the father: lowly as she was, the likely suspects were hardly anonymous figures: Dr. Torrente, Minister Resident Gastreel, J. J. Jump, the British Legation's departed First Secretary, or even that hapless Yankee Indio who'd ruined the country's reputation as a destination for European emigrants. María de las Nieves began visiting Don José Pryzpyz again, and then her favorite booksellers and stationers. She couldn't bring herself to stop into J. J. Jump's photography studio, though, because María Chon had been such a part of that place, and because the image Mr. Doveton had purchased still lived there, at least on a glass negative, like a sleeping but immortal little moth, to say nothing of countless María Chons. J. J. Jump initially assumed it was shame that kept her away, sent her a cheerful postal card ("Old Faithful" he signed it, the name of the great Wyoming geyser pictured on the front), and went ahead and included portraits of María de las Nieves and María Chon, side by side, in his exhibit, *Our 100 Most Popular Beauties*, at the International Exposition in Paris. Many of the distinguished damas and doncellas who made the trip all the way across the ocean especially to see their own images installed amid the modern wonders and natural abundance of the world were disconcerted to find those two dusky young faces displayed along with theirs. (How eccentric is our Señor Jump, a true artist, after all!) As for the fate of María Chon, J. J. Jump was mystified. Had she gone back to her peasant family in the mountains? But that didn't seem likely. Hernán Pedroso seemed relieved that she was gone. Understanding how poorly that reflected on the young man's sour spirit, and that he would never amount to much as a photographer, certainly not as a portraitist of women, J. J. Jump dismissed him.

María de las Nieves didn't reveal the reason for María Chon's disappearance to anyone but Don José (and perhaps, just before he left the country in July, to José Martí, though if she did, he preserved the secret). When six months had passed without any sign of life from her, she wrote to the Chon family to inform them that María had eloped with the returning King of Mosquitia to be his Queen, a romance she tried to cast in the best possible light, and about what had subsequently occurred, though she made no allusion to her own role in the tragedy, and held out the hope that María Chon might yet return. She knew, of course, that the dead almost always appear in dreams soon after they've died, to say good-bye or to reassure their loved ones, or even to leave the living with the burden of a specific or general guilt. The mysterious muchacho had yet to appear in any of her dreams, not in that way—it made sense that even in death the treasonous coward would stay away—but neither had María Chon, and this puzzled her, for no matter how guilty the runaway girl might be feeling, she knew her Mariquita still loved her.

During those months when she'd avoided even Don José, the umbrella mender had been plunged into another sort of mourning: that of a father's helpless grief and worry over a daughter's misfortune. He was hurt and mystified that she'd kept him in the dark regarding all that had apparently occurred, and tremendously missed her companionship. He grieved for his friend Mack Chinchilla too. Once Mr. Doveton had arrived at Don José's shop with two letters from Mack, one for Don José, and the other addressed to Mack's mother in New York City, which the umbrella mender was to mail if Mack was not heard from within three months. Don José had given Mr. Doveton a letter for Mack too, in which he confided the little he knew of María de las Nieves's circumstance. When the three months had elapsed without any further news, he'd dutifully mailed the letter to Mack's mother, and said a Kaddish and lighted a candle for his old friend.

Mack Chinchilla, Don José told María de las Nieves, had died fighting in the War of the Caves, the faraway Indian uprising in the mountains about which so much was rumored and so little known except that it was finished now, thoroughly routed, every last rebel smoked from his cave and hunted down; so it was said and written, anyway, in the capital. But Don José believed Mr. Doveton to have perished in that war too, and María de las Nieves knew that was not true; at least she thought she did. Had the British been aiding the Indians in the mountains without her knowing about it? Had Mack been enlisted somehow by Mr. Doveton or even Wellesley Bludyar in that cause? She knew the British had been supplying the Indians in the ongoing Yucatán uprising for years, mainly via their colony of Belize, but she knew that only because the mysterious muchacho had been told so by Dr. Slam and Mr. Morgan.

"You know, Señor Chinchilla left without saying good-bye to me," said María de las Nieves—a touch ungraciously on her part, all considered, reflected Don José. "I hadn't even realized he was gone. I wasn't paying very much attention, I have to admit." Mack had learned of María de las Nieves's mysterious pregnancy after leaving the city, Don José knew, from his letter. Coming on the heels of the calamity of his Italian immigrant farming colonies, it had bitterly disillusioned him, and Don José worried that Mack had joined the Indian uprising in a spirit of suicidal recklessness. Poor Mack had idealized María de las Nieves far too much.

"That boy wanted nothing more in life than to be your husband, María de las Nieves," said Don José, "and to be able to provide for you in a manner worthy of his affection. Those were his only two dreams."

"That man," she corrected softly. The mysterious muchacho was a boy. She'd had her heart broken twice in one year: where did the allegedly heartbroken Mack Chinchilla fit in alongside that? At least she was not the type who died of heartbreak, she knew that now. But what if poor Mack, if he truly was in love, had died thinking of her? What did she owe his memory then? She placed her hands on each side of her round belly, and after a moment, as if receiving a surprising communication from her womb through her palms, she smiled and said:

"María Chon used to call him Don Cochinilla. She really liked him! That's who *she* should have married. Oh Don José, why did it never occur to me to try to make that happen?" She covered her face with her hands and started to cry.

Mack Chinchilla turned up in one of her dreams a few nights later, standing atop a flat little board that was floating steadily through the night sky, waving good-bye to her, and grinning gleefully. The dream annoyed her because if Mack had been killed months before, then it made no sense, unless he was just endlessly circling the supernatural region of the recently deceased and utterly enjoying himself. Or else a cannonball had hit him in the head and sent him into eternity a grinning idiot! What Don José had told her must have somehow caused that dream, she reasoned, like a conversation you suddenly remember while doing something completely unrelated, and therefore it was not a true dream.

She received a letter under her door one day, and when she opened it read, *God sends misfortune to those he most loves*—it was signed Sor Gloria de los Ángeles. Her first reaction was to scoff: then He must have especially loved the mysterious muchacho, María Chon, Dr. Slam, Mr. Morgan, and Mr. Others. But then she gave in to her amazement to have received this communication from her former sister novice, and had the idea that one of the ways life was superior to novels was its way of sending you totally unforeseen surprises without it seeming in bad artistic taste, or a pitiably strenuous way of resolving a narrative into a moral or sentimental lesson, or at least into a credible ending, and she remembered Martí deriding novels for all those failings, which poetry, of course, does not share. This letter from Sor Gloria de los Ángeles was more like a poem that, once you've read it, goes on expanding inside of you, music turned into thought turned into radiant air. Whether you believe in God or not, she reflected, it's a blessing to have received this message from Sor Gloria, because it's true, there is beauty inside suffering, and the relationship between beauty and suffering is the secret riddle and challenge of secular life too! She sat down that night to a bowl of garbanzo beans in chicken broth, which she'd cooked herself, and wrote Sor Gloria a long letter, and took it the next day, along with another pot of garbanzos, on foot to Jocotenango, for she needed some money anyway, and still had some left with Padre Lactancio. When the shabby, underfed priest saw her coming, her pregnant belly protruding, dressed like any ordinary mengala of the street in flowing shawl and skirt but in cloddish India-rubber boots and carrying the earthenware pot, he clapped his hand over his forehead and exclaimed, "Oh no, Sor Gloria de los Ángeles, I don't want to hear it!" That outcry struck her as a nearly miraculous coincidence—though he quickly recovered, and said, "María de las Nieves, I mean. And, hijita mía, I really *don't* want to hear it!" During that visit she gave the letter to the priest to give to Sor Gloria, trusting that he would know how to deliver it to her, and so began a long and affectionate though not necessarily intellectually or spiritually challenging correspondence, which would continue, though sometimes with lapses of years, long after the novice was finally smuggled out of the country along with Madre Sor Gertrudis and most of her remaining clandestine nuns five years later, in March of 1883, after nearly a decade of hiding in the widow Zazúeta's stable.

In August, María de las Nieves turned eighteen. Later she heard that Mrs. Gastreel's baby had been delivered by the new method of cesarean birth performed by a young physician just returned from studying in Paris. After Queen Victoria's daughter Princess Alice died, the British Legation opened its doors to the public for those who wished to sign the condolence book, and María de las Nieves went. No one but Don Lico noticed her arrival. They exchanged greetings and asked about each other's lives with a shy and amazed formality neither knew how to transcend, and then she stepped into the cold, familiar vestibule and signed her name in the open book; as she left she handed Don Lico a letter for Minister Gastreel, and Don Lico took off his hat and bowed his head to her. In her letter to the Minister Resident she congratulated him on the birth of his son, and asked for any news regarding the fate of María Chon. Two weeks later she received a response by post from Minister Gastreel, penned in his own hand, thanking her, on behalf of himself and Mrs. Gastreel, for her kind note, and wishing her the very best.

On January 14th, 1879, María de las Nieves's daughter was born with an astonishingly full head of soft black curls, a delicately beautiful baby who resembled a minuscule Egyptian Queen. She was given the name Mathilde, for the ambiguous heroine of the novel Martí had mentioned the first time she ever heard him speak; anyway, she liked that name, and there was no one else around but Sarita Coyoy to try to dissuade her from it. Her mother had come from Los Altos to midwife the birth, which was not an easy one. Doña Cristina, still in mourning for both her daughter and her husband, sent a basket filled with pretty clothing for a baby girl that had been worn by her own youngest daughters. Josefa, the broken-toothed servant, arrived with a gift from La Primera Dama, a heavy baby's rattle made of finest sterling silver, the emblem of the Liberal Republic engraved upon it. The first time Don José came to the house to see Mathilde, María de las Nieves answered his knock and then stood in the door gazing rapturously down at the bundled little creature in her arms, speaking as if to herself: "I can't keep my hands off her. I take off her little dress, and I put her in another little dress, and I take off that dress and put her in another little dress. I'm so in love with her I don't what to do." Finally she looked up at him and warmly thanked him for his visit but shut the door before he could even hand her his gift. The baptism was at Padre Lactancio's church in Jocotenango; Don José was godfather, Vipulina Godoy was godmother, no questions asked; the baby girl was baptized Gloria Mathilde Moran. A year went by. The Gastreels returned to England; a new Minister Resident, unmarried, William Locock, replaced him. Sarita Coyoy went home to Los Altos, and came back with the twin boys she'd had by the sheep farmer, Gaspar and Nazareno, whom María de las Nieves found insupportable, eventually banishing all three; soon after, Sarita Coyoy returned alone, and stayed. One windy November evening María de las Nieves stepped into Don José's shop and announced that her daughter was definitely not allergic to wool. Another year passed, and then another. María de las Nieves was working as a private tutor, and sometimes translated documents from Spanish to English or vice versa for lawyers and merchants. Her mother did sewing at home, rolled cigarritos, and helped raise Mathilde, who often accompanied her abuela to church, though María de las Nieves begged her mother, with only a little success, not to fill her daughter's head with wild religious superstitions, Christian or Indian. They were poor, but were not going to starve. Bitterness, loneliness, rage, sarcasm, pessimism, and misanthropy all held places of honor in María de las Nieves's pantheon of personal deities; she intimately knew and respected each, and also feared them, and at times they all rose up together and held her completely in their dominion. Sometimes it was as if every positive thing she'd ever known had fled her forever—let's get away from this monster!— leaving her dangling alone inside a sullen darkness without ceiling, floor, or walls. But often enough that mysterious domain of the positive seemed to win the day, as if deep down inside some natural spring had broken open and the fresh saving water was bubbling up through her, flowing up into her veins, into her heart and brain and spirit as if it would never run out; but then it ran out, or else the demon crab lurking in her depths pushed the black boulder back in place over the source.

One rainy-season afternoon, as her twenty-second birthday approached, dressed in plain black percale and a simple straw *bolerita* with a periwinkle ribbon, and carrying the turquoise, silver-worked umbrella Don José had made for her nearly five years before, María de las Nieves stopped into the reading room kiosk in the Parque de la Concordia and found, for the first time in weeks, a foreign newspaper from someplace other than Panama City: *La Opinión Nacional*, of Caracas, Venezuela. But it's already months old, she reflected as she sat down with it, her eye catching a dateline of Nueva York, February 4 of 1882, before dropping into the column of newsprint, where she read: —The tillers of the soil are happy because the cold snowflakes, like white butterflies, bring to them on their wings, for the good of their crops, all the ammonia in the atmosphere, and they spread themselves over the earth so that all the animal pests will die beneath them, and the salubrious ammonia, which like all that is essence likes to fly, cannot escape from the cultivated soil which so needs it—. Her eyes flitted to the headline, "Letter from Nueva York," and to the subheadings—*Snow, delight and sadness.—Skates and sleds.—The houses of lodging and the taverns.—The year's grand balls.—A terrible fire.—Miserable female workers.—A suffrage congress*—and she went back to where she'd left off and read: The man of the tropics whose cranium resembles a chamber of light that adorns and colors everything wakes on snowy mornings like a man who feeds off hunger and thirst, and cowering like the wolf trapped within the phosphorescent walls of a vast tomb. He imagines that his hair has turned white. He threatens that vast and arrogant enemy with his fist—

Later María de las Nieves would swear that at that instant she saw him, hair a frosty white, standing at his window shaking his fist at the snow, an image that through all the future years would come back to her whenever she woke in a bedroom filled with the blinding light of a morning snow, and that she'd then turned to an inside page of the newspaper and at the bottom of the article there was the name that confirmed her premonition. But might the writer be some other José Martí? It was hardly as rare a name as Pryzpyz. She knew from the Pinkerton report that he'd been trying to find work writing for newspapers. —*within*, she read on, *inside his blazing cranium*, perch the rebellious eagles, frozen and swollen and flapping. But outside all is rejoicing and jubilation . . . noisy sleighs pulled by plumed horses and fast sleds . . . rosy-cheeked children playing in the snow . . . In Central Park the beloved red ball is raised. Now "José Martí'"s prose skated alongside the skaters, spinning, turning, chasing the flirtatious young girls over the ice . . . And then it was festive night, a beautiful January moon shedding its snowy light on the snow, and the chronicler went into the taverns to describe the wretched drunkards trying to keep warm over their drinks, their faces like sickly mushrooms in the poisonous atmosphere, and into the basement lodging houses, and followed a stumbling drunkard into the steaming mass of magnificent horses outside the Academy of Music, and it was the season of elegant society balls and the prose, drawn by the burning light of chandeliers, flowed into the ballrooms, telling what everything looked like, what everyone wore, and then:

—Life and Death wake up together every morning; at dawn one sharpens its scythe and the other takes up its sprig of jasmine, sometimes eaten by worms. Another ball, an inferno of souls. A building next to the tall post office roared with fire that day. It has been a terrible spectacle, but one whose existence didn't disturb the rejoicing lovers of the dance. In that cold night, souls, already liberated from their bodies, crossed the dark and humid space on their path through the silent snow, shivering and sprinkled, wrapping themselves in the flying flakes. (Who else, she thought, would describe souls like that?) The fire was in a building full of newspaper offices. A hundred red tongues came up the staircases and through the corridors. The upper floors, packed with poor office girls and messenger boys, filled with horror and screams. A man standing in flames at a window; another, inside a fiery halo. The firemen's ladders can't reach the upper floors. A poor black woman clambers screaming from a flaming office, curls up on a window frame, roasting as she tries not to fall to the street, her hand on fire, suddenly she straightens up, pulls her skirts between her legs, lets out a shriek, throws herself to the street, her body breaking loudly against the stones. A black, a bootblack in a nearby drinking establishment, heroically and spectacularly saves three lives and, his chest covered in blood, walks off to do more good. A young woman appears in the highest window. Her hands are stained with the glorious ink of her work. Flames bite her hair; she parts the flames with her hands. Her dress ignites and she tears off the burning shreds. She fights hand to hand against the fire. Six yards beneath her is the closest ladder, at the top of which a fireman stands with his arms open, and she lets herself fall, arrogant and serene, and is saved. A man is told to do the same, and he refuses . . . more death, more horror . . . Today all is ash . . . the heroes, honored . . . the newspapers will move to new offices, they are made of spirit, and so do not die in a fire . . . cadavers buried with religious hymns, or buried in the humid ruins. Throughout that rubble, like warriors who've fought well, killed in the midst of battle, are the frames which held the boxes of iron printing type, operated, for a base salary, by frail women. In truth it fills you with pain to see, arriving from the faraway suburbs, in these mornings which resemble dusks, those valiant workers, who having returned home the night before from their rough jobs, reclined their disquieted heads, without time to dream, on their cold and hard pillows. Streetcars and ferries at this hour resemble orphanages. The women arrive with their faded pallor, their reddened noses, their tearful eyes, their swollen hands. They do the work of a man, and their salary is a pittance, much lower than that of a man.

Now María de las Nieves paused to light a cigarrito and ponder this. She was sure she'd never before read such a vivid account of horror; her blood felt quickened. And she was stirred by what Martí wrote about the working girls. Her life was not nearly as hard as theirs; hers seemed lazy in comparison. Those poor women of the city live like Indias of the mountains, she thought: long dawn journeys, endless workdays. From beautiful ice-skaters to elegant balls to girls who died in an inferno clutching red-hot letters of iron type, what a lot to absorb in one sitting, and there was yet more: —the impressive, black-clad damas of the suffragette congress: It's an astonishing thing, wrote Martí, how grace, reason and elegance have come to accompany this cause. The congress of women leaves the impression of a lightning bolt, one that shines, cheers, seduces and illuminates. The women of the congress are like mischievous Cupids, quivers full, aiming their arrows with a fine hand at their perturbed and suspenseful enemies, helpless to protect themselves, turning their faces, lifting their arms to dodge the sure strikes. What lightness of exposition! What brio of feeling! What skill in the arts of combat! What grace in the commotion of their criticisms: "You leave us no choice but between lives of servitude or of hypocrisy! If we are rich, you take our inheritances! If poor, you pay us a miserable salary! If single, you abandon us like broken toys! If married, you brutally deceive us! You flee from us, after you've perverted us, because we are perverted! Now that you've left us alone, give us the means to live alone. Give us the vote." And at this moment, wrote Martí, as if it were a law of this land that the powerful and puerile should always be united, a beautiful lady announced that the George Washington of their cause was in the hall; a famous woman who speaks that language which Americans like because it makes them laugh and possesses in abundance the quickness and brutality of a boxer. Susan Anthony, wearing heavy walking shoes, who that day, rather than give a speech, exhorted the audience to buy her book . . . In Wyoming the women vote and run for office; there a Republican husband ran against his Democrat wife for the same position. Of this last, Martí did not approve: In our lands sharing your lives means truly beginning to enjoy them together. María de las Nieves exploded in silent rancor: Oh, so that's how it is in our sweet little land, is it? Then Mathilde and I will live in Wyoming, and wear heavy walking shoes.

She'd reached the last paragraph: —Reverberating alongside those women's voices are the robust and magnanimous ones of New York's great men, congregated elsewhere to denounce the barbarous treatment the miserable Hebrews are today victims of in Russia—et cetera et cetera—the hearts of all men and women on earth respond to the anguished cries of the men and women of Moses.

It was as if Martí, realizing he was late for an appointment, had handed his pen to Mack Chinchilla to finish his chronicle. A day of unexpected hauntings. As if far away, disappeared and dead friends had decided to call on her in the reading room kiosk via a newspaper, which is made of spirit, so cannot die in a fire. She leafed through the rest of the newspaper as if the spirits of María Chon or the mysterious muchacho or even Wellesley Bludyar might rise from its pages.

From then on, whenever María de las Nieves walked into the park and toward the reading room kiosk, she felt a mounting excitement reminiscent of those long-ago days when she'd always hoped to find Martí sitting inside. Day after day she waited for another *Opinión Nacional* to turn up in the reading room kiosk with another article by him, but none ever did.

It seems plausible enough that María de las Nieves, reading of the tropical man shaking his fist at the snow, had a premonition that the author was José Martí. And maybe she really did think that she'd never before read such poetic and daring prose in a newspaper, and even recognized its revolutionary qualities. Though it's no secret that opportunistic hindsight, however well intentioned, especially among those who'd had personal contact with El Apóstol during his lifetime, was a commonplace of the early Martí scholarship and hagiography. Eventually published in newspapers throughout the Americas (though not in La Pequeña Paris) José Martí's *crónicas* from New York would finally occupy more than three thousand pages of his posthumous *Complete Works.* If not quite in 1882, within a few years, the greatest literary men of the Spanish-speaking Americas would be acclaiming those crónicas in much the same manner as María de las Nieves had in the reading room kiosk that day. For the crónica form, as practiced and developed by certain young writers in Latin-American newspapers at the time, was *the laboratory of the Modernist poetic style.* The Nicaraguan boy genius Rubén Darío, destined to become the greatest Spanish-language poet of his era, wrote that it was while writing for *La Nación* of Buenos Aires, where Martí was a star *cronista*, that he learned to manage literary style. *Martí's United States is a stupendous and enchanting diorama,* wrote Darío. *I'd almost say that it increases the colors of actual vision: . . . a literary Brooklyn Bridge equal to the one of steel; Sioux Indians who speak in Martí's language; snowstorms that make you really feel the cold.*

María de las Nieves tore Martí's crónica from the newspaper that day, folded it, and tucked it into her long sleeve before she went out of the kiosk; as was her manner, she obsessively reread it for weeks.

And one morning there it was, in a clear plastic folder, its soft, barely creased paper and newsprint faded and powdery looking, left for me upon the table at which I worked: that same century-old article, torn by María de las Nieves from the newspaper and carried home by her inside her sleeve. I felt moved, holding it in my hands. It struck me as the most moving thing Mathilde had let me see so far, and I needed a moment to gather myself and remember what we'd been talking about before.

"She never heard from Wellesley Bludyar again, Mathilde?" I asked, there in the library of the legendary mansion—legendary, anyway, to those of us who've grown up in Wagnum, Massachusetts, in the shadow of that baffling, appearing-disappearing family of numberless surnames who founded the Cody Rubber Company so long ago and still own and run it and who for so many years employed so many Wagnum families, who built schools, churches, ball fields, and parks, whose presence in our town is as ubiquitous as the rubber balloons whose manufacturing they pioneered and mysterious as only a lost or suppressed history can be, whether of a family, a business empire, or a long-ago minor episode of political intrigue.

"I think whatever Mr. Bludyar saw or experienced there in the Mosquitia destroyed him. Or maybe whatever he himself *did* there, you know? How did he manage to escape, and not the others? Well, you can look into it if you want"—Mathilde's hands opened and hovered before me in the air like enormous moths—"but you won't find very much. After Minister Gastreel passed on, it seems Mr. Bludyar was close to the widow for a while. But he died alone, in Norfolk. He wrote to my mother only once, when it was many years too late."

"Was María Chon killed with the others?"

"Not even Wellesley Bludyar knew for sure. I assume she was, because she was never heard from again. Maybe she became a *Sukia*. Well, my poor madre liked to think so."

Needless to say, an enormous amount of material was made available to me in Wagnum. Even Mrs. Gastreel's packet of English Christmas cards turned up among María de las Nieves's seemingly inexhaustible trove of papers and artifacts. There I also found a brief article clipped from the French newspaper *Le Figaro* of 1933 concerning the debut of one "Señor Carlos López" at the Theatre Lido in Paris, where he'd just premiered his magic-novelty act of tying inflatable toy rubber balloons into animal figures, with an accompanying photograph showing Señor López, in a black frock coat, holding a rabbit made of white balloons over an inverted top hat. That now unavoidable "party trick" of tying balloons into animals had never before been performed in public in either Europe or the United States. In the photograph Señor López looks like a late middle–aged, albeit darker-skinned and goateed version, of the forty-three-year-old José Martí who, on the 19th of May, 1895, at Dos Ríos, Cuba, rode his horse—in some versions, a runaway horse, and in others, one spurred on a suicidal charge— into a hail of Spanish bullets and eternal glory and martyrdom; in my opinion, the resemblance is strong. The article in *Le Figaro* asserts that Señor López is Mexican, but that is not true. Who is "Señor Carlos López"?

But I was only supposed to clear up the mystery of Mathilde Moran's paternity, and narrate that history as it occurred, and now my task has been more or less completed. Sure, I'll be handing this in nearly thirty years too late, but it turned out to be a much bigger job than any of us had ever imagined it would be. I realize, of course, that there are still some questions that need to be addressed.

ABOARD THE *GOLDEN ROSE*, having carried the brandy snifter from Paquita's stateroom back to her own cabin, and lighted the candle inside its salt-clouded glass box, María de las Nieves was, for the last time on this voyage, sitting down to her copy of the Pinkerton's National Detective Agency office report. The boardinghouse, run by the Mantillas in a four-story rented brownstone on East Twenty-ninth Street, was, according to the operative E.S., though sparely furnished and lacking steam heat, very neatly kept and homey. But E.S.'s small room, down the hall from the Martís' bedroom and sitting room, was dark and airless, with one window facing a wall of brick, a row of strangely reclusive pigeons always lining the sill like feculent grim reapers. Because E.S. had no view of the street, the Pinkertons rented other rooms on that block from which operatives could monitor Martí's comings and goings. It wouldn't have been prudent, of course, for E.S. to scurry after Martí every time he went out. Though Martí usually left the house through the front door on the parlor floor, he often, especially when returning late, entered through the subsidewalk service door. Did the other operatives watching from their rented rooms ever notice if the subject of their surveillance arrived in an especially agitated state? Were they able to tell whether infirm health and strained nerves-heart-mind had combined to deliver the young exile to that door sickly pale and trembling, his torments visible in his eyes like another kind of flower that opens only at night? Were the hilts of *a hundred daggers* protruding from his chest? Did any of those agents spy the hovering glow of a candle inside the door? Was it, by any chance, his landlady who held it? Did she set the candle on the floor, freeing her arms for an embrace? That would be convenient; though, of course, no such thing was reported. María Mantilla, the daughter of Martí's landlady, would be born in late November of that same year, and so she was conceived approximately six weeks before the Pinkerton detectives began their surveillance in April; that is, after Martí had moved into the boardinghouse in January, and before his wife and baby son joined him there in March. In October, one month before María Mantilla's birth, Martí's wife and son would return to Cuba without him.

At the time when I began visiting Mathilde in Wagnum, only a small number of people in the world even knew of the existence of a Pinkerton's National Detective Agency office report on Martí's first year in New York. It's possible that Mathilde, and then me, were the only people still living who had even read it (and she had never read it very thoroughly). A few years later, in 1978, the Center for Martí Studies in Havana, Cuba, published in their journal a French researcher's account of having discovered, in a Madrid archive, the billing records submitted by Pinkerton's agency to the Spanish Legation in Washington, D.C., in 1880. The agency's operatives, identified only by their initials, were required to keep meticulous records of their expenses, to be reimbursed by the Spanish government. Those expense accounts provide a ghostly map and itinerary of that surveillance operation, in which seven operatives were assigned to José Martí alone: On the 21st of April, for example, the operative J.P. filed: *For the weekly rent of a room from which to observe José Martí's residence, $4.00; expenses in a cigar shop at #411 Fourth Avenue in order to be able to watch Martí, 0.20; expenses to be able to stay inside a tavern on Nassau Street and Maiden Lane, watching Martí and Cirilo Pouble, 0.10; April 23rd, breakfast at Delmonico's, while watching Martí and a friend, necessary because that restaurant has two exits . . . ;* and so on, day after day, over four months. Restaurants and taverns with two exits always provided operatives with the pretext for a drink, or a meal, on Spain. E.S. regularly reported buying candy and other gifts for the Mantillas' three children and the Martís' little son, Pepito. He hired Miss Paral to take Spanish lessons. When Martí, claiming to need a bit of rest and seaside air, traveled to Cape May, on the New Jersey shore, from where months before General Calixto García and his men had furtively sailed for Cuba aboard a hired schooner, devoted E.S. arranged to have New York City newspapers delivered to where Martí was staying, and agents trailed Martí there and back on the trains. On twenty-six instances, E.S. recorded buying a bottle of wine for Messrs. Martí and Mantilla.

That discovery of the Pinkerton billing records set off a hunt for the "office report" that would, in keeping with the agency's standard practices, have been submitted to their Spanish clients at the end of the investigation. At least as far as is publicly known, no copy has been found. María de las Nieves kept hers an almost lifelong secret, and then so did Mathilde, apart from the short time when she allowed me to read it. I'm not even sure which of her many heirs has possession of it now. Of course it's possible, even likely, that other copies of the report exist elsewhere, tended as secretly as the one in Wagnum.

—Mrs. Carmita Mantilla is an exceptionally hardworking woman, wrote E.S. in that report about his landlady, her days consumed by myriad domestic chores, tending to her mostly Cuban boarders and raising her three children. She might be a sturdy, pleasant, wide-bottomed Irish maid, if it were not for her Latin features, manners, and the cadence of her walk, which I admit make her another sort of woman entirely, yet there must be a reason I could not resist making that comparison. I merely want, Sir

Superintendent, to draw your attention to certain of Mrs. Mantilla's qualities which others, prejudiced by her dreary circumstances, might overlook.
Mrs. Mantilla encourages me to attempt to befriend our Miss Susan Paral.
"Meester E.S., that ees a cha*rrr*ming señorita, and I see how your eyes
follow her," said Mrs. Mantilla to me yesterday, only moments after our
enchanting Schenectady Southern Belle had again ascended the stairs to
the little sitting room where she takes her Spanish lessons with the Martís.
"Why no I invite for you two a nice cup coffee or chocolate after, we sit
together, and you can get to know, jes?" You can imagine, Sir, how earnestly I desired to prevent that occurrence. My lips, perhaps, struggled to
form a witticism about how pleased I would be to meet that nice cup of
coffee, but—. Mrs. Mantilla took hold of my sleeve: "But why, Señor E.S.,
the intelligent young mans in this country have so much fear of the woman,
while the stupids so bold. Señor E.S., your brow is handsome and pale-ed,
the blue veins like streams under the ice, your blue eyes look as if dream
only of sky. Oh Señor E.S., you need a warm head lie next to yours! I promise you will not be my lonely bachelor boarder forever." In her softly care-
worn face, Mrs. Carmita Mantilla has the lively and expressive dark eyes
of a gypsy girl—. So, thought María de las Nieves, you've fallen for her a bit
too, haven't you, treacherous E.S.?

Manuel Mantilla, some years older than his wife, also owned a small
tobacco-importing company, which brought in an ever diminishing income,
with a little office by the wharves that he no longer attended daily, mainly
for reasons of health, but also, speculated E.S., from demoralization and
perhaps a touch of intrinsic sloth. Manuel Mantilla had a weak heart; his
doctor had ordered him to desist from all vigorous activity, his movements
and breathing were labored, and even walking tired him. In bed at night,
Carmita Miyares de Mantilla had worriedly mentioned to some of the other
boarders, her husband had to sleep nearly sitting up, propped against pillows, for often when he did not he woke choking and gasping like a drowning man. E.S. wrote: Perhaps Mr. Mantilla is just a shadow of the man he
once was, and though that man may never have been a dynamo, I do
sense that he possessed a solid dignity and virility of the tropical and Spaniard kind. His occasional smiles contrast so sharply with his sagging, ill-
complexioned features they seem to contort his face into a ghastly mask of
surprise, which one does warm to, as if sharing with him that unlikely surge

of good feeling and vigor, usually brought on by a few glasses of wine and some animated conversation at the dinner table, or a helping of affectionate doting or a spontaneous caress from his wife, Carmita, as when only the other day she leaned over him as he sat at the table, her arms embracing his ravaged chest, and told us that her husband *is a rooster*. She patted proudly the little bulge beneath her navel. "Mrs. Mantilla is in pregnancy," Martí beamingly told me. Miraculously good news indeed! The Cubanos took turns hoisting their glasses, reciting toasts and even poetry, and eyes grew misty as the talk turned to children born far from their true island home, who are in danger of growing up more accustomed to speaking and writing in English than Spanish, as even the Mantillas' three children, the two boys and the one girl, already show signs of doing. Now another little Mantilla is on the way! The conversation next took up, as so often it does, the latest news of home received by mail, which it is difficult for me to follow, though this contrapuntal chatter does seem to proceed in predictable circles around our table, usually commencing with a lady boarder announcing some señorita's engagement to some young *fulanito* who, *tu sabes*, another voice chimes in, is the brother of *fulanita*, who was married to *fulano*, who is the cousin of *fulana*, who married *fulanito* from Camagüey, whose father was the owner of—now the men add their own brusque but emphatic commentary regarding this apparent scoundrel, son of *fulano*— and so on, Sir, as if Cuba is a place where everybody is always marrying somebody's cousin and everybody knows the secret history of every *fulano* and *fulana* better than they do their actual names, *fulano*, as I'm sure you've deduced, meaning *so-and-so*, though far more variably, for *fulanita* can apparently evoke any girl's name and *fulano* any gallant's. (*So-and-so* is usually Joe, or such.) Why is the life of every *fulano* and *fulana* on the Island of Cuba apparently an open book, while here on the Island of Manhattan some of our exiled *fulanos* lead lives which mystify not only the world's greatest detectives, but the very compatriots with whom they share their domesticity?

Sometimes at our dining table and in our little parlor in the evenings I think I see some of the other boarders, especially the women, but also the men, exchanging distressed and meaningful glances and stares. I have no proof of what they are communicating with those looks, or privately thinking. I have only been able to peer into Mr. Martí's mind, thanks to

Mrs. Dominga Hurley's splendid translations of his personal writings. Like her husband, Mrs. Martí is rarely in a happy mood. Yet anyone watching would think that Mr. Martí loves her desperately, that he is bewitched by this slender, honey-skinned, hazel-eyed, undeniably sensuous young woman, and craves her affection. But Mr. Martí's more exalted perorations are occasionally followed by a brief burst of derisive laughter from his wife, as if she considers him incredible and doesn't care if others perceive it. I often hear excited and exasperated voices rising behind their doors. These Cubans can speak so mellifluously, then so explosively. They are proud, even in the humiliating circumstances of poverty and exile; pride sits inside some like a wise old slave waiting for his interminable life to end. Sir Superintendent, I wonder who the father of Mrs. Mantilla's child actually is? She would have conceived some months before I arrived here. Of course, one cannot rule out the proud, even heroic paternity of "Señor Rooster." What if, five months ago or so, during the winter holiday season, he found himself, after a few glasses of wine, perhaps a little gin or rum punch, feeling chirpy as a cricket in July—?

This was the part of the report, reflected María de las Nieves, that Paquita had referred to, supposedly suggesting that Martí was the father of Carmita Miyares de Mantilla's child. That was all. Paquita must also have been influenced by what E.S. had copied from the notebooks; and also, of course, by the gossip of her friend the Spanish Consul General. Now, off in the night, María de las Nieves heard the beseeching bellow of a passing ship's horn. Sometime tomorrow the *Golden Rose* would dock in San Francisco, and she felt a mixture of excitement and dread, as if she'd been promised that this ship could be her permanent home, and now she'd abruptly been told she had to leave. She leafed ahead in E.S.'s report. Martí was becoming an expert on New York *cock-tails*. Some of the Cuban exiles were wealthy, and gladly offered to pay for their poorer compatriots' drinks. In the taverns Martí preferred to drink gin. He was among the young men who liked to drop in at the fashionable Hoffman House bar, that sumptuous palace of liquors, which didn't even serve beer; and where Martí had, at least once—dogged E.S. was there—ceremonially dropped a rose at the foot of Bouguereau's notorious painting of splendid naked nymphs splashing into a lagoon, coyly fleeing a satyr who is evidently afraid of the water. A perpetual crowd of men stood gawking at that painting, protected from their primitive groping by the silk rope they were forced to stand behind. With a spirited, wondering eye, Martí observed the sweaty spectacle of drunken bankers and Wall Street brokers climbing onto the tables in the July heat, shouting and waving cigars to each other in greeting.

E.S. wrote: We were waiting for his Cubano comrades to arrive, and conversing about President Garfield, when Mr. Martí commented that though everyone seemed to ignore the other paintings covering the walls, there were many worthy pieces. "There is Faustus by a Spanish painter," said Martí, pointing at a gilt-framed portrait near the top of one wall. "Faustus sleep, while Mephistopheles watch with his back to us, because not even he can support the sadness of turn around to see too many wicked young women who come into this place, E.S." Many wicked women do come into that place, maneuvering deftly, swiftly, artfully through the crush of masculine shoulders, many of them quite fetching, slender and tall, with livid complexions and hairdos somewhat disheveled, stray humid strands clinging to their cheeks and their necks, some with frankly satiric and artificial expressions on their faces, and others who know how to look pure and a little abashed or stunned to be there. "So beautiful women," announced Martí, in a tone of earnest regret. "Then how do they end so abandon? Why no can find a good man to love them, E.S., and make a clean home? Where are their brothers, who let them fall?" Absurdly, and not for the first time, Sir, the object of our surveillance had brought a lump to my throat. A moment later he was calling my attention to a porcelain plate hung upon the wall, which depicted a nude ocher-hued young woman carried off on the back of a hulking monster: "But look—she is a Christ," he commented. How was she like our Savior? I asked. The girl depicted on the plate, he said, reminded him of the marvelous depictions of Christ painted by a certain Central American painter of past centuries, because of her long, fine figure, and the expression of fierce delight on her face, which made defiance and submission seem one and sublime. "But what, finally, *are* your views on religion, Mr. Martí?" I asked, with perhaps a note of exasperation. "It is good to study religion for the beauty and the wisdom it can give," said Mr. Martí, "but never should we let it to fill us with fear or fanaticism." "Then you view it as a sort of mythology?" I proposed. "Mythology is for symbols," he answered, "and religion, for aspirations."

"But that is not the same as believing?" I asked. "Aspire is more necessary, more painful than believe, E.S., and is now the work of every free and honest man," he said. In one corner, beneath a small crystal chandelier, perched within an arc of shining bronze, was a parrot. "His name too is Pepe," said Mr. Martí. "Another tropical man, my little brother. Maybe he is from the jungle, and only like to talk when it rain. I ask." He approached the bird and stirringly recited a poem in Spanish, a love ballad, he elucidated, sung by rebel soldiers in Cuba. The parrot spoke, and Mr. Martí responded, "No no, arrogant bird! You are in America!" "But what did that bird say?" I asked, bewildered. "He said, *Je suis anarchiste*," answered Mr. Martí solemnly. "He is not an American bird, and has yet even to learn English, but he carries Old World violence and hatred hiding inside, poisoning his green feathers and yellow eye." Was he having me on, Sir? I do not know. In the opposite corner, wearing a gaudy silk suit, a monkey danced at the end of a gilded leash. "And that wretched creature," said Mr. Martí, "is a spy for Spain." I was much relieved when, a short while after, the Cubano *fulanos* finally arrived. —Oh yes, thought María de las Nieves, I do remember this part. Watch what happens now, she reflected, taking a draw from her cigarrito and hunching over the page. As drinks were consumed, and the conversation grew more excited, only Martí ever remembered to stop and translate from Spanish to English for the young Pinkerton operative. Martí was expounding upon Hamlet: Were the thoughts and emotions that consumed a man in his inner life as *real* as the actions of his outer life? Weren't each as crucial a struggle, and ideally interdependent? Why do so many people believe that only what happens outside is real, and not inside? The inner life should also be heroic! Martí was meeting some heated resistance. A few of the men gathered around Martí were proud and arrogant veterans of the Ten Years' War. They stepped closer to Martí, drawing themselves up, raising and deepening their voices, slapping their own chests and making broad gestures, as if to remind the slight nervous poet of what a vibrating mass of muscle and blood was required to form a true soldier. In the midst of this, Martí generously remembered to turn and provide E.S. with a summary translation.

And I responded, wrote E.S., with this fawning exclamation: "But as you were saying just the other day, Mr. Martí, only those who are denied the privilege of an elevated personality do not recognize the reality of the personal, and isn't that where our sense of the extremely beautiful is born? Haven't we learned to love heroism from those who know how to love beauty?" Then it was as if an electrical switch had been thrown: Martí's expression was like an enormous globe of silently exploding white electricity, through which his mustache and eyebrows blackly shone. I thought: I wonder if am going to have to move from the boardinghouse early in the morning. Sir, I had committed an extraordinary blunder. Mr. Martí had not said any such thing the other day; rather I had copied something very much like it weeks before from one of his notebooks, but had only recently read Mrs. Hurley's translation. Mr. Martí seemed to be staring deeply into my own inner life, which I do not regard as being insensate to either beauty or the heroic. I said, "And I have been pondering your words with profit ever since, Mr. Martí," and smiled like a small-salaried salesman in a furniture house, an employment perhaps now looming in my nearest destiny. For another suspenseful moment, his eyes bored into mine, though I managed to maintain all my composure, until his face finally resolved, for the briefest instant, into a resigned perplexity, and he turned back to his friends, the virile comrades . . . Eventually the hour arrived, as it inevitably does on such nights, when it is difficult for men to keep their eyes off wicked women. Mr. Martí could not, especially off that red-haired one, in a yellow dress, and milky-pale freckled shoulders, and slashing eyebrows, and murky greenish undertow eyes of melancholy yet doubtlessly bewitching suggestion. He said something which made his comrades laugh. The laughter grew, as if Mr. Martí's words discharged successive repercussions, but Mr. Martí barely allowed himself a smile, as his eyes followed pensively the red-haired temptress through the barely diminished crowd. I asked casually, "And what has provoked such merriment?" The wicked though beautiful red-haired woman glanced back again over her bare shoulder, and Mr. Martí, without looking at me, graciously though rather sternly translated, "What noble things we can accomplish with our lives, Señor E.S., if we do not have feed our stomachs. But what about this other stomach which hangs underneath, and has such terrible appetite?" His friends laughed raucously, as if those words were even more astounding in English than in Spanish.

María de las Nieves was unfazed, even amused by what she had just read, her old friend's rare outburst of vulgarity. People would never think me capable of such a thought, she mused, would they—but I am. I just could never speak it out loud. I can go years thinking that it seems impossible that I will ever satisfy that appetite again and then it is easy to satisfy and no one notices or cares, nor does it make me happy, when loneliness surrounds me like water I've already drowned in without dying. I've at least played at being a wicked woman, especially during the little-little while when I was friends with Lola Montenegro. The bohemian poetess, the only female member of the Literary Society of "the Future," also worked as a tutor. A pretty, soft-faced mestiza with Oriental eyes and a small quizzical mouth, Lola resided in a cramped one-room apartment overlooking the plaza where the railroad station was going to be, near the bullring, which had become a popular zone of cantinas, cafés, and revels, a sort of Pequeña Latin Quarter, where a new breed of women, some even from the best families, could indulge in the dangerous nocturnal sport, pioneered by Lola herself, of drinking and smoking in public and knowing how to fall into a spontaneous tryst with a visiting bullfighter, an Italian lyric opera singer, a dissipated young diplomat or naval officer or itinerant merchant or circus acrobat or fugitive confidence man traveling through and who would soon go away. With time those episodes seemed almost not to have occurred, leaving no more than a shadowy tinge on your bones, where no one can see it. Eventually she and Lola Montenegro had fought, over an adorable young poet who was interested in neither of them. And she'd again retreated into her house with her daughter and mother, and then more or less stayed there, sunk in gloom and shame; though the shame, if not the gloom, dissolved quickly enough. But neither the memories nor the appetite go away. They stalk us through our blood, and get lost inside our skin and veins, trying to find a path to our hearts, but their maps are all wrong—no, Lola?

Now and then during those years Paquita had sent money, which María de las Nieves had always returned; baskets of food, which she'd accepted. Eventually she'd fallen into the common habit of the mournfully but resolutely lapsed of occasionally sitting in churches, especially Santo Domingo, where poor María García Granados's funeral Mass had been held and where there was a statue of a young Indian Holy Virgin so brown, pretty, and lively that she couldn't help but think of María Chon whenever she saw it. She began mixing religious books into her reading again, especially saintly *vidas* and theological treatises. After all, they were the most easily available books, by far the most inexpensive, and she enjoyed them. She was worldly and sensual and not impractical; she liked shops. But she'd decided there were aspects of the monastic life that she liked too, and that some little part of her had returned to it, finding truth and solace in austerity and lonely endeavors. Occasionally she recognized some of her former Sisters in Religion passing in the street, hidden under their shawls, shuffling along, coming and going from churches, and sometimes she smiled at them, a slight smile in passing that said, I understand why you live as you do. Once she even recognized Madre Sor Gertrudis walking far ahead down a long avenue, cloaked and hooded, the same figure she'd trailed so many times through the corridors of the convent.

YOU MAY FIND this unbelievable—I know I did, a little—but the table at which I worked at the mansion in Wagnum was the same old oak table where, a century before, little Sor San Jorge had sat reading about Sor María de Agreda and tickling her nose in the novices' study room. The legs were new, I was told, though you couldn't really tell, and though reconditioned, the table's surface, beneath its smooth luster, was scarred and worm-eaten. With the closing of Nuestra Señora de Belén, the table, as well as much of the old religious art that now decorates the library in Wagnum, and the vellum-bound books lining its shelves, had ended up with the convent's majordomo, Don Valentín Lechuga, or with his twin sisters, and had remained in their possession, and then with their descendants. Of course it took money, but even more time, and a nearly fanatical devotion and love, to track all these objects down in the homes of various Lechugas and persuade them to sell and then to transport the recuperated pieces of María de las Nieves's past to Wagnum. The adoring treasure hunter was not, I should add, though I suppose it must seem obvious, María de las Nieves herself.

The light spray patterns of dried droplets across the pages of the books María de las Nieves studied in the convent are like fossil tracks marking the years of wool up her nose and sneezing. The relative spotlessness, in that respect, of the books she read later—even Sainte-Beuve—are proof of how completely she outgrew, or conquered, that addiction. Pencil marks, checks and underlining, show which pages of her edition of Martí's *Complete Works* drew repeated or special attention. Later in life, as an amateur Martí scholar, María de las Nieves would devote herself to writing essays exploring and celebrating her subject's political morality, beliefs, and significance, under such titles as "José Martí: The Infinite Possibility." But the tip of her pencil lingered over, scratched, and nibbled most devotedly at his poetry, his letters, his notebooks, his fragmentary writings, his random attempts at drama and even fiction, anything dealing with the subject of love or allowing a glimpse into his intimate life. How many times, and in how many ways, did Martí say or write that poetry should be drawn from one's own personal life, and written in one's own blood?

—*This is how happiness passes through life: like a cup of snow that melts as it lands.*

—*Carmen: nothing for my own pleasure—all for my duty.*

—*Nothing weighs as heavily as a dead love.*

—*I'm writing calmly today. I'm writing well. Too well! Stay calm. It's death.*

—*I'm scared of not suffering enough before I die.*

—*Those women are like candies which once sucked on, dissolve. But they leave a perfume on your lips. Those who don't leave bitterness.*

These are just a few excerpts from the notebooks kept by Martí during the general period when the Pinkerton operative had infiltrated his boardinghouse. Sometimes he sounds like a nun and sometimes like a libertine, though usually a remorseful one. *The pen should be pure like a virgin!* The inner personal man should be as pure and honorable as the outer political one. In his notebooks, Martí anguished as if he believed his every private failing was also a stain upon Cuba. Eventually his battlefield death transformed him into an Impossible Ideal rather than an Infinite Possibility, beneath which all his private struggles and doubts were submerged, and even forgotten.

Santa Teresa de Ávila, on her wedding day, was given a nail from the Cross as a wedding ring by her Divine Bridegroom. In New York, Martí wore a ring fashioned from one of the links of the chain he'd worn in prison, *Cuba* engraved inside the band. It's not hard to understand that some people have trouble accepting that José Martí might have fathered

María Mantilla, the mother of the man who played the Joker on *Batman*, and the circumstances in which that might have occurred.

After the failure of their first reunion, Carmen Zayas tried twice more to renew her marriage with Martí in New York. The second attempt lasted a little more than a year: the Martís established their own household this time, in Brooklyn, but in March of 1885—only six weeks before María de las Nieves and Mathilde arrived in New York—wife and little son again returned to Cuba, and Martí moved back into the Mantilla boardinghouse, now relocated in Brooklyn also. Carmita's husband, Manuel, had died of heart disease in February. Nobody disputes that the widowed Carmita Miyares de Mantilla was Martí's companion during his last years and that he helped raise her children as if they were his own, especially little María. But Carmita went to her grave without ever once having uttered or written a public word about Martí's paternity of her daughter. Whatever María de las Nieves knew, she also kept to herself; after all, she had also once been the subject of such rumors, and could be again. It was only in 1959, also the final year of María de las Nieves's long life, that María Mantilla, then a nearly eighty-year-old woman living in Los Angeles, California, addressed the issue for the first time outside her immediate family in a confidential exchange of letters with Gonzalo de Quesada y Miranda, the son of Martí's close friend and literary executor. A man had turned up in Cuba claiming to be Martí's grandson. *Who is this man?* she wrote indignantly. *I, as you well know, am Martí's daughter, and my children are the* only *grandchildren of José Martí. I assure you that this matter has caused me great anguish, and realizing that I have only a few years of life left to me, I want the world to know this secret, which I have guarded in my heart with so much pride and satisfaction.* Gonzalo de Quesada answered that if the Quesadas had never publicly confirmed her status, it was only because until now she had never authorized them to. Quesada offered to write an article on the subject for the magazine *Bohemia*. But when the new Cuban Revolution canonized Martí as its highest revolutionary deity, such an article could not appear. María Mantilla's actor son, Cesar Romero, hardly immune to publicity seeking, had, of course, claimed Martí as his grandfather before. But only in 1990, during a debate on the controversy waged over several installments of the literary supplement of a Mexican newspaper, was a letter from María Mantilla to her son, in which she confided that José Martí had been her father, finally revealed. The newspaper published photographs of the letter's most crucial page and of the envelope, postmarked February 9, 1935, from Asbury Park, New Jersey, and addressed to Mr. Cesar Romero at the Hollywood Athletic Club in Hollywood, California. *He was very well known and greatly admired in all the South and Central American countries,* María Mantilla had written. *I want you to know, dear, that he was my father, and I want you to be proud of it. Someday, we will talk a lot about this, but of course, this is only for you to know, and not for publicity. It is my secret.*

In 1895, during the last months of his life, when Martí left New York to join the rebels in Cuba, who hailed him as their Future President, he was writing what would be his masterpiece: the diary of his return to the island he hadn't seen in sixteen years, and in which he at last realized his ambition of fusing poetry and action into a language that incarnates what it describes; the diary was dedicated to little María Mantilla and her sister, Carmita. During those last months of his life he also penned an extravagantly loving series of letters to the two girls, which is often reprinted and excerpted throughout the Spanish-speaking world to this day, especially those to María. In one of those letters Martí told María that he was carrying her photograph over his heart. But in the letter in which she confessed the identity of her father to her Hollywood son, María Mantilla was even more explicit: in Cuba, Martí had carried her photograph over his heart *to protect him from the bullets.* Might that embellishment be a sign of the old woman's tendency to fabricate? Anyway, no such photograph had been recovered from Martí's body after he was killed.

Just as I was finally finishing this work commissioned by Mathilde Moran so many years ago in Wagnum, a discovery was made in a military archive in Spain, a country apparently riddled with archives: the papers Martí had been carrying in the inner pocket of his coat when he was fatally shot off his runaway or charging steed at Dos Ríos, Cuba, recovered by Spanish officers, and subsequently lost for over a century. The packet included letters he'd received from the Mantilla girls and one from their mother, and a rustic little notebook filled with erudite and personal jottings like those he'd kept all his life, and that photograph of María Mantilla.

In one of those final letters to María, like the others obviously written with a presentiment of death and filled with counsel and instructions for living the rest of her life without him, Martí wrote: *Your soul is your silk.*

*Envelop your mother in it, and pamper her, because it is a great honor to have come into the world from that woman. So that when you look inside yourself, and at what you've done, you will find yourself like the earth in the morning, bathed in light.* In none of those letters does Martí invoke the memory of Manuel Mantilla, María's deceased "father." Neither, in their correspondence to Martí, do any of the Mantillas.

At María Mantilla's baptism at St. Patrick's Church in Brooklyn shortly after her birth, "Joseph Martí"—so was his name inscribed in the church's registry book—would serve as godfather, and two days later sail for Venezuela (aboard the ship, he wrote much of *Ismaelillo,* a collection of poems about his son and fatherhood; an attempt to transform that failure, his lost little son, into something ideal and enduring: poetry turned into a father, a father turned into poetry), where he would stay nearly seven months, until expelled by that country's Liberal dictator.

*The sincere man, obligated to hide his love, is converted into a hypocrite,* Martí wrote in one of the many anguished meditations on adultery in his notebooks. *The dignified man, in order to avoid scandals and harm to reputations he can't repair, becomes an undignified man. There is one fixed rule for happiness: don't do in the shadows what won't be applauded in the sun.* Why shouldn't it be assumed that Martí was writing from painful personal experience? How often had he confessed, in his private writings and poetry, his unhappiness?

MISS SUSAN PARAL had finally lured Martí into a meeting in a Broadway hotel. They ordered and drank most of a bottle of champagne, and kissed. So Miss Paral reported to E.S. Aboard the *Golden Rose,* María de las Nieves was accompanying Miss Paral through this disturbing seduction. Of course she had to read between the lines of Miss Susan Paral's subsequent confidences to E.S., her master. Couldn't they all be lies? Or was this Miss Paral's hour of beauty, when spy, student, actress, and lover finally merged. So far she'd supplied E.S. with little but redundant gossip about the Martís' disintegrating marriage; this was her last chance to redeem herself as an operative. She was to interrogate Martí like an adoring lover who wants to share everything: How do the rebels in New York communicate with their compatriots in Cuba? Don't you think I could help, Pepe? Who would ever suspect me? She was succeeding well enough, for here they were, ensconced together in a hotel. "—Coarse, course, curse, curtsy," said the overwrought Martí. "English is so difficult. Chinese is like this. How is told apart?" "Oh Pepe, silly . . ." "Franklin Street. Fraynklan Straight. Frinklin Strit. Frunkln Strut. I never know what are saying the drivers of the streetcar, Susana! Are these all the same stop? No two pronounce the same way." "Pepe, why are you so nervous tonight? Here, another glass of champagne, my darling. You promised to write me a poem, Pepe. Oh, can't you recite it for me? . . ." "But what happened *next*, Miss Paral?" asked E.S., after Miss Paral had fallen silent. "We kissed," said Miss Paral "but he was shaking, and he moved away, and I could tell he wasn't happy, and he said there was too much light in the room, that he needed complete darkness, and I said, Well do you want me to extinguish the lights? And he said, no. He said, No, I can no bed you, Miss Paral."

María de las Nieves has accompanied E.S. through four months of close surveillance, of purloined poetry and notebook confessions. She knows Martí's heart well. She knows him better right now than E.S. or Miss Paral or even María García Granados or Carmen Zayas or Carmita Mantilla has *ever* known him. His pain and turmoil bring her so close to her own that tears start into her eyes when Martí takes the seductress's hand (while also taking María de las Nieves's nervous hand into his delicate, nearly weightless grasp) and tells her that Darwin has written that once a species is extinct, it can never reappear, and asks:

"Is it the same with the emotions? When happiness is extinct within us, can it reappear? If love is extinct, can it reappear?"

"A fire can go out," she answered after a moment. "And then it can be relit."

"But then it is not the same fire," said Martí. "It is as different from the first fire as if Victor Hugo were now sitting on this bed with you, after I have left it."

"Then we are using the language of science and reason when we shouldn't be, Pepe," she said. "The scientist says we are made mostly of water. But Origen said we are more like a river, because we flow on and on, and change every day."

"Origen was also condemned by the Second Council of Constantinople for suggesting that man resurrects in the shape of a sphere."

"But a sphere that contains all that we ever were," she unhesitatingly replied. "Even our scars."

María de las Nieves took a deep drink of brandy. She was astonished at how her hand trembled, and by the feeling and arousal rising within her. She was looking so intently into Martí's eyes that she could see his pupils growing even larger, somehow even blacker, so overflowing with honesty and tender sadness that she felt embarrassed by her own intrusiveness, and she was powerless to pull herself away; she lifted a hand to the standing curls atop his head as if to soothe a nervous cat—

"It's not that you can't love or be happy," she went on. "It's that you've let your soul separate from your body. You worry too much about your soul, Pepe, and forget that it is the body that feels desire, and yearns for God, which is why the body and the soul can only be holy together. The soul may be immortal, but the body is the home of longing, and of love. There are saints and nuns who have explained that better than I can. But I think there is some wisdom in it."

"How is it you know so much, Miss Paral?"

"I was a novice nun in a convent, pues," she answered. "I read enough that one year to last a lifetime. And it seems I have a good memory. Lately, I've been going back to those books a little."

There on the hotel bed, he kissed her again. So it was true: she was Miss Paral, yet she was also still herself. She said, "If you want, Pepe, I will extinguish the lights." He said, "No. I cannot do this, I cannot bed you. Please. I am ashamed. You mentioned scars. I must tell you, I have a wound." He reached stiffly into his pocket and pulled out a few linked rings of iron, which he rattled loosely in his hand. "This is from the chain I wore in prison when I was sixteen. It wounded me in my manhood." His expression was indignant and sorrowful. "I take it with me everywhere."

"Love is a resurrection, Pepe," she said, incredulous that such words were coming from these painted lips. "Let's accept that as a metaphor at least. Jesucristo's scars were turned into rose petals when he was resurrected from death by God's, but also his mother's, love."

"San Bernardo said that no man, once resurrected, can remain pure, because as soon as he sees a woman, corruption enters him," said Martí, but even as he spoke, a playful light flickered into his eyes, sending an excited warmth through her body.

"Oh Pepe, mi amor, please," she murmured. "San Bernardo also said, It is right to call them dearest who are drunk with love. And right now I am drunk with love, and with brandy, and you are drunk, anyway, with champagne."

"I, a Freemason, am brought back to life by a monjita. We never avenge ourselves better or more ruthlessly than we do against ourselves."

"You've always liked monjitas, Pepe, and you know it."

He laughed and they kissed again. She embraced him, and pushed him back on the bed, as if she were the man. She undid her hair, and her long blond locks tumbled down, and Martí's eyes blazed in the dark. Then she was unbuttoning her dress, pulling it down around her shoulders, and cradling his curly head as his mouth began to lavish her large soft breasts. When María de las Nieves finally opened her eyes again, she was no longer in the hotel room and she was no longer Miss Paral: she stared past the curve of the lifeboat, into a sky as thick and radiant with stars as her own body was with satisfied pleasure. Her sailor was no longer José Martí, but he was still moving inside her. Quietly she sang a snatch of an old song and laughed to herself and kissed him again and moved her hands up and down inside his shirt. Her rump and the small of her back ached. How soft his skin was, how hard and lithe and warm his body, so sweetly young. He was as young as they'd both been back then, she and the mysterious muchacho. He was his ghost; but he was already *his own* ghost too. Her sailor boy would mean nothing more to her than that. She wasn't even going to cry. A beautiful adolescent ghost for a lonely woman who has drunk too much brandy and read too deeply and then found something else. She was as happy as she'd been in a very long while. He was done now, and they were both panting, like one body. On her back, her young sailor lying on top of her, between her spread legs, she turned her head sideways and stared across the vast dark expanse of the hurricane deck. The air was chilly. It was nearly dawn. Lights were visible along the California coast. They were almost alone on the deck, and unnoticed, here against the rail, beneath the lifeboats, where she'd made up her mind to lead him as soon as she saw him, when she went up onto the hurricane deck to throw E.S.'s revolting report into the ocean. Now it lay there, inside its cardboard portfolio, just beyond her reach, and she stretched out her arm and turned her body until she touched the manuscript and pulled it toward her. She listened with pleasure to the ocean and the ship moving through it and the low rumble of the engine and the flapping and clinking of the wind in the masts and she looked back up into the stars and told herself she was floating up there too, with all the other celestial heroines . . .

EVER SINCE SHE'D read the writings of Sor María de Agreda as a novice, María de las Nieves had dreamed of experiencing mystical bilocation. Well, maybe now she had. Maybe she'd *trilocated*, the first ever in history to accomplish that feat: Martí, the mysterious muchacho, the young sailor, herself corporeally manifesting with all three! That—according to Mathilde, as confided by her mother—was how the second child, her son Charles/Carlos, alias Señor Carlos López the Mexican, was conceived. That anonymous young sailor who so resembled the mysterious muchacho that he was like his ghost was the physical progenitor, and Martí the mystical one, thus her son's physical resemblance to El Apóstol.

I said, "If you expect me to believe that, you're crazy, Mathilde." Her black eyes widened indignantly at my impoliteness, and I apologized. Though I didn't dare to say so, it seemed obvious to me that this was a ludicrous ruse meant to disguise Martí's paternity of this child, half brother to both María Mantilla and Martí's sole legitimate son, José Francisco (known to Cubans as "the Son of the Statue"). With such a story "for a father," I thought, no wonder Charlie had grown up to become the reclusive inventor of balloon art.

Mathilde asked if I wanted to see the birth certificate. I said, "With Paquita's New York connections, they could have had the certificate fixed to say whatever they wanted it to say. Was he born in a hospital?"

"No, he was delivered at home. Lucy Turner came from Staten Island to be the midwife. She'd married, you know, an oysterman, a Negro."

"Oh, I see," I said sarcastically. "How long was it after María de las Nieves arrived in New York that she found Martí?"

"Not long after. That's true."

"And is that the story little Charlie Junior was told, or did he think Mr. Charles Tree was his biological father too?"

"He was told the truth, but when he was older," said Mathilde. "As far as I know, that is the only explanation my mother ever gave. Anyway, Paquito"—the annoying name she'd taken to calling me by—"this really is *no* concern of yours." She had only hired me, it was true, to compile and narrate the story of her own paternity, not of her half brother's; her two-thirds brother's, if it was a trilocation. Of course, like her mother in her later years, Mathilde usually had a Martí quote on the tip of her tongue to support or explain anything. In one of his notebooks, he'd written, in English: *Stimulate the fancy. The fancy, besides being a source of consolation, is the power of order in the invisible.* "Well, maybe this will help you understand," said Mathilde, and she quoted that. I stubbornly, and not dishonestly, said I had no idea what it meant, and Mathilde actually looked worried for me and softly clucked, "You don't understand?" and then shrugged her ancient, elegant shoulders.

"So that's why E.S.'s report ends there," I finally said. "With Miss Paral's seduction. Because your mother tore out the remaining pages?"

"Yes, I believe so. It happened in August, right at the end."

"But she remembered everything. She remembered what she read every night on board the ship, and what she thought while she was reading it, and everything that was in those missing pages, and later was able to re-create it all—just like Sor María de Agreda rewriting the Virgin's autobiography after she'd destroyed it."

"My mother had a wonderful memory, to her very last day."

"Then how was E.S. exposed in the end?"

"Well, he didn't include that in his report, of course. It ended abruptly, though, as if he'd moved out in a hurry. Martí never wrote, as far as I know, about it either. Why would he have? Whatever he and the others knew, they didn't want anyone else to find out how thoroughly they'd been infiltrated. As you know, General Calixto García had surrendered to the Spanish in Cuba, and Martí had resigned as Interim President of the CRC. Ten years later and more, when he was practically organizing the Cuban Revolution by himself, always traveling between New York and Washington and Florida and the Keys and back to Mexico and Costa Rica and Jamaica and keeping all those secrets up here in his own coco"—Mathilde tapped her forehead with two long fingers—"he used to imagine he saw spies and secret detectives everywhere. But he learned to employ his own secret agents too."

In another plastic folder was preserved the same issue of the *New York Herald Tribune,* dated April 7th, 1885, that María de las Nieves read, already ten days old, in her hotel room her first evening in San Francisco, California, a little more than twelve hours after the episode on the hurricane deck when her son, in accordance with the power of order in the invisible, was allegedly conceived. The newspaper contained an article about El Anticristo's illegitimate son Antonio, who was enrolled at West Point but was now in New York City, in the Windsor Hotel, awaiting further news about his father, whose reputed death in battle he'd learned about in the newspapers. No one from the family or the government had sent him a telegram to tell him that it was true; thus the boy was defiantly clinging to the hope that the reports were a fabrication by his father's enemies. The other news was that Paquita's New York neighbor and friend the former U.S. President General Grant, who lived around the corner from her on Sixty-sixth Street, was on his deathbed, and being fed cocaine by his doctors. In Paquita's own home, the Civil War hero had signed a contract with El Anticristo to extend the Mexican Southern railroad, of which Grant was president, to Central America. As she read these articles, María de las Nieves felt a growing apprehension: how was it that this, her first New York newspaper, had so much news to which Paquita was personally related? As if she was the most crucial personage on earth. Infuriating in a related way was the newspaper's puzzling account of a society marriage between Count Primo Magri, known as Count Rosebud, and Mrs. General Tom Thumb in the Church of the Holy Trinity, to which *only* two thousand celebrants were admitted. Mrs. Thumb's tasteful gown was breathlessly described, down to its last embroidered pearl, but it was also reported that she wore infant-sized gloves, infant-sized lavender slippers, and that the bridesmaid was only forty-two inches high. The bridal gifts included a castle in Italy from the groom, and among the guests were the Mayor and Mrs. Grace, Mrs. Astor, and Mrs. Cornelius Vanderbilt, society people, she knew, who were friendly with Paquita. What sort of count allowed people to call him Rosebud, on his wedding day no less? And why did she care? She was desperate to ask Paquita about this mysterious account of an apparently diminutive aristocracy, but was reluctant to provoke some condescending remark. When she handed Paquita the newspaper later that evening, she said only, "Perhaps you should read this. It has something about your stepson Antonio. He seems to thinks his father is still alive."

Later that night, the dictator's widow announced that on the way east they would stop for a day in Utah to see the bigamists, something she'd always wanted to do—she'd booked all of the train's first-class sleeping and parlor cars for their entourage, and thus the unscheduled stopover had been easy to arrange.

"When María de las Nieves arrived in New York," I said, "Martí was having a hard time again. In a way, it was like 1880 all over again, wasn't it? His wife and child had just left him for the second time. He was in that same mixed-up mood of flagellating himself like a monk and looking for consolation—though not just via his stimulated fancy, hah."

Mathilde tossed back her head and laughed as if my slightly risqué crack was the funniest, most dead-on thing she'd ever heard—but then she stopped and looked at me and said, "Oh I don't know, Paquito. Do you really think?"

Martí's own eyelashes made a sound against his pillow at night, which he compared to the rattling of dry branches in a strong wind, keeping him awake. Occasionally insomnia was kinder, producing golden arabesques of thought that reminded him of moonlight rippling over the night-blackened bay of Havana. He wrote that he knew what it must feel like to be a daisy being eaten by a horse. In a private meeting held in Madame Griffou's Hotel on East Ninth Street with the rebel commanders General Máximo Goméz and the black General Antonio Maceo, Martí broke with them over their plans to subordinate all aspects of the revolution to military rule. "A country is not founded the way a military camp is commanded," he told them. The generals' allies portrayed him as a deserter, but before a raucous Cuban crowd at Clarendon Hall, Martí gave a speech defending himself, and silenced his accusers. For the next two years, he was isolated from the revolution, and for all he knew, might forever be. He worked as a clerk and scribe in commercial and publishing houses. When the newspaper *El Latino Americano* asked his friend Adelaida Baralt to write a short romantic novel for its pages, Martí wrote it for her in a few days, an obscure roman à clef inspired by María García Granados and his year in Central America, published under the pseudonym "Adelaida Ral"; he insisted she keep the payment, even though he now had two households to support, in Cuba and New York. In his private writings, Martí went on wrestling with problems of love, fidelity, and desire. He fell into dreamy raptures over pictures of palm trees, which held a mystic significance for him, always symbolizing either Cuba or María García Granados. He fueled himself with constant drinks of Mariani wine—Bordeaux wine mixed with a strong dose of Peruvian coca; "the Divine Drink" was a favorite of the epoch's workaholics and over-stressed, including Thomas Edison, Émile Zola, Sarah Bernhardt, Queen Victoria, and three successive popes. His wife, Carmen, scorned as an aban-doned woman by her pro-Spanish family in Cuba, wrote asking for more financial help and for truthful talk instead of romance and illusions, and cajoled him to correspond more frequently with his son. He wrote his crónicas; late into the night he wrote his poetry. He taught night-school Spanish, and took on other occasional employments. Cubans spotted him rushing obliviously down the aisles of the elevated trains, his threadbare coat flapping around him as if he barely possessed a body, his arms full of books and newspapers. In the evenings, he was one more office clerk in a black derby hat amid a unanimous multitude of them, boarding the ferry back to Brooklyn. *Everything ties me to New York, at least for a few years of my life: everything ties me to this cup of venom,* he wrote to his closest friend in Mexico City. *You do not know it well, because you haven't battled here as I have battled; but the truth is that every day, as dusk arrives, I feel devoured inside by a poison that forces me to go on. All that I am shatters . . . The day that I might write this poem!—Well, in any case, everything ties me to New York.*

It was mid-April when María de las Nieves and Mathilde arrived, and though Central Park was still littered with patches of snow, and the morn-ings were as cold as the coldest mornings in Los Altos, when a thin layer of ice formed over the puddles, Mathilde would have to wait until the next winter to see the red ball raised in Central Park, signaling that the skating pond was frozen. She wasted no time learning to ride Relámpago, however. Though Paquita had insisted that all her children learn to ride their de-ceased father's war stallion, Mathilde turned out to be an extremely pre-cocious rider, and she and the Historical Horse formed a special bond. Mathilde, often taunted or ignored by Paquita's children, had, by her sec-ond week in New York, taken to spending as much time as she could in the carriage house around the block, where Relámpago had a large stall, and the young groom, Pablo Quej, slept beside him in the straw, though at least now, unlike in the presidential stables at home, he had blankets and a pillow. One afternoon they went riding in the park, Mathilde atop Relámpago, upon a beautifully stitched lavender-and-beige lady's Western saddle, shaped to tilt even a diminutive rider snugly upon her right seat bone. María de las Nieves rode the family's plodding brown mare, Quetzál, and Pablo was on one of the coach horses, a bay named Homero. "Erect posture, Mami, and relaxed hips," scolded Mathilde, already expert and bossy. Anyone seeing them in the park might have assumed that mother and daughter were from the plundering but civilized native royalty of some little-known, primitive corner of the British Empire, they were so fashionably attired in riding costumes provided by Paquita, whose wealth and delighted willingness to spend it seemed limitless. It was the first week of May, everywhere women paraded their new spring hats, the air was delicious, the streams in the park as frothy as mountain streams, all was exuberant fresh green and flowers, and the ground was marshy. They had ridden into the wildest western and northern reaches of the park, where Mathilde had terrified her mother by inducing the muscular white horse to gallop off in a martial charge; now they were heading out of the east side of the park, the horses at a walk. She saw a man entering the park who, despite his strict black coat, looked as wispy as the little girl he was leading by the hand—black derby hat, black tie, black mustache—

"Pepe! Maestro! Señor Martí! What a miracle! Ayyeee—!!" Ringed by three enormous horses, one with a shrieking woman mounted atop, the slight, mustached man glanced up and around in nervous confusion, pulling the girl protectively against him. Without waiting for Pablo to help her dismount, María de las Nieves plummeted from her horse onto her knees in the mud. He stepped toward her with his hands out and helped her to his feet and she looked into his pale, astounded face and said:

"Pepe? Don't you remember me?"

And he let go of her hands and said, "Of course I do, Señorita Moran." For once in his life, Dr. Torrente truly seemed speechless.

How she ached to embrace him! "This is your daughter?" she sang out, shrill with excitement, and she sucked in air in exclamation like María Chon: "She's so pretty, and looks so like her papi! And look, this is my daughter, Mathilde. Mathilde, like the heroine of Stendhal's novel, remember?"

"Who rides in her coach with her lover's head in her lap!" announced Mathilde, looking like a tiny, conquering squirrel atop the war steed.

"This is Señorita María Mantilla," said Martí, his hand on the little girl's shoulder. "The daughter of my dear friends." The slender little girl, unperturbed, more interested in the horses, smiled.

María de las Nieves apologized, and said, "But really you are beautiful, Señorita María Mantilla . . . Mathilde, Maestro Martí was my literary composition teacher. I know you've heard me speak about him many times." She prayed that her daughter would not say something rude or strange.

But Mathilde greeted him pleasantly, and smiled meaningfully, though not at Martí or her mother but at the girl, as if they were both in tune with ironies outside the adults' comprehension, and she told her, in Spanish: "This is the horse the Señor President General was riding on when he was killed in battle. Now it's mine, ve? And we live in his house." She pointed across the street, at a mansard roof and eyebrow windows rising higher than the trees.

"It's true, believe it or not, this very horse," said María de las Nieves.

"I can't think of a better fate for such a horse," said Martí, "than to be ridden in the park by a niña who reads French literature." He's a little paler, she thought (than he was only a few weeks ago, when I was Miss Paral), even thinner, tired around the eyes, his mustache is fuller, his hair has receded. As soon as he starts to talk, he turns into the handsomest, most virile man alive.

"Who pretends to," laughed María de las Nieves, and she added eagerly: "Yes, I think this horse has found its true calling too. Do you think there is some law of nature and history to be elucidated from that?" But even before she'd finished the pretentious phrase, she felt ashamed. Didn't she owe him some explanation, an excuse, for her fraudulent ascension into the world of luxury? What would that explanation be, that she'd sold her soul to Paquita? It was not as if she hadn't accused herself of that repeatedly enough, but somehow doing so had only kept the accusation at a painless distance. It was for her daughter's sake. She'd brought her to the capital of Modernity, where she would have the chance for a life undreamt of at home. She thought, He sees my awful frivolity, my dereliction for not going much deeper into all of this. I have no right to happiness, even less to complacency. Wait until he learns that Paquita surrounds herself with aristocratic Spaniards!

"And how is Carmen?" she asked.

"She is in Cuba, with our son . . . who is about Mathilde's age," said Martí.

"For a visit?"

"No," said Martí. "Perhaps not." She saw him give the little girl's hand a squeeze.

"I think I should explain," said María de las Nieves, realizing that she was launching herself into a speech that she desperately needed to be meaningful though she knew she was following only a vague path into a terrifying vertigo, "that Mathilde and I fall short . . . that is, short of my ideal image of a mother and daughter on horseback." Marti looked quizzical but interested. "On the train coming here, in Wyoming," she continued, and she paused and repeated, "—in Wyoming—the train stopped somewhere, the way trains do, in the middle of nowhere. Then from far across the green plain, I saw a horse galloping toward us. It was only one horse, so we weren't too afraid that it was an Indian raid or bandits. But just like that, it kept coming toward us, Pepe, until it had galloped right up to our window. Isn't that true, Mathilde? I know it sounds strange, but I had the feeling that this horse had spotted us sitting in the train from far across that plain, or even from the hills beyond, and knew it had to bring us its message. Riding on this horse were two girls, just a little older than Mathilde. Two girls of the West, Pepe, of that vast empty space we hear so many terrifying things about. Both with long braids falling over their shoulders, and very rustically dressed, not even wearing hats, and riding like men. One, a bit bigger than the other, was an Indian girl, with chubby rosy cheeks, and the happiest, freshest eyes and smile you can imagine, and the other, sitting in front, almost in the other's lap, was a skinny blond girl, with blue eyes, and just as happy and healthy looking. They rode almost right up to our window, and the four of us all looked at each other. Mathilde said that she wanted to be one of those girls. And the horse rose up onto its hind legs and turned and they galloped away."

Now she was embarrassed, though Martí, speaking carefully, said he could understand why such an arresting incident—her "Wild West Visitation," he sympathetically called it—would speak to her aspirations for her daughter, and for herself too, upon their arrival in this new land. Pablo and Mathilde rode on to the stable, leading the mare. Martí accepted María de las Nieves's invitation to come back to the house with María Mantilla. But what luck, that they had turned into the park at that moment! They'd come uptown to check on the ongoing vigil outside General Grant's house, where the former president remained on his deathbed, reporters and spectators constantly milling outside. Martí had often written about General Grant for the newspapers, and would again: his description a year later of a solemn but excessively extravagant memorial ceremony would end with an image of the tomb crowned by a stuffed white dove, wings spread and olive branch in its beak, a gift of the widow of another President General, Rufino the Just. Now María de las Nieves told Martí about reading his crónica in the reading room kiosk, so effusively praising it that he repeatedly muttered, "Thank you, Señorita Moran. You are so amiable and kind. No, please, enough," and said, "You could do it too. I'm sure you could write an excellent crónica about your journey through the West."

At the house, María de las Nieves, in her mud-smeared riding dress, led Martí and the poised little girl past the medieval suits of armor and palms in the entranceway to the outer drawing room, where they each sat in an enormous armchair. The drawing room was decorated in a fashionable mixture of Louis XVI, Renaissance, and Moorish styles, and needless to say there was not an inch of space that was not covered with some sort of ornamentation: velvet portieres, silk drapes and tassels, gold brocaded tapestries, crystal chandeliers, paintings, brass figurines and curios, and luxurious Oriental rugs over the oaken floors. There were also touches of home, such as a glass display case holding a scene of tropical nature: stuffed quetzal bird, toucan, iguana, baby tigrillo, amid jungle ferns and mosses. The walls were topped by a frieze of hand-painted historical pictures: scenes from the life of Alexander the Great, Julius Caesar, Cortés, Bolívar, Napoleon, Washington, Grant, the Afghan victory over the British in the Khyber Pass, and Rufino the Just leading the Liberal rebels at the battle of Patzicía.

"The purpose of a room like this is to make sure people never run out of things to talk about," said María de las Nieves, after they had been talking about it for some while. Martí was overjoyed by the coffee, fresh from the family plantations, praising it as the strongest and most flavorful cup he'd had in years. And he especially admired a bronze figure, mounted on a rectangular plinth, of a Bedouin warrior in flowing robes, cleaning his long rifle. (I've seen that very piece, in the house in Wagnum.) He was full of curiosity about the West; her story, he said, had given him a delightful image to ruminate on. He'd frequently written about that part of the country in his crónicas, though without having been there—the persecution of the Chinese, the terrible Jesse James—and had decided to write a verse epic about Buffalo Bill and the Indians, not in the light manner in which such subjects were usually treated, but serious and studied.

They agreed to meet three days later, in Madison Square; he would take her to a *salón de lunch,* and to some art exhibitions. With so much to catch up on, a week of nonstop conversation wouldn't be enough! When Paquita came home later that evening and heard about the encounter with the remarkable "Dr. Torrente," she insisted that María de las Nieves invite him to the dinner she was giving for Dr. Matías Romero, the Mexican Foreign Minister, who was coming to New York City to pay a visit to his good friend and railroad partner, President Grant. A few days later one of Paquita's Spanish friends brought her an article clipped from *La Nación* of Buenos Aires in which Martí had written about her late husband, comparing his contemptuous criminal greed to that of Cornelius Vanderbilt, whose sensational new mansion only a few blocks away Martí dismissed as a *dark box.* Paquita apologetically rescinded the invitation, adding that Martí was always welcome for afternoon coffee or tea.

What María de las Nieves really wanted was for Martí to take her to the Bowery, so she could see the neighborhood her late father was from. She arrived in Madison Square more than an hour late; she still did not know her way around. Here a woman was allowed out into the streets by herself, but could not smoke anywhere without inviting sinister consequences. Though she'd dressed as neutrally as possible, in the plainest black dress she'd brought from home, determined to begin a new life of austerity, the ride downtown was disagreeable. Too many New Yorkers had shrewd hard eyes and hard, frightening voices, and some said extraordinarily uncouth things. The shops here were palaces, and Paquita was happy to receive the bill for even the most whimsical purchases, though where would she ever find her doting umbrella mender in this city? But there is no need to catalogue all the ways in which New York could overwhelm. There were as many horses on this island as people, running down the weak, old, infirm, addled, lost, distracted, and foreign in the streets; on that one ride downtown, she witnessed several shockingly violent horse collisions. No wonder Relámpago just wanted to stay in the park playing with niñas! It turned out that she'd taken the wrong streetcar line; Martí told her it was not one that a lady should ever travel on. He was reading newspapers on a bench at the edge of the leafy park at the intersection of clamorous streams of traffic. He was in a cheerful mood: he despised Gotham and he adored it, he told her, though using many more words; he promised her that she would feel the same. "Just look at this marvelous newspaper," he told her. "Every issue of the *New York Herald Tribune* is a sublime poem—though less so today—" He ran his finger over the profusion of headings and subheadings on the densely printed front page, so many different subjects addressed, from all over the world, such originality and verve! "The sublime exists in the secret interrelationship between all things, María de las Nieves," he went on; "that is the secret language of modern poetry, which allows poetry to speak for the universal as well as the individual soul, and it is also the language of modern consciousness, which this newspaper at its best incarnates, though not today, because there is too much news about the backward and savage walking marathon." What a joy it was to be listening to him again! Whoever thought that here in New York City, she would find herself back in the reading room kiosk? What was a walking marathon?

"We will go to a *salón de lunch*, María de las Nieves, where you might well notice that our waiter, even as he pours our cherry cordials, is discussing over his shoulder the new maritime tariffs with another customer, because everything in this city goes forward, and even the waiters are lawyers, but everything goes backward too, as if the more educated and modern a people become, the more riveted they are by the brutal and primitive. Today the newspapers are full of news about the walking marathon in the Madison Square hippodrome, which is in its final day, and is being won by a man named Pérez, a poor Indian from our lands. Even if he wins he will stay poor, for he is surely in debt to his trainers, sponsors, and gamblers, who've entrapped and cheated him. But it gladdens people's hearts to witness these heartless and futile struggles." Even in front of some of the hotels around the park, Martí pointed out, giant canvases and blackboards were displayed, on which the latest results of the walking marathon were posted. The first to walk six hundred miles in a space of six days was the winner; the wretches walked thirty hours at a stretch, slept for a half hour or so, and then continued, as if acting out an eternal Calvary, but with every stumble and fall described in the newspapers. She was only half listening; a new dread was seeping into her, for what if she fell in love with Martí all over again, and ended up just as desolate as the last time, and what if that desolation propelled her into the arms of a new mysterious muchacho, and how was she not going to fall in love, if they were resuming their friendship in this entrancing manner? They would have *lunch*, he said, and go look at art. But couldn't he take her to the Bowery to see where her father was from? she asked. Please, Pepe? No, he would not take her to the Bowery; that was no place for a tender young dama. If she wanted to see Irishmen, said Martí, they would be better off going into the Madison coliseum to see the walking marathon, in which half the walkers would be Irish, and so would many of the ruffians in the stands. But at least there would be police, most of them Irish too, and spectators from every walk of life, even refined ladies of luxury, though now, in the afternoon, it would not be the infernal scene it would be at night, to which he would never think of exposing her. He'd written about the walking marathon last year and didn't think he would again but maybe they could stop in to have a look at this Pérez. "After all, he is one of our own, María de las Nieves, and if he wins we can feel proud, even if the revolting spectacle makes us feel shame for all men."

Martí paid for their tickets; inside, he made her take his arm as they pressed through the multitude toward a seat from which they could see the curving wooden track. He said they should not sit too near, for if they did, he knew from experience, what they would witness would cause nausea and nightmares. There was no precedent in her life for what she was seeing: such a crowded vastness, enough people to populate a whole separate city, as densely packed and roiling as a thick stew of pallid beans and lard cooking in a big sooty pot; and overhead, so spacious and smoky, and the air so noxious. A band played military music, and there, upon an elevated platform, within a gaslit cloud of cigar fumes, reporters and telegraph operators from all the newspapers monitored the race, and atop another perched the scorekeepers, counting the laps each man had circled with white porcelain numerals on a black board. For the six days and nights of the walking marathon, explained Martí, the lights, still mainly gas in this coliseum, would never be extinguished; at four in the morning, observed only by drunkards, vagabonds, gamblers, and criminals, the walkers would be circling the sawdust-covered track like eternally restless souls pacing inside an immense sealed tomb, but tomorrow morning the winner would be celebrated in newspapers as only the winner of a presidential or a great mayoral race was. "Pérez is far in the lead," said Martí. "Unless he is injured, or collapses, he is sure to win!" All in all, as Martí had promised, the marathon was barbarous and pathetic and riveting. At least two of the walkers lay prostrate on the track and hadn't moved at all since María de las Nieves and Martí had arrived; they might be asleep, or even dead; and some were on hands and knees, determined, Martí told her, to keep crawling, for if they did not finish, they would not even earn the minuscule portion of the house proceeds due them. One such man, with a pointy beard, was flopping forward like a seal. A black man walked hunched over, with tiny steps, as if tracking a long line of ants, stepping on them one by one, and was clearly in delirium. Another shuffled along, feet wrapped in bloody rags. Another had bare feet so grimy and swollen they looked like blackened baby pigs pulled from a fire. Some sucked on sponges as they walked, or gnawed at mutton bones. One, tall and emaciated as a walking skeleton, wore a fez, and his long neck bore the terrible pink scar of a knife slash. And there, that black-haired, copper-skinned, squarely built man, churning along, elbows close to his ribs but moving his fists almost as if rowing small invisible oars, in black leather slippers, that must be Pérez the Inca. The other contestants wore the scarves, medallions, and floral buttons that women leaned over the rail to drape around their necks or pin to the soaked fabric over their chests, but Pérez's uniform of green tights and jersey was unadorned, though his name was shouted more than any other, and she could see gaudy women and even women in lavish silks and furs stretching their arms out to him, dangling their offerings as they shouted his name. At one end of the track were the pine-plank private stalls of each competitor, and Martí explained that there was where the trainers, gamblers, doctors, and other human parasites attached to each competitor gathered; that porcine beast with a shaved head looked just like one of the most sadistic Spanish guards of his prison in Cuba—. "But you wanted to see Irishmen, María de las Nieves. That red-haired, bloody-kneed walker, who keeps falling because he is more asleep than awake, poor man, he is surely Irish. Was your father a black-haired Irishman, or red-haired?" Disconcerted that she had to stop and think about it, she finally answered castaño, or chestnut, and Martí said, "The red-haired ones tend to be the roughest." She looked quickly down at the stalls and spotted one that looked neater than the rest, manned only by two brown-skinned young men, in neat dark suits and straw boaters, sitting upon stools, a basket of bananas and oranges at their feet, and as she watched Pérez the Inca turn the corner, driving himself down the stretch of track closest to them, she said, "Here comes Pérez again, Pepe," and Martí said, "Yes, he is going to win. You are enjoying the race, María de las Nieves!" and she said almost placidly, "But I know him. That is Mack Chinchilla. That is my friend Mack, Pepe. Do you remember? The First Secretary of the Immigration Society?" The absurd declaration seemed to disorient them both, as if it had been uttered by some stranger behind them, and they both sat paralyzed a moment, and then she stood up and said, "I must go down to him." With José Martí trailing, María de las Nieves impatiently wound her way through the crowd, enduring many rude comments, until she was finally at the rail, and she waited there, while Martí stood stupefied behind her, repeating into her ear, "Are you sure? His name is Pérez, and they are saying he is a Peruvian Indian," until he was coming around the track again and suddenly she called out at the top of her lungs, "Mack! Mack! It's María de las Nieves!" but he gave no sign of hearing her as he churned past; he circled the track and went past again, and then again. He was clearly in a trance. He was like a supernatural idol, a mud figure into which an indestructible life force has been breathed. His strained, exhausted eyes were big smashed cherries. He had a strangely ecstatic grin, much like the one of her long-ago dream, when he was circling the world between life and death on his little board.

"Mack! Mack!" she cried out, more desperately each time he passed. People were ridiculing her, and Martí was growing uneasy: "María de las Nieves, are you sure? This is Pérez the Inca, who trained by walking across the Andes. Maybe he only resembles your friend."

"Mack! Mack! It's me, María de las Nieves!' she screamed out as he went by again. She looked at Martí with tears of frustration in her eyes.

"Oh, I don't know. Maybe I'm crazy. He doesn't even look over here. Maybe he hates me!"

They left the coliseum soon after. Five days later Mack Chinchilla, who as Pérez the Inca had won the walking marathon by the greatest margin in the sport's heralded New York history, rode the elevated train uptown, in a green-and-black checked suit with a Western string tie, hand-tooled cowboy boots, and a black Stetson hat. He'd also won the greatest purse in the sport's history, and owed little to anyone because he was his own trainer; his assistants were two of the boys who'd escaped the War of the Caves with him, when they had all had to walk through mountain and jungle for even more than six days, two muchachos from the eccentric Pipil Indian-Nahón tribe of Cuyopilín, who lived with him now on a small farmstead in Brooklyn along with his mother, where they earned a modestly reliable living training horses and breeding mules; Mack also had some business in Central America. That, leaving out for the moment the world of schemes in his head, was who Mack was now. Rubén Abensur had perished in that war, as had the *chuchkajawib* Juan Diego Paclom, and even the poor monjitas at the heart of the sacred mountain—the rebels' defeat as absolute and cruel as the fulfillment of an apocalyptic prophecy. For the rest of his life Mack would rarely discuss, certainly not in the presence of María de las Nieves or the children, the terrible scenes he'd witnessed in that war.

Mack had put two and two together. His boys had told him about the skinny woman calling his name. Later he would claim that he *had* heard her calling to him, but had not distinguished that voice from the one inside his trance, driving him on. Anyway, his tongue had been far too swollen for conversation. Francisca Aparicio was listed in the city directory, and he found the house easily; she would at least know where to find María de las Nieves. El Anticristo's troops had massacred rebels and innocents alike, but he wasn't going to allow himself to despise Paquita for her late husband's crimes; he was interested only in María de las Nieves. Mack visited her every afternoon for two weeks, and then, over the next month, nearly as often. He couldn't have been more blunt, nor more dedicated or persistent. His winnings from the race were their future. Yes, their future together was underwritten, and in the black. If she had been able to look inside his stall in the hippodrome, he told her, she would have seen J. J. Jump's old portrait of her, quite a bit the worse for wear after all it had been through, tacked to the wall, and just as Mr. Doveton had done years before, Mack now pulled the precious, cracked, and furled print from the envelope he'd carried uptown that day in the inside pocket of his coat. Wasn't it all meant to be, after all? He was full of ideas and argument about what they would be able to accomplish together, about why they should be together, about what he could offer her, and what he knew she could offer him. As usual, the strategic thoroughness of Mack's presentation could grow overwhelming and tedious, yet she found herself listening to him with a new seriousness and affection; she liked listening to his plans; they were just challenging enough, both far-fetched and feasible, that she found herself constantly mulling them as if they were already partly her own responsibility as well. And she soon realized that she could actually imagine a place for herself and children in the future he described. She trusted Mack; her trust was a tiny sprouting little plant, but one with already deep roots. As she'd known before, no one listened to her more devotedly. Mack took her mind off Martí, and the more time she spent with Mack, the easier it became for her not to fear Martí's renewed friendship. Mack didn't need to hear yes or no just yet anyway. In another month he had to go back to Central America; he was already exporting some raw caucho, gathered by his muchachos from trees that grew wild in the forests, to the United States. It was the industrial material of the future. He had a vision, which his marathon winnings now made possible: his own rubber plantations down there, and eventually, some kind of factory producing some variety of rubber articles up here. Mack wanted to bring Don José Pryzpyz into the enterprise too. Surely the umbrella mender, still living in the capital, would prove indispensable. And he was going to involve as many people from Cuyopilín as he could, especially those with whom he'd survived the war.

"Pérez the Inca" was, for the time being, an extraordinary celebrity among the Latin-American population of New York. Martí told María de las Nieves that even the young Mantilla girls chanted his name. Pérez, Martí confided, had revealed to him a new kind of American beauty and strength through his noble transcending of such squalid enterprise and surroundings. The two men finally met, and went to a tavern together, and spoke long into the night about India-rubber, about the Central American Indians, about Hebrews, and about war. Even Paquita was eager to meet Mack, and invited him to her dinner for Dr. Matías Romero, who, apart from being Mexico's Foreign Minister, was planting his country's first India-rubber plantations in Soconusco, near the southern border, and had written an influential agricultural treatise on the subject. The two men agreed to collaborate, and the distinguished Mexican offered to provide all the help and expertise he could.

Mack went away to Central America without even having yet kissed María de las Nieves, and when he returned three months later, her belly made her state all too obvious. She was consumed with remorse and anxiety that this pregnancy might be too much for Mack to endure. In truth, she was only pretending to be overwrought, because she knew that propriety and respect required her to at least put on such a show; but she also knew Mack. "Now that I've decided I want him, he is going to disdain me forever," she tearfully confessed to Paquita, who also perceived what was in Mack's heart, and had spent eleven years in a world where illegitimate children were nearly the norm. "Yes, you are probably right," said Paquita. "The man who will put up with that in a woman hasn't yet been born, and that is probably a good thing." María de las Nieves had no choice but to tell Mack the truth.

"Which version?" I asked Mathilde. "You mean the shipboard trilocation?"

"She told him the truth," Mathilde repeated sternly.

Mack said, "You could have ten children, María de las Nieves, and I would still want to be your husband." Those weren't exactly his own words, but he spoke them with even more conviction than the ill-fated young man who'd spoken them first.

"Ten children!" she said, with a little gasp. "And what if I have eleven?"

"Well, as long as the eleventh is by me, that's OK."

# Epilogue

ow, Paquito," said Mathilde. "You can go and look for Mr. Cesar Romero in Florida if you want, and ask him yourself whether or not it's true, since I know you've now decided to be skeptical about everything I tell you. He is playing Rex Harrison's role in *My Fair Lady* at a dinner theater in one of those retirement towns—I've received a letter from a friend telling me so. Romero knows that story about the Wyoming girls on that horse from his own mother, María Mantilla, who heard it that day, there in Central Park, from my mother, and never forgot it. Later, I think he put it into one of his Cisco Kid cowboy movies. Butch Romero, a gunslinger, can you imagine?" She looked at me with a hoisted brow. "He is a pansy, you know. No use hiding it, and so was my poor brother, may he rest in peace. Two mama's boys. Well, a man who dedicates his life to making dolls out of balloons, what do you expect?"

There was one article of historical research I'd brought with me when I first went to see Mathilde at the house in Wagnum, and which had first set me down this path: that photograph of "Señor Carlos López," the Mexican who had appeared in 1933 in the Parisian newspaper *Le Figaro* holding a rabbit made from twisted balloons over a black top hat, had been reproduced in the *Wagnum Chronicle* later that same year; I found it while researching some of the town's history when I was a freshman in college. The article published with the photo in the old local paper revealed that Señor López was actually a native of Wagnum, and that his real name was Charles Tree Jr., the son of Mr. and Mrs. Charles Tree, also of Wagnum, and that the elder, late Mr. Tree (Mack Chinchilla) was the founder and owner of the Cody Rubber Company of Wagnum, as well as the inventor, simultaneously with another Massachusetts balloon experimenter from a nearby town, of the mass-produced "specialty balloon," in Mr. Tree's case an inflatable toy balloon in the generic shape of a cat's head (the other inventor's balloon was also shaped like a cat's head, though with pointier ears). The article quoted "Señor López" as saying he'd first learned how to tie balloons into animals from his mother, a trick she'd learned as a girl growing up on her father's jungle coffee plantation in "South America." Young Charlie Tree had slowly mastered and perfected this hobby over many years, during which he'd also assumed his late father's place at the head of their now diverse rubber manufacturing businesses; though it so happens he was later replaced by Mathilde's far more capable son, Leo Nahon, the son of her second husband, Max Nahon, who was, indeed, the half-Indian son of Mack's long-ago murdered friend Salomón Nahón (the modern American Nahons had shed their accents). Mathilde married three times, and had nine children, six of them girls. At the time I met her, Mathilde had nearly forty grandchildren; we won't even count great-grand-children. According to the article in the *Wagnum Chronicle,* "Señor López" now intended to dedicate himself to introducing people the world over to his new art, especially aspiring performers, through the establishment of "Balloon Art" academies, for the more popular this art became the better it would be for balloon manufacturers everywhere. I made a photo-copy and showed it to my Spanish professor, Miss Sommers, actually a graduate student, a pretty red-haired hippie whom I had a terrible crush on, and who remarked on the astonishing resemblance between "Señor Carlos López"/Charles Tree Jr. and the great Cuban hero and martyr José Martí. I had never heard of José Martí. I'd been researching the history of my town because of a rumor that had long interested me concerning the town's early population, especially the first employees of the Cody Rubber Com-pany, most of whom had lived in employee housing in what was then isolated forest—and is now suburban subdivision—behind the factory, beyond the edge of the swamp, and that people in the town used to refer to as the "Az-tec Jungle." Some members of my own family may be partly descended from those workers, though my mother, who is not, knows nothing about it, and my father, a sergeant in the U.S. Marines, was killed in the war in Vietnam in 1965, when I was ten. If you explore the town archives, and old copies of the long-defunct *Chronicle,* and even if you look at some of the old-est photographs of athletic teams displayed in the trophy cabinets in the lobby of the high school gymnasium, you will be struck by this: many of the young people have a look that is not an old New England look. They are fairly dark, and dark-eyed, and have slashing black eyebrows, and broad faces, and though some are curly- and others are straight-haired, they all look a little bit Mayan, that is, like Central American Indians, though the official legend of the Cody Rubber Company has always been that its earliest workers were Middle Eastern Jews, brought from such places as Turkey and Syria by Charles Tree, which of course was only the final pseudonym adopted by that pioneering New England industrialist Marco Aurelio Chinchilla. What Mack, apparently, had had in mind was a symbolic and even superstitious grafting, within that respectable-sounding Yankee surname, of the Hebrew Tree of Knowledge to the Mayan Tree of Creation. He chose Cody as the name for his business because of the natural commercial appeal of that conventional Western name to Americans. (His wife, María de las Nieves, was a fanatic about the West anyway, and was always threatening to move permanently to Wyoming, where Mack eventually bought her a little horse ranch where she went every summer, sometimes staying into the winter.) The forest behind the Cody rubber factory used to be called the Aztec Jungle, but there was also a vague sort of folklore, which only a few very old people in Wagnum might remember now, about "Jewish Aztecs." Why Aztecs? you might ask. Those mysterious, partially hidden foreign workers from Cuyopilín knew who they were and wouldn't have called themselves Aztecs. The name would have been given to them by outsiders, perhaps by the next generation of factory workers, who lived in the town's new working-class neighborhoods rather than in the original worker housing. And now Wagnum is just one of those towns with a mysterious and mostly forgotten history, like that Cape Cod town that is supposedly populated by the descendants of Fiji Islanders, though nobody seems to remember how they landed there either. When the forest was cleared for new neighborhoods back in the forties and fifties, strange artifacts were found where the workers' housing in the Aztec Jungle had been: stone pagan idols, circles of black ash, incense burners, little crystals, petrified beans, and other implements of Indian ritual, left by the Cuyopilín immigrant workers half a century before. Where are the descendants of those workers now? How could such a unique and rich local history have been forgotten so relatively quickly? It reminds me of the complaint some skeptical Martí scholars make about Cesar Romero: Why are his stories, his supposed family memories about Martí, so pedestrian?

How could one family's memories of an intimate coexistence with the immortal Cuban just evaporate from one generation to the next? Why didn't Cesar Romero even speak Spanish? Cesar Romero's sister, in an interview given soon after their mother died, offered this apologetic explanation: the Romeros were raised mainly in the New Jersey suburbs. "This is all very far from us who were born and educated in the United States and grew up as Americans," she said. In all the memoirs written by the Rough Rider and President Theodore Roosevelt about his own heroic role in the eventual liberation of Cuba from Spanish rule, he never once even mentioned José Martí, who made that armed revolution possible. So why should it be surprising that Cesar Romero couldn't speak Spanish, or that the descendants of the first Mr. and Mrs. Tree and that first generation of Cuyopilín Indian–Hebrew immigrant workers knew so little, eventually even nothing at all, of their own history?

I went to high school with Daisy Nahon and her twin sister, Margarita, Mathilde's great-granddaughters. In the current adolescent usage, those two *ruled*. By the time we were in high school, neither was probably much aware of me, though a few years before, when I was at a YMCA summer camp, I'd received a short friendly letter from Daisy, mailed from Nantucket: I remember sitting cross-legged on my upper bunk while outside the screen a soft summer rain fell in the pines and holding that lilac envelope, with its neatly and femininely rounded print in green ink, and the excitement in my heart as I held it to my nose and breathed in that fragrance of a charmed future. I'd sat behind her in seventh-grade English class. She'd thought I was funny. At the end of the school year, we'd traded summer addresses. Maybe I'd even written to her first, I don't remember. Maybe her parents made her write to all of her classmates from Nantucket, as if it were Valentine's Day at school, and the Princess of Wagnum had to show she loved all her subjects equally. She has cinnamon-colored skin, and murky-green eyes that look right through you, and her hair is black, soft, and curly, and she has the long arms and legs of a ballerina, and I guess she did study dance, and she has almost monstrously beautiful hands like her great-grandmother, and of course I realize that whenever I see her, or her twin sister, I am coming as close as I possibly can to seeing the young María de las Nieves alive, at least a dissimilar yet vitally recognizable shade of her. In high school Daisy wore very short skirts and heavy eye makeup; she was the bad twin, and went out for a little while with my friend Robbie Donnelly, the junior-class president, only, it turned out, or so he ungratefully complained later, to clean up her reputation. Margarita never had those problems. The families descended from the founders of the Cody Rubber Company had the sort of wealth that usually sends children to private schools, but it was a point of civic virtue, among those who still lived in Wagnum, to send their children to the public schools, many of which, after all, were named for members of their family. There was even a Chinchilla Road in our town, and a Chinchilla sports complex. They owned the Tennis and Swimming Club too (that was its modest, utilitarian name). It was a kind of middle-class country club, without golf or pretensions, to which people in the town, originally employees of the factory, could easily belong.

The Cody Rubber Company factory, an enormous and crumbling brick eyesore, with broken grimy windows everywhere and the towering smokestacks of a nineteenth-century industrial inferno, was the dominant feature of my childhood landscape, along with the wooded swamp behind the factory, and the pond in front. Cody's was only two hundred yards from my house, at the end of Abensur Road (which at the other end runs into Pryzpyz Circle). The factory made balloons, but also rubber dish-washing gloves and rubber dolls and so on; we'd find the rusting iron axles lined with black molds—rows of black balloon molds, black dolls, black hands— discarded deep in the swamp, where in winter we skated over ice tinged pink, yellow, green, and blue from leaked balloon dyes. It wasn't until the sixties, a decade before it closed, that the factory became fully mechanized: before that its workers had had to hoist those heavy molds with their arms like weightlifters, dip them into vats of liquid latex solution, and hang them up to dry, over and over. We used to play in the factory's fenced-in back lots, a wonderland of industrial squalor: mucky pools of multicolored dyes, sheds overflowing with discarded balloons. Before dances and parties in my sophomore year of high school, we made our sneakers psychedelic, dipping them into the dyes; we climbed onto the tar-paper roof to sit under the smokestacks, smoking marijuana and gazing out over Moran Pond. As children we used to swim in that pond, until everybody started coming down with eye and skin infections, and then swimming in the pond was banned and remains so to this day—no matter how often they drain, treat, and refill it—all these years after the polluting factory was finally torn down, during my junior year, and replaced with condominiums. Cody's wasn't out of business, though; far from it. They had factories all over the world. They still made balloons, and also specialized in medical equipment, latex gloves, and such. They still had their rubber plantations and latex-processing plants throughout Central America. (Later the AIDS crisis would propel a huge boom in rubber farming and natural latex production.) All of that started with Mack Chinchilla, the "father of balloon art."

In the library one day, Mathilde ordered her great-granddaughter Daisy, who had come from her college in upstate New York for Thanksgiving, to set up a film projector. We'd been talking about Cesar Romero, the son of Martí's alleged illegitimate daughter, María Mantilla. Now Mathilde wanted to show me an episode of the *Batman* television show starring Romero as the Joker. The script's original story, she told me, was credited to both Romero and "Señor Carlos López." They had finally met each other. It was young Charlie Tree Jr. who, despite his shyness, had initiated the friendship. The episode was about a battle for the soul of a statue.

Daisy was as beautiful, sultry, and aloof as ever, and hardly acknowledged me; she remembered me as one of Robbie Donnelly's goofy friends, I suppose, and not as the "funny" kid who'd sat behind her in junior high English class; she noticeably adored Mathilde, though, and that made me like her. She could have gone to Paris or anywhere for Thanksgiving, but she'd come to spend it with her widowed great-grandmother. Margarita, a Princeton student, was studying in Paris at the Sorbonne that semester.

Mack and María de las Nieves were married in 1888, but more than a year before she'd moved in with him at the farmstead in Brooklyn. He was often away in Central America, overseeing his first plantations, which had yet to produce caucho in any useful quantity. Sarita Coyoy had sold the house in La Pequeña Paris and joined her daughter and grandchildren in Brooklyn, and then, when Mack was ready to begin the first of his small-scale manufacturing ventures, Don José Pryzpyz had finally closed his shop and headed to New York also. Making rubber stamps was their initial success, but they produced other products, such as India-rubber horse capes. By night, and often by day as well, Don José, Mack, and even María de las Nieves pursued their nearly alchemical obsession: how to make a liquid caucho solution that would adhere to a mold dipped into it, and then cool and harden into an elastic, durable rubber membrane that, when blown into, would expand into a shiny, buoyant sphere, the way an inflated ani-mal bladder or intestine does. They would unveil their first inflatable rub-ber globes at the Paris International Exposition of 1896—a year after the heroic death of José Martí at Dos Ríos in Cuba.

By then, they had already relocated to Wagnum. When Mack had first discovered the town on one of his exploratory missions into New England, where most of the early rubber factories were situated, it resembled a for-saken old English village in a haunted forest. Indeed, the town had a stigma hanging over it: the Scottish farmers who were its first settlers had sent a militia to the Battle of Lexington, but they'd stopped into a tavern on their way, become drunk, and been captured by the British, who'd forced them into setting a murderous trap against another Minuteman militia returning, proud with victory, to their neighboring town. More than a century later, Wagnum still seemed a castigated place of shame and pov-erty. Mack Chinchilla had found exactly what he was looking for: inexpen-sive land with a stream-fed pond, isolated by forest, and relatively protected from scrutiny and prejudice, for how could the demoralized descendants of Scottish cowards and traitors dare to meddle in or protest a nearly clandestine colony of foreign workers who'd come to revive the town with their industry? (They did anyway, but they had no clout.)

Mack and María de las Nieves, with the children, had moved to Wagnum in the autumn of 1890. But she'd remained close to Martí. She turns up in a few published memoirs of those years as the woman who came to La Liga, the night school Martí founded for the mainly black Cuban and Puerto Rican cigar rollers and other workers, to talk to them about the customs and history of the Indians of Central America. She had spent weeks in various New York libraries preparing for that talk. Some-times she and Martí went on long walks with the children, and took them to museums, ice skating, to the roller-skating arenas and other city amuse-ments. In the summers, she visited Martí in Bath Beach, Brooklyn, where Carmita Miyares had a summer boardinghouse.

That summer of 1890, Martí, appointed Uruguayan Consul, had at-tended the American International Conference in Washington, D.C., which he considered a ploy by the United States to extend economic control over all the compliant states of the Americas, at the expense of building hemispheric consensus for the cause of Cuban independence. The tense conference exhausted him, his health collapsed, and his doctor ordered him to the Catskills to relax. It was there that Martí wrote the autobiographical cycle of *versos sencillos*—octosyllables drawing on popular forms of Caribbean song and lyric and even the villancicos of convents—which included several love poems, such as the one about the niña who died of love, whose face he'd loved more than any other, and the poem about seeing her soul leave through her mouth when he said good-bye. Martí's wife and son returned to New York for one last attempt to mend the marriage, but the rapprochement wouldn't even last three months. Carmen Zayas read those *simple verses*, which he intended to publish; soon after, without Martí's consent or even knowledge, she took her son to the Spanish Consulate to arrange their passage back to Cuba. "And to think," Martí told a friend, "that I sacrificed poor María for Carmen, who has climbed the steps of the Spanish Consulate to ask for protection from me." But everyone knows that story.

So María de las Nieves missed being present during those last five years of Martí's most heroic work. Of course, he wouldn't have had much time for her. He'd become a dervish, barely sleeping, riding the trains between New York and Florida, giving speeches, publishing his newspaper, writing, plotting, conspiring, organizing, raising money to buy arms and ships, fueling himself, often until dawn, with sips of Mariani wine. María de las Nieves visited him at his little fourth-story Front Street office whenever she came to New York, though, and as soon as she and Mack had some money to spare, she donated it to the Cuban cause.

She never quite realized her dream of becoming a reporter, of writing crónicas like Martí. She didn't have the time anyway, with two children to raise, and such an agglomerated household to help oversee. The New York newspaper Martí was most involved with, the *Sun*, didn't employ women, and didn't have a women's page. But she found a little job at the *World*. Living with Paquita, María de las Nieves had learned a bit about society and fashion. She was hired to report on the people who attended whatever great party or function was occurring on any given night, to find out what they wore, what was served, how the ballroom was decorated, and so on. She learned to ride a bicycle, and rushed from event to event, and then delivered her reports to the *World*, to the famous lady who actually wrote the society page. She liked riding the bicycle, but not really the job, and after a few months, she resigned.

In the spring of 1891, at an Austrian Embassy ball in Madrid, the widow Francisca Aparicio was introduced by the powerful Spanish Prime Minister, Cánovas de Castillo, to José Martínez de Roda, a young Spanish aristocrat and senator from the country's most conservative and monarchist political wing. He was from Andalusia but had been educated by Catalan Jesuits in Barcelona, and in everything from his dark, sensual good looks and strict martial bearing to his passionate generosity and his reactionary politics, he seemed to incarnate those two region's supposedly opposite traits. They were married a year later in Paquita's home in New York, with special dispensation from the Pope. Queen Isabella of Spain was the wedding's godmother, in absentia, and her gift was to name the couple the Marqués and Marquesa of Vistabella. They moved to Madrid, where for several years Paquita was happier than she'd ever been before. Her salon was the city's most prestigious, invitations to her dinners and balls the most coveted. But her happiness turned out to be the usual cup of melting snow. Both of her sons, interned in the illustrious Jesuit school of Chamartín de la Rosa, died there, one right after the other, of sudden illnesses; shattered and terrified for the lives of her remaining children, Paquita moved her family to Paris. Her older brother, Juanito, was executed in Los Altos by the country's latest tyrant; then her father died in New York; and in 1899, the still young and handsome senator, the Marqués of Vistabella, was riding the *sud-exprès* from Madrid to Paris to spend Christmas with his family when, alone in the bunk of his sleeping car, he suffered a fatal heart attack. Antonio, Rufino the Just's natural son, the former West Point cadet, drank himself to death in a cheap Parisian hotel. Naturally believing herself accursed by a just though unforgiving God for having once been the wife of an excommunicated persecutor of nuns and priests, she never dared to remarry, though she had many suitors. Paquita became extremely religious, though her character was irrepressible and naturally averse to sustained penance. Two of her daughters by El Anticristo eventually married Spanish marquises. Successive European wars drove her from Paris, back to Madrid, and finally to Switzerland. She never set foot in her native country again, though her coffee plantations continued increasing her wealth. For the last forty years of her life, until her death in Lucerne in 1943, Paquita wrote at least one letter to María de las Nieves a week, who wrote back almost as frequently. Thanks to Mathilde, I was able to read that correspondence.

María de las Nieves used to say that Wagnum had become like one of those Indian towns in the mountains where everyone worked at dyeing wool blankets. Mack Chinchilla preferred to compare it to that Swiss town where everyone from childhood studied and then dedicated his or her life to producing one piece, a cog, a spring, a hand, a tiny numeral, for the watches made in the factory there, the finest in the world. The "Trees" grew wealthy. They moved away from their workers' housing in the forest to the imposing house on the outskirts of the town where Mathilde was still living when I found her, a sort of stone-and-stucco château, intentionally somewhat rustic, with broad verandahs and patios, surrounded by sloping meadows littered, to this day, with the collapsed ruins of horse jumps, and by pine forest. For all his wealth "Charles Tree" was denied admission to the Boston Brahmins' and businessmen's clubs because he was assumed to be Jewish. Mack made no effort to deny that; in fact, he heartily played it up, keeping his hat on indoors, lunching alone at the Parker House when he was in the city, asking for his tea to be served in a clear glass, draping his cod fillet with a paper napkin and fastidiously reaching his knife and fork underneath to eat. All he really cared about was María de las Nieves, his business, and, of course, their children, then their grandchildren, and, frankly, trying to expend the nearly inexhaustible energy that seemed to flow through his muscles and veins as if his body had some way of generating electricity from air, and which always made it so difficult for him even to get to sleep. María de las Nieves was impregnated by Mack once, but sadly miscarried. A few years later, without referring to that misfortune, she wrote to Paquita that despite their lack of children, Mack was as tireless in bed as he was in everything else he did. As the years passed, and the wealthier they became, the more devoted María de las Nieves became to the memory of José Martí, to his political and moral ideals especially. She felt her sanity depended on this. She really did try to do *good*, as he would have wanted. Though as the business expanded, and more and more people, whether they were relatives or not, were put into positions of authority, in the factories, in the offices, the warehouses, the plantations, that became a losing cause. Especially after Mack died, in a Boston hospital, from an incurable stomach infection he'd picked up on a visit to the plantations in 1927. Later the family secretly set a ceiling on the amount María de las Nieves was allowed to spend on her charities. As Mathilde's own strong character took shape, mother and daughter became like Penelope, with one constantly trying to undo whatever the other started. María de las Nieves named her charities for loved ones who passed from her life, as of course they all did, one by one, as the years went by and she outlived nearly everyone, though she never named a charity for María Chon, always insisting that there was no proof she was not still alive. She set up a pension in La Pequeña Paris for women forced out of the convents in the decloistering of 1874, and was still contributing to it when she died, sustaining two women who were even older than she, one a former Recollect, the other a Carmelite. She became an ardent *Panamericanista*. Even in the way she dressed she was something of a forerunner of those women you see around nowadays (all those successors and copiers of Frida Kahlo), though more somber—she eschewed loud colors—one of those grand Latin-American damas, the irreverent Queen of her world, with a streak of convent-girl severity and mania. María de las Nieves was known in Martí circles: scholars and historians called on her in Wagnum, but she would discuss only his ideas and achievements, never his personal life, rebuffing such queries with quotes from Martí meant to make her interrogators feel small and mediocre for asking. She kept in touch with that diminishing circle of Cubans and other Latin Americans who'd known him too, whom she'd met in her early New York years. As I've said, she was one of the founders of the statue. She wrote essay after essay, and some were even published, none in any especially prestigious or meaningful journal, though I think at least a few could easily have been, and some, I thought, contained luminous passages, but by now I am biased.

I'm thinking of that November afternoon when Mathilde and the arresting Daisy showed me that episode of *Batman*. Of course, back then there were no video players—even Betamax was a few year away—nor did they have an original film copy. Someone, maybe Mathilde's son Solomon, had filmed and taped the show, coscripted by Cesar Romero and "Señor Carlos López," right off the television. It was projected onto a home movie screen, and synchronized, not too badly, with a reel-to-reel tape recorder. You really couldn't see very well, the characters blurred behind a glare, but it was discernible. The sound was fine, though. It began in millionaire Bruce Wayne's manor, with Robin/Dick, in sweater and tie, practicing his tuba, and the song he was playing, not well but recognizably, was

"Guantanamera." That's the song the folksinger Pete Seeger originally made famous by setting the words of one of Martí's *simple verses* to a melody that was actually brought to the Americas by Spanish conquistadors: *Soy un hombre sincero / De donde crece la palma.* Of course now you hear it in every shopping-mall margarita bar. So Robin/Dick was playing that, and Alfred the butler comes in carrying milk and cookies and says, "Your snack, Master Dick," and then he says, "That's a very peppy song you are playing, sir," and Robin/Dick says, "It's a song by José Martí, Alfred," and the butler asks who that is, and the Boy Wonder explains: he was the great blablabla, known and respected in all the Central and South American countries. "One of the things he believed, Alfred, was that no country can claim to be free if its freedom depends on holding back the freedom of any other." ("Really," snorted Mathilde, "what does *that* mean?") As I'm sure you all know, *Batman* was a very sixties TV show. Anyway, call on the Batphone, Batmobile screaming out of Batcave, pulling up to Gotham City police station. A statue of José Martí has been stolen from the Free Spirit Park. On the chief's desk is a bust of José Martí, sent with a card signed by the Joker. What is the meaning of this provocative clue? It turns out that José Martí's soul is trapped inside just one of the millions of Martí statues on earth. Whoever can break it open and *breathe it in* before it escapes into the air will inherit the Cuban hero's genius and his unmatched oratorical and charismatic powers, a force the Cuban Apostle used for good, but which the Joker has other plans for. The Joker looks a bit like his putative grandfather, with his hair pushed back off the high crown of his forehead; maybe the high whinnying laugh is also an inheritance. The long tails of his frock coat flapping behind him, and powered by his magical ghostly girdle, the Joker flies around the world, to Cuba, Africa, Russia, Miami, New York, and Los Angeles, lifting Martí statues off pedestals in the dead of night with a giant magnet, confounding helpless policemen, park vagabonds, whores and drugged hippies of all ethnicities, and carrying the statues back to his enormous secret warehouse. Batman has to stop him. His rational is explained by another Martí saying: *All men should become orators, so that they won't be so easily led around by orators.* From there the story descends into a predictable sort of Cold War parable. During the fight scene, though you could barely see it as filmed off the television, Mathilde cackled: "Well, they really are all a bunch of pansies, aren't they."

But I thought I knew where María de las Nieves's son, Charlie Tree Jr., "Señor Carlos López," had found the inspiration for that episode. I remembered something I'd read in one of María de las Nieves's unfinished essays, which I'd been struck by without completely absorbing, and now I wanted to see it again, and I excused myself and went into the library. This is a very American story, I sometimes exhort myself. Mack and María de las Nieves practically invented the modern balloon industry, and became wealthy. But how truly American a story is that? For instance, what if Martí really did father a child during his encounter with that naked Indian Venus he found bathing in that tropical stream so long ago, and what if I had instead dedicated all these years to unearthing the story of that forgotten and anonymous child? Wouldn't that be a truer American story?

Then I think: What's more American than balloons? And what's spookier? Caucho, the "blood" of American trees, a sacred substance to American Indians from Mexico to Brazil, who also made sacred balloons, and sacred balloon animals, from intestines and bladders. And what is more ubiquitous now than balloons? Political conventions, birthday and office parties, weddings, or any other kind of similarly forced or sentimental celebration, at all of these, balloons represent our jubilation. In every shopping mall, there is some clown twisting balloons into animal shapes, just as the Mesoamerican Indians originally did with jungle cat intestines a thousand years ago. Mack Chinchilla used to say, "Balloons should only be inflated when you are feeling happy," and you know that he meant it. The company's first advertising slogan was: *Cody Balloons hold your happiness and never leak.* He was drawing on that old idea he'd learned from Juan Diego Paclom, about the mystical breath inside the inflated figure being what made the figure divine. But that was back then, when the balloon industry was very young, during the innocence of balloons. If you allow yourself to think about them in a certain way, balloons have since become one of the more depressing and desperate things around, though it's good to remember, blight that they are, that the natural latex ones are also biodegradable (as every package of Cody Balloons will tell you). Martí statues are also now ubiquitous, also fairly depressing, and not usually biodegradable. In the unfinished essay I was looking for, María de las Nieves had tried to develop her own theory about Martí's death at Dos Ríos, Cuba, on May 19, 1895. Was it a heroic and reckless one-man cavalry charge, or a suicide, or had his horse just run away with him, or something else? The truth can never be known, though people have never stopped speculating and disagreeing about it. Martí's diary shows that he was arguing with the generals over their renewed belief that the military commanders should have predominance over civilians in the revolution. During a meeting in a little field at a sugar mill known as La Mejorana, General Maceo, who could never quite accept the fragile-seeming, voluble intellectual as worthy of the same respect as a true soldier, fought bitterly with Martí, and even told him: *"I no longer love you as I used to."* Martí wrote in his diary: *I understand that I must shake off the role I am to be marked with, as the civilian defender of shackles hostile to the military movement. I hold out, roughly.* He could be rough, when he had to. Later, after he died and the diary was discovered among his belongings at the rebel encampment, someone, probably General Goméz, tore out the next six pages of the diary, in which he'd obviously written about that dispute. (In her library, as if to forever honor those six missing pages that are also a prophecy, María de las Nieves kept a *culantrillo* plant that a Cuban friend had once brought her all the way from that same field at La Mejorana; missing pages that are also a reminder of those María de las Nieves, aboard the *Golden Rose*, tore from E.S.'s report, aborting Miss Paral's account of her seduction, out of a desire, supposedly, to protect Martí's privacy rather than to censor him; but missing pages that also, perhaps out of a similar motive, opened an at least symbolic space in the world for the trilocational conception of Charles Tree Jr.) Other pages in the diary relate Martí's foreboding over the Mambí rebel fighters', many of them peasants and former slaves, excessive willingness to hail him as their President; there has been no election, he reminds them; he is just the Delegate. His groin was so swollen from his old ailment that it was an agonizing struggle for him just to march with the troops, though he tried not to show it, for his pain was nothing compared with his joy. But General Goméz had decided that it was time for the remarkable adventure to end, that Martí could do more good as the revolution's civilian leader off the island. Martí insisted that he wouldn't leave until he'd experienced combat at least twice. On May 19th, at a ranch called Dos Ríos, by the banks of the Contramaestre River, General Goméz mounted an ambush against a column of Spanish troops. He ordered Martí to stay well back from the line of fire, and assigned a young soldier named Ángel de la Guardia to look after him. But Martí insisted on advancing, perhaps prudently at first. Then his horse bolted forward and charged toward the Spanish troops. He was trailed by Ángel de la Guardia, whose horse took twenty-six bullets. Martí was hit in the neck, and fell. A Spanish scout appeared, who happened to be a Cuban mulatto. "What are you doing here, Don Martí?" asked the scout, and he lifted his Remington and shot Martí dead.

In the last paragraph of her unfinished essay, María de las Nieves wrote:

Some say that José Martí has already been turned into a statue. But doesn't Saint John Chrysostom remind us that statues and images of saints are not gods, but are more like books, their pages open to all? Often I find myself reading Martí as if his writings constitute an autonomous language, one I've spent years studying in order to be able to express myself in a way that wouldn't have quite the same meaning or flavor in any language other than "Martí." In one of his crónicas I read, for example: *Sentences have their luxuries as we have clothing; some wear wool, and some wear silk.* Because of my own personal history, the word *wool* loomed as a secret question posed solely to me, which I sought to answer by once again turning to the Maestro's words. *Words have a layer that envelops them,* he wrote, *which is their usage: it is necessary to go to the body of words. One should use words in their deepest sense, in their real significance, etymological and primitive.* I spent that whole day meditating on the significance of wool in my life, and came to many private recognitions. Often I wonder, What did Martí think when that young rebel soldier introduced himself as Ángel de la Guardia? Elsewhere he'd written that angels are the most beautiful of all human creations. But there are all sorts of angels. Hebrew mystics believed you could create angels just by speaking sacred words. What, to Martí, was the deepest sense of the word *angel?* What was the body of that word to him? Some believe that your Guardian Angel is not a spirit outside you but is actually your Perfect Self. That is what resurrects and goes to heaven. In Luke Jesus says that in resurrection we are equal to the angels. The young soldier told Pepe that his name was Ángel de la Guardia. When he understood *the body of that word,* he spurred his horse and rode to meet his Perfect Self, which resurrected as an Angel: the infinity of words he left us, their infinite possibilities. Which words shall you choose? Some wear silk, some wear wool.

# Acknowledgments

Clark Colahan's magnificent translations and research in his *The Visions of Sor María de Agreda* were indispensable to the chapter in which María de las Nieves discovers the writings of that seventeenth-century nun. Mr. Colahan is this book's true "Fray Labarde." T. D. Kendrick's book on Sor María was also essential for that chapter, as was Antonio Rubial García's *La santidad controvertida;* also many thanks to Prof. Dolores Bravo, of the UNAM.

I am grateful for the generous support of the New York Public Library's Cullman Center for Scholars and Writers; the Guggenheim Foundation; Beatrice Monti della Corte and the Santa Maddalena Foundation; I am especially indebted to Sharon Dynak and Elizabeth Guheen, who provided two crucial stays at the wonderful Ucross Foundation, in Ucross, Wyoming.

In the course of learning about José Martí, I profited from the research, writings, and conversation of a great many scholars and writers, but I especially wish to acknowledge Cintio Vitier, Carlos Ripoll, José Miguel Oviedo, Julio Ramos, Luis García Pascual, Roberto Fernández Retamar, Antonio José Ponte, Mario Montefiore Toledo, Nydia Sarabia, Doris Sommer, Rafael Rojas, Paul Estrade, and Guillermo Cabrera Infante, especially his introduction to the *Diarios.* Susana Rotker's pioneering work on Martí's New York crónicas stands alone. I also wish to thank the staff (especially Javier and Minorkis) at the Centro de Estudios Martíanos in Havana, Cuba. Nearly all of the translations of Martí's writings that appear in *The Divine Husband* are my own, but I profited immensely from the example and friendship of Martí's greatest English-language translator, Esther Allen.

I also want to thank Jaime Abello, and Oswald Loewy, president of Sempertex SA, Barranquilla, an unsurpassable guide to the balloon industry; Professor Barbara Benedict and my colleagues in the Trinity College

English Department; and la familia Jauregui, and all who contributed to our cover image of Fleeing Girl with Batmancita.

For his unwavering support, I can't thank my editor and friend, Morgan Entrekin, enough; likewise all my friends at Grove/Atlantic, and Amanda Urban.

# The Divine Husband

# Francisco Goldman

## ABOUT THIS GUIDE

We hope that these discussion questions
will enhance your reading group's exploration
of Francisco Goldman's *The Divine Husband*. They are
meant to stimulate discussion, offer new viewpoints,
and enrich your enjoyment of the book.

More reading group guides and additional information, including
summaries, author tours, and author sites, for
other fine Grove Press titles, may be found on
our Web site, www.groveatlantic.com.

## QUESTIONS FOR DISCUSSION

1. Francisco Goldman has written an extensively researched historical novel full of real-life details that intermingle with invented ones. There are the historical documents and events—José Martí's writings, Cesar Romero's television appearance claiming Martí as his grandfather, the hagiography of Sor María de Agreda, the espionage plot involving Dr. Slam, and the broad outlines of the life of the real Francisca Aparicio. And there are Goldman's inventions: José Martí's spoken dialogue, the Pinkerton report, the *Batman* episode, and María de las Nieves. What was your reaction to Goldman's richly textured novel?

2. Goldman has called the historical novel "pure humbug . . . it's ridiculous to pretend you're actually giving a realistic depiction of how things were. To me the past is pure fiction." In what sense is the past "pure fiction"? Why is fiction even relevant to an exploration of history? What can fiction do that "pure" history cannot?

3. In *The Divine Husband* the narrator strives to uncover the paternity of Mathilde, with a particular eye to José Martí. To what extent would you call this question of paternity the novel's subject? Or would you describe Goldman's subject in wholly other terms?

4. According to the narrator, an "historic vow" (p. 6) made by two thirteen-year-old convent girls "influence[s] the history of that small Central American republic" (p. 3). What is Goldman suggesting about the place of women and domestic concerns in history? Who in the novel makes history?

5. How did you feel about the novel's portrayal of José Martí? Though he is its most historically important character, and his significance hovers over the novel, he gets very little time to speak and act for himself. In fact, Goldman had researched José Martí extensively enough to write a book simply on him, but arguably it is María de las Nieves who provides the book its center of gravity. What does Goldman's choice suggest about his subject? What did it say to you about the knowability of great historical heroes? About the concerns Goldman was interested in engaging in his novel?

6. On the first page Goldman proposes an analogy: "What if love, earthly or divine, is to history as air is to a rubber balloon?" (p. 3). How important is this idea in the novel? And how important is love in *The Divine*

*Husband*? How does love affect history, not only our personal histories but also our political histories?

7. Convents fall under the ultimate critique—elimination—within the course of the novel (although more than secular ideology drives their closure). The convent is often portrayed as a harsh, unyielding environment that suppresses young women, body and soul. How does Goldman depict the cloistered religious life, so censured by the modern age?

8. Why does María de las Nieves rebel against the convent? What did her obsession with sneezing, and her wool allergy, represent? What might it mean that she has a quasi-religious vision, and that her wool allergy returns at the baths at Don Ky's, when she does not yet know she is pregnant?

9. José Martí tells María de las Nieves, "You represent the new American intelligence, María de las Nieves. You will be a mother of our new America" (p. 217). What do you take these words to mean? What idea of the "new America" surfaces in the book?

10. How does the book use María de las Nieves as a personification of our tendency to "keep secrets" in order to idealize great historical figures—as was certainly the case among those who were close to José Martí? How do you interpret María de las Nieves's story of trilocation during the conception of Carlos Lopez, and her evolution into one of the very scholars responsible for Martí's idealized image?

11. What is the place of revolutionary movements in the novel? Of violence? How would you characterize Goldman's depiction of El Anticristo? Of Paquita? How does the novel handle the question of Paquita's guilt by association?

12. *The Divine Husband* is full of religions of all different sorts. Catholicism predominates, but native animism, shamanism, Judaism, and the Popol Vuh are all alluded to. After Mack Chinchilla leaves La Pequeña Paris, he even participates in the War of the Caves with a shaman who has created his own blend of several of these faiths. What is the place of religion in the novel? How does Goldman portray religion in the modern world?

13. Goldman creates a vivid sense of the exploding possibilities of capitalism and industry in *The Divine Husband*, for example, the Jewish florists

who set up shop in La Pequeña Paris and the coffee-importing firm for which Mack Chinchilla works in New York. What is the role of work in the novel? How do the nineteenth-century changes Goldman describes—the secularization of governments, increases in international trade—influence the nature of work? How does the novel illuminate the relationship between the United States and its neighbors to the south?

14. The novel takes place in an era when international travel, while possible, was extremely arduous. Yet there are many adventurers in the book seeking a better life by traveling to countries with greater opportunity—for example, Don José, the Nahon brothers, the shipload of Italians, Sor Gertrudis, and Mack Chinchilla. What are each of these characters seeking, in spite of the hardship of travel? How is Paquita and María de las Nieves's journey to New York of a different type than these other journeys?

15. La Pequeña Paris, in the novel, is a cosmopolitan metropolis, peopled with Indians, Spaniards, Spanish-Indian mestizos, North Americans, Europeans, tearaways from the Jewish Diaspora, even a random family of what we might today call German hippies. There are also several characters who change their names—Mack Chinchilla and Don José Przyzpyz, for example. What do you think about the way Goldman handles ethnicity in the book?

16. When speaking about the structure of *The Divine Husband*, Francisco Goldman paraphrased Flaubert: "The right structure only comes along when the illusion of the subject becomes an obsession." Goldman went on to say that you "follow the story that's emerging, and eventually, in a very slow motion kaleidoscope, the form begins to take place." As a reader, what was your experience of the book's movement through time? How might a more linear structure have changed the experience of the book and even its meaning?

17. Francisco Goldman has said the following about *The Divine Husband:* "I wanted to write an antirealism, as opposed to, say, even a magic realism. I was dreaming of going hunting for that strange beast of a novel that's like none we've ever seen before." What do you think he meant? Is *The Divine Husband* a "strange beast"? Is it antirealistic? How is it distinct from the magic realism of a writer like Gabriel García Márquez? How would you describe the mystical bilocation in the novel—as magic realism, antirealism, or something else?

18. Finally, the title *The Divine Husband* accrues considerable complexity by the end of the book. It refers in a literal sense to Jesus Christ, the Divine husband that nuns are "married" to. But in the book, María de las Nieves renounces the divine husband she is promised to and goes back out into *el Siglo*, the world. Who, in the universe of the novel, is María de las Nieves's real "divine husband"? Does the novel have a definition of true love? Did its final romantic resolution satisfy you?

# ABOUT THE AUTHOR

Francisco Goldman's first novel, *The Long Night of White Chickens*, was awarded the Sue Kaufman Prize for first fiction from the American Academy of Arts and Letters. *The Ordinary Seaman*, his second novel, was a finalist for the International IMPAC-Dublin Literary Award and the *Los Angeles Times* Book Prize in Fiction. Both of his novels were finalists for the PEN/Faulkner Award and have been translated into nine languages. He has been the recipient of a Guggenheim Fellowship and a Fellow at the New York Public Library Center for Scholars and Writers. His fiction and journalism have appeared in the *New Yorker, Harper's, The New York Times Sunday Magazine, Esquire, The New York Review of Books, Outside*, and many other publications.